U0587147

民族文字出版专项资金资助项目

𖹀𖹁𖹂𖹃

Langaxihe

傣译汉◎普学旺　岳小保
刘　琳　万德美
汉译英◎毕晓红

云南出版集团
云南美术出版社

图书在版编目（CIP）数据

兰嘎西贺 / 普学旺等傣译汉；毕晓红汉译英. --
昆明：云南美术出版社，2023.3
ISBN 978-7-5489-5111-7

Ⅰ. ①兰… Ⅱ. ①普… ②毕… Ⅲ. ①傣族－史诗－
中国 Ⅳ. ① I222.7

中国国家版本馆 CIP 数据核字 (2023) 第 068113 号

责任编辑： 张湘柱　赵关荣　赵　婧
封面设计： 高　伟
责任校对： 魏　薇　魏于清

兰嘎西贺

傣译汉 / 普学旺　岳小保
　　　　刘　琳　万德美
汉译英 / 毕晓红

出版发行：云南出版集团 云南美术出版社
印　　刷：云南出版印刷集团有限责任公司华印公司
开　　本：787mm × 1092mm　1/16
字　　数：150 千
印　　张：30.75
版　　次：2023 年 3 月第 1 版
印　　次：2023 年 3 月第 1 次
书　　号：ISBN 978-7-5489-5111-7
定　　价：280.00 元

序

普学旺

《兰嘎西贺》是一部傣族家喻户晓的民间叙事长诗，广泛流传于云南省西双版纳、德宏、临沧、普洱、保山等州市的傣族地区。长诗以阿罗替雅王国（或勐沓达腊塔）朗玛满和勐兰嘎王国十头王争夺西达公主为线索，展开了一场错综复杂而又曲折尖锐的斗争，歌颂了坚贞不渝的爱情和正义战胜邪恶的美好愿望。长诗内容异常广阔，结构庞大，主题鲜明，立意深邃，故事情节引人入胜，富有神话传奇和浪漫主义色彩，深受傣族人民喜爱。

傣语“兰嘎西贺”的意思是“兰嘎地方长有十个头的国王”，学者认为，“兰嘎”即斯里兰卡的古称“兰卡”，因长有十个头的“十头王”奢淫无度，导致人神共愤，所以有人又将它译为《十头魔王》。《兰嘎西贺》与印度史诗《罗摩衍那》具有密切的源流关系，如《罗摩衍那》的男主人公叫罗摩，《兰嘎西贺》中叫朗玛满；女主人公前者叫悉多（或息多），后者叫西达；神猴将领前者叫哈奴曼，后者叫阿奴曼……故事情节亦大体相似，《兰嘎西贺》的故事情节在《罗摩衍那》中都能找到。明显可以看出，《兰嘎西贺》取材于印度史诗《罗摩衍那》，随佛教的传播而从斯里兰卡经缅甸、泰国等国传入了中国傣族地区。

值得注意的是，从篇幅看，《兰嘎西贺》只有《罗摩衍那》的五分之一左右；从情节看，前者舍弃了后者的许多情节而又增加和丰富了许多内容。《兰嘎西贺》不是对《罗摩衍那》的简单翻译，而是经过了傣族人民的艺术加工、改编和再创造，历经上千年的流传后，现已成为傣族自己的作品。因此，《兰嘎西贺》是中印文化交流的成果，它对后世的傣族文学有着深远的影响，在傣族文学史上具有重要地位，在新时代进行面向南亚东南亚辐射中心建设方面具有重要研究价值和开发利用价值。

在我国傣族地区流传的《兰嘎西贺》有两种抄本，一种抄本篇幅较大，有一万五千行以上，称为“大兰嘎”；另一种抄本篇幅相对简略，约三千至五千行，是大兰嘎的缩写本，又称“小兰嘎”。迄今大兰嘎抄本已翻译出版多次，并已于2022年入选云南省第五批非物质文化遗产保护名录，但小兰嘎抄本至今尚未有人翻译出版。本次翻译出版的抄本即为小兰嘎类，是我们于2011年在保山市昌宁县湾甸傣族乡万德美家发现的抄本，此书现由万德美和万建国收藏保护，已有一百五十多年历史。从这部长诗中，我们可以看出不同地区的《兰嘎西贺》亦随其传播路径的不同而有一些新的变化。如《兰嘎西贺》在西双版纳地区被作为英雄史诗看待，而此次出版的小兰嘎抄本则已演变为阿銮叙事长诗了。因此，本书用傣、汉、英对照出版，以丰富傣族文学研究的内容，并为考察南亚东南亚文化传播史提供更多新颖资料。

本书得到国家民族文字出版专项资金资助，得到云南美术出版社的大力支持，谨致谢意。

2022年10月6日于昆明

Preface

By Pu Xuewang

Langaxihe is a famous narrative Dai folk epic circulating widely in Dai regions such as Xishuangbanna, Dehong, Lincang, Pu'er, Baoshan of Yunnan Province. With the clue of fighting for the Princess Xida between Langmaman, the King of the Kingdom Aluotiya (or Mengtadalata) and the Ten-headed King of Kingdom Menglanga, the epic tells about a complex and tortuous struggle, singing the praise of unswerving love and the good wish of triumph of justice over evil. Full of myths and legends and tinged with romanticism, the epic is rich in content, huge in structure, clear and profound in theme, compelling in storyline, which is deeply loved by the Dai people.

The Dai "Langaxihe" means "the king with ten heads in Langa". According to some scholars, "Langa" is "Lanka", the ancient name for Sri Lanka. As the Ten-headed King is greedy and wicked, which annoys both man and god, the epic is also translated as *The Ten-headed Evil King*. There is close relation between *Langaxihe* and the Indian epic *Ramayana* in origin. For instance, the heroes in *Ramayana* and *Langaxihe* are called Rama and Langmaman respectively; while the heroines in *Ramayana* and *Langaxihe* are called Sita and Xida respectively; and the divine monkey generals in the two epics are called Hanuman and Anuman respectively. There are also many other similarities between *Langaxihe* and *Ramayana* in terms of the storyline. Apparently, *Langaxihe* is based on *Ramayana.* Later with the spread of Buddhism, it was introduced from Sri Lanka through Myanmar, Thailand and other countries into the Dai region of China.

It is worth noting that *Langaxihe* is only about one fifth of *Ramayana* in terms of length and many plots in *Ramayana* are abandoned in the former with enriched content. Therefore, *Langaxihe* is not the translation of *Ramayana.* Through the artistic processing, modification and recreation by the Dai people over thousands of years of circulation, *Langaxihe* has become the own work of the Dai people. *Langaxihe* is one of the achievements of Sino-Indian cultural exchange. It has a profound impact on the Dai literature of later generations, and it also has an important position in the history of Dai literature. Besides it has important research value and development and utilization value in building Yunnan into an international hub facing South and Southeast Asia in the new era.

There are two kinds of transcripts of *Langaxihe* circulating in China's Dai regions. The one with more than 15,000 lines is comparatively longer in length and is known as the "Major Langa" ,while the other one, an abridged version of the Major Langa, with 3,000 to 5,000 lines is comparatively short and is called "Minor Langa". So far, the transcript of Major Langa has been translated and published many times and was included into the fifth batch of intangible cultural heritage protection list of Yunnan Province in 2022. Nevertheless, the transcript of Minor Langa hasn't been translated and published yet. What we translated and published this time belongs to the category of Minor Langa, which was found at Wan Demei's house, Wandian Dai Township, Changning County, Baoshan City in 2011. The transcript now is collected by Wan Demei and Wan Jianguo and it has a history of over 150 years. We will find some new changes to *Langaxihe* due to the different propagation paths, for instance, *Langaxihe* has been regarded as a heroic epic in Xishuangbanna while the Minor Langa has evolved into an Aluan narrative poem. Therefore, the book will be published in Dai, Chinese and English to enrich the research content of the Dai literature and to provide more new materials for research of cultural communication history in South and Southeast Asia.

We are grateful to the National Special Fund for Publication in the Ethnic-minority Languages for funding and Yunnan Fine Arts Publishing House for its great support.

In Kunming, October 6, 2022

目录

兰嘎西贺

Langaxihe

兰嘎西贺：傣语音译，意为“兰嘎地方长有十个头的国王”，因十头国王贪婪奢淫，故又名《十头魔王》。

Langaxihe: transcribed from the Dai language, literally meaning “The Ten-headed King in the land of Langa. As The Ten-headed King is greedy and wicked, this epic is also entitled *The Ten-headed Evil King*.

听吧，慈祥的老人，
听吧，善良的乡亲，
这是一个古老的故事，
这个故事已说不清流传了多少年。

我双手合十礼敬先师苏拉萨帝①，
礼敬普天之下各门类的师父。
请先师们加持于弟子，
让弟子今日里文思敏捷。
我要唱述兰嘎西贺的故事，
让这个故事传遍傣乡四面八方。

Listen, my beloved elders with loving smiles,
Listen, my kind fellows with kindly hearts,
Listen to this old story from old time,
As old as our old homeland.

I put my palms together and pray to the Great Master Sulasadi①,
Pray to the Masters of all kinds under the Heaven.
Please enlighten me as your disciple at the authoritative position,
Please empower me as your disciple to be a ready story-teller now.
I would like to tell the story of Langaxihe,
To spread the story around the land of our Dai people.

① 苏拉萨帝：傣族传说中文学、武术、舞蹈等艺术门类的祖师。

①Sulasadi: the Dai people's legendary great master of art in literature, martial art, and dance, etc.

第一章

Chapter One

话说在那遥远的时候，
先是开天辟地大火烧天，
接着是洪水泛滥淹大地，
山川河谷开始慢慢形成。

后来天神降临大地上，
天神将大地分成四大块，
地上就有了东南西北四方。
地上有了山岗、森林和湖海，
高山峻岭是动物们的乐园，
平川和坝子是人们繁衍生息的地方。

当初天下不太平，
没有和谐相处的规矩。
人们以山为界各自为政，
分不清善与恶的界限在哪里。

后来有人离家进入森林里修行，
他们在山里清净修行做雅细[①]，
他们慢慢地智慧超众生，
他们能明辨是非善恶。

Long long ago, there was a time,
When heaven was separated from earth,
Followed by the engulfing of the flood,
Gradually forming mountains, rivers and valleys.

Afterwards the God befell on the earth,
And divided the earth into four pieces,
Forming the east, south, west and north.
There were mountains, forests, lakes and seas,
With lofty mountains and steep hills being the paradise of animals,
And the plain and basin being the place for reproduction of human beings.

Initially, it was not peaceful,
And there were no rules for harmonious coexistence.
People took mountains as boundaries,
And no one knew where the boundary between the good and evil lied.

Subsequently some people left home and entered the forest,
As Yaxi[①] who cultivated themselves peacefully in the mountains.
Gradually, they transcended over all living creatures,
And they could distinguish the right and wrong, good and evil.

①雅细：傣语音译，出家在深山里修行的得道者。一般造诣很高，传说有的已获得神通。

①Yaxi is transliterated from Dai, which means the spiritual leader who cultivates himself or herself in the mountains. Generally these people are learned and it is said some have supernatural power.

话说当时有一个王国名叫勐兰嘎，
坐落在大海的正中央。
王国地域宽广望不见边际，
山清水秀人口密集。
王国风调雨顺，
人民百姓安居乐业。

国王是一位真龙天子，
王位已说不清传了多少代人。
国王集中精力来施政，
聪慧的王后服侍在他身旁。
国王有大臣们在朝中议事出主意，
王国的威名传遍四面八方。

俗话说富翁也会缺酸腌菜，
王宫里虽应有尽有，
但有一件事让国王和王后难安眠，
没有生育一个儿女让他们很闹心。
国王夫妇想到了雅细，
因为有一位雅细年年岁岁修行在大山中。

国王和王后带着珍贵的供养品，
来到山里虔诚供养雅细。
国王夫妇滴水[①]祈祷诸神，
雅细为他们念诵求子经典。

There was a kingdom named Menglanga,
Situated in the middle of the sea.
The kingdom boasted a boundless territory,
With picturesque scenery and dense population.
The kingdom and its people were enjoying peace and prosperity then.

The king was the true son of Heaven.
No one could tell for how many generations the throne had passed down.
The king focused on governance of the kingdom,
With his intelligent queen attending to him by his side.
With the assistance of the ministers in the court,
The fame of the kingdom spread far in all directions.

As the saying goes, even the rich need pickled vegetables.
Though there was everything under the sun in the palace,
There was one thing that made the king and queen sleepless,
That was they had no children.
The royal couple thought of Yaxi,
Because there was a Yaxi cultivating himself in the mountains year after year.

The king and queen brought precious offerings,
To sacrifice to Yaxi in the mountains.
The royal couple prayed to deities by practicing Dishui[①],
And the Yaxi recited the scripture for children for them.

①滴水：将清水装在壶里使之慢慢流出滴在地上，是傣族民间一种祈福仪式。

①Dishui is a praying ritual of folk Dai, in which clean water is put in a pot and drips to the ground slowly.

国王夫妇供养完毕，
他们带着期望回到王宫中。
国王夫妇在王宫里亦天天祈祷，
他们的虔诚终于感应了大天神混西迦[①]。

After the sacrifice, the royal couple returned to the palace with hopes.
The royal couple prayed every day in the palace,
And eventually their piety moved the Supreme God Hunxijia[①].

王后不多久就有了身孕，
让国王和王后悲喜交加。
国王让王后养好身子，
不要辜负勐兰嘎王国人民。

The queen soon got pregnant,
Which was a mixed blessing to the king and queen.
The king asked the queen to keep fit,
And not let the people of Menglanga Kingdom down.

王后怀胎十月后分娩，
她生下了一位不同寻常的女婴。
国王知道后万分高兴，
他离开宝座来看女儿。

The queen gave birth to an extraordinary female baby after 10 months of pregnancy.
The king was very happy to hear that,
And he left the throne to have a look at his daughter.

因为公主身上有野姜花的清香，
国王为女儿取名叫冒雅。
侍女们精心照顾王后和公主。
她们轮流拥抱公主不离王后身旁。

The daughter was named Maoya by the king,
Because the princess has the fragrance of wild ginger flowers on her body.
The maidservants took intensive care of the queen and princess,
And held the princess in rotation without leaving the queen's side.

公主一天一天在长大，
不知不觉已经长成一位大姑娘。
公主到了谈婚论嫁的年龄，
国王唤公主来到身旁：
“我心爱的宝贝女儿啊，

Day by day, the princess grew up,
Unconsciously, the princess became a big girl,
Who reached the age of marriage.
The king summoned the princess to his side and said,
"My beloved daughter, you are the pearl in the palms of

① 混西迦：傣语音译，天上的最高主宰神。

①Hunxijia is transliterated from Dai, meaning the Supreme God in Heaven.

你是父王和母后的掌上明珠，
我欲招一位驸马进王宫协助你，
要将王位让你来继承，
让你成为国人的大榕树。”

your father and mother.
I want to recruit a son-in-law into the palace to assist you,
So as to let you succeed to the throne,
And become the big banyan tree of the countrymen".

公主回答说她不当国王，
国王再怎么劝也没有用。
国王万万没想到，
女儿心里早已有了主张。

The princess said in reply that she wouldn't be the queen,
Regardless of how hard the king persuaded.
Out of the king's expectation,
The princess had her own ideas.

国王忍无可忍地说道：
“既然我的话你一句都不入耳，
你就给我离开王宫吧！
我不想再看到你，
我眼不见心不烦。”

Driven beyond forbearance, the king said,
"Since you don't listen to me,
Get out of the palace,
And I won't see you,
For out of sight is out of mind."

公主决心不继承王位，
她亦不想解释理由。
她伤心地离开了王宫，
她来到了深山老林中。

The princess was determined not to succeed to the throne,
Neither would she like to explain.
She left the palace sadly,
And came to the thickly forested mountains.

这座大山名叫达撒季利，
深山里住着一位修行的雅细。
公主来到雅细修行的洞府，
她想在洞府里修行。

The mountain was called Dasajili,
In which a Yaxi was living.
The princess came up to the cave where the Yaxi was cultivating,
She wanted to cultivate herself in the cave.

雅细让公主住下来，
雅细教她念诵经文。
冒雅公主念诵经文不马虎，
字字句句记在心间。

Yaxi asked the princess to stay in the cave.
And he taught her to recite the scriptures.
Princess Maoya was very careful when reciting the scriptures,

	With every word and verse kept in mind.
公主常到山中摘野果，	The princess often picked wild fruits in the mountains,
供养雅细于洞府中。	To feed Yaxi in the cave.

有一天公主又去山里找水果，
她来到一棵杧果树下边。
有一树枝上挂着十个熟杧果，
公主折断树枝摘下杧果。
公主用十个杧果供养雅细，
雅细为公主念诵吉祥经。

One day, the princess went to the mountains for fruits.
She came up to a mango tree.
There were ten ripe mangos on a branch.
The princess broke the branch and picked the ten mangos,
With which the princess fed Yaxi.
Yaxi recited the scripture of auspiciousness for the princess.

公主双手合十虔诚祷告：
“供养杧果的功德请诸神记下，
鄙女很想生儿育女，
因为有了子女方能托付终生。”

The princess prayed by putting her palms together.
“Deities, please remember the merits and virtues of
provision of mangos,
I am eager to bear children,
For only with children, can one entrust the whole life.”

由于公主有一颗虔诚心，
公主的祈祷使大天神混西迦有了感应。
大天神混西迦俯瞰大地，
看见公主修行在深山中。
她虽没有异性朋友，
但是她很想有子嗣。

Since the princess was so pious,
That the supreme God Hunxijia was moved.
God Hunxijia overlooked the earth,
And he saw the princess was cultivating in the mountains.
Though she had no male friends,
She was eager to have offspring.

混西迦派天神扁玛法下凡，
天神同情地对公主把话谈：
“冒雅公主啊，
你居住在深山老林中，
心里却存有生儿育女的欲念。
我是大天神混西迦派来的天神，

Hunxijia sent the God Bianmafa to earth,
The God said to the princess sympathetically,
“Princess Maoya,
Though you are living in the mountains,
You have the desire to bear children.
I'm the one of the Gods sent by the Supreme God
Hunxijia.

你就把我当同修[1]吧。”

公主看见天神下凡尘十分高兴，
公主与天神如同同修一见如故。
天神用手轻轻拍打公主的脊背三下，
眨眼工夫天神就不见了影踪。
从此公主有了身孕，
公主小心翼翼地乐在其中。

冒雅公主怀胎已满十月，
到了吉日良辰那一天，
公主开始分娩，
她生下了一个儿子。
奇怪的是这个儿子长有十个头颅，
公主就像被人推进万丈深渊。

冒雅公主终于想通了原因，
也许这是一种缘分，
因为她供养雅细的杧果是十个，
所以她生出来的孩子有十个头颅。
不管是善是恶，
她都得把这个孩子养大。

公主开始疼爱这个儿子，
感觉自己有了依靠。

①同修：共同在一起修行的僧人。

Let me be your Tongxiu[1].”

The princess was very happy to see the God's descending to the world.
The princess and the God felt like old friends at the first meeting.
The God tapped at the back of the princess for three times.
Suddenly, the God disappeared.
From then on, the princess got pregnant,
And she was carefully leading a happy life.

Princess Maoya had been pregnant for ten months.
When the auspicious day came,
She started to deliver,
And gave birth to a son.
It was very strange that her son had ten heads.
The princess was desperate as being pushed into abyss by someone.

Maoya finally figured out the reason.
Perhaps it was destiny.
Since the amount of mangos she provided to Yaxi were ten,
The child she born had ten heads.
She had to raise the child,
For good or evil.

The princess started to dote on her son,
Feeling she had someone to depend on.

①Tongxiu means the monks who are cultivating together.

因为十个杧果来自达撒季利山，
公主给孩子起名叫达撒季利。
公主希望十头儿子能出人头地，
就像巍峨无垠的达撒季利大山一样雄壮威风。

Because the ten mangos were from the Mount Dasajili,
The child was named after Dasajili by the princess.
The princess wanted her son to be somebody in future,
Just like the magnificent and mighty Mount Dasajili.

儿子天天跟着母亲游逛在山里，
儿子身相越长越庄严英俊。
十头儿子满一周岁，
公主又想生第二个孩子。
公主来到贡帕甘腊山，
这是一座有花有果的花果山。
公主看见了一棵杧果树，
她折断结有一个杧果的树枝，
她带着杧果返回到洞府中。

Day in and day out, the son followed his mother,
Wandering about in the mountains.
When the ten-headed son was one year old,
The princess wanted to give birth to the secondchild.
The princess came to the Mount Gongpaganla,
Which was a mountain with flowers and fruits.
The princess saw a mango tree,
And she broke a branch with only a mango.
She brought back her mango to the cave.

公主将杧果供养雅细，
她在心中暗暗祈祷，
希望能够再生一个孩子。
她离开洞府时，
天神又从天宫下来轻轻拍了她后背三下，
天神返回到天宫中。

The princess offered the mango to Yaxi,
And prayed by herself,
For the birth of one more child.
As she was leaving the cave,
The God descended from the heavenly palace again to tap her back for three times,
And then he returned to the heavenly palace.

公主身孕满十个月，
她又生下了一个孩子。
因为这一次的杧果来自贡帕甘腊山，
公主给儿子起名贡帕甘腊。
公主希望第二个儿子，
就像这座巍峨的贡帕甘腊大山一样厚实。

After ten months of pregnancy,
The princess gave birth to a child.
Because this time the mango came from the Mount Gongpaganla,
The son was named after Gongpaganla.
The princess wanted her second son to be outstanding,
As firm as the magnificent Mount Gongpaganla.

贡帕甘腊满一周岁，
公主又想生第三个孩子。
公主来到毕披山，
这座山上一年四季瓜果飘香。

When Gongpaganla was one year old,
The princess wanted to have the third child.
The princess came to the Mount of Bipi,
With various melons and fruits available all year round.

公主看见了一棵杧果树，
她折断结有一个杧果的树枝，
带着树枝回到洞府中。
公主将杧果供养雅细，
她在心中虔诚祈祷，
希望能够再生一个孩子。
天神扁玛法又再次出现，
天神用手轻轻拍公主后背三下，
天神又返回天宫中。

The princess saw a mango tree,
And she broke the branch with a mango,
And returned to the cave with the branch.
The princess offered the mango to Yaxi,
And prayed piously by herself,
For the birth of one more child.
The God Bianma appeared again,
And tapped the princess's back for three times,
And then he returned to the heavenly palace.

公主身孕满十月，
公主生下了第三个孩子。
因为这次的杧果来自毕披山，
公主给第三个孩子起名叫毕披。
公主希望第三个儿子也能够出人头地，
就像毕披山一样顶天立地。

After ten months of pregnancy,
The princess gave birth to the third child.
Because this time the mango was from the Mount Bipi,
The third child was named after the Mount Bipi.
The princess wanted her third child to be outstanding,
As mighty as the Mount Bipi.

母子四人生活在深山里，
三兄弟在慢慢长大。
陪伴三兄弟的只有母亲而不见父亲，
三兄弟感到很奇怪。
三兄弟决心向母亲问清楚，
为何不见他们的父亲。

The princess and the three sons lived in the mountains.
The three brothers grew up slowly.
The three brothers felt very strange,
As they had never seen their father.
The three brothers decided to ask their mother about this.

三兄弟跪拜在母亲脚下：
“我们尊敬的妈妈啊，

The three brothers knelt down before their mother,
"Our respected mother,

您的养育之恩比天高比地厚。
可是我们不能只有母亲而没有父亲啊，
不知我们的父亲在哪里？
请妈妈告诉我们。”

Nothing can be equal to your affection of upbringing.
But we can't live without our father,
Please tell us where our father is."

公主知道这件事情回避不了，
还不如早早就向三个儿子讲明白：
“聪明的孩子们啊，
我们的故乡不在山里，
我们的王国不是一般的地方，
我们的王国是勐兰嘎。
勐兰嘎有一百多个附属国，
是一个强盛的国家。

The princess knew it was inevitable.
Then she told the three sons,
"intelligent children,
Our hometown is not in the mountains.
Our kingdom is not an ordinary place.
Our kingdom is Menglanga,
Which has more than 100 dependent states.
It's a powerful country.

“王宫里宽敞壮丽，
王宫里应有尽有。
成百上千的侍女个个美若天仙，
将军和卫士个个威武似天兵天将。
勐兰嘎王国富饶美丽，
国家富强人民安居乐业。

"The palace is spacious and magnificent,
With everything under the sun.
There are hundreds of fairy-like maidservants in the palace.
The generals and soldiers are as mighty as heavenly generals and soldiers.
The Kingdom of Menglanga is fertile and beautiful,
With the country being prosperous and people living in peace and harmony.

“你们的外公是那里的国王，
他就在那里治理江山。
当时外公外婆无子女，
盼望子女就像盼星星盼月亮。
因为没有子女就没有了接班人，
勐兰嘎王国的前途看不见曙光。

"Your grandfather is the king of the kingdom,
Governing the country there.
Having no children,
Your grandfather and grandmother are eager to have children.
If they have no children, they have no successors.
The Kingdom Menglanga has no prospects.

"后来外公外婆向雅细做供养，
他们进山里祈求天神赐子女。
外婆终于生下了我，
外公和外婆十分高兴。
众侍女精心照看我，
让我寸步不离她们身旁。

"Afterwards your grandfather and grandmother offered food to Yaxi,
And they went to the mountains to pray to the god for offspring.
Your grandmother finally gave birth to me.
They were very happy.
The maidservants took intensive care of me,
Keeping me at their elbows all the time.

"你们的外公给我起名冒雅。
意思就是美丽的花朵。
你们的外公要让我接替王位，
还要找一位精干聪明的驸马来辅佐。
我无论如何也不接受，
我就这样冒犯了你们的外公。
拒接王命是要杀头的啊，
就这样我被赶出了王宫。

"I was named Maoya by your grandfather.
It means beautiful flowers.
Your grandfather wanted me to succeed the throne.
He also wanted to find a smart son-in-law to assist me.
I refused to accept no matter how hard he persuaded,
Which offended your grandfather.
Defying king's edict can be beheaded.
I was driven out of the palace.

"我跑到深山里，
只想找一个可以安身的地方。
深山里住着一位雅细，
他长年修行在洞府中。
雅细见我很可怜，
他就教我念诵神咒，
他收容我在洞府中学经文。

"I ran into the mountains,
To find a place to stay.
There was a Yaxi,
Who was cultivating himself in the cave all the year round.
Yaxi thought I was so poor.
He taught me to recite scriptures.
He received me at the cave for the learning of scriptures.

"我念经学咒求子嗣感动天神，
天神下凡让我圆心愿。
后来生下你们三兄弟，
母亲在山里不再寂寞孤单。
感恩雅细收容了我，

"God Hunxijia was moved by my praying for offspring.
God Bianmafa descended to the world to help accomplish my wish.
Afterwards I gave births to your three brothers.
Your mother is no longer alone.

我们一家才有了安身立命的地方。”

I'm grateful to Yaxi for receiving me,
And for offering us a place to settle down to a tranquil life."

三兄弟听完母亲的话惊奇又感动，
他们双手合十跪拜母亲：
原来我们的母亲是圣女啊，
三兄弟亦知道了自己是天根。
如此看来住在深山里不是长久之计，
勐兰嘎王国才是故乡。

The three brothers were surprised and moved by their mother's words.
They put their palms together and knelt down before their mother.
Originally our mother was a saintess.
The three brothers knew that they were sons of the king.
It was not a long-term policy to live in the mountains,
Kingdom Menglanga was our hometown.

三兄弟希望母亲能请天神下凡尘，
他们想找天神改变处境走出大山。
三兄弟期盼心切，
母亲只好把神咒传授三兄弟。

The three brothers wanted their mother to invite the God father to descend to this mortal world.
They wanted to resort to the God father to walk out of the mountains.
The three brothers were so eager to change their situation.
Their mother had to teach the three brothers the sacred incantation.

三兄弟对神咒很熟悉，
因为他们出世前是神脉天根。
八万年前他们曾经念诵这些神咒，
母亲传授的神咒三兄弟一点就通。

The three brothers were very familiar with the sacred incantation,
As they were the holy veins and heavenly roots before they were born.
They once recited these sacred incantations 80,000 years ago.
With some advice from their mother, the three brothers quickly mastered these incantations.

三兄弟念诵神咒的声音似神箭传到天庭，
天神父亲扁玛法离开天庭下凡尘。
天神扁玛法对三兄弟说道：

The voice of the three brothers' recitation was passed on to the heavenly court as a divine arrow.
God father Bianmafa left the heavenly court for this world.

"你们三兄弟需要什么尽管开口，
我让你们如愿以偿。"

God Bianmafa said,
"You three brothers, please feel free to ask for help,
I'll have your wished fulfilled."

十头儿子虔诚跪拜，
他双手合十求天神父亲：
"请天神父亲传我本领，
让我落水如履平地，
让我下火海犹如树下乘凉，
不要让天灾人祸接近我身。
儿子就有这些要求，
请天神父亲传授我这些大本领。"

The ten-headed son knelt down piously,
And pleaded the father of God by putting his palms together,
"God father, please endow me with the capabilities of,
Landing on the surface of water like on the ground,
Jumping into the sea of fire like enjoying the cool under the tree,
Staying away from natural calamities and man-made misfortunes.
I just have these requests,
God father please endow me with these capabilities."

天神父亲回答十头儿子道：
"孩子你的愿望父亲都给你满足，
唯有三样不能让你去征服：
一是用两脚行走的人类，
二是在森林中度日的猴子，
三是开天辟地时留下的一把神弓。
神弓是阿銮①的武器，
它在等待主人的出现。
除了这三种本领不能传，
其他本领父亲都传给你。"

The God father replied,
"I'll help fulfill your wishes,
Except for the following three things that you are not allowed to conquer:
First, mankind that walks on two feet.
Second, monkeys that live in the forest.
Third, the magic bow passed down from the time when heaven was separated from earth.
The divine bow was the weapon of Aluan①.
It is waiting for its master.
I'll endow you with all capabilities except for the above three."

①阿銮：傣语音译，傣族传说阿銮是集智慧、勇敢、仁爱、善良、英俊、诚实于一身的英雄人物。后人将阿銮作为优秀男子的美称。

①Aluan is transliterated from Dai, which refers to a legendary intelligent, brave, kindness, handsome and honest hero. Aluan is regarded as the laudatory title for excellent men.

十头儿子对天神父亲所传都心领神会，
十八般武艺样样得到真传。
十头儿子既可以飞上天，
又能入地钻海底。
十头儿子顶礼膜拜天神父亲，
他心花怒放喜气洋洋。

The ten-headed son understood tacitly of what the God father taught,
Mastering various kinds of skills.
The ten-headed son could fly to the sky,
And dive to the bottom of the sea.
The ten-headed son worshipped the God father.
He was bursting with joy and happiness.

天神又来到二儿子贡帕甘腊面前，
他向二儿子问道：
“力大无穷的贡帕甘腊，
你的心愿是什么尽管与父亲明说。”

The God father came to the second son Gongpaganla,
And asked the second son,
“The super strong Gongpaganla,
Please tell me your wishes.”

“尊贵的天神父亲啊，
我们三兄弟在山里衣食住行不如人，
儿子只想美美地睡上一觉，
睡够了再说其他事情。”

“Distinguished God father,
We three brothers live in the mountains with poor clothing, food and shelter.
For me, I don’t want to talk about anything before I have a sound sleep.”

因为贡帕甘腊力大无比，
如他学到太多本领将对众生不利，
天神父亲就给他睡大觉，
让他美美地进入梦乡。

Since Gongpaganla was a man of extraordinary strength,
If he gained more skills, it would be unfavorable to all living creatures.
The God father made him sleep,
Allowing him to fall into a dream.

天神又来到三儿子毕披面前，
天神父亲对三儿子说道：
“仁慈智慧的小儿子毕披，
你有什么愿望尽管与我说。”

The God father came up to the third son Bipi,
And said,
“Merciful and intelligent son Bipi,
What wishes you want me to help you fulfill.”

毕披听到父亲的声音十分高兴，

Bipi was very glad to hear his father voice,

他虔诚跪拜在父亲面前： “神力无边的父亲啊， 儿子需要的是聪明和智慧， 就让我身心清净有智慧， 在人间行善奉献为众生。”	He knelt down before his father piously and said, “Almighty father, What I need are intelligence and wisdom. Please allow me to enjoy inner peace and tranquility as well as wisdom, To do good deeds and sacrifice on earth.”
天神向小儿子传授智慧， 小儿子毕披默默念诵天书记心间。 天神父亲将知识传授完毕， 眨眼工夫就消失得无影无踪。	The God father passed on the wisdom to the third son. The third son Bipi recited the divine scriptures quietly and kept them in mind. Soon after the God father passed on the knowledge, He disappeared completely.
三兄弟学到了真本领， 他们欲回王宫寻找外公。 十头哥哥达撒季利不愿回王宫， 他派三弟毕披先回王宫去。	The three brothers gained their real skills, And wanted to return to the palace for their grandfather. The ten-headed brother Dasajili didn’t want to return to the palace. He sent the youngest brother Bipi to return to the palace first.
三弟向母亲拜别， 母亲对三儿子说道： “儿子要向外公说出前因后果， 说清楚从前外公外婆无子女， 曾经虔诚供养雅细于大山中， 是上天赐给了他们一位公主。	The youngest brother bid farewell to his mother. His mother told him, “You need tell your grandfather about the antecedents and consequences, Telling them that they had no children before. But they once offered food to Yaxi in the mountains. It was the god that bestowed a princess to them.
后来公主长大外公欲让她继位。 公主拒绝继位后被赶出王宫。 从此公主居住在深山里，	Later the princess grew up and your grandfather wanted her to succeed to the throne. The princess was driven out of the palace after she refused

用清净心虔诚供养神明和雅细。
公主的虔诚感动了天神，
天神赐公主三个儿子。
三个儿子在大山里长大，
现在欲回到王宫中。”

the succession.
Since then, the princess had been living in the mountains,
Offering food to deities and Yaxi with pure mind and pious heart.
Moved by the princess's piousness,
The god bestowed three sons on the princess.
The three sons grew up in the mountains.
Now they want to return to the palace.”

三儿子毕披告别母亲忙赶路，
他来到勐兰嘎王国的皇城。
他将来意告诉给门卫，
门卫速速赶去王宫禀报国王。
国王闻讯很吃惊，
让门卫速速领毕披面见国王。

The third son Bipi bid farewell to his mother and hurried on with his journey.
He came to the imperial city of Menglanga Kingdom.
After he told the entrance guard of his intention,
The guard hurried to report to the king.
The king was surprised at the news.
He told the guard to lead Bipi to him quickly.

毕披看见国王外公忙跪拜，
他将母亲的话语告诉国王外公：
“尊贵的外公啊，
母亲在山里生下我们三兄弟，
大哥名叫达撒季利，
二哥名叫贡帕甘腊，
三弟是我名叫毕披，
我们都是您的外孙。”

Having met the king, Bipi busied himself kowtowing.
He told the king what his mother said,
“Distinguished grandfather,
Our mother gave births to our three brother.
The eldest brother is Dasajili,
And the second elder brother is Gongpaganla.
The third elder brother is me Bipi.
We are all your grandchildren.”

国王听得目瞪口呆。
他抱住毕披泪涟涟。
“我的孙子啊，
你们长年累月住在深山里，
你们靠野果山芋来充饥。

The king was dumbfounded by Bipi's words.
He hugged Bipi with tears in his eyes,
“My grandchildren,
You have lived in the mountains over the years,
Depending on the wild fruits and sweet potatoes to stay

你们母子风吹雨淋又饥寒交迫。
外公外婆欠你们实在太多。"

your hunger.
Your mother and three brothers suffered from poor shelter and food.
We your grandparents owed you a lot."

毕披亦伤心哭诉道：
"尊敬的外公外婆啊，
即使是富翁腰缠万贯，
出门在外还难免缺金少银。
想想我们母子过的日子，
我们从未见过半粒米，
因为我们住在深山老林中。"

Bipi also cried sadly,
"Distinguished grandparents,
Even if the rich,
They may suffer from lack of gold and silver,
When staying away from home.
Think of life we lived,
We have never seen any rice,
Since we are living in the mountains."

国王传下王命，
要派仪仗队伍迎接女儿和外孙回王宫。
队伍和彩车浩浩荡荡出门去，
战象和战马走在最前方。

The king decreed an order,
That a team of honor guard be sent to meet his daughter and grandchildren.
The team and float were marching with great strength and vigor,
With war-elephants and horses at the front.

不知走了多少日子，
队伍来到山脚下。
毕披让队伍在山脚下停下来，
他要先进山里报告十头兄长。

No one knew how many days had passed,
Before the team reached the foot of the mountain.
Bipi had the team stop at the foot of the mountain.
He would report to the ten-headed brother first.

十头兄长看见三弟忙问道：
"三弟回去见外公外婆是否如愿，
他们是否愿意把我们接回王宫中？"
"外公外婆很高兴，
外公已派队伍来接我们回王宫。"

The ten-headed brother asked the third brother,
"Have you seen our grandparents ?
Are they willing to bring us back to the palace ?"
"Our grandparents were very happy,
Grandfather has sent a team to bring us back to the palace."

三弟又把话来讲：	The third brother said,
“弟弟唯恐战象战马糟蹋果树，	“I made the team station at the foot of the mountain
山脚下场地宽阔队伍好驻扎，	for fear that the war-elephants and horses will destroy fruit trees,
我让队伍驻在山脚下，	
弟弟先回山中来报告哥哥。”	I came back to report to you first.”
“我就暂时不回王宫里，	“I will not go back to the palace.
我要出去寻找心仪的女人。	Instead, I will go and find my beloved woman.
母亲和两位弟弟随队伍先回王宫，	Our mother and you two brothers go back to the palace first,
你们先回王宫见外公外婆。”	To see our grandparents.”
母子三人向雅细跪拜道别，	The mother and two sons bade farewell to Yaxi by kowtowing.
母子三人坐上彩车回宫。	The three went to the palace by the float.
仪仗队伍来到城门外，	Tens of thousands of people were already waiting there,
成千上万的人们等待在那里迎接。	When the team of honour guard arrived outside the city gate.
母子三人进入王宫里，	After the mother and two sons entered the palace,
母亲控制不住热泪盈眶。	The mother couldn't help having her eyes run over with tears.
离别时的情境不堪回首，	It was unbearable to recall the parting,
因为冒雅公主也想念父母亲。	Because the Princess Maoya missed her father and mother too.
父母与女儿分离已有十余载，	It had been more than ten year since the parting.
如今重逢时外孙已长大成人。	The grandchildren had grown up when they met again.
父母抱着女儿痛哭悲喜交加，	The parents hugged their daughter and cried bitterly.
国王高兴得双眼泪涟涟：	The king wept tears of joy.
“本以为王国已无人继承王位，	“I thought no one would succeed to the throne.
谢天谢地外孙已经长大成人！”	Thank god the grandchildren have grown up.”
因为国王没有看见长外孙，	The king asked Bipi why the eldest grandson didn't come,

国王问毕披为何长外孙没有回来。
毕披回答说哥哥要去寻找心仪的人。
找到有缘合意的妻子就回王宫中。

As he didn't see the eldest grandson.
Bipi said his elder brother would look for his beloved.
He would return to the palace after he found a congenial wife.

国王听后一时很生气，
但细细想想长外孙的想法也在情理中。
因为寻找妻子是终身大事，
找到心仪的妻子才能成家立业。

Initially the king was very angry to hear that.
But after he thought it carefully, he found his eldest grandson's thought was reasonable.
Because finding a wife and getting married is a lifelong business,
Finding a desirable wife is prerequisite to establishment of a family and starting a career.

女儿和外孙们回到王宫里，
勐兰嘎举国上下家喻户晓。
人们为国王有了接班人而欢欣鼓舞，
国王和王后更是喜笑颜开。

The news that the daughter and grandchildren returned to the palace,
Was known to all the people of Menglanga.
People were elated at the kingdom's successor.
The king and queen smiled radiantly.

十头公子具有的大本领，
天神父亲早已传授他这些神通。
十头公子听说尚拎[①]王国有美丽的公主，
他来到尚拎王国中。

The ten-headed prince had great skills,
Which were taught by the God father.
After the ten-headed prince heard there was a beautiful princess in the Kingdom of Shanglin[①],
He came to the Kingdom of Shanglin for the princess.

国王把美丽的公主献给他，
让公主与十头公子配成双。
尚拎王国的国王还送他许多金银珠宝。
一百多位侍女服侍在他们身旁。

The king bestowed the beautiful princess on him,
Making the princess and the ten-head prince get married.
The king of the Kingdom of Shanglin also sent them a deal of gold, silver and jewelry.
More than 100 maidservants were tending beside them.

---

① 尚拎：传说是远在天边的一个神国。

①Shanglin: It is a legendary divine kingdom situated at the edge of heaven.

十头公子要离开尚拎王国。
他要带着公主回到勐兰嘎。
外公外婆知道长外孙要回宫非常高兴。
万人空巷出来迎接十头外孙。

The ten-headed prince wanted to leave the Kingdom of Shanglin.
He wanted to go back to Menglanga with the princess.
The grandparents were very delighted to know that their eldest grandson would come back to the palace.
The whole city turned out to meet the ten-headed grandson.

勐兰嘎国王挑选吉祥的日子，
为尚拎国公主重新起名叫丽穆莎。
国王为长外孙和公主举行婚礼，
又让十头外孙继承王位耀祖光宗。

The king of Menglanga chose an auspicious day,
And renamed the princess of Shanglin Kingdom as Limusha.
The king held the wedding ceremony for the eldest grandson and the princess,
And made the ten-headed grandson succeed the throne to bring honour to the ancestors.

腊嘎[①]国王也来为十头王献公主。
大鹏鸟王国亦不甘落后于别国。
一些小王国亦来献公主。
这是十头王前世修来的大福报。
勐兰嘎王国开始了十头王时代。
从此十头王名扬四方。

The king of Laga[①] came to sacrifice the princess to the Ten-headed King.
The Kingdom of Roc was unwilling to lag behind other kingdoms.
Some small kingdoms also came to sacrifice their princesses.
It was the blessing that the Ten-headed King cultivated through former generations.
It had ushered in the Era of the Ten-headed King.
Since then the Ten-head King had became famous throughout the land.

一年光阴不算久长，

One year was not long.

①腊嘎：傣语音译，传说蛇修行一千年但还未完全变成龙时，它的头上会长出红冠，人们称它为腊嘎。腊嘎与龙一样亦能呼风唤雨，变化多端。腊嘎也有自己的王国。

①Laga is transliterated from Dai. According to the legend, if a snake remains to be a snake instead of a dragon after one thousand years of cultivation, there will be red crown on its head. People call it Laga, which is as capable and versatile as a dragon, and it has its own kingdom.

丽穆莎公主在人间已经习惯。
丽穆莎公主生下了一个女儿，
王宫上下个个欢欣。
曾外祖父为小公主起名叫密哈纳，
密哈纳的美名传遍勐兰嘎四面八方。

The Princess Limusha had got used to the world,
And she gave birth to a daughter.
All people in the palace were very happy.
The princess was named Mihana by her great-grandfather.
The reputation of Mihana was widely spread to every corner of Menglanga.

话说尚拎国国王苏腊与大天神有心结未了，
这是前世积下的仇怨。
苏腊要率兵去与大天神混西迦开战，
苏腊国王希望女婿十头王来助战。
女婿十头王闻讯兴奋不已，
因为他有天神父亲传授的神功。

There was emotional entanglement between Sula, king of Shanglin Kingdom and the Hunxijia, the Supreme God.
It was hatred accumulated through previous generations.
King Sula wanted to lead troops to start a war against Hunxijia.
He wanted his son-in-law, the Ten-headed King to assist in fighting.
The son-in-law was so excited to hear the news,
Since he had the superb skills passed on by the God father.

苏腊国王与女婿有备而来，
他们率队伍升空与大天神开战。
战争的结果是大天神被打败，
苏腊和十头王凯旋。

The King Sula and his son-in-law were well prepared,
They led the troops to ascend to fight against Hunxijia.
The result of the war was the defeat of Hunxijia,
Sula and the Ten-headed King returned in triumph.

十头王不久又得到神明的恩赐，
丽穆莎公主生下一位王子。
王子身相十分庄严，
宛如天神下凡一般。

Before long the Ten-headed King was bestowed by god,
The Princess Limusha gave birth to a prince.
The prince looked very solemn,
As if he were a deity descending from heaven.

丽穆莎公主每次生产的时候，
天空就会电闪雷鸣。
四面八方隆隆巨响，
人们都知道这个日子不寻常。

Every time when Princess Limusha delivered,
There was thunder and lightning in the sky.
When rumbles happened in all directions,
People knew it would be an unusual day.

勐兰嘎老国王说这是王国大福报，
他给王子起名为英大腊吉达。
曾外祖父和曾外祖母十分欣慰，
冒雅奶奶亦很开心。
从此勐兰嘎王国越来越强大，
王国名声传遍所有天下人。

The old king of Menglanga said it was a blessing for the kingdom.
The prince was named Yingdalajida Lajida by the old king.
The great-grandparents felt very gratified,
The grandmother Maoya was also very pleased.
Since then, the Kingdom of Menglanga was getting stronger and stronger,
Making its name known to everyone under heaven.

勐兰嘎王国的王宫雄伟壮丽，
天堂一般的宫殿金光闪闪。
宫内珠宝玉器琳琅满目，
就像天宫而非人世间。

The palace of Menglanga Kingdom was magnificent,
Glittering as if it were in the heaven.
The palace was full of jewelry and jade articles,
As if it were in the heaven instead of on earth.

宽阔的护城河有七条，
犹如七层铁壁铜墙护着王宫。
护城河的河床用宝石镶嵌，
夜晚在月光下会闪闪发蓝光。

There were seven broad moats around the city,
As if seven-tiers of iron walls guarding the palace.
The riverbeds of the moats were inlaid with gems,
Which shone with blue light in the moonlight at night.

王城四方有七个莲花湖，
无数鱼群在湖中游乐。
这不是天然湖泊，
莲花湖完全是靠人工挖成。

There were seven lotus lakes in the four directions of the imperial city,
Numerous fish swam in the lakes freely.
These lakes were not natural lakes,
They were dug out by manual.

王城周围是宜人的景色，
四方种有宝树和檀香木。
这些宝树非地上物种，
树种来自遥远的神邦。
宝树上有金银珠宝做点缀，

The imperial city was surrounded by pleasant scenery,
Precious trees and sandalwood were planted in the four directions of the imperial city.
These precious trees were not the species on the land,
These species of the trees were from the remote divine

不分昼夜闪闪发光。	kingdom. Decorated with gold, silver, jewelry, The precious trees shone all day and night.
每当月亮最圆的时候， 天上的众仙女就会下凡光临王城。 守天柱山的四位天神， 亦来守护王城的东南西北四道城门。	Every time when the moon was fullest, The fairies of Heaven would come down to earth to visit the imperial city. The four gods guarding the Heavenly Pillar Mountain, Would also come to guard the east, south, west and north gates of the imperial city.
勐兰嘎王城庄严华丽若天界， 天神也时常下凡在人群里同乐。 成群的金翅鸟从天而降， 它们在人群中起舞翩跹。 整个王城昼夜人山人海， 乐声歌声传遍王城四方， 热闹场面犹如一窝发旺的大土蜂。	The imperial city of Menglanga was solemn and magnificent as Heaven, The gods often descended to the world to enjoy the good time together. Flocks of garudas descended from Heaven, Dancing among people. The whole imperial city was full of people day and night, The voice of music and songs spread to every corner of the city, The bustling scene was like a swarm of annoyed bumblebees.
十头王的功德如此巨大， 大象和犀牛也来投奔。 飞禽走兽从森林倾巢出动， 纷纷奔来向十头王庆贺。	The Ten-headed King had such great merits and virtues, That elephants and rhinoceros also came to him for shelter. Birds and animals turned out from the forest, To rush to convey congratulations to the Ten-headed King.
十头王开始忘乎所以， 各种已发霉的水果吃下肚， 有毒的野花戴头顶。 王国的规矩早已丢脑后，	The Ten-headed King started to get himself, He ate various moldy fruits, With poisonous wild flowers on head. He already forgot the rules of the kingdom,

雅细传授的五戒[①]早已成耳边风。
十头王像一个疯子，
十头王昼夜癫狂。
十头王走进深山野林中，
飞禽走兽看见他就四处逃散。

十头王来到森林里，
森林中的野果被他糟蹋。
森林中的野果是雅细们的食粮，
雅细们在山里已经无法居住下去，
雅细们只好逃到阿罗替雅王国，
来到异国的深山老林里修行。

十头王在王宫里昏庸无道，
他在王宫里如醉汉一般。
他已将所有规矩抛之脑后，
他忘记了做国王的十条原则[②]。

他把眼光投向国内所有美女，
只要是被他看见就受糟蹋。
即使是有夫的妇女，
他狂言美女住在他的地盘就要归他。

And the five precepts[①] taught by Yaxi.
The Ten-headed King was like an insane,
All day and night.
When the Ten-headed King walked into the forest in the mountains,
Fowls and beasts fled in all directions at the sight of him.

When the Ten-headed King walked into the forests,
The wild fruits in the forests were ruined by him.
The wild fruits in the forests were food for Yaxi,
Who were unable to live in the mountains.
They had to flee to the thickly forested mountains,
In the Kingdom of Aluotiya for cultivation.

The Ten–headed King was fatuous and tyrannous in the palaces,
Spending his life like a drunkard.
He already forgot all the rules and proprieties,
He also forgot the ten precepts[②] for being a king.

He focused on the domestic beautiful women,
The beauties would be occupied by him as long as he saw them.
He bragged that beauties living in his territory belonged to him.

---

①五戒：即不杀生、不偷盗、不邪淫、不妄语、不饮酒。

②傣族阿銮叙事长诗里认为，当国王要坚持十条原则：一是要布施，二是要行持五戒，三是要一心为公，四是要公正，五是要怀慈悲心，六是要率先垂范，七是要不存嗔恨心，八是要不打压异己，九是要能忍让，十是要服务人民。

①Five precepts: namely, no killing, no stealing, no adultery, no lying, no drinking.

②In Aluan Epic of the Dai ethnic group, a king must adhere to the following ten precepts, namely, first is donation, second is practice of Five Precepts, third is devotion to the public interests, fourth is justice, fifth is compassion, sixth is setting examples, seventh is no hatred, eighth is no suppressing the alien, ninth is forbearance, tenth is serving the people.

每当十五月亮最圆时， 他就坐上神奇的飞行器飞行在天空。 他在白云端俯瞰大地， 许多美女就这样落入他的魔爪中。	Every time when the moon was fullest on the fifteenth day of the lunar calendar, He flew to the sky by his magic craft. He overlooked the land from the clouds, Many beauties turned into his prey this way.
话说有一尊天神名叫甘塔腊， 他的女儿是莲花公主。 莲花公主向诸神祈祷发誓： “若是有缘遇到持戒清净者， 甘愿做他的妻子守护一生。 如是无缘遇到持戒清净者， 甘愿孤身一人隐居修行在深山中。”	There was a God called Gantala, His daughter was the Princess Lotus. The Princess Lotus prayed to gods and swore, “If I'm lucky enough to meet someone who observes commandment, I am willing to be his wife to take care of him. But if not, I'd like to live in seclusion alone for cultivation in the mountains.”
莲花公主走在深山老林里， 恰遇十头王在空中游荡。 十头王发现一美女在森林中， 他落地抱住莲花公主就向空中飞去。	As the Princess Lotus was walking in the forest in the mountains, She saw the Ten-headed King wandering about in the sky. The Ten-headed King found a beauty in the forest, He descended to the ground to catch the Princess Lotus and flew to the sky.
莲花公主挣脱十头王的双手， 独自飞向另一边。 十头王亦紧跟莲花公主飞奔而去， 得不到莲花公主誓不罢休。	The Princess Lotus shook off the Ten-headed King's hands, And flew to another side alone. The Ten-headed King closely followed the Princess Lotus, He would never give up until he got the Princess Lotus.
莲花公主对十头王说道：	The Princess Lotus spoke the Ten-headed King,

"我是持戒的修行女，
请你别跟在我后边。
为了修行我才离开父母，
独自一人来到森林中。"

"I am the girl who observes the commandments,
Please don't follow me.
I left my parents for cultivation,
And came to the forest alone."

虽然莲花公主如此拒绝，
十头王仍然不放过她。
莲花公主默默在心中祈祷：
"请诸神替我记下誓言，
若是十头王对我行为不轨，
就让他犹如果熟落地自我毁灭，
从此以后生生世世，
十头王要在地狱受罪欲出无期。

Though the Princess Lotus rejected him like this,
The Ten-headed King was not willing to let her go.
The Princess Lotus prayed silently in her heart,
"Gods, please memorize what I swear today,
If the Ten-headed King bullies me,
Let him ruin by himself as the ripe fruits fall down on the ground,
Henceforth, generation after generation,
The Ten-headed King will suffer in the hell forever.

"若是天神听到我的誓言，
烈火立即呈现在我面前。
我将跳进烈火堆里，
以证明我是清净无染的修行身。
请诸神助力于我，
让我来践行我的诺言。"

"If gods hear my swear,
Let a fire appear in front of me.
I will jump into the fire,
To testify my purity of cultivation.
Gods please help me,
With the implementation of my promise."

突然旁边出现一堆熊熊烈火，
莲花公主缓缓走进烈火中。
十头王看见此情此景吃惊不小，
他认为公主还会从火堆中走出来。

Suddenly there appeared a blazing fire beside her,
The Princess Lotus walked slowing into the fire.
The Ten-headed King was surprised to see this,
Thinking that the princess would come out of the fire.

十头王让几个魔鬼日夜守候在火堆面前，
交代说如她变成男子出来就立即打死，
火堆中走出来的若是女子，
就速速抓她送到王宫中。

The Ten-headed King ordered several devils to guard the bonfire day and night,
Telling that if she turned into a man and walked out of the fire, beat him death,

If a woman walked out of the fire,
Seize her and send her to the palace as quickly as possible.

十头王交代完毕就返回王宫里，
他又醉生梦死于美女群中。
十头王在王宫里昼夜荒淫无度，
他的恶行已经天怒人怨。

The Ten-headed King returned to the palace after he told this.
He led a befuddled life again with beauties.
The Ten-headed King indulged himself in sensual pleasures day and night,
The gods were annoyed and people were resentful at his bad conduct.

这是流传久远的故事，
神奇的故事才刚刚开篇。
父老乡亲们啊请别走开，
往后的情节更精彩。
我们的长诗告一段落，
精彩的情节还在下一章中。

This was a story told for years,
The magic story has just begun.
Please do not walk away my fellow countrymen,
The following plots will be more wonderful.
This is the end of the first chapter of the epic,
Splendid plots are included in the next chapter.

第二章
Chapter Two

话说大海边有数座大山，
一群猴子居住在大山中。
山中的猴子无法计数，
几座大山都是他们的乐园。

There were several mountains by the sea,
A group of monkeys were living in the mountains.
The mountains were paradise to the countless monkeys.

猴王的名字叫巴力莫，
他英勇无比力量不平凡。
他的妻子是达纳公主，
协助猴王管理着猴国大森林。

The Monkey King's name was Balimo,
Who was brave and powerful.
His wife was Princess Dana,
Who assisted the Monkey King with the management of the forest in the Kingdom of Monkey.

猴王巴力莫变化多端神通广大，
他可以变身高达五个眼程[①]，
他可以眨眼工夫飞到五十个眼程的地方。
巴力莫变化的功夫人们无法想象，
他的其他本领更是无人知晓。

The Monkey King Balimo was infinitely resourceful,
He could turn into someone with the height of 5 eye-reaches[①],
He could fly to a place with 50 eye-reaches in a blink of an eye.
His capability of change was beyond people's imagination,
No one knew his other skills.

有一天猴王巴力莫来到大海边，
他要去祭拜太阳神。
祭拜太阳神是猴国的传统，
也不知道传承了多少年。

One day, the Monkey King Balimo came to the sea,
To sacrifice to the God of Sun,
Which was one of the traditions for the Kingdom of Monkey.
No one knew for how many years it had been handed down.

这一天十头王也要去森林里游逛，
他骑着飞行器飞行在空中，

The Ten-headed King wanted to wander in the forest on that day.

①眼程：长度单位。一个眼程即一眼所能看到的距离。

①Eye-reach refers to a length unit. One eye-reach is the distance that one can see.

正好从猴王巴力莫头顶上飞过。
巴力莫容不得别人比自己强，
此事让猴王心里很不悦：
“十头王胆敢从我头上飞过，
你如此癫狂真是太不把猴国放在眼中。
你以为你是天下的老大啊，
今天我要让你开开眼界。”

He was riding his craft in the sky,
Just flying overhead of Monkey King Balimo.
It was unbearable for Balimo to have someone stronger than him.
The Monkey King said angrily,
"The Ten-headed King is so bold as to fly overhead.
You are so defiant and the Kingdom of Monkey is nothing in your eyes.
You think you are the dominator of the world.
I'm going to make you know who I am."

猴王往空中一跃就赶上了十头王，
猴王用双手抱住十头王的头，
又用尾巴缠绕十头王的脖子七圈，
猴王拉着十头王在大海上空快速转圈圈。
十头王头晕目眩呕吐不止，
十头王几乎要断气命归黄泉。

The Monkey King caught up with the Ten-headed King in one leap,
And hugged the Ten-headed King head with his hands.
The Monkey King also twined his tail around the Ten-headed King's neck for seven laps,
And dragged the Ten-headed King for circling over the sea.
The Ten-headed King felt dizzy and kept vomiting,
And almost died from it.

十头王突然想起当年天神的教诲，
猴类、人类和一把神弓自己无法征服，
今天差一点死在猴王手下，
十头王快快抱拳施礼低头认错：

Suddenly the Ten-headed King remembered what the God taught him.
Monkeys, mankind and a magic bow were the things that he could not conquer.
He almost lost his life today.
The Ten-headed King made a boxing ceremony quickly and lowered his head to apologize,

“本领高强的猴王啊，
你的本领真是不一般。

"The mighty Monkey King,
You have extraordinary skills.

我本是有天神赐予了神通，
天上和地下任我独来独往。
就是大鹏鸟神国和腊嘎王国我也不怕，
谁见我都要俯首称臣。

I was endowed with supernatural power,
And I can fly to the sky and go through the ground freely.
I am not even afraid of Kingdom of Roc and Kingdom of Laga.
Anyone who sees me should bow his head in submission.

“我十头王不论飞到哪里，
都有人献金银供美女。
今天遇见你神通广大，
请求你饶恕我的罪过。
我俩就交个朋友吧，
我俩的名声一定传遍远方。
一切灾祸一定离我俩而去，
看见我俩的人都会五体投地称臣。”

“Wherever I the Ten-headed King fly,
There are people sacrificing gold, silver and beauties to me.
Today I found you infinitely resourceful,
Please forgive my sins.
Let's make friends,
Our reputation will certainly spread far and widely.
All disasters will stay away from us.
Those who see us will prostrate themselves before us in admiration and be loyal to us.”

猴王巴力莫回答十头王道：
“自从天神赐予你神通，
你在天地间实在太狂妄。
猴类、人类和开天辟地神弓你征服不了，
你却不把天神的话放在心中。
凭你今天犯下的罪过，
我就可以将你碎尸万段。
你回去反省自己，
待你有了醒悟我才与你做朋友。”

The Monkey King Balimo replied,
“Ever since the God endowed you with magic power,
You have been extremely conceited in heaven and on earth.
Monkeys, mankind and the magic bow are the things that you can not conquer.
But you just ignored what the God said.
For the sins you committed today,
I will tear you to shreds.
Go back and introspect yourself.
I won't be your friend until you come to realize the error.”

猴王教训了十头王，
十头王红着脸怏怏离去。
眨眼的工夫十头王消失在云层里，
十头王回到了王宫中。

The Monkey King taught the Ten-headed King a lesson.
The Ten-headed King blushed and left sullenly.
In a moment, the Ten-headed King disappeared in the clouds.

The Ten-headed King returned to the palace.

本章讲了海边的猴国，
唱述猴王教训十头王的故事。
阿銮故事结构相似，
但内容各不相同。
父老乡亲们啊，
我们要听故事的核心点，
就是光明与黑暗的斗争，
亦是善与恶的。
我们的长诗告一段落，
后面的情节更精彩。

This chapter tells about the Kingdom of Monkeys by the sea,
Describing how the Monkey King taught the Ten-headed
King a lesson.
With similar structure of Aluan stories,
They are different in content.
My fellow countrymen,
The core part of the tale,
Is the struggle between brightness and darkness,
As well as a battle between the kind and the evil.
This chapter has come to an end,
The following chapter will be more wonderful.

第三章
Chapter Three

话说这里是阿罗替雅王国，
国家富强版图广大。
百余个附属国岁岁献金银珠宝，
王国的声名传遍四面八方。

There was Kingdom Aluotiya.
It was prosperous with vast territory.
More than one hundred dependent states contributed gold, silver and jewelry every year.
The kingdom's reputation has been spread to all directions.

国王的名字叫达撒腊塔，
他当国王已不知多少年。
国王乐善好施爱民如子，
全国上下无不拥护爱戴。
国王智慧又聪明，
人们赞扬他是会治理江山的明君。

The king's name was Dasalata,
He had been king for so many years.
The king was always ready to help others and loved the subjects as if they were his own children.
People throughout the kingdom loved and supported him,
Praising him as a wise king who was good at governance of the kingdom for his wisdom and intelligence.

国王拥有三位王后，
大王后名叫万纳公主，
她心善貌美是某一国王的宝贝心肝。
二王后是苏迪塔国王的女儿，
她的名字叫苏米达纳，
她心地善良貌若天仙。
三王后是果嘎律国王的女儿，
她的名字叫吉西公主，
她待人宽厚身材婀娜多姿。

The king had three queens.
The first queen was called Princess Wanna,
Who was kind and beautiful and the sweetheart to a king.
The second queen was the daughter of King Sudita.
Her name was Sumidana,
Who was kindhearted and fairy in appearance.
The third queen was the daughter of King Guogalü.
Her name was Princess Jixi.
She was generous and graceful in figure.

王城中央是富丽堂皇的宫殿，
国王与三位王后在王宫里亲密无间。
王宫里有侍女一千六百人，
她们人人貌美赛天仙。
只惋惜国王有一个不尽人意的心病，
国王没有可以继位的儿女。

In the middle of the imperial city, stood the magnificent palace.
The king and the three queens were on very intimate terms with each other in the palace.
There were 1,600 maidservants in the palace,
With each of them as beautiful as fairy maiden.

The only secret trouble to the king was,
He had no offspring to succeed.

国王拥有神速的飞行器，
国王上天游览很方便。
国王常到四面八方游玩，
人间各地他都已经游遍。

With the swift craft,
It was convenient for the king to tour in the heaven.
The king often went everywhere to play,
He had visited all the places under heaven.

有一天混西迦与尚拎王国又再次开战，
消息不胫而走传到了人世间。
达撒腊塔国王与大天神是好朋友，
大天神请国王速速去助战。

One day, the war between Hunxijia and Shanglin Kingdom broke out,
The news spread quickly like wildfire to the human world.
King Dasalata and the Supreme God were good friends,
The Supreme God asked the king to assist in haste in fighting.

国王速速飞到天宫里，
协助大天神攻打尚拎王国敌军。
尚拎王国的军队被打败，
大天神酬谢达撒腊塔神箭神弓。

The king flew to heaven in hurry,
Assisting the Supreme God in fighting the enemy troops of Shanglin Kingdom.
The enemy troops of Shanglin Kingdom were defeated,
As a reward, the Supreme God gave Dasalata the magic bow.

战争虽然已经胜利结束，
但国王还是身受箭伤回到王宫中。
达撒腊塔养伤于三王后宫里，
得到吉西王后日夜精心照料。
国王箭伤很快痊愈，
国王欲重赏吉西王后表达感激之情。

Though the emperor won the war,
He returned to the palace with archery wound.
Dasalata was healing his wounds in the palace of the third queen,
With the intensive care by Queen Jixi day and night.
The king soon recovered from the archery wound,
He wanted to give Queen Jixi a large reward to convey his gratitude.

吉西恭敬有礼地说：
"尊敬的国王啊，
金银首饰妹妹柜里有，
妹妹不需要大王任何的奖赏，
唯愿大王将妹妹记在心中。
今后如有妹妹需要大王帮助时，
妹妹一定请求大王帮忙。"

Jixi replied politely,
"Distinguished king,
There are gold, silver and jewelry in my cupboard,
I don't want any of your reward,
Except for keeping me in mind.
In future, I will ask you king for help,
If I need your help."

"本王一定将你的话记在心里，
本王一定说话算数，
今后妹妹需要帮助时，
妹妹随时可以告诉本王。"

"I will keep your words in mind,
And I will also keep my words,
In future, feel free to tell me at any time,
If you need my help."

国王要去测试天神赠送的神弓，
国王让大臣准备车辆。
国王要进森林里去围猎，
大臣苏曼达将国王送到森林中。
森林里居住着雅细师徒，
他俩修行在大山中。
由于老雅细有眼疾行动不方便，
由徒弟小雅细在洞府里照料他。

The king was going to test the magic bow given by the God,
He asked ministers to prepare the carriage.
The king was going to encircle and hunt in the forest,
Minister Sumanda sent the king into the forest.
In the forest, lived Yaxi, the master and his student,
Who were cultivating in the mountains.
Since the senior Yaxi suffered from eye disease and he had difficulty in walking,
The younger student Yaxi took care of him in the cave.

小雅细天天用罐子去河里打水，
有时候会到河边的沙滩玩。
这一天他到河里去洗澡，
然后又到沙滩上玩乐。

The young Yaxi went to the river to fetch water with pots every day,
Sometimes he would play on the sand beach of the river.
One day, he went swimming in the river,
And then played on the sand beach.

国王听见有响动声，

Hearing the noise,

他以为是野兽在河边戏水，
国王在树丛里射箭，
神箭不偏不倚射中了小雅细。

The king thought that beasts were playing beside the river bank,
He discharged an arrow from the woods.
The magic arrow hit the young Yaxi without deviation.

小雅细大声哭叫：
"我是修行的小雅细，
我从来不招惹任何人，
是谁在向我射箭？
我死了不足惜，
只是担心我年迈的雅细师父，
从今往后没有人服侍他。

The young Yaxi cried in loud voice,
"I am the Yaxi who is cultivating,
And I've never offended anyone.
Who is shooting arrow towards me ?
My death is not to be regretted,
I'm worried about my elderly master Yaxi,
From now on, he has no one to take care of him.

"人们都说杀大象是为了取象牙，
杀老虎是为了取虎皮，
但我身卑体贱，
杀死我没有什么用处。

"People say killing of an elephant is for ivory,
Killing of a tiger is for the tiger skin.
I'm such a humble person,
It's useless to kill me.

"我死了靠谁送水给师父？
我死了靠谁摘野果给他吃？
我死了靠谁给师父洗衣服？
这分明是一箭射死二个人。

"Who will fetch water for him if I'm dead ?
Who will pick wild fruits for him if I'm dead ?
Who will wash his clothes for him if I'm dead ?
It makes no difference to kill two people with an arrow.

"我恩重如山的师父啊，
那空土罐还等我用它来打水，
那山里的野果还等我去采摘，
那些旧衣服还等我去洗，
可是今天我要走了，
不知是谁要把我射死在沙滩。"

"My benefactor master,
The empty clay pot is still awaiting me for water,
The wild fruits are there for me to pick,
And the old clothes are there for me to wash.
But I have to leave today,
I don't know who is going to shoot me to death on the sand beach."

国王听到有人在哭喊，
他向河边赶过去。
国王看见一个小雅细挣扎在沙滩上，
一阵阵的不安涌上心头。

Hearing someone crying,
The king rushed to the riverside.
He saw a young Yaxi struggling on the sand beach.
Waves of uneasiness welled up in his mind.

国王不知所措地向小雅细说：
“小雅细师父啊，
我是阿罗替雅国国王。
是天神送我一套弓和箭，
我才来测试弓箭于大山中。
是我把你看成野兽来喝水，
我才急忙开了弓。
万万没想到神箭射中了修行的雅细，
灾难怎么会这样降临在深山中！”

Out of his wits, the king said to the young Yaxi,
“Young Yaxi master,
I'm the king of Aluotiya Kingdom.
It was the God who sent me a set of bow and arrows,
I came to test the bow and arrows in the mountains.
It is me that view you as a beast coming to drink water,
That's why I discharged an arrow in haste.
It has never occurred to me that the magic arrow hit the cultivating Yaxi,
How can a disaster befall like this in the mountains !”

小雅细回答国王道：
“我是雅细的徒弟，
我们师徒修行在大山中。
我死了不足惜，
但从此以后没人来服侍我师父。”

The young Yaxi replied,
“I'm the student of Yaxi,
My master and I are cultivating in the mountains.
My death is not to be regretted,
But since then my master has no one to take care of him.”

“你的师父由我替你来服侍，
我可以将照顾事务安排给宫里人。
我也可以将师父接到王宫去养老，
让师父在宫里颐养天年。”

“I will take care of your master for you,
I will arrange people in the palace to take care of him.
Also I can take your master to the palace,
To enjoy the happy life in the palace.”

小雅细向国王说：
“请国王快快将我送回山里，
让我去看一眼我的师父。”
国王抱着小雅细向洞府走去，

The young Yaxi said to the king,
“Please send me to the mountain fast,
To allow me to have a look at my master.”
The king carried the young Yaxi and headed for the cave,

国王将小雅细安放在洞府中。

The king placed The young Yaxi in the cave.

国王去拜见老雅细：
“修行在大山中的尊者啊，
在下是阿罗替雅国国王。
不久前大天神送我神弓神箭，
今天我来山里练箭试弓，
我把师父的徒弟错看成猎物，
不幸将他射倒在沙滩上。”

The king went to visit the senior Yaxi,
“Respected Yaxi who cultivate in the mountains,
I'm the king of Aluotiya Kingdom.
Not long ago, the God sent me a set of magic bow and arrows,
Today I came to test the bow in the mountains,
I mistook your student for the prey,
And shoot him down on the sand beach.”

“我可怜的徒弟啊，
灾祸怎么来得如此突然！”
老雅细伤心地流下眼泪。
国王跪在雅细面前忏悔道：
“从今以后由我来供养师父，
我亦与师父修行在大深山。”

“My poor student,
How can the disaster befall so suddenly !”
The senior Yaxi shed tears sadly.
The king knelt down before the senior Yaxi and prayed,
“From now on, I'll provide food to the master,
And I will cultivate myself with the master in the mountains.”

国王又继续说：
“我可以将师父接到王宫里，
让师父在宫里安享晚年。
我也可以派心腹来服侍师父，
让师父修行在深山老林中。”
尊者雅细摆手拒绝，
此时他只想去看自己的徒弟：
“你领我去见徒弟吧，
这孩子真可怜。”

The king continued saying,
“I can take you to the palace,
And have you enjoy the old age.
I can also send a trusted subordinate to attend on you,
To let you cultivate in the mountains.”
The respected Yaxi turned him down by waving hand.
He just wanted to see his student,
“Take me to see my student,
What a poor child.”

国王领老雅细去看小雅细，
小雅细向师父说：

The king led the senior Yaxi to the young Yaxi,
The young Yaxi said to his master,

"我尊敬的师父啊，
徒弟要先走一步了！
莫怪徒弟不孝，
因为我在人世间的食物已用完。"
小雅细说完就断了气，
老雅细不像凡人哭嚎泪涟涟。

"Respected master,
I have to leave first !
Don't blame me for impiety,
Because I have used up the food in the human world."
The young Yaxi died soon after he finished his words,
Unlike the mortal, the senior Yaxi wept with tears in his eyes.

老雅细对国王说道：
"万人之上的国王啊，
你将来也会和我一样悲伤，
你的悲伤也是为了孩子，
只是我俩的现实我在先。"

The senior Yaxi said to the king,
"His Royal Majesty,
You will be sad like me in future.
You will grieve for your children.
The only difference is my grief is ahead of yours."

国王向老雅细愧疚地说：
"尊者啊，
在下现在无儿无女，
不知道今生有何业障，
至今尚无王位继承人。"

The king said to the senior Yaxi,
"The venerable,
I have no offspring,
I don't know what karma I have in this life,
Which causes the situation that I have no successor to the throne so far."

老雅细开示国王道：
"大王若是想要得到子女，
就去求一位雅细吧！
他住在遥远的天边，
从此到彼地有几十个眼程的距离。
他长发绕头十几圈，
他是一位得道的雅细。"
老雅细说完亦断了气，
两位修行者就这样离开了人世间。

The senior Yaxi said to the king,
"If you want to have offspring,
Go and pray to a Yaxi,
Who lives in the remote horizon,
The distance from here to that place is dozens of eye-reaches.
His long hair coils around his head for over ten circles,
He is a Yaxi who attains the highest state of spiritual enlightenment."
The senior Yaxi died as he finished his words,
The two Yaxi left this human world this way.

大臣苏曼达来到山里寻找国王，
看见国王后他知道了发生的这一切。
国王和苏曼达找来干柴火，
将两位修行者荼毗①于大山中。
国王和苏曼达恭敬跪拜三次，
国王和苏曼达回到彩车旁。

The minister Sumanda came to the maintains to look for the king,
After he met the king, he knew what was going on.
The king and Sumanda found some dry firewood,
They cremated the two Yaxi in the mountains (It's called Tupi① in Pali).
The king and Sumanda kowtowed respectfully for three times,
And then they returned to the float.

国王对苏曼达说道：
“雅细开示说我亦将为子女而死去，
但我现在没有一儿一女。
雅细让我去求另一位雅细，
他就住在遥远的天边。”

The king said to Sumanda,
"The Yaxi told me that I would die for my offspring,
But I don't have a son or a daughter.
The Yaxi asked me to pray to a Yaxi,
Who was living in the remote horizon."

“能够得到求子嗣的消息，
哪怕有十个二十个眼程的距离也无妨。
有儿有女是大王和王国的大事，
我们现在就出发！”

"As long as we can get the news of praying for children,
10 eye-reaches or 20 eye-reaches will never discourage us.
It's a great event for the king and the kingdom to have sons and daughters,
Let's set out now !"

国王与苏曼达抵达雅细住处，
国王用鲜花水果供养雅细：
“修行得道的尊者啊，
在下是阿罗替雅国国王。
只因神国开战，
大天神赐我一套神弓神箭。

The king and Sumanda arrived at the dwelling of the Yaxi,
The king provided flowers and fruits to the Yaxi and said,
"Respected Yaxi,
I'm the king of Aluotiya Kingdom.
Due to the war,

①荼毗：巴利语音译，佛教僧人死后，将尸体火葬叫荼毗。

①Tupi means the cremation of the body after a Buddhist monk dies.

孤王去山里练箭试弓，
不料误将雅细的徒弟射死在河边。
后来老雅细亦死去，
孤王与大臣将他们荼毗于大山中。

The Supreme God gave me a set of magic bow and arrows.
I went to the mountains to test the magic bow,
Only to find that I shot Yaxi's student to death at the riverside by mistake.
Afterwards, the senior Yaxi also died,
I and the minister cremated them in the mountains.

“孤王与雅细在交谈中得到开示，
本王未来亦将为子女而死亡。
孤王虽为国王至今无子女，
请尊者予以开示。
老雅细说让在下来求教尊者，
请让孤王不虚此行。”

“I got enlightened during my conversation with the Yaxi,
I will die for my offspring.
Though I'm the king, I have to offspring,
The respected, please enlighten me.
The senior Yaxi asked me to pray to you,
Then my trip will be worthwhile.”

雅细盘腿入座，
他用天眼观察到了国王的未来：
国王将有四个儿子，
长子将来威震四方。
雅细观察到长子还与十头王有纠纷，
他们将打打斗斗没个休停，
胜利与失败都会发生，
最终长子会获得无上荣光。

The Yaxi sat cross-legged,
And observed the future of the king through the Divine Eye.
The king was going to have four sons,
The eldest son would be famous in future.
The Yaxi also observed the disputes between the eldest son and the Ten-headed King,
There would be endless fighting between the two,
With victory and failure.
Eventually, the eldest son would win the supreme glory.

雅细把观察到的结果告诉了国王，
随手又拿两个芭蕉递给国王。
国王高兴得心花怒放，
他虔诚跪拜雅细。
国王双手合十拜别了雅细，
与苏曼达返回到王宫中。

The Yaxi told the king what he had observed,
And passed two bananas to the king.
The king was extremely delighted,
He kowtowed to the Yaxi piously.
Having bid farewell to the Yaxi by putting his palms together,
The king and Sumanda returned to the palace.

两个芭蕉三个王后，
国王知道不好分配。
国王欲把芭蕉分给大王后和三王后，
但二王后那里就会落空。
国王将分配难题交给了苏曼达，
希望他把好主意告诉国王。

There were two bananas and three queens,
The king knew it was difficult to divide.
The king wanted to give the bananas to the first queen and third queen,
But the second queen had nothing.
The king left the difficult problem of division to Sumanda,
Hoping he could come up with a good idea.

“万人之上的大王啊，
您是我们的绿色保护伞。
微臣认为要给大王后一个芭蕉，
三王后和二王后分吃另一个芭蕉，
这样既合理又公平。”

“Your Majesty,
You are our green protective umbrella.
I think we should give a banana to the first queen,
The third and second queens share the other banana,
It’s reasonable and fair.”

国王欣喜地夸苏曼达道：
“苏曼达你有智慧，
这样就既不伤莲花又不让水浑，
既不打死蛇也救了蛇嘴里的青蛙。”

The king praised Sumanda with joy,
“Sumanda, you are really intelligent.
This way, it’s neither damaging the lotus nor muddying the water.
The frog in the mouth of the snake will be saved without killing the snake.”

国王回到王宫里，
国王内心里还是在犯愁。
因为三王后对自己很好，
不给三王后一个芭蕉不顺心。

The king returned to the palace,
The king was still worried.
Because the third queen was very nice to him,
The king felt uncomfortable without giving a banana to the third queen.

国王换了正装坐在宝座上，
他让侍从把大王后和三王后叫进宫里，
国王将一个芭蕉送给大王后，

The king put on the imperial robe and got seated on the throne,
He asked his attendants to call in the first and third

又将另一个芭蕉送给三王后。

queens.
The king gave a banana to the first queen,
And the other to the third queen.

大王后和三王后拿到芭蕉，
她们向国王诚心拜谢。
她们告别国王退出宫廷，
大王后和三王后激动又犯愁。

Getting the bananas,
The first and third queens thanked the king sincerely.
They bid farewell to the king and withdrew from the court,
The first and third queens were excited and anxious.

在路上大王后对三王后说道：
“芭蕉只给我俩不给二王后，
于情于理都说不通。
我们三姊妹是平起平坐的啊，
两个芭蕉应该共同分享。
我俩一人分一截芭蕉给二王后，
两个芭蕉三人吃。”

On the way, the first queen said to the third queen,
"The two bananas were divided among you and me except for the second queen,
It's unreasonable.
We three sisters are equal,
The two bananas should be shared.
Each of us divides a section of the bananas to the second queen,
This way, the two bananas are shared by three people."

两个芭蕉三个王后共分享，
成群侍女在旁做见证。
两个芭蕉实为圣物，
预示三个王后将生产王子。

The two bananas were shared by the three queens,
With the witness of hordes of maids.
The two bananas were indeed holy things,
Which indicated that the queens would give births to princes.

话说勐兰嘎王国已经一派乱象，
因为十头王当国王治理江山乱作为。
十头王无恶不作，
国民已经怨声载道。

The Kingdom of Menglanga was in chaos,
Due to the Ten-headed King's arbitrary behaviors in governance of the empire.
The Ten-headed King did all manner of evil,
There were rumblings of discontent throughout the

kingdom.

十头王的暴行已经让地方神很反感，
地方神明集会议论道：
“勐兰嘎国王如此下去我们将无安身处，
他一定会糟蹋我们居住的森林。”

The Ten-headed King's evil deeds made the local gods disgusted.
The local gods got together and commented,
"If the Menglanga Kingdom goes on like this, there may be no place for us to settle down.
He will surely damage the forest where we live."

地方神去找天神玛哈律禀报：
“十头王已把勐兰嘎王国搅乱，
不少国民已经不行正道，
无数国民已经流离失所，
勐兰嘎王国已经动荡不安。
如是让十头王继续当国王，
人们一定不再供养我们诸神。”

The local gods went to report to the God Mahalü,
"The Ten-headed King has messed up the Menglanga Kingdom,
Many citizens have taken the low road,
Numerous citizens have been homeless,
The Menglanga Kingdom is in turmoil.
If we continue to make the Ten-headed King the king,
People will not provide food to our gods."

听到地方诸神如此控诉，
天神玛哈律去找大天神混西迦：
“至高无上的天尊啊，
在下有一件急事要禀报，
十头王在勐兰嘎王国作恶多端，
大地生灵涂炭，
王国已经动荡不安。
不能让十头王如此猖狂下去，
我们请求大天神快快作主张。”

Having heard the local gods' complaints,
The God Mahalü went to the Supreme God Hunxijia and said,
"The Supreme God,
I have an urgent matter to report,
The Ten-headed King did all manner of evil in Menglanga Kingdom.
People are in great misery.
The empire is in turmoil.
We shall not allow the Ten-headed King to go on like this,
We request the Supreme God to make a decision as soon as possible."

大天神混西迦感到吃惊，
他回答玛哈律道：
“这事只有天神扁玛法知道，
待我去找扁玛法问问。”

The Supreme God Hunxijia was surprised at this,
He replied to Mahalü,
“No one knows this except for God Bianmafa,
Let me ask Bianmafa first.”

大天神速速来到神邦，
他找到扁玛法大神：
“十头王无恶不作，
不知你赐给了他什么本领？
人间已经怨声载道，
诸神已经不满他的胡作非为。”

The Supreme God came to the Holy State in haste,
He asked Bianmafa,
“The Ten-headed King did all manner of evil,
I don't know what skill you have endowed him.
There are rumblings of discontent throughout the empire,
Gods are disgusted with his evil behaviors.”

扁玛法回答大天神混西迦道：
“水域和陆上我都让他去统管，
他不能战胜的是人类和猴类，
还有那把开天辟地时留下的神弓。”

Bianmafa replied to the Supreme God Hunxijia,
“I have him in charge of water area and land,
He can conquer neither mankind and monkeys,
Nor the magic bow handed down from the creation of the world.”

大天神混西迦听了扁玛法的回答，
他用神眼观察神界各方。
他看见阿銮在朵细达神国[①]享受天乐，
大天神决定派阿銮下凡尘。

Having heard Bianmafa's reply,
The Supreme God Hunxijia observed the divine world with the divine eyes.
He saw Aluan enjoying the heavenly happiness in divine Duoxida Kingdom[①],
The Supreme God decided to send Aluan to descend to the earthy world.

大天神找到阿銮说：
“十头王在人间无恶不作，
再这样下去天界和人间将不得安宁。
天下人非他对手，

The Supreme God came to Aluan and said,
“The Ten-headed King did all manner of evil in human world,
If it goes like this, there will be no peace between heaven

① 朵细达神国：天上的一个神邦。

①The Divine Duoxida Kingdom is a divine state in heaven.

请您下凡走一程。
只有您才能够战胜他的恶行，
天下地上才有希望获得平安。”

and earth.
People of the world are not a match for him,
Please descend to the human world.
Only you can defeat him,
And then there will be peace under heaven."

阿銮俯瞰天下，
看见阿罗替雅王国最称心。
达撒腊塔在那里当国王，
人民安居乐业国泰民安。

Aluan looked down at the earth,
He found the Kingdom of Aluotiya the most satisfactory.
With Dasalata being the king,
The empire enjoys prosperity and the people live in peace.

国王有三个王后，
大王后内心清净身相端庄。
阿銮决定投胎于大王后，
他要带三个助手下凡尘。
一个助手投胎吉西王后，
另外两个助手投胎二王后腹中，
三亿八千万猴民是后盾，
他们居住的深山是靠山。
阿銮告别了大天神混西迦，
他带三个助手投胎下凡间。

The king had three queens,
The first queen was quiet in mind and dignified in appearance.
Aluan decided to reincarnate as the child of the first queen,
He would descend with three assistants.
One assistant would be reincarnated as the child of Queen Jixi,
The other two assistants would be reincarnated as the children of the second queen,
380,000,000 monkeys were the prop,
The huge mountains where they lived were the prop,
After Aluan bid farewell to the Supreme God Hunxijia,
He descended to the human world for reincarnation with his three assistants.

三个王后十月胎龄已满，
阿銮他们四兄弟将出生在人世间。
大王后生下一位王子，
他生相端庄如十五的月亮。

After ten months of pregnancy,
The three queens would give births to the four brothers in the human world.
The first queen gave birth to a prince,

阿罗替雅王国王宫上下欢欣鼓舞，
下凡投胎的阿銮被起名为朗玛满。

With elegant appearance as the moon on the 15th day of the lunar calendar.
People in the palace of Aluotiya Kingdom exulted at the news,
Aluan was reincarnated as the prince named Langmaman.

三王后吉西亦生下一位王子，
这位王子起名帕腊达。
二王后生下一对双胞胎，
其中一个王子被起名叫纳哈腊。
因他与兄长同属一个芭蕉果，
他将协助兄长朗玛满跟随左右。
另一个王子被起名沙达鲁嘎纳，
因他与帕腊达同属一个芭蕉果，
他俩天生就是一条心。

The third queen Jixi gave birth to a prince,
Who was named Palada.
The second queen gave birth to a twin.
One of the princes was named Nahala.
Because the prince and his elder brother belonged to the same banana,
He would assist his elder brother Langmaman by following him.
The other prince of the twin was named Shadalugana.
Because he and Palada belonged to the same banana,
The two were born with one mind.

四位王子渐渐长大，
成群侍女争相服侍在他们身边。
国王喜欢四位王子不舍离开半步，
就像穷人捡到金银一样开心。
国王像如饥似渴者突然获得饭菜，
亦像戴枷锁者突然获得特赦一般，
国王激动的心情无法用言语表达。

The four princes grew up gradually.
Groups of maids competed with each other for attending to them.
The king liked his four princes so much that he couldn't bear to leave half a step,
As if the poor had found gold and silver.
The king was so hungry as if the starveling suddenly got food.
The feeling was no less than a criminal with shackles being pardoned.
The king's excitement was beyond words.

话说当时跳进火堆的神女莲花公主，

The Goddess Princess Lotus who jumped into the fire,

现在她变为一个婴儿重生在火堆中。
她被十头王安排守候火堆的魔鬼抓住，
魔鬼们要将莲花公主交给十头王。

Now became an infant reborn in the fire.
She was caught by the devils who were arranged by the Ten-headed King beside the fire,
The devils took the Princess Lotus to the Ten-headed King.

十头王对魔鬼们说道：
"如果莲花公主重生成一个男人，
他将来一定会来把我杀死。
现在她已经重生为一个女婴，
我们也不能放过她，
要趁树未长大拔草除根！"

The Ten-headed King said to the devils,
"If the Princess Lotus is reborn into a man,
He will come to kill me in future.
Now she was reborn into a female infant,
However, we shall not let her go,
We should remove her when she is still young !"

十头王让魔鬼们将女婴关在铁笼里，
用一把铁锁锁住笼口后丢进大海里边。
海浪把铁笼冲到大海的对岸，
铁笼停泊在扎腊王国地盘的沙滩上。

The Ten-headed King asked the devils to lock the female infant in the iron cage,
He had the cage locked up and thrown into the sea.
The iron cage was carried by the waves to the other side of the sea,
The iron cage stopped on the beach of Zhala Kingdom.

却说扎腊王国的国王没有儿女，
国王到深山里供养雅细积功德。
雅细知道国王在求儿女，
雅细用慧眼观察到了国王的未来。

The king of the Zhala Kingdom had no offspring,
So he came to the mountains to provide food to Yaxi to accumulate merits and virtues.
The Yaxi knew that the king was praying for the offspring,
Through enlightening eyes, the Yaxi perceived the king's future.

雅细把观察到的结果给国王说：
"国王你有一个神赐的公主，
她就在你的王国大海沙滩上。

The Yaxi told the king about what he had perceived,
"Your Majesty ! You have a princess blessed by the god.
She is right on the beach of your kingdom.

你速速派人赶黄牛车去寻找，
这公主就是你的宝贝心肝。”

Send someone to get her in haste by driving the cattle cart,
The princess is your beloved baby.”

国王带人赶着黄牛车去寻找，
一群宫人跟在牛车后边。
国王和大臣们一路走一路看，
他们仔细观察大海边。

The king took some people and drove the cattle cart for the princess,
Maids in the imperial palace followed the cart.
The king and the ministers searched as they were walking,
They checked the beach carefully.

他们来到一片沙滩上，
人们看见铁笼里面关着一个女婴。
国王亲自打开铁锁，
铁笼里的女婴体相可爱又端庄。
她的五官就像春天的花朵一样漂亮，
人们赞扬她貌美赛天仙。

As they came to a beach,
They saw a caged female infant.
The king unlocked it by himself,
The female infant looked lovely and elegant.
She was as beautiful as the flowers in spring,
People praised her as a fairy.

国王将女婴抱回王宫里，
让侍女们精心陪护在她身边。
国王给女婴起了一个好听的名字，
西达公主将名扬四方。

The king carried the female infant back to the palace,
And asking the maids to attend to her intensively.
The female infant was named Xida by the king,
Princess Xida would become famous throughout the land.

国王为公主修建了一座宫殿，
成百的侍女服侍在她身边。
宫内设施应有尽有，
公主身心快乐如天仙。

The king built a palace for the princess,
In which hundreds of maids attend to her.
The palace boasted every facility that one expected,
The princess was physically and mentally happy as a fairy.

西达公主已经长成一位少女，
公主的美名传遍四面八方。
人人知晓的勐兰嘎王国，
也知道了西达公主的芳名。

Princess Xida had grown into a maiden,
She was famous throughout the kingdom.
The princess's name Xida was spread to the Menglanga Kingdom.

各国王子纷纷前来求亲，
都想娶到这位天下无双的大美人。
国王收到许多求亲礼，
金银和绸缎堆积如山包。

The princes of various kingdoms came to propose the marriage,
and wanted to marry the unparalleled beauty.
The king received many betrothal gifts,
The gold, silver, silks and satins were piled up like a hill.

公主的婚事已经成为大难题，
国王六神无主。
国王在夜里念诵吉祥咒，
虔诚祈祷天神来帮忙解除困苦。

The princess's marriage had become a big problem,
The king was out of his wits.
The king recited the auspicious incantations at night,
Praying piously to gods for removing the hardship.

天神在夜里来到国王的宫殿，
国王把自己的困惑讲给天神听：
“我有一位公主端庄美丽，
各国王子都想娶小女为妻，
许给谁不许给谁都有战争隐患，
请求天神帮助开示。”

The God came to the king's palace at night,
The king told the God about his confusion,
“I have an elegant and beautiful princess.
The princes of various kingdoms want to marry my daughter.
There is risk of war in marrying any of them.
Please help me with the decision.”

天神用神眼观察公主的未来，
朗玛满就是她这一生的夫君：
“国王无需纠结，
我送神弓给你解围，
有谁能将此神弓拉动，
国王就让谁与公主成亲。”
国王惊醒在龙床上，
果真看见一把神弓挂在龙床边。

The God observed the princess's future with his divine eyes.
Langmaman would be her lifelong husband,
“Your Majesty, don't sweat it,
I'll send you the magic bow to get you out of the trouble,
Whoever can pull the magic bow,
You have him marry the princess.”
The king woke up with a start in the king's bed,
Only to find there was a magic bow hanging beside the bed.

我们的长诗越来越精彩，
就像吃橄榄慢慢回味无穷。

Our epic is getting more and more wonderful,
Just like chewing phyllanthus emblica which will bring

父老乡亲们啊请慢慢聆听，
后面的故事扣人心弦。

you endless aftertaste.
Dear fellow countrymen, just enjoy the epic,
The following stories will be more thrilling.

第四章
Chapter Four

话说有一位雅细在大山里修行，
森林里的野果是他的食物。
有一天一只巨型乌鸦飞来到大山里，
它的身体有黄牛一般粗壮。

There was a Yaxi cultivating in the mountains,
The wild fruits in the forest were his food.
One day, a huge crow flew to the mountains,
which was as strong as cattle.

森林里的野果被乌鸦吃尽，
乌鸦糟蹋了这片原始森林。
仁慈的雅细非常生气，
他决心要把乌鸦赶走。

The wild fruits in the forest were eaten up by the crow,
The crow had destroyed the primitive forest.
The benevolent Yaxi was very angry,
He was determined to drive away the crow.

雅细用慧眼观察，
能克巨型乌鸦者唯有朗玛满。
但他生活在王宫里，
他是国王的宝贝心肝。

Yaxi observed through enlightening eyes,
And found that only Langmaman can defeat the huge crow.
However, he was living in the palace,
He was the sweet baby of the king.

雅细来到王城边，
他坐在东边的大城门旁。
守门人回去向国王禀报，
国王知道如无大事雅细不会走出森林。

The Yaxi came to the edge of the imperial city,
He sat beside the East City Gate.
The gate keeper went to report to the king,
Who knew that Yaxi would not walk out of the forest without important matter.

国王让守门人请雅细到王宫里，
国王离开宝座前往迎接。
国王双手合十虔诚跪拜雅细，
用水果、牛奶、糍粑和汤圆供养雅细。

The king asked the gate keeper to lead the Yaxi to the palace,
He left the throne to meet the Yaxi.
The king put his palms together and kowtowed to Yaxi piously,
He provided fruit, milk, glutinous rice cake and sweet dumplings to the Yaxi.

国王向雅细问道：

The king asked Yaxi,

"不知尊者有何要事进城来?
请尊者明示本王。"
"近来有一只巨型乌鸦来到森林里,
它把整个森林破坏得一无是处,
今天贫修来城里找国王,
请您让大王子去赶走乌鸦。"

"I wonder if your respected have important matter to
cope with in the city.
Please show me."
"Recently, a giant crow has come to the forest,
And it has destroyed the whole forest, good-for-nothing,
Today I, the humble stylite came to your Majesty,
Please send your first prince to drive away the crow."

国王故意岔开话题,
因他舍不得自己的宝贝儿子出门。
雅细又向国王复说一遍,
请国王派大王子去赶走乌鸦。

The king intentionally digressed from the topic,
Because he was not reluctant to send his be-loved son out.
The Yaxi told the king again,
Please send the first prince to drive away the crow.

"智慧的尊者啊,
王子朗玛满还幼小,
赶乌鸦的大事他实难承担,
还是本王随您去赶乌鸦吧。"

"Respected Intelligent,
The prince Langmaman is too young to undertake the
task of driving away the crow,
Let me follow you to drive away the crow."

雅细不接受国王随他前往,
因为雅细知道只有朗玛满才能赶走乌鸦。
国王又说派士兵去把乌鸦赶出森林,
雅细仍然不答应。
雅细无奈地离开了国王,
他要回森林再想其他办法。

The Yaxi did not accept his proposal,
Because he knew that no one can drive away the crow
except for Langmaman.
The king added that he would send soldiers to expel the
crow from the forest,
The Yaxi didn't accept either,
And reluctantly left the king.
He would return to the forest for other solutions.

国王静静一想,
森林出了问题或是坝区出了灾祸,
国王都应该去关心处理,
因为这是他管辖的地盘。

The king thought,
If there were problems in the forest or disasters in plain
areas,
The king should be concerned about and should cope

with these problems.
Since the king was in charge of the territory.

国王让大臣苏曼达请雅细回来，
雅细又回到国王身边。
国王向雅细说：
“请尊者少安毋躁，
本王就是担心王子幼小，
能否赶走乌鸦还是问他自己吧，
稍后请尊者与他交谈。”

The king had Minister Sumanda invite Yaxi back.
The Yaxi returned to the king's side again.
The king said to the Yaxi,
"Please remain patient venerable,
I'm just worried about the prince's youngness.
Whether he can drive away the crow or not,
Please talk to him later."

苏曼达将朗玛满和纳哈腊请到大殿里，
兄弟俩虔诚跪拜雅细。
国王向大王子说：
“朗玛满啊，
你是我们王国的希望，
你是父母的心肝。
今天尊者有重要事来王宫里，
只因巨型乌鸦破坏了大森林。
尊者欲让你去将乌鸦赶出森林，
不知道你有没有办法。”

Sumanda invited Langmaman and Nahala to the palace.
The two brothers kowtowed to the Yaxi piously.
The king said to the first prince,
"Langmaman,
You are the hope of our kingdom,
As well as your parent's sweetheart.
Today the venerable came to the palace for some important matter.
The giant crow has destroyed the forest.
Therefore, the venerable wants you to drive the crow out of the forest.
I don't know if you have any ideas."

“此事请父王莫担心，
巨型乌鸦孩儿能赶走。
请父王派孩儿前往，
一定将巨型乌鸦撵出森林。”

"Father, please don't worry about it.
I can drive away the giant crow.
Father, please send me there.
I'll definitely drive out the crow from the forest."

国王听了王子的话很高兴，
国王跪拜雅细说：

The king was pleased to hear the prince's words.
The king kowtowed to the Yaxi and said,

“请尊者将王子带走， 让他去把巨型乌鸦赶出森林。” 纳哈腊王子亦急忙向父王跪拜： “请父王让孩儿一同前往， 我去协助哥哥把乌鸦撵出森林。”	“Your venerable, please take the prince there, To drive out the giant crow from the forest.” Prince Nahala also kowtowed to the king and said, “Father, please allow me to go there together To assist my elder brother in driving out the crow from the forest.”
“只要尊者答应带你去， 两兄弟一起出行父王也放心， 出门要听雅细的吩咐， 一定要把巨型乌鸦赶出森林。”	“As long as the venerable agrees to take you there, I'll be relieved for you two brothers' traveling together. Being away from home, you should listen to Yaxi's instructions. You must drive the giant crow out of the forest.”
朗玛满和纳哈腊两兄弟向母亲拜别， 他们要出门去把巨型乌鸦赶出森林。 王宫上下人们很激动， 赞扬朗玛满两兄弟是干大事的人。	Langmaman and Nahala bid farewell to their mother. They were going to drive the giant crow out of the forest. People in the palace were very excited, Praising the two brother as persons who do great things.
两兄弟将母亲的脚抬过头顶行辞行礼， 母亲祝福他们赶走乌鸦奏凯旋。 哥哥让弟弟去取弓箭， 两兄弟带着弓箭整装待发。	The two brothers did farewell-bidding ritual by holding their mother's feet over their heads. Their mother wished them success in driving away the crow. The elder brother had the younger brother take the bow and arrows. The two brothers were ready with bow and arrows.
雅细与国王鞠躬道别， 带着两兄弟回到了森林。 雅细交代说不能射死乌鸦， 射箭吓唬它离开森林就是目的。 不能让乌鸦再来搞破坏，	The Yaxi bid farewell to the king by bowing down, And returned to the forest with the two brothers. The Yaxi told them not to shoot the crow dead. The purpose was to frighten the crow out of the forest. We shall not allow the crow to destroy the forest anymore.

要让这片森林郁郁葱葱。

雅细教朗玛满念诵神咒，
又将咒语加持在神箭上。
不一会儿巨型乌鸦飞过来，
朗玛满向乌鸦射出了箭。
乌鸦慌忙向远方飞去，
但神箭不停地跟踪追击，
击中了乌鸦的眼睛。
乌鸦飞回来向朗玛满求饶：
“请朗玛满留我一条性命，
从此我再也不来糟蹋森林。”

乌鸦的一只眼睛还插着神箭，
朗玛满将神箭拔了下来。
从此巨型乌鸦就瞎了一只眼睛，
它看东西要扭头晃脑。
直到现在乌鸦看东西还要扭头晃脑，
因为它有一只眼睛看不见前方。
朗玛满兄弟赶走了危害森林的乌鸦，
他们的威名传遍四面八方。

朗玛满将结果告诉雅细，
雅细对两兄弟的本领给予赞扬。
雅细拿出诸多新鲜水果，
让两兄弟在洞府中享用。

朗玛满跪拜雅细道：
“智慧的尊者啊，
为了能够战胜邪恶，

We shall make the forest lush.

The Yaxi taught Langmaman magic incantations,
Which were enchanted to the magic bow.
Before long, the giant crow came over.
Langmaman shot an arrow at the crow.
The crow flew away hurriedly.
But the magic arrow kept tracking the crow,
And hit the crow' eyes.
The crow flew back to beg Langmaman for mercy,
“Please spare my life, Langmaman.
I will never come to destroy the forest again.”

The arrow was till inserted in one of the crow's eye.
Langmaman pulled out the magic arrow.
From then on, the giant crow has been blind in one eye.
It would wag its head when watching something.
Until now, a crow will wag its head as it views,
Because the single-eyed crow can see the front.
The Langmaman brothers drove away the crow that
jeopardized the forest.
They became famous throughout the kingdom.

Langmaman told the Yaxi about the result.
The Yaxi praised the two brothers for their skills.
He took out a lot of fresh fruit,
To treat the two brothers in the cave.

Langmaman kowtowed to the Yaxi and said,
“Your Intelligent venerable,
In order to defeat the evil,

请尊者传授我们战胜邪恶的神咒，
让我们兄弟本领高强力大无穷。”

Please teach us the magic incantations.
With it, we two brothers will be infinitely resourceful in
magic powers”

听到两兄弟的请求，
雅细高兴在心中。
他知道朗玛满将来是国王，
是人民的大靠山。

Hearing the two brothers' request,
The Yaxi was delighted,
Because he knew Langmaman would become the king.
He would be the people's great backer.

雅细朝云端飞去，
他要去寻找战无不胜的神咒。
雅细得到各种神咒，
他把神咒传给两兄弟。
雅细说两兄弟未来之路艰难险阻，
过完漫漫黑夜方能见阳光。

The Yaxi flew towards the clouds,
To seek the invincible magic incantation.
The Yaxi got various magic incantations.
He passed on the magic incantations to the two brothers,
And said the road to the future for the two brothers
would be difficult and dangerous.
The sun could only be seen after the long dark night.

我们的长诗告一段落，
后面的故事情节纷繁复杂。
欲知两兄弟将来如何，
父老乡亲们请听下一章。

It has come to the end of the chapter.
The following chapters are complex in plots.
If you want to know what will happen to the two brothers
in the future,
Dear fellow countrymen, please listen to the next chapter.

第五章

Chapter Five

话说扎腊王国疆土辽阔富庶又美丽， 西达公主的到来让王国名扬四方。 各国王子都想来攀这门亲事， 公主的婚姻大事国王没了主张。 国王决定举行拉神弓比赛， 用拉神弓比赛选驸马。	Zhala was a prosperous and beautiful kingdom with vast territory. The arrival of Princess Xida made the kingdom famous throughout the land. Princes of all kingdoms wanted to marry the princess. The king did not have his own opinion for the marriage of his princess. Therefore, the king decided to hold a magic bow-pulling competition, To select the son-in-law.
一百多个大小王国知道了消息， 各国王子都想来试运气。 国王搭建了一座神弓楼， 将神弓安放在楼台上。	Having got the message, Princes of more than one hundred kingdoms wanted to try their luck. The king built a magic bow tower, Where the magic bow was placed.
国王又修建了上百间供王子们居住的房屋， 各国王子集中到王城中。 各国王子都不想错过这一次机会， 十头王亦来到了王城中。	The king built more than one hundred houses for the princes to stay. The princes gathered in the imperial city. They didn't want to miss this chance. The Ten-headed King also came to the city.
雅细把事情告诉了朗玛满两兄弟， 两兄弟非常激动开心。 雅细带两兄弟来到扎腊王国， 国王安排雅细住进了客房。	The Yaxi told the Langmaman brothers about it. The two brothers were very excited and pleased. The Yaxi led the two brothers to the Kingdom of Zhala, The king arranged the Yaxi to stay in the guest room.
国王举行拉神弓选女婿活动， 王城里人山人海盛况空前。	The king held the magic bow-pulling competition to select a son-in-law,

因为公主实在太美丽，
谁都在做美梦要与公主成亲。

There were huge crowds of people in the imperial city.
Everyone wanted to marry the princess,
Because the princess was so beautiful.

所有参赛者个个摩拳擦掌，
他们做梦都在想着公主大美人。
公主在一旁偷偷观望，
但公主没有看见一个心仪的人。

All the competitors were ready to have a try.
They dreamed about the beautiful princess.
The princess watched secretly.
But she didn't see a man of her favor.

十头王第一个冲上前来试神弓，
但十头王始终没有拉动神弓。
十头王丢尽了脸面，
他在人群中满脸通红。

The Ten-headed King was the first one to try the magic bow.
However, he had never pulled the magic bow.
The Ten-headed King had to eat crow.
His face flushed bright red among the people due to embarrassment.

十头王心里在想，
自己拉不动的神弓别人也休想拉动。
不管国王答应与否，
公主非自己莫属。
他认为没有人与公主般配，
他一定要将公主抢到手中。

The Ten-headed King thought,
That no one could pull the magic bow that I could not pull.
Whether the king agreed or not,
The princess only belonged to me.
He thought that no one could match the princess.
He must seize the princess.

所有王子都没有能力将神弓拉动，
他们只好灰溜溜地叹息。
朗玛满想去试运气，
他请雅细去向国王禀报。

All the princes were unable to pull the magic bow.
So they groaned in dismay.
Langmaman wanted to try his luck.
He invited the Yaxi to report to the king.

雅细向国王作了禀报，
国王同意让朗玛满来试神弓。
朗玛满向雅细跪拜，

The Yaxi reported to the king,
Who agreed to have Langmaman try the magic bow.
Langmaman kowtowed to the Yaxi.

他请求雅细加持让自己成功。

He asked the Yaxi for blessing to make himself successful.

朗玛满缓缓走上试弓台，
王子们看见他就讥笑起哄。
西达公主看见了朗玛满，
她突然眼睛一亮感觉无上荣光。

Langmaman walked slowly onto the bow-trying stand.
The princes started to jeer and create disturbance as soon as they saw him.
The Princess Xida saw Langmaman,
Who turned her on suddenly and the princess felt so honored.

西达公主认为他不需来拉神弓，
他就是自己的心仪之人。
公主向诸神祈祷，
她祈望这位小伙轻轻就拉动神弓。

The Princess Xida thought he did not need to pull the bow,
He was her beloved.
The princess prayed to gods,
She prayed that the youngster would pull the magic bow easily.

"他只是雅细的侍者，
居然也敢来拉神弓。"
"你就是在山里吃野果的命，
别在人群中献丑。"
王子们议论纷纷，
他们对眼前的朗玛满不屑一顾。

"He is just one of Yaxi's attendants.
How dare he come and pull the magic bow."
"You were born to eat wild fruits in the mountains,
Don't show yourself up in the crowd."
The princes discussed,
They looked on Langmaman with contempt.

朗玛满对他们大声说道：
"王子们不要看不起人，
拉神弓比赛只是小事一桩。
但凡人间大事难事拦不住我，
即使大天神的金斧霹雳我亦无妨！"

Langmaman said to them loudly,
"Don't look down upon people, princes.
Magic bow-pulling competition is just a small matter.
All the difficulties in the world will not stop me.
Even if the Supreme God's golden axe and thunderbolt won't stop me !"

朗玛满的一句话将起哄声压了下去，
他站在高台将弓线轻轻拉动，

The noise from the disturbance was suppressed by Langmaman's words.

神弓渐渐要拉满时，
人们已经感觉到地动山摇。

Standing on the platform, he pulled the bow easily.
When the magic bow was about to be drawn full,
People felt the earth shaking.

突然天上发出一声巨响，
电光闪闪如雷霆万钧。
在场的人个个惊慌失措，
人们忙着去寻找可以躲避的地方。

Suddenly there was a loud noise in the sky,
Followed by lightning and thunderbolt.
People present were panic-stricken.
They were busy looking for places to hide.

朗玛满接着将神弓折断，
之后离开试弓台回到雅细身旁。
十头王默默念诵神咒，
他在用慧眼观察朗玛满的前世。

Langmaman continued to break the magic bow.
And then he left the bow-trying platform and returned to Yaxi.
The Ten-headed King chanted the incantations silently.
He was observing the previous life of Langmaman with enlightening eyes.

十头王用慧眼知道了朗玛满的底细，
他心里自言自语道：
"眼前这个朗玛满，
他虽没来与我争抢公主，
但这位扎腊王国的美丽公主，
她的缘分在朗玛满一边。"
十头王只身骑上飞行器离开广场，
闷闷不乐地回到王宫中。

The Ten-headed King learned about the background of Langmaman with his enlightening eyes.
He spoke to himself,
"Though the guy in front of me,
Didn't come to compete with me for the princess.
The beautiful princess of the Kingdom Zhala,
Her fate is on Langmaman's side."
The Ten-headed King got on the craft and left the square alone.
He went back to the palace sullenly.

扎腊国国王也很纳闷，
因为王子们都无力将神弓拉动，
未料雅细的侍者却拉动了神弓。
国王觉得选侍者为婿不合适，

The king of Zhala Kingdom was also sad,
Because the princes were unable to pull the magic bow.
Unexpectedly, Yaxi's attendant pulled the magic bow.
The king thought it was not suitable to select an attendant

感觉自己丢尽了脸面，
国王也闷闷不乐地回到王宫中。

as the son-in-law.
Feeling humiliated,
The king went back to the palace sullenly.

雅细向国王说明了情况：
“尊敬的大国王啊，
这位小伙并非贫僧的侍者，
他是达撒腊塔国王的长子，
是他帮我从森林中赶走巨型乌鸦，
我才带他来大王的试弓场看热闹。
未料到他拉满了弓线，
还惊动了天宫大神们。”

The Yaxi explained the situation to the king,
“Your Majesty,
This youngster is not my attendant,
He is the eldest son of King Dasalata.
It was him who drove away the giant crow from the forest.
That's why I brought him to the bow-trying site to have a look.
Unexpectedly, he pulled the bow full.
It also shocked the gods of the Heavenly Palace.”

国王听了雅细的介绍后十分高兴，
国王将朗玛满叫到他面前：
“你驱逐巨型乌鸦于森林里，
尊者又把你带到本王面前。
这是你的功德和缘分在感召，
西达公主与你有姻缘，
今后你俩就在这里治理江山。”

The king was very happy after hearing Yaxi's introduction.
He called Langmaman to him and said,
“You drove away the giant crow in the forest,
The venerable brought you to me.
This is your merit and destiny.
Princess Xida and you will be bound by marriage,
You two will govern the kingdom here from now on.”

朗玛满跪拜国王说道：
“本人并非为娶公主来这里，
我只想与众王子比赛拉神弓。
是王子们欺人太甚，
我才折断了神弓。
还请国王勿怪罪小人，
因为我眼里容不得沙尘。”

Langmaman kowtowed to the king and said,
“I didn't come here to marry the princess.
I just want to compete with the princes to pull the magic bow.
It was the princes who went too far in bullying me.
I just broke the magic bow.
Please don't blame me, your Majesty.
Because I can't stand dust in my eyes.”

国王对朗玛满说：
“今天不谈其他事，
今天就谈你与公主做一对新人。”
朗玛满回答国王道：
“万人之上的国王啊，
我们弟兄有四个人，
您欲嫁女就要嫁四位公主，
我们四兄弟有盟誓要同一天成婚。”

The king said to Langmaman,
“We won’t talk about anything else today.
Let’s talk about you and the princess as a couple today.”
Langmaman replied to the king,
“Your Majesty,
There are four of our brothers.
If you want to marry your daughter, you have to marry your four princesses.
We four brothers have pledged to marry on the same day.”

“真是缘分啊，
我家正好还有三个侄女，
她们是我三个弟弟的女儿，
三个弟弟是国王我的副手，
真是有缘千里来相会。
只是两国之间距离太遥远，
这桩喜事让谁去转达你父王？”

“It’s fate.
I happen to have three nieces.
They are the daughters of my three brothers.
The three brothers are my assistants.
Separated as we are thousands of miles apart, we come together as if by predestination.
It’s just that our two kingdoms are far away from each other.
Who will tell your father about this happy event ?”

朗玛满将书信写在贝叶里，
又将贝叶捆绑在神箭上，
他把神箭射向远方，
他要让神箭将书信送给父王。

Langmaman wrote the letter in the pattra leaves,
And tied the pattra leaves to the magic arrow.
He shot his magic arrow into the distance,
He wanted the magic arrow to send the letter to his father.

达撒腊塔国王看到书信后十分高兴，
他下令组织庞大的迎亲队伍，
包括象队、马队、车辆和金银绸缎，
还有大臣、将军、侍女和陪郎。

The King Dasalata was very happy when he received the letter.
He ordered to organize a huge welcoming team,
Including elephants team, horses team, carriages, gold, silver and silk.
There were also ministers, generals, maids and escorts.

达撒腊塔国王与大臣坐在彩车里，
浩浩荡荡的队伍一路走向前方。
他们跋山涉水，
他们走过茫茫原始森林。
他们抵达扎腊王国的王城，
扎腊国王已组织大队伍等待在王城门前。

The King Dasalata and his ministers were sitting in the floats.
The mighty team marched forward all the way.
They crossed mountains and rivers,
They walked through the vast primeval forest,
They arrived at the royal city of Zhala Kingdom.

王城里举行四对新人的婚礼，
王宫里整整热闹了七夜七天。
国王同一天嫁公主和三个侄女，
新娘的母亲们在卧室里泪涟涟。

Four couples were married in the royal city.
The palace was full of excitement for seven nights and seven days.
The king married the princess and three nieces on the same day.
The bride's mothers wept in their bedroom.

隆重的婚礼庆典结束，
阿罗替雅王国的大臣向国王禀报，
因为路途遥远国中不能无国王，
迎亲队伍要快快返程。

The grand wedding ceremony ended.
The minister of Aluotiya Kingdom reported to the king.
Because it's a long way to go and it will not be a kingdom without a king.
The welcoming team should return quickly.

扎腊国王答应了他们的请求，
国王对来道别的女婿和女儿祝福道:
"祝福你们互敬互爱，
同心协力治理江山。
两个王国都要由你们统一管理，
祝福你们威名传遍四面八方。"

King Zhala agreed to their request,
The king wished his son-in-law and daughter,
"Bless you for your mutual respect and love,
May you work together to govern the kingdom.
Both kingdoms will be under your unified governance,
May your fame spread all over the world."

迎亲队伍返程的礼炮响彻云霄，
锣鼓号角威震四方。
迎新队伍向深山里挺进，
排成长龙的大队伍彩旗卷山风。

The salute of the welcoming team's return rang out in the sky.
The gongs, drums and horns were powerful.
The welcoming team marched into the mountains,

象吼马鸣声回荡在山谷里，
野兽和鸟群忙着向远方逃窜。

Long queues of colorful flags rolled in the mountain breeze.
The sound of roaring elephants and horses reverberated in the valley.
Beasts and birds were busy running away.

西达公主跟着朗玛满走了，
别国的王子们怀恨在心中。
几个王子在议论：
“他抢走了美丽的公主我们不服输，
我们要联合起来把公主抢回来！”
有一位王子回答道：
“那把神弓谁都拉不动，
他却轻轻拉动了神弓，
这是缘分啊，
西达公主是他的人！

Princess Xida left with Langmaman.
Princes of other kingdoms held a grudge against it.
Some princes were talking,
“Though he took the beautiful princess, we won't admit defeat.
We need to unite to get the princess back !”
A prince replied,
“Nobody could pull that magic bow.
However, he pulled the magic bow easily,
It is the fate,
Princess Xida is his woman.

“依我看还是罢了，
他一定是圣者阿銮。
他拉动了神弓，
还将神弓折断。
如他心狠手辣把我们全射死，
我们都要遗臭万年。
我们不是他的对手，
我们还是各自回家吧。”

“In my opinion, let's give up.
He must be Aluan, the sage.
Because he pulled the magic bow,
And broke the magic bow.
If he were ruthless, he would have shot us all to death.
We will all be notorious forever.
We are not his opponents,
Let's go home separately.”

突然有一位国师冲出来说：
“各种神咒我们都有，
进攻和防卫的神咒我们也一样不缺，
只要我们各国同心协力，

Suddenly a Guoshi (advisor, title conferred by a king) rushed out and said,
“We have all kinds of magic spells.
We have the magic spells of attack and defense.

我们不怕他是圣者或是阿銮。”	As long as we unite in a concerted effort. We don't care whether he is sage or Aluan."
国师联合各国王子们追上来， 他们在朗玛满的队伍后面大喊大叫。 朗玛满的父王有一些担心， 朗玛满对父王说道： “父王请您尽管放心， 我不怕国师带来的王子兵。 即使是各国军队联合起来追上来， 他们亦无法打败我们。”	Princes mobilized and united by the Guoshi caught up. They were yelling at the back of Langmaman's team. Langmaman's father was a little worried. Langmaman said to his father, "Father, please don't worry, I am not afraid of the imperial soldiers brought by the Guoshi. Even if the armies of all kingdoms got united and caught up, They won't defeat us."
朗玛满对弟弟纳哈腊说道： “弟弟把你的嫂子接到你车上， 你领大伙找个地方先休息。 你要保护好父王， 不能让敌人伤害了四位新娘。”	Langmaman said to his brother Nahala, "My younger brother, take your sister-in-law to your carriage. You lead them to a place to take a break first. You should protect our father, Don't let the enemy hurt the four brides."
朗玛满将车横挡在道路上， 他对追来的国师说道： “国师你为什么要追赶我， 难道你要与我比高低？”	Langmaman blocked his carriage on the road, He said to the chasing Guoshi, "Why are you chasing me, Guoshi ? Do you want to compete with me ?"
国师听到朗玛满大声说话， 国师急忙念诵他的神咒。 森林上空顿时出现熊熊火光， 朗玛满变出瓢泼大雨将烈火熄灭。	Guoshi heard Langmaman speak loudly. Guoshi hurriedly recited his mantra. The sky above the forest suddenly burst into flames. Langmaman had there be a pouring rain to extinguish the fire.

国师又变出阵阵狂风，	The Guoshi had there be gust of wind,
欲让狂风吹刮朗玛满。	To let the strong wind blow the Langmaman.
朗玛满变出闭风器，	Langmaman had there be wind closing device,
将狂风包围在森林中间。	To enclose the strong wind in the middle of the forest.
朗玛满在车里安然无恙，	Langmaman was safe in the carriage,
周围的森林又恢复了鸟语花香。	The surrounding forests had regained peace.
国师将宝物抛向空中，	The Guoshi threw the treasure into the air,
宝物突然变成烈火烧森林。	The treasure suddenly became a fire burning the forest.
战象战马和将军士兵都恐惧，	War elephants and horses, generals and soldiers were frightened,
争先恐后要逃离队伍。	And they Struggled to escape the team.
国师以为胜利在望，	Guoshi thought victory was in sight.
他咬牙切齿地吼道：	He gnashed his teeth and roared,
“看你怎么对付我，	“See how you deal with me.
我看你的魔法已经用完！”	I think your magic has been used up !”
朗玛满在默默虔诚祈祷：	Langmaman prayed silently and devoutly,
“如果我从前的神咒没有破灭，	“If my old mantra hasn't been broken,
就让大火立即进入我嘴里，	Let the fire enter my mouth immediately,
让大火变化成水清凉我全身！”	And let the fire change into water to cool my body.”
大火突然进入朗玛满的嘴里，	The fire suddenly entered Langmaman's mouth.
朗玛满却微笑着坐在车中。	But Langmaman sat in the carriage smiling.
国师看见如此情景，	Seeing such a scene,
他在心里不得不服输：	The Guoshi had to admit defeat in his heart,
“如是朗玛满向我动怒，	“If Langmaman were angry with me,
我们早就命归黄泉了！”	We would have been dead !”
国师抱着装有圣水的白螺向朗玛满走来，	The Guoshi came to Langmaman with a white conch filled with holy water.
他将白螺送给朗玛满以示臣服。	

He gave the white conch to Langmaman to show his
obedience.

国师叩拜朗玛满说：
“您是人间伟大的阿銮，
您的本领超过所有人。
您是高山大海，
我们只是渺小的一粒沙尘。
只求尊者从今往后莫计较，
把我们当成是无知的信徒包容在心中。
祈望圣者阿銮珍重，
祝您威名传遍四面八方！”
国师与朗玛满道别，
国师带着王子们各自回到了故乡。

The Guoshi kowtowed to Langmaman and said,
“You are the great Aluan in the world.
Your skills exceed all others.
You are a mountain and a sea,
While we are just a tiny grain of sand.
I just hope that you will never mind from now on,
And embrace us as ignorant believers.
Take care Aluan, the sage.
May your fame spread far and wide !”
Having bidding farewell to Langmaman,
Guoshi led the princes to their own hometown.

迎亲队伍回到阿罗替雅王国，
国王为四对儿子儿媳举办七天大庆典。
一百多位附属国国王来到王城，
金银和绸缎堆满了王宫。

The welcoming team returned to the Kingdom of Aluo tiya.
The king held a seven-day celebration for his four sons and
daughter-in-law.
More than 100 kings of affiliated kingdoms came to the
royal city.
The palace was full of gold, silver and silk.

我们的故事越来越精彩，
我们的长诗还要继续念诵。
就像英雄行走在道路上，
目的地还在遥远的前方。

Our story is getting more and more wonderful.
We should continue to recite the epic,
Like a hero walking on the road,
With the destination still being far ahead.

第六章

Chapter Six

话说果嘎律王国的国王逝世，
噩耗传到了阿罗替雅王国。
因为他是三王后吉西的父亲，
吉西想让儿子帕腊达前往吊丧。

The death of the King of the Kingdom of Guogalü,
Reached the Empire of Aluotiya.
As he was the father of the third queen, Jixi,
Jixi wanted his son Palada to go to the funeral.

父王交代帕腊达快去快回，
因为众王子没有娶到西达公主，
他们心有不甘，
国王担心他们会来偷袭行凶。

The father told Palada to come back soon.
As the princes didn't marry Princess Xida,
They were not satisfied.
The king was afraid that they would come and attack.

帕腊达去拜别三位兄长，
朗玛满亦让弟弟快去快回。
朗玛满安排沙达鲁嘎纳一同前往，
希望两位弟弟快快出发。

Palada went to pay farewell to the three elder brothers,
Langmaman also asked his brother to come back quickly.
Langmaman arranged Shadalugana to go with him,
Hoping the two brothers could leave soon.

两兄弟赶着车跋山涉水，
他们跨过了数座森林和山梁。
果嘎律王国的舅舅知道外甥来吊丧，
让大臣们快快接他们进王宫。

The two brothers were driving across mountains and rivers.
They crossed several forests and ridges.
Knowing that his nephew was coming mourn,
The uncle of Guogalü Kingdom had the ministers take
them to the palace quickly.

舅舅安排人们准备丰盛的饭菜，
迎接外甥回到王国中。
舅甥双方多年不见，
他们谈天说地问寒问暖。

The uncle arranged people to prepare rich meals,
To welcome his nephew back to the kingdom.
The uncle and his nephew had not seen each other for
many years,
They chatted and inquired after each other's life.

国王去世后舅舅已继承王位，
王国繁荣富强国民安居乐业。
国王舅舅对外甥的才貌很欣赏，

After the king died, his uncle succeeded to the throne.
The kingdom was prosperous and strong, and the people
lived in peace and contentment.

他向两兄弟介绍许多异国风情。

The uncle appreciated his nephew's talent.
He introduced many exotic customs to the two brothers.

话说阿罗替雅王国版图宽阔无边，
国家历史悠久至今已有数万年。
国王的四个儿子个个威武出众，
他们的身相与天神没有两样。
长子朗玛满非常孝敬父母，
他爱国爱家体贴人民。

The Kingdom of Aluotiya was vast in territory,
With a long history of tens of thousands of years.
The king's four sons were all powerful,
They were no different from the gods.
Langmaman, the eldest son, was very filial to his parents.
He loved his country, his family and the people.

自从扎腊国国王用拉神弓方式招女婿后，
朗玛满的名声已传遍四面八方。
因为众王子无人能将神弓拉动，
唯有朗玛满拉动了神弓。
朗玛满天下第一，
他与西达公主真是天配的一双。

Since the king of Zhala recruited his son-in-law by pulling the magic bow,
Langmaman's reputation has spread all over the world.
Because none of the princes could pull the magic bow,
Only Langmaman pulled the magic bow.
Langmaman was the best in the world.
He and Princess Xida were a perfect match.

阿罗替雅王国国民反映强烈，
他们迫不及待地希望朗玛满当国王。
一大伙人已集中在王城东大门，
他们要向国王进谏推荐朗玛满当国王。

The citizens of Aluotiya Kingdom had a strong response,
They could not wait for Langmaman to be the king.
A group of people had gathered at the east gate of the city,
They were going to recommend Langmaman to the king as the new king.

国王让苏曼达请大伙到王宫里，
大伙排成行向国王跪拜。
国王微笑着问众人：
“大伙有什么要事尽管说出口，
我们一起好商量。”
大伙推选出来的代表能言善道：
“尊贵的国王啊，

The king asked Sumanda to invite everyone to the palace.
Everyone lined up to kneel down to the king.
The king smiled and asked the people,
"If you have anything important, just let me know,
Let's discuss it together."
The representative elected by the people had a silver tongue,

您是我们的绿色保护伞，
亿万人民在宝伞下乘凉。
我们的王国宽阔美丽，
不管是城镇或是乡村，
不管是居民或农夫，
不管是渔民或商贾，
男女老幼个个体健安康。

"Your Majesty,
You are our green protective umbrella.
Hundreds of millions of people enjoy the cool under the umbrella.
Our kingdom is vast and beautiful.
Whether it's a town or a village,
Whether residents or farmers,
Whether fishermen or merchants,
Men and women, the old and young, they all enjoy good health.

"我们的四位王子如天神一般，
朗玛满王子与众不同。
他有过人的智慧和本领，
普天之下无人能及。

"Our four princes are like gods,
With Prince Langmaman being different from others.
He has great wisdom and skills,
Who is equaled by no one in the world.

"国王您已经年老体弱，
我们希望您安度晚年。
我们希望朗玛满继承王位，
让他治理阿罗替雅王国的江山。
请国王考虑我们的建议，
我们不是胆大包天。"

"You are getting old and weak.
We hope you can spend your old age in peace.
We hope Langmaman will succeed to the throne,
To let him govern the land of Aluotiya.
Please consider our proposal.
We are not bold as you please."

国王他也在心中思虑，
因为大家的建议很合理，
这是人民对自己的关心，
也是为王国的前途着想。

The king was also thinking.
Since the people's suggestions were reasonable,
This was the people's concern for themselves.
It was also for the future of the kingdom.

国王的面容很严肃，
整个王宫鸦雀无声。
个个都捏着一把冷汗，

The king looked serious.
The whole palace was silent.
Everyone was in a cold sweat.

他们的内心非常担心。

They were very worried.

国王慢慢地微笑起来，
大家才松了一口大气。
国王向人们缓缓地说道：
"这是你们关心王国的善举，
本王接受你们的建议。"

The king began to smile,
Everyone was relieved.
The king said slowly to the people,
"This is your kindness to the kingdom.
I accept your suggestion."

国王让苏曼达请朗玛满来到大殿，
朗玛满跪拜父王问道：
"父王有何吩咐请明示，
儿子即刻去完成！"

The king asked Sumanda to invite Langmaman to the main hall.
Langmaman knelt down to his father and asked,
"Do you have any mission for me, Father ?
I'll go to finish it immediately !"

"朗玛满你是长子，
你们四兄弟已经长大成人。
人们进王宫来向我提建议，
他们希望让你继承王位。
父王已经想好要让位养身，
已经做好了准备。
待到吉日良辰的时候，
我们举行继位仪式以示天下人民。"

"Langmaman, you are the eldest son.
You four brothers have grown up.
People came to the palace to give me suggestions,
They wanted you to succeed to the throne.
I've decided to step aside for my health,
Everything is ready.
When the auspicious day comes,
We will hold a succession ceremony to show the people of the world."

消息即刻传遍王宫上下，
接着传遍王城和乡村。
国人个个十分激动，
因为朗玛满即将当大国王。
朗玛满将消息向母亲禀报，
三个王后都非常开心。

The news immediately spread all over the palace,
And then spread all over the royal city and the countryside.
Everyone in the kingdom was very excited,
Because Langmaman was about to become the king.
Langmaman reported the news to his mother,
The three queens were very happy.

国王让国师们挑选最吉祥的日子，
就选定在五月十五月圆那一天。
王宫里要举行新国王继位仪式，
全国各地都要举办大庆典。

The king asked the Guoshi to choose the most auspicious day.
It was fixed on the full moon day on the 15th day of the 5th lunar month.
The new king's succession ceremony would be held in the palace.
Celebrations would be held in all parts of the kingdom.

国王当着众大臣和将军的面说道：
“朗玛满王子啊，
国王的担子一定不轻，
不是让你享福高高在上，
是让你来做国人牢固的篱笆桩。

The king said in front of the ministers and generals,
“Prince Langmaman,
The burden of a king must be heavy.
It's not for you to enjoy yourself,
It is for you to be a solid fence post for all subjects.

“当国王要坚持十条原则，
要事事以善良为先。
要将全国的孩子当亲生子，
要把所有长辈当双亲。

“To be a king, he should adhere to the ten principles,
And be kind in everything.
He should treat children from all over the kingdom as his own children.
He should treat all elders as his parents.

“调解纠纷要有一杆称，
该赏该罚理据要公平。
对犯大罪者先说教为主，
如能改正惩罚要放宽。
若遇国民犯死罪，
若能改正就要免死改坐牢房。

“Mediation of disputes requires a steelyard.
The reason for reward and punishment should be fair.
Priorities should be given to preaching to those who commit serious crimes,
The punishment shall be relaxed if it can be corrected.
If a subject commits a capital crime,
If he can correct it, you should change the penalty from death to jail.

“对大臣、将军和年长者要尊重，
对三个弟弟须当成一娘所生。

“You should respect ministers, generals and seniors,
And treat the three brothers equal.

三个母后你要孝顺，
不可厚此薄彼有话说。
若要人知道你必须先懂，
欲叫人做你必须先行。

You should be filial to the three mothers,
Don't be partial to one another.
You should understand first before you require other people to understand,
If you want someone to do it, you must do it first.

“你不能当初三或三十的月亮，
你要做十五的明月照亮四方。
做王须懂理有礼貌不能作威作福，
要学会与邻国友好往来共同富强。”
朗玛满虚心接受父王教诲，
他双手合十跪拜谢父王。

"You can't be the moon on the 3rd or 30th day of the lunar calendar,
You should be the bright moon on the 15th of lunar calendar to light up the world.
To be a king, you must be reasonable and polite, and you must not be domineering.
You should learn to make friendly exchanges with neighboring countries and become prosperous together."
Langmaman accepted his father's teachings modestly,
He knelt down with his palms putting together to thank his father.

大臣将军们皆赞同朗玛满继位，
三位王后也欢喜赞同。
全国上下欢欣鼓舞，
因为这是国家富强的大决策。

Ministers and generals all agreed with the succession of Langmaman.
The three queens also agreed happily.
There was rejoicing at the news throughout the empire,
Since it was an important decision for the country's prosperity.

王子继位的消息全国人人皆知，
唯有阿婷还蒙在鼓里。
她是三王后吉西最亲近的丫鬟，
阿婷知道消息后很气愤，
她速速去与三王后说：

The news of the prince's succession was widely known throughout the kingdom,
Except for Ating.
She was the closest servant girl of the third queen Jixi.
Ating was very angry when she learned the news.

“我亲爱的三王后啊，
人家要把你卖了你都不知道！
朗玛满就要当国王，
你怎么能无动于衷！”
“朗玛满当国王是一件大好事啊，
全宫上下都认为这是国王的正确决策。
朗玛满善良又智慧，
他当国王一定会一碗水端平。”

She quickly went to tell the third queen,
“My dear the third queen,
You don’t even know they’re going to sell you.
Langmaman is going to be the king.
How can you be indifferent !”
“It’s a good thing that Langmaman succeeds to the throne,
People in the whole palace believed that this was the right decision of the king.
Langmaman is full of kindness and wisdom,
When he is king, he will be even.”

“三王后你真是一只憨兔子啊，
你已经被别人要得团团转了还不知道，
你为什么不叫国王让你儿子继位？
你儿子当国王我们就会拥有一切。

“You are really a silly rabbit.
You’ve been fooled around by others.
Why don’t you ask the king to let your son succeed?
If your son succeeds to the throne, we will have everything.

“你不会是忘记了吧，
当年国王受箭伤在你宫里养伤，
你服侍他如用人一般。
当时国王就要给你奖赏，
你回答说等你需要的时候再说。
当时国王就答应了你，
现在你就让国王奖赏你王位，
就让你儿子当国王，
你儿子一定能够管理好王国的江山！

“Don’t you forget that the king was wounded by an arrow and was healing his wound in your palace.
You attended to him like a servant.
At that time, the king was about to give you a reward,
You replied that you would wait until you needed it.
Then the king promised you,
Now you can request the king to reward you the throne.
If your son succeeds to the throne,
He must be able to govern the kingdom well !

“你让国王给你儿子当国王十二年，
这个期间就让朗玛满到深山里居住十二年。
十二年以后我们再做打算，
你就与国王求这个奖赏。”

“You request the king to make your son the king for 12 years,
During this period, you have Langmaman live in the mountains for 12 years.

We will make plans in 12 years,
You ask the king for this reward."

阿婷丫鬟这样教唆三王后，
三王后吉西突然感觉此话在情理中。
三王后说她不好意思去向国王禀报，
阿婷就教她装生病。

Ating, the servant girl abetted the third queen like this.
The third queen suddenly felt that this was reasonable.
The third queen said she was embarrassed to report to the king,
Ating taught her to pretend to be sick.

阿婷出鬼主意让三王后装生病，
她还说待国王来看望时就开口要奖赏。
国王说出的话不可能再收回，
这件事要找机会有的放矢。

Ating had such a nasty idea to let the third queen pretend to be sick,
She also said that when the king came to visit, she would ask for a reward.
What the king said can't be recalled,
This matter needed to be targeted.

这一天是五月十四日，
国王要去看望三王后。
大王后和二王后的宫殿干干净净，
都在为大王子继位做准备，
各种装饰都重新布置了一番。
三王后吉西的宫殿却反常寂静，
丫鬟阿婷也不在三王后旁边，
只有三王后吉西独自在房间哭泣。

On the 14th day of the 5th lunar month,
The king was going to see the third queen.
The palaces of the first queen and second queen were clean,
They were preparing for the succession of the first prince,
All kinds of decorations had been rearranged.
The palace of the Queen Jixi was unusually quiet.
The servant girl Ating was not beside the third queen.
Only Jixi, the third queen cried alone in the room.

国王走到三王后身边她也没反应，
国王坐下来问三王后道：
“心肝宝贝你是生病了吗？
哪里不舒服就告诉我，
是否需要让太医来看看？”

When the king came to the third queen, she didn't respond.
The king sat down and asked the third queen,
"Darling, are you sick ?
Tell me if you feel uncomfortable.
Do you need to go to see the imperial physician ?"

“我是生病了，
但这是国王您给我生的病啊！
微臣患的是心病，
唯有国王您才能让我逢凶化吉。”

“I'm sick.
But this is the disease you gave me.
I have a secret trouble,
Only you, the king can make my fortune come true.”

“既然如此你就尽管开口吧，
只要你的病能康复，
本王可以掏出我的心给你，
本王一定能够说到做到。”

“Since it is so, feel free to tell me,
As long as you can recover from your illness,
I can give you my heart.
I mean it.”

“今天是个好日子啊，
大湖里的金莲花都在开放迎宾客。
国王说的话是金口玉言，
国王您一定要说到做到。
国王您现在就奖赏我吧，
我要我们的儿子当国王。”
国王差一点就昏倒过去，
国王满脸通红地问道：
“吉西你不是在随便说说吧？
不是谁都可以当国王！”

“Today is an auspicious day.
The golden lotus flowers in the Great Lake are in bloom to welcome guests.
What the king said were previous words,
You must keep your words.
Your Majesty, please reward me now.
I want our son to be the king.”
Hearing it, the king almost fainted.
The king asked with a flushed face,
“Jixi, are you kidding me ?
Not everyone can be a king !”

“请大王先息怒啊，
大王您回想一下当年。
您去帮助大天神与尚拎王国开战，
您受箭伤在我宫中疗养。
我为您洗伤口敷良药，
您说伤好后要奖赏我，
当时我就说待我需要时再奖赏，
当时国王已答应了微臣，
现在我需要国王兑现诺言。”

“Please calm your anger first.
Your Majesty, think back to those days.
You went to help the Supreme God fight against the Kingdom of Shanglin.
You were wounded by an arrow and recuperated in my palace.
I washed your wound and applied good medicine.
You said you would reward me when you recovered.
At that time, I said I would wait until when I needed.

At that time, your Majesty had promised me.
Now I need you to keep your promise."

国王顿时感觉天崩地裂，
他一时手足无措：
"我的三王后宝贝啊，
这是万万不行的啊！
人们都知道朗玛满是阿銮，
他的威名传遍四面八方。
这是人民和大臣们的选择，
明天朗玛满就要继任国王。"

The king suddenly felt that the sky was falling apart.
And he was at a loss,
"My third queen baby,
This is absolutely impossible.
People know that Langmaman is Aluan,
Whose fame spread far and wide.
This is the choice of the people and ministers,
Tomorrow Langmaman will succeed to the throne."

"尊贵的大王啊，
您一定要让我的儿子当国王。
他当国王只要十二年，
这十二年就让朗玛满进深山里修行，
十二年后就让朗玛满回来当国王。
我相信国王您会践行诺言，
明天就让我儿子当国王。"

"Your Majesty,
You must make my son king.
He will be the king only for 12 years.
In these 12 years, let Langmaman cultivate in the mountains,
Let Langmaman come back to be the king in 12 years.
I believe you will keep your promise, your Majesty.
Let my son be king tomorrow."

大臣和国师们都在大殿里，
因为新国王继位仪式事务要商量，
各位大臣都在大殿里等待着国王的出现。
大臣苏曼达很着急，
他不相信国王还在卧室中，
他出出进进就是找不到国王。

Ministers and Guoshi were in the main hall,
Because the succession ceremony of the new king needed to be discussed.
All the ministers were waiting in the hall for the king.
Minister Sumanda was very worried.
He didn't believe the king was still in his bedroom,
He went in and out, but he could not find the king.

苏曼达和朗玛满到处寻找国王，
他们来到三王后的宫殿里。

Sumanda and Langmaman searched everywhere for the king.

他们看见了国王和三王后，	They came to the palace of the third queen,
朗玛满跪拜在父王面前：	Seeing the king and the third queen.
“父王和娘娘为何有愁容？	Langmaman knelt down before his father,
请当面给儿子明说。	“Why are father and mother so sad ?
父王需要什么请告诉我，	Please tell me in person.
就算是需要龙宫的珍珠宝贝，	Please tell me what father needs.
儿子也可以取来放在您面前。	“Even if you need the pearl treasure of the Dragon Palace, I can take it and put it in front you.
“即使父王想要天神的宝座，	“Even if father wants the throne of God,
儿子也可以搬到王宫中。	I can also move it to the palace.
若是父王需要尚拎王国的夜明珠，	If father needs the luminous pearl of Shanglin Kingdom,
儿子也可以取来献给父王。	I can also take it for you.
即使让儿子去住在深山里修行受苦，	Even if you let me go to live in the mountains for cultivation.
儿子亦感到无上荣光。”	I will feel great glory.”
三王后开口说话：	The third queen said,
“朗玛满啊，	“Langmaman,
你是你们四兄弟中的长兄，	You are the eldest among the four brothers,
我要把一件大事与你讲，	I want to tell you something important,
希望你作为长子能做出让步。	Hoping that you can make concessions as the eldest son.
当年你父王协助天神与尚拎王开战，	In those days, your father helped the God fight against King of Shanglin.
你父王受箭伤后在我宫中养伤。	Your father was wounded by an arrow and was healing in my palace.
我如丫鬟一般服侍他疗伤，	I attended to him like a servant girl to heal his wounds,
无微不至费尽苦心。	With great care.
“当时你父王答应我，	“At that time, your father promised me
我需要什么以后一定有奖赏。	That what I needed would be rewarded later.
现在娘娘需要王位，	Now I need the throne,

娘娘希望你父王立你四弟当国王。
你是兄长希望你宽宏大量，
你四弟当国王只当十二年。
十二年里你就居住在深山里，
居住山里修行可以益寿延年。”

I want your father to make your fourth brother king.
As the eldest brother, I hope you are generous,
Your fourth brother will be the king for only 12 years.
You are supposed to live in the mountains for 12 years,
Living and cultivating in the mountains will prolong your life.”

朗玛满听到此话后很淡定，
他给父王和三王后回答道：
“请父王和娘娘不要为难，
父王说话要言而有信，
儿子可以去住在深山老林里，
明日我就去深山里居住，
就让四弟继位当国王。”

Langmaman was calm after hearing this.
He replied to his father and the third queen,
“Please don’t be embarrassed.
Father, you should be true to your word,
I can go and live in the mountains.
I will live in the mountains tomorrow,
Let the fourth younger brother become king.”

朗玛满拜别父王与吉西娘娘，
他回到寝宫中。
他对西达公主说道：
“我美丽的西达公主啊，
你的美名已经传遍整个人世间。
只因父王与吉西娘娘曾经有约定，
要让四弟帕腊达当国王。
明日哥哥要去森林里修行，
我走后你要安心在宫里等我回来。

Langmaman bid farewell to his father and the Queen Jixi,
He returned to his sleeping palace.
He said to Princess Xida,
“My beautiful Princess Xida,
Your reputation has spread all over the world.
Only because my father and Queen Jixi had an agreement,
That is to let the fourth younger brother Palada be the king.
Tomorrow I will go to cultivate in the forest.
After I leave, you should wait for me in the palace.

“你服侍父母要经常问寒问暖，
对父母要孝顺体贴关心。
你对众侍女要视同亲姊妹，
随时随地都要把自己看作平凡人。

“You should inquire after their life when you serve our parents,
Be filial and considerate to our parents.
You should treat the maids like sisters,
And always treat yourself as an ordinary person.

“你所吃所用诸物不能小气， 遇到苦难者要和和气气地施舍。 初一十五是圣洁的日子， 你要保持一颗清净心。 王宫所有兄弟姐妹， 你须当作同母所生一家人。 如是宫里难以待下去， 你可以回到父母身边。”	“Don’t be stingy with what you eat and use. Give arms kindly to those suffering. The first and fifteenth days of the lunar calendar are holy days, You should keep a clean heart. For all brothers and sisters in the palace, You must treat them as family members with the same mother. If it’s hard to stay in the palace. You can go back to your parents.”
公主回答朗玛满道： “哥哥说的话难入妹妹耳里， 哥哥为何要妹妹回娘家？ 即使落水妹妹也要与你一起湿， 即使下火海妹妹也要跟着你， 哥哥进山我也要跟在后面， 住在深山里兄妹一起赏山花。”	The princess replied to Langmaman, “I don’t like what you said. Why do you want me to go back to my parents’ home ? Even if you fall into the water, I would like to get wet with you. Even if you step into the sea of fire, I would like to follow you. I’ll follow you as you enter the mountain. Living in the mountains, we two will enjoy the mountain flowers together.”
公主的表白让朗玛满很感动， 他向公主表白自己的内心： “赛过仙女的公主啊， 哥哥这样说并非不爱你， 因为深山里的情景确实不如王宫。 饿了吃的唯有野果， 渴了喝的是山泉。 夜晚住宿就在窝棚或大树下。	Langmaman was moved by the princess’s confession. He confessed to the princess, “The princess who has surpassed the fairy in beauty. What I said does not mean that I don’t love you, Because the situation in the mountains is really inferior to the palace. There are only wild fruits when you get hungry, You can only drink the spring when thirsty.

魔鬼和野兽是山中霸王，
有时它们还会来伤害人。

You have to stay under the shelter or big trees at night.
The devil and beasts are the overlords in the mountains,
Sometimes they come to hurt people.

“山里生活一定艰苦，
风吹雨淋只能躲在树林里边。
长年累月不见半粒米，
我们的粮仓就是深山老林。
山里的树叶是我的被褥，
绿色草皮是我的垫子。
山里与王宫差别大，
妹妹你鲜嫩的肌肤不适合在大山中。

“Life in the mountains must be hard,
You have to hide in the woods in windy and rainy days.
You can't see half a grain of rice for years,
Our granary lies in mountains and forests.
The leaves in the mountains are my bedding,
The green turf is my mat.
There is a big difference between the mountain and the palace.
Your delicate skin is not suitable for mountains.

“妹妹的双脚洁白若棉花，
哥哥不想让妹妹踏进深山老林。
你的手掌洁白似山顶上的雪，
哥哥不想让你去抓茅草和树干。

“Your feet are as white as cotton,
I don't want you to step into the mountains.
Your palms are as white as the snow on the mountain top,
I don't want you to catch the grass and tree trunks.

“哥哥爱你永远不变心，
哥哥爱你不只是这一辈子，
几生几世哥哥与你心连心。
哥哥就是不想让你去受苦，
希望你住在宫殿里，
让你天天与双亲生活在王宫中。”

“I will love you forever,
I love you not only for the rest of my life,
My heart will be with you for generations.
I just don't want you to suffer,
I hope you live in the palace,
So that you can stay with your parents every day.”

“哥哥所言不入妹妹的耳朵，
妹妹和哥哥心连心不能分离。
如是太阳没有了光芒，
它就无法照亮人世间。
如是大火没有了火焰，

“I don't like what you said,
We two can't be separated from each other.
If the sun has no light,
It can not illuminate the world.
If there is no flame in a big fire,

它就无法给人们温暖。
开荒种果正是硕果累累时，
园主没有理由离开果园。
既然命运让哥哥和妹妹走到一起，
哥哥没有理由舍妹妹独自到深山中。

it can not warm people.
When there is a good harvest in the orchard, the owner has no reason to leave the orchard.
Since fate bring you and me together,
You have no reason to leave me for the mountains.

“妹妹一定要跟您走，
妹妹服侍您日夜在身边。
哥哥口渴时妹妹去打水，
哥哥饥饿时妹妹去摘野果在深山。
只要能够和哥哥在一起，
千难万险我不怕。
森林里有美丽的风景，
在那里一定会益寿延年。”

“I must go with you,
I serve you day and night.
I'll go to fetch water when you are thirsty,
I'll pick the wild fruits in the mountains when you get hungry.
As long as I can stay with my brother,
I am not afraid of all kinds of difficulties and dangers.
There is beautiful scenery in the forest,
Where you will surely live longer.”

公主的话语句句发自肺腑，
公主的话打动了朗玛满的心。
朗玛满答应带公主一道前行，
公主欢喜笑开颜。

Every sentence was from the bottom of the princess's heart,
Langmaman was moved by the princess's words.
Langmaman promised to take the princess along,
The princess smiled happily.

纳哈腊来到宫殿里，
他真心跪拜在哥哥面前。
他请求哥哥让他也一同前往，
他说要去服侍哥哥在深山老林。
朗玛满让他去与母亲商量，
纳哈腊跪拜在母亲足前：
“我尊贵的妈妈啊，
大哥要去深山里修行，
我也要跟他进大山里，
我要天天守护在大哥身边，

Nahala came to the palace.
He sincerely knelt down before his elder brother,
And asked his elder brother to let him go together.
He said he would serve his elder brother in the mountains.
Langmaman asked him to consult with his mother.
Nahala knelt at his mother's feet,
“My honorable mother,
My elder brother is going to cultivate himself in the mountains,

请妈妈答应我同行。”

I also want to follow him into the mountains,
To guard my elder brother every day.
Mother, please allow me to go.”

“孩子啊，
这是前世修来的缘分。
你母亲我也想去服侍阿銮，
我也想常在阿銮身边。
我的儿子你就去吧，
你和你的哥哥住在深山里，
你也如同在持戒修行。
祝福你们事事如意，
祝福你们在深山老林里无病无灾。”

“My child,
This is the fate of the previous life.
I also want to serve Aluan,
And stay with him.
My son, you can go with him,
You and your elder brother live in the mountains,
You are also cultivating yourself by observing the commandments.
I wish you two all the best.
I wish you two a disease-free life in the mountains.”

纳哈腊去告诉哥哥朗玛满，
告诉说母亲二王后乐意让他同行。
朗玛满让弟弟去带弓箭，
朗玛满答应弟弟一路同行。
纳哈腊快快去拿神赐的弓箭，
他又回到哥哥身边。

Nahala went to tell his elder brother Langmaman
That his mother, the second queen was willing to let him go together.
Langmaman asked his younger brother to take the bow and arrow,
Langmaman promised his younger brother to go together.
Having got the bow and arrow from God quickly,
Nahala returned to his elder brother.

朗玛满带公主和弟弟来到宫殿里，
他们过去与母亲拜别：
“生我养我的妈妈啊，
只因父王与吉西娘娘有言在先，
要让帕腊达弟弟继承王位。
儿子要去深山里修行，
时间只是十二年。”

Langmaman brought the princess and younger brother to the palace.
They bid farewell to their mother,
“Mother, you gave birth to me and raised me.
Because father and Queen Jixi have previously pledged their word,
That they want to let Palada succeed to the throne.

I'm going to cultivating myself in the mountains,
For only 12 years."

母亲双手抚摸着朗玛满的脸，
母亲悲喜交加。
母亲泪流满面，
但她没有一丝的悲伤：
"我的儿子啊，
人们说你是一位阿銮，
你要走的路艰难险阻，
妈妈相信你会用智慧排除万难。
你肩上的担子与众不同，
妈妈相信你有超人的能力。
你将为众生铲除邪恶，
还天下一个明媚的艳阳天。"

The mother touched Langmaman's face with her hands,
She was filled with sorrow and joy.
But she didn't have a trace of sadness,
"My son,
People say you are a Aluan,
Thought the road you have to take is difficult and dangerous,
I believe you will overcome all difficulties with wisdom.
The burden on your shoulders is different,
I believe you have superior ability.
You will eradicate the evil for all beings,
To give the world a sunny day."

朗玛满的母亲为他们祈福，
祈愿他们前行道路无阻，
十二年转眼就会过去，
十二年后再回到王宫中。
冬去春来一年又一年，
祝愿战胜邪恶奏凯旋。

Langmaman's mother prayed for them,
Wishing them all the best,
12 years would pass in an instant,
You would be back to the palace in 12 years.
Spring follows winter year after year,
I wished you victory in the fight against the evil.

十二年时间不短暂，
喜怒哀乐不可臆测。
朗玛满已经坚定了信心，
朗玛满要用胜利回报人世间。

12 years were not short,
It was impossible to speculate about happiness, anger and sadness.
Langmaman had been more confident and determined
In rewarding the human world with victory.

朗玛满他们要启程，
国王和大臣们都来送行。

Langmaman and other people were about to leave,
The king and ministers came to see them off.

前来送行的还有成千上万的人民，
人们舍不得与他们分别。

Besides, thousands of people came to see them off,
People were reluctant to part with them.

国王对朗玛满依依不舍，
国王含泪目送朗玛满前行。
朗玛满他们向前方走去，
国王昏倒在宫殿前。

The king was reluctant to part with Langmaman,
He watched Langmaman walk forward with tears.
Langmaman and others were marching forward,
As the king fainted in front of the palace.

大王后用圣水涂抹国王面部，
国王才慢慢苏醒过来。
国王醒过来就喊朗玛满的名字，
但朗玛满的身影已消失在前方。

After the first queen daubed the king's face with holy water,
The king slowly came to himself.
When the king woke up, he called Langmaman's name.
But Langmaman's figure had disappeared in front.

国王与大伙回到王宫里，
国王一直想念朗玛满，
因为前方是野兽出没的原始森林，
国王总是放心不下。
十二年的时间不短暂，
国王的日子将会度日如年。

The king and other people returned to the palace.
But the king has been missing Langmaman,
Because there were beasts in the primeval forest ahead,
The king was always worried.
12 years would not be short,
The days of the king would pass like years.

朗玛满他们来到深山里，
他们临时搭建了两间窝棚。
朗玛满与公主住在里间，
纳哈腊与苏曼达住外间。

Having arrived at the mountains,
Langmaman and others people established two temporary shacks.
Langmaman and the princess stayed in the inner shack,
While Nahala and Sumanda stayed in the outer shack.

朗玛满安排苏曼达回王城去，
苏曼达不舍地说：
“此次出来我的任务就是服侍您，
我要永远陪伴在您身边。”

Langmaman arranged for Sumanda to return to the imperial city.
Sumanda said reluctantly,
"My task is to serve you this time,
I will stay with you forever."

朗玛满悲伤地说道：
“有的人说爱我只是嘴上讲，
但我知道你的爱发自内心。
你是一位忠诚的大臣，
你还是快快回去报告父王我们一切平安。”
苏曼达跪拜朗玛满后离去，
朗玛满与公主和纳哈腊又开始启程。

Langmaman said sorrowfully,
“Some people say they love me just by mouth,
But I know you love me from the bottom of your heart.
You are a loyal minister,
You'd better go back quickly and tell our father that we are safe.”
Sumanda left after he knelt to Langmaman,
Langmaman, the princess and Nahala set out again.

此时大天神混西迦已有感应，
他让助手宇肃忠天神下凡帮助朗玛满。
宇肃忠下凡施法变出鲜花水果布满深山，
施法完毕他又回到天宫中。

At this time, the Great God Hunxijia had already felt,
He asked his assistant Yusuzhong to come down to earth to help Langmaman.
Yusuzhong came down to earth to cast magic for flowers and fruits all over the mountains,
He returned to the heavenly palace after he finished casting magic.

朗玛满他们行走在深山里，
公主的嫩脚被刺戳伤，
她疼痛得哭泣泪涟涟。
朗玛满心疼地对公主说：
“哥哥让你留在王宫里，
你却执意要跟我进大山中。
我们的路程才开始，
不知道还要走几天。”
他们走走停停又向前走，
他们走进了另一座大山中。

The princess's tender foot was stabbed,
As Langmaman and other people were walking in the mountains.
She cried in pain.
Langmaman said to the princess sorrowfully,
“I asked you to stay in the palace,
But you insisted on following me into the mountains.
It's just the beginning of our journey,
I don't know how many days we will have to walk.”
They walked for distance, stopped and then continue to walk.
They walked into another mountain.

山里住着一位得道的雅细，
纳哈腊礼敬跪拜雅细足前。
雅细开口问：
“施主是何方人士？
你们的根底深厚非同一般人。”

There lived a virtuous Yaxi in the mountain,
Nahala knelt at Yaxi’s feet.
Yaxi asked,
“Who is the benefactor ?
Unlike ordinary people, you have good morality.”

“聪明智慧的尊者啊，
我们的父亲是国王达撒腊塔。
我们有四个弟兄，
大哥名叫朗玛满，
身相庄严无人能及。
我是弟弟名叫纳哈腊，
此次跟随大哥进山是为了修行。”

“Your intelligent venerable,
Our father is the King Dasalata.
We have four brothers,
The eldest brother is Langmaman.
No one can match his dignified appearance.
I’m Nahala, the younger brother.
This time, I followed my elder brother into the mountain
to cultivate myself.”

雅细听后开口道：
“如此说来你们皆为我晚辈孙，
要我帮什么忙尽管开口。”
纳哈腊将前后原因向雅细诉说，
又请雅细指点落脚处。
朗玛满向雅细行告别礼，
虔诚跪拜又谢恩。

Hearing it, Yaxi said,
“So you are all my junior grandchildren,
Please feel free to ask, if you need any help.”
Nahala told the Yaxi about the reasons,
And asked Yaxi to point out a temporary lodging.
Langmaman bade farewell to Yaxi,
And thanked Yaxi by kneeling down piously.

雅细对朗玛满说道：
“你年纪轻轻就能够为父王解难题，
离开王宫居住大山中。
你的功德已经巨大无比，
将来你的威名留人间。”

The Yaxi said to Langmaman,
“You can solve difficult problems for your father at such a
young age,
By leaving the palace for the mountains.
Your show great merits and virtues.
In the future, your reputation will remain in the world.”

纳哈腊进山去砍树，

Nahala went into the mountains to cut trees

他们在雅细居住地附近搭建窝棚。	To set up shacks beside Yaxi's residence.
大山深处好风景，	There is beautiful scenery in the mountains,
渴了饮山泉饿了吃野果。	They drank spring water when thirsty and ate wild fruits when hungry.
十二年的光阴将在这里度过，	They would spend the 12 years here,
他们将与野兽为伍鸟语伴花香。	They would keep company with wild animals Along with singing birds and fragrant flowers.
无数国人怀念朗玛满，	Countless subjects missed Langmaman,
他们踏着朗玛满的足迹来到大山中。	They followed Langmaman's footsteps to the mountains.
他们看见了大臣苏曼达，	They saw Minister Sumanda,
但没有看见朗玛满和公主。	But they didn't see Langmaman and the princess.
人们呼唤着朗玛满的名字，	People were calling the name of Langmaman,
有人在偷偷流泪不停地哽咽。	With some secretly sobbing in tears.
人们没找到朗玛满，	People didn't find Langmaman,
陆续回到王城中。	They returned to the royal city one after another.
苏曼达回到王宫向国王跪拜禀报：	Sumanda went back to the palace to kneel down and report to the king,
“微臣已将朗玛满送到深山里，	"I've sent Langmaman to the mountains,
一路上皆为顺利平安。	We've been safe along the way.
微臣欲陪他在深山里居住，	I wanted to accompany him to live in the mountains.
是朗玛满让微臣返回王宫中。	It was Langmaman who asked me to return to the palace.
他说国王的身体最要紧，	He said the king's health was the most important thing,
国王是他最大的担心。”	The king was his biggest concern."
国王担心地对苏曼达说道：	The king said to Sumanda anxiously,
“你去把帕腊达王子叫来我这里，	"Go and fetch Prince Palada to me,
本王虽是夕阳无限好，	Although the setting sun is infinitely good,
但不可回避已是近黄昏。”	But it's almost dusk."

国王又忧愁地继续说道：
“这件事完全是怪我，
是我听信了女人的谗言，
我完全是在引火烧身。
我把朗玛满派到深山里居住，
我今生也许就再也不能见到朗玛满。”

The king went on sadly,
“It's all my fault.
I listened to the slander of women,
I'm totally on fire.
I sent Langmaman to live in the mountains,
I may never see Langmaman again in this life.”

国王让人叫来了大王后，
国王双手拉住大王后的手说道：
“朗玛满是个好儿子，
他住在深山老林中，
本王也想念朗玛满，
不知何时才能再相见。”
国王才把话说完，
就闭上双眼驾崩在大王后怀中。

The king had someone call in the first queen.
The king took the queen's hand and said,
“Langmaman is a good son,
He is living the mountains,
I also miss Langmaman,
I don't know when we can meet again.”
The king closed his eyes and died in the first queen's arms,
Soon after he finished his words.

这是十头王的故事，
我们的故事一环扣一环，
往后的内容更精彩，
预想不到的情节就在下一章中。

This is the story of the Ten-headed King,
Our story is linked one by one,
The following chapters will be more wonderful,
The unexpected plot is in the next chapter.

第七章

Chapter Seven

前一章结束后一章又开始，
一章更比一章牵动人心。
话说大臣们在商议如何料理国王的后事，
认为请帕腊达回来继承王位是上策。
因为四个王子都不在王宫里，
大臣们唯恐他国趁机发动战争。
大臣们让苏曼达去请帕腊达王子，
要请帕腊达速速回到王宫。

A new chapter started with end of the previous chapter,
The story became more and more thrilling.
The ministers were discussing about how to deal with the king's funeral affairs.
They thought it was the best decision to invite Palada back to succeed to the throne.
Because the four princes were not in the palace,
The ministers were afraid that other countries would take the opportunity to start a war.
The ministers asked Sumanda to invite Prince Palada
To come to the palace in haste.

帕腊达王子与国王舅舅拜别，
他与苏曼达坐车往回走。
路上有许多反常现象，
车前出现狐狸自左跑向右，
又见老鹰自右飞向左，
还有一只老雕紧紧跟在彩车后。

Prince Palada bid farewell to his uncle,
He and Sumanda took the carriage back.
There were many anomalies on the way.
A fox appeared in front of the carriage, running from left to right,
And the eagle flew from right to left,
There was also an old eagle closely following the float.

帕腊达王子有一种不祥的预感，
他的心里开始担心父王。
他向苏曼达问道：
“你出来时王宫里出了什么事？
父母他们是否都安康？
大臣、将军和宫里人，
是否人人都平安？”
苏曼达大臣回答道：
“我离开王宫时一切都安好，
请王子尽管放心。”

Prince Palada had a foreboding,
He began to worry about his father.
He asked Sumanda,
"What happened to the palace when you came out ?
Are both parents safe and healthy ?
Are all ministers, generals and people in the palace safe ?"
Minister Sumanda replied,
"Everything is OK when I left the palace,
Please don't worry, prince."
Palada was not convinced after hearing this.

帕腊达听后心里不太相信，
他的心里在忐忑不安。

He fell into in a state of uneasiness.

彩车快要回到王城，
路上的百姓议论国事乱纷纷：
“本来是要朗玛满继承王位，
就是三王后吉西在作梗，
她是要她的儿子当国王，
朗玛满不得不舍王位躲进深山中。
老国王就是为此事操心才舍命，
不知以后谁来做国王。”

The float was about to return to the imperial city.
The people on the road talked about the state affairs in disorder,
“It was supposed that Langmaman would succeed to the throne,
It is the third Queen Jixi who made trouble,
She wanted her son to be the king.
Langmaman had to give up the throne and hide in the mountains.
The old king died because he was so worried about it.
I don't know who will be the king in the future.”

帕腊达质问苏曼达，
要他告诉真实情况。
苏曼达只好如实回答道：
“大臣、将军、国师和百姓，
他们都要求朗玛满继位当国王。
因为三王后与国王从前有约定，
三王后一定要让您当国王，
十二年后朗玛满才能回来继承王位。
朗玛满王子已经离开王宫，
他带着妻子和二王子到森林里修行。
现在国王已经去世，
大臣们派我出来请您回去当国王。”

Palada interrogated Sumanda,
Asking him to tell the truth.
Sumanda had to answer truthfully,
“Ministers, generals, Guoshi and civilians all asked Langmaman to succeed to the king.
Because there was an agreement between the third queen and the king,
The third queen must make you king
And it will be 12 years before Langmaman returns to the throne.
The Prince Langmaman has left the palace.
He brought his wife and the second prince to the forest for cultivation.
Now the king has passed away.
The ministers sent me here to invite you back to be the king.”

帕腊达心里很清楚，
他的母亲也很喜欢哥哥朗玛满，
她为什么突然要自己去当国王？
这里肯定有人在捣鬼。
他决心一定要弄清楚，
因为哥哥朗玛满最适合当国王。

Palada knew very well,
His mother also liked his brother Langmaman,
Why did she suddenly want her son to be the king.
Someone must be doing something here.
He was determined to figure it out,
Because his elder brother Langmaman was the most suitable for the king.

帕腊达到达王宫里，
他速速去拜见母亲：
“我尊贵的母亲啊，
我哥哥为什么躲进深山里？
父王为什么这个时候去世？
请母亲告诉我，
儿子回王宫里身心不安宁。”

After Palada returned to the palace,
He went to see his mother quickly,
“My noble mother,
Why did my elder brother hide in the mountains ?
Why did my father die at this time ?
Please tell me, mother,
I went back to the palace feeling restless.”

在一旁的阿婷插话道：
“我们高贵的王子啊，
大臣、将军和百姓都要朗玛满当国王，
婢女我知道后犹如刀割五脏，
是婢女给三王后出主意，
国王才改变主意让您继位当国王。”

Ating who was nearby cut in,
“Our noble prince,
The ministers, generals and civilians all wanted Langmaman to be king.
Having known it, I was torn with grief,
It was me who gave advice to the third queen,
The king changed his mind to let you become the king.”

帕腊达听后发怒火，
他一把揪住阿婷的头发往门外拖，
阿婷痛得哇哇哭叫忙认错，
帕腊达将她赶出了王宫。

Palada got very angry after hearing this,
He grabbed Ating’s hair and dragged it outside the door,
Ating was so painful that she cried and apologized.
Palada drove her out of the palace.

帕腊达来到大殿上，

Palada came to the hall,

他召集大臣们料理国王的后事。
到了庄严吉祥的日子，
人们将国王的遗体火化在坟场中。

He summoned the ministers to deal with the king's funeral affairs.
On a solemn and auspicious day,
The king's body was cremated in the cemetery.

国王的后事料理结束后，
帕腊达向大臣、将军和国师们说道：
“尊贵的大臣们啊，
我哥哥朗玛满聪颖又智慧，
我哥哥朗玛满仁慈又善良。
我哥哥朗玛满还活在世上，
让我当国王就是叫我下地狱。
如今我哥哥还活在这世上，
我坚决不当这个国王。
我们现在速速做准备，
快去深山里迎接哥哥朗玛满，
请他回来做我们的国王。”

After the king's affairs were finished,
Palada said to the ministers, generals and Guoshi,
“Distinguished ministers,
My elder brother, Langmaman is intelligent and wise,
My elder brother Langmaman is merciful and kind.
My elder brother Langmaman is still alive,
To make me king was to make me go to hell.
My elder brother still lives in this world.
Therefore, I am determined not to be the king.
Let's get ready now,
Go to meet my elder brother Langmaman in the mountains,
Invite him back to be our king.”

大象、马车和士兵组成大队伍，
还有大臣、将军、王后和侍从，
浩浩荡荡的队伍向大山进发。
队伍来到深山老林里，
鼓声、号声和礼炮声回荡在森林中。

Elephants, carriages and soldiers formed a large team.
There were also ministers, generals, queens and attendants.
The mighty troops were marching towards the mountains.
The team came to the mountains and forests,
The sound of drums, trumpets and salutes reverberated in the forest.

纳哈腊正在深山里找野果，
他听见了隆隆大炮声。
他速速回到窝棚里，
他将情况告诉了兄长朗玛满。

Nahala wsa looking for wild fruits in the mountains,
He heard the rumble of cannon.
He quickly returned to the shack,
He told his elder brother Langmaman about the situation.

朗玛满问弟弟道：

Langmaman asked the younger brother,

“是不是有人要来抢西达公主，	“Is someone coming to grab Princess Xida ?
难道这支大队伍是带着阴谋来到大山中？	Does this team come to the mountain with a plot ?
弟弟你爬到树上去观察，	Brother, you climbed up a tree and observe,
如有情况就射神箭吓唬他们。”	If there are circumstances, shoot magic arrows to frighten them.”
纳哈腊看得很清楚，	Nahala could see clearly,
前来的大队伍原来是自己人。	The team approaching turned out to our people.
纳哈腊跑回窝棚对哥哥说道：	Nahala ran back to the shack and said to his elder brother,
“我尊贵善良的哥哥啊，	“My noble and kind brother,
弟弟已经看清楚，	I’ve seen clearly,
前来的队伍是王宫里的人。	The troops coming are from the palace.
也许是来接我们回去，	Maybe they come to bring us back,
也许是王宫里出了什么事情。”	Maybe something happened in the palace.”
王宫里来的大队人马来到山里，	The group of people from the palace came to the mountain.
帕腊达跪拜在朗玛满面前：	Palada knelt before Langmaman and said,
“我尊贵的哥哥啊，	“My noble brother,
弟弟终于找到您了，	I finally found you,
弟弟前来迎接哥哥，	I come to meet you,
我们请哥哥返回王宫中。”	To invite you to return to the palace.”
“我贤德的弟弟啊，	“My virtuous brother,
难道是王宫里发生了什么意外？	Did something happen to the palace ?
弟弟才带大队伍来到大山中。	That’s why you are leading a group of people to the mountain.
弟弟你要说实话，	Brother, you should tell me the truth.
要不然哥哥就不跟你回王宫。”	Otherwise, I won’t go back to the palace with you.”
“哥哥啊，	“Brother,
王宫里真是发生了意外，	There was an accident in the palace.

自从您离开王宫出门去修行，	Since you left the palace and went out to cultivate yourself,
父王日夜在为王国忧愁。	The king has been worried about the kingdom day and night.
父王厌倦了钩心斗角的王宫生活，	He has been tired of the palace life of intrigue.
他已离开我们去了神邦。”	He has left us for Heaven."

王后她们走进窝棚里，	The queens and other people went into the shack,
她们忍不住哭泣。	They couldn't help crying.
大王后号啕诉衷肠：	The first queen wailed,
“我仁慈善良的儿子啊，	"My merciful and kind son,
快快回到生你养你的王宫吧，	Come back quickly to the palace where you were born and raised,
那里吃穿诸事不用愁，	Where you don't have to worry about your food and clothing,
成群的侍女服侍在身旁。	Where groups of maids are attending to you.
你们在山里用树叶当被褥，	You use leaves as bedding in the mountains,
靠野果当饭吃，	Eat by wild fruits.
你们已经历尽万般艰辛，	You have gone through all kinds of hardships.
谁人见了都会哭断肠。”	Anyone will cry sorrowfully when he sees this."
众人个个伤心地流下眼泪，	Everyone wept sadly,
哭泣声回荡在大山中。	With the crying echoing in the mountains.
雅细坐在窝棚里，	Yaxi was sitting in the shack,
人们纷纷前去跪拜雅细。	People went to kneel down to Yaxi.
雅细向人们传授经文，	Yaxi taught scriptures to people,
让人们经常背诵。	Asking them to recite often.
雅细劝化人们弃恶从善，	Yaxi persuaded people to abandon evil and be good.
朗玛满将经文全部记在心中。	Langmaman kept all the scriptures in mind.

朗玛满拿水果来把雅细和父王供养，	Langmaman provided fruit for Yaxi and the king.
父王突然显像在高空中：	The king suddenly appeared in the sky and said,
“朗玛满你供养的诸水果，	"Langmaman, I have received the fruit offered by you,

父王已经全部领受。
父王已经来到神邦，
祝福你好好修行早结善果。”

I've been in the heaven.
I wish you good cultivation and good results."

帕腊达激动地说道：
“尊贵的父王啊，
我们在王宫里做了诸多供养，
但是父王就是没有显像，
今天哥哥供养水果，
父王就显像于天空中。
说明父王信任哥哥朗玛满啊，
我们一定要让哥哥回去当国王。”
帕腊达开始责怪母亲吉西，
认为一切皆由她引起。
吉西向朗玛满认错：
“聪明智慧的朗玛满啊，
您是我们全国的希望，
您的智慧超过所有人！
是娘娘做错了事情，
请您谅解愚蠢的娘娘。
尊贵的朗玛满啊，
您是春天的雨露，
请您去滋润人间万物。
多大的伤痛也请您忍耐，
请您别放在心中。
全国民众都期待您回去继承王位，
娘娘我已无脸在王宫中。
请您原谅娘娘这一次吧，
从今往后娘娘我不再犯错误，
我将为这次过错忏悔一生。”

Palada said excitedly,
"Distinguished father,
We made many offerings in the palace,
But you have never shown.
Today my brother offered fruit,
And then you appear in the sky.
It shows that you trust my brother Langmaman,
We must have my brother go back to be the king."
Palada began to blame his mother Jixi,
Thinking she caused everything.
Jixi apologized to Langmaman,
"Intelligent and wise Langmaman,
You are the hope our kingdom.
Your wisdom surpasses all others.
I made a mistake,
Please forgive me.
Distinguished Langmaman,
You are the rain and dew of spring,
Please moisten the world.
Please bear whatever pain you have,
Please don't take it to heart.
People of the kingdom are looking forward to your succession to the throne.
I have no face in the palace,
Please forgive me this time.
From now on, I'll never make mistakes,
I will repent my life for this mistake."

帕腊达哭着劝朗玛满道：
“请哥哥跟我们回王宫去，
等待哥哥的是宝座和王宫。
如是哥哥不回王宫里，
弟弟我也要陪哥哥修行在大山中。
弟弟每天用野果把哥哥来供养，
洗漱用水弟弟负责端到哥哥面前。
只要哥哥不嫌弃弟弟，
弟弟宁愿服侍哥哥一生。”

Palada cried and persuaded Langmaman,
"Brother, please go back to the palace with us,
The throne and palace await you.
If you don't return to the palace,
I will also accompany you to cultivate in the mountains,
Offering wild fruit to you every day.
I will be responsible for carrying the water for you for washing.
As long as you don't dislike me,
I will serve you all my life."

朗玛满思前又想后，
朗玛满想得很周全：
“如是我和帕腊达都不回王宫去，
王宫就是摆设的花篮。
如是我违背与父王的约定回去当国王，
我就违反了父王的金口玉言。
把我踩踏过的路边小草带回王宫中，
因为那些小草上有我的足迹，
你们把我的足迹供奉在宝座上，
这样就如同我坐在宝座上边。

Langmaman thought back and forth to himself,
Langmaman was thoughtful,
"If neither Palada nor I go back to the palace,
The palace is a decorated flower basket.
If I break the agreement with my father that I will go back to be the king,
I violated my father's oracular words.
Take the roadside grass I stepped on back to the palace,
Because those grass have my footprints.
You put my footprints on the throne,
It's like I'm sitting on a throne.

“如是大臣和将军们违了规矩，
小草就会在宝座上训话。
如是人人依章办国事，
小草就会安静地待在宝座上边。
帕腊达弟弟啊，
你就按哥哥的话去做吧，
哥哥与你们永远心连心。”

"If ministers and generals break the rules,
The grass will lecture on the throne.
If everyone handles state affairs according to regulations,
The grass will stay quietly on the throne.
Palada, my brother,
Do as I told you.
My heart will always be with you."

朗玛满说出了这样一番话，
众人哭泣着将朗玛满“足迹”拢在一起，
他们用各种鲜花祈请朗玛满的“足迹”，
众人与朗玛满依依道别在大山中。

Hearing the words above by Langmaman,
People were crying to gather the “footprints” of Langmaman,
They prayed for Langmaman’s “footprints” with all kinds of flowers,
People said goodbye to Langmaman in the mountains.

浩浩荡荡的大队伍回到王宫里，
众人将“足迹”供奉在宝座上，
国师们念诵吉祥语滴水祝福，
以示朗玛满已继位当国王。
王宫内外人们载歌载舞，
歌声炮声回荡在王城上空。

The mighty team returned to the palace,
People enshrined the “footprints” on the throne.
Guoshi recited the auspicious scriptures for blessing,
To show Langmaman had succeeded to the throne.
People inside and outside the palace sang and danced.
The sound of singing and gunfire reverberated over the imperial city.

帕腊达王子后来也离开了王宫，
他来到另一座大山上修行。
这座大山名叫季里玛那山，
这座山像一座王宫会闪闪发光。
他与三哥沙达鲁嘎纳在山里生活，
这里是山清水秀的地方。
我们的长诗告一段落，
我们的故事环环相扣。
我们的长诗就像一座长廊，
许许多多的人们要到这里相会。
相会的人们就像赶集一样你来我往，
故事的情节就像丝线一样穿来穿去。
下面的情节更引人入胜，
请父老乡亲们等待念诵精彩的下一章。

Prince Palada left the palace afterwards,
He went to another mountain for cultivation.
The name of this mountain was Mount Jilimana,
The mountain glittered like a palace.
He lived in the mountains with his third brother, Shadalugana,
It was a beautiful place.
This is the end of the chapter,
Our stories are interlinked.
The epic is like a corridor,
Where many people meet.
People meet each other like going to the market,
The plot of the story goes through like silk thread.
The following plot is more compelling.
My fellow countrymen, please wait for the next wonderful chapter.

第八章
Chapter Eight

话说在那由数座大山连成的大森林中，	In the big forest connected by several mountains,
居住着三亿八千万只猴子。	Inhabited 380 million monkeys.
他们来自朵细达神国，	They were from Duoxida Kingdom of God.
他们是阿銮的护卫军。	They were the escort troops of Aluan.
猴国中有一只猴子最特别，	There was a unique monkey in the Kingdom of Monkey.
他英勇威武神通不凡，	He was brave, powerful and supernatural,
他会将身体变长十五个眼程，	Having the ability to lengthen his body by 15 eye-reaches,
他快活在宽阔无边的原始森林中。	He was enjoying himself in the vast primeval forest.
有一天太阳从东方出来金光闪闪，	One day, the sun rose in the east and was shining brightly.
他以为是一个水果挂在天空中。	He thought it was fruit hanging in the sky.
他纵身一跃就来到苍穹里，	He jumped into the sky,
他抓住了太阳车的轮子不让太阳前行。	He grabbed the wheel of the solar car to keep the sun from moving.
太阳公子告到大天神混西迦处：	The Sun God reported to the Great God Hunxijia,
“至高无上的大王啊，	“The supreme Emperor,
我有急事要向您禀报，	I have something urgent to report to you.
有一个怪物跳到天上来，	A monster jumped into the sky,
他牢牢抓住了我的车轮。”	And grabbed my wheel firmly.”
大天神混西迦用金斧砍过去，	The Great God Hunxijia hacked through with his golden axe,
砍断了那只猴子的下巴，	The monkey’s chin was cut off.
猴子掉落大地上，	The monkey fell to the ground,
他如死了一般。	As if he were dead.
猴王上天求救：	Monkey King went to heaven to ask for help,
“至高无上的大天神啊，	“The supreme Great God,
请您救救猴国的一只猴子吧，	Please save a monkey from the Monkey Kingdom,
他是猴国的得力助手，	He is the right assistant of the Monkey Kingdom.
还要让他服务于猴国。”	

I want him to serve the Monkey Kingdom."

大天神混西迦下凡救猴子，
还赐给了他三大神通：
让他落水如履平地，
让他下火海时犹如游泳一般清凉。
天上和人间百般武器，
不会伤害到他的身体。
大天神还给他赐名阿奴曼，
三大神通让这只猴子享用终生。

The Great God Hunxijia descended to earth to save the monkey.
He also gave him three magic powers, namely,
Making him fall into the water like walking on the ground,
Making him step into the fire as if swimming in the coolness,
Making him invulnerable to various weapons in heaven and on earth.
The Great God also gave him the name Anuman.
The three magic powers enabled the monkey to enjoy his life.

有一天几位雅细去师父处学经文，
他们路过这片大森林。
阿奴曼看见了数位雅细，
他手疾眼快地抢走了雅细的经卷，
他把经卷撕碎在大森林中。

One day, several Yaxi went to their master to learn scriptures,
They went through the forest.
Anuman saw the Yaxi,
And snatched Yaxi's scrolls of scriptures with great agility.
He tore up the scrolls of scriptures in the forest.

雅细向师父诉苦：
"圣贤智慧的师父啊，
一只猴子将我们的经卷撕得粉碎，
然后大摇大摆跑进大森林中。"
师父用天眼观看四方，
方知这只猴子有三大神通，
他能够在天上人间为所欲为。

Yaxi complained to their master,
"Sage and wise master,
A monkey tore our sutras to pieces,
And then swaggered into the forest."
The master observed with his heavenly eyes
And knew that the monkey had three magic powers.
He could do whatever he wanted in heaven and on earth.

雅细们离开师父集中到一座山上，
他们集体念诵神咒，

Yaxi left their master and gathered in a mountain.
They recited the mantra together,

他们诅咒猴类只能居住在森林里：
“龙王住在水里也害怕凡人，
各种猛兽住在森林里也害怕人类，
猴类只能生活在森林里，
猴类的智力要永远低于人类，
要让猴类见到人就惊恐万分。”

Cursing the monkeys to confine themselves to the forest,
"The Dragon King lives in the water and is afraid of mortals.
All kinds of beasts live in the forest and are afraid of humans.
Monkeys can only live in the forest.
The intelligence of monkeys is always lower than that of humans.
We shall make monkeys panic when they see people."

自从雅细们念诵神咒，
阿奴曼就萎靡不振，
他全身疼痛难忍，
他的本领已经大不如前。
他百思不得其解，
他行走在地上就非常胆小，
他只想快快躲避凡人。

Since Yaxi recited divine mantras,
Anuman had been depressed.
His whole body ached unbearably,
His skills were not as good as before.
He was puzzled.
He was very timid when he walked on the ground.
He just wanted to evade the mortal.

阿奴曼突然想出一个主意，
他要去找占布曼，
因为占布曼是猴医。
“占布曼啊，
从前我的力量巨大无人能及，
现如今却软弱无力。
我落在地上就会惊恐万分，
我很害怕看见凡人。”

Anuman suddenly had an idea,
He wanted to find Zhanbuman,
Because Zhanbuman was a monkey doctor.
"Zhanbuman,
Once I was so powerful that no one could match me.
Now I'm weak and feeble.
If I fall on the ground, I will be terrified.
I'm afraid of seeing the mortal."

猴医占布曼有神通长天眼，
他一看便知道阿奴曼做了什么事情：
“你是得罪了众位尊者，
是尊者们对你念诵了神咒真言。”

The monkey doctor Zhanbuman has magic powers and heavenly eyes.
He knew at a glance what Anuman had done,
"You have offended the honorable ones.

“求你帮我破解神咒，
让我的体力和神通恢复如前。”

It was the venerable ones who recited the mantra to you.”
“Please help me break the magic spell,
To restore my strength and magic power as before.”

“那是万万使不得啊，
你要用野果鲜花去供养众尊者承认错误，
求他们将你的体力和神通恢复如从前，
你要虔诚真心才能见效。”

“That’s absolutely impossible.
You have to offer wild fruits and flowers to the venerable and apologize to them,
Praying to them for restoring your strength and magic powers as before.
It won’t work unless you are devout and sincere.”

阿奴曼去找雅细，
阿奴曼跪拜在雅细们面前说道：
“博学智慧的尊者啊，
千错万错都是我的错，
现在我虔诚跪拜忏悔，
请尊者把我的体力和神通恢复到从前。”

Anuman went to Yaxi,
He knelt before Yaxi and said,
“Learned and wise venerable,
I should be responsible for all this.
Now I sincerely kneel down to repent.
Venerable, please restore my strength and magic powers as before.”

雅细们一起商议道：
“如是让他恢复神通与体力，
他会耀武扬威目中无人。”
雅细们对他说道：
“有一位阿銮名叫朗玛满，
某年某月的某一天，
他会带着他的随行从你身边路过，
你们会相遇在深山老林中。

Yaxi discussed together,
“If his magic powers and strength are recovered,
He will be arrogant with his nose in the air.”
Yaxi said to him,
“There is an Aluan called Langmaman.
On a certain day of a certain month in a certain year,
He will pass you with his entourage.
You will meet in the mountains.

“阿銮会用他的手掌拍打你身体，
你的神通和体力就会恢复到从前。
到那时从森林到勐兰嘎你可以飞来飞去，

“Aluan will slap you with his palm.
Your magic powers and strength will be restored as before.
Then you can fly freely from the forest to Menglanga.

一切灾难不沾你身。”
从此阿奴曼日夜愁眉苦脸，
他期盼阿銮快快出现在他面前。

我们的长诗告一段落，
我们的故事正精彩。
长诗要慢慢来念诵，
长诗要细细聆听才记得牢。
父老乡亲们啊请耐心期待，
精彩的情节还在下一章中。

You will be free from all disasters."
Henceforth, Anuman had been melencholic.
He expected Aluan to appear in front of him soon.

This is the end of the chapter,
Our story is in the prime time.
The epic should be recited slowly,
The epic should be carefully listened to before it can be remembered.
My fellow countrymen, please wait patiently,
For the wonderful story in the next chapter.

第九章

Chapter Nine

前一章结束后一章又开始，
一章更比一章牵动人心。
话说大山中的猴王是巴力莫，
他横行霸道不讲兄弟情。
巴力莫将弟媳占为己有，
还以弟弟苏嘎林要篡位为由将其赶出了猴邦。

The end of the previous chapter is followed by a new chapter,
The stories are getting more and more compelling.
The Monkey King in the mountain was Balimo,
He was a bully and didn't talk about brotherhood.
Balimo took his sister-in-law as his own,
He also drove his younger brother Sugalin out of the Monkey Kingdom on the pretext that he wanted to usurp the throne.

朗玛满他们三人住在深山里，
光阴荏苒已有十二年。
他们离开了原始森林，
他们迁往辽阔的大海边。

Langmaman and other two people had lived in the mountains
For 12 years.
They left the primeval forest,
For the vast seaside.

这里是十头王的领地，
他管辖着这里的陆地与高空。
这里居住着一个名叫哈达的魔女，
她的两个儿子也经常游荡在大山中。
两个魔子在海边森林游荡，
看见朗玛满他们三人闲坐在森林边。

This was the territory of the Ten-headed King,
He was in charge of the land and the sky here.
There lived a witch named Hada,
Her two sons also often wandered in the mountains.
As they were wandering in the forest by the sea,
They saw Langmaman and other two people sitting beside the forest.

魔子想对朗玛满他们下毒手，
大模大样走近他们好几次。
朗玛满怒斥魔子，
魔子更加疯狂放肆。

The two sons of the witch wanted to kill Langmaman and other two people,
They walked up to them arrogantly for several times.
After Langmaman angrily rebuked the witch's two sons,
They became crazier and more unrestrained.

朗玛满让纳哈腊弟弟用箭射魔子，
魔子突然飞上了天空中。
神箭在追赶魔子，
魔子还是用刀挡开了神箭。

Langmaman asked his younger brother Nahala to shoot the witch's two sons with bow.
The witch's two sons suddenly flew into the sky.
The magic arrow was chasing the two sons,
The devil sons blocked the magic arrow with his knife.

魔子突然变化出成百上千的魔鬼，
魔群向朗玛满他们扑过来。
朗玛满用神箭射向魔子，
魔子两兄弟中箭身亡。

The devil sons suddenly changed into hundreds of demons.
The demons rushed at Langmaman and other people.
Langmaman shot at the devil sons with magic arrows,
The devil brothers were killed by arrows.

魔女看见两个儿子死去，
她发誓一定要为儿子报仇。
她看到了朗玛满两兄弟，
看见了美丽的西达公主，
她决心快快过去报告十头王，
她要让十头王把公主抢到手中。

The witch saw her two sons die,
She vowed to avenge her sons.
She saw Langmaman and his brother,
As well as the beautiful Princess Xida.
She was determined to report to the Ten-headed King in hurry.
She wanted the Ten-headed King to seize the princess.

魔女飞过茫茫大海，
来到了十头王的王宫：
“大王啊大王，
我有好消息要报告您，
朗玛满他们就在我们的地盘上。
那个西达公主美丽得无人能比，
她配大王简直就是天设的一对。

The witch flew across the vast sea,
And arrived at the palace of the Ten-headed King,
"Your Majesty,
I have good news to report to you,
Langmaman and other people are on our territory.
The Princess Xida is so beautiful that no one can match,
She is a perfect match for you.

“我的两个儿子已经被朗玛满杀死，
您一定要为我儿子报仇。
我们先把朗玛满两兄弟杀死，

"My two sons have been shot to death by Langmaman,
You must avenge my sons.
Let's kill Langmaman brothers first,

然后将西达公主抢到手中。
大王我们就来个突然袭击，
把朗玛满两兄弟杀死在大山中。”

And then grabbled Princess Xida.
Your Majesty, let's make a surprise attack
To kill Langmaman brothers in the mountains."

十头王有几分担忧地说道：
“你不要高兴得太早，
朗玛满是阿銮不是平凡人。
当年进行拉神弓比赛时，
所有公子王子均败在他手下。
他拉动了神弓才得到了西达公主，
你就不要痴心妄想。”

The Ten-headed King said anxiously,
"Don't be happy too soon.
Langmaman is Aluan, not ordinary person.
At the magic bow-pulling competition,
He defeated all other princes.
He pulled the magic bow to get Princess Xida,
Don't be paranoid."

魔女不罢休又出主意道：
“大王啊大王，
我有一个最好的主意，
我想办法让朗玛满离开公主，
您就趁机把公主抢到手中。”

The witch did not want to give up and said,
"Your Majesty,
I have a perfect idea.
I'll try to have Langmaman leave the princess,
You just take the opportunity to seize the princess."

十头王认为魔女的主意可行，
他俩速速飞出王宫。
十头王悄悄躲在树林中，
等待着机会的到来。

The Ten-headed King thought the idea of the witch was feasible,
They two flew out of the palace quickly.
The Ten-headed King hid quietly in the forest,
Waiting for the opportunity.

魔女哈达进入森林里，
她变化成一只小羚羊。
小羚羊从朗玛满他们住的窝棚边走过，
小羚羊装成寻找母亲的样子“咩咩”叫。

The witch Hada walked into the forest,
And changed into a gazelle.
When the gazelle walked by the shack where Langmaman and other people stayed,
The gazelle pretended to be looking for its mother and bleated.

西达公主让朗玛满去抓小羚羊：
“请哥哥去抓小羚羊给我玩，
这只小羚羊妹妹喜欢。
我要将小羚羊拴在窝棚里抚养，
我要让小羚羊陪伴妹妹在大山中。”

Princess Xida asked Langmaman to catch the gazelle,
"Please go to catch the gazelle for me to play.
I like the gazelle.
I will tie the gazelle in the shack and raise it in the shack.
I want the gazelle to accompany me in the mountains."

“羚羊不会来我们这里，
一定是魔鬼变成羚羊来诱惑。
妹妹不能要小羚羊，
哥哥不能把小羚羊抓给你玩。”

"Gazelles will not come to this place.
The devil must have turned into a gazelle to tempt us.
You can't have the gazelle.
I can't catch the gazelle for you to play."

“妹妹在大山里寂寞，
我想拿草来喂小羚羊。
平时我在王宫里也与羚羊做伙伴，
哥哥外出时我与羚羊在窝棚里多开心。”

"Since I am lonely in the mountains,
I want to feed the gazelle with grass.
Gazelles used to be my companions in the palace.
How happy I will be in the shack with the gazelle when you are out."

朗玛满交代弟弟纳哈腊：
“弟弟你在窝棚里陪你嫂子，
我去抓那只小羚羊。
你不要让你嫂子走出窝棚外，
走出外面有危险。”

Langmaman told his brother Nahala,
"Brother, you stay with your sister-in-law in the shack.
I'll catch the gazelle.
Don't let your sister-in-law go out of the shack.
It's dangerous to go out."

朗玛满走出窝棚去追小羚羊，
羚羊跑得越来越快。
朗玛满拉弓射羚羊，
羚羊发出像人一般的哭叫声。
羚羊的叫声传到窝棚里，
西达公主感觉朗玛满遇难在大山中。
西达公主吩咐纳哈腊去救朗玛满：
“弟弟你快去看看你哥哥，

Langmaman went out of the shack to chase the gazelle.
The gazelle was running faster and faster.
Langmaman drew the bow to shoot at the gazelle.
The gazelle made a human like cry.
The cry of the gazelle came to the shack.
Princess Xida felt that Langmaman was killed in the mountains,
Princess Xida told Nahala to save Langmaman,

你哥哥可能遇难在大山中。”
“大嫂啊，
哥哥交代让我陪你在窝棚中，
山里的魔鬼变化多端，
我们不能中了魔鬼的圈套。”

“Brother, you go to see your elder brother.
Your brother may have been killed in the mountains.”
“Sister-in-law,
My elder brother told me to accompany you in the shack.
The devil in the mountain is changeable,
We can't be trapped by the devil.”

“弟弟啊我求你了，
如果你哥哥回不来怎么办，
你就快快去看看他吧，
我一定不走出窝棚。”

“Brother, I beg you,
What if your brother can't come back.
Go and see him quickly.
I will not go out of the shack.”

纳哈腊画地为圈念神咒：
“大嫂你不能走出圈子外，
走出圈外很危险，
我和哥哥很快就会回到窝棚中。”

Nahala drew a circle on the ground and chanted a magic spell,
“Sister-in-law, you can't go outside the circle.
It's dangerous to get out of the circle.
I and Langmaman will be back to the shack.”

纳哈腊走出窝棚，
他走进森林找哥哥朗玛满。
朗玛满看见弟弟时很吃惊：
“弟弟你怎么能离开你嫂子啊？
现在她的处境很危险，
因为魔鬼们诡计多端！”

Nahala walked out of the shack.
He went into the forest to find his brother Langmaman.
Langmaman was surprised when he saw his brother,
“How can you leave your sister-in-law, brother ?
Now she's in danger.
Because the devils are devious !”

“我是牢牢记住了哥哥的吩咐，
但听见有个声音在呼喊我的名字，
我嫂嫂说是你的声音，
她催我快快进山里来找你。
我在地上已画神咒圈将她围护，
她在圈子里魔鬼不能接近她身。”

“I firmly remember your instructions.
But I heard a voice calling my name.
My sister-in-law said it was yours.
She urged me to come into the mountains to find you.
I have drawn a magic circle on the ground to protect her.
The devil can't get close to her,

Because she's in a circle."

兄弟俩在大树下歇息，
周围吹来凉爽的山风。
十头王躲在树梢上，
他看见朗玛满他们已离开窝棚。
西达公主一个人在窝棚里，
但十头王无法走进窝棚里的神咒圈。

While the two brothers were relaxing under the tree,
A cool wind blew from around.
The Ten-headed King hid on the top of the tree,
He saw Langmaman brothers leave the shack.
Though Princess Xida was alone in the shack,
But the Ten-headed King could not enter the magic spell circle in the shack.

十头王变成一位雅细，
他手持金钵走近窝棚。
公主看见雅细喜出望外，
她手捧水果走出了窝棚。
十头王抱起公主就向他的王宫飞去，
西达公主哭喊在半空中。

The Ten-headed King changed into a Yaxi,
He approached the shack with a golden bowl in his hand.
The princess was overjoyed to see Yaxi,
She walked out of the shack with fruit in her hands.
The Ten-headed King scooped up the princess and flew to his palace,
Princess Xida cried in mid air.

十头王将西达公主带到王宫里，
让她坐在高床上。
他派勇士守在四周围，
又让成群侍女服侍在身旁。

The Ten-headed King took Princess Xida to the palace,
Having her sit on the high bed.
He sent warriors to keep watch around,
And let a group of maids serve her.

十头王对西达公主说道：
“我美丽的公主啊，
你的丈夫朗玛满已死在大山中，
你就安心住在王宫里，
从此与我有享不尽的快乐。”

The Ten-headed King said to Princess Daxi,
"My beautiful princess,
Your husband Langmaman has died in the mountains,
You can live in the palace at ease.
From then on, we will enjoy endless happiness."

“你这个专横跋扈的魔鬼，
难道你不知道我丈夫的威德。

"You despotic devil,
Don't you know my husband's powerful and benevolent

他的威名传遍四面八方，
他会让你的宫殿变成废墟。”

rule.
His fame spread far and wide.
He will turn your palace into ruins.”

十头王无法接近西达公主，
十头王想起当年她走进火堆时，
他也无法接近她，
十头王新恨旧恨涌上心头。
十头王把公主关在御花园里，
他让魔女哈达看守她。
他又安排一群侍女服侍公主，
不许她们离开西达公主半步。

The Ten-headed King couldn't get close to Princess Xida.
He remembered when she walked into the fire,
He couldn't get close to her either.
The Ten-headed King's new and old hatred welled up in his mind.
He locked the princess in the imperial garden
And had the witch Hada guard her.
He arranged for a group of maids to serve the princess.
He did not allow them to leave Princess Xida even for a half step.

朗玛满兄弟回到窝棚里，
西达公主已不在窝棚中。
朗玛满一时昏迷过去，
控制不住两眼泪涟涟。

When Langmaman brothers returned to the shack,
Princess Xida was not in the shack.
Langmaman passed out for a moment,
And couldn't help shedding tears.

朗玛满苏醒过来，
兄弟俩到处寻找西达公主。
朗玛满呼喊着公主的名字，
就是没有听到公主的回音。

After Langmaman came to life,
The two brothers searched everywhere for Princess Xida.
Langmaman shouted the name of the princess,
But there was no response from the princess.

两兄弟到处去寻找，
已经跑遍了几座大山和森林。
朗玛满祈祷诸神，
希望知道偷走公主的是谁。
他希望诸神快快告诉他，
西达公主现在是否平安？

The two brothers searched everywhere,
Covering several mountains and forests.
Langmaman prayed to gods for knowing who stole the princess,
Hoping that the gods would tell him quickly.
Is Princess Xida safe now ?

朗玛满兄弟已经跑得很累，
他俩在一棵大树下休息。
朗玛满的头靠在弟弟的腿上睡着了，
一只母鸡大的树苍蝇咬住了纳哈腊。

The Langmaman brothers were very tired.
They relaxed under a big tree.
Langmaman fell asleep with his head on his brother's leg.
A tree fly the size of a hen bit Nahala.

弟弟担心打树苍蝇会把哥哥惊醒，
弟弟只好忍住疼痛不吭一声。
苍蝇的叮咬让弟弟流出鲜血，
弟弟纳哈腊就是纹丝不动。

The younger brother was worried that the beating of the fly would wake his elder brother up.
Therefore, the younger brother had to endure the pain without saying a word.
The bite of the fly made the younger brother bleed.
The younger brother Nahala was absolutely still.

一只猴子在树上见此情景，
被感动得两眼泪涟涟。
猴子的眼泪滴在朗玛满脸上，
朗玛满从梦中醒过来：
“弟弟为什么流眼泪？
寻找你嫂嫂不要太着急。”
弟弟回答说自己没有流眼泪，
但见水珠从树上滴下来。
朗玛满睁开眼看见树上有一只猴子，
朗玛满开口骂猴子是魔鬼。

A monkey saw this scene in a tree.
It was moved to tears.
The monkey's tears dropped on Langmaman's face,
Langmaman woke up from his dream and said,
"Why did you shed tears ?
Don't be too anxious to find your sister-in-law."
The younger brother replied that he didn't cry,
But he saw water dripping from the tree.
Langmaman opened his eyes and saw a monkey in the tree.
Langmaman started to scold the monkey as the devil.

朗玛满正准备射箭，
猴子急忙解释道：
“我不是魔鬼，
我就是在此等候圣者您啊，
我是猴王巴力莫的弟弟苏嘎林，
他乱伦霸道夺走了我的妻子，
还把我赶出了猴国。

When Langmaman was ready to shoot an arrow,
The monkey explained in a hurry,
"I'm not the devil.
I am waiting for you, the sage here.
I'm Sugalin, brother of Monkey King Balimo.
Being incestuous and tyrannical, he took my wife.
He also drove me out of Monkey Kingdom.

我看见你们兄弟俩如此亲密互爱，
让我感动得泪涟涟。”

I saw you two brothers so close and loving each other,
I was moved to tears.”

朗玛满听到后很感动，
他对苏嘎林说道：
“看得出来苏嘎林你有情有义，
我们都是受人排挤才落难他乡。
今后自有王位等你坐，
我一定要让你益寿延年。”

Hearing it, Langmaman was very moved.
He said to Sugalin,
“You look like a sentimental and righteous guy,
We are all excluded from our homeland.
There will be a throne waiting for you in the future.
I must make you live longer.”

猴子苏嘎林下树向朗玛满跪拜，
他将所见缓缓道来：
“如是圣者让我坐猴国王位，
我会兢兢业业报大恩。
公主已经被十头王劫持，
我看见十头王带着公主从我头上飞过。
公主口口声声呼唤圣者的名字。
她说抢走她的是十头王。
这一经过我看得清清楚楚，
我才在大树枝上等您，
请圣者不要忧愁苦恼，
小弟我可以让西达公主回到您身边。”

Monkey Sugalin descended from the tree and knelt down before Langmaman.
He went into details about what he had seen,
“If you let me sit on the throne of Monkey Kingdom,
I will do my best to repay my great kindness.
The princess has been kidnapped by the Ten-headed King.
I saw the Ten-headed King flying over my head with the princess.
The princess kept on calling your name.
She said it was the Ten-headed King who stole her.
I witnessed this clearly.
That’s why I’m waiting for you in the tree.
Saint, please don’t worry.
I can make Princess Xida come back to you.”

朗玛满两兄弟听后很高兴，
他们在树下畅所欲言。
苏嘎林对两兄弟说道：
“我的哥哥名叫巴力莫，
他身体魁梧可以变成一座大山。
他可以升高到十五个眼程，

Langmaman brothers were very pleased to hear that,
They spoke freely under the tree.
Sugalin said to the two brothers,
“My elder brother is Balimo.
He has a big body and can turn into a mountain.
He can rise to 15 eye ranges.

他住在大海岸边的森林中，
他在那里称王称霸。”

He lives in the forest beside the sea shore.
He was the king there.”

朗玛满听后说道：
“莫说他可以变成一座大山，
就算他高若天柱山①。
他也不可能超过我，
你就等着看我射一箭，
这神箭稀罕力量无穷。”

Langmaman said,
“Let alone he can turn into a mountain.
Even if he is as tall as Tianzhu Mountain①.
He is unable to surpass me,
You just wait to see me shoot an arrow.
This rare magic arrow has infinite power.”

朗玛满举手即射箭，
神箭声音隆隆如地覆天翻。
神箭射倒七棵参天大树，
神箭又自动回到朗玛满的箭筒中。
猴子苏嘎林看后高兴得欢天喜地，
他对朗玛满赞叹不已。
苏嘎林带领朗玛满两兄弟向原始森林走去，
他们来到了猴王巴力莫住处附近。
朗玛满对苏嘎林说道：
“如是我们与猴国开战，
一定会毁灭许多生灵。
你去把你哥哥巴力莫引出洞府，
我躲在附近森林中，
用神箭将他射死。”

Langmaman raised his hand to shoot an arrow.
The sound of the magic arrow rumbled like the earth shaking.
He shot down the seven big trees with the magic arrow,
The magic arrow returned to Langmaman's quiver automatically.
Monkey Sugalin was highly delighted when he saw that,
He was full of praise for Langmaman.
Sugalin led Langmaman brothers to the primeval forest,
They came near the residence of Balimo the Monkey King.
Langmaman said to Sugalin,
“If we are at war with Monkey Kingdom,
Many lives will be destroyed.
Go and lead your brother Balimo out of the cave,
I will hide in the nearby forest,
And will shoot him to death with the magic arrow.”

苏嘎林走近他大哥大声喊话：
“你这个该死的巴力莫，
快快出来，我要一口咬死你！

Sugalin walked up to his elder brother and shouted,
“You god damned Balimo,
Come out quickly, and I will kill you !

①天柱山：传说中支撑苍天的大山。

①Tianzhu Mountain, a mountain that supports the heaven.

你把我妻子占为己有，	You took my wife for yourself,
你做王不讲伦理。	Judging by the ethics, you are not a good king.
你敢出来我就把你杀死，	I'll kill you if you dare to come out,
我来接替你当猴王！”	I'll succeed you as the Monkey King !"
巴力莫听后火冒三丈，	Balimo became furious to hear that,
他从宫殿里跑出来与弟弟撕咬起来，	He ran out of the palace and bit his brother.
两兄弟互相撕咬双方都受了伤。	The two brothers tore at each other and both were injured.
因为兄弟俩长得一模一样，	Since the two brothers looked exactly alike,
朗玛满无法辨别谁是兄谁是弟，	Langmaman could not tell from each other.
朗玛满正在犹豫徘徊中。	Langmaman was hesitating.
弟弟苏嘎林力量不如哥哥巴力莫，	The younger brother Sugalin was not as powerful as the elder brother Balimo,
苏嘎林退回到朗玛满身旁。	Sugalin retreated to Langmaman.
“您怎么不射神箭？	"Why don't you shoot magic arrows ?
我已经快敌不过他了。”	I can't beat him."
“你俩长得一模一样啊，	"You two look exactly alike.
我无法分辩谁是兄谁是弟。”	I can't tell from each other."
朗玛满用槟榔汁将苏嘎林的屁股涂红，	Langmaman painted Sugalin's ass red with areca juice.
从此猴子的屁股成了红色。	Since then, the monkey's ass has become red.
苏嘎林信心满满地冲向巴力莫，	Sugalin rushed to Balimo with confidence.
巴力莫冲出来也怒气冲冲。	Balimo rushed out angry too.
兄弟俩又在撕咬起来，	The two brothers were biting again.
苏嘎林频频翘尾巴告诉朗玛满。	Sugalin stuck his tails up frequently to tell Langmaman.
朗玛满看清了哪个是巴力莫，	After Langmaman identified Balimo clearly,
他拿神箭向他射出去。	He shot at Balimo with his magic arrow.
朗玛满的神箭射中了巴力莫，	Langmaman's magic arrow hit Balimo.
猴王巴力莫吼叫着寻找箭主：	Monkey King Balimo roared to find the archer,

"你从何处蹿到我这里来?
我没有去你的王国捣乱,
你为什么来射杀我?
你出来告诉我是何原因!"

"Where did you come from ?
I didn't go to your kingdom to make trouble.
Why did you shoot me ?
You come out and tell me why !"

朗玛满跳下树来回答道:
"我是达撒腊塔国王的儿子,
我在阿罗替雅王国当国王,
我的使命是惩办乱伦的坏人!
今天与你相遇在大山中,
我要除掉你这个猴国的败类,
我要让你弟弟苏嘎林当猴王!"

Langmaman jumped down the tree and replied,
"I'm the son of King Dasalata.
I am the king of Kingdom Aluotiya.
My mission is to punish the bad people of incest !
I met you in the mountains today.
I want to get rid of you, the scum of Monkey Kingdom.
I will make your brother Sugalin the Monkey King !"

"苏嘎林帮你做了什么好事?
让你不远万里来到森林里杀我。
如此大的决心从何而来?
你不能让我死得不明不白。"

"What good did Sugalin do for you ?
Let you come all the way to the forest to kill me.
Where did such determination come from ?
You can't let me die without knowing."

"如你是一个正直公道的王者,
我不会对你射出神箭。
我从天界投胎人世间,
就曾发下坚固的誓言。
凡是遇到有违公德的乱伦者,
我都要一箭送他到黄泉。"

"If you are a righteous king,
I will not shoot an arrow at you.
When I was born into the world from heaven,
I made a firm pledge.
Every time when I meet an incest that violates social morality,
I will kill him with an arrow."

巴力莫明白自己已经没有退路,
他速速跪拜朗玛满恳求道:
"来自天界的圣者啊,
我有一事相求,
你让我弟弟苏嘎林做王也可以,

Balimo knew he had no way out,
He quickly knelt down to Langmaman and pleaded,
"Sage from the heaven,
I have a request.
You can make my brother Sugalin king.

我有一个儿子名叫旺果，
请你让他在苏嘎林手下做帮手。”

I have a son named Wangguo,
Please let him work as an assistant under Sugalin.”

朗玛满接受了巴力莫的请求，
巴力莫再次跪拜朗玛满谢恩。
朗玛满示意请巴力莫一路走好，
巴力莫慢慢断了气息。

Langmaman accepted Balimo's request,
Balimo knelt down again to Langmaman to express his gratitude.
Langmaman asked Balimo to go all the way,
Balimo slowly lost his breath.

我们的长诗告一段落，
我们的长诗还没有结束。
我们的长诗像一只大麻袋，
里面装满了各种各样的水果，
各种味道的水果都在里边，
各种美味需要慢慢来品尝。
欲知朗玛满和猴子苏嘎林的关系如何，
请等待念诵下一章。

This chapter has come to an end,
Our epic is not over yet.
Our epic is like a big sack,
Which is filled with all kinds of fruits.
Fruits with various flavor are in it,
All kinds of delicious food need to be tasted slowly.
If you want to know the relations between Langmaman and the Monkey Sugalin,
Please wait for the next chapter.

第十章

Chapter Ten

前一章结束后一章又开始，
一章更比一章牵动人心。
话说朗玛满已让苏嘎林当上猴国国王，
又让苏嘎林的侄子旺果任副手。
猴王叫来了所有猴民，
三亿八千万猴民挤满数座大山。

The previous chapter ends and the new chapter starts,
The plots are getting more and more compelling.
Langmaman had made Sugalin the king of Monkey Kingdom,
And made Sugalin's nephew Wangguo the assistant.
The Monkey King called all the monkeys.
Several mountains were crowded with 380 million monkeys.

苏嘎林跪拜朗玛满说道：
“圣者阿銮啊，
小弟认为救公主宜早不宜迟，
我们从此岸要搭建一座桥到彼岸，
要跨过这茫茫的大海洋。”

Sugalin knelt down before Langmaman and said,
“Saint Aluan,
I think it's better to save the princess sooner than later.
We will build a bridge,
Across the vast ocean.”

“如此宽阔的大海洋，
要到彼岸有一百多个眼程的距离，
兄弟你如何来搭桥？”
“我让三亿八千万猴民齐动手，
要搬山上的石头填大海，
从海底填到海面就大功告成。”

“For such a vast ocean,
There are more than 100 eye ranges between here and the other shore.
Brother, how do you build a bridge ?”
“I will ask 380 million monkeys to join hands
To move rocks from the mountains to fill the sea,
From the bottom of the sea to the surface of the sea.”

“兄弟你这样做没把握，
我担心西达公主不在十头王的王宫中。
还是你先派人去查探，
了解清楚后我们再动工。”

“Brother, this is risky.
I'm afraid that Princess Xida is not in the palace of the Ten-headed King.
You'd better send someone to detect.
We can start construction after we confirm it.”

苏嘎林要拿出价值高昂的物品做奖赏，

Sugalin would give something of high value as a reward.

动员令发到每一户猴民：	The mobilization order was sent to every monkey family.
有谁能够飞过大海洋去查看实情，	The reward would go to the one who could fly across the ocean to check the truth.
这个奖赏就给谁。	
这个奖品价值高昂，	The prize is of high value
可以养活几代子孙。	And can feed generations of descendants.
有几个勇士主动来报名，	Several brave men volunteered to sign up.
有的说能飞二十个眼程，	Some said they could fly 20 eye ranges,
有的说能飞二十五个眼程。	While some said they could fly 25 eye ranges.
猴医占布曼说他能飞行三十个眼程，	Zhanbuman, the monkey doctor said he could fly 30 eye ranges.
报名的英雄能力都相当。	The heroes registered were well-matched in capabilities.
占布曼跪拜朗玛满禀报：	Zhanbuman knelt down before Langmaman and said,
“尊贵的圣者啊，	“Distinguished saint,
我们有一位高手叫阿奴曼，	We have a master named Anuman,
飞过海面他能行。”	Who can fly across the sea.”
朗玛满不相信地说道：	Langmaman said in disbelief,
“阿奴曼身体瘦小，	“Anuman is thin and small.
看他那身体哪来的力气！”	Just look at his body! Where does his strength come from?”
朗玛满的话音引得猴群哄堂大笑，	Langmaman's words made the monkeys roar with laughter,
笑声回荡在森林中。	The laughter reverberated in the forest.
朗玛满又对占布曼说道：	Langmaman said to Zhanbuman again,
“那些身体魁梧者都飞不过去，	“Those strong people can't fly across,
阿奴曼身体瘦小如甘蔗，	Anuman is as thin as sugarcane,
勐兰嘎王国不在对面那山上。”	Menglanga Kingdom is not on the opposite mountain.”
占布曼跪拜朗玛满解释道：	Zhanbuman knelt down to Langmaman and explained,
“圣者请您听我说，	“Please listen to me, saint.
阿奴曼不是森林里的普通猴子，	Anuman is not an ordinary monkey in the forest.

他的本领不一般。
有一天阿奴曼看见太阳挂在天空，
他以为那是一个熟透的水果，
他看见了就嘴馋。
他跳到天空双手抓住就不放，
太阳公子把他告到大天神那里。

His ability is extraordinary.
One day Anuman saw the sun hanging in the sky.
He thought it was a ripe fruit,
He was greedy at the sight of it.
He jumped into the sky and grasped with both hands,
The Sun God complained to the Great God.

"大天神抓起神斧砍下去，
一斧子砍断了他的下巴掉地上，
猴王见状去求大天神帮忙医治，
大天神告知他将来有任务，
等到朗玛满带兵开战时，
他将参与帮大忙。

"The Great God grabbed the magic axe and cut it down,
His chin was cut off and fell to the ground.
The Monkey King saw this and asked the Great God to help heal him.
The Great God told him that he had a mission in the future.
When Langmaman led the troops to fight,
He would be a great help.

"大天神下凡为他救治，
还为他赐名阿奴曼，
天神还赐给他三大神通：
一是所有灾祸远离他而去，
二是烈火不能接近他身体，
三是落水犹如走在平地上。"

"The Great God came down to heal him,
And gave him the name Anuman.
The Great God gave him three magic powers.
First, the ability to be free from all the disaster.
Second, the fire can't get close to his body.
Third, falling into the water is like walking on the flat ground."

占布曼还讲了其他经过，
包括他遇雅细将经文撕毁，
阿奴曼被雅细们念诵经咒控制了本领，
阿奴曼只有言听计从。
天神让他等待与圣者朗玛满相遇，
到那时阿奴曼的体力就会恢复到从前。

Zhanbuman also told other stories
Including his meeting of Yaxi and tearing of the scriptures.
Anuman's skills were controlled by Yaxi's chanting of sutras.
Anuman had to act upon whatever Yaxi said.
The God asked him to wait for meeting the saint Langmaman.

By then, Anuman's strength would be restored.

朗玛满听后十分高兴，
他唤阿奴曼来到身边。
朗玛满用手掌拍打他的脊背，
阿奴曼就恢复了全部神通：
"尊贵的圣者朗玛满啊，
人间和天上随我自由上下，
即使有诸鬼神把路阻挡，
救不出西达公主我不回来。

Langmaman was very happy to hear that,
He called Anuman to his side.
Langmaman slapped his back with his palm,
And then Anuman regained all his powers.
"Langmaman, the distinguished saint,
I can fly to the heaven and go down to the world freely,
Even if ghosts and gods block the way.
I won't come back if I can't get Princess Xida out.

"圣者朗玛满啊，
只要阿奴曼还活着，
救西达公主一事包在我身上，
圣者您尽管放心。
我将飞过茫茫大海洋，
不久就返回到您身边。"

"Langmaman, the saint,
As long as Anuman is alive,
I'm responsible for saving Princess Xida.
Saint, don't worry.
I will fly across the vast ocean,
And return to you soon."

这是阿奴曼的真诚表白，
朗玛满听了很高兴：
"你能够飞过大海去我很高兴，
但西达公主的模样如何你不知道，
我说出来你要记在心中。
公主的脑门与双目犹如天神画成，
她的头发乌黑着装合体，
她腰细胸满与天宫仙女一般。

This is Anuman's sincere expression.
Langmaman was very happy to hear that,
"I'm glad you can fly across the sea.
But you don't know what Princess Xida looks like.
I'll tell you and you should keep it in mind.
The princess's forehead and eyes are like that of the gods painted,
Her hair is black and her dress fits.
With a thin waist, she is full and round like fairy in the Heavenly Palace.

"她肌肤嫩白美丽，
她红唇两片美舌薄如簧，

"With two red lips, a beautiful thin tongue and white delicate skin,

她就像十五的月亮光彩夺目，
她如七仙女闪闪发光在人间。

She is as beautiful and bright as the moon on the 15th day of lunar calendar,
As well as the seven fairies shining in the world.

“你去救她她不会相信，
你就告诉她我从前的经历，
我曾在森林里追赶巨型乌鸦，
她的父王举行拉神弓择驸马，
是我战败所有参赛人。
还有父王要让我继承王位，
是三王后吉西出鬼主意篡夺王位。
如说这些她还不相信，
你就让她看这只金戒指。”

“If she does not believe you when you go to save her,
Just tell her about my past experience.
I once drove away the giant crow in the forest.
Her father organized a magic-bow pulling competition to select her husband.
It's me who defeated all competitors.
And the king wanted me to succeed to the throne.
It was the third Queen Jixi who came up with the idea of usurping the throne.
If she does not believe you,
Show her the gold ring.”

阿奴曼拜谢朗玛满后要出发，
猴民们准备花篮花环前来送行。
阿奴曼将身体变粗壮，
忽然他的身体就要顶到蓝天。

Anuman thanked Langmaman and was about to depart.
The monkeys brought with them flower baskets and garlands to see him off.
Anuman had his body get stronger,
Suddenly his body would reach the blue sky.

赠送阿奴曼的花篮花环不计其数，
阿奴曼对大家说道：
“如是我寻找不到西达公主，
我就不回到你们身边。”

There were countless flower baskets and garlands presented to Anuman.
Anuman said to everyone,
“If I can't find Princess Xida,
I will not come back to you.”

猴民们说道：
“我们个个踮脚站立等候你，
等着你带好消息回到我们身边。”

The monkeys said,
“We will be standing on tiptoes waiting for you,
Waiting for your return with good news.”

阿奴曼救公主的决心让人们感动，
森林里如盛典一般。
阿奴曼要向勐兰嘎出发，
猴民们的祝福声祈祷声响彻森林中。
姆利腊哈纳神女住在此海中，
她变成一座大山在大海中间。
阿奴曼用尾巴将山尖打断，
他以为是魔鬼变山把路拦。

Anuman's determination to save the princess moved people.
It was like a grand ceremony was going on in the forest.
Anuman was going to set out for Menglanga.
The blessing and prayer of monkeys resounded through the forest.
The Goddess Mulilahana lived in this sea,
She became a mountain in the middle of the sea.
Anuman broke the mountain peak with his tail,
He thought it was the devil who turned into the mountain to block the road.

神女急忙出来说道：
“我不是魔女，
我是神女驻守在大海中，
你为朗玛满出门办事，
我变一座花山送你出行。”

The Goddess hurried out and said,
"I'm not a witch,
I'm the Goddess living in the sea.
Since you work for Langmaman,
I'll conjure a flower mountain to see you out."

阿奴曼听到后心情舒畅，
他用手轻轻触摸一下花山便一飞而去，
他飞到了大海的对岸，
来到了勐兰嘎王国的王城边。

Anuman was pleased to hear that.
He touched the flower mountain with his hand and flew away.
He flew to the other side of the sea.
He arrived at the suburb of the imperial city of Menglanga Kingdom.

阿奴曼在细细盘算，
如是大大咧咧走进王宫里，
自己一定会引火烧身。
他决定变成一只小猫，
太阳落山后走入王宫中，
轻手轻脚才能够瞒过宫里人。

Anuman was considering carefully.
If he walked into the palace carelessly,
He himself would get everyone's attention.
He decided to change into a cat,
And walked into the palace after sunset.
Only by walking gently, could he hide from the people in the palace.

夜深后王宫里静悄悄无一点声响，
阿奴曼来到十头王的卧室中。
他看见十头王一只手搂抱着十个美女，
他与一群美女合睡在一张大床上。
尚拎王国的公主最美丽，
她睡在十头王身旁。

It was quiet late at night without a sound.
Anuman came to the bedroom of the Ten-headed King.
He saw the Ten-headed King holding ten beautiful women in one hand.
He was sleeping in a big bed with a group of beauties.
The princess of Shanglin Kingdom was the most beautiful.
She was sleeping beside the Ten-headed King.

尚拎公主与西达公主长得很相似，
阿奴曼在心里想来想去，
难道西达公主已经和十头王睡在一起，
难道西达公主已经变了心?
阿奴曼不相信自己的眼睛，
因为西达公主不是那种人。

The princess of Shanglin looked very similar to Princess Xida.
Anuman thought about it over and over again.
Was it possible for Princess Xida to sleep with the Ten-headed King ?
Did Princess Xida change her mind ?
Anuman didn't believe his eyes,
Because Princess Xida was not that kind of person.

阿奴曼找遍了整个王宫，
他又找遍了整个王城。
不见西达公主他内心焦虑，
因为无数猴民还等候他带回好消息。

Anuman searched the whole palace,
And the whole imperial city.
Without seeing Princess Xida, he was worried,
Because countless monkeys were waiting for him to bring back good news.

阿奴曼累得在凉亭里睡着了，
他梦见许多鲜花在开放，
梦见公主在花园中。
阿奴曼来到御花园里，
十头王的花园宽阔无边。
阿奴曼看见了西达公主，

Anuman was so tired that he fell asleep in the pavilion.
He dreamed that many flowers were blooming,
He dreamed of the princess in the garden.
Anuman came to the Imperial Garden.
The Ten-headed King's garden was vast and boundless.
Anuman saw the Princess Xida,

原来公主被关在御花园中。

She was locked in the Imperial Garden.

公主虽然打扮靓丽，
但是公主愁眉苦脸。
阿奴曼相信公主不会变心，
因为公主与朗玛满的姻缘是上天的安排。

Although the princess was beautifully dressed,
She wore a long face with knitted eyebrows.
Anuman believed that the princess would not change her mind,
Because the marriage between the princess and Langmaman was arranged by the god.

十头王与美女们开始起床，
他们洗漱后要用早餐。
十头王收拾打扮戴金冠，
他威风凛凛似天神。
十头王的美女们有的穿红色绸缎，
有的全身穿绿色，
有的全身戴满金银首饰，
个个美丽得楚楚动人。

The Ten-headed King and the beauties started to get up.
They would have breakfast after washing up.
The Ten-headed King dressed himself up and put on a golden crown.
He was as majestic as a god.
Some of the Ten-headed King's beauties were wearing red silks and satins,
Some green all over,
While some were wearing gold and silver jewelry all over.
Everyone was beautiful and attractive.

阿奴曼正要靠近西达公主，
危险已经来到他面前。
西达公主看见十头王走进花园里，
她躲进树丛把身藏。
她就像小鸡躲老鹰，
亦像小鹿躲狮子。

As Anuman was approaching Princess Xida,
The danger had come to him.
Princess Xida saw the Ten-headed King walk into the garden.
She hid herself in the bushes.
She was like a chicken hiding from an eagle,
Or a deer hiding from a lion.

十头王看见公主就笑着说道：
“我的大美人啊，
跟我回宫才是上策，

The Ten-headed King said with a smile when he saw the princess,
“My super beauty,

数万侍女中让你做老大，
整个王宫里让你做领头人。
我当用人服侍你，
只要你从我在我身边。
你父王那里我会去打理，
我们都是一家人。
进出宫殿你我是一对，
我们成双坐彩车逛花园。”

The best policy is to go back to the palace with me.
In the palace, you are the boss of tens of thousands of maids.
I'll make you the leader in the whole palace.
I'll have maids serve you,
As long as you stay with me.
I'll take care of your father,
Since we are all a family.
In and out of the palace, you and I are a couple.
We'll take floats to the garden in pairs."

十头王用甜言蜜语劝公主，
他胡编乱造欺骗人：
“你别指望你丈夫来找你，
你就别想你俩旧梦再重圆。
魔鬼已经把他杀死在深山里，
皮肉骨头早已变为灰尘。”
西达公主骂十头王道：
“你为什么这样说朗玛满，
朗玛满威名传遍四面八方。
当年我父王举办拉神弓比赛，
你这个魔鬼就拉不动神弓，
你们两个相比他在天上你在地上，
你想害死他天地不容。

The Ten-headed King persuaded the princess with sweet words.
He made up the following story to deceive her,
"You can't expect your husband to come to you.
It's impossible for you two to reunite.
The devil has killed him in the mountains.
The skin and bones have turned into dust."
Princess Xida scolded the Ten-headed King,
"Why did you say that about Langmaman ?
Langmaman's fame spreads all over the world.
In those years, my father held the Magic Bow-pulling Competition.
You devil couldn't pull the bow.
Of you two, he's in heaven, you're on earth.
You want to kill him.
Providence will not forgive.

“如是你迟迟不放我回去，
他一定会来把你的王国踏平。
你的无数国民将陪你去死，

"If you don't let me go back,
He will surely come to level your kingdom.
Your countless subjects will die with you.

你会在地狱里煎熬无期。

You will suffer forever in hell.

“你若听我一句劝放我出去，
朗玛满一定会原谅你，
让你活在人世间。
如你仍然执迷不悟，
小心神箭穿透你的心。
若你将我送回到朗玛满身边，
你的所有罪过一笔勾销。”

“If you listen to my advice and let me out,
Langmaman will forgive you,
And let you live in the world.
If you are still stubborn,
Be careful that the magic arrow pierces your heart.
If you send me back to Langmaman,
All your sins are cancelled.”

十头王听后十分气愤，
他对那些守花园的魔鬼骂道：
“你们这些该死的魔鬼，
为什么还让她活在人间。
七天后如她还不从我，
你们就吃了她。
你们把她的肉用火烤着吃，
她的肉一定又甜又香！”

The Ten-headed King was very angry after hearing this.
He cursed the demons guarding the garden,
“You goddamn devils,
Why do you let her live in the world ?
If she won't do as I told her in seven days,
You eat her.
By roasting her meat over the fire.
Her meat must be tasty !”

十头王气得咬牙切齿，
他的脸色变绿又变红。
尚拎公主担心十头王移情别恋，
她对十头王说道：
“王宫里不缺她这个美女，
你想爱谁就爱谁，
那些美女不是孔雀就是金凤凰，
大王何必如此把她放心上。

The Ten-headed King gnashed his teeth angrily,
And his face turned green and red.
The princess of Shanglin was worried that the Ten-headed King would transfer his affections from her to someone else.
She said to the Ten-headed King,
“There are many beauties in the palace.
You can love whoever you like.
Those beauties are either peacocks or golden phoenix.
Why do you miss the whole forest because of a tree.

“这个妖女不是人间的公主，

“This witch is not a princess on earth.

人间的公主不会这样一派胡言。
她一定是吃人的魔女，
大王不能与她一般见识。
王宫里成群美女随你挑，
王宫里你一天可以爱好几个人。”

The princesses on earth will never have these nonsenses.
She must be a cannibal witch.
What you and she perceive is like comparing apples and oranges.
You are free to choose the beautiful women you like in the palace.
And you can favor several beautiful women in a day in the palace.”

尚拎公主说完就去牵十头王的手，
十头王闷闷不乐返回王宫中。
魔鬼们个个张牙舞爪，
来到西达公主面前疯狂怒吼道：
“小女子你别敬酒不吃吃罚酒，
你快快答应我们大王还来得及。
我们忍耐有限，
七天后就送你去见阎王！”

After the princess of Shanglin finished her words, she went to hold the Ten-headed King's hand.
The Ten-Headed King returned to the palace in dismay.
The demons bared their teeth.
They came to Princess Xida and shouted crazily,
“Don't you know how to show some appreciation of favor ?
It's not too late to do what the king has said.
We won't be patient forever.
We'll send you to hell in seven days !”

魔鬼们要动手，
西达公主跑进花丛中。
她伤心地哭诉道：
“我的夫君啊，
七天后我将死在魔鬼手中。
你是我的圣者阿銮啊，
你怎么还不来救我走出魔窟。
虽然我在魔鬼手里，
但你日夜都在我心中。
看来灾难已经无法避免，
我将死在魔鬼手中，
哥哥你何时才能来到我身旁，

The demons were about to seize her.
Princess Xida ran into the flowers.
She cried sadly,
“My husband,
I will die in the hands of the demons in seven days.
You are my saint Aluan.
Why don't you come to get me out of here ?
Although I am in the hands of the devil,
You are in my heart day and night.
It seems that the disaster is unavoidable.
I will die in the hands of the demons.
Darling, when will you come to me ?

妹妹期待再见一次你的尊容。”

I'm looking forward to seeing you again."

公主在花丛里伤心哭诉，
西达公主想到了远方的父母亲，
她禁不住泪水夺眶而出：
“我远方的父母啊，
也许你们还认为女儿很幸福，
其实女儿已落难在魔窟中。
也许这是女儿前世种下的恶业，
才让我远离亲人来到这鬼地方。”
西达公主已经哭干了眼泪，
西达公主看不见一线生的曙光。

The princess cried in the flowers.
Thinking of her parents far away,
Princess Xida couldn't help bursting into tears,
"My parents far away,
Maybe you still think your daughter is happy.
Actually, your daughter has been stranded in the devil's cave.
Maybe this is the evil karma that your daughter planted in her previous life.
That's why I came to this place far away from my relatives."
Princess Xida has dried up her tears.
Princess Xida could not see the dawn of life.

我们的长诗告一段落，
我们的长诗还将继续念诵。
山上的草木有花开花落，
唱长诗要唱完一章歇一口气。
父老乡亲们请莫走开，
精彩的情节还在下一章中。

This is the end of the chapter,
We will continue to recite our epic.
The grass, trees and flowers in the mountains luxuriate and wither.
We need to take a breath after finishing a chapter in chanting the epic.
Dear fellow countrymen, please don't go away.
The wonderful plot is coming in the next chapter.

第十一章
Chapter Eleven

前一章结束后一章又开始，
一章更比一章牵动人心。
话说在御花园里负责守公主的魔女哈达，
昨晚做了一个奇特的噩梦。
次日清早天还没亮，
她就把几个魔鬼叫到身边。

The previous chapter ends and the new chapter starts.
The plots are getting more and more compelling.
Hada, the witch who was in charge of guarding the
princess in the imperial garden,
Had a strange nightmare last night.
She called the demons to her side
The next morning when it was still dark.

魔女急匆匆地对魔鬼们说：
“昨晚我做的梦好奇怪啊，
这个噩梦很反常。
也许这是现实的预兆，
也许灾难就要到来。”

The witch hurriedly said to the demons,
“What a strange dream I had last night !
This nightmare is abnormal.
Maybe this is the presage of reality.
Maybe disaster is coming.”

魔鬼们迫不及待地问魔女，
缠着魔女快快把梦讲出来听听：
“我的梦惊心动魄，
我梦见十头王被人们捆绑，
梦见王后脖子上挂着铁链，
梦见他们被人们赶出了王城。

The demons couldn’t wait to ask the witch
To tell them about the dream,
“It is a breath-taking dream.
I dreamed that The Ten-headed King was tied up by
people.
I dreamed that there is a chain around the queen’s neck.
I dreamed that they were driven out of the imperial city.

“梦见勐兰嘎王国王宫变成火海，
御花园里也是一片哭喊声。
我惊醒后坐在床上，
吓得我虚汗满身。
我梦见了朗玛满，
还有西达公主和纳哈腊，
他们个个穿着盛装，
他们三人坐在彩车上向王宫走来。

“I dreamed that the palace of Menglanga Kingdom turns
into a sea of fire.
There was also a lot of crying in the imperial garden.
I woke up and sat on the bed.
Scared, I was sweating all over.
I dreamed of Langmaman,
Pincess Xida and Nahala.
They are all in splendid attires.

They three came to the palace on the float.

“也许这是我们十头王国王的明天，
也许灾难将会发生在我们面前。
如是谁想安然无事，
去服侍西达公主也许是上策。
这是我昨晚做的噩梦，
我们要注意管好自身。”
魔鬼们听后开始害怕，
谁也不敢接近魔女身边。

“Maybe this is the future of our Ten-headed King.
Maybe the disaster will happen in front of us.
Whoever wants to be safe,
It’s the best policy for him to serve Princess Xida.
This is my dream last night.
We should attach great importance to it.”
The demons started to fear after hearing this.
Nobody dared to approach the witch.

阿奴曼藏在花丛中，
他看见了西达公主，
也看见了那些魔鬼。
魔鬼与公主有一段距离，
阿奴曼悄悄走过去与公主说：
“美丽的西达公主啊，
我不是魔鬼请你不要害怕。
自从公主与朗玛满分别，
朗玛满已经心力交瘁，
他与纳哈腊在到处找你，
刮大风下大雨他们也没有停下来，
他们为找你躲雨在树下两眼泪汪汪。

Anuman was hiding in the flowers.
He saw Princess Xida
And the demons.
There was a distance between the demons and the
princess.
Anuman walked over quietly and said to the princess,
“Beautiful Princess Xida,
I’m not the demon, please don’t be afraid.
Since the princess and Langmaman parted,
Langmaman has been exhausted.
He and Nahala have been looking for you everywhere,
Even during the windy and rainy days.
They cried under a tress shelter from the rain.

“因为寻找不到公主，
他们才派小弟前来王宫里探听，
小弟我找遍城里城外，
好不容易才在花园中找到公主。”

“Because they could not find the princess,
They sent me to the palace for the princess.
I searched all over the city,
and found the princess in the garden.”

公主听到话音后一点也不诧异，

The princess was not surprised at all when she heard the

因为这是十头王常玩的花招。
公主看见一只猴子藏在花丛中，
公主愤愤地说道：
“你就收起你的伎俩，
除了朗玛满的话其他我都不相信。”

voice.
Because this is a trick often played by the Ten-headed King.
Seeing a monkey hiding in the flowers,
The princess said angrily,
“You put away your tricks.
I don’t believe anything except for Langmaman’s words.”

“成群的魔鬼我已见习惯，
你们的伪装我当耳边风。
现在你还来这一套，
你让我怎么能够相信你。
如果你是朗玛满派来找我，
你有什么证据说出来给我听听。”

“I’ve been used to seeing crowds of demons.
I won’t be cheated by your disguise.
Now you still do this.
How can I trust you ?
If you are sent to me by Langmaman,
Show me what evidence you have.”

阿奴曼在花丛中回答：
“美丽的公主啊，
就数你对朗玛满最喜爱最忠贞。
朗玛满出生在阿罗替雅王国，
那里土地肥沃国强民富。
那里年年风调雨顺，
那里户户百姓阖家欢乐。

Amuman replied in the flowers,
“Our beautiful princess,
You are the most faithful princess who likes Langmaman most.
Langmaman was born in the Aluotiya Kingdom.
The land there is fertile, the kingdom is prosperous and the people are rich.
There is favorable climatic weathers each year.
People in the kingdom enjoy peace and happiness.

“朗玛满的父王名叫达撒腊塔，
是天神赐给了他四位王子，
个个身相如天神，
他们聪明过人本领不一般。
三王后吉西的儿子名叫帕腊达，
还有二王后的儿子纳哈腊心地善良。

“Langmaman’s father is Dasalata.
It was god who gave him four princes.
Everyone looks like a god.
They are very smart and talented.
The name of the son of the third queen is Palada.
And Nahala, the son of the second queen, is kind-hearted.

沙达鲁嘎纳也是二王后所生，
四位王子成长在王宫中。”

Shadalugana is also the son of the second queen.
The four princes are growing in the palace.”

阿奴曼又讲述朗玛满的过去，
讲了朗玛满追赶巨型乌鸦的事情，
讲了雅细领朗玛满去参赛拉神弓，
讲了十头王拉神弓败下赛台，
讲了多少王子退出赛场。
是国王举行拉神弓选驸马，
朗玛满才把公主娶到身边。

Anuman also told about Langmaman's past.
He told about Langmaman's driving of the giant crow out of the forest.
He also mentioned Langmaman's participation in the magic bow–pulling competition.
The Ten-headed King was defeated in the competition.
Many princes withdrew from the competition.
It was through the magic bow-pulling competition that Langmaman had the change to marry the princess.

阿奴曼讲述了所有的经过，
他又拿出金戒指说道：
“如是公主不相信，
你就看看这只金戒指。”
阿奴曼将金戒指拿给公主，
公主看见自己的戒指激动万分。

Anuman told all the story.
He took out the gold ring again and said,
“If you don't believe, princess,
Just look at this gold ring.”
Anuman gave the gold ring to the princess.
The princess was very excited at the sight of her ring.

公主亲切地对阿奴曼说道：
“没想到哥哥是朗玛满派来的啊，
真是让我感到喜从天降。”
阿奴曼变化成一位帅小伙，
他跪拜在公主面前。
他将遇到朗玛满的经过告诉了公主，
告诉她朗玛满就等候在大海那边。

The princess kindly said to Anuman,
“I didn't expect that you were sent by Langmaman.
It really makes me feel happy.”
Anuman turned into a handsome boy,
And knelt down before the princess.
He told the princess how he met Langmaman.
He added the Langmaman was waiting at the other side of the sea.

阿奴曼又对公主说道：
“是圣者朗玛满派我来救你，

Anuman said to the princess again,
“It's the saint Langmaman who sent me to save you.

我从一百多个眼程的那边飞过来，
我现在就带你回到朗玛满身边。”

I flew from the side of more than one hundred eye ranges.
I'll take you back to Langmaman now."

“哥哥你说的话我相信，
但我想还是行不通。
我和朗玛满哥哥心连心在一起，
除了朗玛满谁都没法靠近我身。
十头王曾经对我说，
他要把权力交给我，
满宫的嫔妃随我使唤，
他甘愿为奴将我服侍，
十头王说的这些我已全部拒绝。
他让魔女来看守我，
七天以后我就会死在御花园中。

"I believe what you have said.
But I don't think it will work.
I and Langmaman are together heart to heart.
Nobody can get close to me except for Langmaman.
The Ten-headed King once said to me
That he would hand over the power to me.
The concubines in the palace would follow my orders.
He was willing to serve me as a slave.
I have refused all the things the Ten-headed King said.
He had the witch guard me.
And I'll die in the imperial garden in seven days.

“尚拎公主给十头王进谗言，
十头王恼羞成怒脸发红。
七天后群魔要将我放在火炕上烤，
群魔要用我的肉当饭吃。
这是十头王给我的最后通牒，
他们不会轻易放了我。

"The princess of Shanglin offered slanders to the Ten-headed King.
The Ten-headed King became angry with embarrassment and flushed.
Seven days later, the demons will put me on the fire to roast.
The demons will eat my meat.
This is the ultimatum given to me by the Ten-headed King.
They won't let me go easily.

“请你快快回到哥哥身边，
把这里的情况向朗玛满哥哥禀报。
为了让我早日脱离苦海，
期盼哥哥早日将我救回到他身边。”

"Please go back to Langmaman quickly
And report the situation here to Langmaman.
In order to get me out of the sea of misery,
I hope he will come to rescue me back to him as soon as possible."

阿奴曼跪拜公主要返程，
他把御花园里的花草踩得粉碎，
还打伤了几个魔鬼，
魔鬼们疼得大声呼叫。

Anuman knelt down to the princess to return.
He crushed the flowers and plants in the imperial garden
And wounded some demons.
The demons cried out in pain.

阿奴曼飞行在高空上，
王城上下人心惶惶。
魔鬼回去给十头王禀报，
说是一只猴子已将勐兰嘎王国搅乱。
十头王听说猴子是朗玛满的手下，
顿时他暴跳如雷。
十头王把自己的长子叫来，
让他去将此事解决。

Anuman flew high in the sky.
The people in the imperial city were in a panic.
The demons went back to report to the Ten-headed King,
Saying that a monkey had messed up the Menglanga Kingdom.
The Ten-headed King heard that the monkey was Langmaman's subordinate.
Suddenly he was furious.
The Ten-headed King called his eldest son to deal the matter.

十头王的长子赶到御花园里，
他看见猴子还在半空中。
阿奴曼认为这样逃走还不行，
他要知道十头王有何打算，
他又降落到御花园里让十头王长子捆绑自己，
他让十头王长子拉他来到王宫。

The eldest son of the Ten-headed King rushed to the imperial garden.
He saw the monkey still in the air.
Anuman thought it was not enough to escape like this,
He wanted to know what the Ten-headed King planed to do.
He descended in the imperial garden and let the eldest son of the Ten-headed King tie him up.
He asked the eldest son of the Ten-headed King to bring him to the palace.

十头王看见阿奴曼后大声问道：
“你这妖猴从何而来，
为何来糟蹋我的御花园？”
“我是朗玛满的手下，

The Ten-headed King asked loudly when he saw Anuman,
“Where did you come from, demon monkey ?
Why do you come here to ruin my imperial garden ?”
“I work for Langmaman.

是他派我来寻找西达公主，
昨晚我到处寻找就是不见公主，
原来是你们将她藏在花园中。
如是圣者朗玛满发话，
你的王宫早就被我踏平！”

He sent me to find Princess Xida.
Last night, I searched everywhere but couldn't find the princess.
So you hid her in the garden.
If the saint Langmaman gives me instructions,
Your palace has probably been levelled by me !"

十头王气得浑身发抖：
“立即将这只疯猴处死，
把他的肉放在火炕上烤吃，
再用大锅将他的骨头熬成汤喝！”

The Ten-headed King trembled with anger and said,
"Put the mad monkey to death immediately.
Put his meat on the fire to roast it.
Then boil his bones into soup in a big pot !"

十头王的长子一伙立即动手，
他们将猴子拉去绑在树桩上，
数把刚刀一起砍向猴子，
但始终杀不了猴子。
他们又用大火烧开水烫猴子，
猴子不但没死还反过来讥笑他们。

The eldest son of the Ten-headed King and his gang immediately started.
They pulled the monkey and tied it to the tree stump.
Several steel knives were chopped at the monkey.
But the monkey was still alive.
They also boiled monkeys with hot water.
The monkey didn't die.
On the contrary, he laughed at them.

十头王对手下人大声吼道：
“你们一定要将疯猴杀死，
杀不死他不要来见我！”
阿奴曼笑着说道：
“你们这样是杀不死我的啊，
你们要用数百丈土布裹我身体，
土布上面浇上芝麻油再烧我，
才能把我烧死在你们王宫中。”

The Ten-headed King shouted at his servants loudly,
"You must kill the mad monkey.
Otherwise, don't come to see me !"
Anuman smiled and said,
"You can't kill me like this.
You should wrap my body with hundreds of Zhang(a Zhang is about 3.33 meters) of handwoven cloth,
And pour sesame oil on the cloth and burn me.
This way, I will be burnt to death in your palace."

十头王下达命令快快动手，
从王宫里搬出许多土布来。
几十匹土布裹猴身，
土布上面又泼上芝麻油。
土布顿时燃起熊熊烈火，
猴子突然变化飞至白云端。
阿奴曼在宫殿之间跳来跳去，
整个王城忽然变成大火海。

The Ten-headed King gave an order to get it moving quickly.
They took out a lot of handwoven cloth from the palace.
Dozens of Pi(a Pi is about 13.2 meters)of handwoven cloth was rapped around the monkey.
The sesame oil was sprinkled on the cloth,
The cloth suddenly ignited.
The monkey suddenly changed and flew to the top of the cloud.
Anuman jumped from palace to palace,
The whole imperial city suddenly became a raging fire.

阿奴曼在空中说道：
“十头王你的末日即将来临，
你将如熟透的水果掉落大地上，
我的伙伴与我一样有本事，
累计数量达三亿八千万只。
你的王城容不下猴国兵马，
所有后果由你来承担！”

Anuman said in the air,
“The Ten-headed King, your doomsday is coming.
You will fall on the earth like a ripe fruit.
My companions are as capable as me.
The cumulative number reaches 380 million.
Your imperial city is unable to accommodate the troops of Monkey Kingdom.
You will bear all the consequences !”

阿奴曼说完就跳入大海里，
他挣脱掉身上的层层土布。
他又来到了御花园里，
他跪拜在西达公主面前。
他将情况一一向公主述说，
公主听后激动万分。
公主拔下七根长发递给阿奴曼，
让他尽快回到朗玛满身边。

After that, Anuman jumped into the sea.
He got rid of the layers of handwoven cloth.
He came to the imperial garden again
And knelt before Princess Xida.
He told the princess about the situation in details.
The princess was very excited to hear that.
The princess pulled out seven long hairs and handed them to Anuman,
And asked him to return to Langmaman as soon as possible.

阿奴曼飞过大海回到对岸，
他跪拜在朗玛满面前。
朗玛满问他情况如何，
阿奴曼将所有经过向朗玛满叙述。
阿奴曼将七根公主的头发递给朗玛满，
朗玛满见头发如见其人。

Anuman flew across the sea to the other side.
He knelt before Langmaman.
Langmaman asked him about his detection trip.
Anuman narrated all the experiences to Langmaman.
Anuman handed over the princess's seven hairs to Longmaman.
At the sight of the hairs, Langmaman seemed to have seen the princess.

朗玛满伤心地哭道：
“我美丽无比的西达公主啊，
我俩就像一对鸳鸯在湖中走散。
你如雌鸳鸯被魔鬼劫持而去，
我如雄鸳鸯在湖中游荡孤孤单单。
你落在魔掌里我该怎么办，
我已为你心力交瘁没人替我分担。”

Langmaman cried sadly,
“My beautiful Princess Xida,
We two are like a pair of mandarin ducks lost in the lake.
You were kidnapped by the devil like a female mandarin duck.
I am like a male mandarin duck wandering alone in the lake.
What should I do if you fall into the hands of the demons.
I have been haggard for you, and no one has shared it for me.”

阿奴曼对朗玛满说道：
“花园里那些魔鬼多数已被处死，
王宫里的宫殿也已成火海，
探清虚实后我才回到圣者朗玛满身边。”
朗玛满听后十分高兴，
他命令苏嘎林召集猴群在海中建桥。

Anuman said to Longmaman,
“Most of the demons in the garden have been executed.
The palace in the city has also become a sea of fire.
I returned to you after I found out the truth.”
Langmaman was very delighted to hear that.
He ordered Sugalin to gather monkeys to build a bridge in the sea.

数千万的猴子搬石头在海中建大桥，
无数石头投入大海中。
有一只巨型螃蟹在海底，

Tens of millions of monkeys were carrying stones to build the bridge in the sea.
Countless stones were thrown into the sea.

它的两把钳子又大又长。
阿奴曼已看清楚，
巨蟹在用双钳将一个个石头推开，
不收拾了它猴群就白忙活。

There was a giant crab at the bottom of the sea.
Its two pincers were big and long.
Anuman saw the giant crab pushing away stones with its two pincers.
If it was allowed to develop like this, the monkeys would work in vain.

阿奴曼对大家说道：
“我们在上面辛苦搬石头，
巨蟹却在海底搬走石头。
我要到海底去找它，
我以摇动尾巴为信号，
看见摇尾你们就把我拉上来。”

Anuman said to the monkeys,
“We are working hard to move stones on the top,
but the giant crab is moving away stones at the bottom of the sea.
I'm going to the bottom of the sea to find it.
Pull me up when you see the wagging tail.”

阿奴曼说完就将尾巴作变化，
他的尾巴有一百二十个眼程长。
他一头钻入海底，
他在海底到处寻找巨蟹。
巨蟹正在海底推开猴群丢下来的石头，
推开一个石头石桥就下沉一层。
阿奴曼抓住巨蟹的两只钳手，
阿奴曼又将自己的尾巴摆动传信号，
猴群把阿奴曼拉到岸上来。

Anuman then changed his tail,
Which was 120 eye ranges long.
He dived into the sea
Searching for the giant crab at the bottom of the sea.
The giant crab was pushing away the stones thrown by monkeys at the bottom of the sea.
The stone bridge would sink one layer when a stone was pushed away.
Anuman grabbed the crab's two pincers.
Having seeing Anuman swinging his tail, the monkeys pulled Anuman to the shore.

巨蟹也被拉上了岸边，
朗玛满觉得巨蟹很可怜。
他让猴群把巨蟹的一只钳打断，
又把巨蟹放回大海中。
从此螃蟹的双钳就一长一短，

The giant crab was also pulled to the shore.
Langmaman felt sorry for the giant crab.
He asked the monkeys to break one of the crab's pincers
And sent the crab back into the sea.
Since then, the crab's pincers have been long and short,

这一切都与阿奴曼有关。	which is related to Anuman.
七天后石桥已修到彼岸，	Seven days later, the stone bridge had been built to the other side,
就像一条巨龙横跨大海中央。	Which looked like a giant dragon across the sea.
朗玛满命令在桥的中间建一座大凉亭，	Langmaman ordered to build a large pavilion in the middle of the bridge.
猴群在凉亭里唱歌跳舞锣鼓喧天，	The monkeys sang and danced in the pavilion, and the sound of gongs and drums resounded in the sea.
热闹声音回荡在大海里，	
也惊醒了勐兰嘎国王城的国民。	It also awakened the subjects of Menglanga Kingdom.
十头王听到吵闹声后问道：	The Ten-headed King asked after hearing the noise,
“这是哪里传来的吵闹声？	“Where is the noise coming from ?
是谁胆子大得目中无人。”	Who is so bold as to be arrogant ?”
十头王的儿子回答道：	The son of the Ten-headed King replied,
“威震四方的父王啊，	“Your Majesty,
这是朗玛满在大海上建大桥，	Langmaman is building a bridge above the sea.
他们在唱歌跳舞庆祝胜利，	They are singing and dancing to celebrate their victory.
也许是要来找西达公主，	Maybe they will come to find Princess Xida.
也许他们要围攻我们的王城。”	Maybe they will besiege our imperial city.”
十头王狂妄自大地说道：	The Ten-headed King said arrogantly,
“这是给我们的魔友们送美食来了，	“They will be the delicious food to us.
我们的魔友可以饱餐一顿。	We can have a good meal.
大家不必慌张，	Don't panic.
他们一定进不了我们的王城。”	They will never enter our royal city.”
朗玛满与猴王苏嘎林说道：	Langmaman said to Sugalin, the Monkey King,
“我们已在海中建成大桥，	“We have built a bridge in the sea.
十头王仍然躲在王宫中。	But the Ten-headed King is still hiding in the palace.
我们不能与十头王大规模开战，	We should neither fight the Ten-headed King on a large

不能让尸体堆满王城。
不如先派出几个得力干将，
进去王城里探个虚实再商量。”

scale,
Nor let the corpses fill the city.
Why don't we send some go-getters to the royal city to explore the truth and then discuss ?"

苏嘎林跪拜朗玛满说道：
“圣者朗玛满啊，
我侄子旺果他机灵又勇敢，
这个任务旺果可以完成。
十头王认识我哥哥猴王巴力莫，
旺果是最合适的人选。
当年十头王骑飞行器到处游逛，
他不小心就从我哥哥头顶上飞过，
我哥哥巴力莫追上去抓住他不放，
还用尾巴缠住他的脖子在空中转了几大圈，
十头王怕死就不得不急忙认错，
我哥哥看他可怜才放了人。”

Sugalin knelt down and said to Langmaman,
"Your saint Langmaman,
My nephew Wangguo is smart and brave.
He is able to complete the task.
The Ten-headed King knows my brother Balimo, the Monkey King.
Therefore, Wangguo is the most suitable person.
In those days, the Ten-headed King rode around on the craft.
He accidentally flew over my brother's head.
My brother Balimo ran after him and caught him.
He also wrapped his tail around his neck and spun around in the air.
The Ten-headed King was afraid of death, so he had to apologize in hurry.
My brother let him go because he was pathetic."

朗玛满听了很高兴，
希望旺果马到成功。
旺果感恩地跪拜朗玛满，
他告别朗玛满飞上了蓝蓝的天空。

Langmaman was very happy to hear that,
Hoping Wangguo will succeed soon.
Wangguo knelt down to Langmaman thankfully.
He said goodbye to Langmaman and flew into the blue sky.

十头王坐在宝座上，
长子和大臣们围坐在他身旁。
旺果从高空缓缓落地，
他卷着尾巴坐在宫殿中。

The Ten-headed King was sitting on the throne,
With the eldest son and the ministers sitting around him.
Wangguo descended slowly to the ground.
He sat in the palace with his tail coiled.

十头王看见他后大声问道：
“你这毛猴从何而来？
是谁派你来这里，
不声不响就闯进王宫中。”

At the sight of it, the Ten-headed King said in loud voice,
“Where did you come from, monkey ?
Who sent you here into the palace
Without making a sound.”

旺果回答十头王道：
“是圣者朗玛满派我来找你，
你当国王的时间已经不久长。
我的父亲是猴王巴力莫，
几座猴山都是我的故乡。
我的父亲虽已作古，
但你不会忘记过去吧，
你与我父亲相遇在空中，
我父亲拖着你转圈圈，
你当场老老实实认错，
我父亲可怜你才放你回王宫中。

Wangguo replied to the Ten-headed King,
“It's the saint Langmaman who sent me to find you.
Your reign as a king will not last long.
My father is Balimo the Monkey King.
Several Monkey Mountains are my hometown.
Though my father is dead, you won't forget the past, will you ?
You encountered my father in the air.
My father dragged you around.
Since you apologized sincerely,
My father had pity on you and let you go back to the palace.

“朗玛满是当今圣者，
他仁爱友善待众生。
如是你还想活在人世上，
现在你就跟我去找朗玛满认错称臣。

“Langmaman is the saint today,
Who is kind to all beings.
If you still want to live in the world,
You can go with me to apologize to Langmaman.

“我们已将御花园的魔鬼杀死一大半，
他们因为作恶才横尸花园中。
宽阔无边的大海上，
我们已经建成一座大桥通两边。
如你怕死就快快把西达公主送回来，
还有贵重礼品一并送到朗玛满身边，
这样做也许你的王国还能平安无事。
如是你痴迷不悟狂妄自大，

“We have killed more than half of the demons in the imperial garden.
They died in the garden because they did evil.
We have built a bridge across the vast sea,
If you are afraid of death, send Princess Xida back quickly to Langmaman,
Along with the valuable gifts.
Maybe your kingdom will be safe in this way.

如是你不把西达公主送回来，
你的身体一定被神箭射穿！”

If you are infatuated with arrogance,
If you don't send Princess Xida back,
Your body will surely be pierced by a magic arrow !"

十头王拳击桌子发怒火，
十头王立即站起来全身发抖怒吼道：
“立即将这只疯猴子砸死，
别让他在此欺负人！”

The Ten-headed King punched at the table in anger.
He immediately stood up, trembling and roared,
"Kill this crazy monkey immediately.
Don't let him bully people here !"

十头王的两个儿子抓住旺果，
欲将他拖出宫殿外边。
旺果左右手各抓起一个人，
他将两人高高举到半空中，
又从空中将他们砸在地上。

The two sons of the Ten-headed King seized Wangguo.
They wanted to drag him out of the palace.
Wangguo grabbed one son with each hand.
He lifted the two sons high in the air,
And then smashed them to the ground from the air.

十头王顿时很痛心，
他战战兢兢地说道：
“猴国的军队已进入我们的领土，
猴兵犹如滚滚海水漫王城。
我们怎么对付他们啊？
谁有主意快快说出来！”

The Ten-headed King was very sad.
He said trembling,
"The army of Monkey Kingdom has entered our territory.
The monkey soldiers are like billowing sea water flooding
the imperial city.
How can we deal with them ?
Anyone with a good idea, just let me know !"

十头王的弟弟毕披真诚跪拜说道：
“当年天神父亲赐本领给哥哥时，
天上和地下都让你随便出入，
但有三样不让你战胜：
一是用两脚行走的人类，
二是在森林中度日的猴子，
三是开天辟地时留下的一把神弓。

Bipi, the Ten-headed King's younger brother knelt down
and said,
"Our father gave you the skills
With which you could fly into the skies and come down
to the earth at will.
Except for the following three things:
First, mankind that walks on two feet.
Second, monkeys that live in the forest.

Third, the magic bow passed down from the time when heaven was separated from earth.

“如是我们与猴类硬碰硬，
吃亏的肯定就是我们。
我们不如与朗玛满他们和好，
将西达公主送还他。
这样做对双方都有好处，
这是最妙的主意了，
全国人民都可以平安无事。”

"If we fight with monkeys,
We will be the losers.
Why don't we make up with Langmaman ?
And send Princess Xida back to him.
It's good for both sides.
This is the best idea.
The whole kingdom will be safe."

十头王立即站起来骂道：
“你这个吃里爬外的家伙，
就算立即杀死你也无人可怜！”
十头王用脚猛踢毕披头部，
弟弟毕披很伤心。

The Ten-headed King immediately stood up and cursed,
"You live on me while helping Langmaman secretly.
Even if I kill you immediately, nobody will feel sorry !"
The Ten-headed King kicked Bipi's head with his feet.
Bipi, the brother was very sad.

毕披又说道：
“是哥哥你让我们出主意，
我认为这是最好的谏言。
你却这样发怒火，
你让我们忠臣伤心欲断肠！”

Bipi said again,
"It was you that made us come up with ideas.
I thought it was the best advice.
But you are so angry.
You made the loyal officials sad and heartbroken !"

大臣们都赞同毕披的主意，
但十头王就是不赞成。
毕披说完就冲出王宫，
毕披跑到了朗玛满身边。

The ministers all agreed with Bipi's idea,
Except for the Ten-headed King.
After that, Bipi rushed out of the palace,
And ran to Langmaman.

毕披向朗玛满跪拜后说道：
“尊贵的圣者啊，
您就像一只狮王安祥住在深山中，

Bipi knelt down to Langmaman and said,
"Your distinguished saint,
You are like a lion king living in the mountains peacefully.

我今天就来投靠您身边俯首称臣。
如是我不诚心怀恶意，
就让诸神把我拖入黄泉永不投生。”

I'm coming to join you today and bow down to you.
If I am not sincere and malicious,
Let the gods drag me into the netherworld and never reincarnate."

朗玛满开口问道：
“你为何离开你的兄长，
为何要跑来投靠在我身边？”
“十头王要我们出主意，
我就讲了我的想法和主张，
我说双方不能用武力对抗，
要把西达公主送回您身边。
天神父亲赐给他本领时，
天上和地下允许他自由来往，
在王国里任他做国王，
但有三样本领天神没有赐给他，
一是用两脚行走的人类，
二是在森林中度日的猴子，
三是开天辟地时留下的一把神弓。

Langmaman asked,
"Why did you leave your brother ?
And come here to join me ?"
"The Ten-headed King asked us for advice.
I told him my thoughts and opinions,
Saying that the two sides could not confront by force.
On the contrary, we should send back Princess Xida to you.
Our God father gave him the skills
With which he could fly to the skies and come down to the earth freely.
He could be the king as long as as he wished.
Except for the following three skills:
First, mankind that walks on two feet.
Second, monkeys that live in the forest.
Third, the magic bow passed down from the time when heaven was separated from earth.

“现在这三样正在向王国逼近，
只有送回西达公主才有望解除危机。
这是我的心里话，
十头王却听不进去。
他不占理还用脚踢我头部，
我只有来投靠在您身边。
请您一定收下我，
我来投奔圣者是一片真心。”

"Now these three are approaching the kingdom.
Only when Princess Xida is sent back can the crisis be solved.
This is what I really mean,
But the Ten-headed King wouldn't listen.
He was in the wrong and kicked me in the head.
I have to come to join you.
Please accept me.
I'm sincere to join you the saint."

朗玛满听后很赞赏，	Langmaman was very appreciative at this.
朗玛满问苏嘎林毕披这个人怎么样，	He asked Sugalin about his opinions on Bipi.
苏嘎林缓缓把话谈：	Sugalin said slowly,
“毕披是一个真正的汉子，	“Bipi is a real man.
他守戒清净对人真诚，	He keeps the precepts and is an honest man.
圣者可以大胆让他当助手，	You can make him your assistant and
他一定能够为圣者争光。”	He will definitely win honor for you.”
朗玛满将毕披叫到面前说道：	Langmaman called Bipi to him and said,
“我相信你的诚心诚意，	“I believe in your sincerity.
如是你帮助我们将你哥哥十头王打败，	If you help us defeat your brother the Ten-headed King,
我就让你当勐兰嘎国王。”	I will make you the king of Menglanga Kingdom.”
毕披向朗玛满真诚跪拜，	Bipi sincerely knelt down to Langmaman.
从此毕披紧紧跟在朗玛满身旁。	From then on, Bipi had been following Langmaman closely.
旺果已把勐兰嘎王城寻遍，	Wangguo had searched every corner of the imperial city of Menglanga Kingdom,
包括宫殿、花园和池塘。	Including the palaces, gardens and ponds.
他看见了无数仙女般的侍女，	He saw countless fairy maids.
他看见了宫殿里无数的金银珠宝。	He saw countless gold, silver and jewels in the palace.
他看见了御花园里被困的西达公主，	He saw Princess Xida trapped in the imperial garden.
愁眉苦脸的公主让他同情。	The sad princess made him sympathize.
旺果回到了朗玛满身边，	After Wangguo came back to Langmaman,
他跪拜朗玛满说道：	He knelt down and said to Langmaman,
“圣者朗玛满啊，	“You saint Langmaman,
您派我前往勐兰嘎王国探虚实，	You sent me to Menglanga Kingdom to explore the truth.
我与十头王争辩不休，	I argued with the Ten-headed King.
但他听不进我的半句话。	But he wouldn’t hear a word from me.
他派两个儿子要处死我，	He sent the two sons to put me to death.

我将两个王子从空中砸在地上。
我飞到空中俯瞰侦察，
整个王城开有东南西北四道城门。”

I smashed the two princes to the ground from the air.
I flew into the air to look down on reconnaissance,
Finding that there are four gates in the east, south, west and north of the royal city.”

朗玛满听后说道：
“因为十头王没有把公主送回来，
我们只有一条路就是跟他拼！
他认为我们无本事，
我们要将王城踏成烂泥丸。
旺果将军啊，
你就去集合我们的队伍吧，
你已经摸清了情况，
你安排部署要周全。”

Hearing that, Langmaman said,
“Because the Ten-headed King did not send the princess back,
We have to fight with him.
He thinks we are incompetent.
We will turn the royal city into a muddy pill.
General Wangguo,
Assemble our troops.
Since you have found out the situation.
You are the most suitable person to deploy the troops.”

旺果开始调动猴兵，
东南西北四座城门已被猴军围住。
北城门的队伍由纳哈腊挂帅，
东城门的队伍由朗玛满负责，
阿奴曼和占布曼亦在其中。
四座大城门已被猴军堵死，
一场大战正在来临。

Wangguo started to mobilize the monkey soldiers.
Four gates in the east, south, west and north had been surrounded by the monkey troops.
The troop at the North Gate was led by Nahala.
Langmaman was in charge of the troop at the East Gate.
Anuman and Zhanbuman were among the troops.
Four city gates had been blocked by the monkey troops,
And a war was coming.

十头王让他的儿子率队伍迎战，
让他们将猴群杀光：
“把跑进王宫的猴子养在宫里，
给宫女们当玩物。
那个朗玛满与纳哈腊，
就抓去与西达公主关在大花园中。

The Ten-headed King had his son lead the troops to fight
To kill all the monkeys,
“Keep the monkeys running into the palace
As a plaything for maids in the palace.
For Langmaman and Nahala,
Seize them and lock them in the garden with Princess Xida.

我们万众一心， 要让朗玛满溃败在我们王城。”	Let us all unite To defeat Langmaman in our royal city."
十头王的儿子接到了命令， 他调兵遣将雷厉风行。 他带来的大将军多达一千人， 跟着他的骑兵有上亿人。 骑兵后面兵卒九千万， 还有七万的大象骑兵。	Having received the order, The son of the Ten-headed King mobilized his troops vigorously. He brought as many as 1,000 generals. There were hundreds of millions of cavalry under his command, Which was followed by 90 million soldiers, And 70,000 elephant cavalry.
猴军看见敌方阵势很害怕， 他们跑到朗玛满身边。 朗玛满问毕披道： “毕披兄弟啊， 敌方率军当先锋的是何人？ 他年少有精力， 他的相貌也是可爱可亲。”	The monkey soldiers were scared when they saw the enemy's formation. They ran to Langmaman. Langmaman asked Bipi, "Brother Bipi, Who is leading the enemy troops ? He is young and energetic. His appearance is also lovely and amiable."
“他是十头王的长子， 他的外公是尚拎神邦的国王。 尚拎国王曾与大天神交战， 当年十头王亦曾前往助战。 这个儿子起名为英大腊吉达， 勐兰嘎王国大事均让他承担， 现在他是勐兰嘎王国的副国王。”	"He is the eldest son of the Ten-headed King. His grandfather was the king of Shanglin Kingdom. The King of Shanglin once fought with the Great God. The Ten-headed King also went to help in the war. This son was named Yingdalajida. He is responsible for all the important events of Menglanga Kingdom. Now he is the deputy king of Menglanga Kingdom."
朗玛满呼喊英大腊吉达的名字：	Langmaman shouted the name of Yingdalajida,

"英大腊吉达啊，
战争会伤害无辜生命，
现在我俩对射弓箭，
不要让一兵一卒有伤亡。"

"Yingdalajida,
War will hurt innocent lives.
Now we two shoot arrows at each.
Don't let a soldier die."

猴王苏嘎林跪拜朗玛满说道：
"我们已经站在他们的王国土地上，
他骑大象我们也不能不如敌人，
圣者您就骑在我背上与他比试，
我们的朗玛满一定能取胜获荣光！"

Sugalin, the Monkey King knelt down to Langmaman and said,
"We are now standing on the land of their kingdom.
He is riding an elephant, we are not inferior to the enemy.
You saint can compete with him on my back.
Our Langmaman will win and be honored !"

朗玛满骑在猴王背上，
朗玛满欲用神箭射向对方。
英大腊吉达先向朗玛满射箭，
朗玛满亦立即用神箭射向对方。

Riding on the Monkey King's back,
Langmaman wanted to shoot at the other side with magic arrows.
Yingdalajida shot arrows at Langmaman first.
Langmaman also immediately shot at the other side with magic arrows.

英大腊吉达的箭在空中被折断，
英大腊吉达立即变化成蛇类腊嘎，
腊嘎正向朗玛满冲过来。
朗玛满亦变化成大鹏鸟，
咬住腊嘎尾巴欲把他消灭在空中。

Yingdalajida's arrow was broken in the air.
Then he immediately became a snake, Laga,
Which was rushing towards Langmaman.
Langmaman also changed into a roc bird.
It bit Laga's tail in an attempt to kill him in the air.

英大腊吉达让空气变成熊熊烈火，
朗玛满让空气变暴雨将大火熄灭。
英大腊吉达躲在彩车里，
朗玛满变暴风将彩车刮翻。

Yingdalajida turned the air into a raging fire,
While Langmaman turned the air into a rainstorm to extinguish the fire.
Yingdalajida hid in the float.
Langmaman turned into a storm to turn over the float.

英大腊吉达又立即想出一招，
他速速飞到半空中，
他在空中大声说道：
“朗玛满你已无法脱身，
你看看什么在闪闪发光。”
英大腊吉达将法器从空中砸下来，
朗玛满看到了腊嘎的法绳。
朗玛满才将法绳砍断，
腊嘎的毒气已扩散到他体中。

Yingdalajida came up with another trick immediately.
He flew fast into the air
And said in the air in loud voice,
“You can’t get away.
Look, what’s shining.”
Yingdalajida dropped the divine instrument from the air.
Langmaman saw the magic rope of Laga.
Soon after Langmaman cut off the magic rope,
The poison gas of Laga had diffused into his body.

朗玛满中毒后疼痛难忍，
英大腊吉达开始十分狂妄：
“朗玛满你就等死吧，
改日我扛你的尸体去展示给猴群看，
再把你的尸首送到西达公主面前！”

The pain of Langmaman was unbearable.
Yingdalajida began to be very arrogant,
“Langmaman, you wait to die.
I will carry your body to show the monkeys some day.
And send your body to Princess Xida !”

英大腊吉达振臂高呼，
夸耀自己战无对手。
英大腊吉达仰面朝天狂笑，
带着浩浩荡荡的队伍凯旋回王宫。

Yingdalajida shouted loudly,
Boasting that he was invincible.
Yingdalajida laughed on his back,
And returned to the palace with a huge team.

朗玛满中毒后疼痛难忍，
苏嘎林问猴医占布曼能否医治，
占布曼说腊嘎的毒气已渗透到血脉，
克毒药就长在遥远的深山老林中。

The pain of Langmaman was unbearable.
Sugalin asked the monkey doctor Zhanbuman whether he could cure Langmaman.
Zhanbuman said that the poison gas of Laga had penetrated into his blood.
The antidote grows in the mountains.

猴王让阿奴曼去取药，
阿奴曼说多远的地方他都能到达，
只是担心分不清哪棵是克毒药。

The Monkey King asked Anuman to get the antidote.
Anuman said he could reach as far as he could.
He was just worried that he couldn’t tell which one was

the antidote.

占布曼将药的形状细细讲：
“克毒药的叶是金黄色，
树干和叶柄绿茵茵。
一定要在太阳落山前取药到手，
然后快快赶到我房间。”

Zhanbuman detailed the shape of the medicine,
“The leaves of the antidote are golden,
While the tree trunk and petiole are green.
Be sure to get the medicine before sunset,
And then hurry to my room.”

阿奴曼飞速来到森林里，
他认真寻找克毒药。
阿奴曼采药飞回来，
朗玛满的身体药到病除。
朗玛满恢复健康如从前，
朗玛满感激猴臣占布曼，
又夸阿奴曼本领高强。

Anuman hurried to the forest,
And began to search for the antidote carefully.
Anuman flew back with the medicine,
Langmaman was cured with medicine.
He has recovered as before.
Langmaman was very grateful to Zhanbuman,
He also praised Anuman for his superior skills.

朗玛满不解地问毕披道：
“毕披兄弟啊，
我的弓箭皆为天神所赐，
但英大腊吉达在半空中我就无法对付，
不知该如何对付十头王父子？”

Langmaman was puzzled and asked Bipi,
“Brother Bipi,
I got the bow and arrow from God,
But I could not defeat Yingdalajida in midair.
I don’t know how to deal with the Ten-headed King and his son.”

毕披跪拜朗玛满后回答道：
“我至尊的圣者啊，
要对付十头王父子也有捷径，
要寻找一位长时间未正视过女子面容的男人，
不正视女子面容的时间要达十二年。
无论十头王他们躲到天上或海底，
让他向他们射击一定百发百中。”

Bipi knelt down to Langmaman and replied,
“Your venerable saint,
There is also a shortcut to deal with the Ten-headed King and his son,
We can find a man who hasn’t faced a woman for a long time,
The time should be at least 12 years.
The man will shoot the Ten-headed King and his son,
No matter where they hide.”

朗玛满听后愁眉苦脸， 朗玛满叹一口气说道： “天下本是男爱女欢的红尘世界， 天下没有不看女子面容的男人。 这个难题我难解， 虽然我不敢说是荒唐。”	Langmaman frowned after hearing that. He said with a sigh, “This is the world of men and women, There is no man who does not like to look at a woman’s face. This problem is difficult for me to solve, Although I dare not say it is absurd.”
弟弟纳哈腊跪拜哥哥后说道： “请哥哥勿忧愁， 弟弟我就是十二年不看女子面容的男人。” 朗玛满不解地问道： “弟弟啊， 我们三个人一起住山里十二年， 你天天服侍我和你嫂子， 你怎么会是不正视女子面容的人？”	The brother Nahala knelt down to Langmaman and said, “Brother, don’t worry about that, I’m the man who hasn’t seen a woman’s face for 12 years.” Langmaman asked in bewilderment, “Brother, We three people have lived in the mountains for 12 years. You serve me and your sister-in-law every day. How can you be a person who hasn’t faced a woman’s face ?”
“十二年来我们三人住在深山里， 外出时我走在我嫂子后边， 住在窝棚里时我只面对你， 你和嫂子在一起我当父母看待， 我从来没有正眼看过嫂子的容颜。”	“We three have lived in the mountains, I walked behind my sister-in-law when we were out. In the shed, I only faced you. I regard you and my sister-in-law as my parents, I have never seen my sister-in-law’s face.”
朗玛满又问弟弟纳哈腊道： “我们在山里转来转去， 你不看你嫂子如何走在她后边？” “我行走在山里不看我嫂子， 我只看嫂子脚后跟， 十二年来均是如此， 我管好身口意已有十二年。”	Langmaman asked Nahala, “We walked around the mountains. How could you walk behind her without looking at your sister-in-law ?” “When I was walking in the mountains, I never looked at my sister-in-law’s face, I only saw my sister-in-law’s heel.

朗玛满听后十分感动，
他赞扬弟弟修行有进展。

It has been like this for 12 years,
I have controlled my body and mind for 12 years."
Langmaman was moved by his words,
He praised his brother for his progress in cultivation.

朗玛满又对阿奴曼说道：
“你曾把神女变的金山打断，
你要去修补还原那座金山。”
阿奴曼不愿意去修复那座山，
朗玛满批评阿奴曼做错了事就要改正。
阿奴曼很不情愿地跑过去，
他抱起被他打断的山峰丢下去，
虽然山峰与山体已连接在一起，
但那座山就成了一座歪斜的金山。

Langmaman said to Anuman again,
"You once broke the golden mountain changed by the Goddess,
You need to repair and restore the golden mountain."
Anuman was unwilling to repair the mountain,
Langmaman said that if one did something wrong, he or she should correct it.
Anuman ran over reluctantly.
He picked up the peak broken by him and dropped it.
Although the peak and the mountain were connected,
The mountain has become a skewed golden mountain.

相隔十二个眼程的距离，
阿奴曼一跃即到达。
猴民看见阿奴曼有大本领，
猴国个个欢呼雀跃。

Anuman arrived at a distance of 12 eye ranges
In one leap.
Finding that Anuman had great skills,
Everyone in the Monkey Kingdom cheered.

英大腊吉达看见朗玛满还活着，
英大腊吉达很吃惊。
他一跃就来到了太阳底下，
他用巨大的身体遮住了阳光，
人间突然就像黑夜。
他正准备往下射神箭，
纳哈腊跪拜朗玛满请来神箭，
纳哈腊向英大腊吉达怒吼道：
“上一次你将我哥哥蒙骗，

Yingdalajida was surprised to see Langmaman alive.
He jumped in the sun.
He covered the sun with his huge body.
The world suddenly looked like a dark night.
He was about to shoot a magic arrow.
Nahala knelt down to Langmaman to ask for the magic bow.
Nahala roared at Yingdalajida,
"Last time you lied to my brother.

现在我让你尸首分离在天空中。"

Now I will kill you in the air."

纳哈腊说完就射出神箭去，
神箭一路电光闪闪飞向天空，
神箭的声音犹如雷霆万钧。
在空中得意的英大腊吉达顿时全身分离，
尸体伴随轰隆巨响掉落在大地上。
英大腊吉达的队伍哭喊声震天，
那情形犹如就要地覆天翻。

Nahala then shot the magic arrow,
Which flew into the sky with lightning all the way
With a thunderbolt-like sound.
The proud Yingdalajida in the air suddenly separated,
The body fell to the ground with a loud noise.
The team of Yingdalajida cried loudly,
As if it was about to turn upside down.

英大腊吉达的队伍将尸首拉回王宫里，
十头王夫妇哭得死去活来。
他们认为此后将无人来继承王位，
勐兰嘎王国花谢后再无花开。

The team of Yingdalajida brought the body back to the palace.
The Ten-headed King and his wife cried their eyes out.
They thought that no one would succeed to the throne,
Flowers in Menglanga Kingdom would never bloom after it withered.

人们将英大腊吉达的尸体拉去焚烧在坟地，
勐兰嘎王国全国上下悲痛万分。
十头王咬牙切齿下定决心，
他要活吞朗玛满的骨肉，
不能让他活在人世间。

People carried Yingdalajida's body to the cemetery for cremation.
The whole Menglanga Kingdom was in great sorrow.
The Ten-headed King gnashed his teeth and made up his mind.
He wanted to eat Langmaman's flesh and blood alive,
And would not let him live in this world.

十头王命令祭拜诸神明求保佑，
祭品有猪鸡鸭鹅并牛羊，
还有水果、米饭加白酒，
还有钱币、宝旗、宝伞和纸凉亭。
周围燃烧数十堆熊熊烈火，
浓烟滚滚卷到高空中。

The Ten-headed King ordered to worship the gods, asking for blessings.
The sacrifice included pigs, chickens, ducks, geese, cattle and goats,
Along with fruits, rice and liquor.
There were also coins, flags, umbrellas and paper

pavilions.
There were dozens of blazing fires around,
And the smoke rolled up into the sky.

毕披跪拜朗玛满报告道：
“圣者啊，
勐兰嘎王国上空浓烟滚滚，
这是十头王在祭拜诸大神。
他在求诸神保佑，
他一定是要来找我们报仇。”

Bipi knelt down to Langmaman and said,
“You saint,
Smoke billowed over Menglanga Kingdom,
This was the Ten-headed King worshiping the great gods,
And asking the gods to bless him.
He must come to us for revenge.”

朗玛满知道后暗暗高兴，
他命令阿奴曼去看看：
“阿奴曼兄弟啊，
你快快前往十头王祭拜神明处，
捣毁他们的祭场，
速去速回动作快如风！”

Learning of it, Langmaman was very happy.
He ordered Anuman to go and have a look,
“Brother Anuman,
Go to the place where the Ten-headed King was sacrificing to gods.
Destroy their sacrificial field. Go and return quickly !”

阿奴曼受命向勐兰嘎飞去，
他立即将所有祭台全部捣毁，
又释放全部家禽和牛羊。
所有在场的人员遭拷打，
人们抱头四处逃散，
不少抵抗者一命呜呼尸横祭场里，
阿奴曼完成任务后又飞回到朗玛满身旁。

With the order, Anuman flew towards Menglanga.
He immediately destroyed all the sacrificial altars,
Freeing all poultry, cattle and goats.
All people present were tortured.
People ran around holding their heads.
Many resisters died in the sacrificial field.
Anuman flew back to Langmaman after he finished his mission.

十头王的队伍看见阿奴曼返回去，
十头王命令手下人说道：
“快去叫我弟弟贡帕甘腊过来，
让他去收拾猴群。”

Seeing Anuman returning,
The Ten-headed King said to his men,
“Go and ask my brother Gongpaganla to come here.
Let him deal with the monkeys.”

十头王的士兵敲响咚咚大鼓，
但贡帕甘腊深睡不醒，
人们又用木棍戳他的耳朵，
但他仍然呼呼大睡。
人们用白酒灌他的双耳，
贡帕甘腊才苏醒过来。

The soldiers of the Ten-headed King beat the big drum,
But Gongpaganla couldn't wake up.
Some people were poking his ears with sticks,
He was still in a sound sleep.
Some people irrigated his ears with liquor,
And Gongpaganla woke up.

人们告诉贡帕甘腊说有猴群来捣乱，
猴群多得不计其数。
贡帕甘腊站起来向猴群跑去，
他的身体粗壮得直径有五百米。
猴群看见他后十分恐惧，
猴群集聚到朗玛满身旁。
如是被贡帕甘腊抓到真是不堪设想，
一时间猴群害怕得乱哄哄。

People told Gongpaganla that monkeys were making troubles.
There were countless monkeys.
Gongpaganla stood up and ran to the monkeys.
His was so strong that its diameter was 500 meters.
The monkeys were scared when they saw him.
They gathered around Langmaman.
It was inconceivable if the monkeys were caught by Gongpaganla.
For a moment the monkeys were in a panic.

朗玛满骑在阿奴曼背上，
他用神弓一箭射中贡帕甘腊，
贡帕甘腊当场气断身亡。
贡帕甘腊的尸体横躺在那里，
就像一座巨大的山峰。
十头王的士兵和魔鬼们纷纷往后逃，
他们要去缩在十头王身边。

Riding on the back of Anuman,
Langmaman shot Gongpaganla with the magic bow.
Gongpaganla died on the spot.
The corpses of Gongpaganla lay there like a huge mountain peak.
The soldiers and devils of the Ten-headed King fled one after another,
And they wanted to shrink behind the Ten-headed King.

猴群将贡帕甘腊的尸体拖进大河里，
尸体把大河堵得严严实实，
上游流下来的水流不下去，

The monkeys dragged the body of Gongpaganla into the river.
The body blocked the river tightly.

下方河床变成一片沙滩。

The water flowing from the upstream could not go down,
And the river bed below became a beach.

十头王气得浑身发抖，
十头王穿上戎装，
珠宝金银佩戴王冠上，
他要亲自上战场。

The Ten-headed King trembled with anger.
He put on his military uniform,
And the crown decorated with jewelry, gold and silver.
He would go to the battlefield in person.

十头王的女人多得不计其数，
他的儿女大大小小上万千。
儿女都跟母亲过日子，
每个母亲带着儿女一大群。

There were countless women of the Ten-headed King.
He had thousands of children of all ages.
The children lived with their mothers,
And each mother had a large group of children.

十头王的队伍数量无法估算，
将军们骑马骑象走在前。
十头王挥手走在最前方，
浩浩荡荡的队伍从东门出发。
整个王国几乎没有一处空地，
东南西北处处是士兵。

The number of the Ten-headed King's teams could not be estimated.
The generals rode horses and elephants in front.
The Ten-headed King waved his hand and walked in the front.
The mighty team started from the east gate.
There was hardly any open space in the whole kingdom,
And soldiers were everywhere in the east, south, west and north.

朗玛满信心十足，
他对十头王说道：
“荒淫无度的十头王啊，
你的福报真不小，
金银珠宝堆满宫殿里，
出门就坐飞行器到处游荡。
天下美女你掌控，
儿女多得像人世间的一窝马蜂。

Langmaman was very confident.
He said to the Ten-headed King,
"The decadent king,
What a great blessing you have.
The palace was full of gold, silver and jewelry.
When you were away from home, you rode in the craft to wander about.
You control all the beautiful women in the world.

但是今天你的末日已来临，
你将陪葬士兵死在战场中！”

There are as many children as a nest of hornets in the world.
But today your doomsday is coming.
You will be buried with the soldiers killed in battle.”

朗玛满手持弓箭，
他用神箭向十头王射去，
不偏不倚射中了十头王的王冠。
王冠落地十头王吃惊不小，
无数士兵紧张得围在他身旁，
十头王惊慌失措返回王宫中。

Holding the bow and arrow,
Langmaman shot at the Ten-headed King with his magic arrows.
He shot the crown of the Ten-headed King.
The Ten-headed King was surprised to see the crown falling on the ground.
Countless soldiers surrounded him nervously.
The Ten-headed King returned to the palace in panic.

十头王向队伍解释道：
“今天我们出师东门不吉利，
改日我们出师南城门。
我们的队伍比猴群多数倍，
我要把朗玛满的尸体拉到西达公主面前。”

The Ten-headed King explained to his troops,
“It's unlucky for us to depart from the East Gate today.
We will depart from the South Gate another day.
Our troops are several times that of the monkeys.
I'm going to bring Langmaman's body to Princess Xida.”

十头王的队伍浩浩荡荡向前移动，
朗玛满的队伍已经堵挡在前方。
苏嘎林猴王对十头王说道：
“罪恶滔天的十头王啊，
我们只等朗玛满下达命令，
我们一定把你们消灭光。”

The Ten-headed King's troops moved forward with great strength and vigor,
While Langmaman's troops had blocked ahead.
Sugalin, the Monkey King said to the Ten-headed King,
“The Ten-headed King of heinous crimes.
We are just waiting for Langmaman's orders.
We will destroy all of you.”

朗玛满用神箭射向十头王，
顿时天空中隆隆作响。
但十头王的身体硬如磐石，

Langmaman shot at the Ten-headed King with the magic arrow.
Suddenly the sky rumbled.

神箭纷纷掉落在地上。
十头王眼明手快拉弓箭出，
一箭就射中朗玛满，
朗玛满倒地几乎要身亡。

But the Ten-headed King's body was as hard as a rock,
The arrows fell to the ground one after another.
The Ten-headed King was quick to draw the bow and arrow.
The first arrow hit Langmaman.
Langmaman almost died when he fell to the ground.

十头王走出飞行器，
他要把朗玛满抬去交给西达公主，
但十头王怎么使劲都抬不动，
朗玛满躺在那里就像一座石山。

The Ten-headed King walked out of the craft,
He was going to take Langmaman to Princess Xida.
But the Ten-headed King couldn't lift it with any effort,
Langmaman was lying there like a rock mountain.

阿奴曼跑过来抱住十头王，
两人在那里你推我打，
阿奴曼用拳头揍十头王，
十头王的战服被撕得粉碎。

Anuman ran to hold the Ten-headed King.
The two were fighting with each other.
Anuman beat the Ten-headed King with his fist.
The Ten-headed King's battle clothes were torn to pieces.

十头王被士兵扶进彩车里，
十头王在车里唠叨道：
“这个朗玛满真奇怪，
我怎么用力就是抱不动他，
不知道是何路神仙在帮他。”

The Ten-headed King was carried into the float by soldiers.
The Ten-headed King nagged in the float,
"This Langmaman is really strange.
Though I tried my best, I could not move him.
I don't know who is helping him."

阿奴曼对十头王说道：
“我猴国阿奴曼不怕你，
我只是把你当作牙签！
我明天就要把你的宫殿全捣毁，
待朗玛满有令我就送你进阴间！”
十头王听到阿奴曼侮辱自己，
就像一把火烧到了他的心肝。

Anuman said to the Ten-headed King,
"I'm not afraid of you.
You are nothing in front of me.
I will destroy your palace tomorrow.
I will send you to the underworld as long as Langmaman gives an order."
Finding that Anuman was insulting him,

The Ten-headed King burst into anger.

朗玛满也奇怪地说道：
“我用神箭射十头王，
但为何射不死十头王？”
在旁的毕披回答朗玛满道：
“当初天神赐本领时就说得清楚，
天上地下十头王均可掌控，
所有动物包括腊嘎王也在里边。

Langmaman also said in confusion,
"Why couldn't I shoot the Ten-headed King to death with the magic arrow ?"
Bipi nearby replied to Langmaman,
"The God had made it clear when he gave you the skills.
The Ten-headed King could manage anything in the heaven and on earth,
All the animals including the King of Laga.

“十头王不能掌控的只有三样，
一是用两脚行走的人类，
二是在森林中度日的猴子，
三是开天辟地时留下的一把神弓。”

"There are only three things that the Ten-headed King can't control.
First, mankind that walks on two feet.
Second, monkeys that live in the forest.
Third, the magic bow passed down from the time when heaven was separated from earth."

朗玛满拿出开天辟地神弓要射十头王，
猴群开始欢欣鼓舞。
十头王很敏感，
他知道自己死期已来临。
他知道朗玛满要用开天辟地神弓射自己，
他已经没有还手之力。

Langmaman took out the magic bow to shoot the Ten-headed King.
The monkeys began to rejoice.
The Ten-headed King was very sensitive.
He knew his death was coming.
Though he knew that Langmaman was going to shoot him with the magic bow,
He had no strength to fight back.

十头王在空中向朗玛满求情：
“圣者朗玛满啊，
都怪我有眼无珠，
对抗您是我的大错误。

The Ten-headed King begged Langmaman in the air,
"Saint Langmaman,
It's all my fault.
It's my big mistake to confront you.

就当我是顽童闹街巷， 请您如心怀慈悲的老人包容我。 就当我是刚入寺院的小和尚， 您是精通佛理的老僧人容下小徒。	Just think of me as a naughty boy. Please forgive me like a merciful old man. Think of me as a young monk who has just entered the temple. You are an old monk who is proficient in Buddhism.
“您将成为三界众生大尊师， 请您收下我做徒弟。 待到您要修成正果， 请您别将我甩在后边。 现在我向您真心承认错误， 请您别把过去的恩仇记在心中。”	“You will become the great teacher of the three worlds. Please accept me as your disciple. When you succeed in cultivation, Please don't leave me behind. Now I sincerely admit my mistakes and apologize to you. Please don't keep the past gratitude and hatred in mind.”
十头王在假装认错， 他的内心朗玛满看得清楚。 朗玛满手拉神弓将神箭射出去， 正中十头王脖子中间。 十头王尸首落地隆隆巨响， 犹如海风扫落叶落入森林间。	The Ten-headed King was pretending to admit his mistake. Langmaman knew what the Ten-headed King was thinking. Langmaman pulled the magic bow to shoot the magic arrow, Which hit the middle of the neck of the Ten-headed King. The corpse of the Ten-headed King fell to the ground with a rumbling sound, Like the sea breeze sweeping the fallen leaves into the forest.
十头王的队伍如一盘散沙， 人们见状四处逃散。 朗玛满的队伍追杀十头王的队伍， 十头王的队伍被追得溃不成军。	The Ten-headed King's troops were in a state of disunity. People fled everywhere when they saw this. Langmaman's troops were chasing the Ten-headed King's troops, Which were completely routed.
战争终于取得胜利， 猴群没有一只伤亡。 数亿猴民欢欣鼓舞，	The war was finally won. Not a single monkey was killed. Hundreds of millions of monkeys cheered for

欢呼圣者朗玛满战胜十头王。	The victory of the saint Langmaman over the Ten-headed King.
回到勐兰嘎王城，	Back to Menglanga royal city,
朗玛满决定举行庆典盛会七天。	Langmaman decided to hold a seven-day celebration.
庆典盛会人山人海，	There were huge crowds of people at the celebration
还有猴国士兵和当地人民。	Including soldiers of the Monkey Kingdom and the local people.
我们的长诗告一段落，	This is the end of the chapter.
我们的长诗还没有结束。	Our epic is not over yet.
父老乡亲们啊请耐心等待，	Please be patient, our fellow countrymen.
精彩的情节还在下一章的字里行间。	The plot in the following chapter will be more wonderful.

第十二章

Chapter Twelve

前一章结束后一章又开始，
一章更比一章牵动人心。
话说十头王已被朗玛满射死，
全国上下一片欢欣。

While the previous chapter ended, a new chapter unfolded,
It was getting more and more thrilling.
The Ten-headed King was shot to death by Langmaman.
People throughout the country exulted at the news.

十头王的弟弟毕披跪拜请求：
“圣者朗玛满啊，
我哥哥十头王已离开人界，
我欲将他火化在坟山中。”

The Ten-headed King's brother Bipi knelt down and begged,
"Saint Langmaman,
My elder brother, the Ten-headed King has left the secular world,
I am going to incinerate him in the graveyard."

“我忠诚的弟弟啊，
你就快快去料理吧。
十头王的罪过由他自己带走，
勐兰嘎的未来一定国泰民安。”

"My faithful brother,
You go and take care of it quickly.
The sins of the Ten-headed King should be taken away by himself.
The future of Menglanga must be prosperous and peaceful."

朗玛满安排毕披担任勐兰嘎国王，
让他在勐兰嘎治理江山。
让他成为勐兰嘎国民的大宝伞，
让勐兰嘎王国繁荣富裕威名传四方。

Langmaman made Bipi the King of Menglanga Kingdom,
Letting him govern Menglanga,
Letting him become the national protective umbrella of Menglanga,
Letting Menglanga Kingdom become prosperous and famous.

人们前往御花园，
人们去接美丽的西达公主。
西达公主年轻又美丽，
西达公主终于回到朗玛满身边。

People went to the imperial garden,
To pick up the beautiful Princess Xida.
The young and beautiful Princess Xida,
Final returned to Langmaman.

朗玛满怀疑公主是否忠贞：
“西达公主啊，
不要怪我怀疑你，
我俩分离各自在一方，
从前你说海枯石烂不变心，
我是否还能相信你？
我忙忙碌碌在寻找营救你，
听说你被关在御花园中。
你守忠贞何以为据？
你说出来让大家听一听。”

Langmaman was suspicious of the princess's chastity,
“Princess Xida,
Don't blame me for doubting you.
We were separated and on our own side.
Once you said you would never change no matter what happened.
Can I still trust you ?
I have been busy looking for and rescuing you.
It's said that you were locked in the imperial garden.
What is the evidence for your chastity.
Let's listen to it.”

西达公主双手合十跪拜朗玛满，
恭恭敬敬向朗玛满表真心：
“哥哥啊，
你怀疑我也在情理中，
因为我们各自在一方。
其他证据妹妹没有，
现在请哥哥烧起一堆大火，
让妹妹走进大火中。
如是妹妹不忠就一定会死在火堆里，
如是妹妹忠心就一定会完好无伤。”

Princess Xida put her palms together and knelt down to Langmaman,
To show her sincerity to Langmaman.
“Brother,
It's reasonable for you to doubt me,
Because we were separated from each other.
I have no other evidence for my chastity.
Brother, please make a fire.
I'll walk into the fire.
If I'm not faithful, I'll die in the fire.
If I'm faithful, I'll be intact.”

朗玛满命令烧起一堆大火，
大火顿时升起熊熊火光。
公主默默虔诚祈祷诸神来做证：
“如我忠心就让烈火烧不化身体，
若我有异心就让我死在火堆中。”

Langmaman ordered a big fire to be set on.
The fire immediately burst into flames.
The princess silently and piously prayed to gods for testifying,
“If I'm loyal, let me be fireproof.
If I'm not loyal, let me die in the fire.”

西达公主很严肃，	Princess Xida was very serious.
公主祈祷完毕就走进火堆里。	After praying, the princess walked into the fire.
朗玛满问她为何如此认真，	Langmaman asked her why she was so serious.
公主向朗玛满表达久违的真心：	The princess expressed her long lost sincerity to Langmaman,
“自从妹妹离开哥哥，	“Since I left you,
妹妹没有一天不挂心。	I've been thinking of you.
庆幸七天的死期内哥哥来救我，	Fortunately, you came to save me in seven days.
相信与哥哥有缘感激在心中。”	I'm grateful for being destined for you.”
朗玛满回答西达公主道：	Langmaman replied to Princess Xida,
“十头王已被哥哥射死，	“The Ten-headed King has been shot to death by me.
勐兰嘎王国的故事说不完。	The story of Menglanga Kingdom is endless.
王城四大城门无损坏，	The four gates of the royal city are undamaged.
所有一切完好无损交还国民。	Everything was returned to the subjects intact.
“勐兰嘎王国是天神光顾的地方，	“Menglanga Kingdom is a place where the gods visit.
我已委任毕披当国王。	I have appointed Bipi the king.
毕披离开十头王来归顺我，	Bipi left the Ten-headed King to submit to me.
此次双方开战他立大战功。	This time he won honor in the war between the two sides.
他已前往王宫料理国事，	He has gone to the palace to manage state affairs.
来不及看妹妹尊容。”	He has no time to see you.”
西达公主离开熊熊烈火走出来，	Princess Xida left the raging fire and came out.
公主扶着朗玛满哭诉道：	The princess held Langmaman and cried,
“重见哥哥犹如在梦里，	“Seeing you again is like a dream.
没有想到还有这样一天。	I didn't expect such a day.
自从十头王把妹妹劫持，	Since the Ten-headed King kidnapped me,
哥哥寻找妹妹走遍深山。	You have been searching for me in the mountains.
你在大山中把妹妹名字来呼唤，	You call my name in the mountains,
遇到猴王在树梢才知音讯。	And you don't know until you meet the Monkey King at

the top of the tree.

"猴王说妹妹已被十头王劫走，
哥哥知道后万分痛心。
猴王下树诉说自己家的不幸，
告诉说他的妻子被他哥哥霸占，
他哥哥还把他赶出猴群。
自此哥哥和猴子建友谊，
你帮猴王消灭了他哥哥，
你让他当王统领猴群。
你又发动猴群建桥跨大海，
为救妹妹哥哥下了最大决心。"
朗玛满听完西达公主的倾诉，
他感动得热泪盈眶。

"The Monkey King said I had been robbed by the Ten-headed King.
You were very sad to learn about that.
The Monkey King went down the tree to tell about his family's misfortune,
Saying that his wife was taken over by his brother.
His brother drove him out of the monkeys.
Since then, you have built friendship with monkeys.
You helped the Monkey King kill his brother.
And you made him the leader of the monkeys.
You also mobilized the monkeys to build a bridge across the sea.
In order to save me, you have made the utmost determination."
Langmaman was moved to tears
By Princess Xida's words.

毕披跑来跪拜朗玛满道：
"弟弟我要跟随哥哥一辈子，
我要服侍哥哥至寿终。"
朗玛满听后开示道：
"弟弟的心意我领了，
但眼前事与心愿实在两难全。
愚痴人即使同住一室亦如相隔千山，
哥哥与弟弟无论多遥远犹如在一室。"

Bipi came to kneel down at Langmaman and said,
"I want to follow you all my life.
I will serve you until your death."
Langmaman said,
"I appreciate your kindness.
But it's a dilemma.
Even if a fool lives in the same room, it is like a thousand mountains apart.
No matter how far away I and you are, we are like in the same room."

毕披接受朗玛满的教导，

Accepting Langmaman's teaching,

毕披再次跪拜以示谢恩。
朗玛满继续开示道：
“毕披弟弟啊，
你是勐兰嘎王国的栋梁，
爱护百姓要如亲生父母，
一句好话如蜂蜜甜透心，
要让人赞扬你是好国王。

Bipi knelt down again to show his gratitude.
Langmaman continued to point out,
“Brother Bipi,
You are the backbone of Menglanga Kingdom,
And you should love the people as your own parents.
A good word is as sweet as honey.
You should have people praise you as a good king.

“对待那些偷盗作恶多端者，
惩罚处分要公平得当。
团结各方民众力量大，
这是大道理你须记在心。
对待大臣将军要和蔼，
国家大事要开诚布公共协商。
尖锐矛盾勿拖延，
水溢坝垮时更费心。

“Those who steal and commit crimes
Should be punished fairly and appropriately.
Great strength comes from the unity of the people of all parties.
You must keep it in mind.
You should be kind to ministers and generals.
National affairs should be openly and jointly discussed.
Sharp contradictions should not be delayed.
It is more difficult when the dam overflows.

“四面八方要因地治宜，
王国上下要提防内乱在先。
做王关键要关注民心，
只有民安百姓才来拥护你，
民安全国才能百业旺，
国家强大你也才会得民心。

“All sides should be governed according to the local conditions,
And the whole kingdom should be wary of civil strife.
The key to being a king is to pay close attention to the well-being of the people.
Only when people are at peace, can the people support you.
Only when people are at peace, can the kingdom be prosperous.
Only when the kingdom is strong, can you win the hearts and minds of the people.

“慈悲施舍永牢记，

“Always remember the merciful almsgiving,

维护寺院敬僧人。 各种戒律永行持， 要教诲国人弃恶从善。 上述诸条请弟弟牢记， 祝福弟弟威名传人间。”	And maintain the temple and respect for monks. All kinds of commandments must be kept forever. You should teach people to forsake evil and learn to do good. Please remember the above commandments. I wish you a great reputation in the world.”
朗玛满嘱托毕披已完毕， 呼唤大家要启程。 朗玛满让西达公主梳妆打扮， 他俩和纳哈腊坐彩车上， 他们缓缓起步走向大山。 阿奴曼紧紧跟在车辆后面， 浩浩荡荡的队伍过桥跨海洋。	After this, Langmaman called for everyone to leave. Langmaman had Princess Xida dressed up. He and Princess Xida were on the float, Heading for the mountain slowly. Anuman followed closely behind the float, And the huge team crossed the bridge and the sea.
走过桥后朗玛满命令搬石头， 上亿猴民将石头搬到岸边。 长长的海上石桥已撤除， 苏嘎林和阿奴曼欲紧跟朗玛满前行， 还有猴医占布曼跟在后边。 朗玛满好言相劝， 朗玛满说已经牢记他们的功劳， 劝他们各自回到快活的深山老林。	After crossing the bridge, Langmaman ordered to move the stones. Hundreds of millions of monkeys move stones to the shore. The long stone bridge across the sea had been removed. Sugalin and Anuman wanted to follow Langmaman closely. And the monkey doctor Zhanbuman was behind. Langmaman was very persuasive. Langmaman said that he had remembered their contributions, And advised them to return to the happy mountains.
苏嘎林又跪拜朗玛满说道： “因为道路坎坷行车不方便， 请让我们把道路先修通。”	Sugalin knelt down to Langmaman and said, “Since the road is bumpy and inconvenient for carriages, Please let us build the road first.”

朗玛满仍然拒绝，
劝他们回到各自的故乡。
大多数猴兵都回到各自的住地，
他们跳跃在各自熟悉的深山中。
唯有阿奴曼执意要跟随朗玛满左右，
他要终身陪伴在朗玛满身边。
毕披也回到王宫里，
他召集大臣和将军们议国事，
他们要让勐兰嘎王国繁荣强大，
要让王国的美名传遍四方。

Langmaman still turned down their proposals,
And advised them to return to their hometown.
Most of the monkey soldiers returned to their places of residence.
Jumping in the familiar mountains.
Only Anuman insisted on following Langmaman.
He wanted to accompany Langmaman all his life.
Bipi also returned to the palace.
He summoned ministers and generals to discuss state affairs.
They wanted to make Menglanga Kingdom prosperous and powerful.
And let the kingdom's reputation spread all over the world.

朗玛满他们来到帕腊达修行的地方，
朗玛满让弟弟前去告知王宫里，
包括王母和王宫里所有人。
大臣、将军和国师皆欢喜，
人们走街串巷奔走相告。
朗玛满离别王宫已满十二年，
国人欢迎朗玛满来坐镇，
人们拥护朗玛满当国王。

Langmaman and other people came to the place where Palada cultivated.
Langmaman asked his brother to report to the people in the palace,
Including the queen and all the people in the palace.
The ministers, generals and Guoshi were all happy,
And people walked through the streets to tell each other.
It has been 12 years since Langmaman left the palace.
The fellow countrymen looked forward to Langmaman's succession of the throne.
People support Langmaman as a king.

王城上下筹办欢迎仪式，
彩旗飘扬锣鼓声震天。
多辆彩车和大象齐出动，
三位王母坐在彩车里，
她们与大队伍走出王城。

People in the royal city were preparing for a welcoming ceremony.
With colorful flags flying, gongs and drums resounding.
Many floats and elephants set out simultaneously.
The three queens were sitting in the float.

队伍向大山里进发，
他们来到了雅细的住地，
朗玛满他们也来到了大山中。

They walked out of the royal city with a big team,
Marching towards the mountains.
They came to Yaxi's residence.
Langmaman and other people also arrived at the mountains.

朗玛满看到了三位王母，
朗玛满激动地跪拜在母亲足前。
三位母亲伤心哭泣，
双方问寒问暖诉说苦与辛。

Seeing the three queen mothers,
Langmaman knelt down to his mothers in excitement.
The three mothers cried bitterly,
And the both sides were solicitous about each other's hardship and sufferings.

自从分别后各种伤心事，
样样苦楚诉与母亲听。
庆幸苦事难事已成过去事，
现在终于母子得团圆。

All kinds of sad things,
As well as sufferings were told to the queen mother.
Thankfully the hardship and sufferings had passed.
Now the mother and son were finally reunited.

王后抱住西达公主哭泣：
"我美丽的儿媳啊，
我们以为你们都健康平安，
未曾想过你们曾如此艰辛。
若不是诸神来护佑，
也许你们早已遇难在深山老林中。"

The queen hugged the Princess Xida and cried,
"My beautiful daughter-in-law,
We thought you were healthy and safe,
I've never thought you have experienced such a great of hardships.
If the gods had not come to protect you,
You might have been killed in the mountains."

王后问西达公主道：
"当年十头王将公主偷到王宫中，
是否对公主下毒手？
公主如何过此难关？"
"我尊敬的母后啊，
我们三人的苦难说不尽道不完，

The queen asked Princess Xida,
"That year, when the Ten-headed King grabbed you to the palace,
Did he lay murderous hands on you ?
How did you get through this difficulty ?"
"My venerable queen mother,

我们日日以野果当饭吃，	We three suffered a lot.
尝遍了百果所有苦酸甜。	We have wild fruits as food every day,
	Tasting all the bitter and sweet fruits.
“当年十头王把我带到王宫里，	“That year, the Ten-headed King brought me to his palace,
他要让我与他同床。	And he wanted me to sleep with him.
我发誓对朗玛满的忠心不变，	I swore my loyalty to Langmaman will remain unchanged.
十头王无法接近我身。	The Ten-headed King couldn't get close to me.
我说莫说你是一个十头魔鬼，	Even if the Great God comes to beg me,
就是大天神来求我，	I only love Langmaman,
我也只把朗玛满一个人爱在心中。	Let alone you are a ten-headed devil.
“除了朗玛满，	“Nobody can take a hair from me except for Langmaman.
谁都别想拿走我一根毫毛。	The Ten-headed King locked me in the imperial garden.
十头王把我关在御花园里，	He had the devils monitor me,
安排那些魔鬼来监视，	Threatening me that if I didn't listen to him,
威胁我说若是不听他使唤，	He would let the devils eat me as delicious meal in seven days.
七天后就让魔鬼们把我当美餐。	
“我尊贵的三位母后啊，	“My distinguished three queen mothers,
我的苦难道不尽说不完。	I've endured endless hardships.
今天我们能在王宫相见，	It was a narrow escape
真是死里逃生！”	That we could meet in the palace today !”
听到公主伤心哭诉，	Hearing the princess's sad cry,
王后突然昏迷倒地，	The queen suddenly fell into a coma.
公主把她抱在怀里。	The princess held her in her arms.
王后边哭边说道：	The queen cried and said,
“诸神为何不护佑我家公主啊，	“Why didn't the gods protect my princess ?
怎能让我家公主遭受的苦难超过所有人。	How can we make our princess suffer more than everyone else ?

"我家公主如此忠贞守节，
找遍天下四大洲没有第二个人。
天下人间唯有我家公主受的苦最多，
受苦整整十二年。"

"Our princess is so loyal.
There is no second person in the four continents.
Only our princess suffered the most in the world
For 12 years."

帕腊达跪拜在哥哥面前，
哥哥问弟弟道：
"十二年来是否风调雨顺国泰民安，
十二年来是否丰衣足食，
全国城乡男女妇幼富翁和百姓，
是否生活幸福户户美满？"

Palada knelt down before his brother.
Langmaman asked Palada,
"Did the kingdom prosper and the people enjoy peace with adequate clothing and food in the past 12 years ?
Were the rich, women and children in urban and rural areas and the common people living happily ?"

帕腊达听后回答道：
"十二年来哥哥住在深山里，
哥哥以野果为食过完每一天。
今天哥哥却关心国民是否丰衣足食，
哥哥以民为怀感动弟弟在心中。
回想哥哥十二年的艰苦日子，
真让弟弟实在心酸。

Palada replied,
"You have lived in the mountains for 12 years.
You live on the wild fruits every day.
Today, you are concerned about whether the people are well-fed and well-clothed.
I've been moved by your concern about the welfare of the people.
Reviewing the hard life that you experienced in the past twelve years,
I feel really sad and sorry.

"十二年来国民日子都幸福，
家家户户均有吃有穿。
风调雨顺庄稼饱满，
无天灾人祸民富国强。
无旱无涝山清水秀，
竹木成林处处清风徐徐。"

"In the past 12 years, people have been happy,
With ample food and clothing.
There were favorable weather and good harvests.
Without natural or man-made disasters,
The people were rich and the kingdom was prosperous.
Without drought or waterlogging, the mountains were green and the water was clear.

Bamboo and trees were everywhere with breezing wind."

朗玛满听后对弟弟说道：
"弟弟啊，
晌午时让我们一起吃一顿团圆饭，
每人一杯玉液就足够，
备好午餐送到大家面前。"

Hearing that, Langmaman said to his brother,
"My brother,
Let's have a reunion lunch at noon.
One glass of jade liquid is enough for each person.
Prepare lunch and deliver it to everyone."

帕腊达以为是得罪了哥哥，
他又跪拜在哥哥面前。
朗玛满对弟弟说道：
"我的好弟弟啊，
在深山里吃野果未必就含辛茹苦，
天下所有飞禽和走兽，
谁不是以野果为食度过每一天。

Palada thought he offended his brother.
So he knelt down before his brother.
Langmaman said to his brother,
"My good brother,
Eating wild fruits in the mountains is not necessarily painful.
All birds and animals in the world
Live every day on wild fruits.

"往生极乐的佛菩萨超过沙粒数，
他们亦靠供养水果滋养仁慈心。
我问你国民是否丰衣足食，
因为民以食为天。
哥哥说的玉液其实是山泉水，
各种动物与水离不开。"

"The Buddha and Bodhisattva who enjoyed the bliss of passing away exceeded the number of sand grains.
They also nourish their benevolence by providing fruits.
I asked you if the people were well-fed and well-clothed,
Because food is the most important thing for people.
The jade liquid I mentioned is actually the spring water.
All kinds of animals are inseparable from water."

朗玛满与人们坐在一起，
十二年来第一次与宫里人共餐。
餐饮结束朗玛满欲去供养雅细，
备齐供品与大伙前往洞堂。

Langmaman was sitting with people,
For the first meal with the people in the palace over the past 12 years.
After the meal, Langmaman wanted to provide food to Yaxi.
He prepared food and went to the cave with the people.

朗玛满和西达公主跪拜雅细足前，
雅细接受供品并予以祝福：
“祝福朗玛满顺利坐上王位，
统领一方水土恩泽一方人民。
做王最重要的是爱人民，
关爱大臣、将领和士兵。
真心孝敬赡养你三位母后，
西达公主是你终生的伴侣，
从勐兰嘎王国回到你身边不容易，
对她说话不能刺心。

Langmaman and Princess Xida knelt down to Yaxi
Who accepted the offerings and give blessings,
“I wish Langmaman a smooth succession to the throne
To govern the kingdom and benefitting the people.
The most important thing to be a king is to love the people,
Caring for the ministers, generals and soldiers.
You should sincerely support your three mothers,
Princess Xida is your lifelong companion.
It's not easy to come back to you from Menglanga Kingdom,
You should be careful with your words when talking to her.

“三个弟弟你要好好呵护，
大事与他们和睦协商别偏心。
做王要遵守佛法和人道，
天时地利人和万事顺心。”

“You should take good care of the three brothers,
And negotiate with them on important issues in a harmonious way without bias.
To be a king, you should abide by the Buddhist doctrine and humanity.
With right time, right place and right people, everything will go smoothly.”

朗玛满将雅细的开示记心里，
朗玛满再三跪拜谢恩。
供养结束后离开洞府，
人们坐车离开深山。
抵达王宫有十六个眼程的距离，
朗玛满终于回到王宫中。

Langmaman kept Yaxi's words in mind,
Langmaman knelt down to Yaxi again to express gratitude.
After the provision of food, people left the cave
And the mountains by carriage.
It was 16 eye-range away from the palace,
Eventually Langmaman arrived at the palace.

八位国师、大臣和将领，
共同协商朗玛满继位大事。
十二年前继位时间定在五月十五，

Eight Guoshi, ministers and generals
Discussed about Langmaman's succession to the throne.
Twelve years ago, the succession was scheduled for 15th

中途出意外朗玛满进深山。
现在国师们观察天上星象，
又查大地山川景象选吉日，
四月十五卦书里称为大安最吉祥。

day of the 5th lunar month.
Accidentally, Langmaman entered the mountains in the middle.
Now the Guoshi observed the stars in the sky,
And checked the landscape of the earth, mountains and rivers to choose an auspicious day.
According to the divination, the 15th day of the 4th lunar month was the most auspicious.

朗玛满继位的大喜日子，
就是四月十五这一天。
这一天是金凤凰开鸣的日子，
这一天是金角龙送珠的日子，
锣鼓号角声声传四方，
王城举行盛大的大庆典。
人们载歌载舞还表演木偶剧，
大象马车成纵队出场，
姑娘小伙放歌把朗玛满国王来赞扬。

The day of Langmaman's succession,
Was the 15th day of the 4th lunar month.
It was the day when the golden phoenix sang.
It was the day when the Golden Horn Dragon sent pearls.
The sound of gongs, drums and horns spread everywhere.
A grand celebration was held in the royal city.
People sang, danced and performed puppet shows,
Elephants, carriages came out in columns.
The girls and boys sang praises to King Langmaman.

国师们的声声祝福伴滴水，
祝福朗玛满和西达公主长寿平安。
祝福千灾万难远远离去，
祝福颗颗福星照国人。
祝福年年岁岁风调雨顺，
祝福座座山峰变金山。
祝福国人安居乐业，
祝福家家户户有美好家园。

The Guoshi's blessings were accompanied by the water-dripping ceremony.
The people wished Langmaman and Princess Xida a long life and peace,
As well as a disaster free life.
They wished the people good luck,
Favorable weather and wealthiness,
Peaceful life in contentment,
And a beautiful home.

国师们的祝福人人欢喜，
朗玛满和公主双双坐入王位，

Everyone was happy with the Guoshi's blessings.
After Langmaman and the princess sat on the throne,

大臣、国师、将领和百姓齐跪拜，
人们真心向国王和王后求吉祥。

The ministers, Guoshi, generals and the common people knelt down together,
To pray for blessings for the king and the queen.

国王和王后用金银施舍，
祝福国民健康长寿，
祝福国家蒸蒸日上，
祝福民富国强国泰民安。

The king and the queen gave gold and silver as alms,
Wishing the people long and healthy lives,
Wishing the kingdom a prosperous future,
Wishing the people and kingdom wealthiness, prosperity and peace.

朗玛满的弟弟帕腊达被委以副国王，
其他两位弟弟亦委以重任。
朗玛满顺利继承国王位，
人们期待王国繁荣富强。

Palada, the brother of Langmaman, was appointed as the deputy king.
The other two brothers were also entrusted with important responsibilities.
Langmaman successfully succeeded to the throne.
People expected the kingdom to be prosperous and strong.

数月后西达公主有身孕，
侍女们欢天喜地热闹非凡。
侍女们问十头王长什么模样，
公主画十头王的像展示在侍女们面前。
侍女们看见地板上的画像惊恐万分，
侍女们说十头王长得就不是人形。

A few months later, Princess Xida was pregnant,
The maids were very happy with the news.
And they asked the princess what the Ten-headed King looked like.
The princess drew a picture of the Ten-headed King and showed it to the maids.
The maids were terrified when they saw the portrait on the floor,
The maids said that the Ten-headed King was not a human being.

此时朗玛满来到西达公主卧室里，
十头王的画像没有擦干净，

At the moment, Langmaman came to the bedroom of Princess Xida,

朗玛满看见了十头王的画像，
朗玛满顿时感觉被粪水泼湿了全身。

The portrait of the Ten-headed King was not wiped clean.
When Langmaman saw the portrait of the Ten-headed King,
He felt sick.

朗玛满一时起疑心生烦恼：
十二年来自己离开王宫在山里，
不知道人们在如何议论自己，
自己是否还有脸见人。

Langmaman became suspicious and worried,
In the past 12 years, I left the palace and lived in the mountains,
I don't know how people talk about me,
Do I have the face to see other people ?

朗玛满欲回自己卧室，
他离开公主的宫殿就听到有人在吵架，
原来是两夫妇在吵嘴，
他俩是王宫里的守象人。
守象人的妻子吵着说要回娘家去。
她边走边说：
“古往今来夫妻都和睦同住一屋，
你却天天骂我太欺负人！
你以为我还会回到你身边，
我不是那种人！”

Langmaman wanted to return to his bedroom.
When he left the princess's palace,
He heard a quarrel between a couple,
Who were the elephant keeper in the palace.
The wife of the elephant keeper said loudly that she would return her parents'home.
She said as she walked,
“Since ancient times, a husband and a wife have lived in the same house in harmony,
But you scold me every day for bullying you too much !
You think I'll come back to you.
I'm not that kind of person !”

她的丈夫也大声说道：
“你不回来我更高兴，
你以为只有你才是女人？
你以为我和国王朗玛满一样？
西达公主让别人抢走，
国王派兵征战才把公主救回来，
现在公主又成为王后夫人。”

Her husband also said loudly,
“I'll be happier if you don't come back.
Do you think you're the only woman ?
Do you think I'm just like the King Langmaman ?
Princess Xida was taken away by other people.
Only when the king sent troops to fight, was the princess rescued.

Now the princess becomes the queen again."

守象人的话说得朗玛满很痛心，	What the elephant keeper said made Langmaman very sad.
朗玛满回到卧室思绪万千。	After he returned to his bedroom, he thought a lot.
天亮后朗玛满问公主道：	After daybreak, Langmaman asked the princess,
“西达公主啊，	"Princess Xida,
自古以来孕妇都爱吃酸。	Since ancient times, pregnant women like to eat sour food.
不知公主想吃何种水果？	I wonder what kind of fruit you would like to eat.
请公主告诉我，	Please feel free to tell me.
我让你满愿顺心。”	I'll meet your demands."
西达公主回答道：	Princess Xida replied,
“我在雅细住处时，	"When I was in Yaxi's residence,
吃过一次椰子味道特别甜。	I once had coconut, which tasted very sweet.
自那以后再也没吃过那种果味，	Since then, I have never tasted that fruit again.
回想起来犹如在昨天。”	It seems like it was just yesterday."
朗玛满听后非常生气，	What the princess said made Langmaman very angry.
他叫纳哈腊备车到面前：	He asked Nahala to get his carriage ready,
“公主还在思念雅细，	"The princess is still missing Yaxi.
你就快快备车送她到深山里。	You are expected to get a carriage to take her to the mountains as soon as possible.
你将她送到雅细住处，	You send her to Yaxi's residence,
你把她丢在那里就返回来。”	And you drop her there and return."
纳哈腊将公主送到雅细住处，	Nahala sent the princess to Yaxi's residence.
雅细看见后问他们有何事情。	Yaxi saw them and asked what he could do for them.
纳哈腊回答雅细道：	Nahala replied to Yaxi,
“公主怀念山里的椰子味道，	"The princess misses the taste of coconut in the mountains.
朗玛满国王让我将公主送到您面前。”	King Langmaman asked me to send the princess to you."
纳哈腊又跪拜西达公主：	Nahala knelt down to Princess Xida,

"因为国王哥哥让我返回去， 你就住在雅细这里， 等你想王宫时再回到朗玛满身边。"	"Because the king, my brother asked me to go back, You will live in Yaxi's residence, Till some day when you want to live with Langmaman in the palace."
西达公主听到此话就流下泪水： "回想当初我落难大山中， 十二年后回到王宫终得平安。 以为要荣华富贵在王宫里， 未料会再次落难似在梦里边。	Princess Xida wept when she heard this, "When I was trapped in the mountains, I couldn't imagine returning to the palace in 12 years. I thought I would live a rich and noble life in the palace, But I didn't expect to be in trouble again. It seems like I was in a dream.
"我小时遇难大海边， 是国王救了我的性命。 我长成少女亭亭玉立， 消息传到千里外边。 求婚王子无法计数， 是国王举行拉弓比赛选驸马， 所有王子无人能拉动神弓， 唯有跟随雅细的朗玛满胜过所有人。 父王将我嫁与朗玛满， 我与朗玛满成为夫妻乐人间。 也许是我前世造下罪孽， 不得不反复受苦受难超过天下人。"	"I almost died at the seaside when I was young. It was the king who save my life. I grew up into be a beautiful young lady. The news spread thousands of miles away. Countless princes came to propose marriage. It was the king who held a bow-pulling contest to select his son-in-law. None of the princes could pull the bow, Except for Langmaman who followed the Yaxi. My father-king married me to Langmaman. I and Langmaman became husband and wife and lived a happy life. Maybe I committed a sin in my previous life. So I had to suffer more than other people in the world."
西达公主在深山里忧伤哭泣， 纳哈腊回到了朗玛满身边。 朗玛满看见弟弟回来也是五味杂陈， 只因种种缘故让朗玛满太心烦。	Princess Xida was crying in the mountains. Nahala returned to Langmaman. Langmaman had mixed feelings when he saw his brother coming back.

For various reasons, Langmaman was so upset.

西达公主胎龄渐满心力交瘁，
有一日双胞儿出世在人世间。
公主抱着儿子喜出望外，
她给大儿子起名叫诺腊，
给弟弟起名叫果腊。

As the pregnancy developed, Princess Xida was getting
mentally and physically exhausted.
One day the twins were born.
The princess was overjoyed with her sons.
She named her elder son Nuola,
And the younger son Guola.

草木更新日月轮回，
兄弟俩渐渐长大成人。
兄弟俩已有十五岁，
身相与他们的父亲一模一样，
清秀的样子像天神下凡尘。

Year in and year out,
The two brothers grew up.
The two brothers were 15 years old.
They looked exactly like their father.
With elegant appearance, they looked like gods who
descended to the earthly world.

兄弟俩开山种地，
甘蔗和芭蕉水果绿满园。
他们砍甘蔗和芭蕉供养雅细，
傍晚又从地里回去看望母亲。
兄弟俩天天如此度日月，
母子三人习惯了深山老林。
朗玛满继位很顺利，
这一天他提出来一个怪问题，
他向大臣们问道：
“天下有没有人能够与我抗衡？
可以举行一次拉弓比赛，
让天下人知道谁最威风。
我想知道谁能够超过我，
若发现这样的人就请他住王宫中。

The two brothers opened up wasteland for cultivation.
The garden was full of sugarcane, plantain and other fruits.
They cut sugarcane and plantain to offer to the Yaxi.
At dusk, they went back to see their mother.
The two brothers spend every day like this.
The mother and the two sons have been used to the
mountains.
Langmaman's succession went on smoothly.
One day he asked a strange question.
He asked the ministers,
“Is there anyone who can compete with me ?
Let's hold a bow-pulling competition
To see who is the strongest in the world.
I want to know who can surpass me.
If there are such kind of people, invite them to live in the

palace.

“扎腊国王当年赛弓嫁公主，
天下王子无人能拉动神弓。
当众能将神弓拉动者，
唯有我朗玛满一个人。
三亿多猴民本事大，
被我调动出来战十头王。
勐兰嘎王国威名扬四方，
金光闪闪的宫殿有七座。
腊嘎王和龙王都要向十头王敬贡，
尚拎国王献公主给他做第一夫人。
十头王的力量超过我百倍，
他的威力无人能及，
十头王神通广大，
超过所有天下人。
但是十头王仍然中了我的神箭，
落地死在战场中间。
本王欲寻找超过我的能人，
这事如何操办请诸位共同出主张。”

“The King Zhala married off his princess by holding the bow-pulling competition.
No prince in the world could pull the magic bow.
I was the only one who could pull the magic bow in public.
More than 300 million monkeys had great abilities,
And I had mobilized them to fight against the Ten-headed King.
The fame of Kingdom Menglanga spread far and wide.
There are seven glittering palaces.
King Laga and Dragon King had to pay tribute to the Ten-headed King.
The King of Shanglin offered his princess to the Ten-headed King as his first wife.
The power of the Ten-headed King was a hundred times greater than mine.
His power was unmatched.
The Ten-headed King had great power,
Surpassing all the people in the world.
But he was hit by my magic arrow,
And fell to the ground and died in the middle of the battlefield.
I want to find someone who can transcend over me.
I'd like to hear from you for proposal to handle this matter.”

忽然有大臣跪拜朗玛满后说道：
“至尊的智者朗玛满国王啊，
古时有让骏马寻找圣者的办法，
我们可以用此方法寻找能人。”

Suddenly, a minister knelt down and said,
“The venerable and wise king,
In ancient times, there was a way for steeds to find saints.
We can use this method to find capable people.”

朗玛满听后觉得有道理，
命令选骏马做彩车。
人们找来好骏马，
又做彩车把马装扮得美丽庄严。
朗玛满书写文字藏在马鞍里，
告诉说胆小之人不要碰骏马，
谁敢比赛弓箭就拉住骏马来宫中。

Langmaman thought it was reasonable,
And he gave orders to choose steeds for the floats.
People found good steeds,
And made the floats to dress the horses beautiful and solemn.
Langmaman's writing was hidden in the saddle.
He emphasized that the coward should not touch the horse.
Whoever dares to compete with bows and arrows, pull the horses to the palace.

人们将骏马和彩车备好，
让骏马带路走在前。
纳哈腊驾车跟在骏马后，
还有朗玛满的弟弟沙达鲁嘎纳，
还有大臣、将领和其他人。
浩浩荡荡的大队伍出城去，
路上的人们避让在道路边。
富翁们在路旁捐银两，
贫穷百姓看热闹站两边。

People prepared steeds and floats,
Having the steeds lead the way.
Nahala drove behind the steeds,
Along with Langmaman's brother Shadalugana,
Ministers, generals and other people.
A huge team went out of the city,
and people on the road yielded to them.
The rich donated silver on roadside,
While the poor people were looker-ons standing on both sides.

庞大的队伍向前方走去，
人们看见十八位僧人在前边。
纳哈腊避让僧人继续走，
骏马来到一条大河边。
对岸的芭蕉香味扑鼻，
骏马走过河后走进了果园里边。

The huge team moved forward.
People saw eighteen monks in front.
Nahala yielded to the monks and kept moving.
The steed came to a big river.
There was a fragrance of plantains coming from the opposite bank.
The steed walked into the orchard after crossing the river.

守果园的诺腊看见骏马，
他拉住骏马拴在窝棚前。

Seeing the steed, Nuola who was watching over the orchard
Pulled the steed and tied it to the shack.

他心里在想这匹马的主人欺人太甚，
随便放马来到我们的果园中。
他看见马鞍上有字条，
他看懂了字里行间的内容。

诺腊用芭蕉和芭蕉叶喂马，
他准备牵马离开果园。
雅细看见后来劝阻道：
“那是一匹从王宫里出来的骏马啊，
你不要随便牵马离开果园。”

诺腊对雅细说道：
“智者此话你休讲，
你怎么能将这匹马与王宫扯在一起？
你的好名声传遍四面八方，
你不能样样都护着宫里人！

“天下规矩皆相同，
胜者为尊败者为卑。
如是马主人找上门来比武艺，
这个果园我愿意送给他。
如是马主人胆小吃败仗，
这匹骏马就归我所有。
世界上的事情就该这样，
请智者将我的话记在心间。”

宫里人跟踪马的足迹来到果园里，
他们看见一位小伙牵马欲离开果园。
宫里人开口骂小伙道：
“小伙你怎么不知此马如蛇毒性大，

He thought that the owner of this horse went too far in bullying others that he let the horse into the orchard.
He saw a note on the saddle,
And he read between the lines.

Nuola fed the steed on plantains and plantain leaves.
He was about to lead the horse out of the orchard.
Seeing this, Yaxi came to dissuaded him,
“It is a steed from the palace.
Don’t lead the steed out of the orchard.”

Nuola said to Yaxi,
“No more words, wise man !
How can you connect this steed with the palace ?
Though your good reputation has spread all over the world,
You can’t protect everyone in the palace !”

“All rules are the same.
Success supposedly justifies any actions.
If the owner of the steed comes to compete with me in feat,
I’d like to give him the orchard.
But if the owner of the steed was a coward and he lost the competition,
This steed belongs to me.
Things in the world should be like this.
Please keep my words in mind, wise man.”

The people from the palace followed the steed’s footsteps to the orchard.
They saw a young man leading the steed out of the orchard.
The people from the palace scolded the boy,

你还敢抓蛇尾巴玩？
天下人皆恐惧国王神威，
小伙你怎么不怕引火烧身？
这是国王的骏马啊，
敢牵此马者天下无一人！”

“Why don't you know that this steed is poisonous like a
snake ?
How dare you catch the tail of a snake !
Everyone in the world is afraid of the king's invincible might.
Why aren't you afraid of it ?
This is the king's steed.
No one dares to lead it !”

宫里人如此骂诺腊，
诺腊手持弓箭骂宫里人：
“你们这些看马人怎能胆大包天，
来到他乡随便开口就骂人？
不管是不是国王的骏马，
骏马进了我的果园是事实。
即使它是一匹天神骏马，
你们也休想夺回！”

Hearing the people from the palace scold him like this,
Nuola cursed them with a bow and arrow in his hands,
“How can you be so bold
To swear someone as you like in an alien place.
Whether it is the king's steed or not,
It is true that the steed entered my orchard.
Even if it is a divine steed,
You can't take it back !”

宫里人对他说道：
“你怎么不怕死啊，
还敢用大话吓唬人！”
诺腊听后非常气愤，
他用力拉弓射出一箭去，
宫里人有人被射死受伤者数人。

The people from the palace said to him,
“Why aren't you afraid of death ?
How dare you scare people with big talk !”
Nuola was very angry after hearing this.
He pulled his bow and shot an arrow.
Some people from the palace were killed and several injured.

宫里人跑回去禀报纳哈腊：
“骏马跑进芭蕉园里，
一个小伙射死我们好几个人。
看他相貌与朗玛满很相似，
他的脸型像西达公主，
体型就像国王朗玛满一般。
此人相貌天下难寻第二个，

The people from the palace ran to report to Nahala,
“The steed ran into the plantain garden.
A guy shot several of us to death.
He looks very similar to Langmaman.
His face is like Princess Xida,
While his body is like King Langmaman.
It's hard to find the second person like him in the world.

他勇敢又胆大超常人。”

纳哈腊坐车前往果园里，
他看见诺腊就问道：
“你是谁家孩子在这里，
难道深山里只有你一人？
看你相貌如王子，
怎么独自离开家人在大山中？”

诺腊回答道：
“你怎能这样不礼貌地追根问底，
怎么能问我父母是何人。
如是双方欲开战，
就不该问对方根底有多深。”

纳哈腊走上前一步，
仔细观察那个守园人。
这人怎么长得像自己的哥哥一样，
言行举止与哥哥丝毫无差别，
他胆大勇敢亦如朗玛满，
越看越感觉与他哥哥是一个人。

诺腊拉弓对纳哈腊射箭，
纳哈腊射箭动作比他快，
射中诺腊昏迷倒在果园中。
人们将诺腊抬进车里，
他们要将他拉回到国王身边。

He is brave and extraordinarily courageous."

Nahala went to the orchard by carriage.
When he saw Nuola, he asked,
"Who are you ?
Are you alone in the mountains ?
You look like a prince.
How can you leave your family alone and stay in the mountains ?"

Nuola replied,
"How can you raise one question after another in such an impolite way ?
How can you ask who my parents are ?
If both sides want to fight.
Don't ask the other side's background."

Nahala stepped forward
And carefully observed the garden keeper.
This man looked exactly the same as his brother.
His behavior was the same as his brother's.
He was as brave as Langmaman.
The more he observed, the more he felt like they were the same person.

Nuola drew the bow to shoot at Nahala.
Nahala shot arrows faster than him.
Nuola was shot to faint and fell down in the orchard.
People carried Nuola into the carriage.
They wanted to bring him back to the king.

雅细将这一切回去告诉西达公主：
“你的儿子诺腊胆子大，
他把王宫的骏马拴在果园里边。
王宫里的人们调来许多士兵，
已将他射倒在果园中。
宫里人还用彩车将他拉走，
不知道他还能不能回到你身边。”
西达公主号啕大哭道：
“儿子啊，
你是妈妈的心头肉，
住在深山已经够辛苦，
你怎么能把妈妈丢下就走人！”

Yaxi told Princess Xida all this,
“Your son Nuola was so bold
That he tied the royal steed in the orchard.
People from the palace brought in many soldiers,
And shot him down in the orchard.
People from the palace took him away by a float.
I wonder if he can come back to you.”
Princess Xida wailed,
“My son,
You are my sweet heart.
It's hard enough to live in the mountains.
How can you leave your mother behind !”

弟弟果腊从远处回来看见妈妈在哭泣，
他问妈妈为何如此伤心？
西达公主回答儿子道：
“你哥哥独自一人去看守果园，
有人放带信马来糟蹋果园。
你哥哥准备把马牵回家，
官兵把你哥哥射倒在果园中。
官兵已将你哥哥拉走，
不知他是否还能生还。”

Brother Guola came back from afar and saw his mother crying.
He asked his mother why she was so sad.
Princess Xida replied to her son,
“Your brother went to watch over the orchard alone.
Someone sent a messenger horse to spoil the orchard.
As your brother was about to take the horse home,
The soldiers shot your brother down in the orchard.
They have taken him away by the float.
I wonder if he will survive.”

果腊听到后就拿定主意，
他要前往王宫救哥哥：
“哥哥没有带任何武器，
不带武器会吃亏在眼前。
请妈妈给我武器，
我和哥哥一定能平安。”
公主给儿子祝福：

Guola made up his mind after hearing this.
He was going to the palace to save his brother,
“Without bringing any weapons with him,
He would suffer.
Please give me weapons, mother.
My brother and I will be safe.”
Princess Xida prayed for her son,

"虽然朗玛满赶我出门送山里，
但我始终无怨言。
我的忠心丝毫没有改变，
我犹如日日在朗玛满身边。
祝福我儿无灾无祸，
祝福我儿说话如阵阵春雷，
听到者皆恐惧在心里，
纷纷前来美言讲和平。"

"Though Langmaman drove me out of the palace and sent me to the mountains,
I never complained.
My loyalty has not changed at all.
I feel like I am around Langmaman every day.
May my son be free from disasters and misfortunes !
May he speak like spring thunder
That make those who hear scared,
And make those who hear speak words of peace."

公主祈祷完毕将弓箭交给儿子，
儿子跪拜母亲快速离开森林。
果腊改走一条直路，
他已赶在纳哈腊的彩车前边。
他大声喊叫彩车停下来，
所有在场人皆吃惊观看，
个个睁开大眼睛看着来人。

After the praying, the princess gave the bow and arrows to her son.
Guola knelt down to his mother and left the forest quickly.
Since Guola changed to a straight road,
He overtook Nahala's float.
He shouted at the float to stop.
All the people present were surprised,
Looking at Guola.

纳哈腊问小伙你是谁，
果腊回答说自己是车上那个人的弟弟，
纳哈腊手握弓箭关注对方，
因为他担心来者不善。
果腊气愤地大声说道：
"你们为何杀害我哥哥，
为何不明不白就把人拉走？
你们要道歉赔偿！"

Nahala asked the boy who he was.
Guola said he was the brother of the person in the carriage.
Nahala stared at Guola with a bow and arrow in hands,
Because he was worried that the other party was ill-intended.
Guola shouted angrily,
"Why did you kill my brother ?
Why did you take my brother away without telling any reasons ?
You should apologize and compensate !"

果腊说完就连射数箭，
顿时尸横大地血流深山。

After Guola said that, he shot several arrows in succession.
Immediately, the field was littered with corpses with blood

纳哈腊吃惊地问道：
“你为何不讲道理啊，
为何射死我们这么多人？”

everywhere in the mountains.
Nahala asked in surprise,
“Why don't you be reasonable ?
Why did you shoot so many of us ?”

“人欲伐大树必先砍掉周边小树，
欲去征服他国要先消灭士兵，
这是先辈留下的名言。
我是遵循古训，
要把阻挡去路的兵卒斩杀为先。”

“If you want to cut down a big tree, you must first cut down the small trees around.
To conquer other countries, we must destroy the soldiers first.
This is a famous saying from our ancestors.
I'm just following the ancient maxims that the soldiers who block the way should be killed first.”

果腊说完又摆出射箭姿势，
纳哈腊手持弓箭站立在彩车前方。
果腊手疾眼快射出一箭去，
纳哈腊从彩车上掉落地上血染身。
果腊还在大声骂对方，
他还欲放箭射人。
哥哥诺腊在彩车上苏醒过来，
兄弟俩相见在道路边。

Guola finished that and then took an archery posture.
Nahala stood in front of the float with the bow and arrow in hands.
Guola shot an arrow quickly.
Nahala fell from the float and became bloody.
Guola was still shouting abuse at the other party.
He wanted to shoot arrows at other people.
The brother Nuola came back to life in the float.
The two brothers met at the side of the road.

王宫来的兵卒四处逃散，
有的赶回去禀报国王：
“大王啊大王，
纳哈腊大臣已中神箭，
跌下彩车倒地犹如气断身亡。
只因骏马走进芭蕉地里，
一位小伙拉住骏马就不放，
我们去找他索要骏马，

The soldiers froм the palace fled everywhere,
And some rushed back to report to the king,
“Your Majesty,
Nahala has been hit by a magic arrow.
He fell to the ground as if he had died.
Only because the steed walked into the plantain field.
A young man held the steed and wouldn't let it go.
We went to him to ask for the steed.

小伙追打我们还有伤亡。

There are still casualties when the young man chased and attacked us.

“还有一事更奇特，
两兄弟相貌酷似国王。
高矮胖瘦一个模样，
胆大英勇也相当，
兄弟俩有使不完的力量，
看得出来今后是一方国王。”

“There is one more strange thing.
The two brothers look like you
In appearance and figure
As well as courage.
The two brothers have endless power.
I can see that they will be a king in the future.”

国王听后微笑说道：
“纳哈腊弟弟拥有过人的本领，
也许是疲劳过度昏迷一时，
没人能够把他打翻。”

The king smiled and said,
“Nahala has excellent skills.
Maybe he was so exhausted and fell into a coma.
Nobody can knock him down.”

手下人继续跪拜说道：
“至尊的大国王啊，
您是国人的金宝伞，
您的威名传遍四面八方。
我们看到有危险才来报告您，
纳哈腊已昏死在彩车旁。”

The subordinate continued to kneel down and said,
“The supreme king,
You are the golden umbrella of the kingdom.
Your reputation spreads everywhere.
We came to report to you as we saw the danger.
Nahala has fallen into a coma beside the float.”

朗玛满听后思索片刻，
他要召集队伍前去看究竟。
帕腊达弟弟率队走在前，
阿奴曼与国王坐彩车在后边。

After listening to this, Langmaman thought for a while.
He wanted to muster troops to see what happened.
Palada led the troops in the front.
Anuman and the king sat in the float at the back.

朗玛满的队伍来到道路上。
朗玛满看见弟弟纳哈腊躺在道路边。
遇到能人朗玛满吃惊不小，
国王朗玛满高兴又伤心。

Langmaman's troops marched forward on the road.
He saw his brother Nahala lying by the road.
Langmaman was very surprised to meet the capable man.
King Langmaman was happy and sad.

国王微笑着问两位小伙道：
“两位小伙年轻力壮相貌不凡，
你们为何住在深山中？
请两位小伙告诉我，
你们的父母是何人？”

The king smiled and asked the two boys,
“You two are young and strong and look extraordinary.
Why do you live in the mountains ?
Please tell me who your parents are ?”

两兄弟跪拜国王后说道：
“统领王国的大国王啊，
您是一国之主不该来到深山中，
国王还是养精蓄锐少操心，
集中精力统领人民才是您分内事。”

The two brothers knelt down to the king and said,
“The king who rules the kingdom,
You are the head of a kingdom and should not come to the mountains.
The king still needs to keep his strength and worry less.
It's your job to concentrate on leading the people.”

国王觉得兄弟俩说话有暖意，
兄弟俩相貌如天神一般。
他俩面目与西达公主很相似，
国王开始怀疑两兄弟是西达公主所生。

The king felt that the two brothers spoke with warmth
And they looked like gods.
With similarity in appearance between the two brothers and Princess Xida,
The king began to suspect that the two brothers were born to Princcss Xida.

国王对两兄弟说道：
“两位小兄弟啊，
我的问话你们怎么不回答？
无论你俩有何过错，
我不会伤害你们俩。”

The king said to the two brothers,
“Two little brothers,
Why didn't you reply to me ?
No matter what fault you two have,
I won't hurt you.”

听到国王如此说话，
两兄弟感觉国王对他俩没有防范之心。
两兄弟商议不把国王杀害，
但要让国王昏迷在车上就当警告。

Hearing these words,
The two brothers felt that the king was not on guard against them.
The two brothers discussed not to kill the king,

But to make the king fall into a coma in the carriage as a warning.

两兄弟快速拔箭向国王射去，
国王两眼发黑昏倒在彩车中。
国王没有断气，
只是两眼模糊头脑发昏。

The two brothers quickly drew arrows to shoot at the king.
The king fainted in the carriage.
He did not die,
But felt dizzy with eyes blurred.

两兄弟又商议，
认为空手去告诉母亲一定不相信，
脱下国王衣服回去是上策。
他俩来到彩车上，
兄弟俩将国王衣服脱下来，
要带国王的衣服返回大山中。

The two brothers discussed again.
They thought the best policy was to bring the king's attire back to their mother.
Otherwise their mother wouldn't believe if they returned empty-handed.
The two brothers got on the float
And took off the king's attire.
They would bring the king's attire back to the mountains.

阿奴曼在细思量，
两兄弟也许是朗玛满的亲人。
阿奴曼决定要跟在两兄弟后面，
他决心要把两兄弟的底细搞清。

Anuman was pondering.
The two brothers might be the relatives of Langmaman.
Anuman decided to follow the two brothers.
He was determined to find out the details of the two brothers.

阿奴曼跟在后面来到深山里，
看见他们走进窝棚中。
两兄弟跪拜母亲说道：
“只因有母亲的威德来护佑，
我们两哥弟打败了国王的宫里人，
现在回到母亲身边。
马匹和彩车我们已带到深山里，
还带回来了国王的衣服。”

Anuman followed them to the mountains
And saw them enter the shack.
The two brothers knelt down to their mother and said,
"With the blessing of our mother's prestige and morality,
We two brothers defeated the people from the palace.
Now we are back to our mother.
We have brought the horses and floats to the mountains,
Along with the king's attire."

西达公主仔细来观看，
这是朗玛满国王的衣服。
阿奴曼看见了西达公主，
他急忙走出来跪拜在公主面前。
西达公主几乎要昏迷过去，
未曾想到这一切会发生在大山中。

Princess Xida made a careful identification to the attire.
It was the attire of King Langmaman.
Seeing Princess Xida,
Anuman hurried out and knelt down before the princess.
Princess Xida almost fainted,
She didn't think it would happen in the mountains.

公主看见国王的衣服哭泣道：
“我的儿啊，
我把你俩生在森林中，
你们都未曾见过父亲，
这个国王就是你俩的父王。
你们两兄弟杀害了自己的父亲，
你们将堕地狱投胎无期。”

The princess saw the king's attire and cried,
"My sons,
I born you two in the forest.
You have never seen your father.
This king is your father.
Your two brothers killed your father.
You will be reincarnated to the hell for an unlimited duration."

“我俩在果园遇到官兵，
当时国王要追根问到底，
追问谁是父母亲。
本来我俩准备告诉他，
但是我俩生活在深山里不便讲，
我俩就把国王射伤昏迷在彩车上。”

"We met officers and soldiers in the orchard.
At that time, the king kept asking such questions
As who our parents were.
Originally, we wanted to tell him.
But we live in the mountains, it's inconvenient to talk about it.
So we shot the king unconscious on the float."

西达公主听后伤心哭泣，
公主对儿子说道：
“儿子你们真是错了！
快快去请雅细救你父王！”

Hearing that, Princess Xida wept bitterly.
She said to her sons,
"Sons, you are really wrong.
Go and ask Yaxi to save your father immediately !"

两兄弟去见雅细跪拜说道：

The two brothers knelt down to Yaxi and said,

“尊敬的智者啊，
由于我两兄弟无知犯下大错，
我两兄弟射伤了我们的父王。
请智者快去救国王，
我们两兄弟要认父亲。”

“Distinguished wise man,
We have made big mistakes due to our ignorance.
We wounded our father with an arrow.
Wise man, please go and save the king.
We are going to recognize our father.”

雅细知道出了大事，
他拿着咒水跟着两兄弟去看国王。
雅细口中念念有词，
他用咒水滴撒在国王身上。

Knowing something thorny had happened,
Yaxi followed the two brothers to see the king with the mantra water.
Muttering incantations,
Yaxi sprinkled the mantra water on the king.

国王慢慢苏醒过来，
国王的弟弟纳哈腊亦被救活。
国王跪拜雅细问道：
“尊贵的智者啊，
两个小伙相貌堂堂，
这两个小伙来自何处？
他们怎么会住在深山里，
说话声音让我喜欢。
他们勇敢值得赞扬，
我想知道他们来自何方。”

The king came to life gradually.
Nahala, the king's brother was also saved.
The king knelt down to Yaxi and asked,
“Distinguished wise man,
The two boys are very handsome.
Who are these two guys ?
Why are they living in the mountains ?
I like their voice.
They are brave and worthy of praise.
I wonder where they come from.”

雅细告诉国王道：
“两兄弟就是国王的骨肉啊，
当年国王赶公主出宫时已有孕在身，
两兄弟是双胞胎同一天出世。
你看他们的相貌就知道，
他们长得与国王一个模样。

Yaxi told the king,
“the two brothers are your sons.
When the king drove the princess out of the palace, she was pregnant.
They are the twins.
You can tell from their looks,
They look the same as the king.

“哥哥名字叫诺腊，	“The elder brother is Nuola.
弟弟起名叫果腊，	And the younger brother is Guola.
你看两个相貌多威武，	With the powerful appearance,
相貌堂堂就像一对天神。”	They look elegant like a pair of gods.”
国王听后悲痛自责，	The king remorse himself in grief,
抱住两兄弟痛苦泪涟涟。	And held the two brothers in tears.
国王对两个儿子说道：	The king said to his two sons,
“你俩仿佛天神下凡界，	“It seems that you two are the gods descending to the earth.
来到深山出世是天神巧安排。	Your birth to the mountains is an ingenious arrangement by the gods.
母亲对你两兄弟恩深似海，	Your mother is very kind to you two.
两兄弟赡养母亲一定要无微不至。	You must be meticulous in supporting your mother.
从今往后要弃恶从善，	From now on, only by shunning evil and doing good deeds,
保家卫国方能长寿平安。”	And safeguarding the homeland, can you live a long and safe life.”
国王跪拜雅细说道：	The king knelt down to Yaxi and said,
“过去是我错怪西达公主，	“I used to blame Princess Xida,
以后我一定改正做好人。	I will correct and be a good person in the future.
请智者领我去见公主，	Wise man, please lead me to the princess,
还请求在公主面前替我美言。	And please speak for me in front of her.
我要领他们兄弟俩回王宫中，	I will take the two brothers back to the palace.
他俩就是我的王位继承人。	They are my heirs to the throne.
“请智者原谅我的过错，	“Wise man, please forgive my fault.
让我脱离苦海凡心。	You help me get out of the sea of misery.
请智者成为菩提树，	May you be the Bodhi tree,
让我在下面乘凉发忏悔心。	And let me repent in the shade under the tree.
本王犹如鲜花在凋谢，	I'm like a flower withering.
请智者成为甘露滋润花树根。”	May you become the dew to moisten the roots of flowers.”

雅细回答国王道：	Yaxi replied to the king,
“我去说和不容易，	“It was not easy for me to make peace.
只怪当时国王你存疑心和毒害他人心。	It was only because you were so suspicious.
西达公主本来无过错，	Princess Xida was innocent.
你却把她冤枉得一塌糊涂。	But you wronged her completely.
你把一个孕妇赶进深山里，	You drove a pregnant woman into the mountains,
你的过错百口难辩。	There is no possibility to explain to your fault.
公主的心就像秋日里的干稻草，	The princess's heart is like dry straw in autumn,
再浇水也难复苏。	Which is hard to recover.
我不敢为你去劝公主，	I dare not persuade the princess for you.
我不希望以后公主再受苦。”	I don't want the princess to suffer again."
国王听后跪拜雅细道：	Hearing that, the king knelt down to Yaxi and said,
“智慧的雅细啊，	"Intelligent Yaxi,
本王只有求您了，	I have to beg you.
无论如何请您发发慈悲心。	Please be merciful anyway.
除了智者您出面，	There is no second person in the world
能助我者天下没有第二人。	who can help me except for you.
若往后智者有求于我帮忙，	If you ask me for help in the future,
我会速速赶进山里来。	I will rush into the mountains.
“公主生养长大的两个儿子，	"I will take the two sons who were born and brought up by the princess back to the palace as the heir.
我要领回王宫做继承人。	
请智者让公主跟我回去，	Wise man, please ask the princess to go back with me.
本王一定牢记智者一番苦心。	I'll keep your words in mind.
本王在此发誓不再出大错，	I hereby swear that I will not make any major mistakes again,
也请诸神替我记录在案。	And ask the gods to record it for me.
帕腊达兄弟你也记在心里，	Brother Palada, you also remember that the day I swear is today."
我发誓的日子在今天。”	

雅细听后领国王去见西达公主，
公主悲伤地向朗玛满跪拜。
国王心里忏悔不尽，
存疑心是祸根：
“我亲爱的西达公主啊，
你在深山里受尽了人间诸苦。
今天我请你跟我回王宫去，
享受荣华富贵在王宫中。
我将让你统管王宫诸事务，
我让他们两兄弟继任国王和将军。”

After hearing this, Yaxi led the king to Princess Xida.
The princess knelt down to Langmaman in grief.
The king was very regretful.
Suspicion is a curse.
“My dear Princess Xida,
You have suffered all human sufferings in the mountains.
Today I ask you to come back to the palace with me,
To enjoy the splendor and wealth in the palace.
I'll let you take charge of all the affairs of the palace,
And make the two brothers the king and general.”

“我不想回到王宫里，
因为是你把我撵进大山中。
十头王劫持我去王宫里，
他把我关在御花园中。
后来你把十头王打败，
接我脱离苦海走出魔王的御花园。
夫妻才团圆你又怀疑我，
逼我走进熊熊烈火中示清白。”

“I don't want to go back to the palace,
Because you drove me into the mountains.
The Ten-headed King kidnapped me to the palace,
And he locked me in the imperial garden.
Later, you defeated the Ten-headed King
And took me out of the sea of misery and out of devil's imperial garden.
It was not long before you doubted me.
You forced me to walk into the raging fire to show my chastity.”

“熊熊大火没把我烧死，
诸神护佑我这苦难女人。
后来我已经有了身孕，
你又怀疑我把我赶出王宫送进深山老林。
现在你欲把我接回王宫里，
我没有那么厚的脸皮面见众人。

“I was not burnt to death in the raging fire.
The gods protect me, a poor woman.
Later, when I was pregnant,
You suspected me and drove me out of the palace to the mountains.
Now you want to take me back to the palace.
I don't have the cheek to meet people.

"当时你认为我怀的是私生子，
你认为是十头王的孽种在我腹中。
我忍辱负重把两个儿子生在大山中，
艰难困苦把他们抚养长大。
如今你可以把他们带走，
我愿意住在大山中修行一生。

"At that time, you thought I was pregnant with an
illegitimate child.
You thought it was the Ten-headed King bastard.
I endured humiliation and gave birth to my two sons in
the mountains,
And brought them up with great difficulties.
Now you can take them away.
I am willing to live in the mountains to cultivate all my life.

"即使我往后成了乞丐到处乞讨，
我也不会到你的王宫中去讨饭。
我宁愿饿死在大山里，
也不愿让人冷眼看我清洁身。
我俩的夫妻缘分让它在山里结束，
我的清净心已经硬如钻石。
人有脸面树有皮，
我不想再受你污损。
我在山里与花鸟为伴度一生，
你在王宫里享荣华富贵做你的大国王。

"Even if I become a beggar and beg everywhere,
I will not beg in your palace.
I would rather starve to death in the mountains
Than be looked at my clean body coldly by other people.
Let our marital predestination end in the mountains.
My pure mind is as hard as a diamond.
People have faces and trees have barks.
I don't want to be stained by you.
I spend my life with flowers and birds in the mountains.
As the king, you shall enjoy your high position and great
wealth in the palace.

"我已看破一切红尘事，
我的命就该如此。
你我姻缘命里注定，
要不然当年你不会把我赶进大山中。

"I have seen through everything in the world,
And it's my fate.
Our marriage is destined to end.
Otherwise, you wouldn't have driven me into the mountains.

"国王你的甜言密语自己收回去，
我知道你只是在哄骗我的一颗真心。
婢女再愚痴也能看透你的心，
国王你不必接二连三哄骗人。"

"Please take back your sweet words yourself,
I know you're just kidding me.
No matter how stupid I am, I can see through your heart.
You don't have to cheat one after another."

国王内心有愧地苦苦哀求公主：
“俗话说船头走船尾跟着走，
你不能让两个孩子走了自己却待在大山中。
公主啊，我是真心向你认错，
你就给我一次改错的机会吧，
看在我们夫妻缘分上，
请你发出比大海宽广的慈悲心原谅我。
我向天地诸神发誓，
如我疑心不改就让雷公劈让大地吞没。”

The king begged the princess in guilt,
“As the saying goes, if the bow moves, the stern will follow.
I won't take away the two children and let you stay in the mountains alone.
Princess, I sincerely apologize to you.
Please give me a chance to correct my mistake.
For the sake of our marital relationship,
Please forgive me with a great compassion.
I swear to the gods of heaven and earth
That if I keep suspecting, I shall be struck by lightning.”

雅细走过来为他们开示道：
“活在世上个个是凡人，
世上没有十全十美的人。
唯有放下诸多无明烦恼，
往生才能顺利到达极乐天。

Yaxi came to them and pointed out,
“Everyone in the world is mortal,
And there is no perfect person in the world.
Only by letting go of many delusions and worries
Can we successfully reach the pure land.

“一切因果前世已造下，
公主今生因此落难在大山间。
公主的最佳选择还是回王宫去，
互相揭短只会伤身又伤人。
国王已经面对诸神天地发大誓，
公主就要放下烦恼嗔恨心。”

“All karmas have been created in the previous life.
Thus, the princess is in trouble in the mountains.
The best choice for the princess is to go back to the palace.
Exposing each other's shortcomings is detrimental to both sides.
Since the king has made a vow to the gods,
The princess should let go of your worries and resentment.”

听完雅细慈悲开示，
公主顾全大局放下嗔恨心。
国王伸出手去牵西达公主，
双双跪拜在雅细面前。

Hearing Yaxi's merciful revelation,
And taking the overall situation into consideration, the princess let go of her hatred.
The king held the hand of Princess Xida
And knelt down with the princess to Yaxi.

朗玛满国王和西达公主告别雅细，
他们缓缓走向彩车前。
国王的两个弟弟紧紧跟在后面，
还有诺腊和果腊随后前行。

After King Langmaman and Princess Xida bid farewell to Yaxi,
They walked slowly to the float.
The king's two brothers followed closely,
Along with Nuola and Guola.

彩车开始移动缓缓向王宫驶去，
浩浩荡荡的队伍离开深山。
大臣和王城的人们早已在王宫前等候，
王城周围早已人山人海彩旗飘扬。

The float moved slowly towards the palace,
And the mighty procession left the mountains.
The ministers and people of the royal city had been waiting in front of the palace.
There were already a lot of people around the royal city,
With colorful flags flying.

一百多个属国到王宫献礼，
欢迎王后和王子回王宫中。
长子诺腊被委以副国王重任，
次子果腊任元帅协助长兄。
三位国叔亦均委以要职，
大臣和将军们都被重用晋升。
一百多个属国国王个个受奖赏，
从此阿罗替雅王国国泰民安。

More than 100 vassal kingdoms came to the palace to present their gifts,
And welcomed the queen and prince back to the palace.
The eldest son Nuola was appointed as the deputy king,
and the second son Guola served as the marshal to assist the elder brother.
The three uncles were also appointed to important positions,
And the ministers and generals were all promoted.
More than 100 vassal kings were rewarded,
And since then the Kingdom of Aluotiya has enjoyed peace and stability.

王国军队数量无法计数，
国力强大威名传四方。
国王面向军队来开示：
平时苦练战时少出血，
军队是人民的大靠山。

With countless troops in the kingdom,
The prestige of the kingdom spread far and wide.
The king revealed to the troops,
The more we sweat in peacetime, the less we bleed in wartime.

号召将军士兵练好武艺，
卫国护民显威风。

The army is the great support of the people.
He called on the generals and soldiers to practice martial arts well,
And show their prestige in defending the country and protecting the people.

王宫事务又恢复常态，
国王对两个儿子开示道：
“当王要心明眼亮，
佛法经典永远记在心中。
不能自私自利贪心重，
五戒十戒融在言行中。
做王要将国民当父母，
得民心者得天下威名自在人心中。”

The affairs of the palace returned to normal.
The king revealed to his two sons,
"As a king, you should be clear-minded and keep the Buddhist scriptures in mind forever.
Don't be selfish and greedy.
The five precepts and ten precepts should be embodied in words and deeds.
To be a king, you should take the people as your parents.
Those who win the hearts of the people will win the world, and their fame will be in people's hearts."

阿罗替雅王国国强民富今非昔比，
国王和王后安享晚年在王宫中。
他们双双高寿均超过父辈，
两老作古后又享受安乐在神界中。

The Kingdom of Aluotiya was stronger and the people were richer than ever.
The king and the queen enjoyed their old age in the palace.
Both of them lived longer than their parents,
And enjoyed peace in the divine world after their death.

后来人们推选诺腊继承国王位，
国家强盛人民安居乐业。
诺腊国王遵行当国王的十条原则，
睦邻友好国富民强。
后来诺腊国王晚年安然仙逝，
他的阳寿岁数超过他的父王。
阿罗替雅王国旧址今犹在，

Later, Nuola was chosen to succeed to the throne.
The kingdom was prosperous and the people lived and worked in peace and contentment.
King Nuola followed the ten precepts of being a king.
The kingdom was enjoying good neighborly and friendly relations with other kingdoms.
Later, King Nuola died peacefully in his late years,

可惜已变成高耸入云的巍巍岩石城。

And his longevity exceeded that of his father.
The former site of Aluotiya Kingdom still exists today,
But it has become a towering rock city.

兰嘎西贺的故事记录在贝叶经典里，
代代艺人抄录传四方。
这是十头王的神话故事，
几乎传遍所有傣乡。
各地都有不同抄本，
故事情节基本相同。
少数情节有差异，
文中诗句各地抄本亦不同。
我们将长诗典籍收进藏书柜里，
把慈爱善良的种子播撒在人们心中。

Recorded in the Pattra-leaf scriptures,
The story of the Ten-headed King of Langa has been transcribed and spread far and wide by generations of artists.
This is the fairy tale of the Ten-headed King,
Which has spread to almost all Dai villages.
The transcripts vary from place to place.
The story is basically the same.
With slight difference in some plots.
The transcripts of the verses also vary from place to place.
We put the ancient epics and books in the bookcase,
In a desire to spread the seeds of love and kindness among people.

《兰嘎西贺》古籍原图

Orignal picture of ancient *Langaxihe*

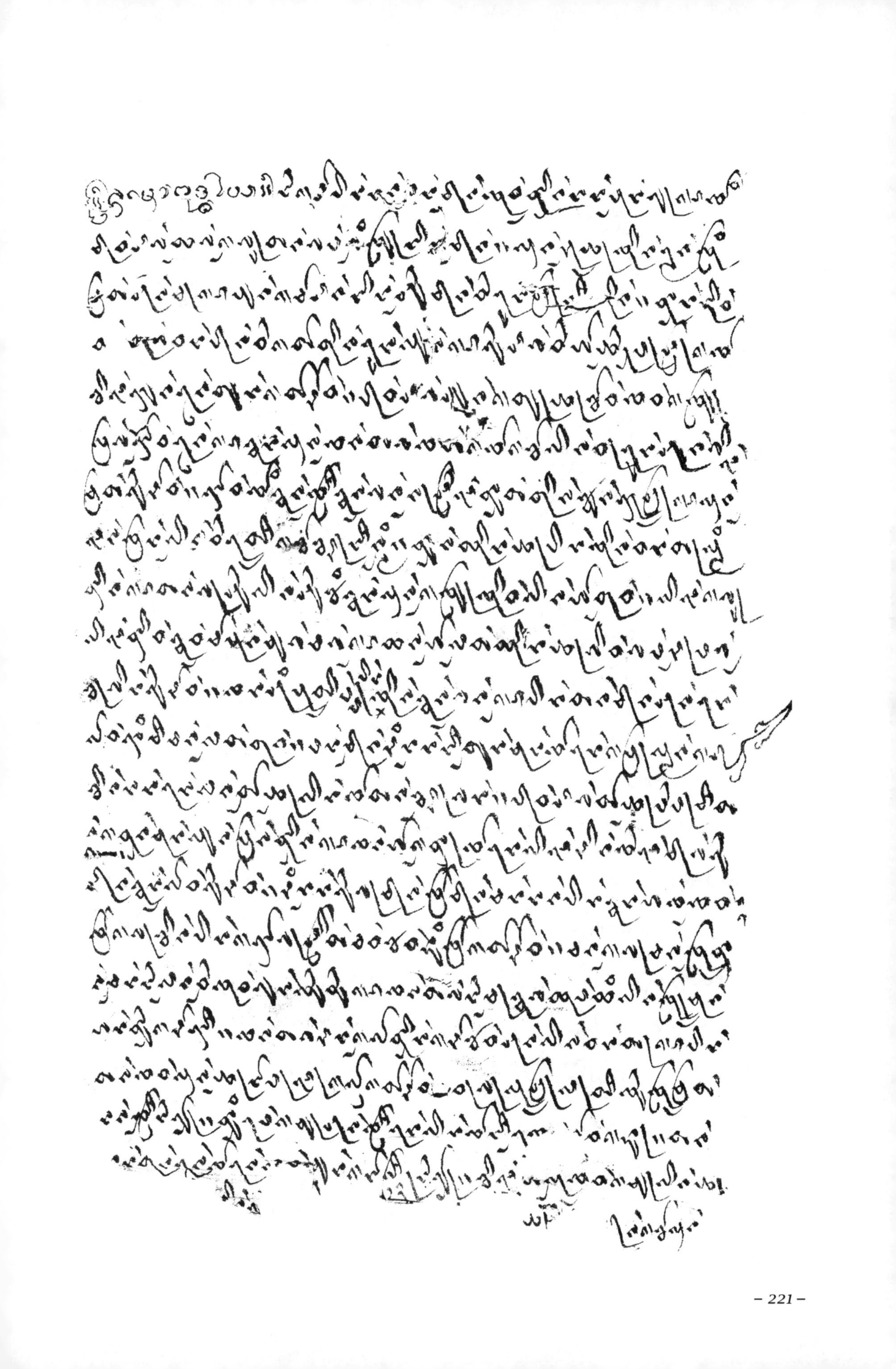

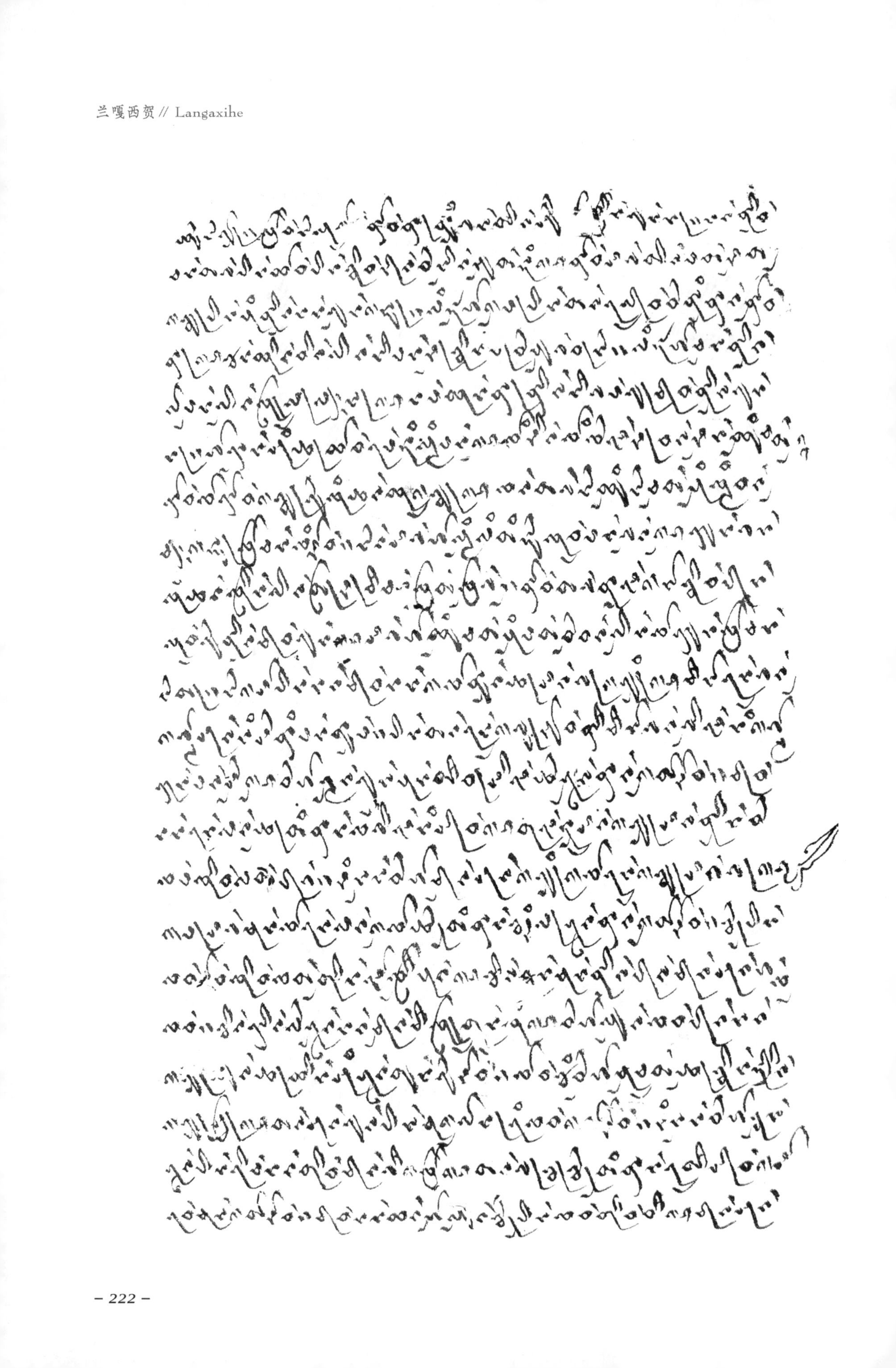

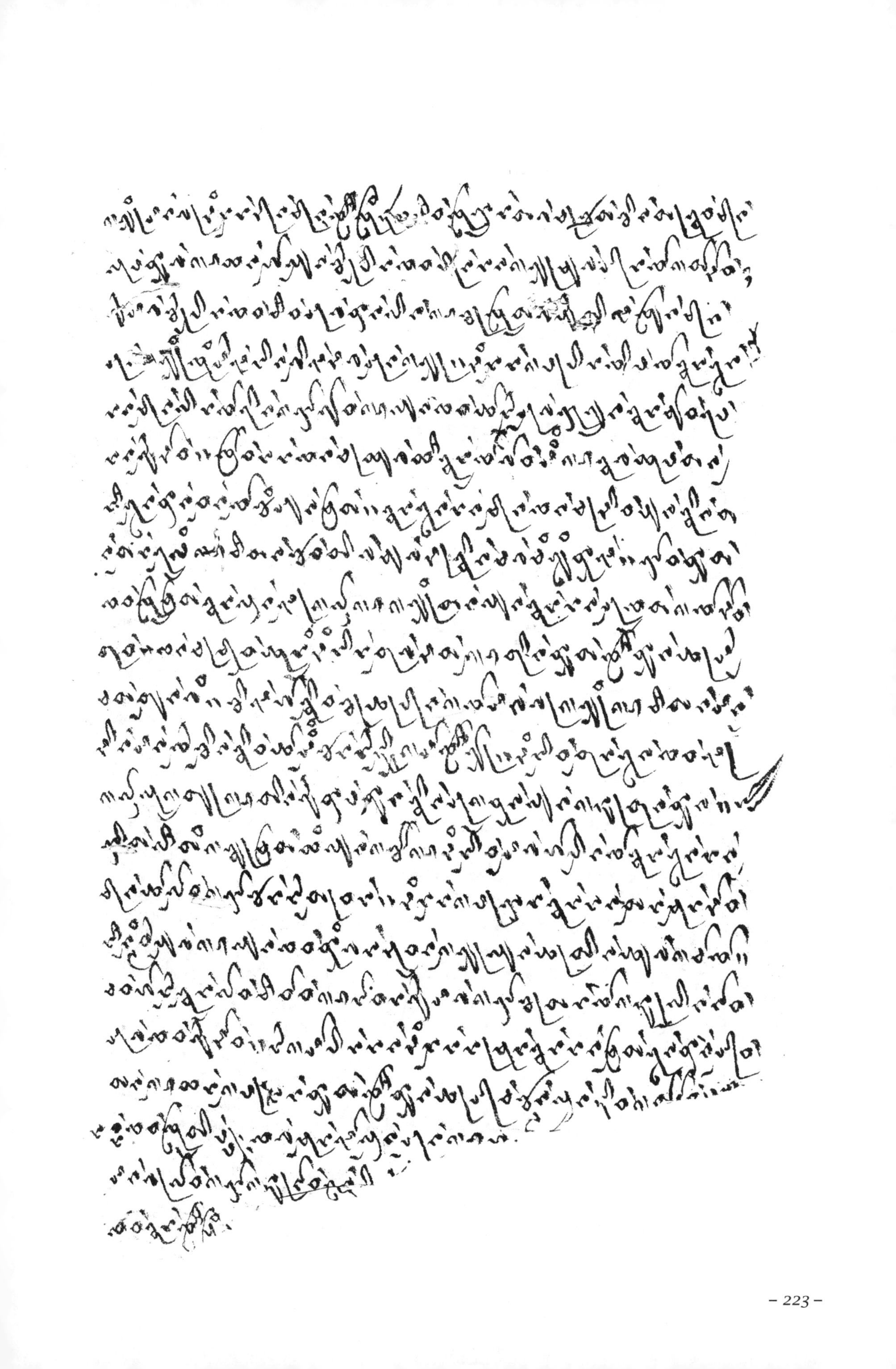

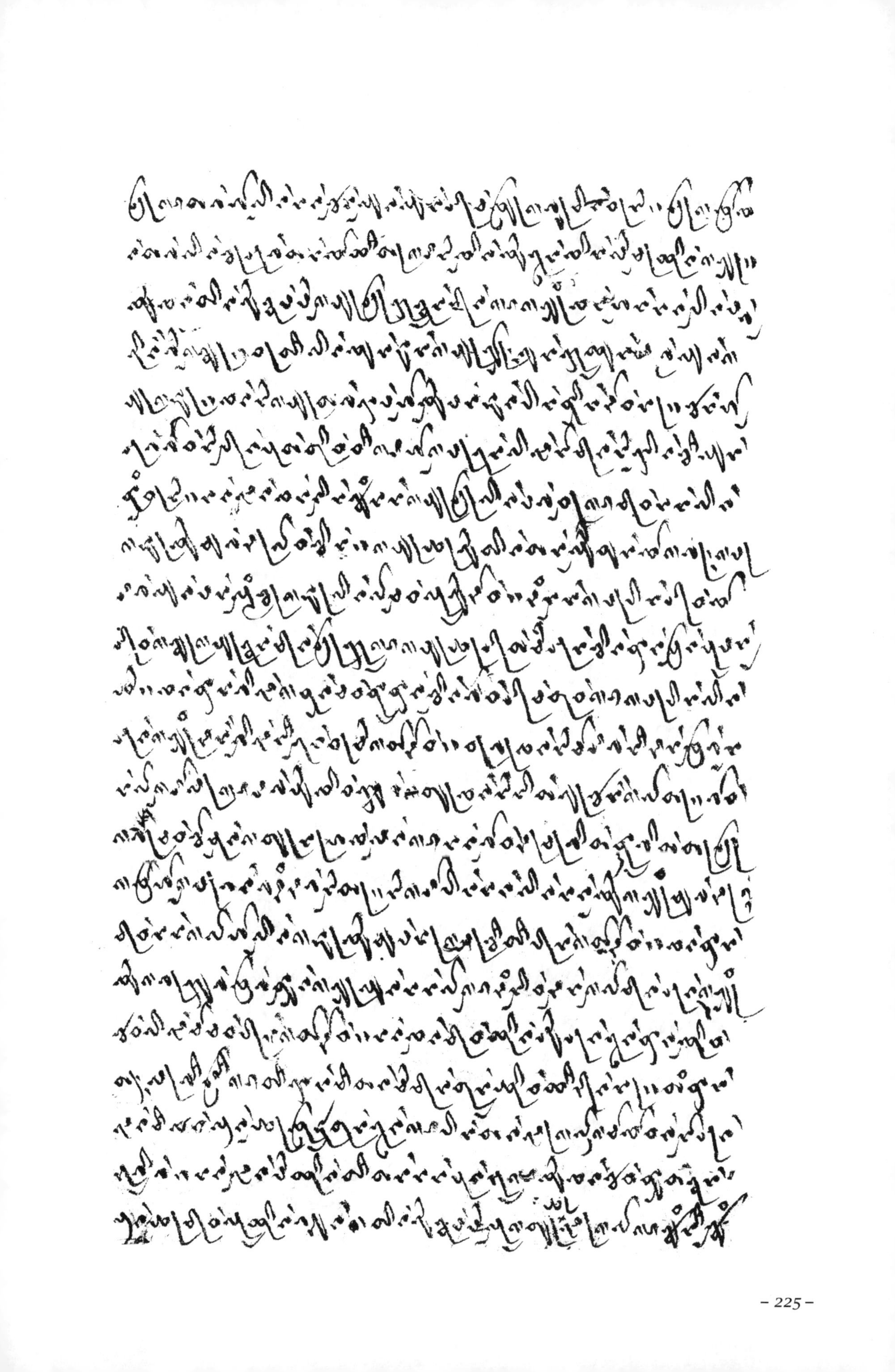

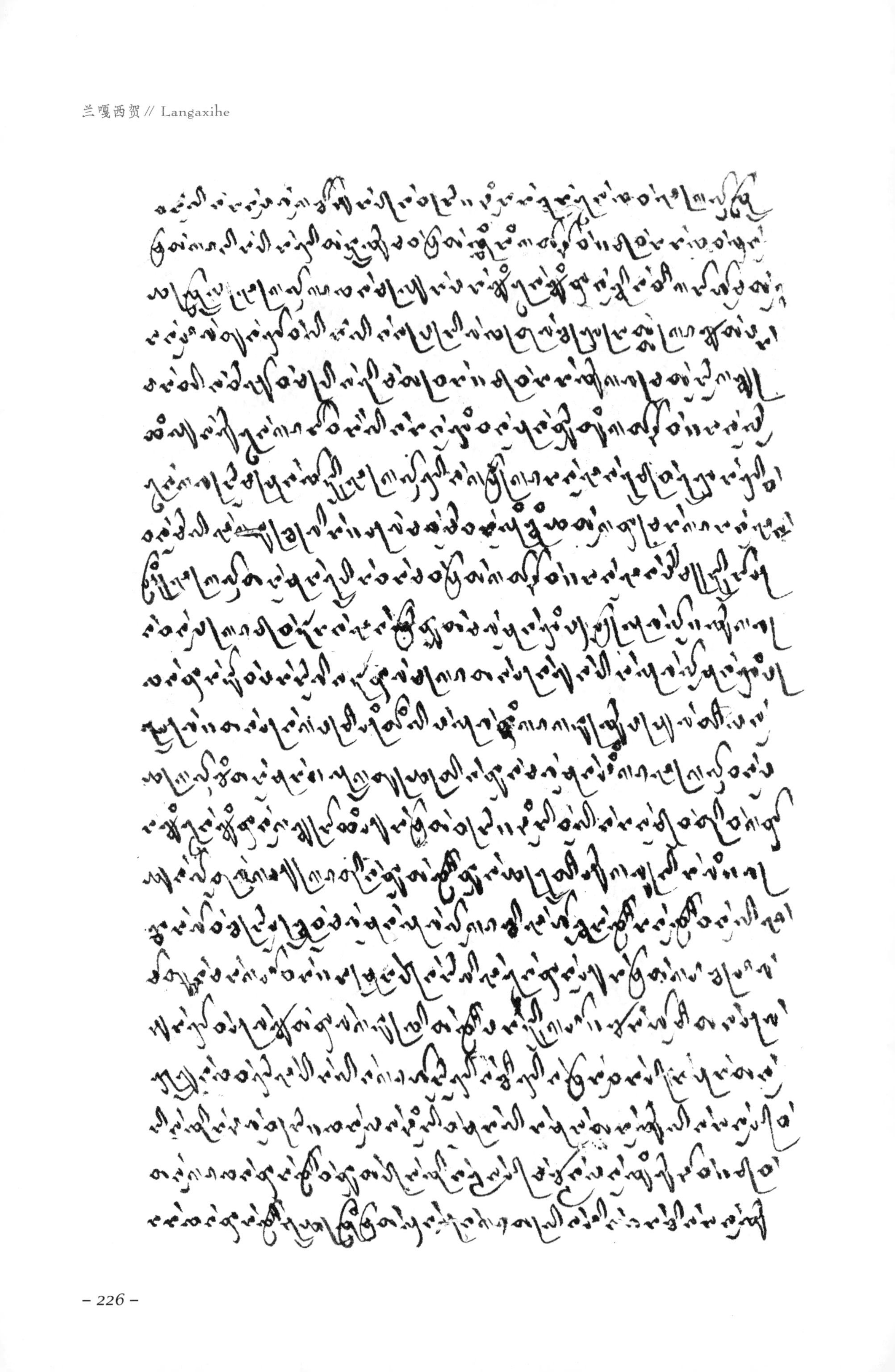

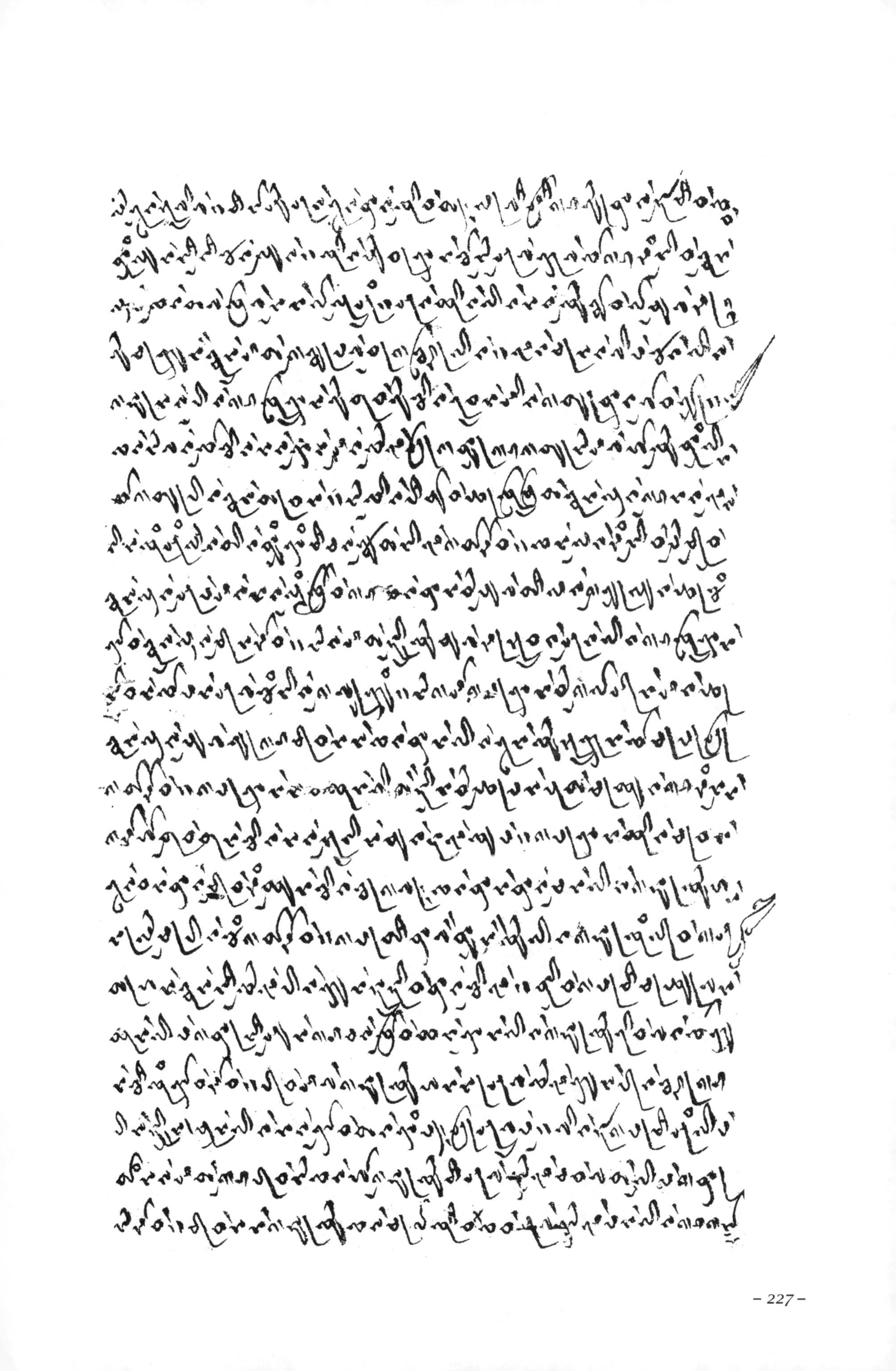

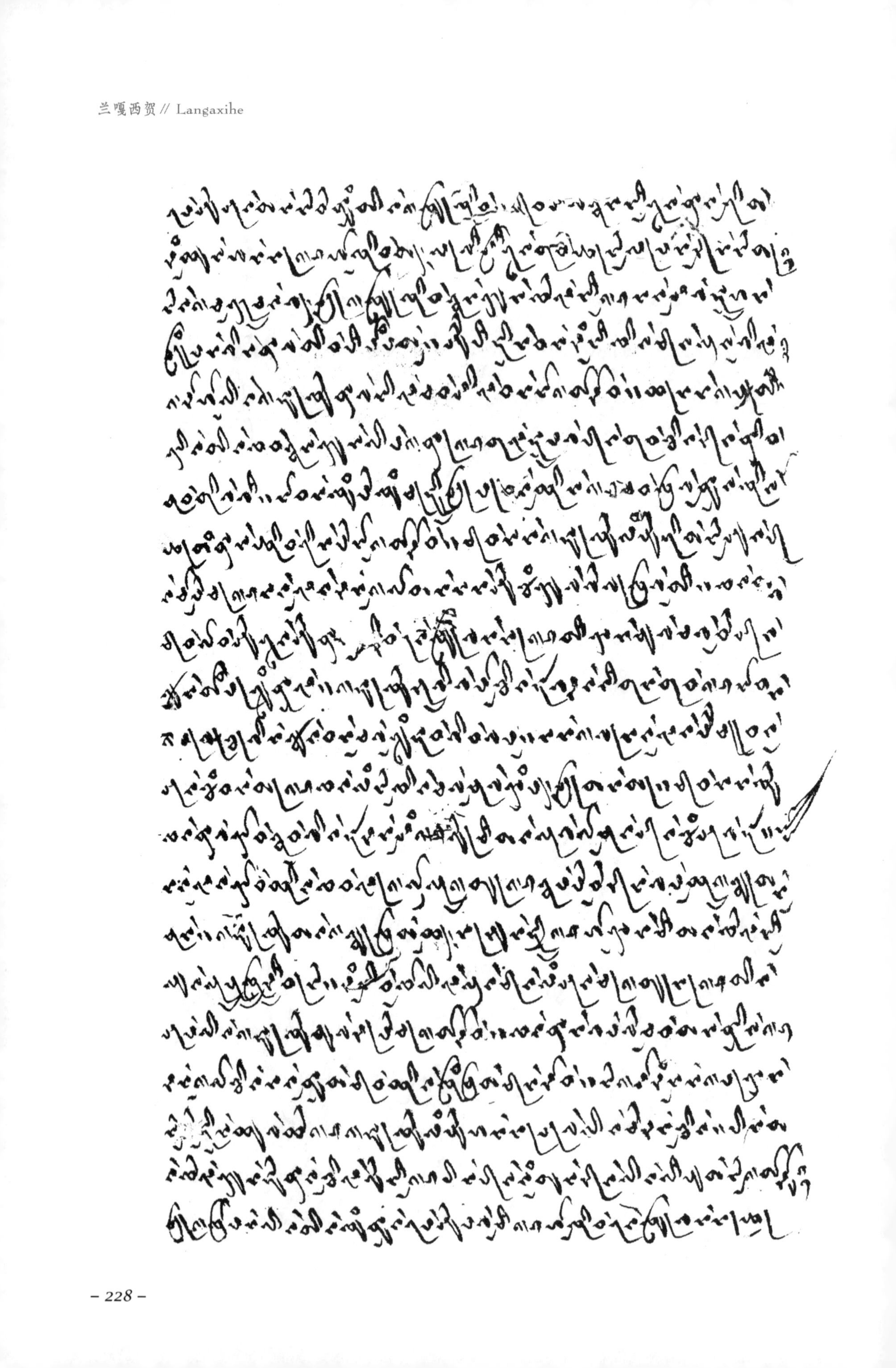

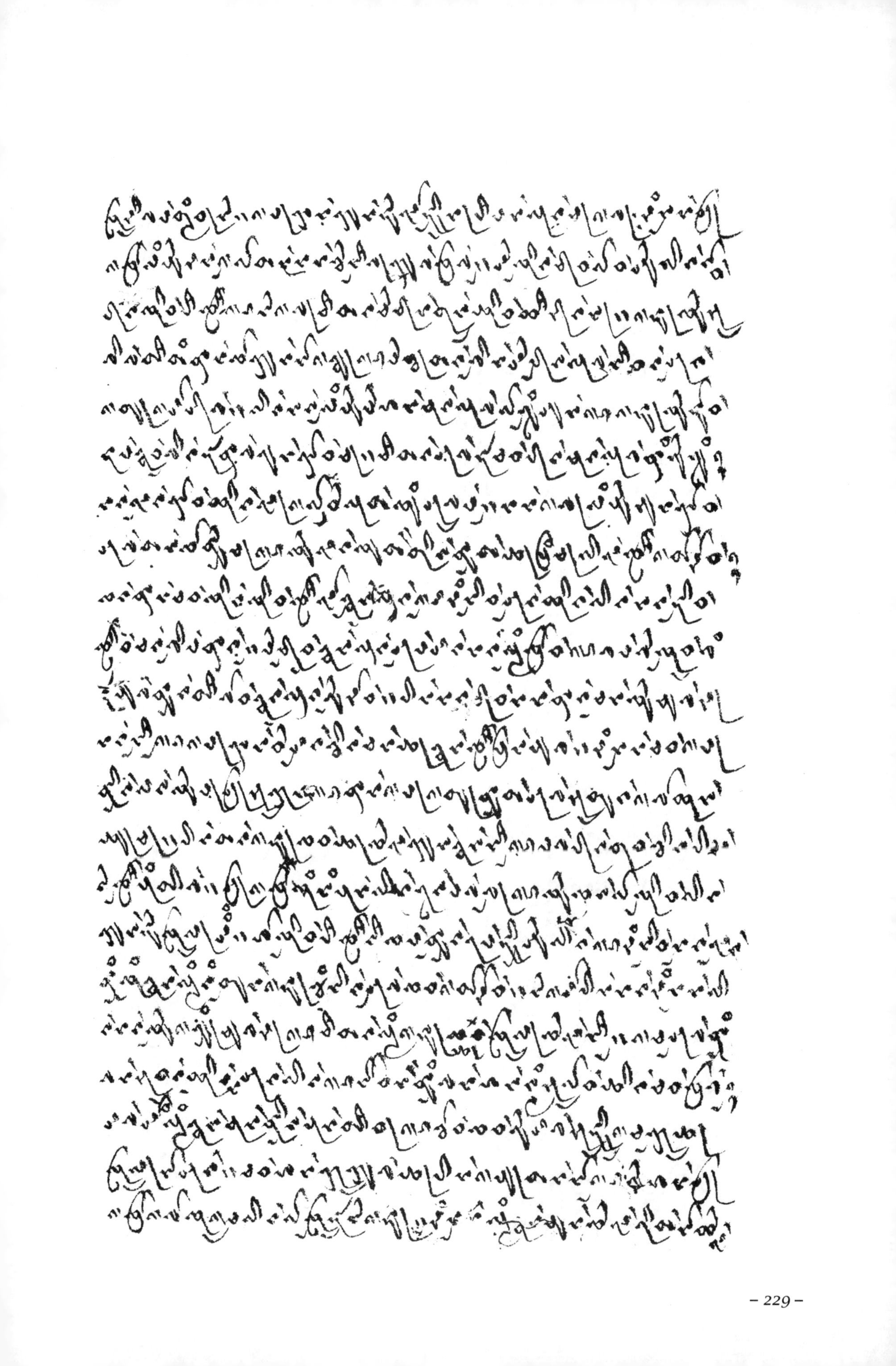

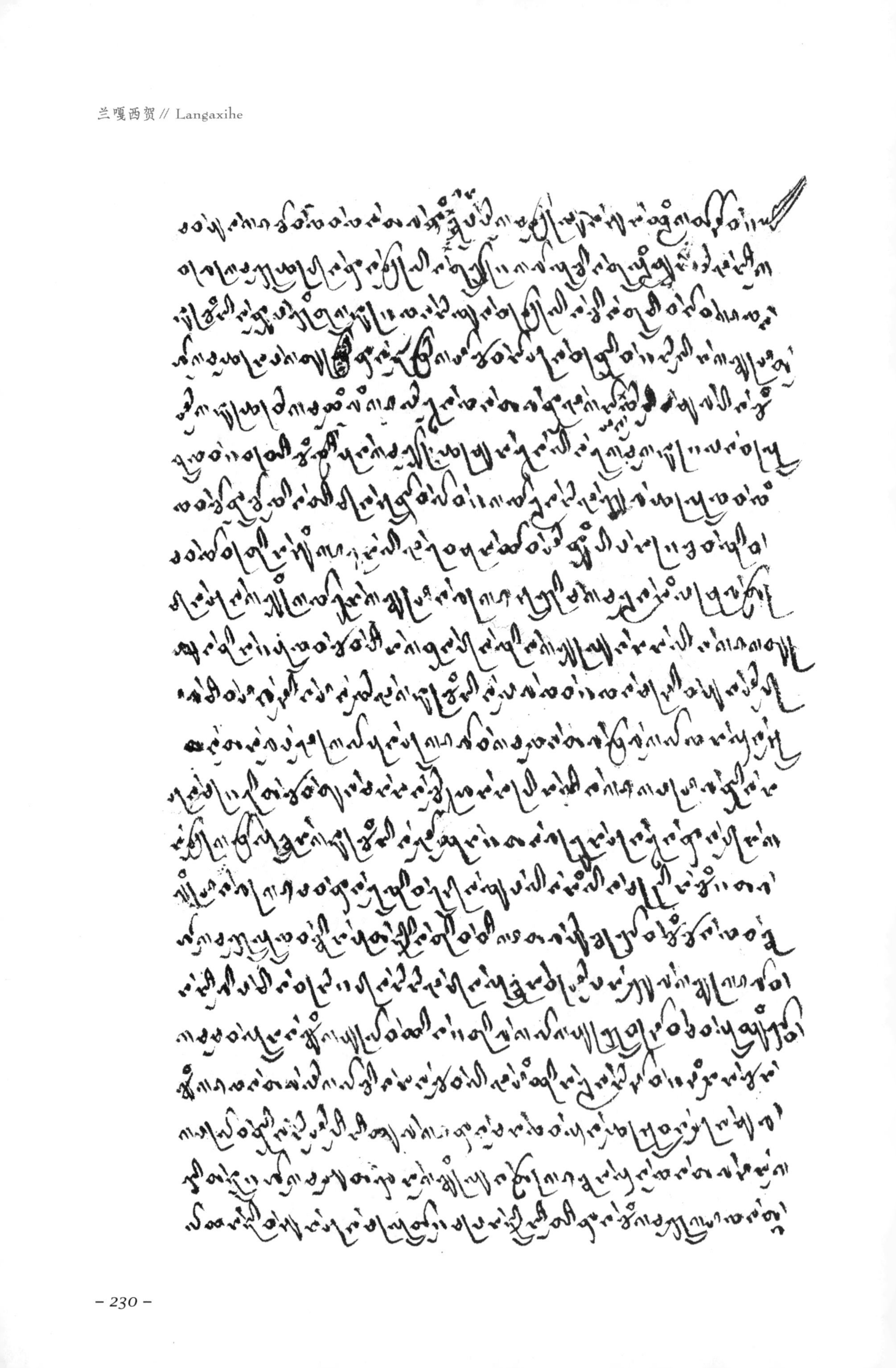

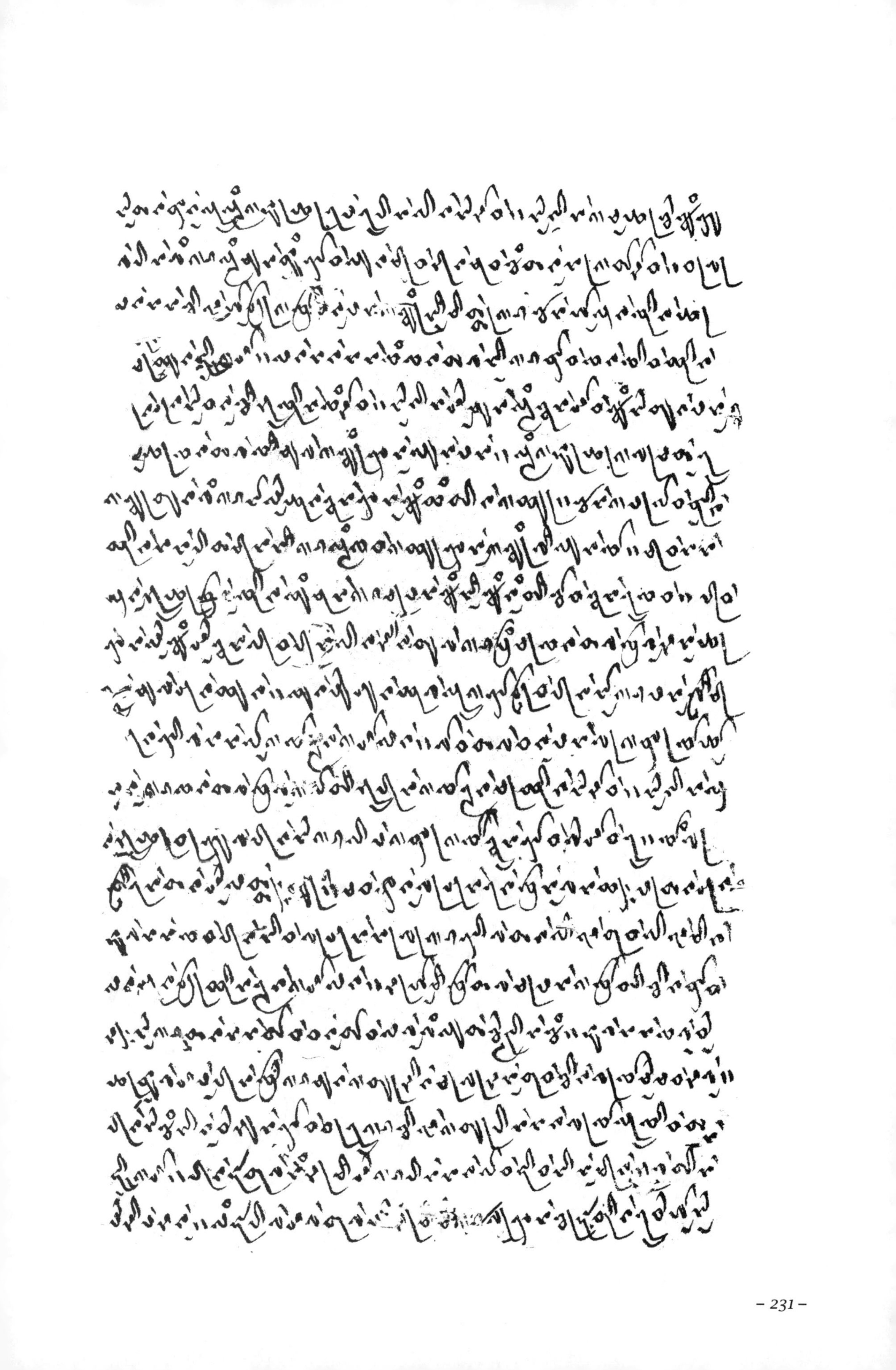

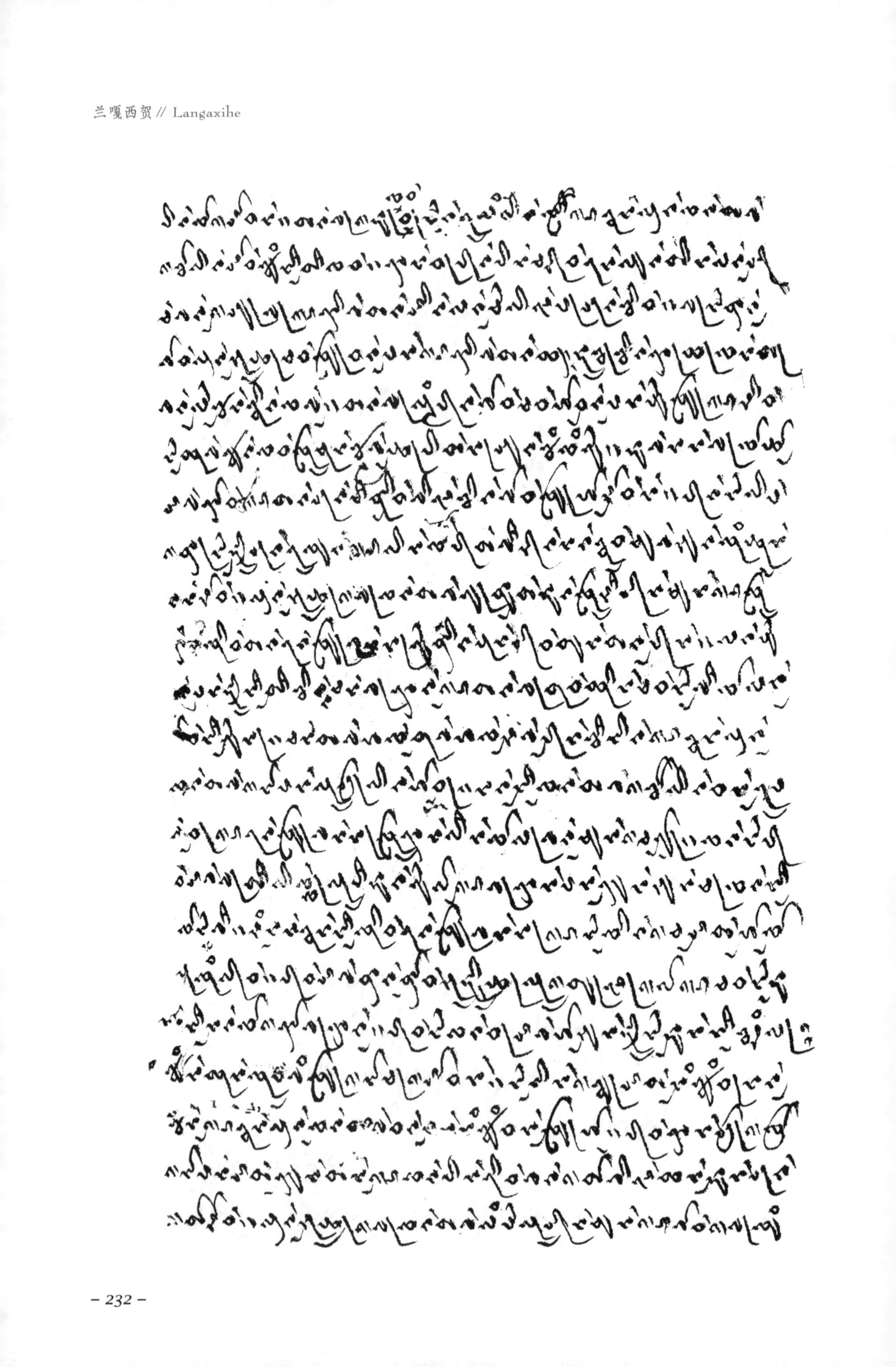

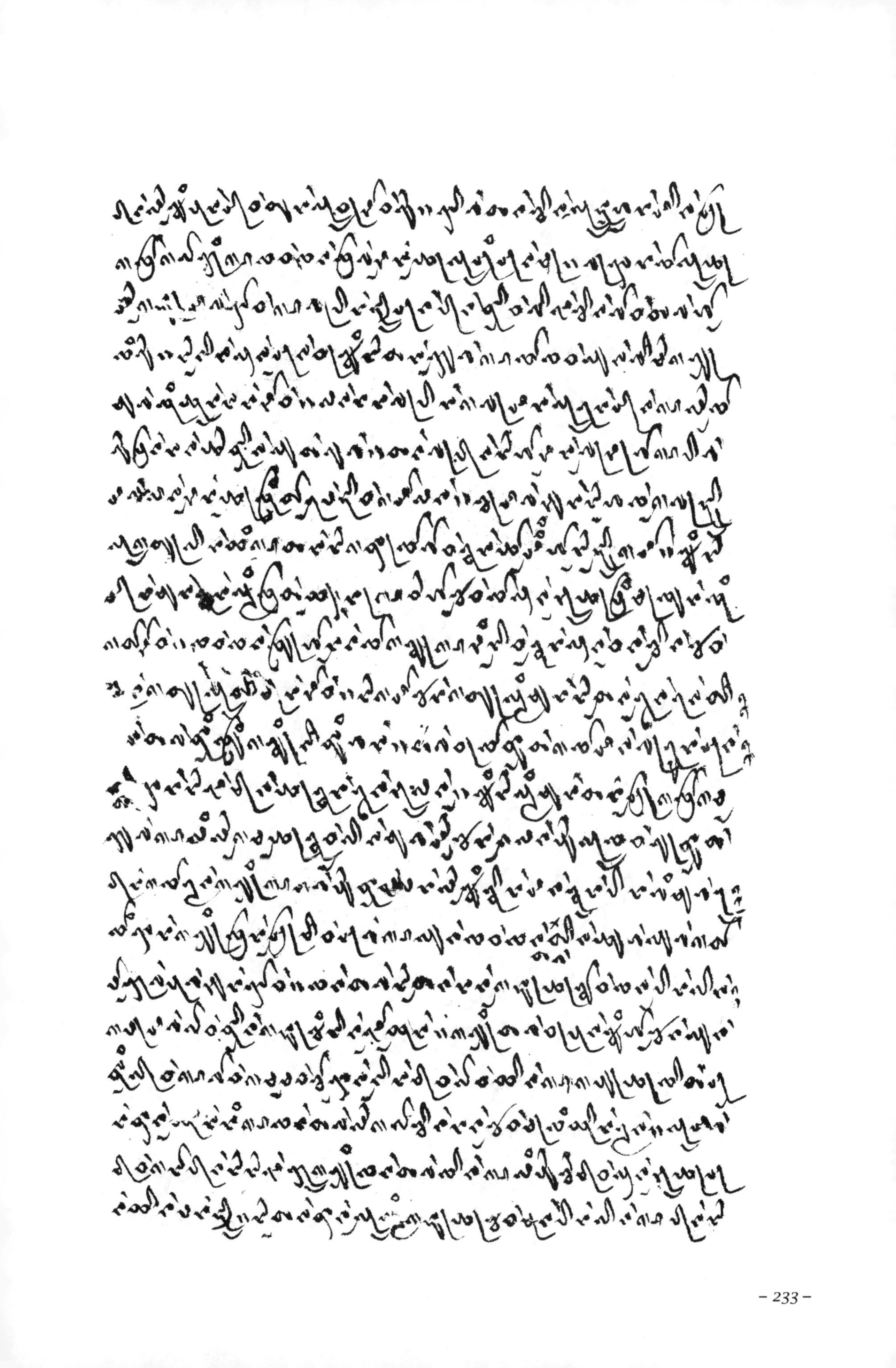

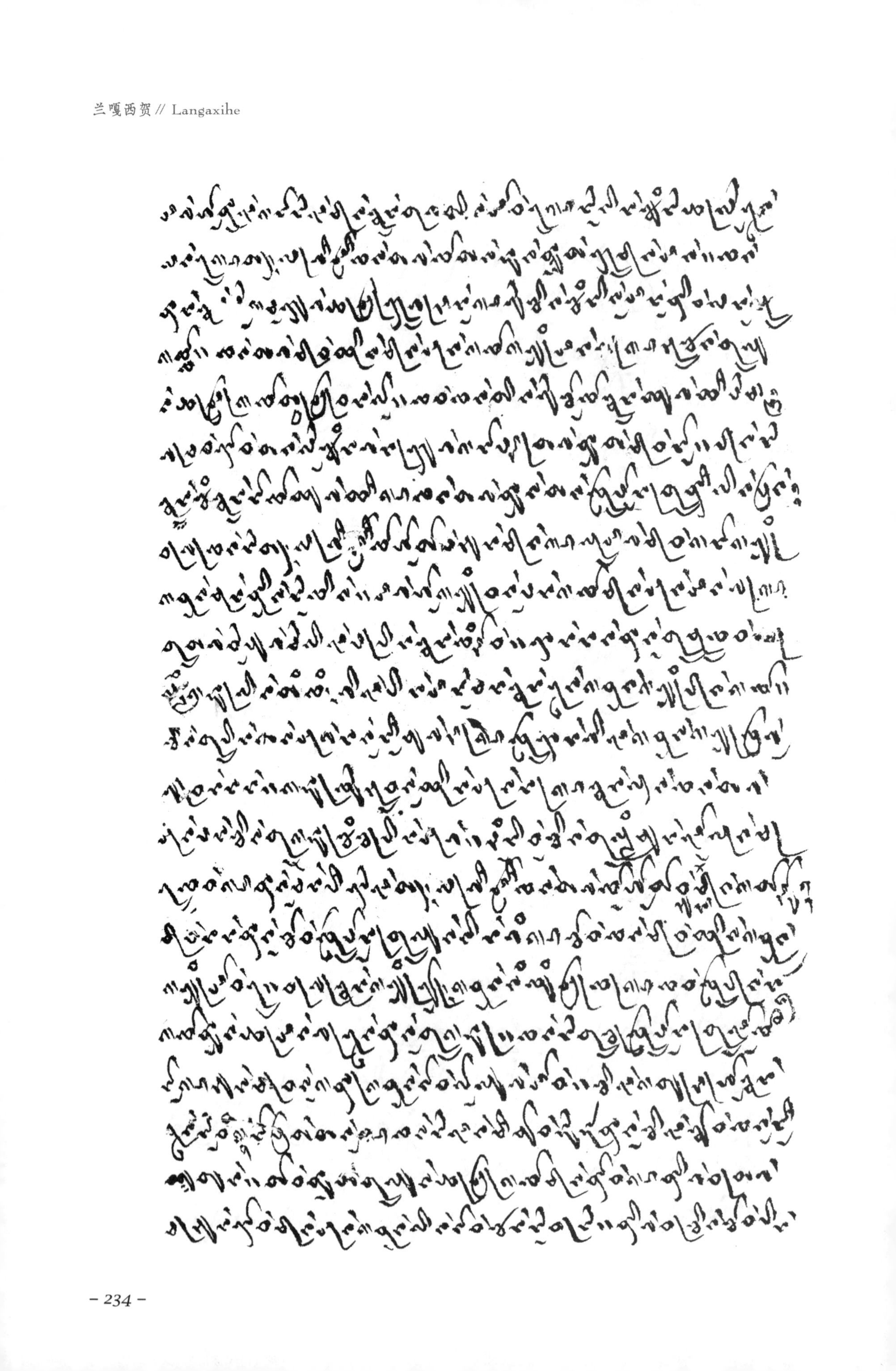

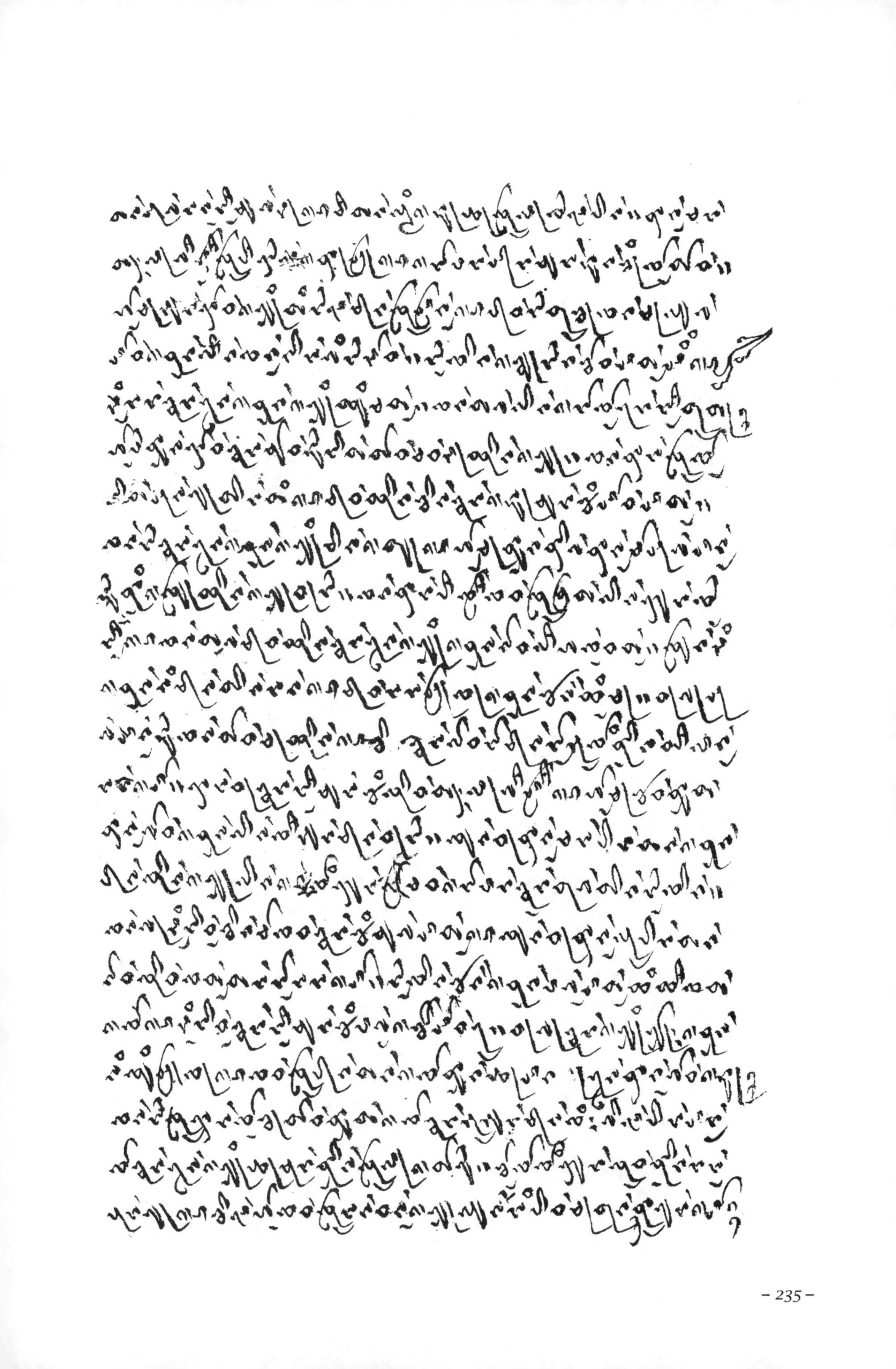

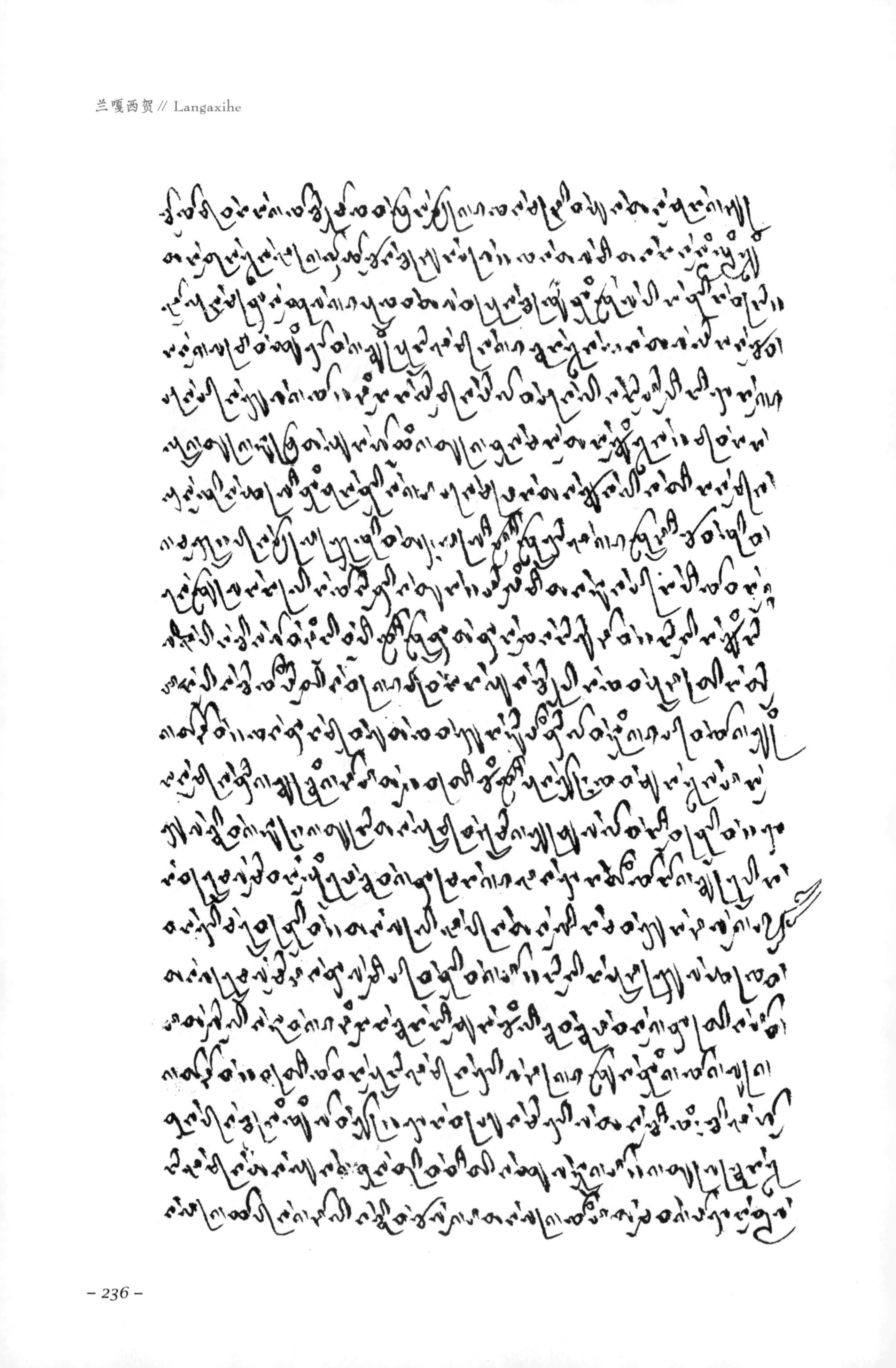

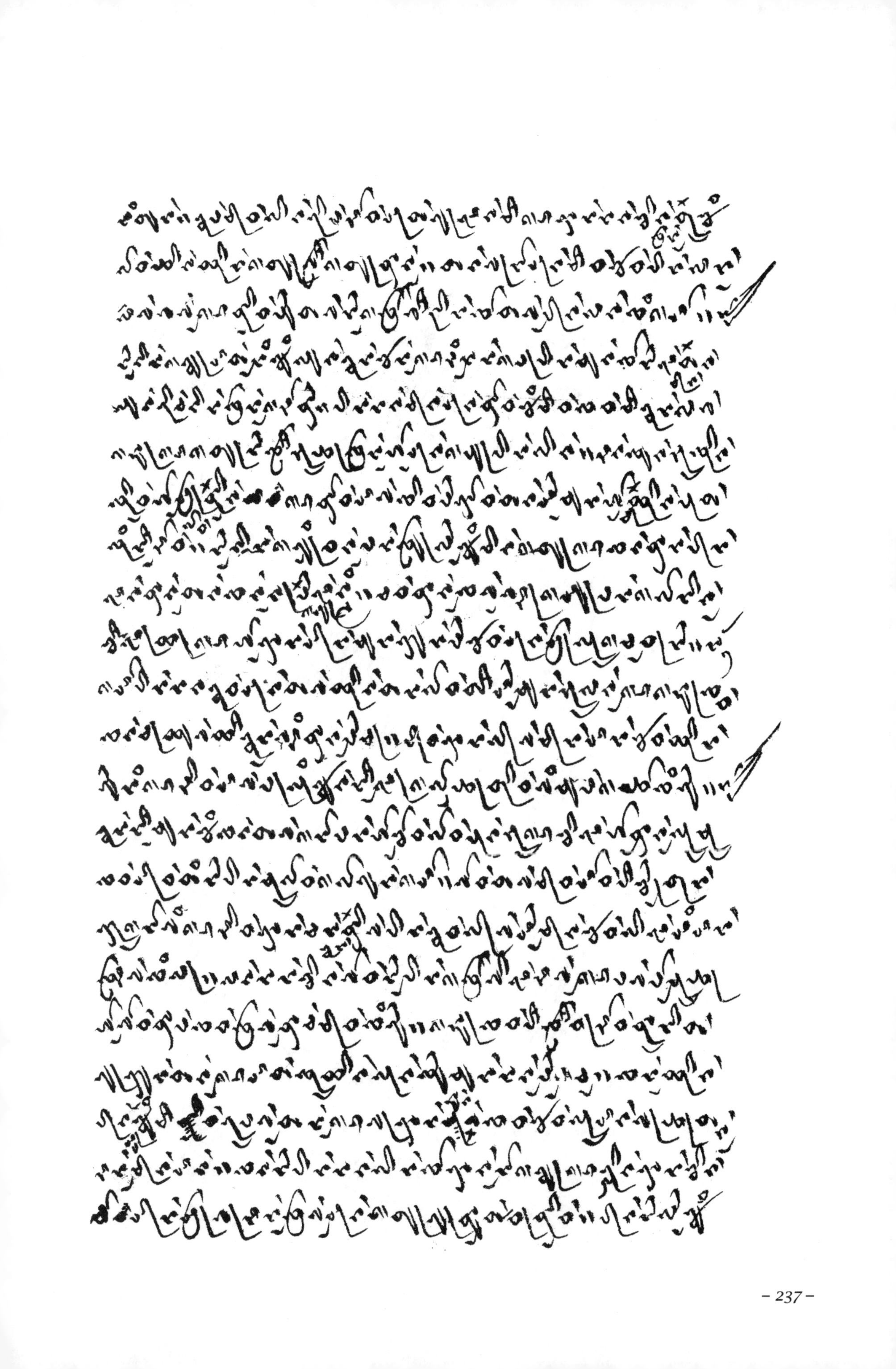

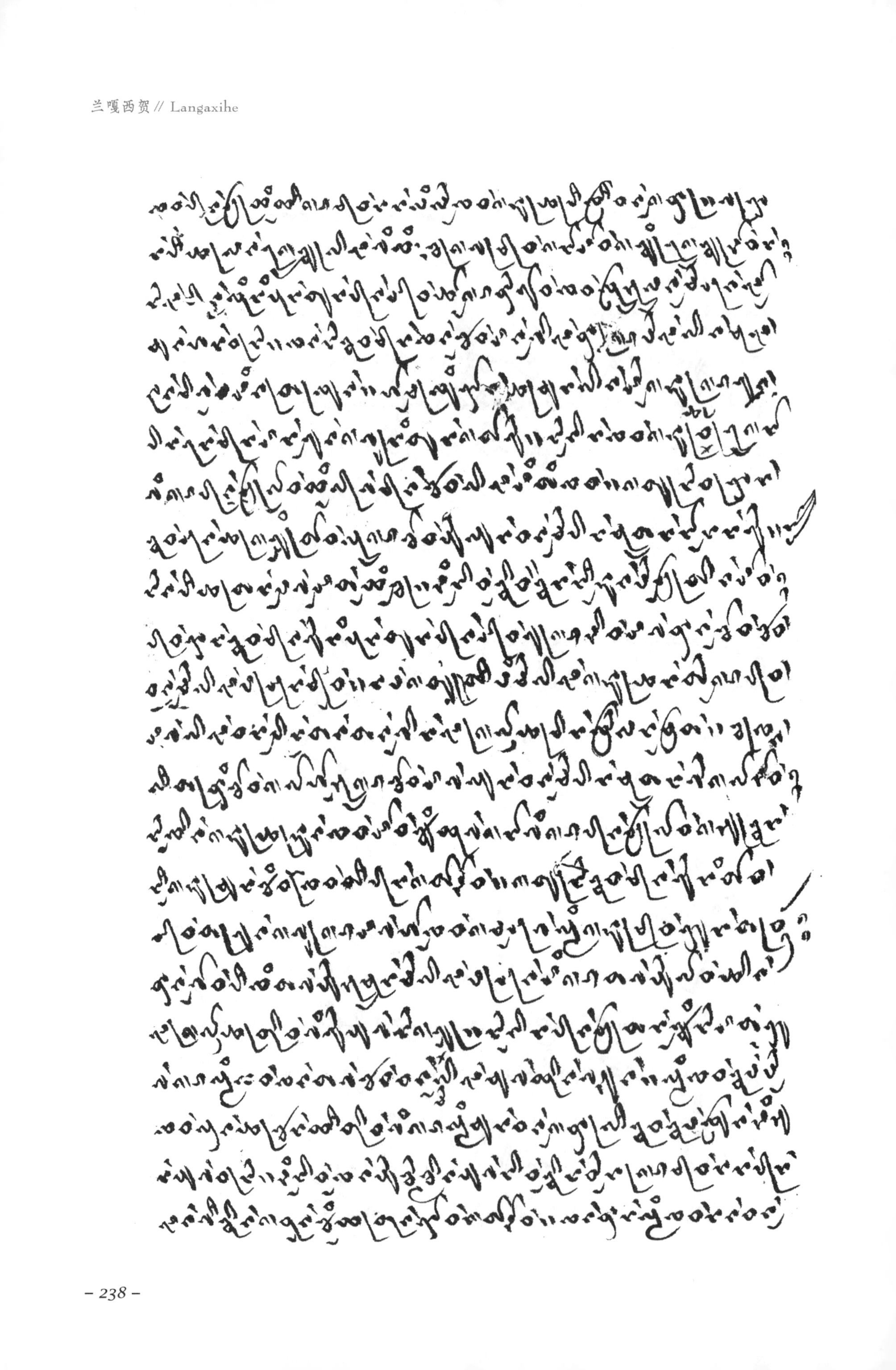

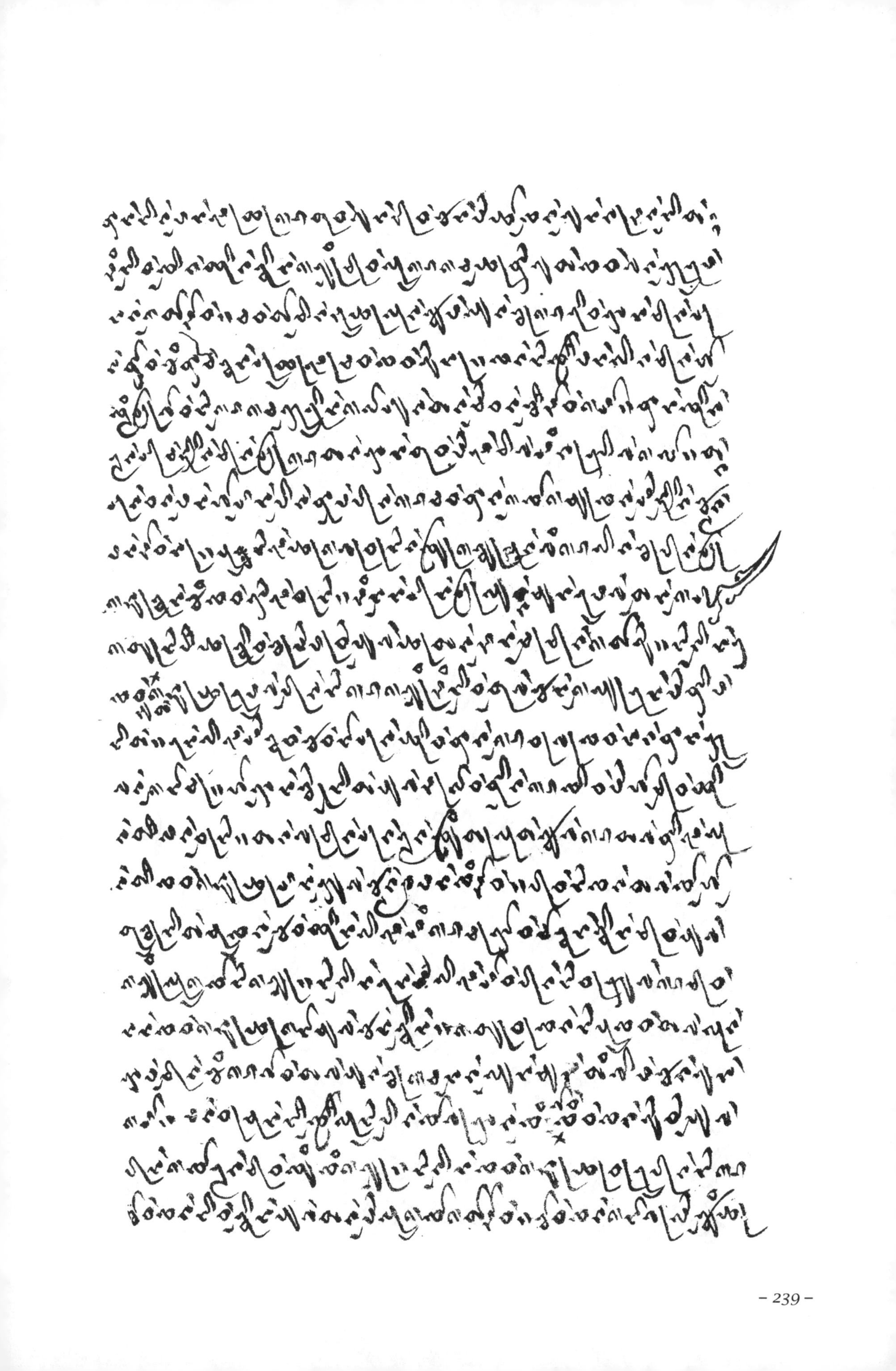

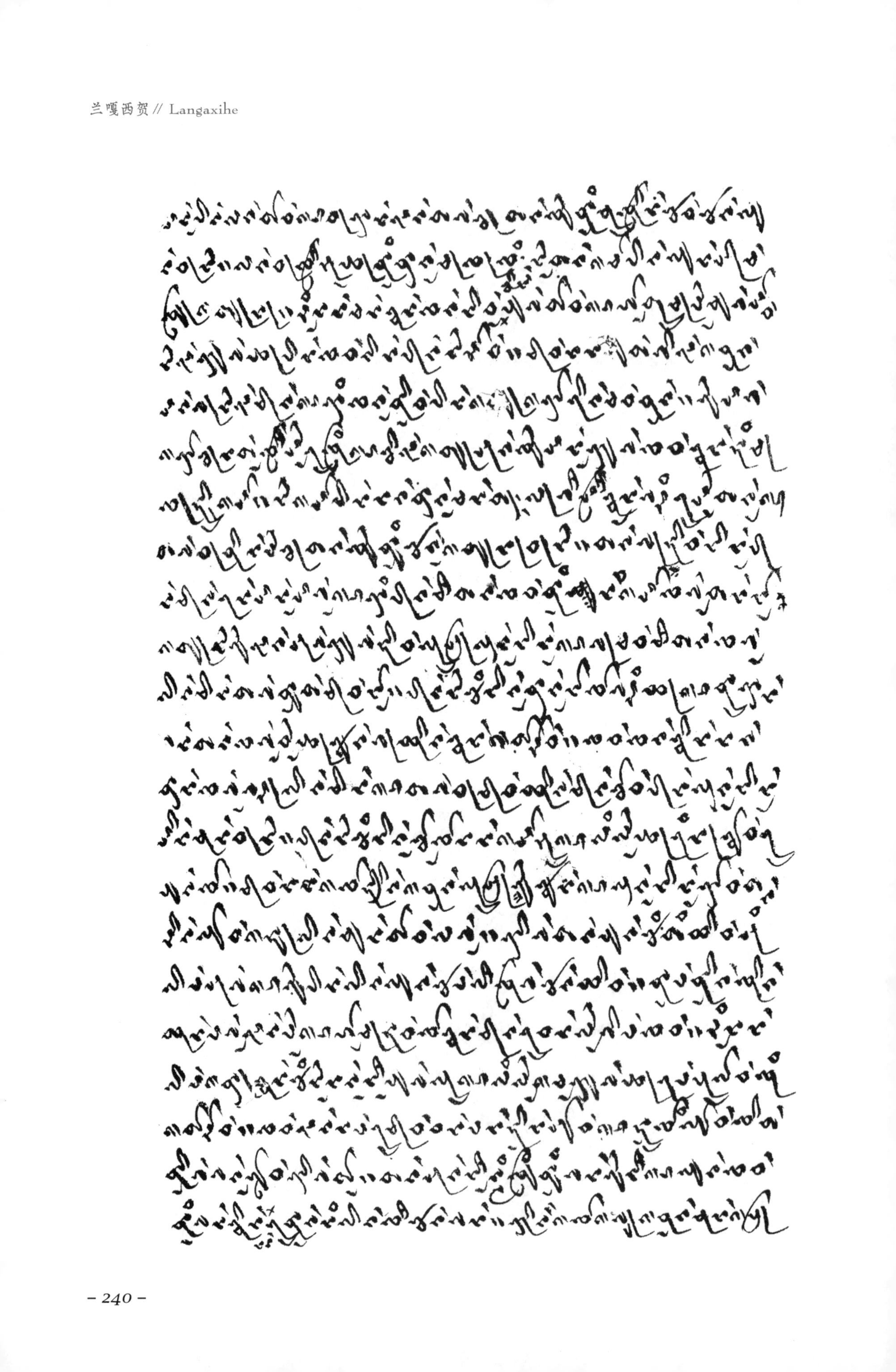

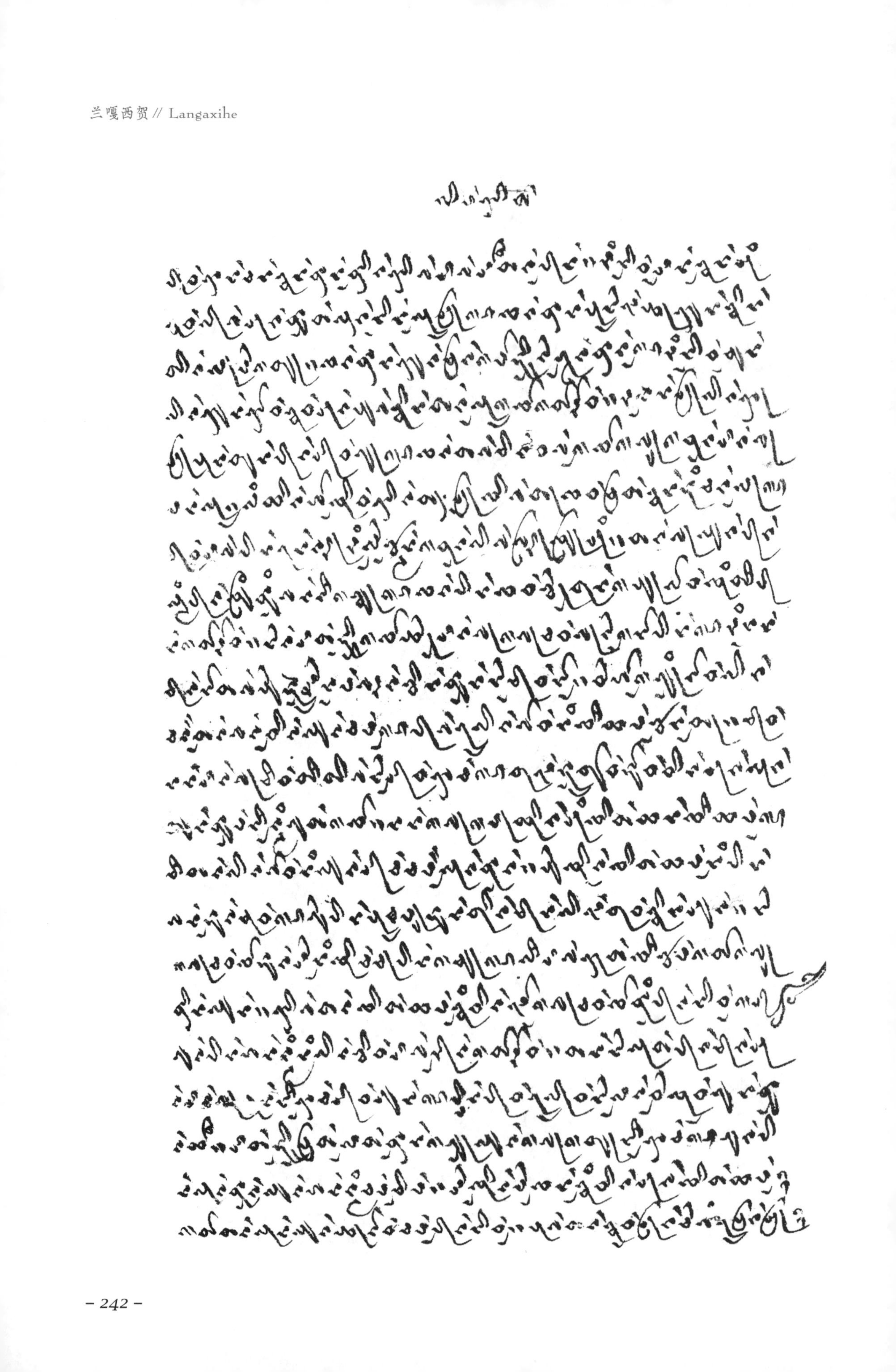

[illegible]

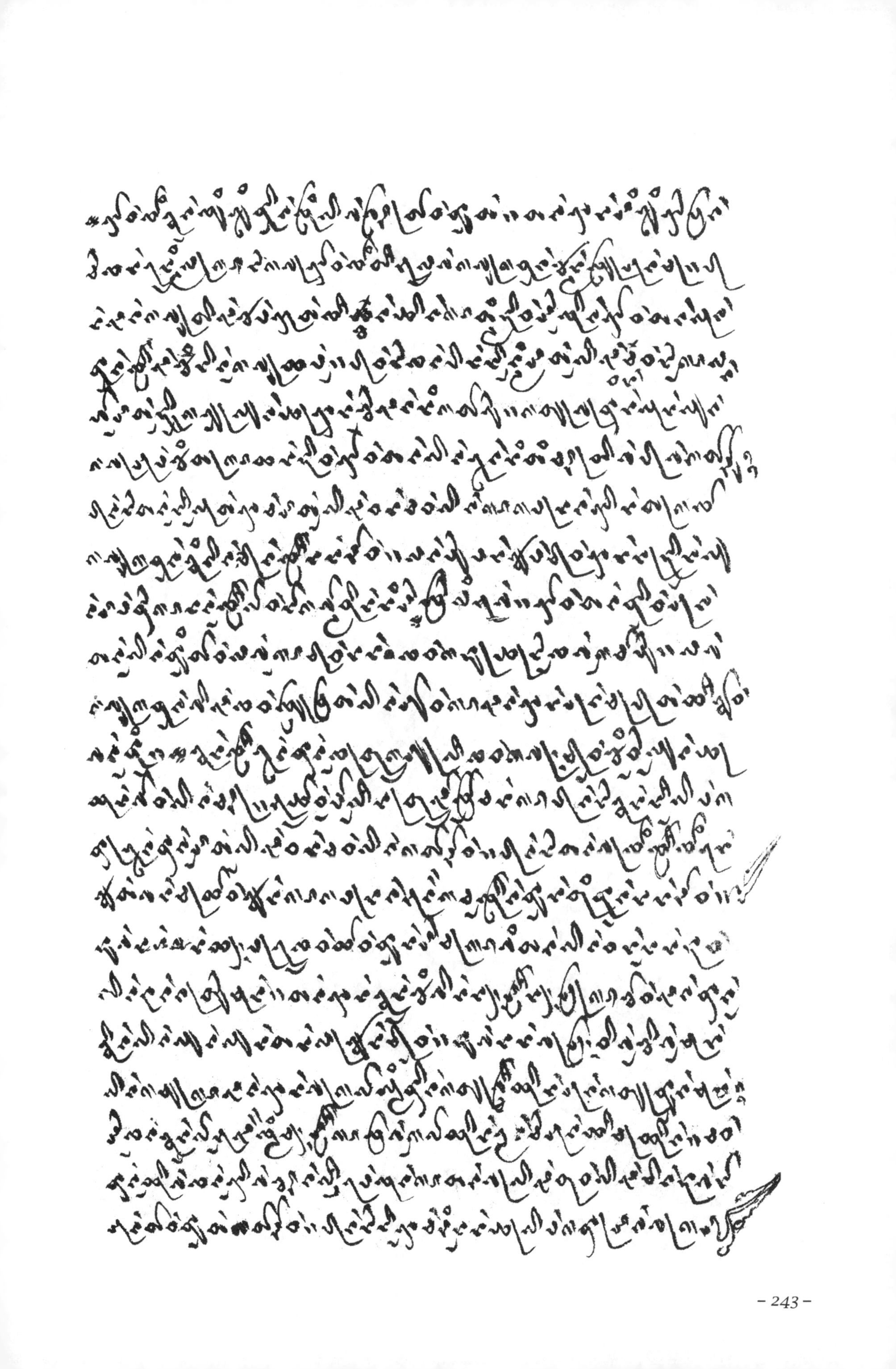

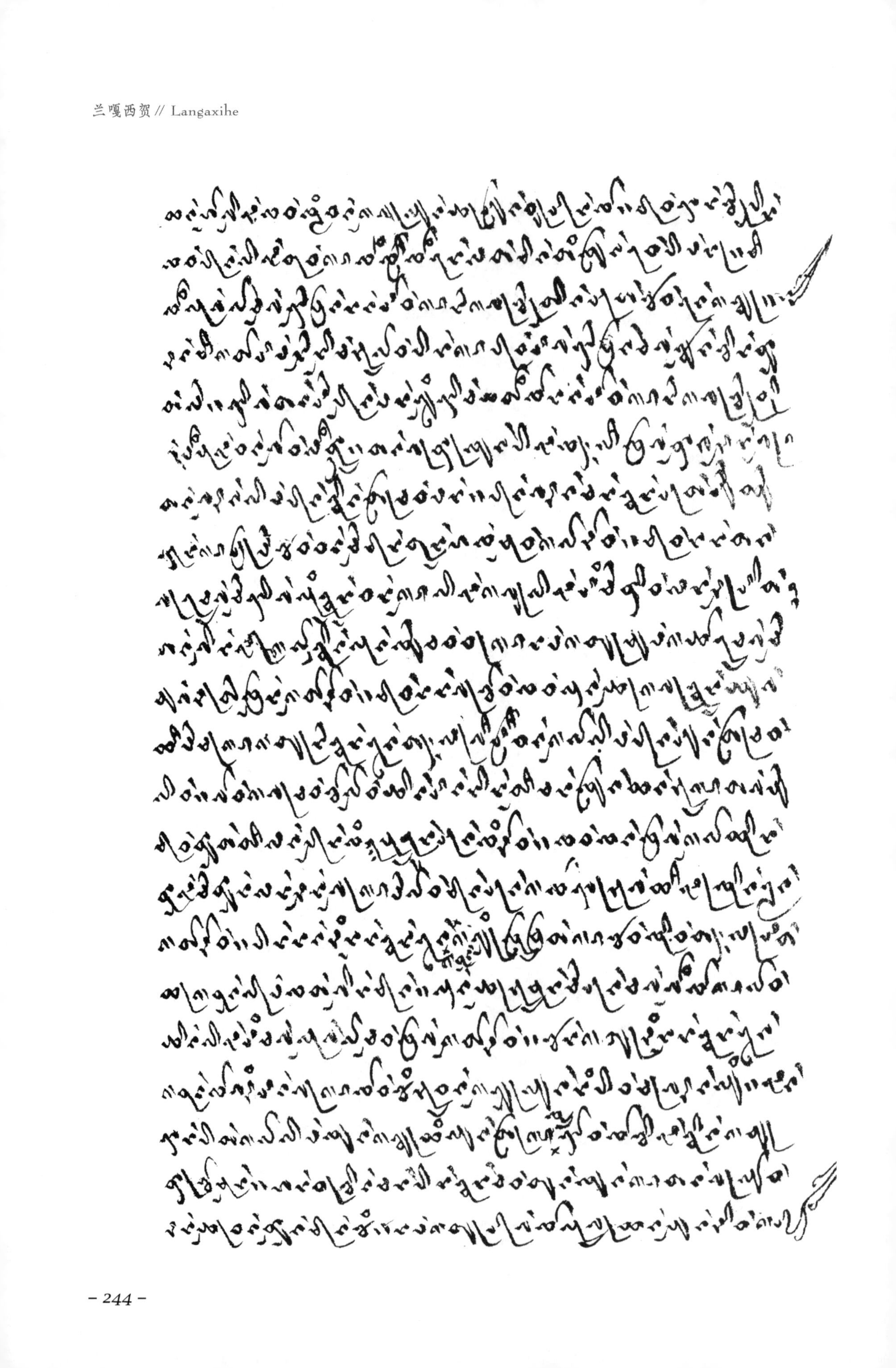

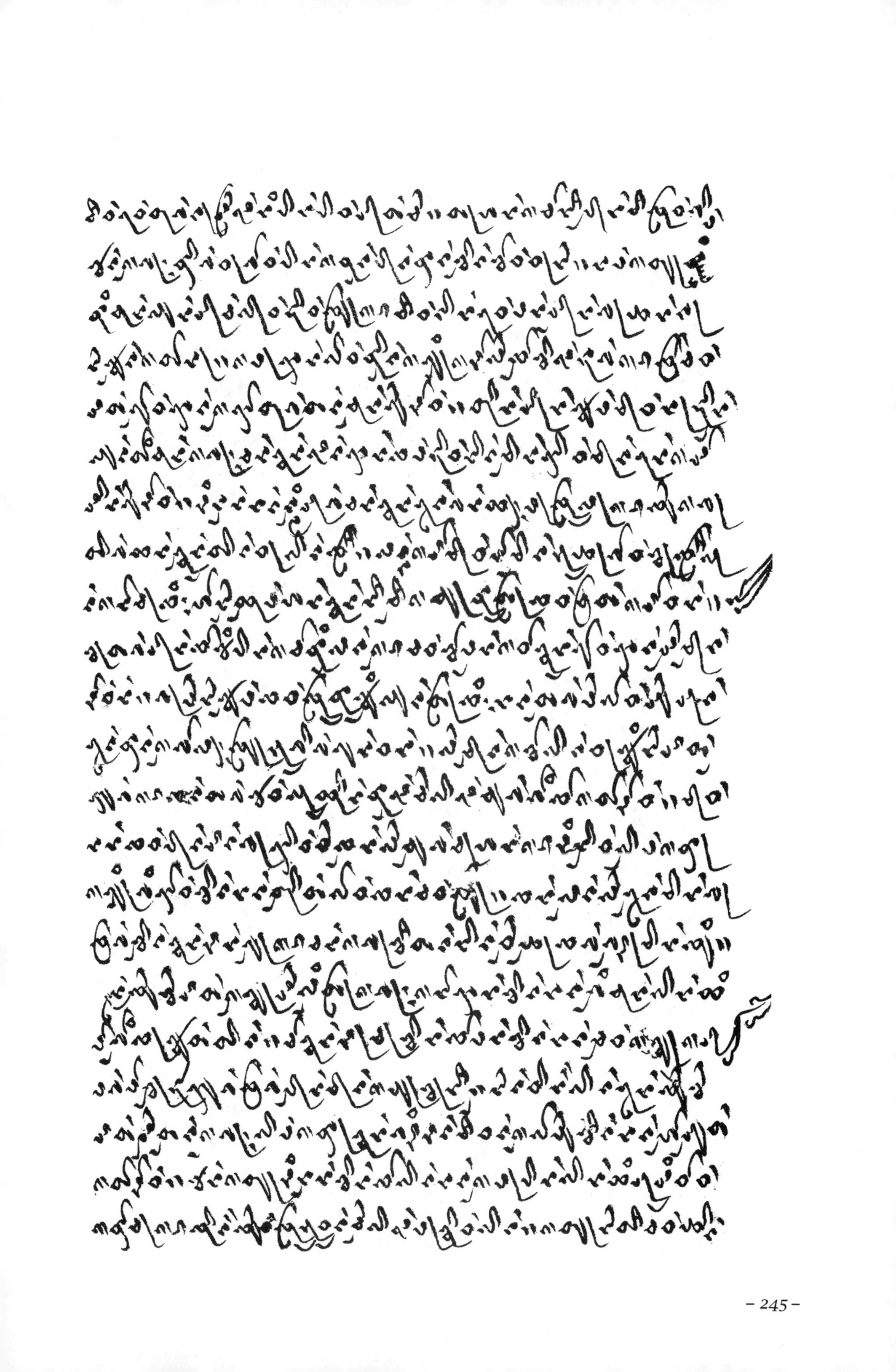

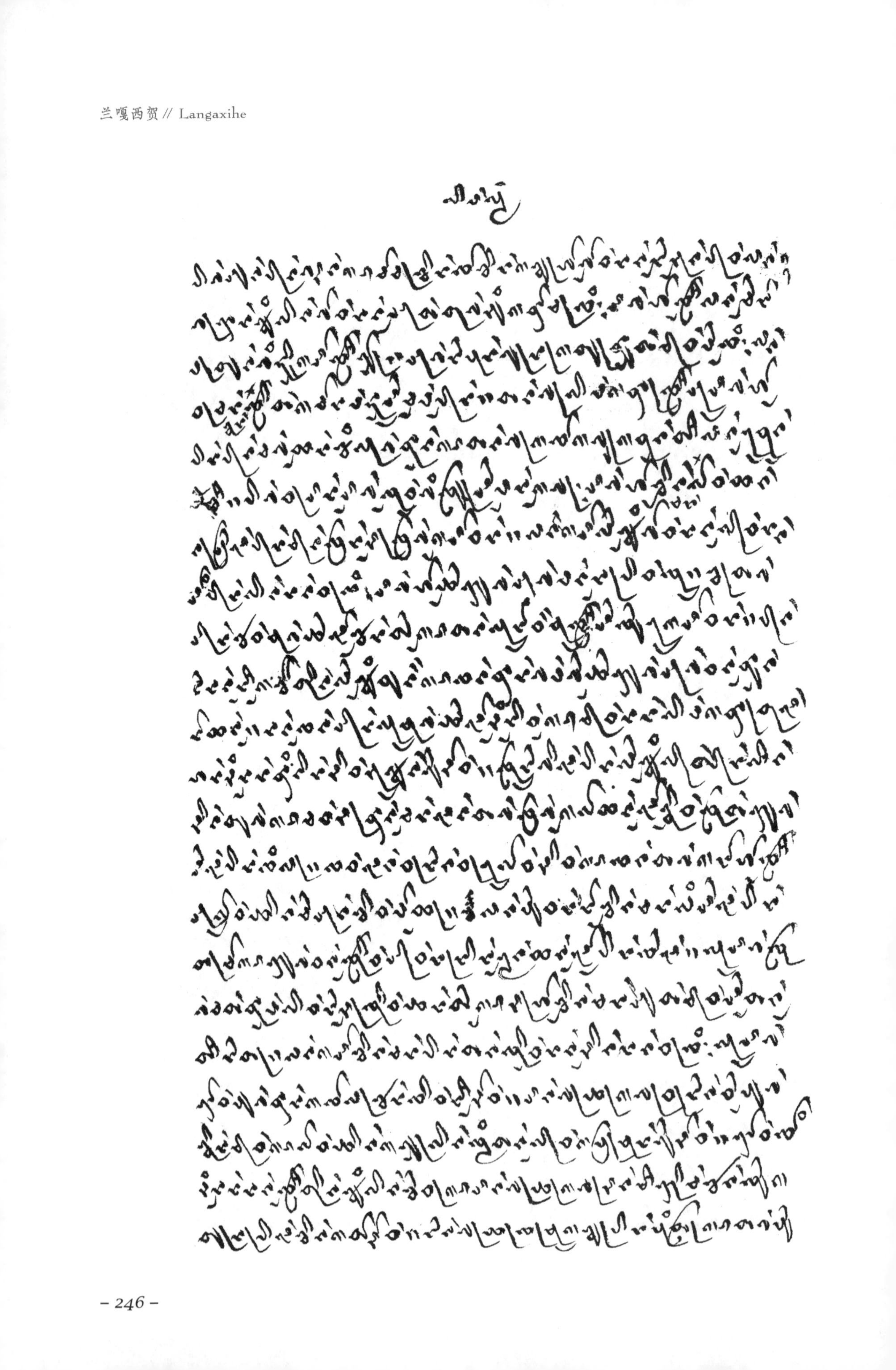

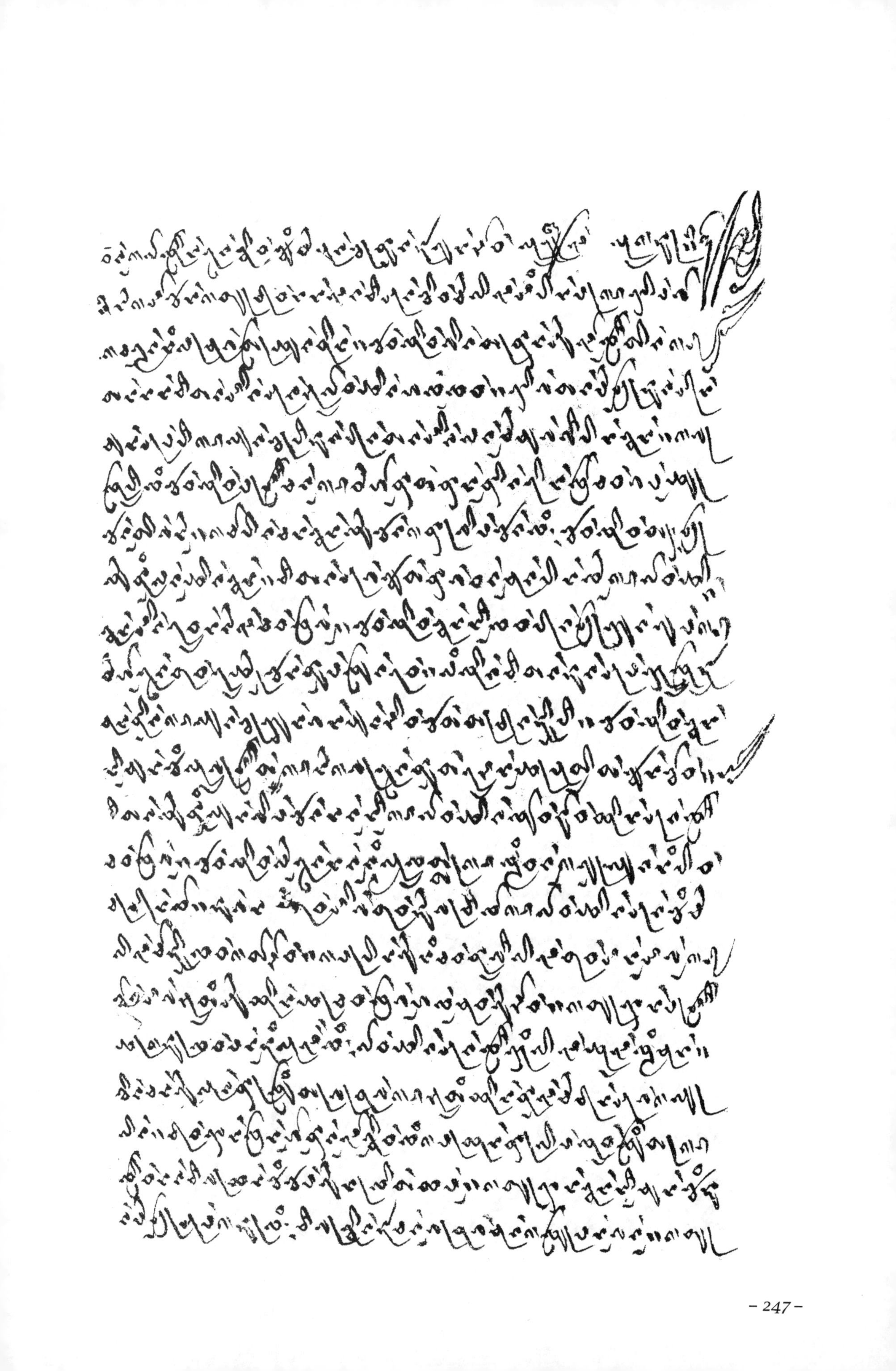

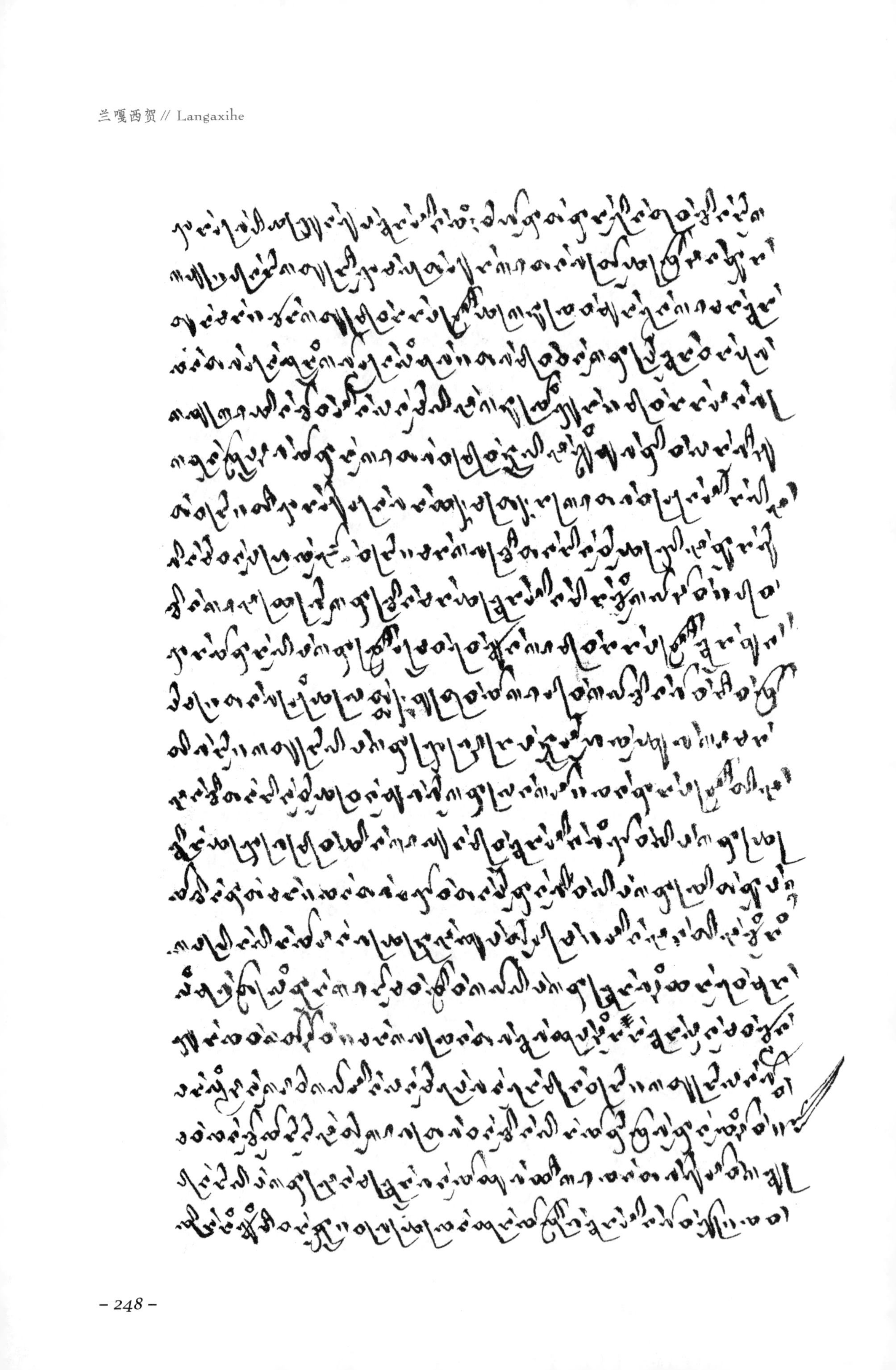

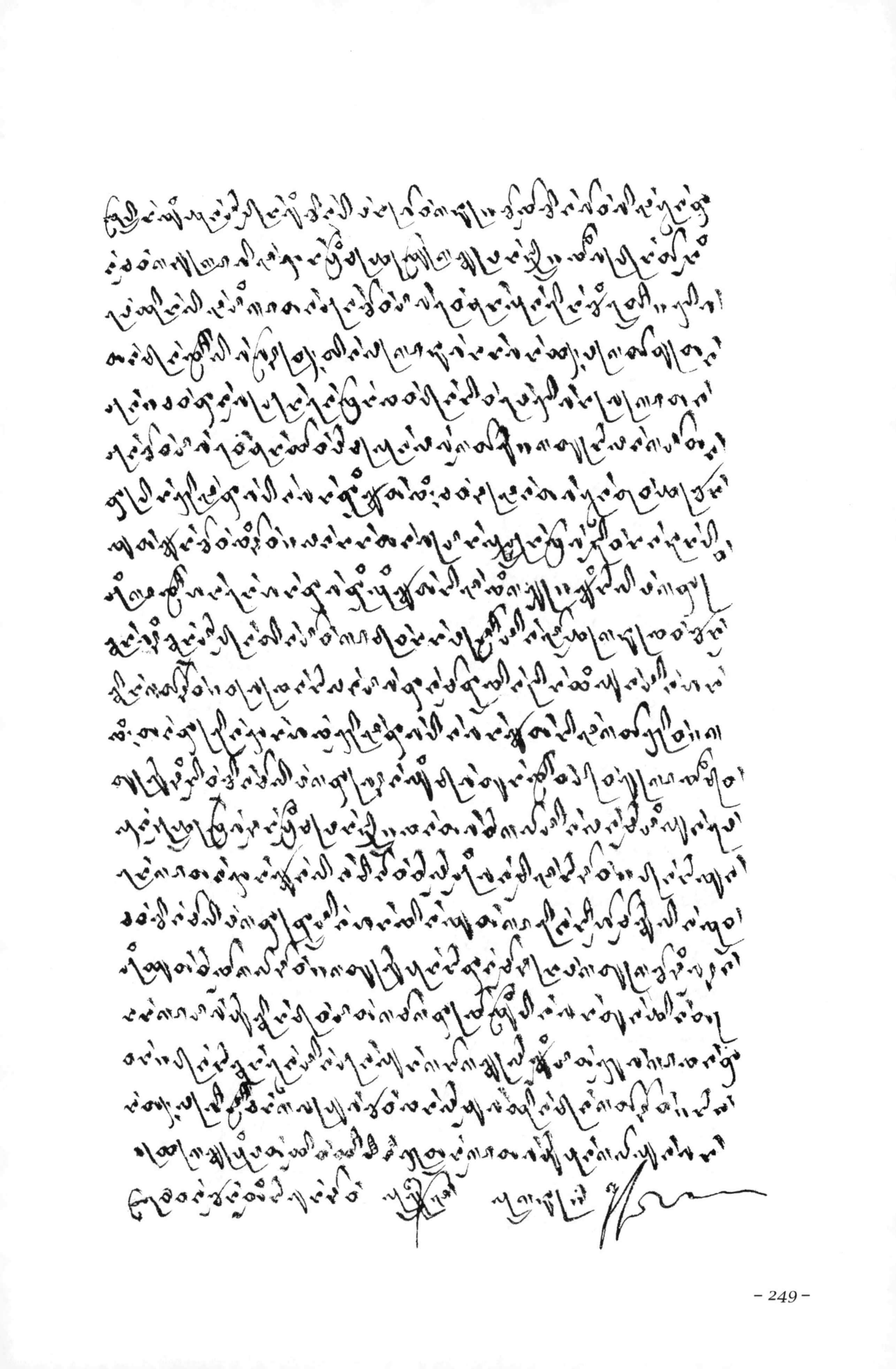

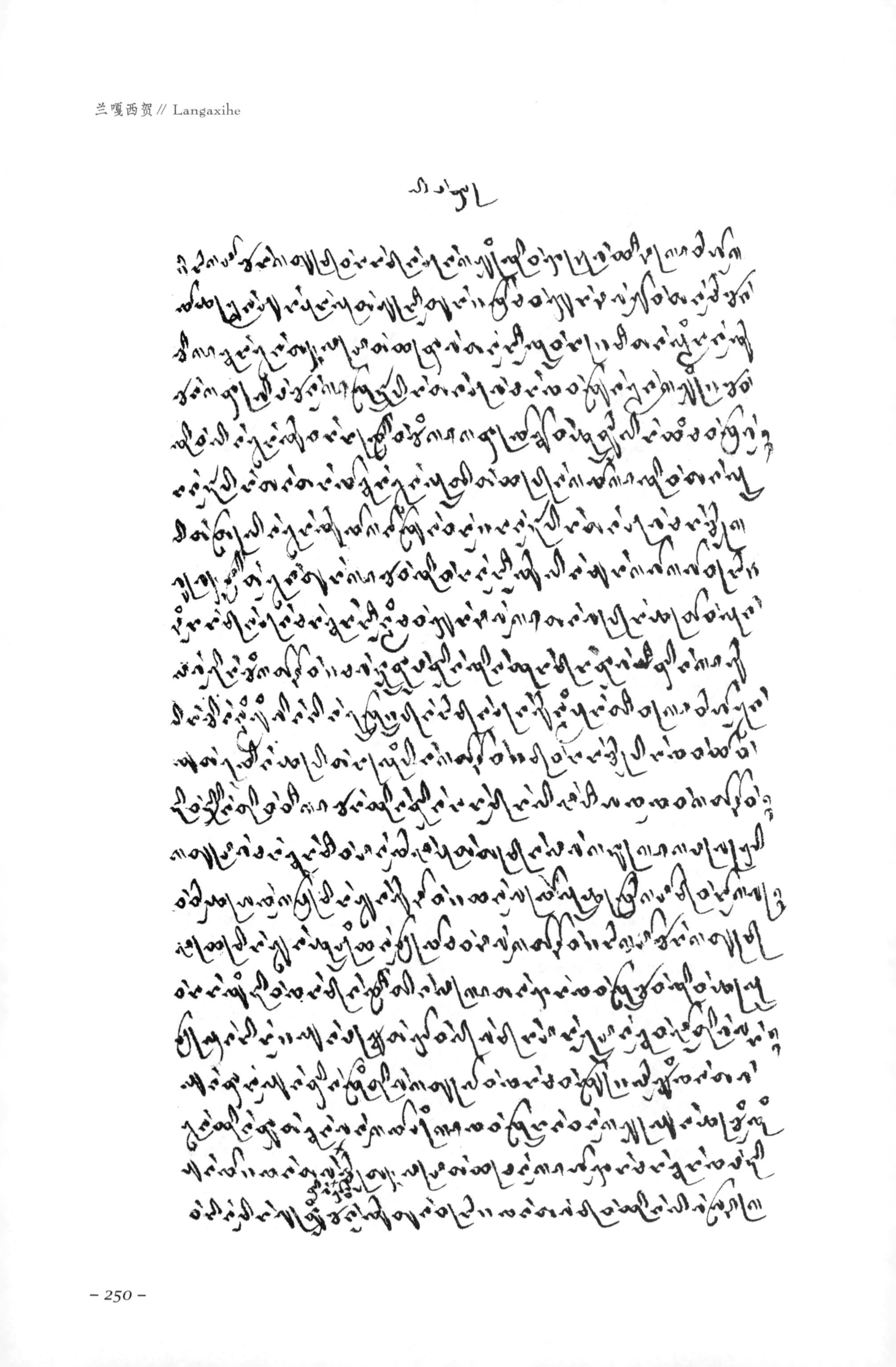

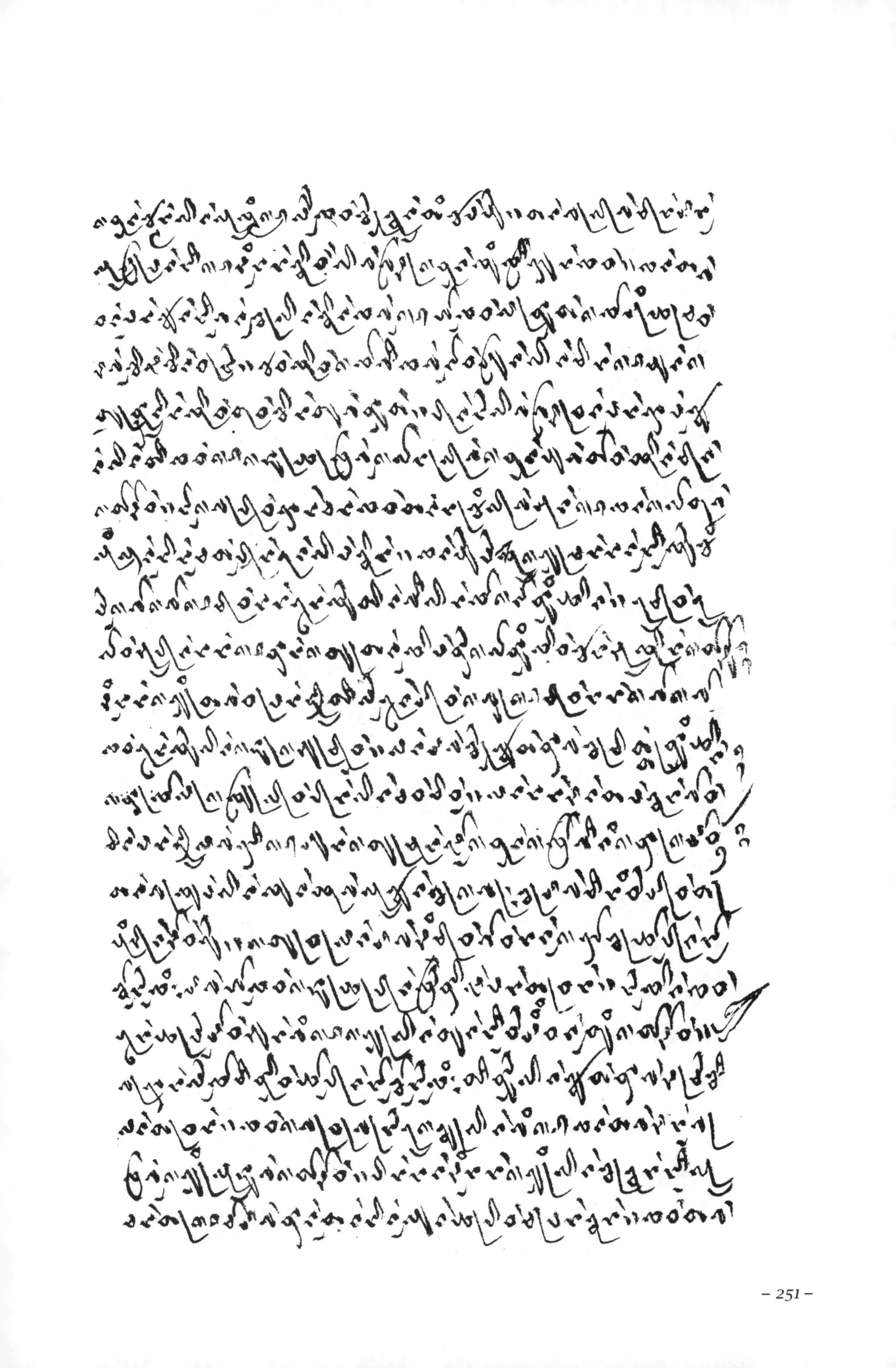

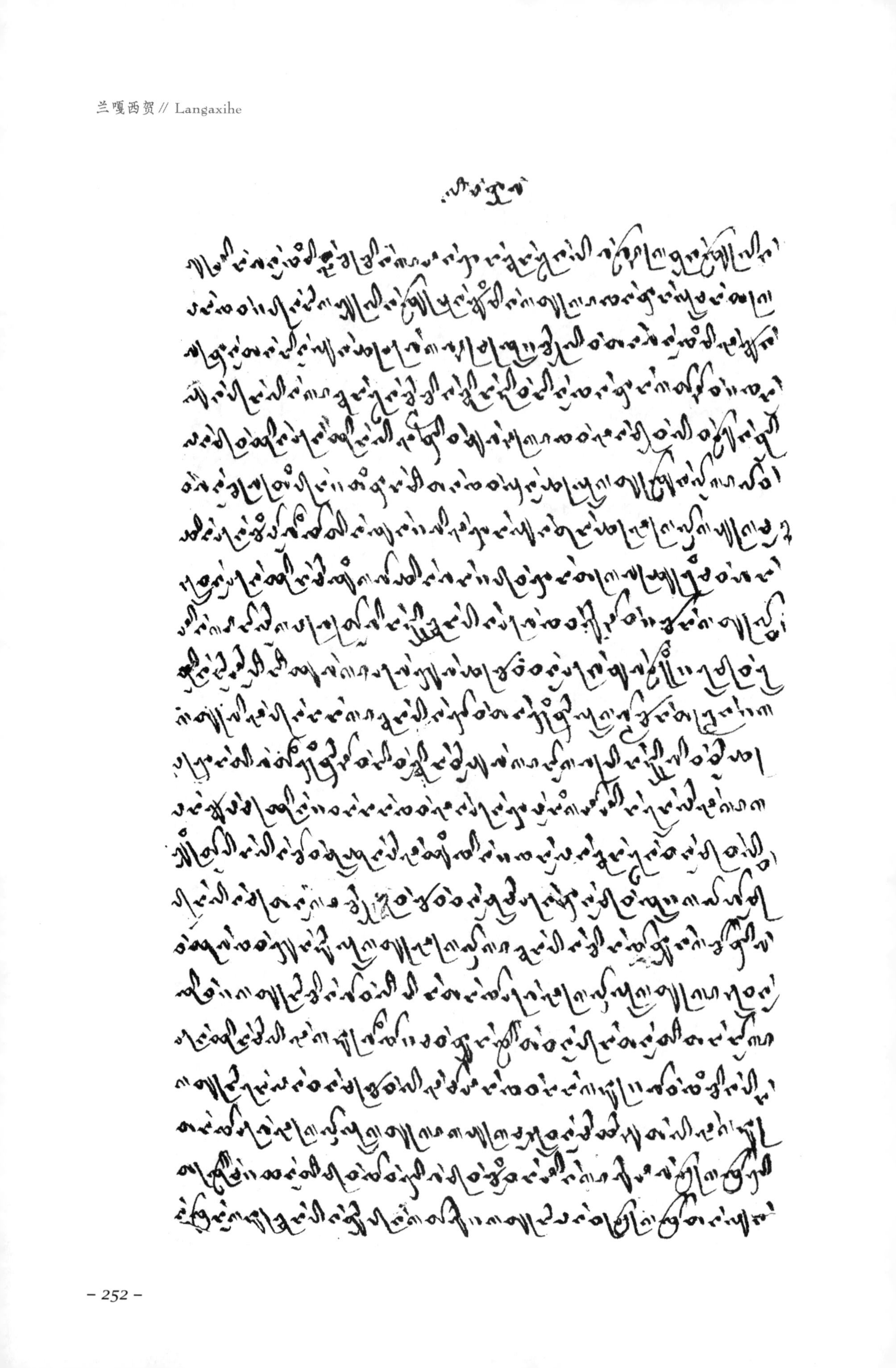

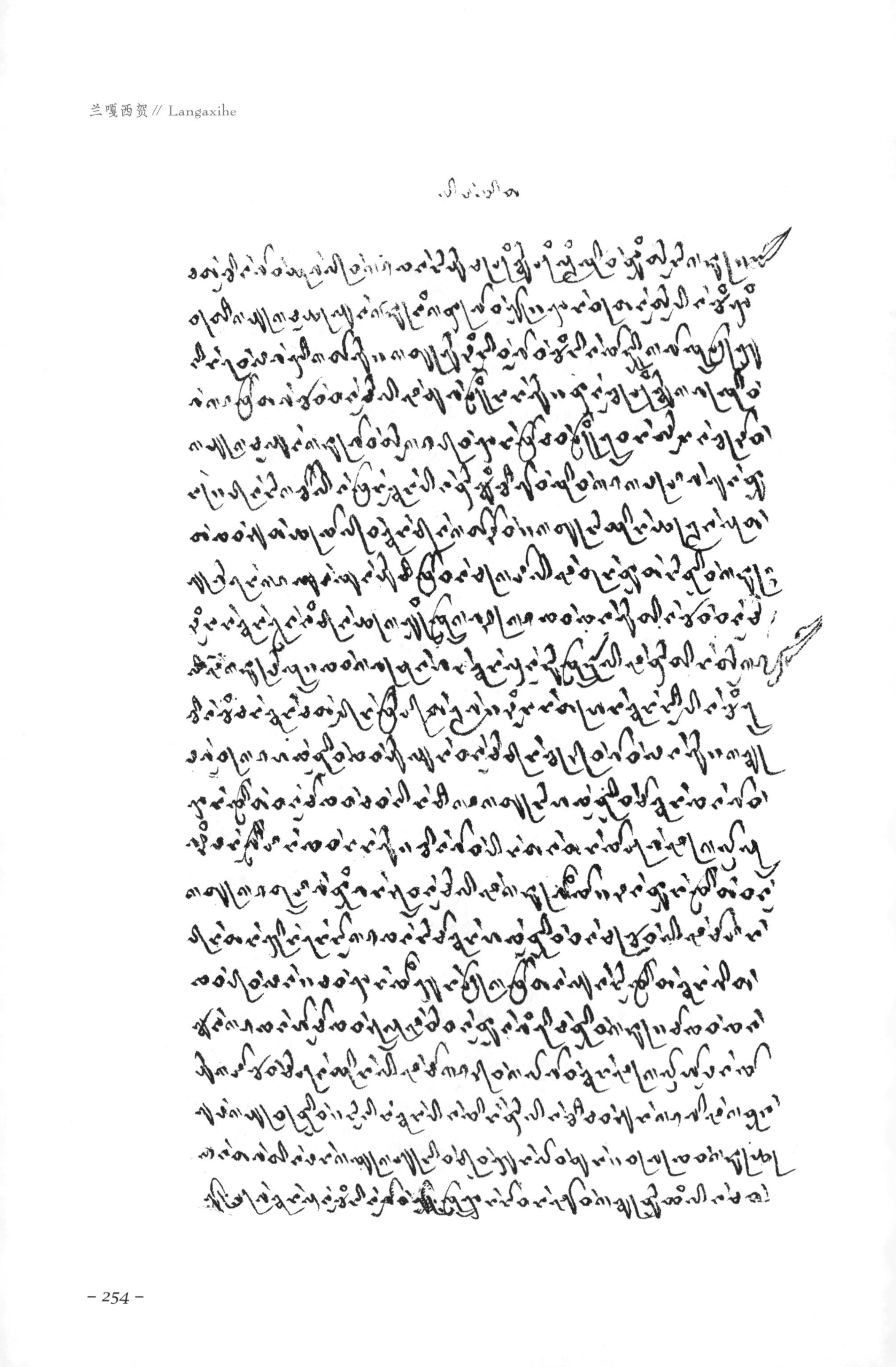

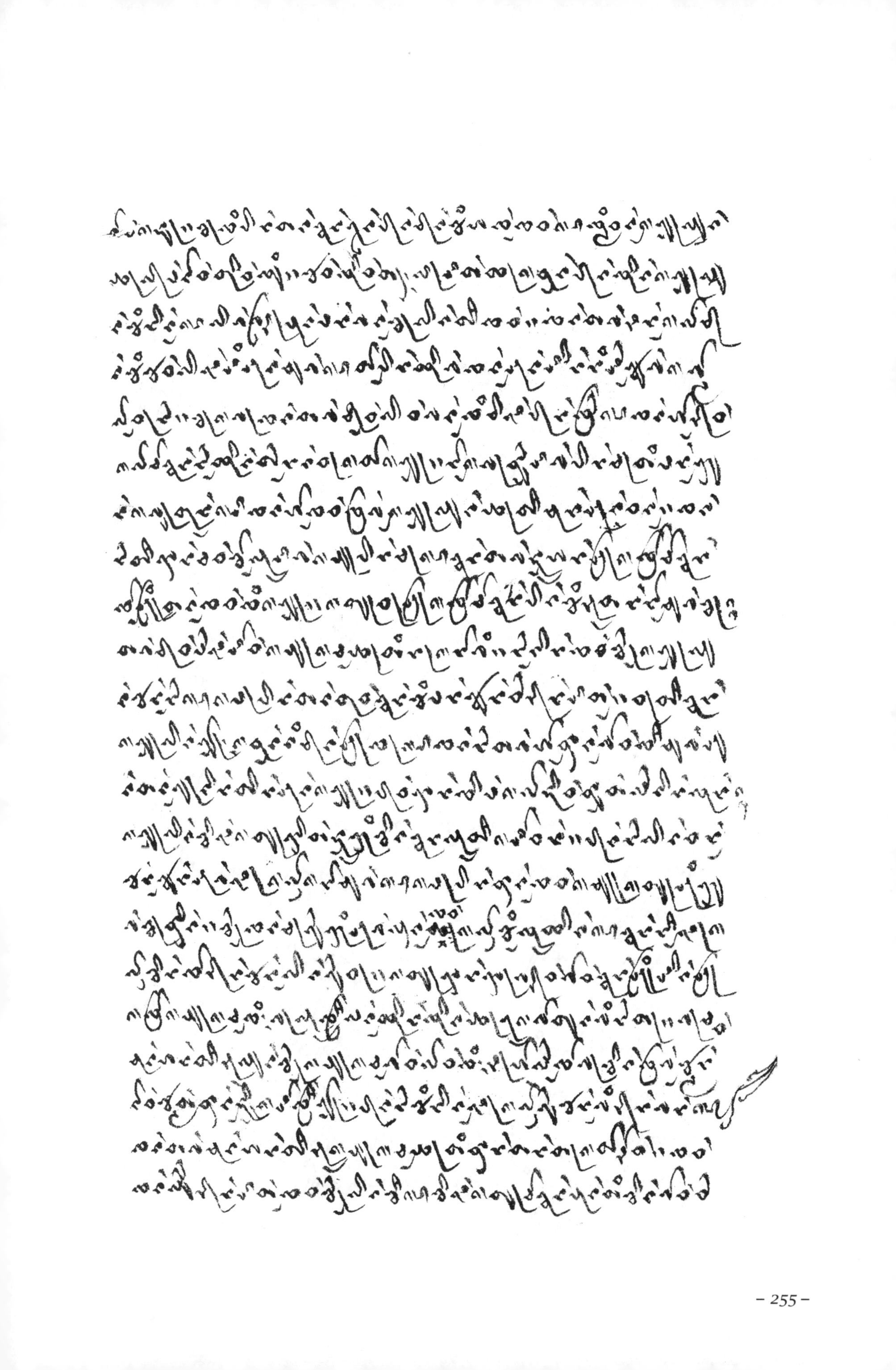

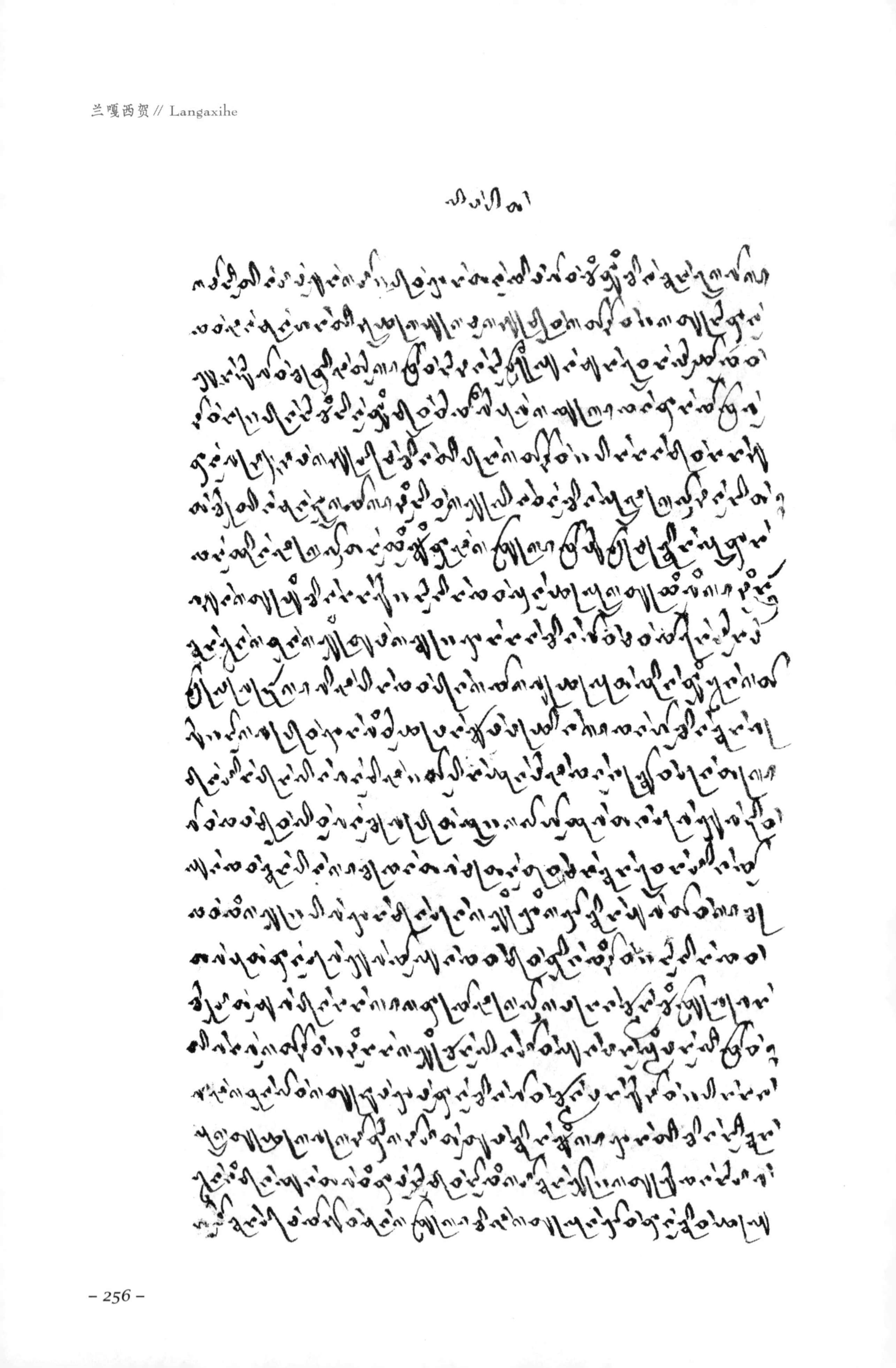

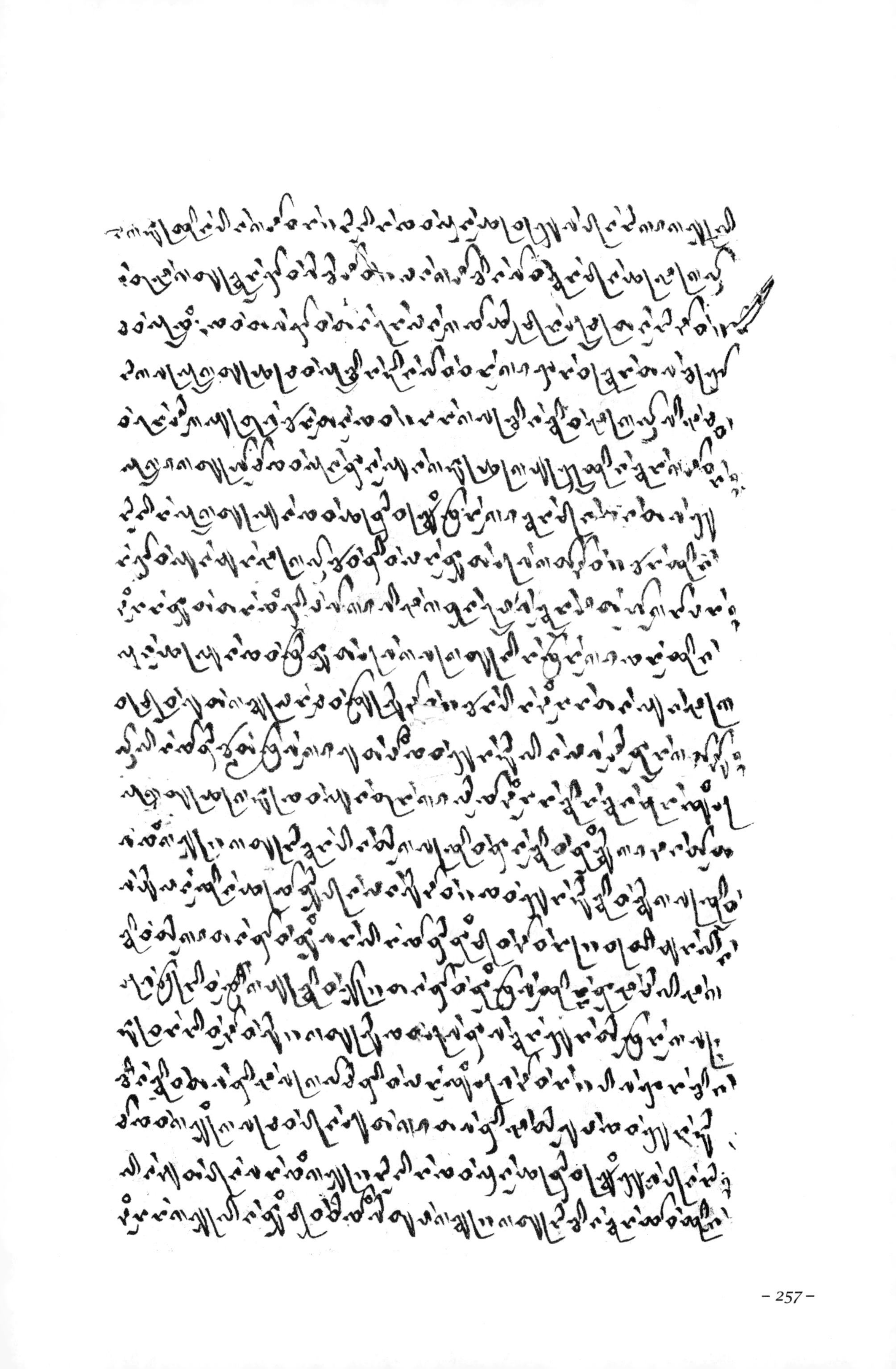

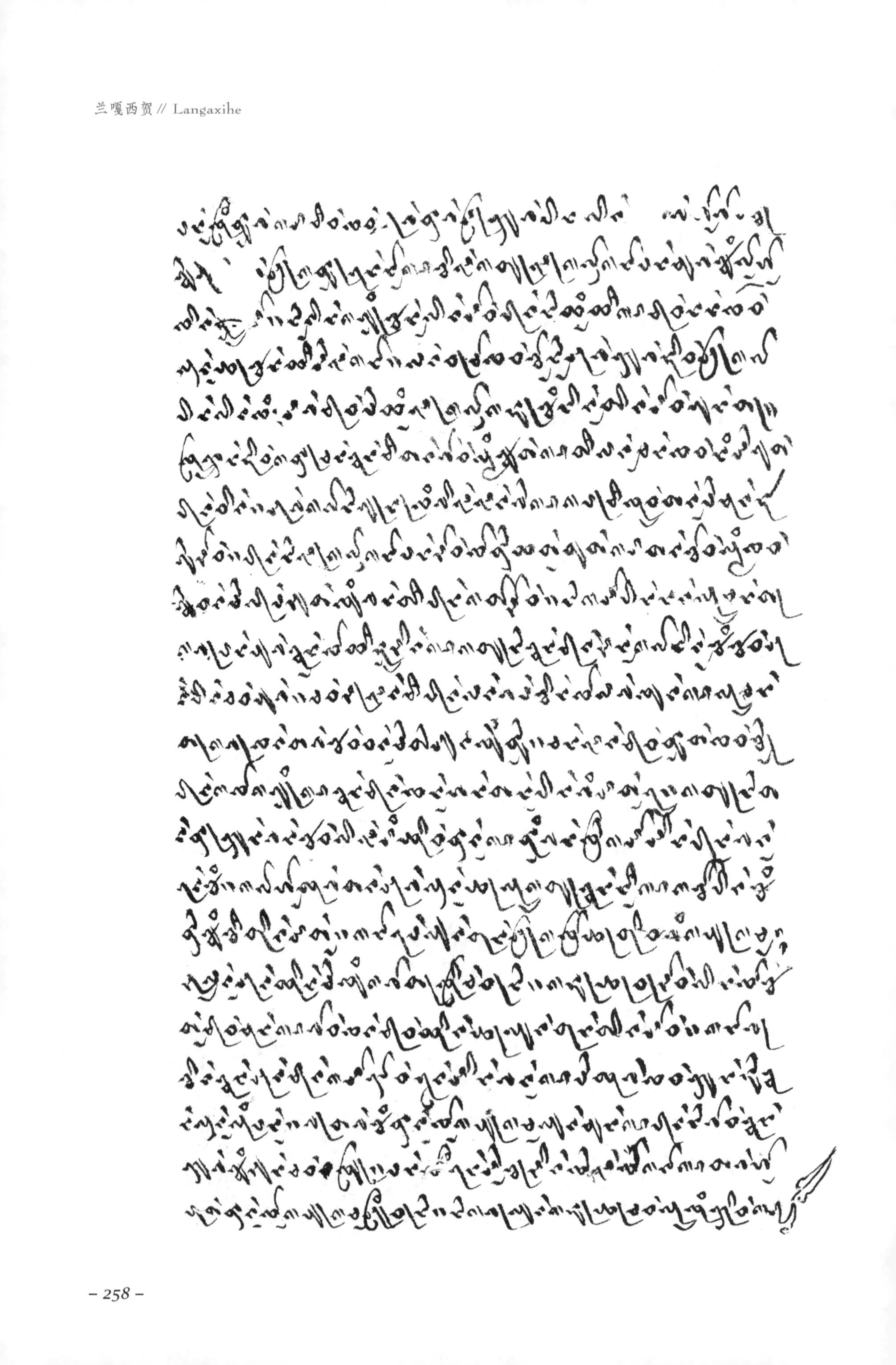

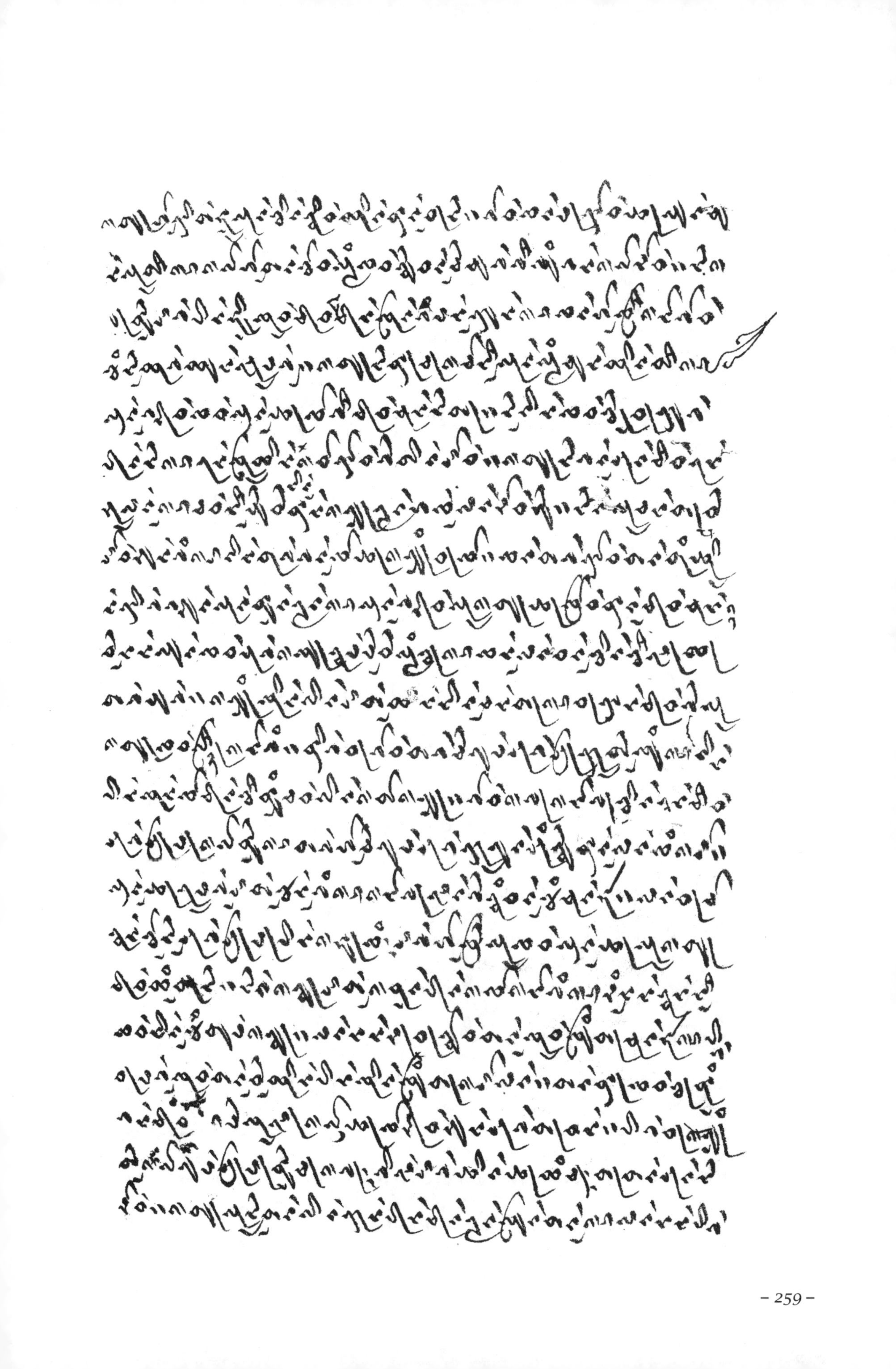

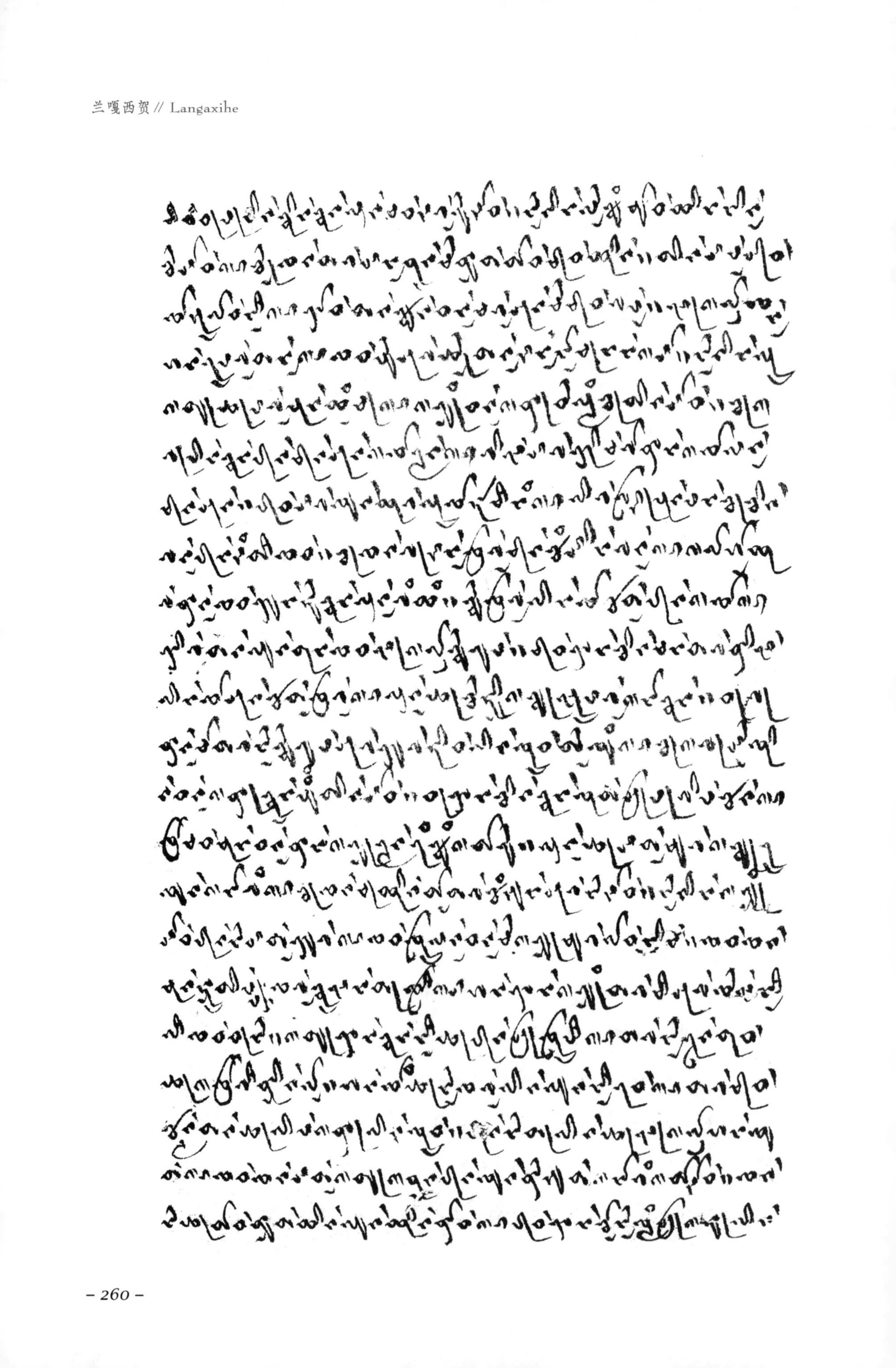

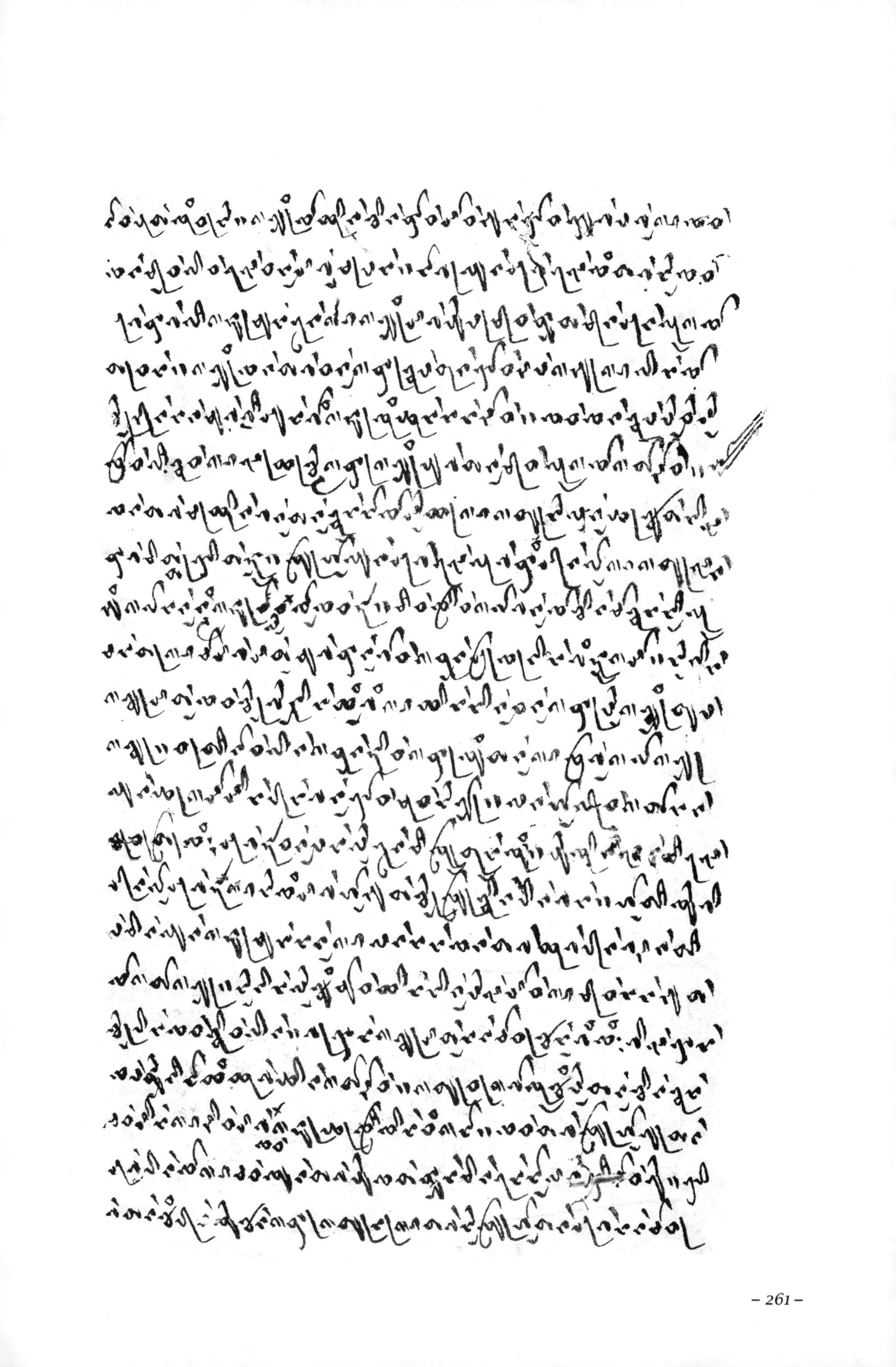

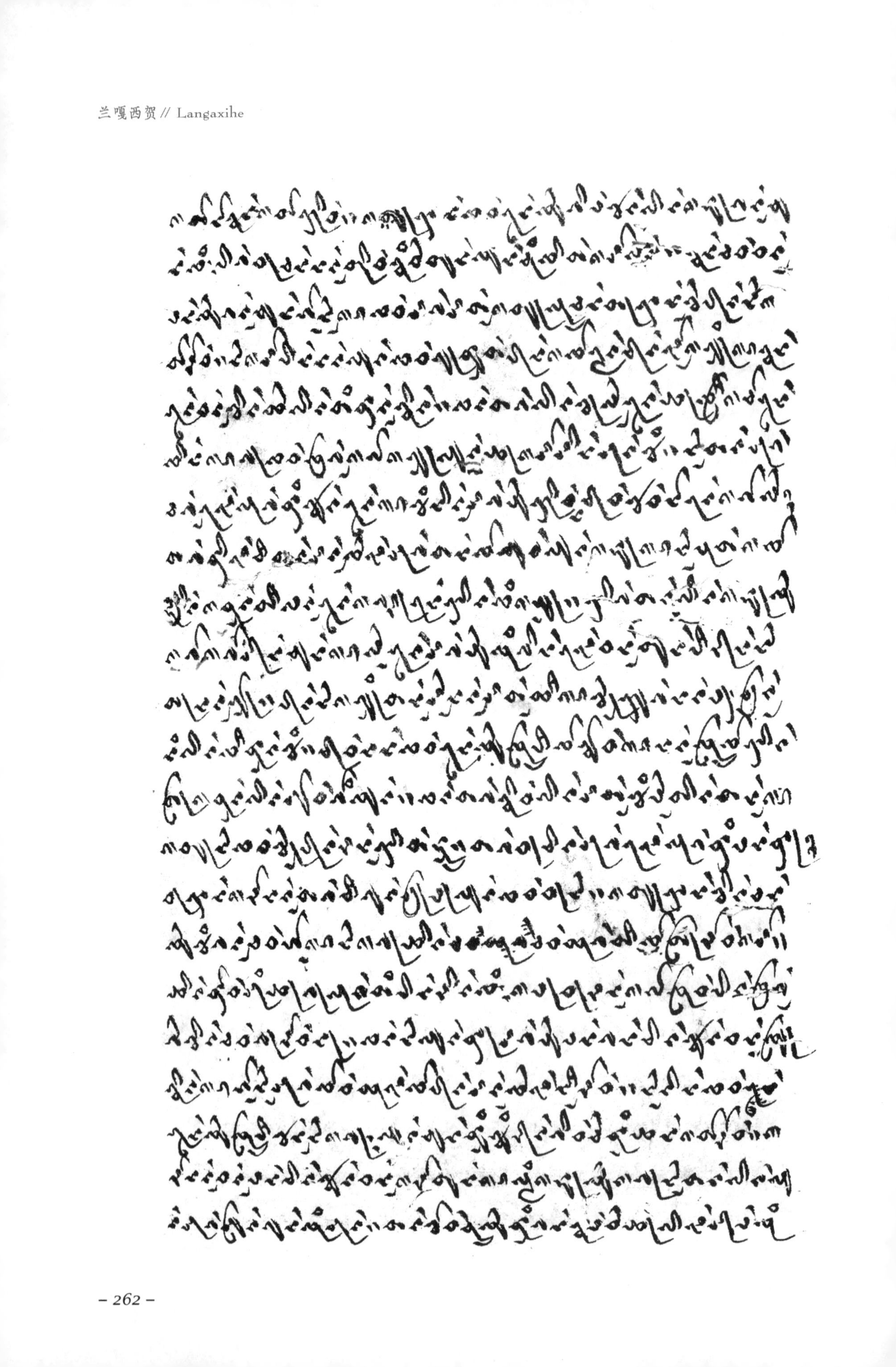

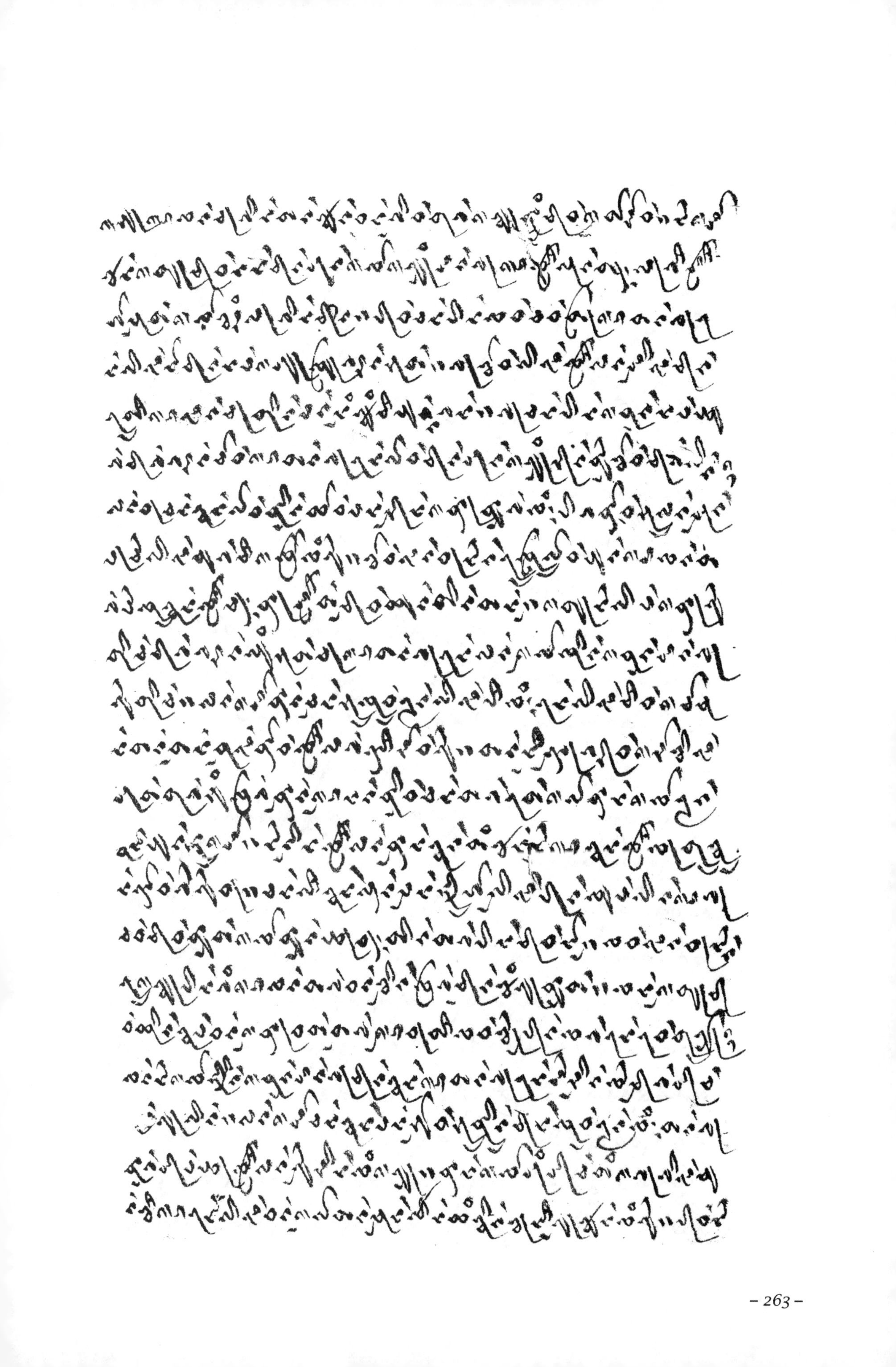

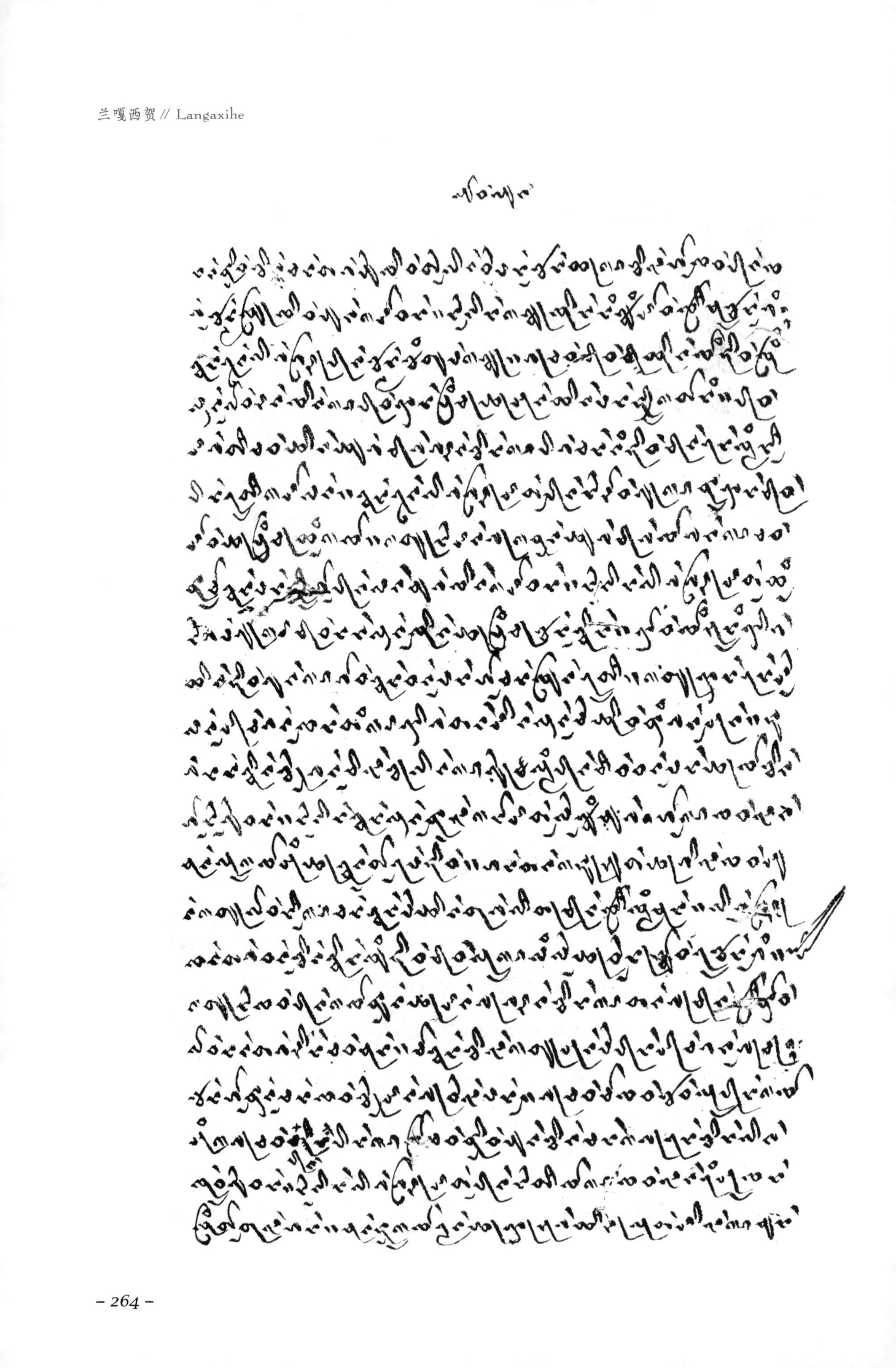

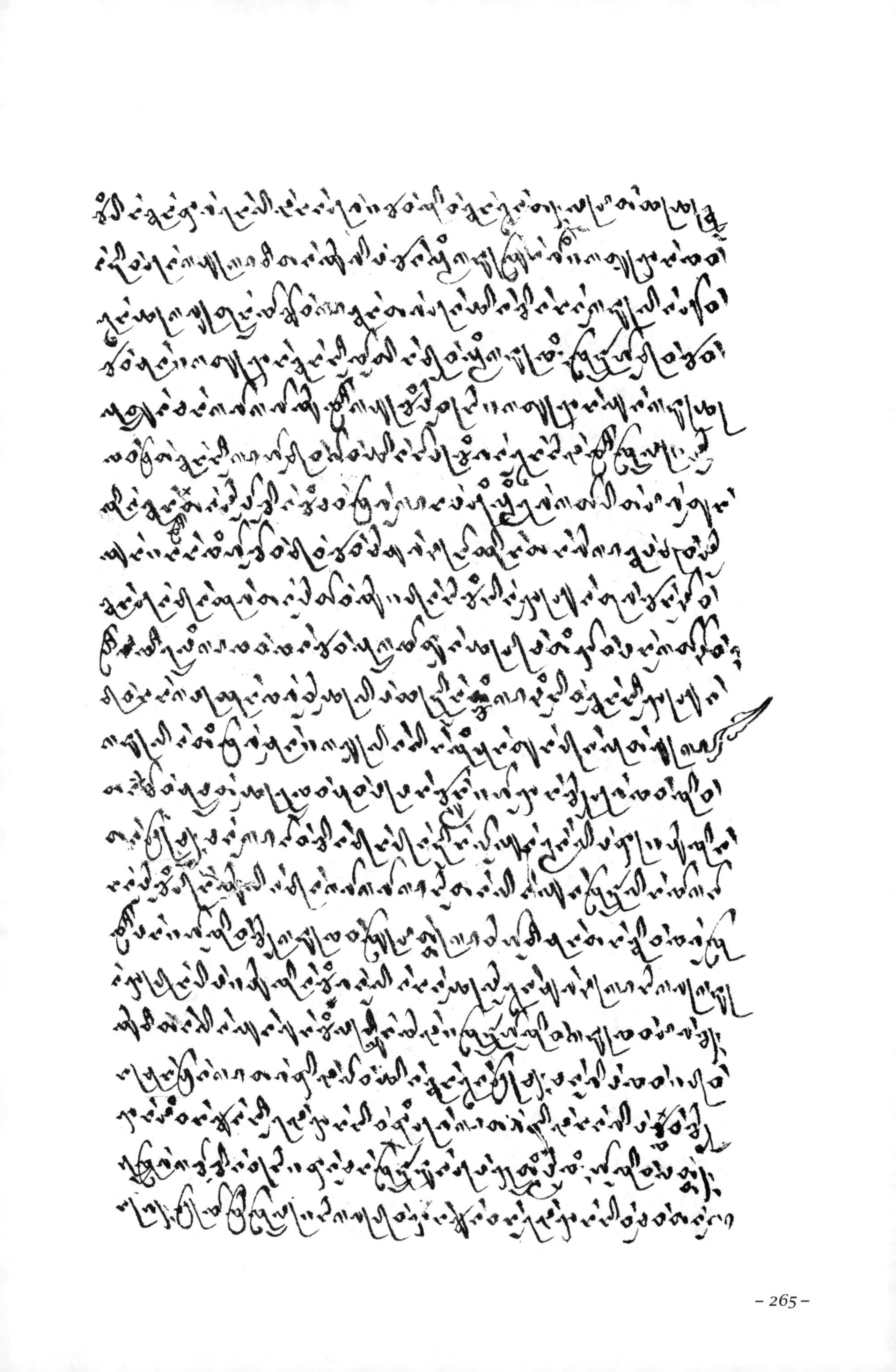

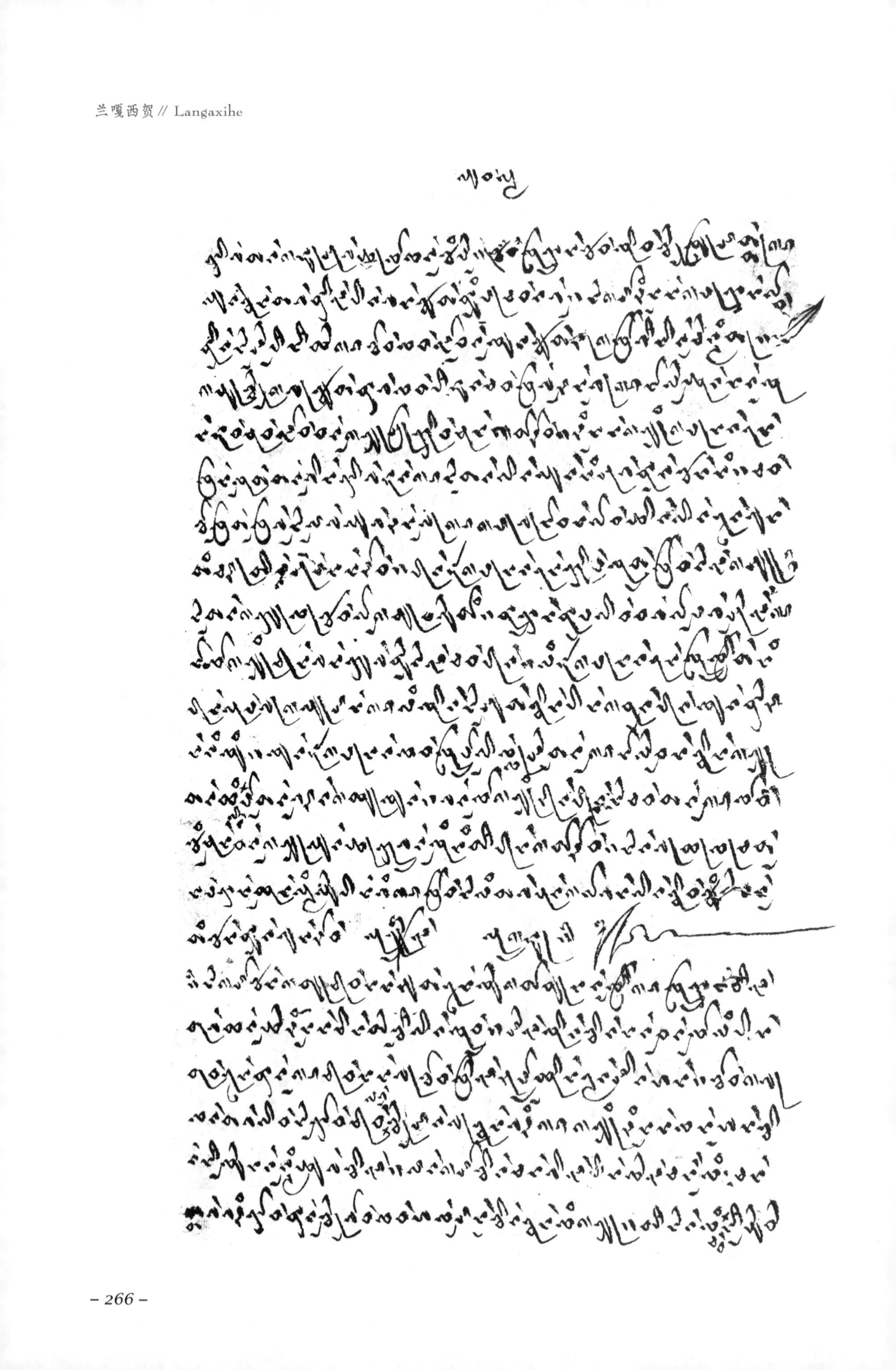

[illegible]

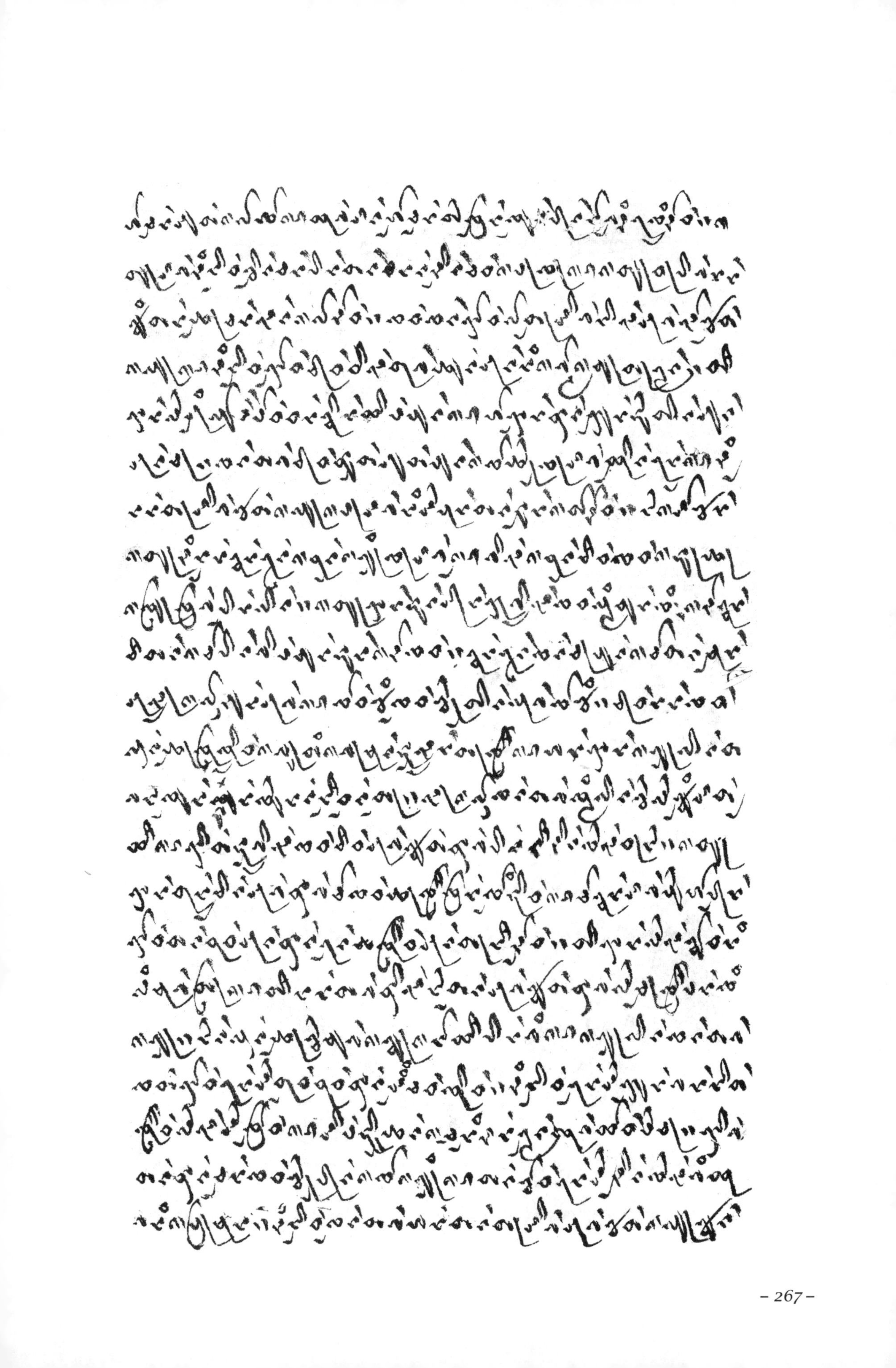

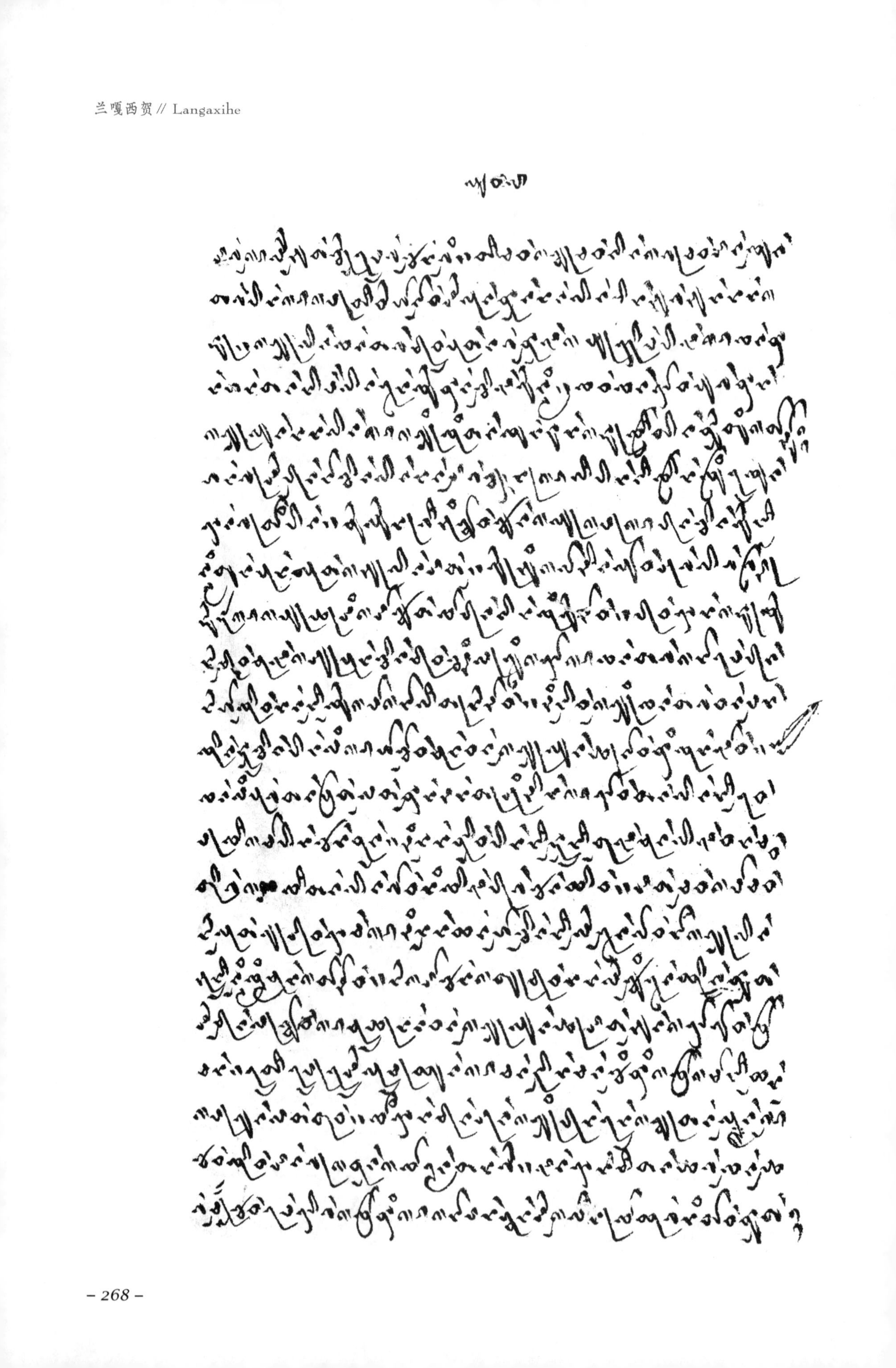

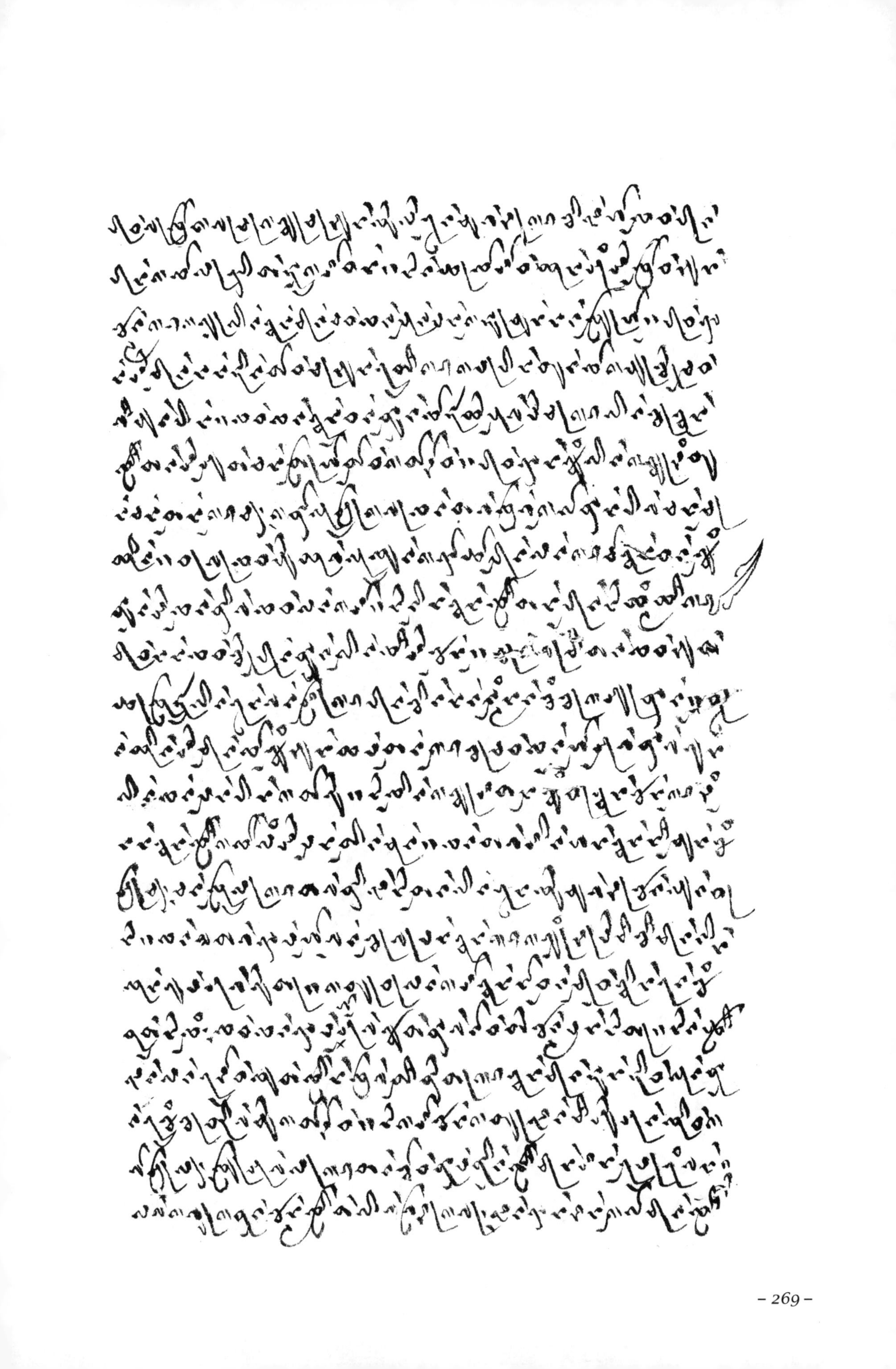

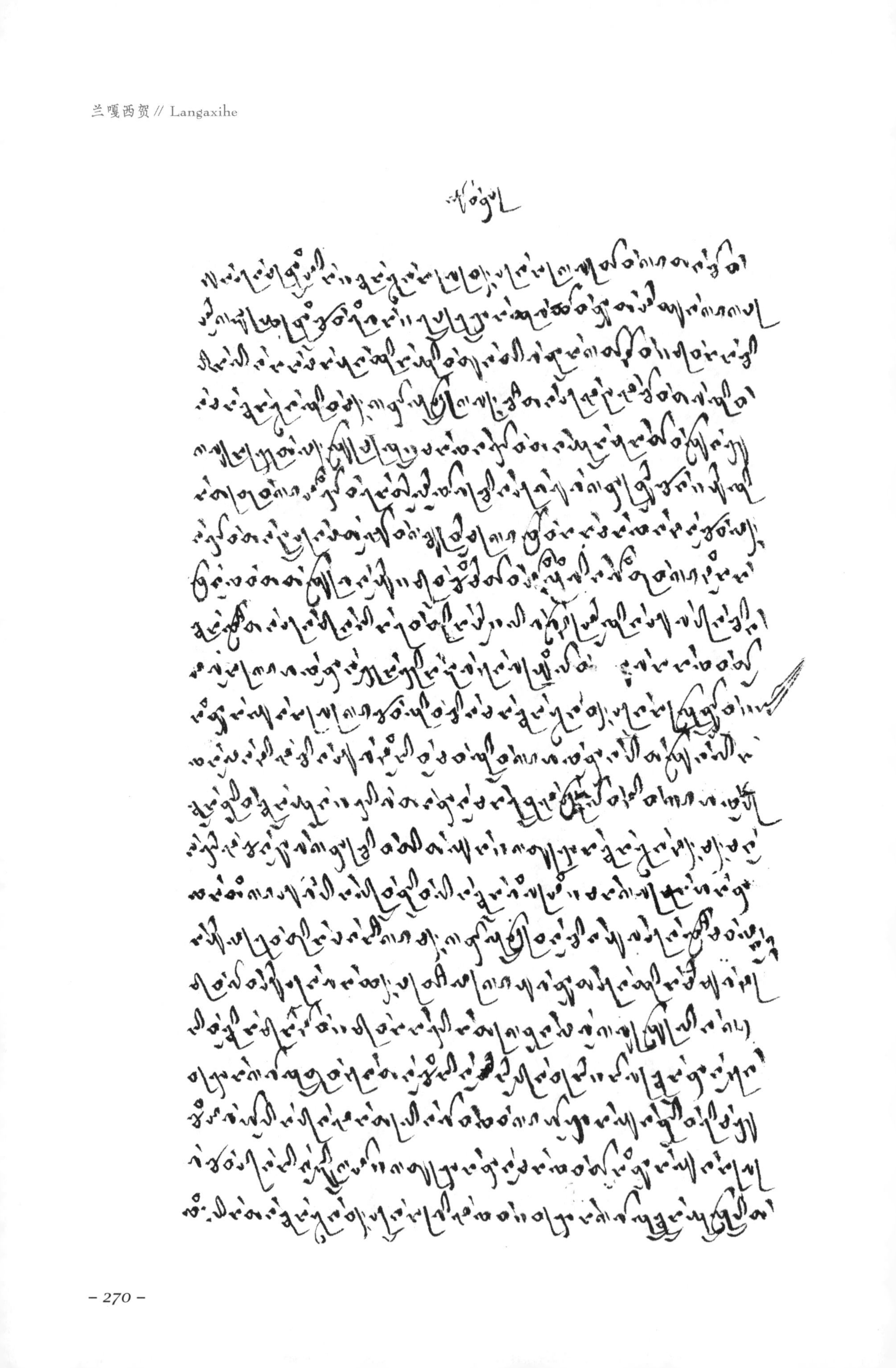

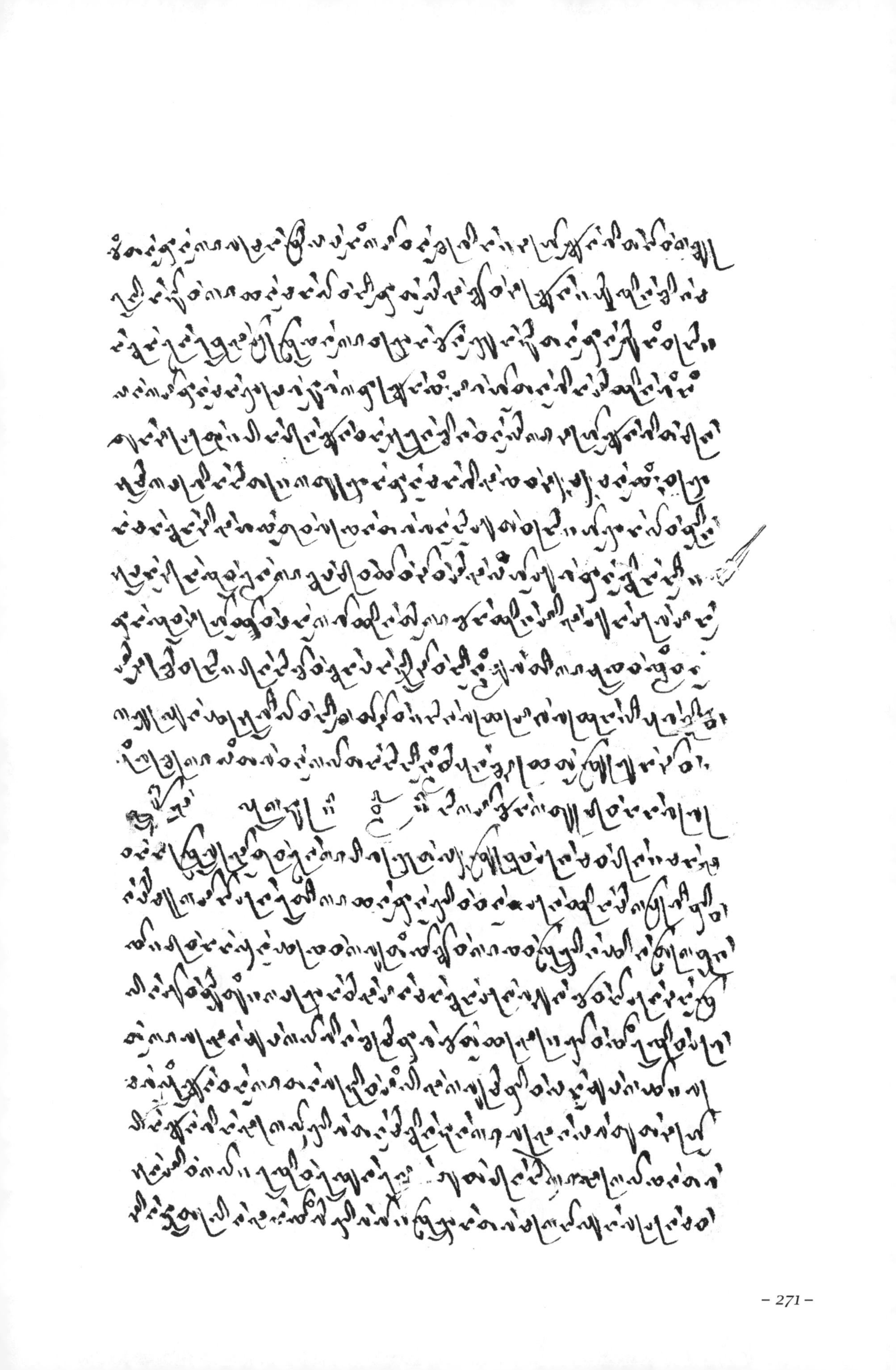

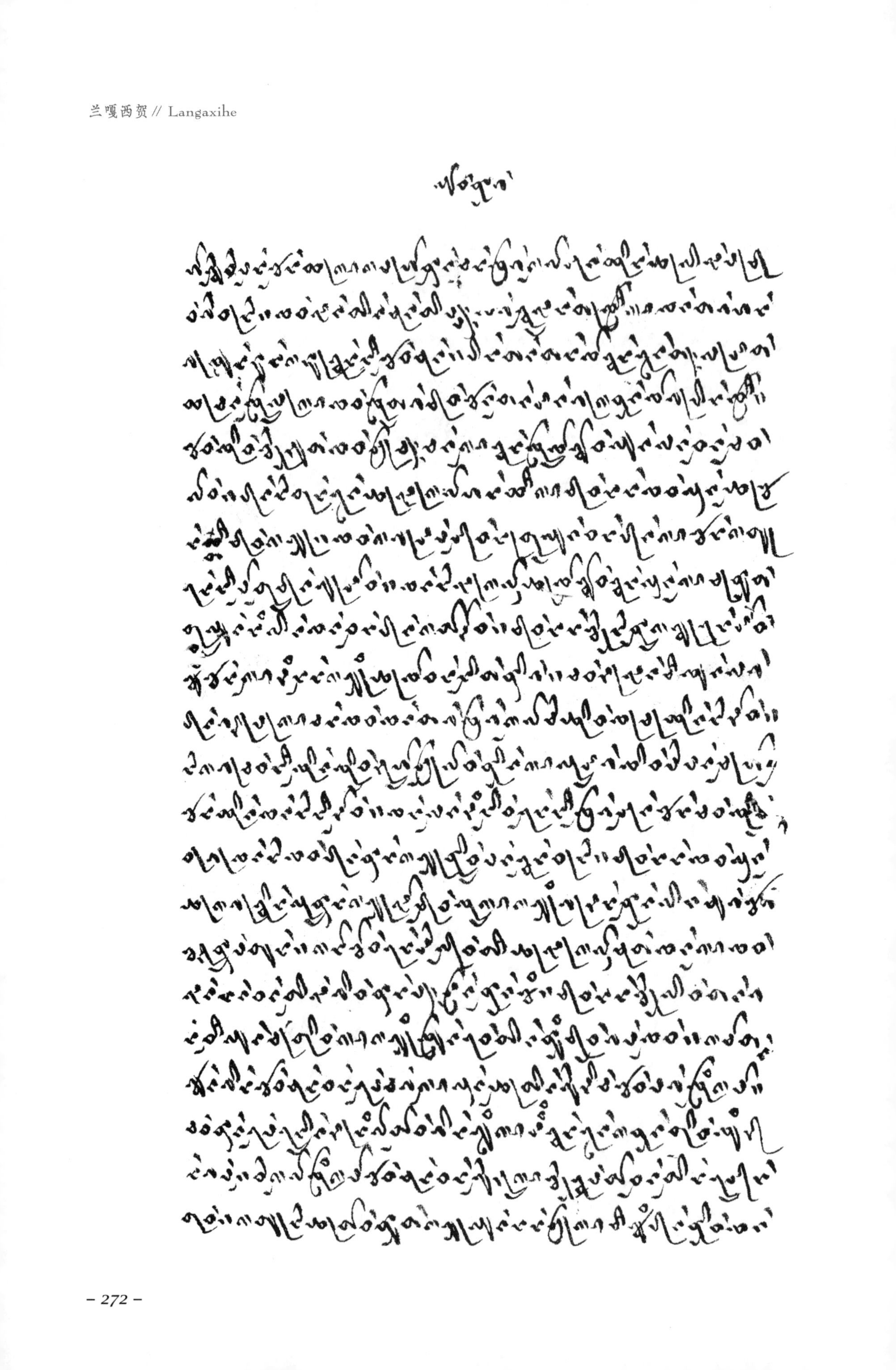

[illegible]

[illegible]

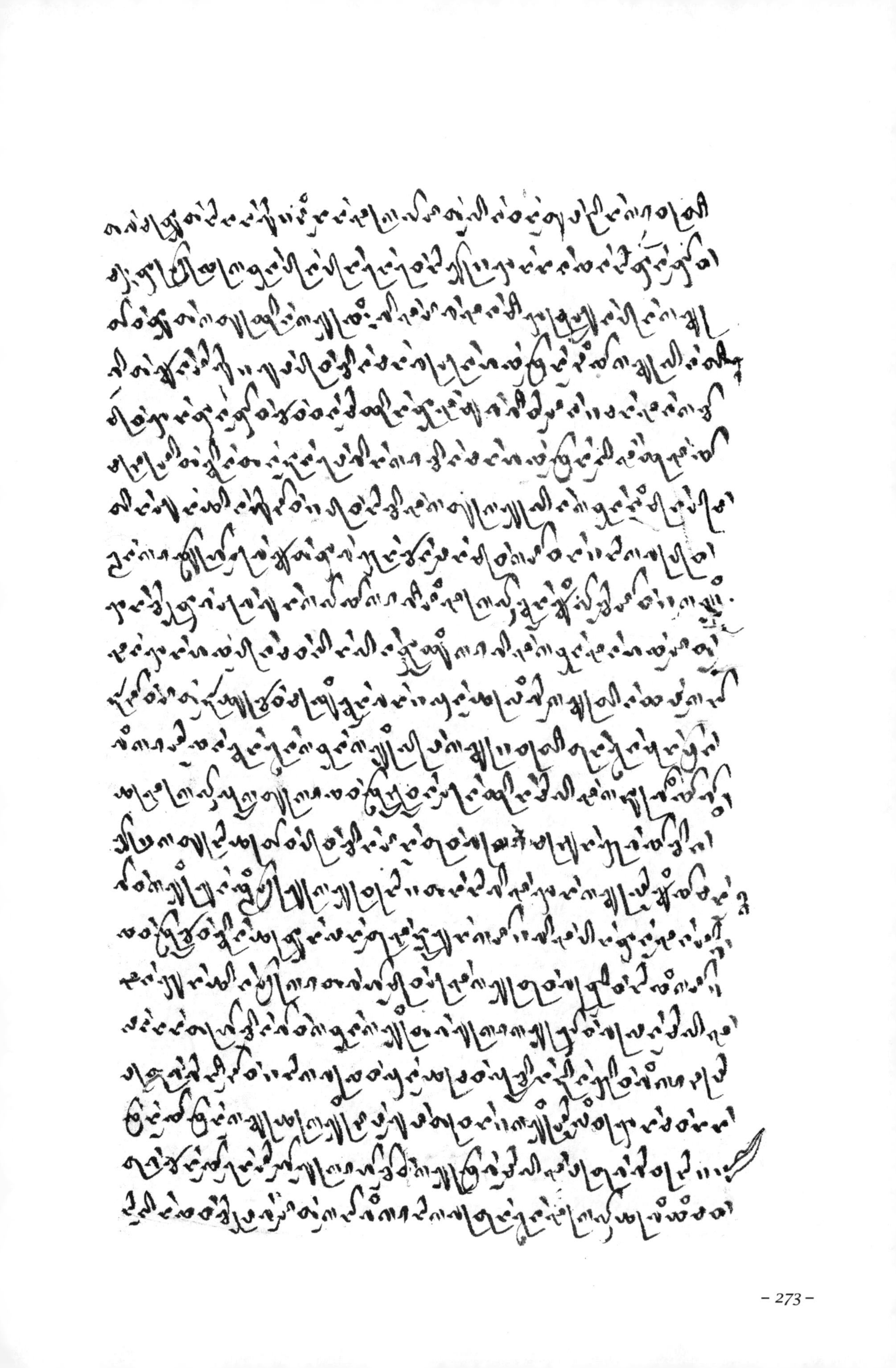

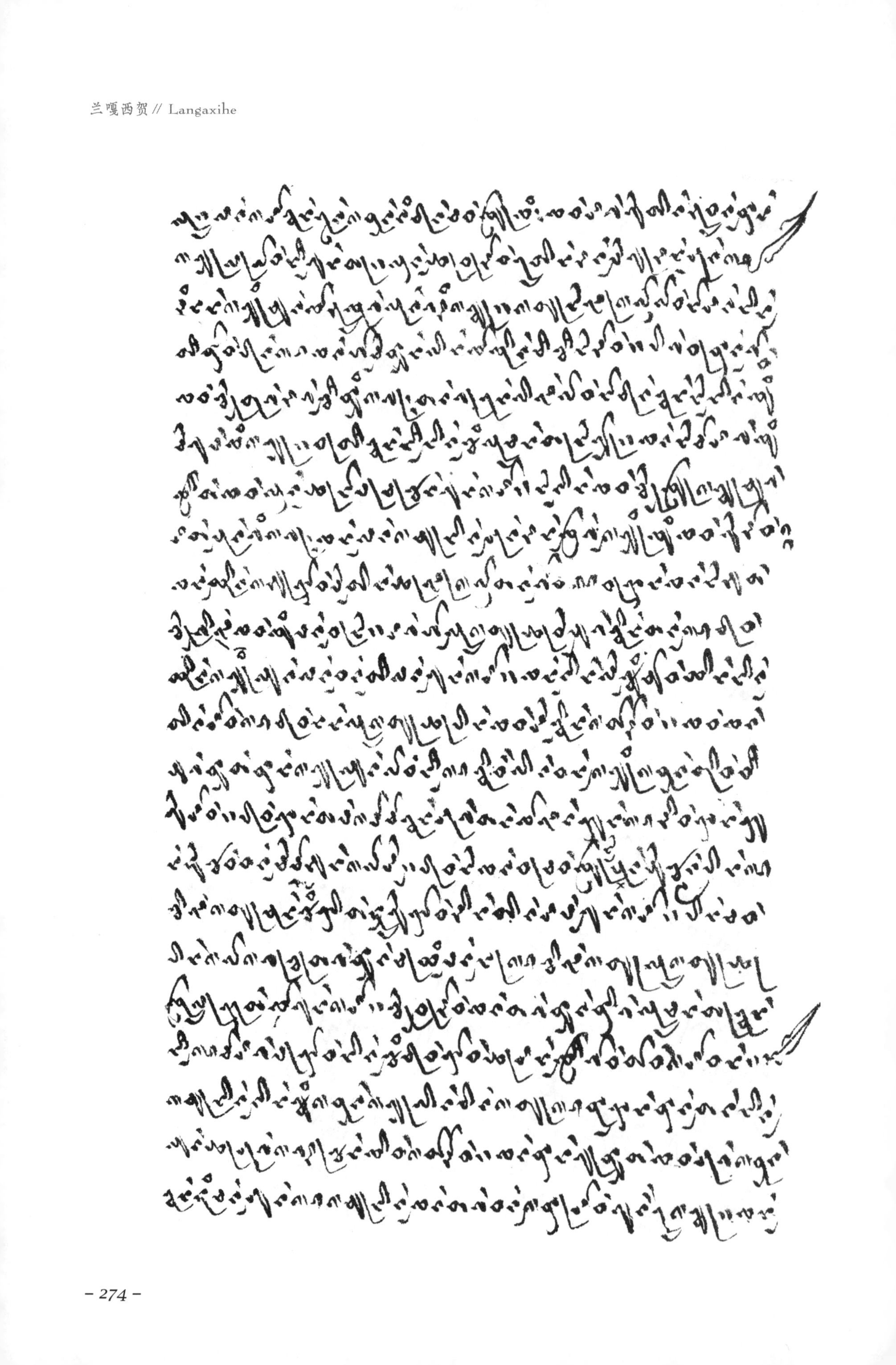

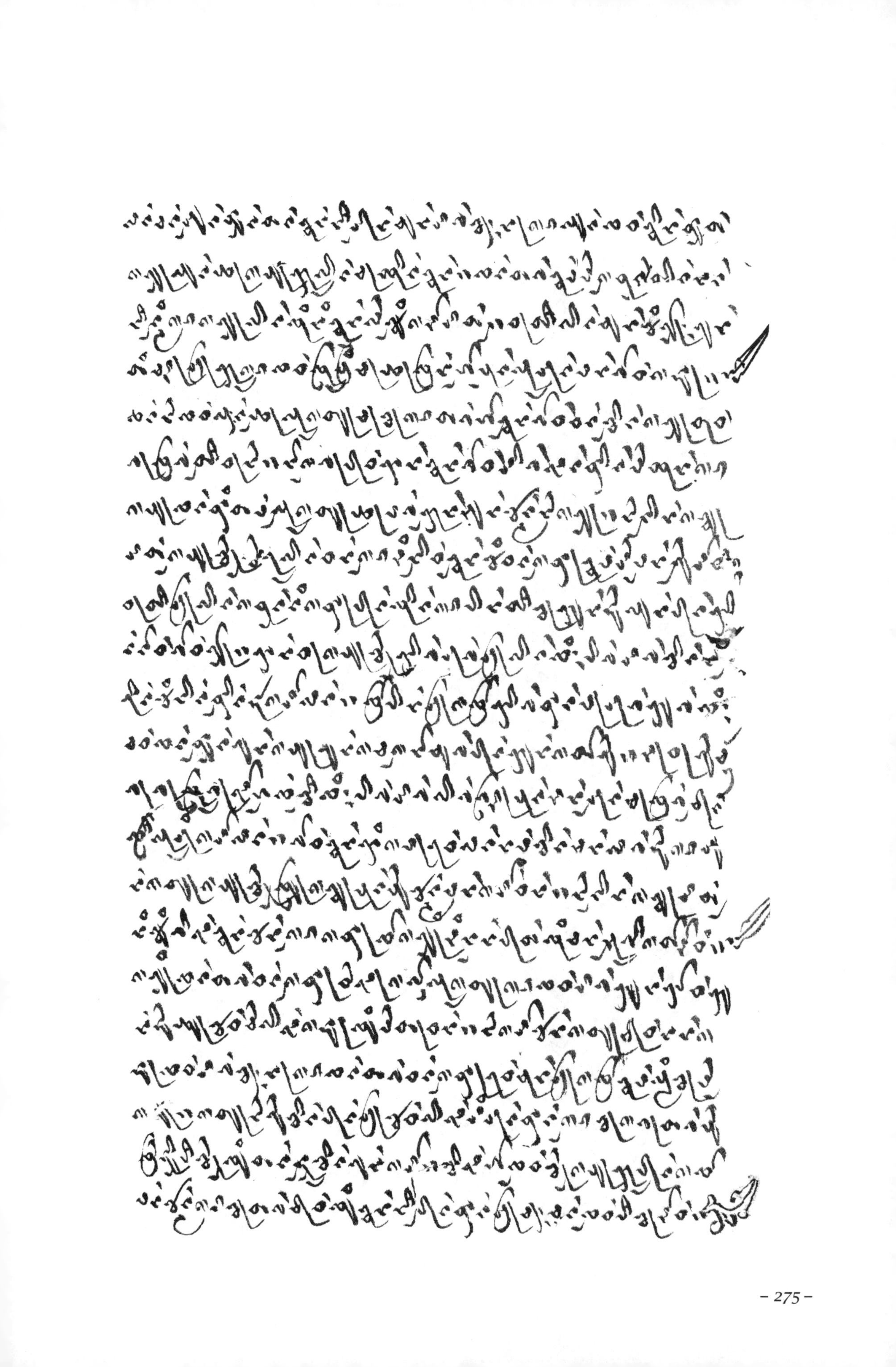

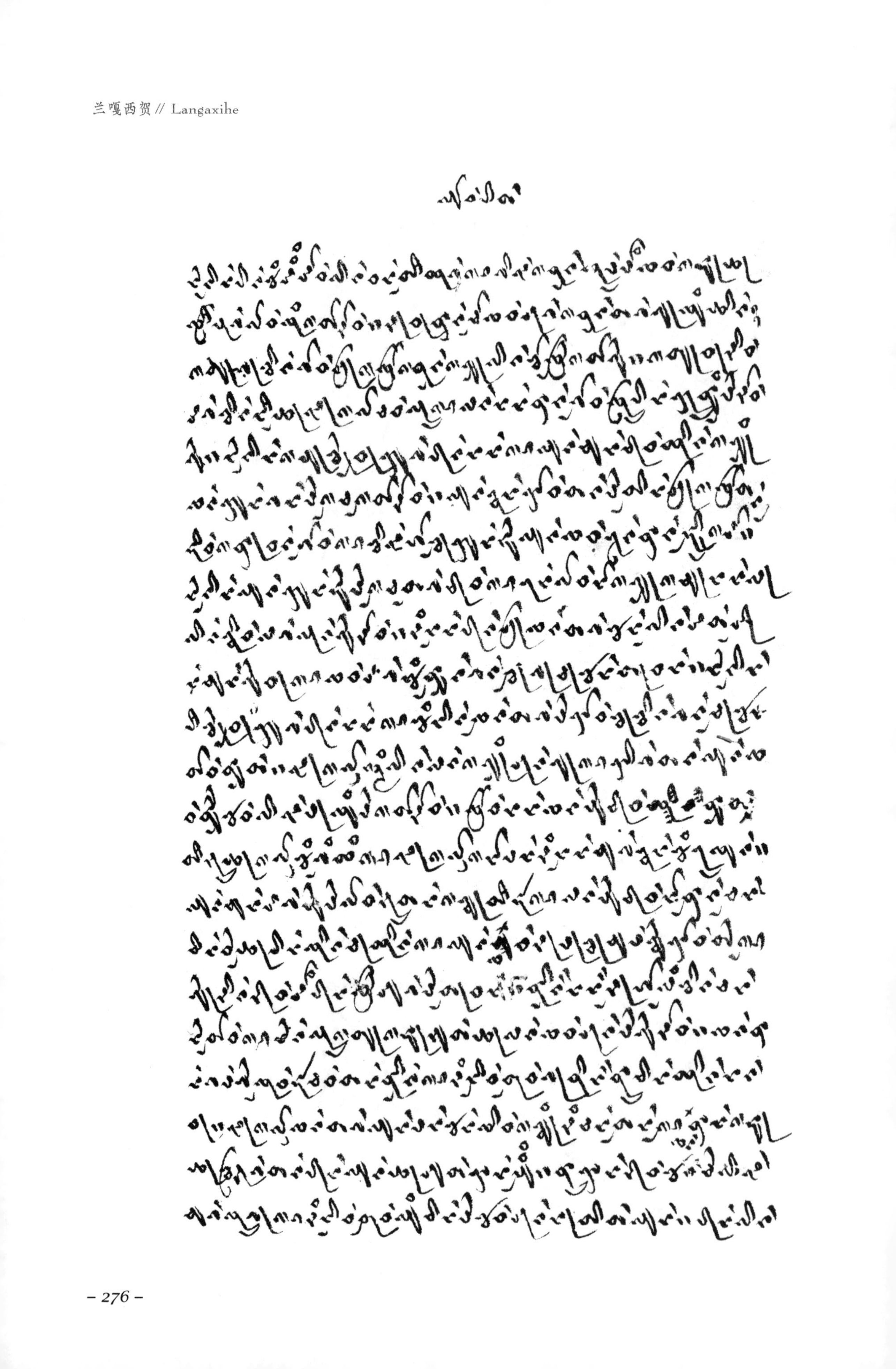

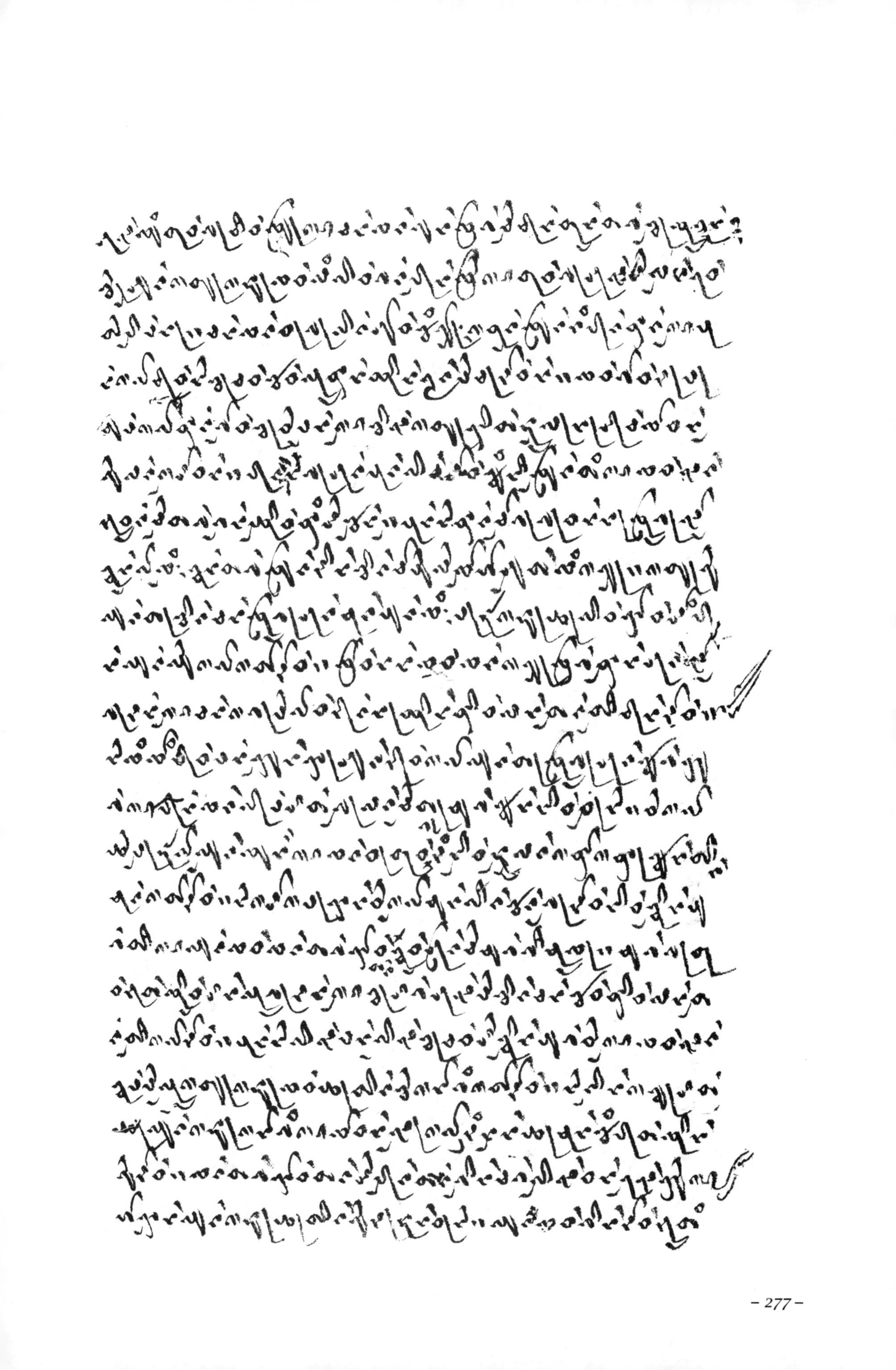

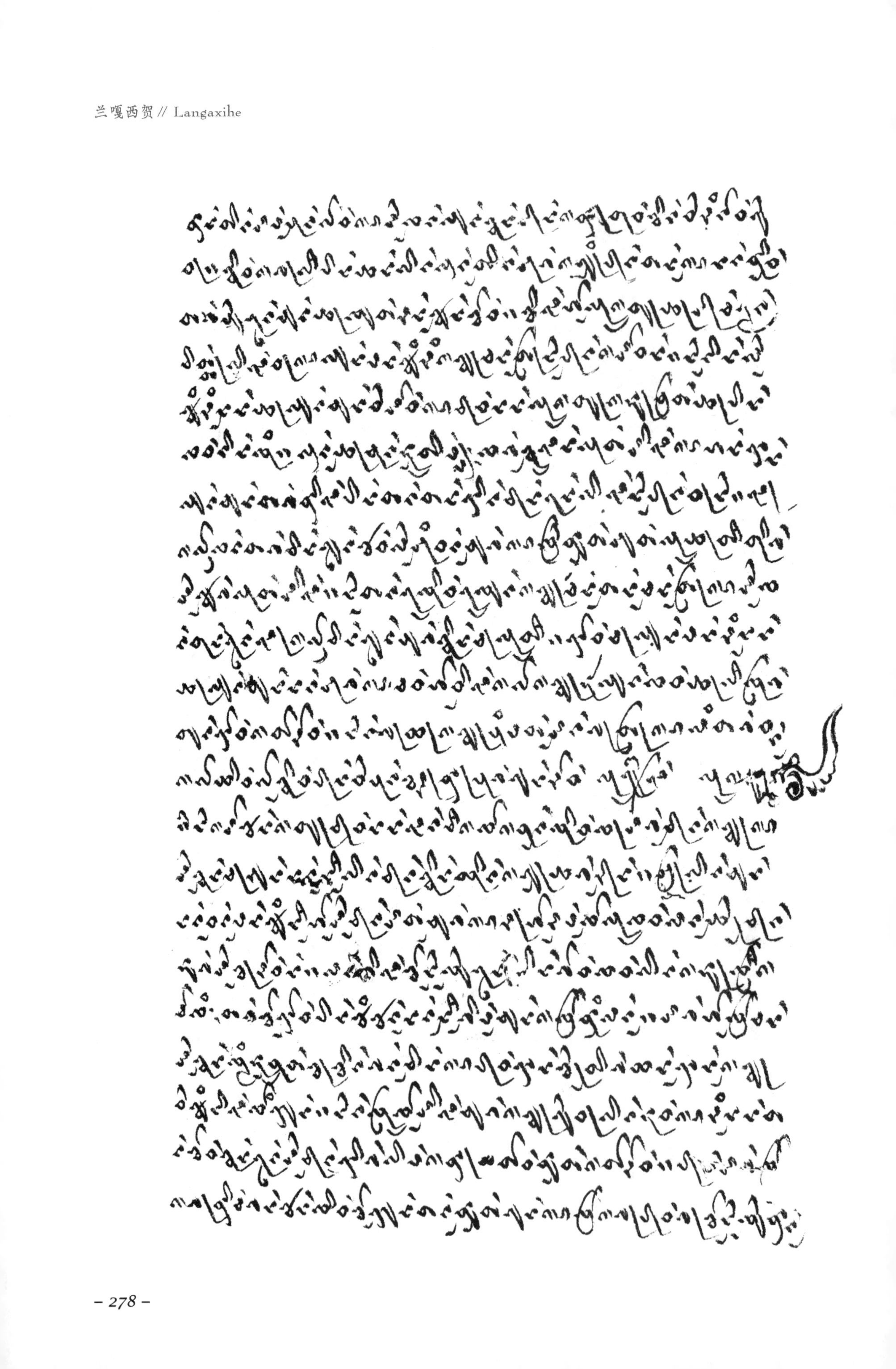

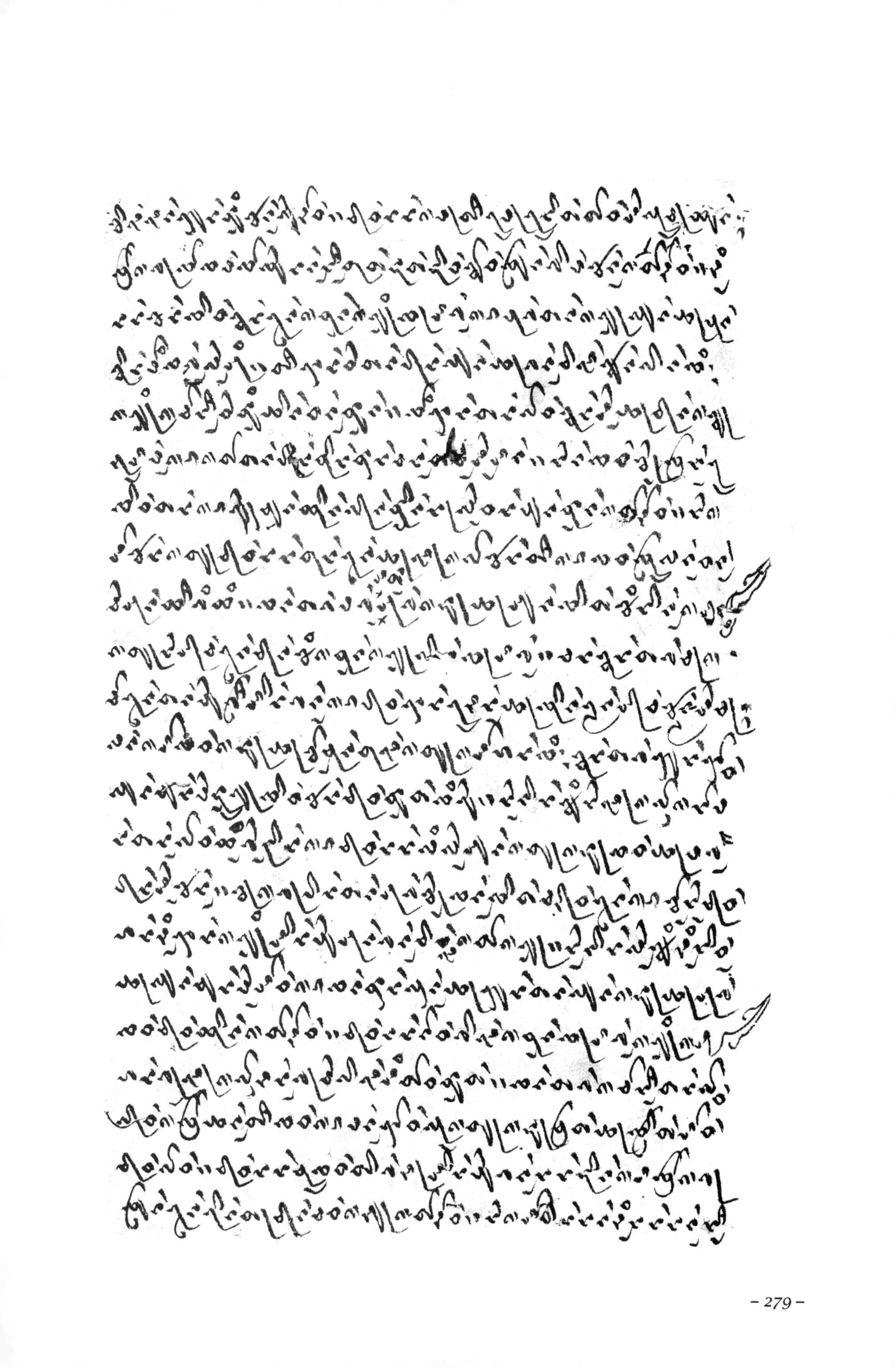

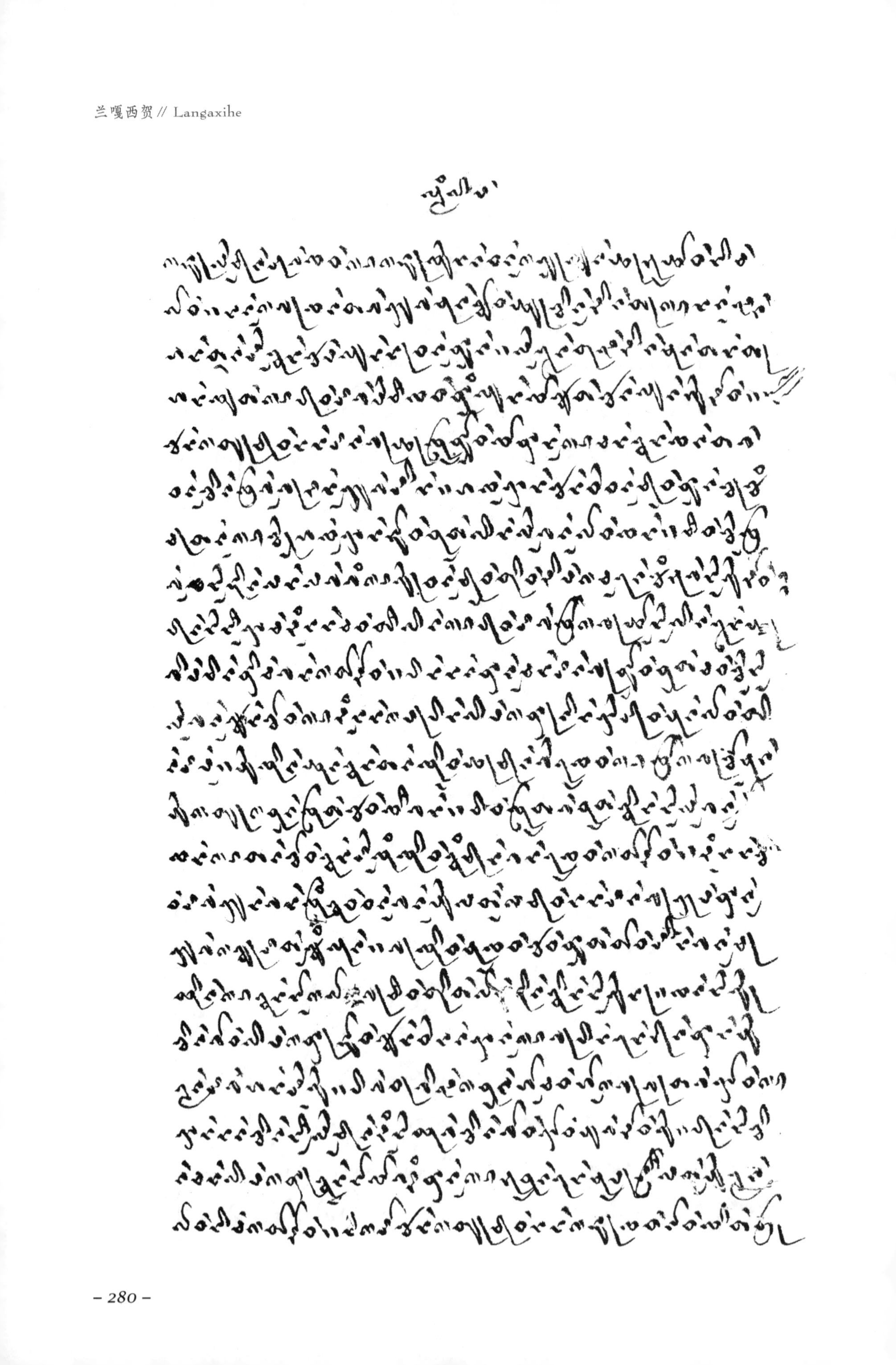

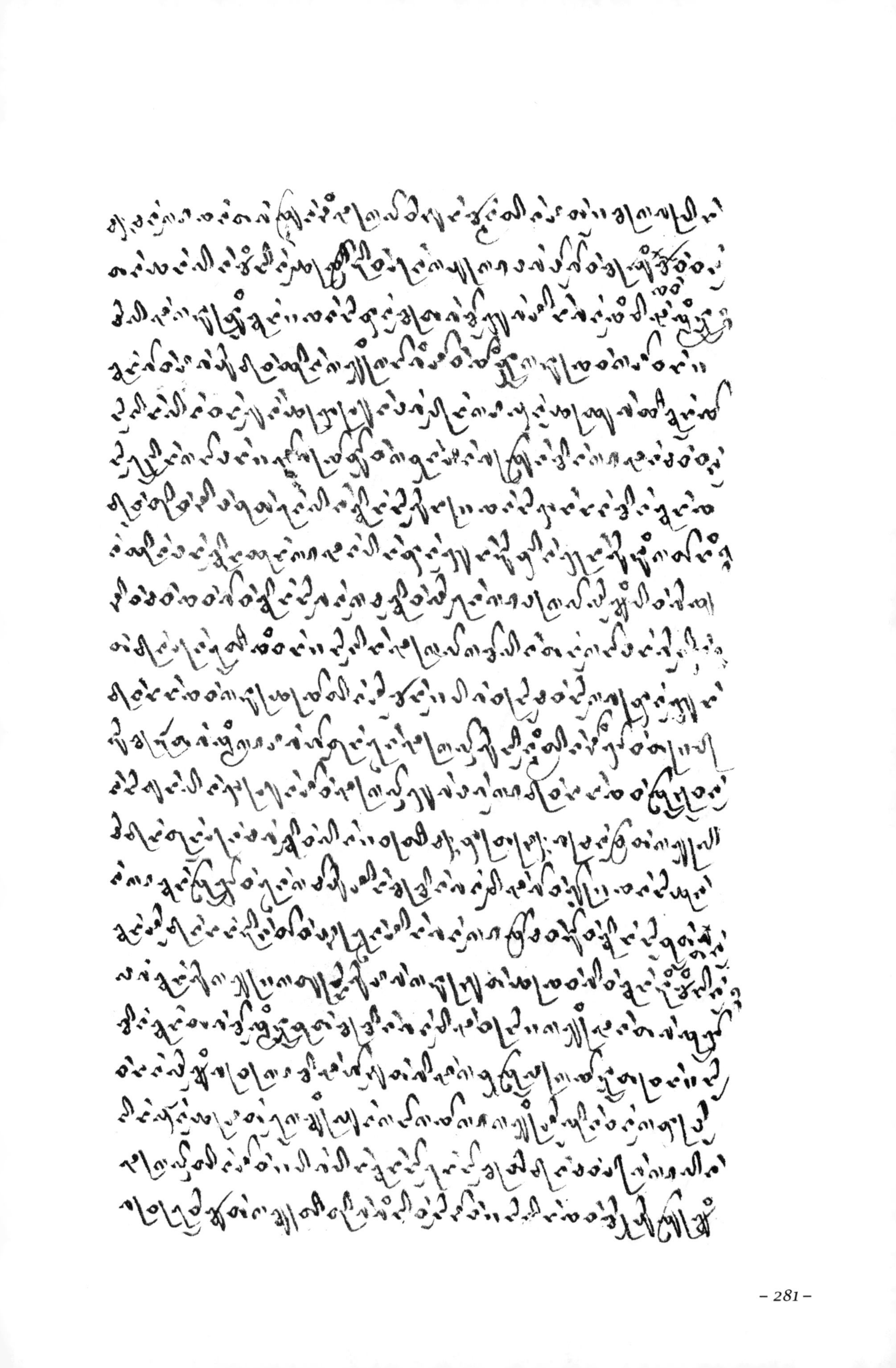

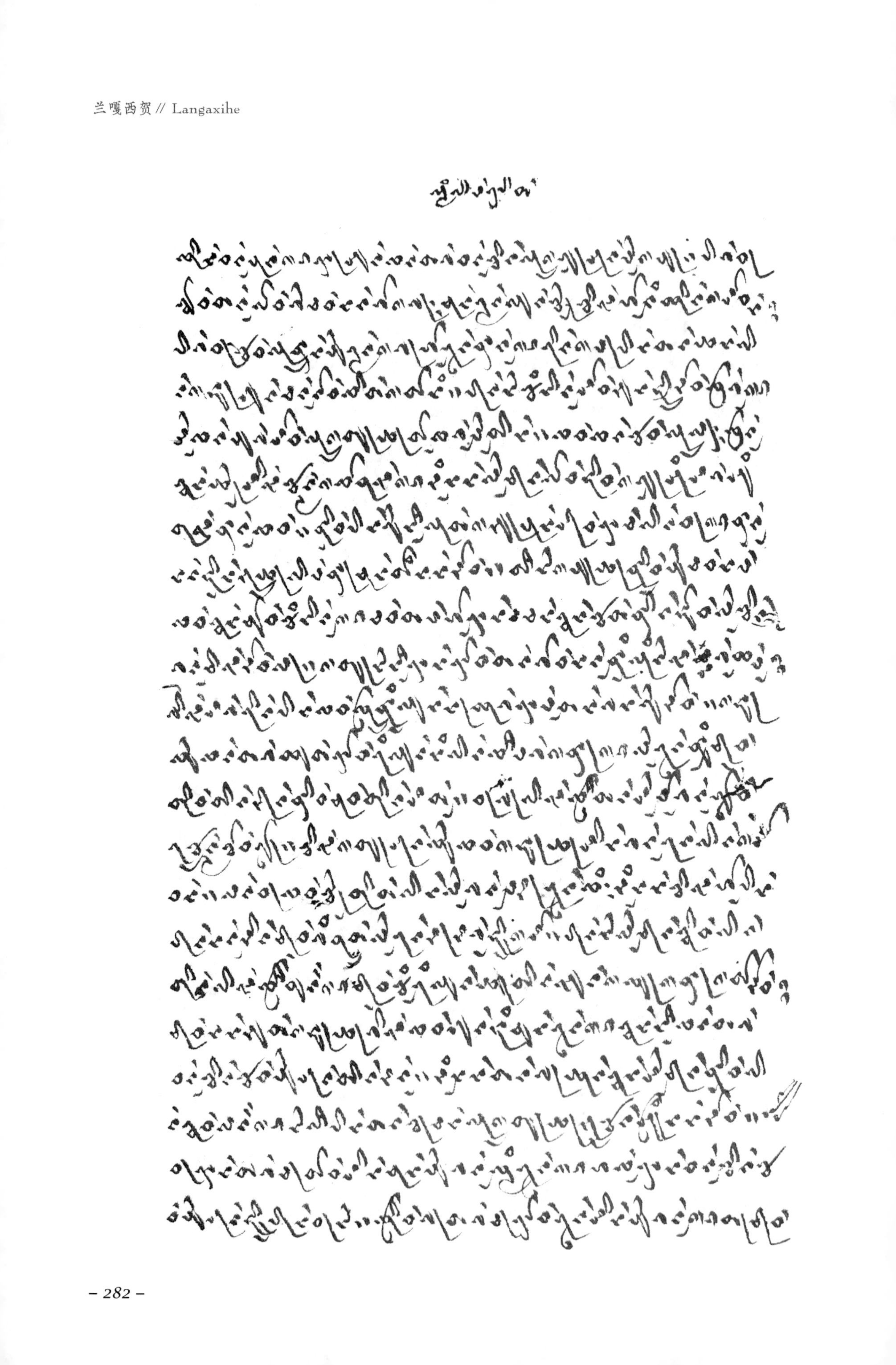

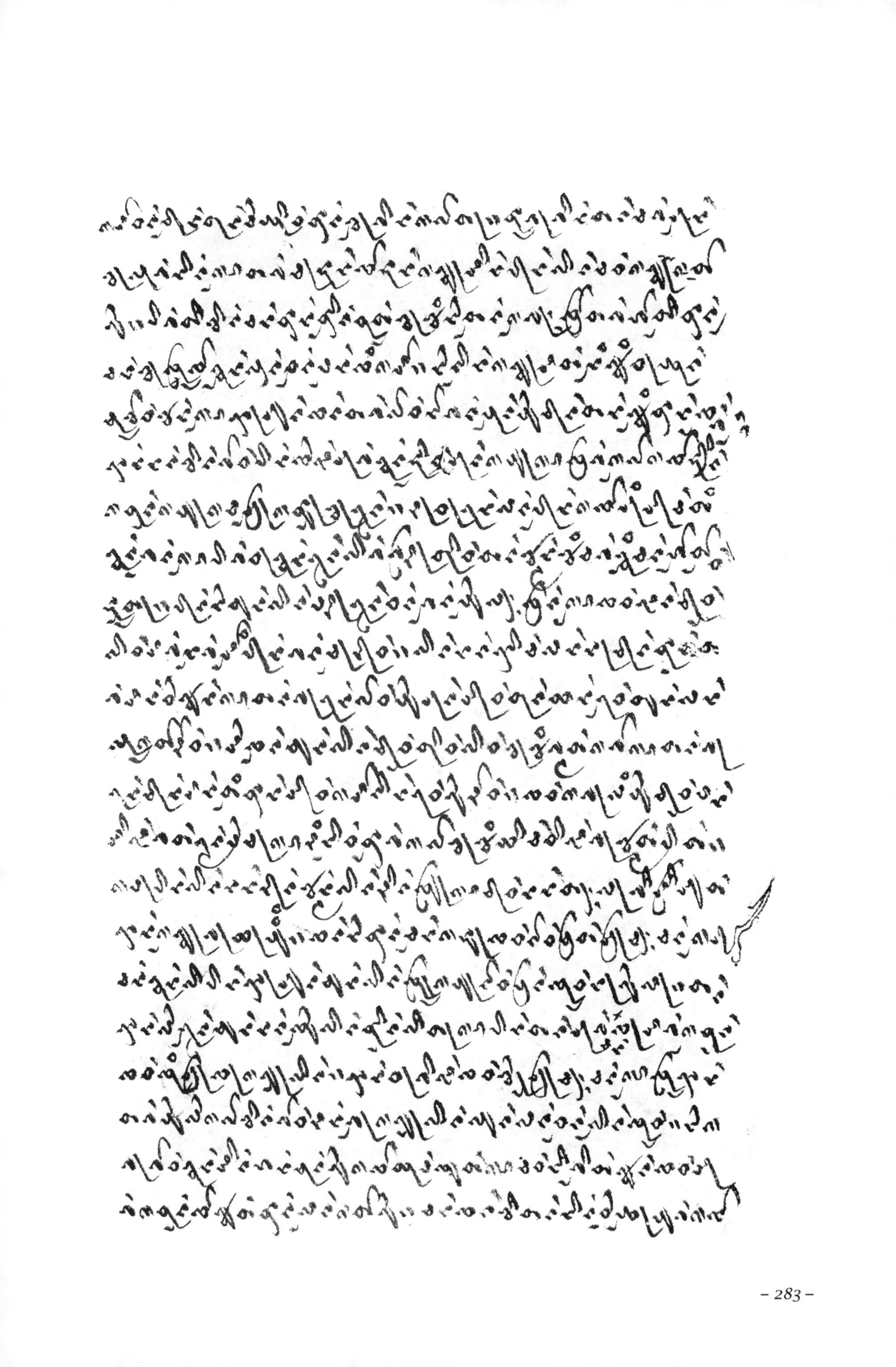

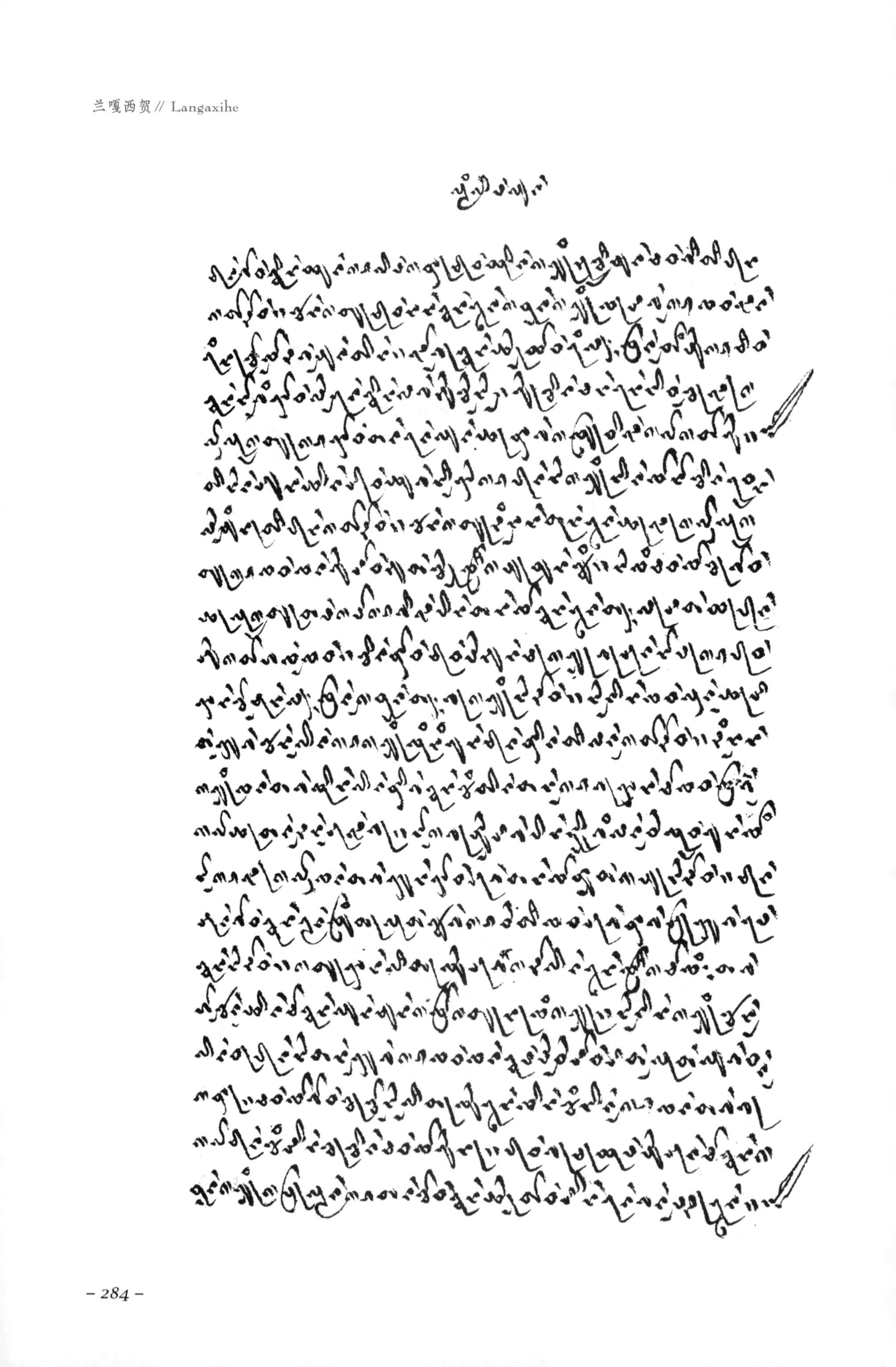

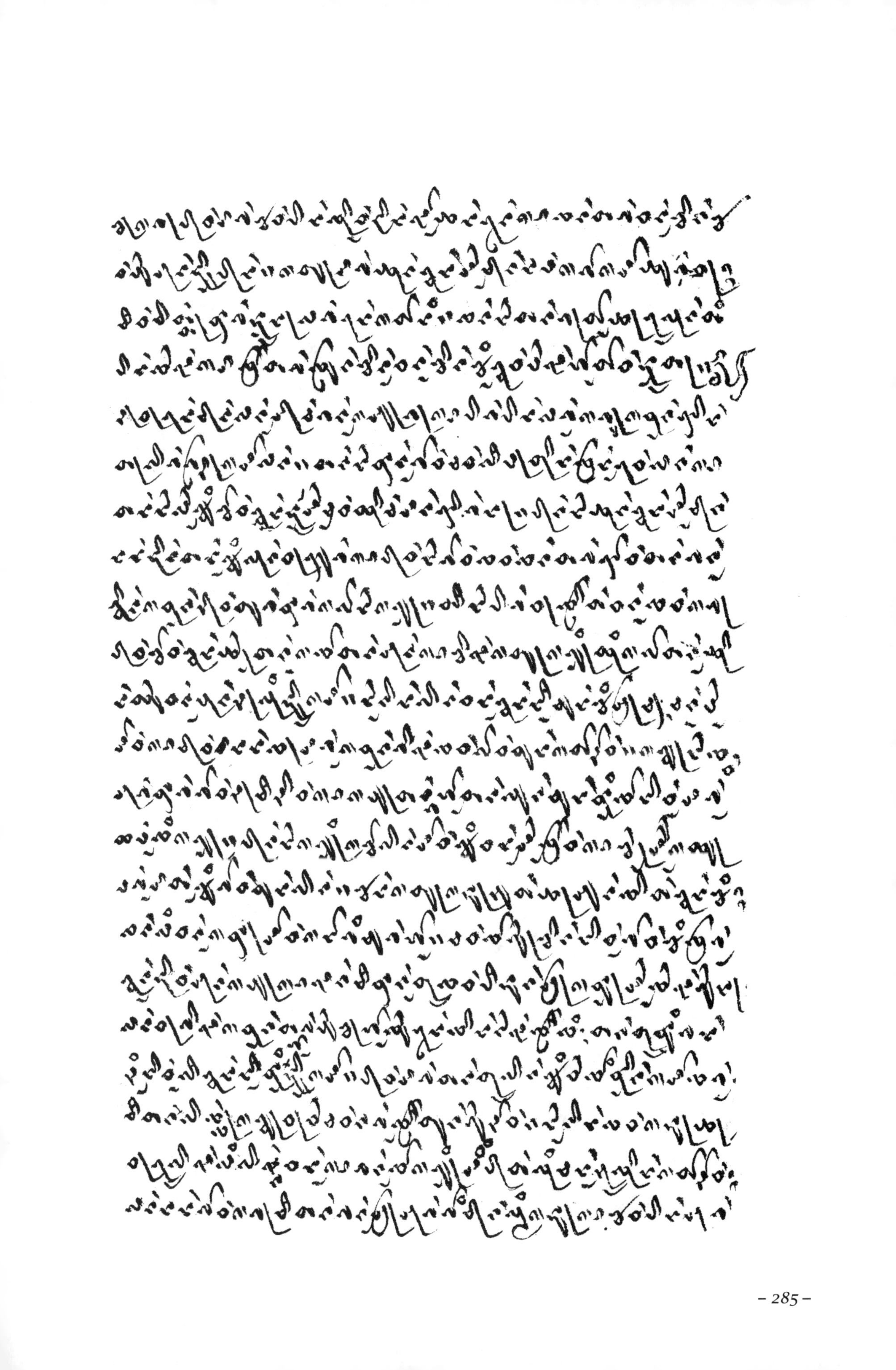

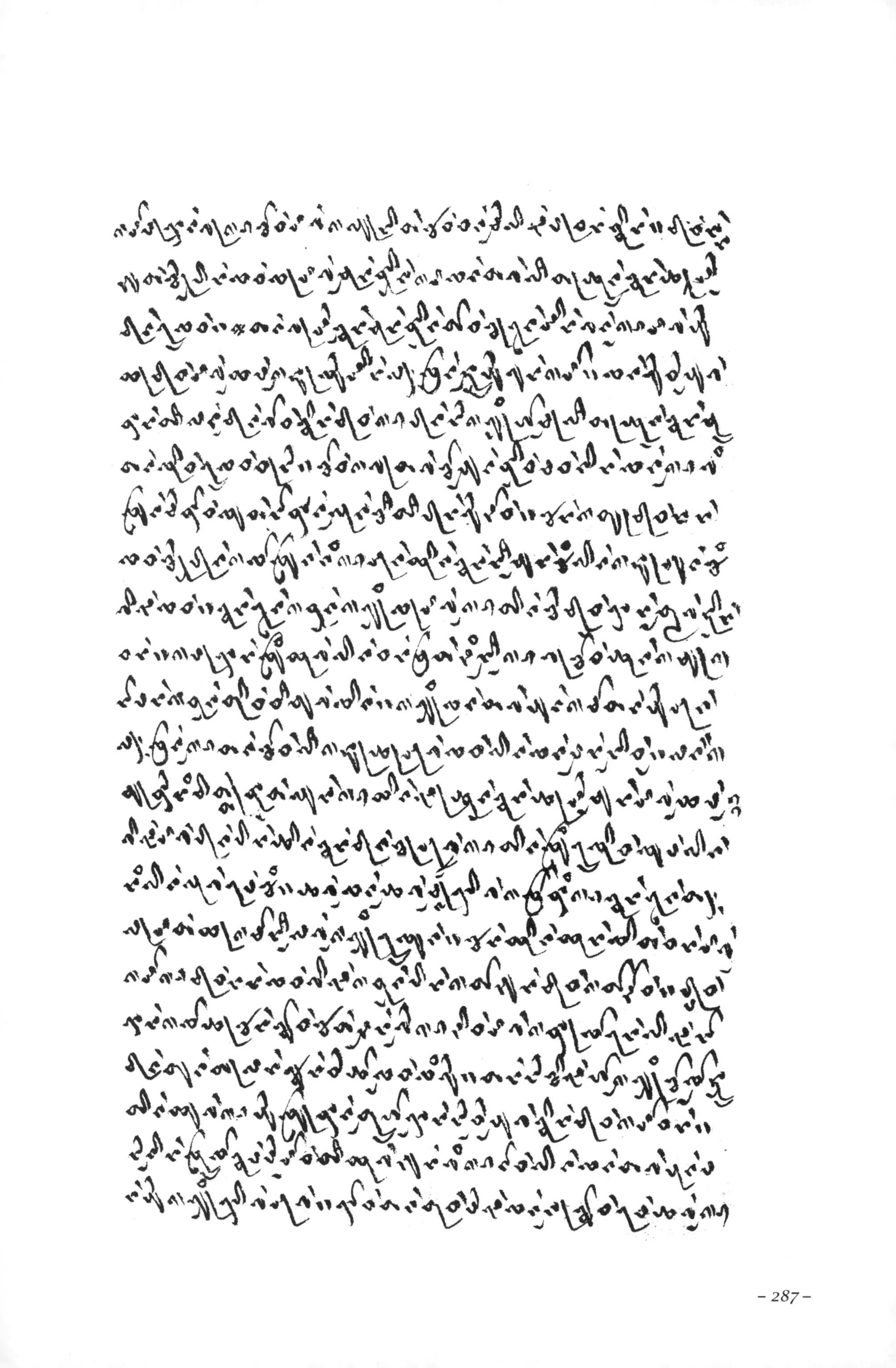

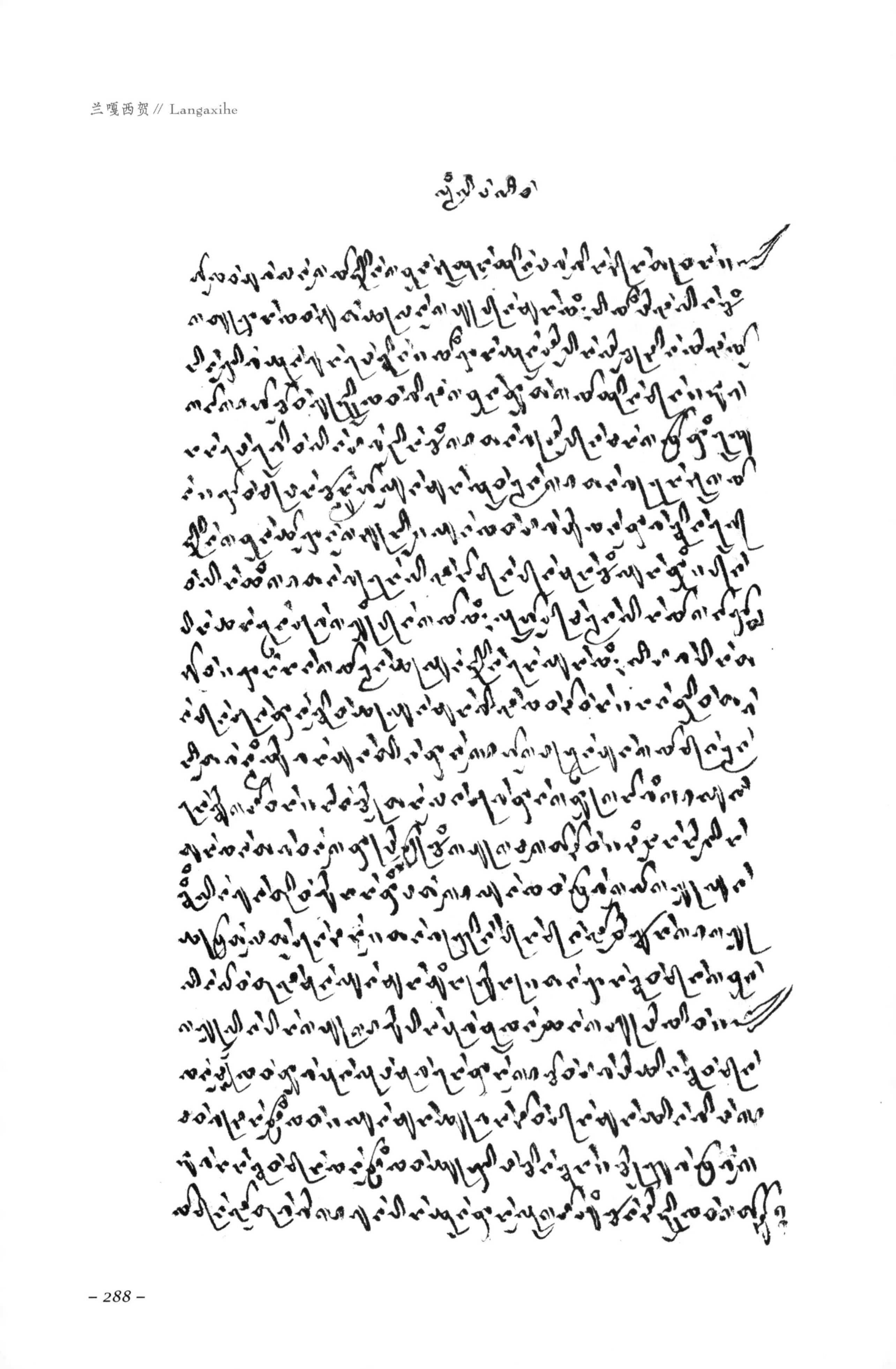

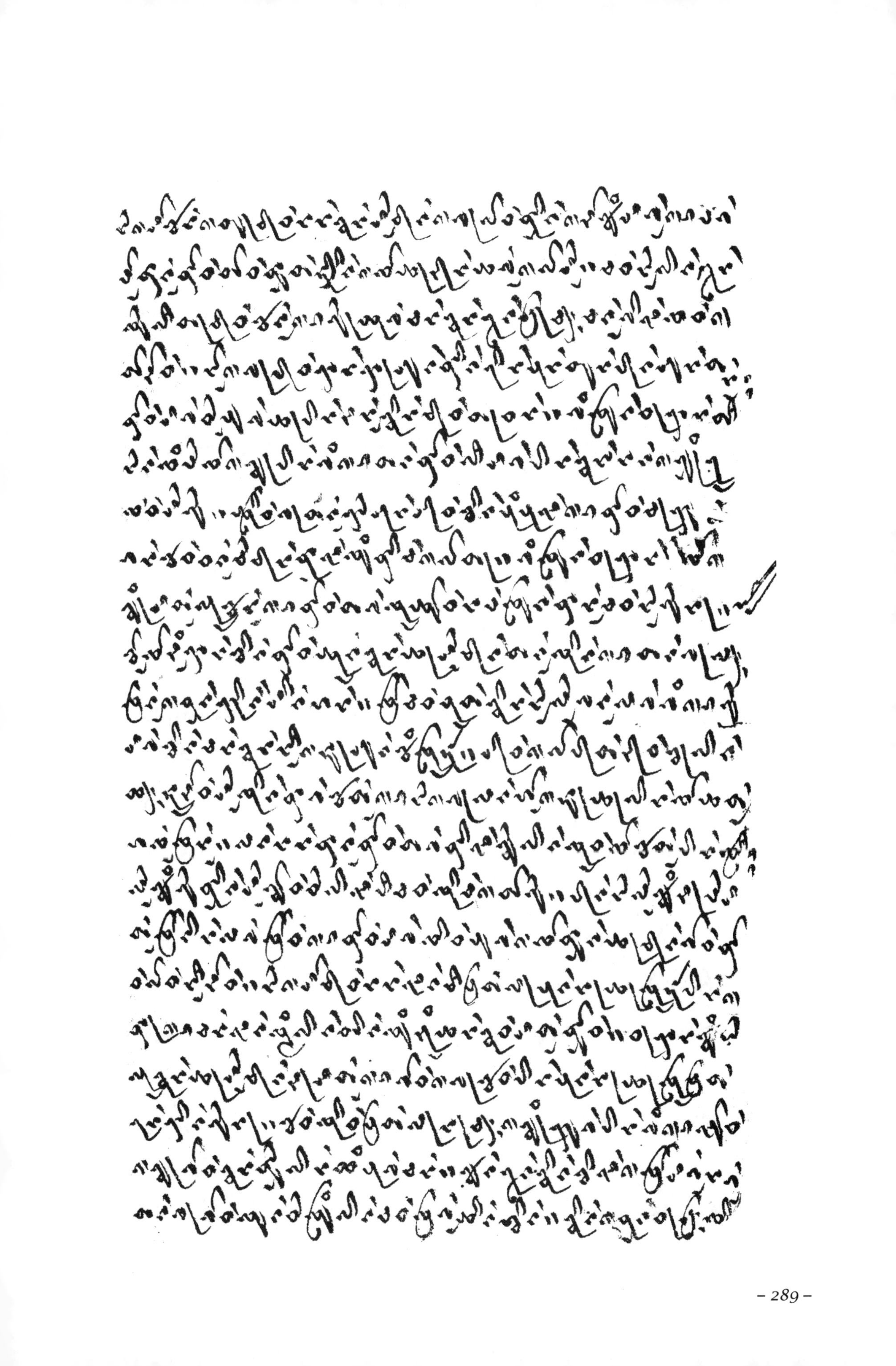

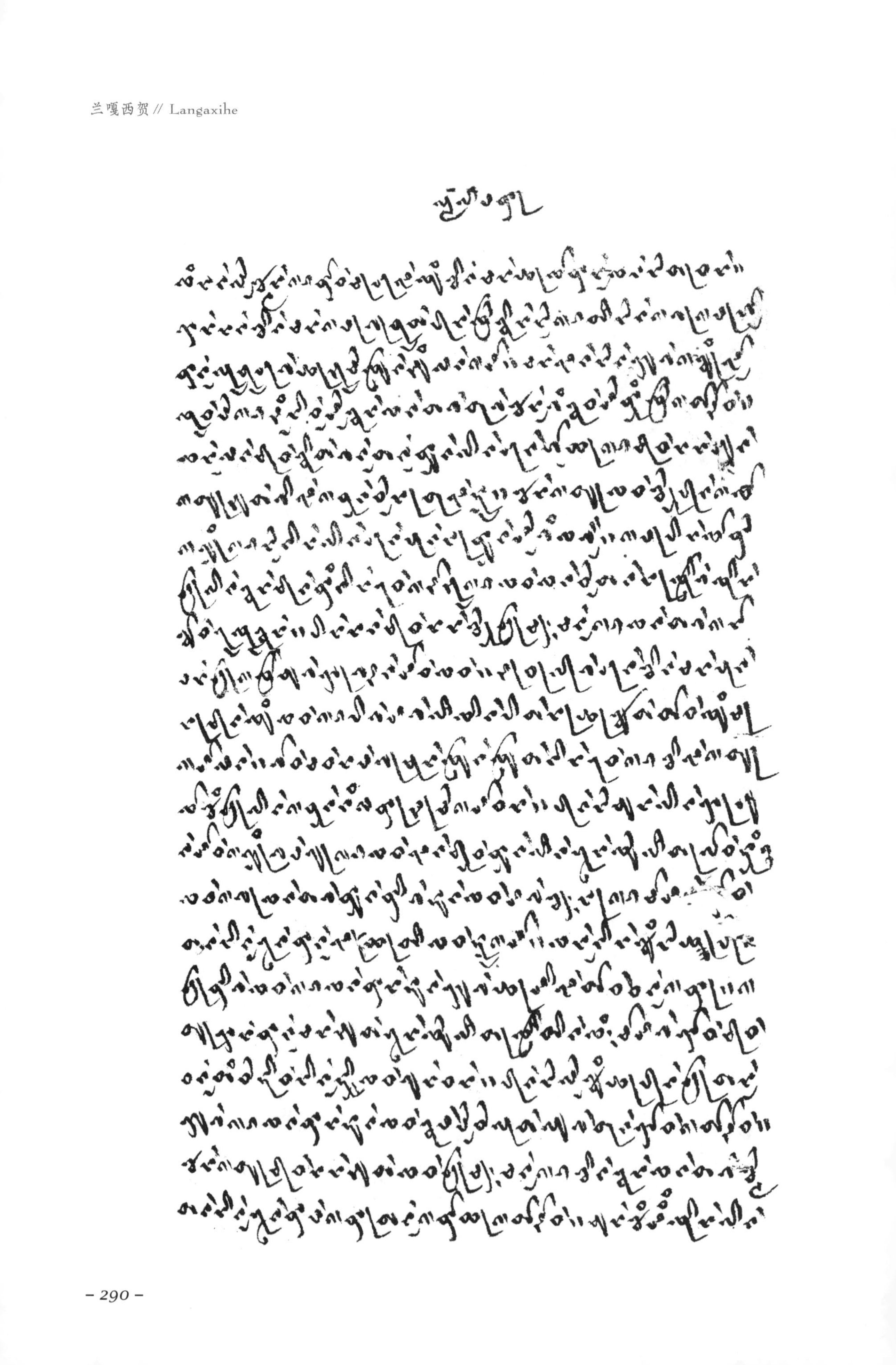

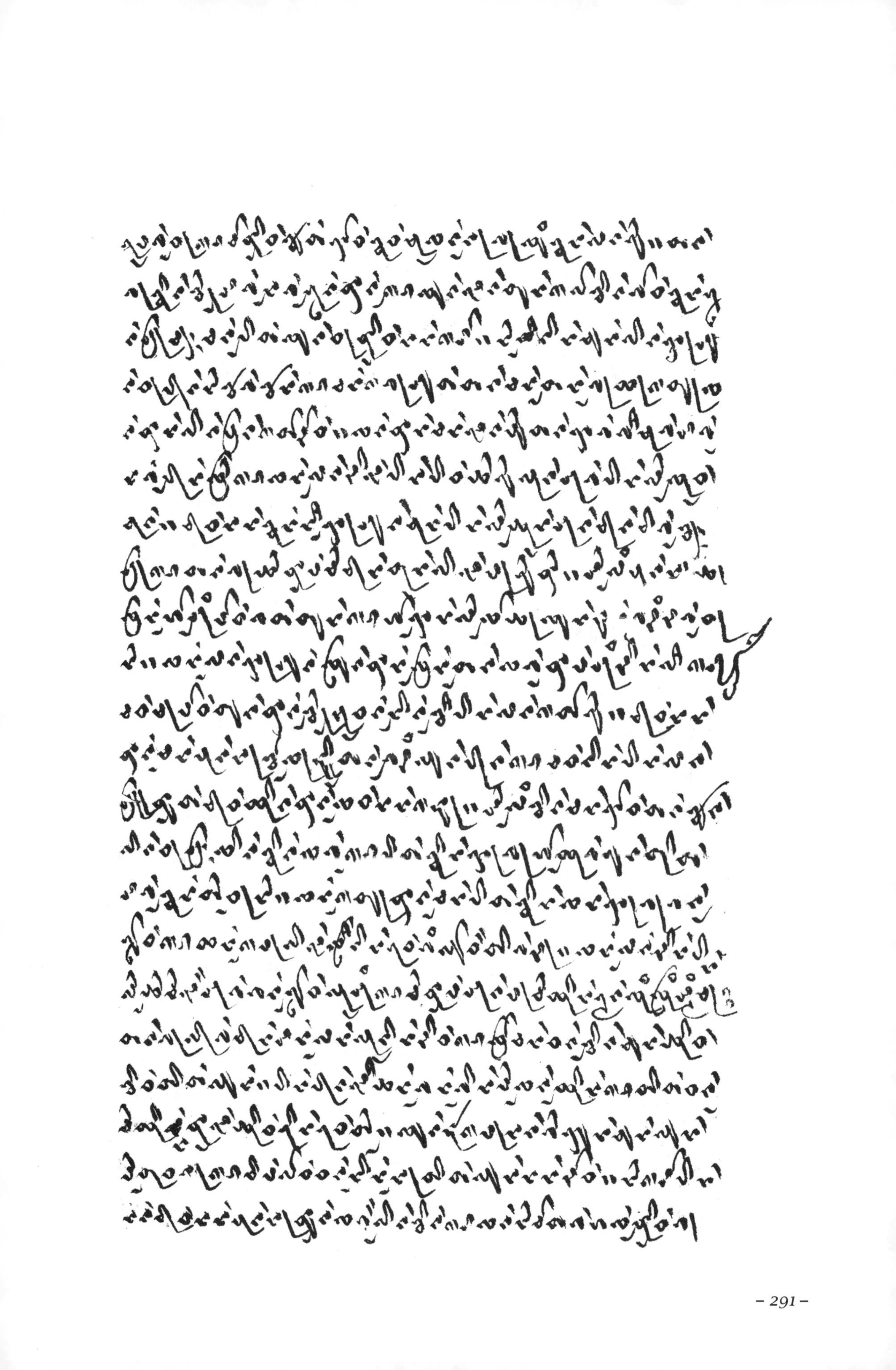

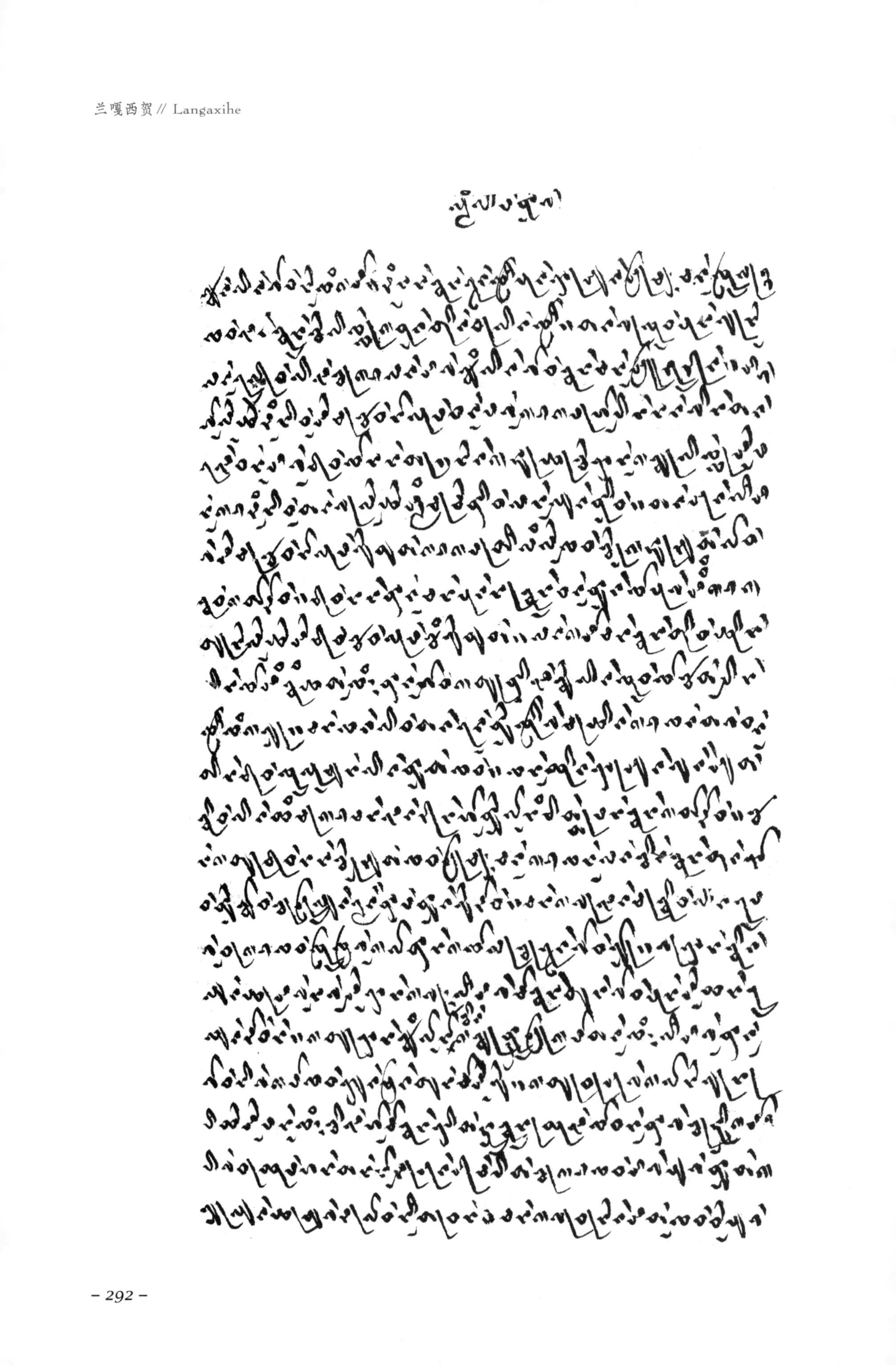

[illegible]

[illegible]

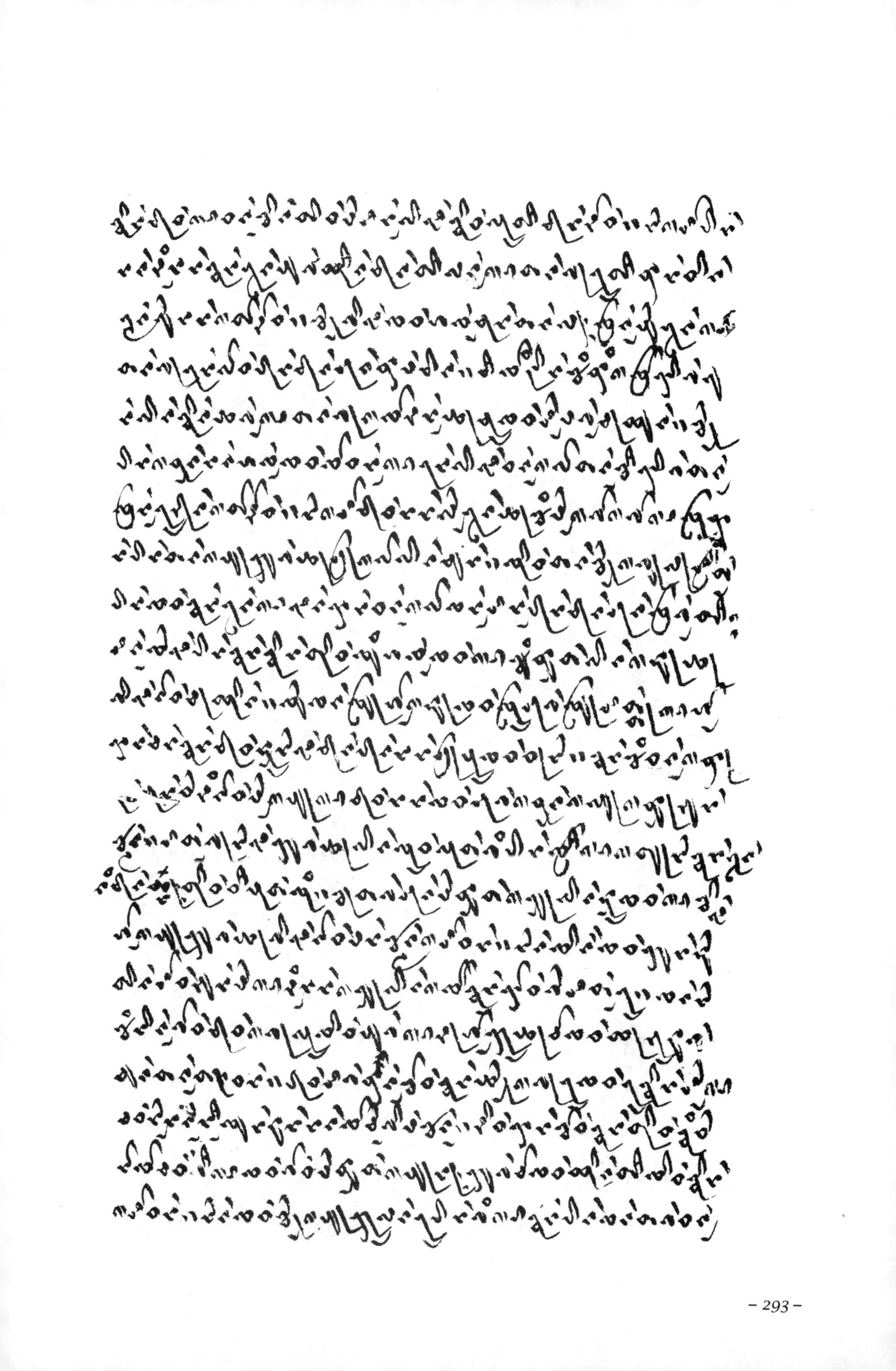

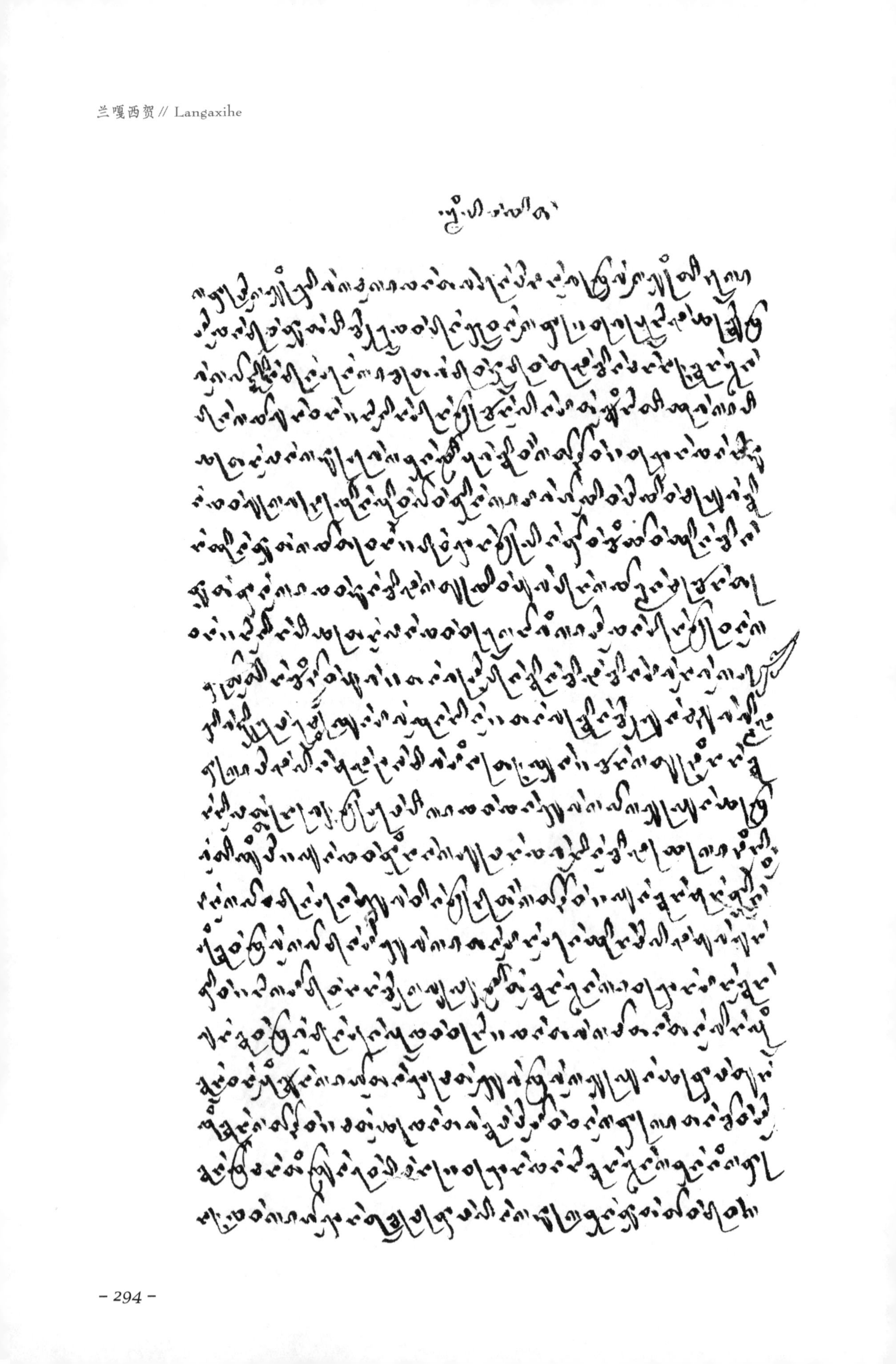

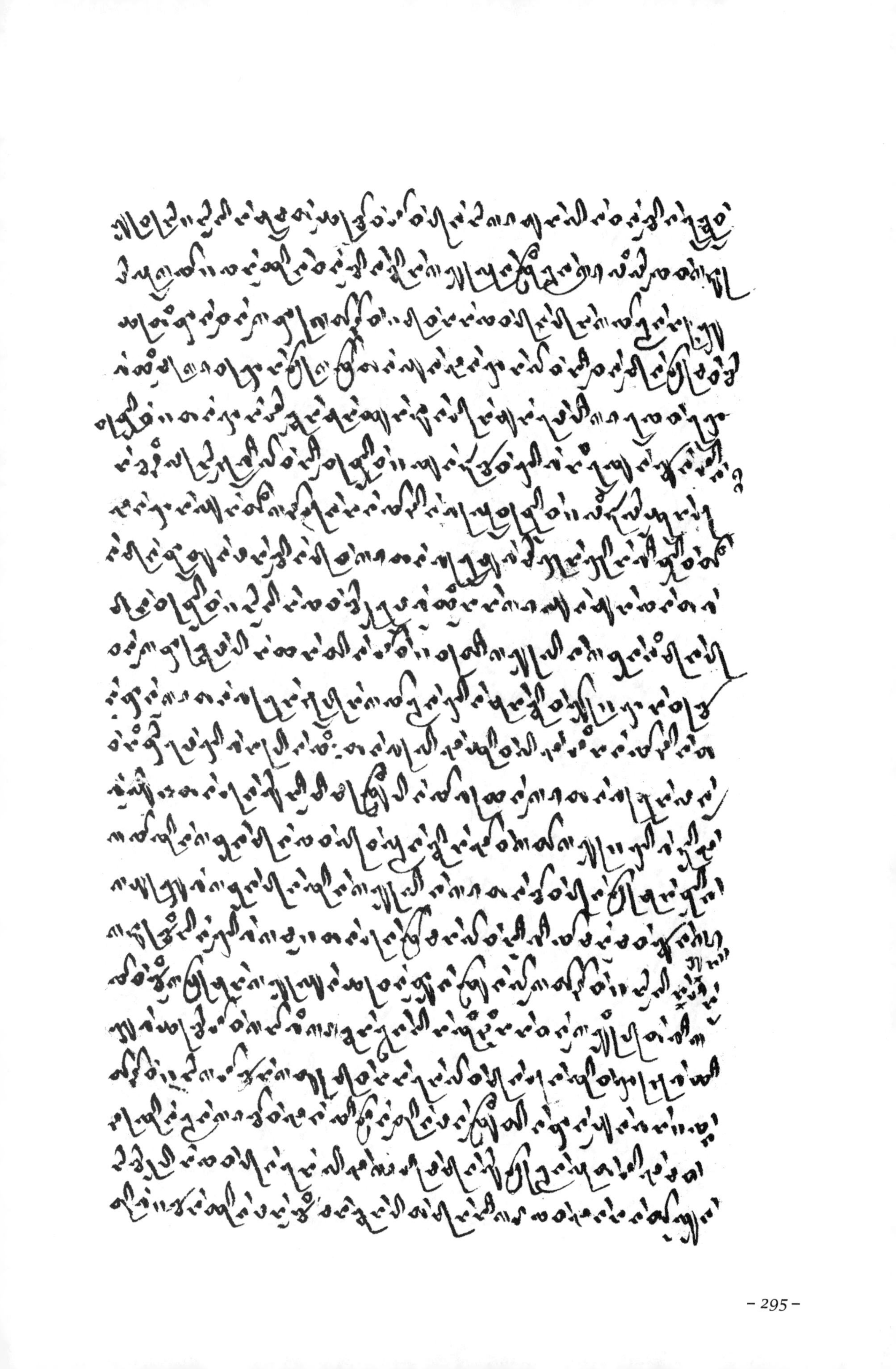

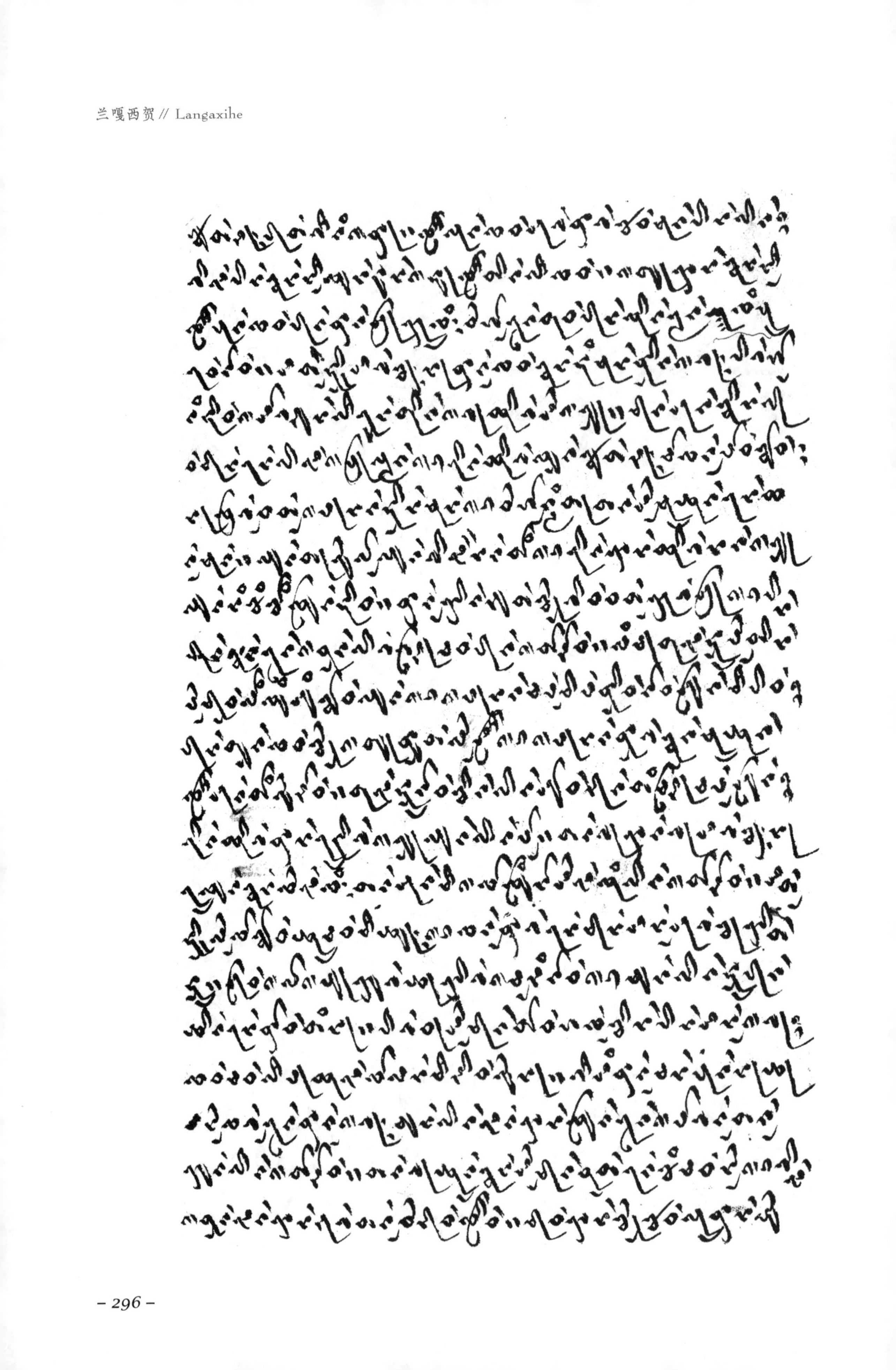

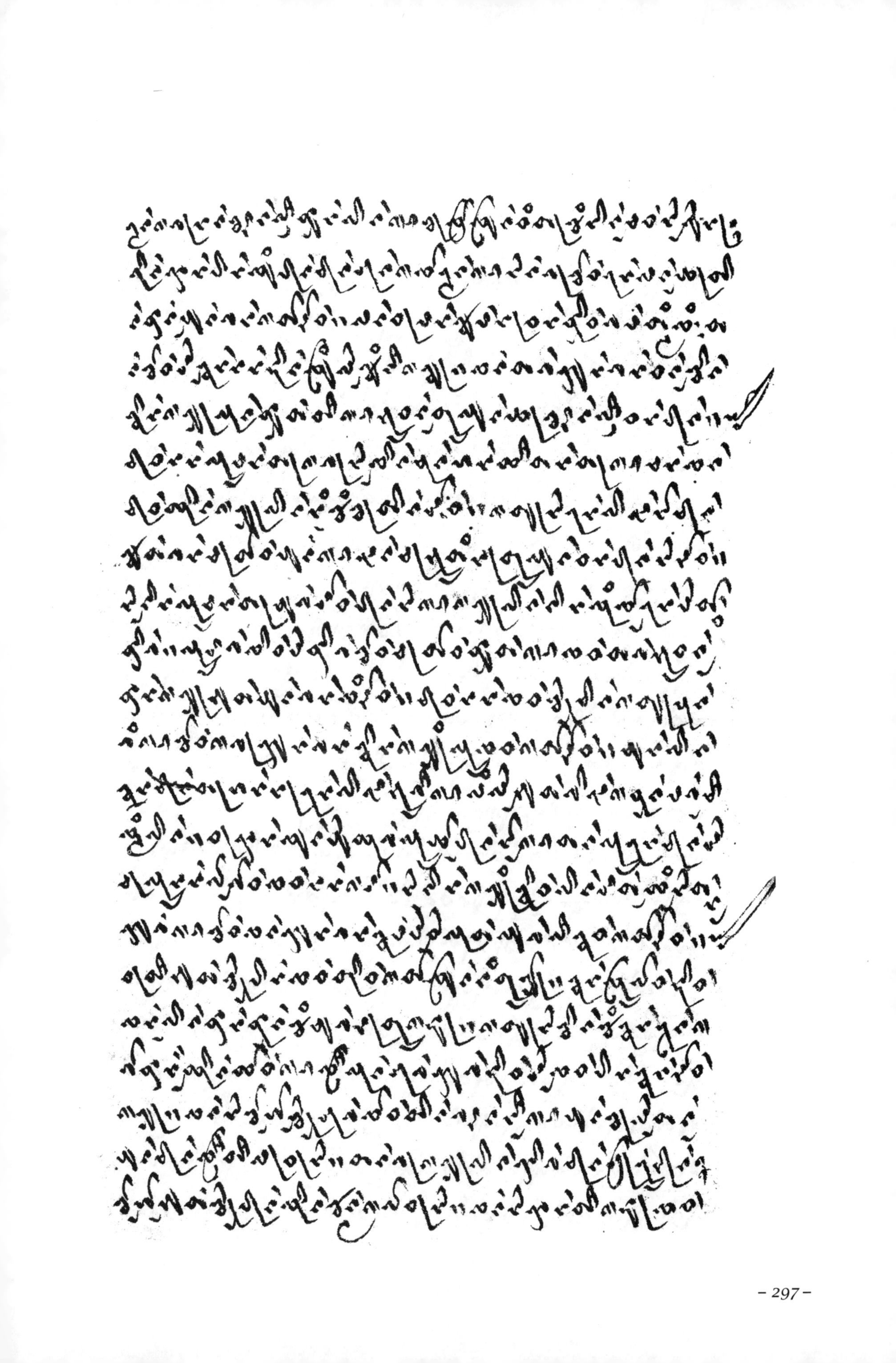

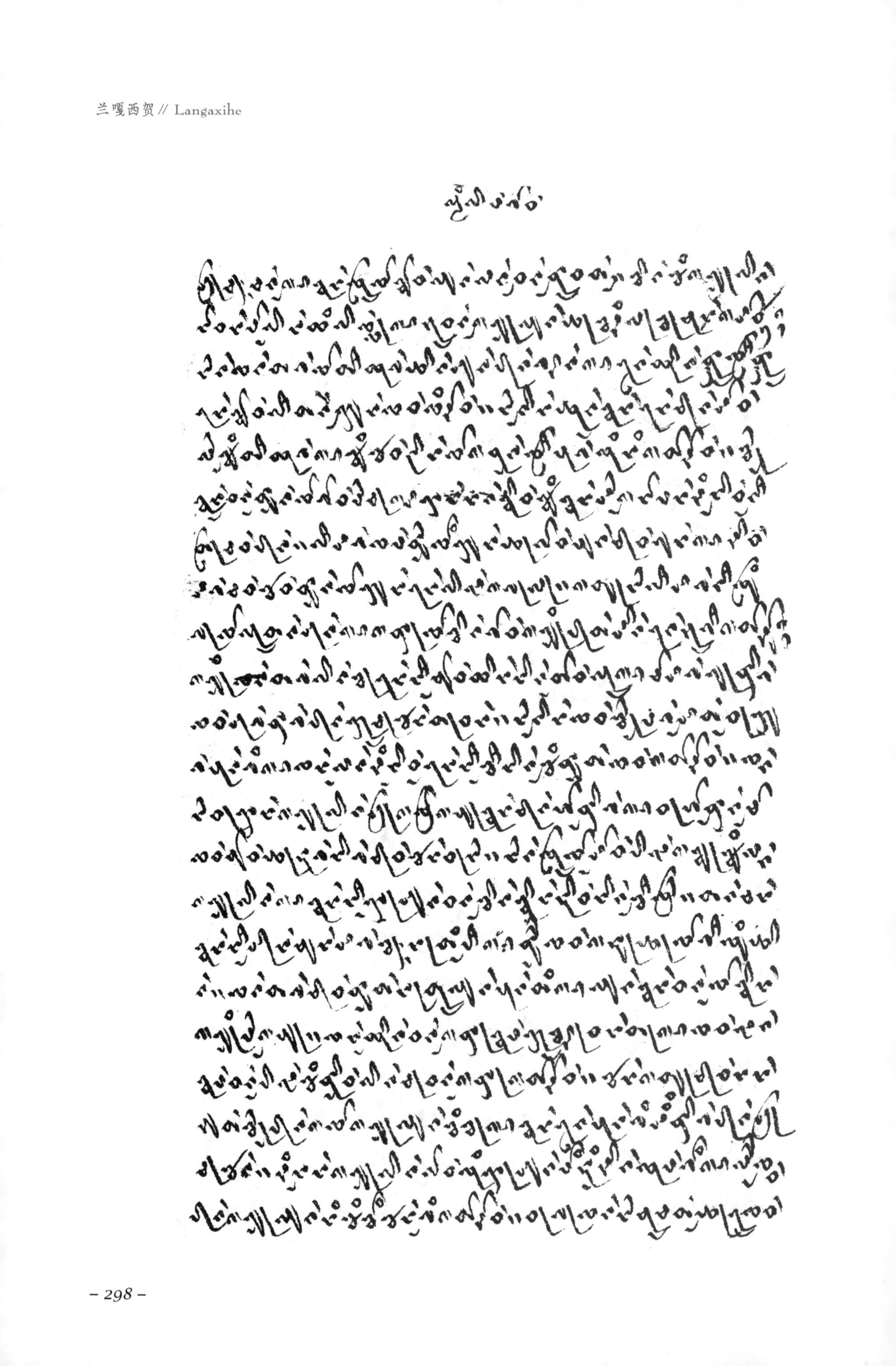

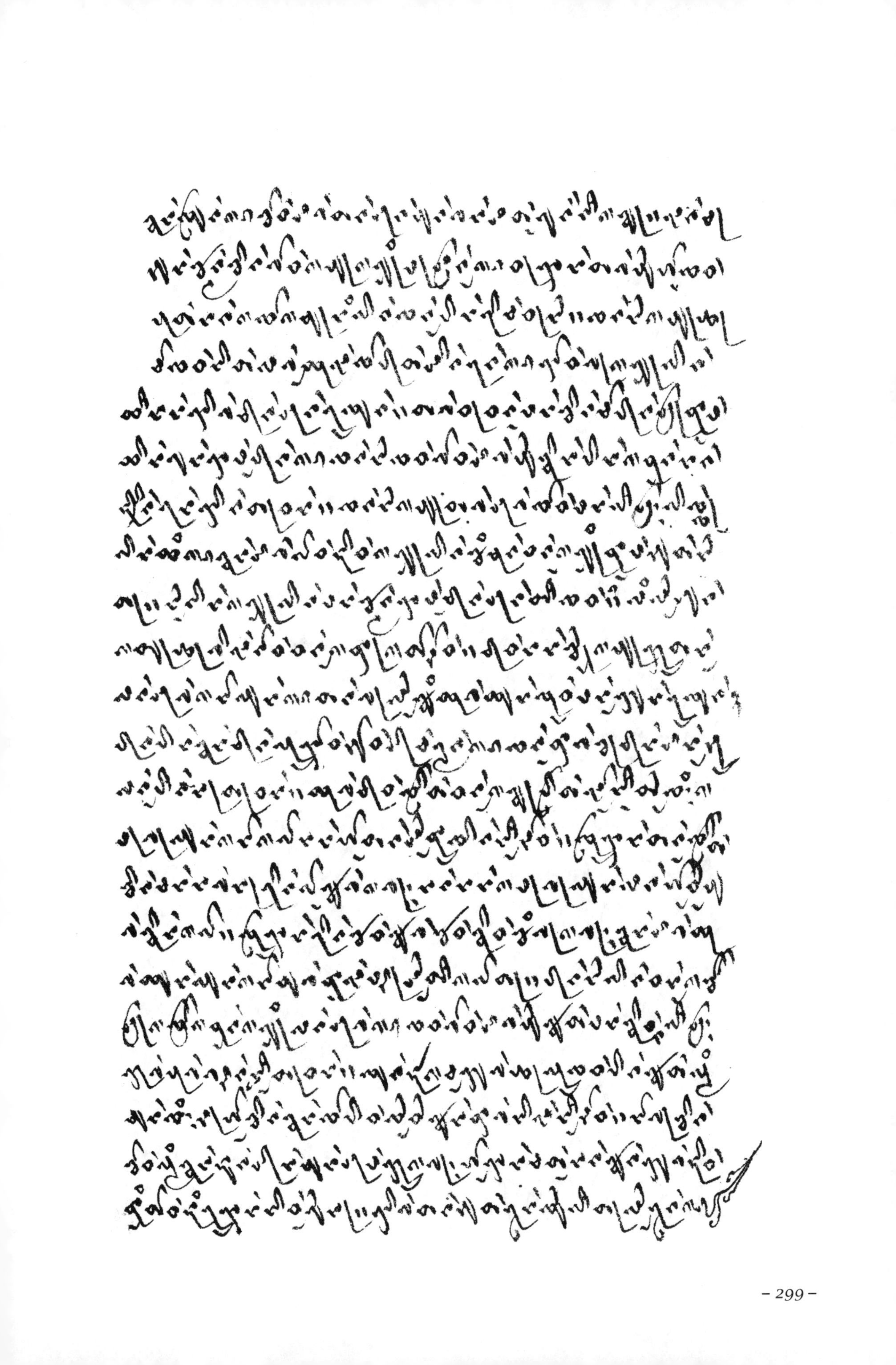

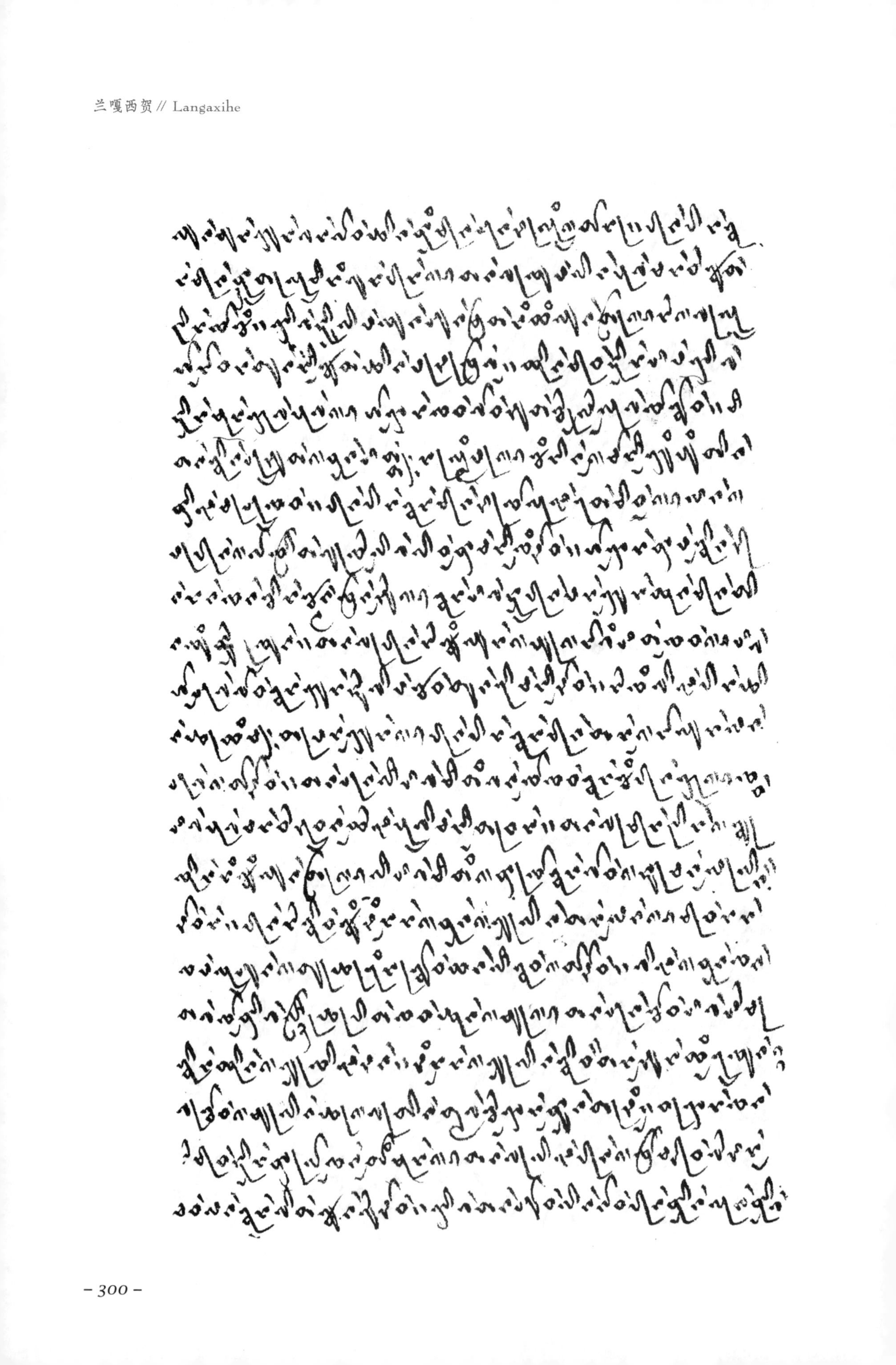

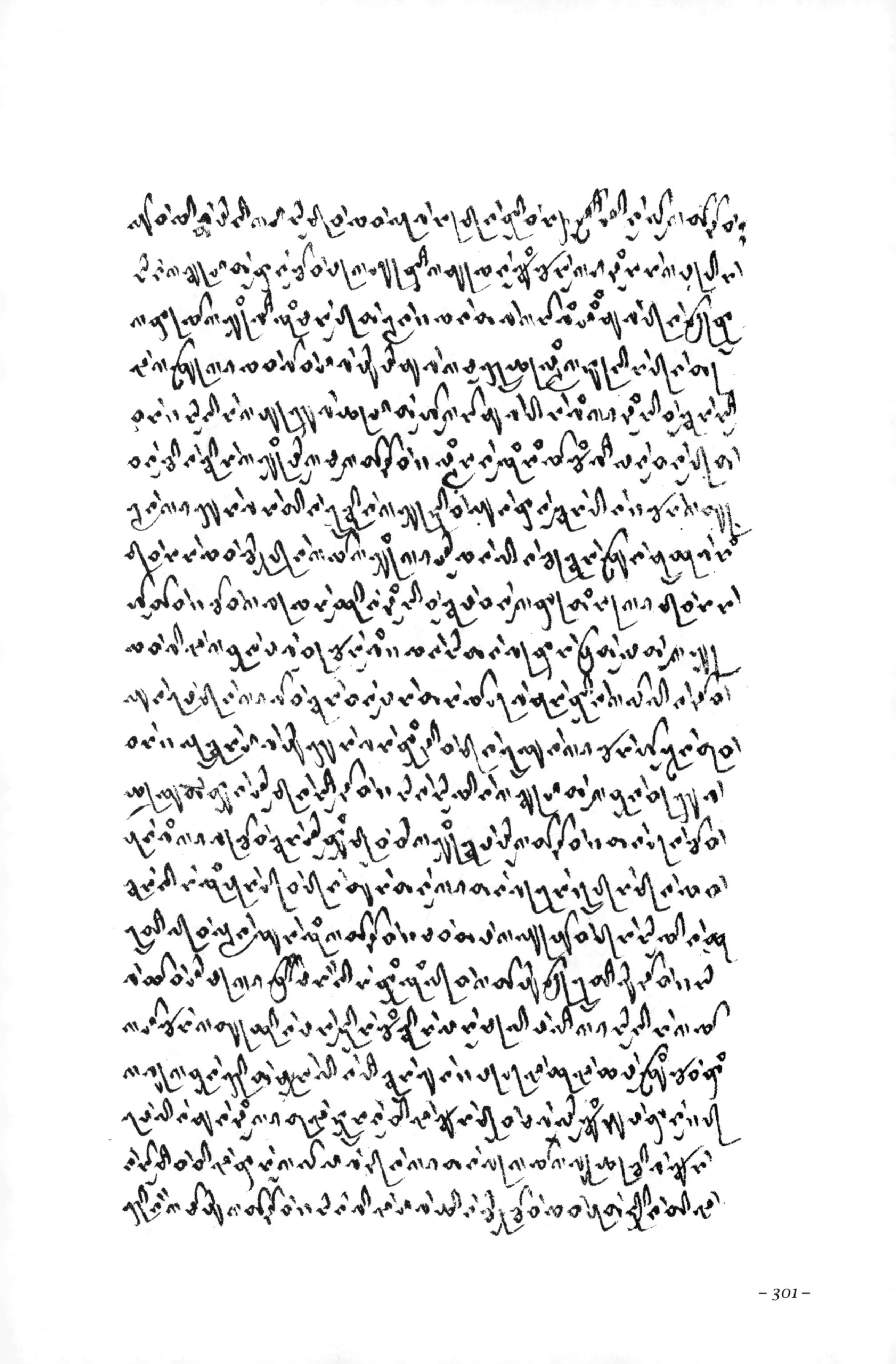

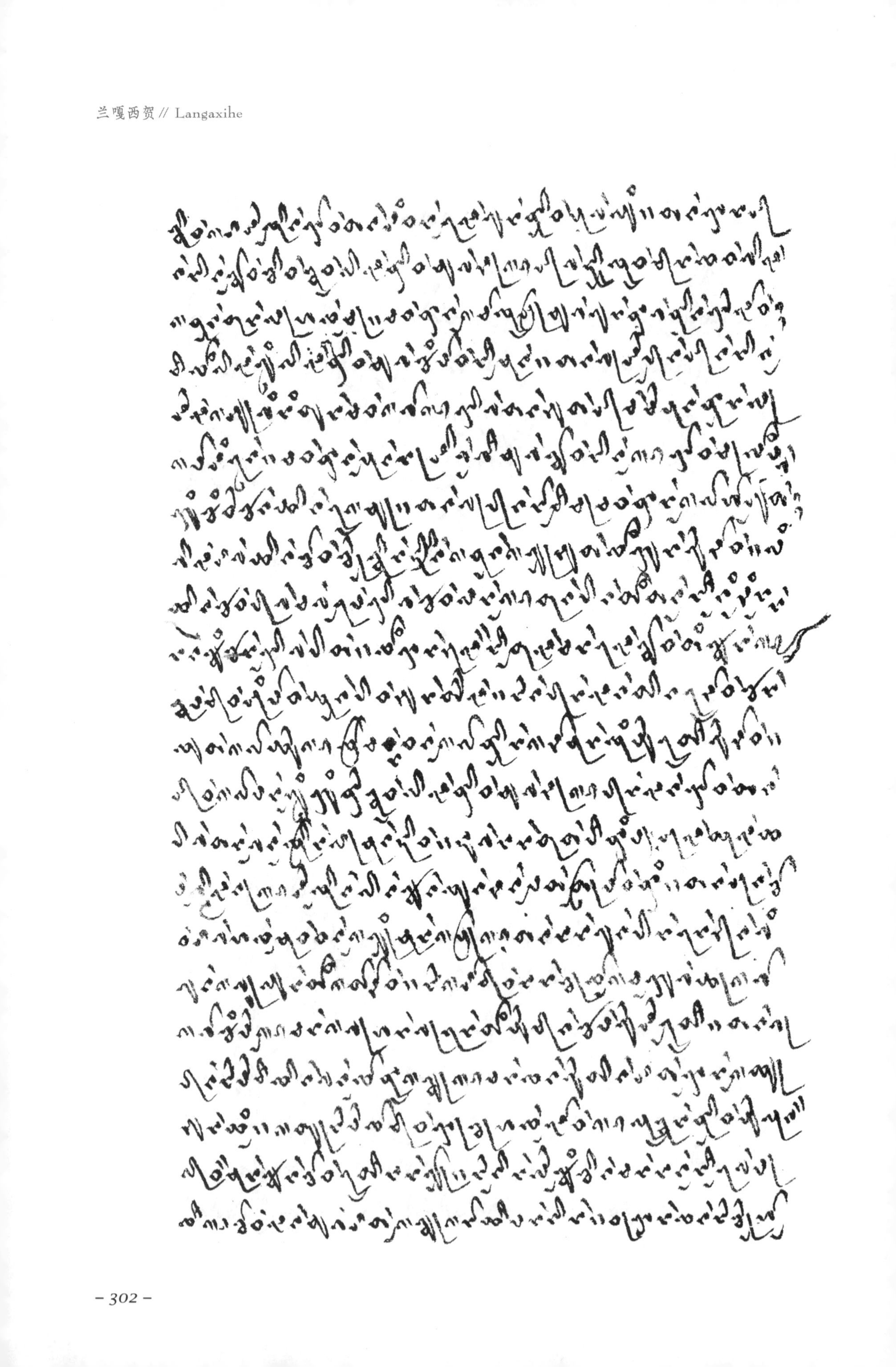

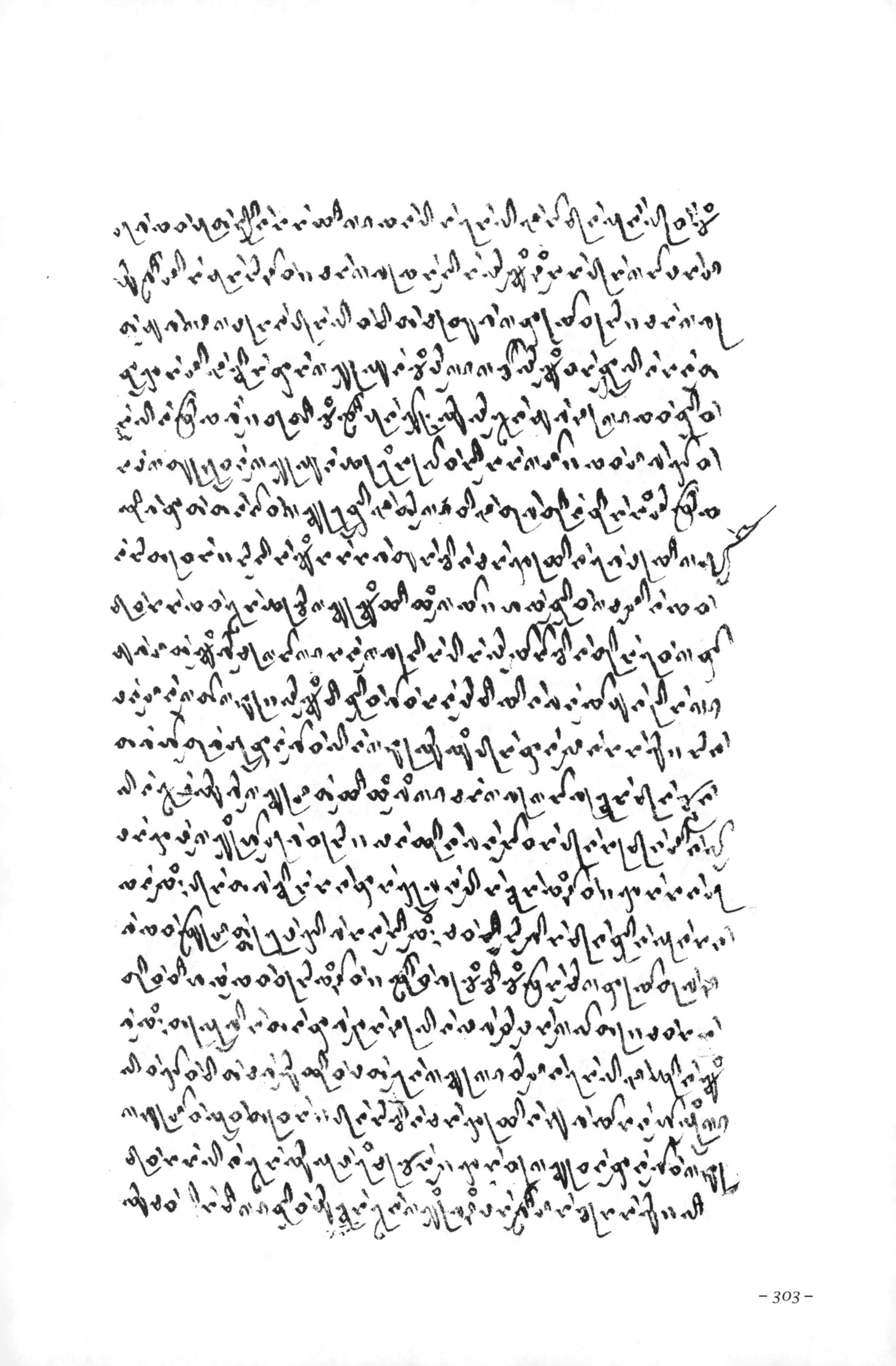

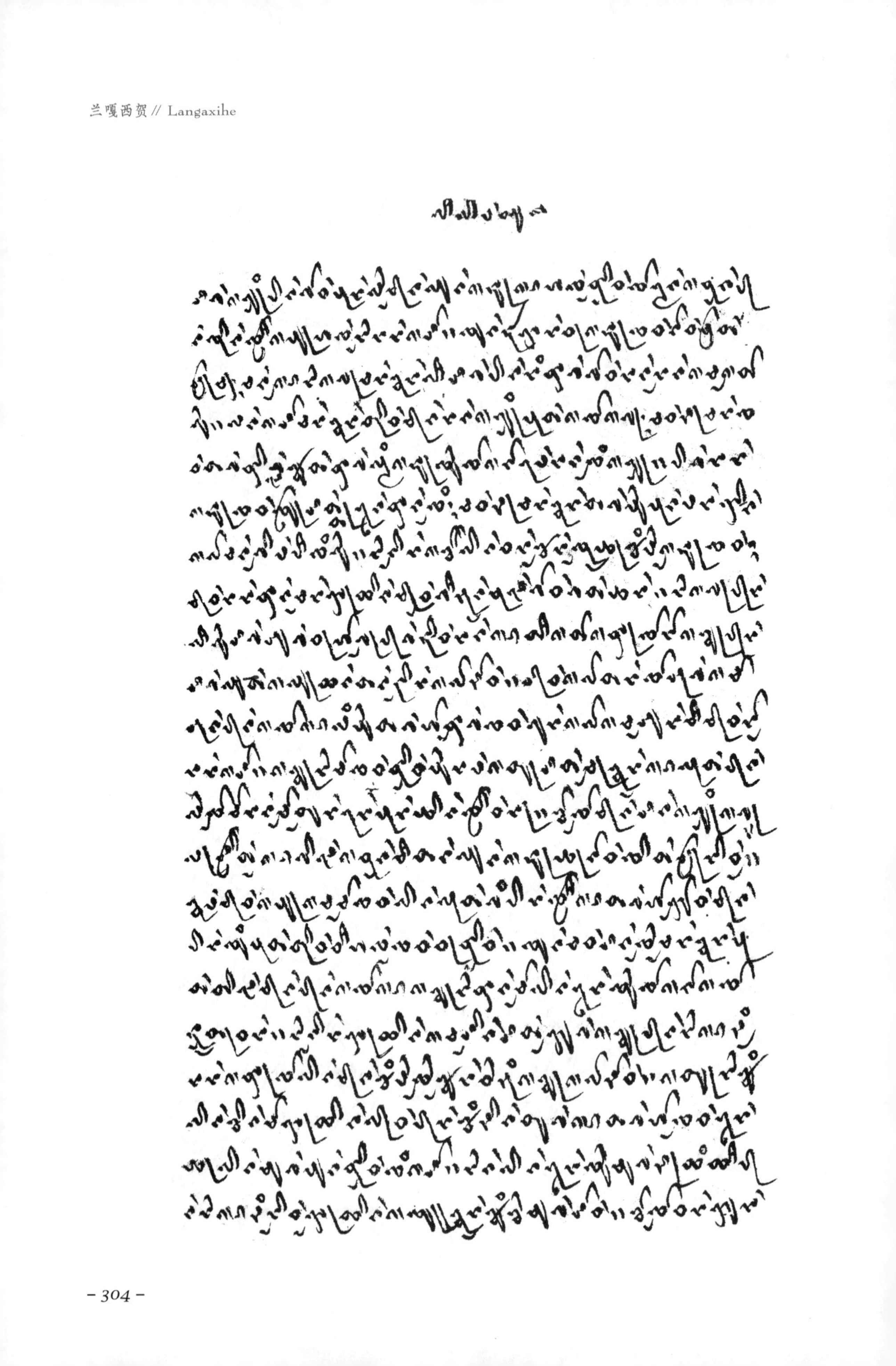

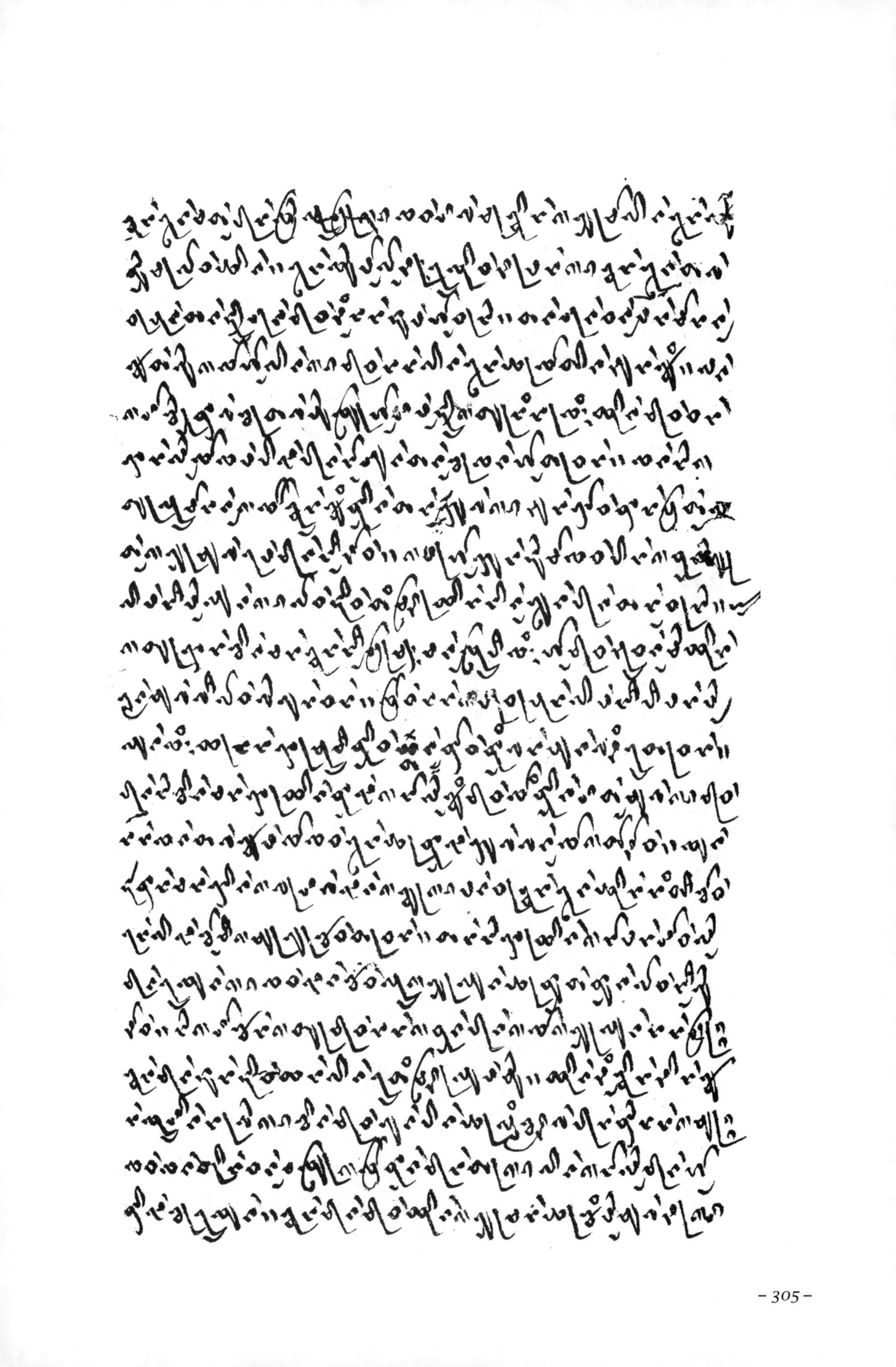

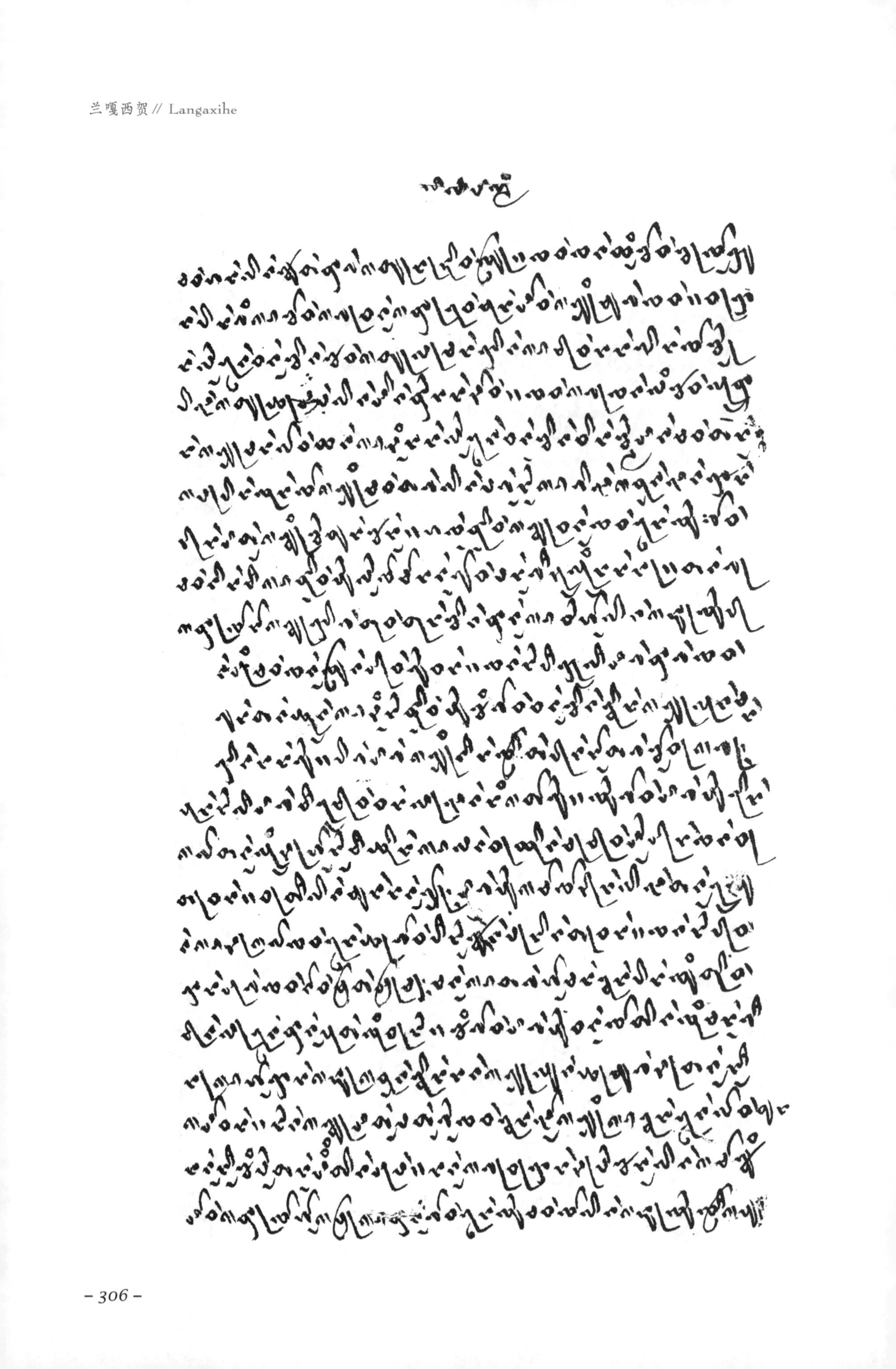

[illegible]

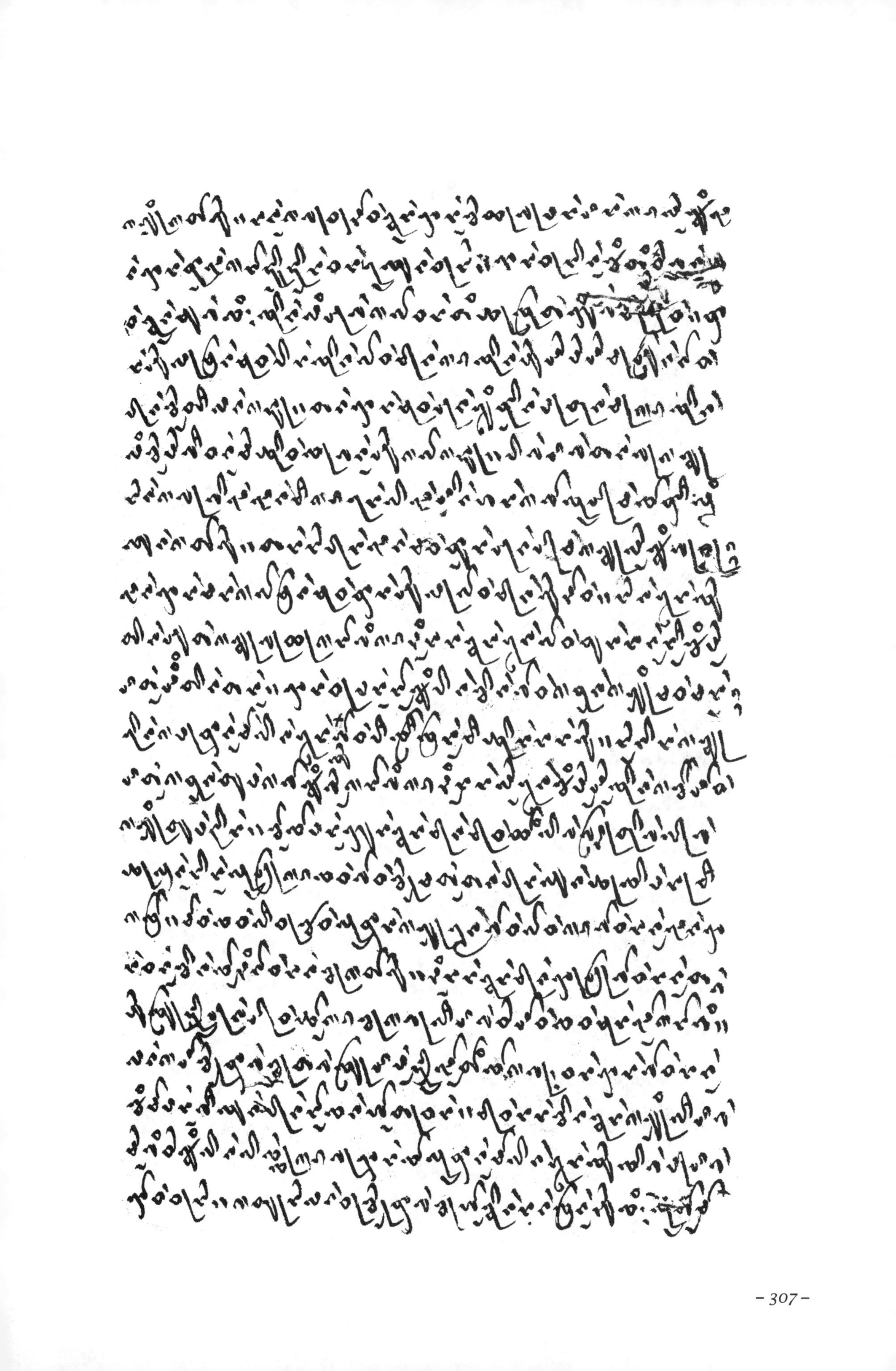

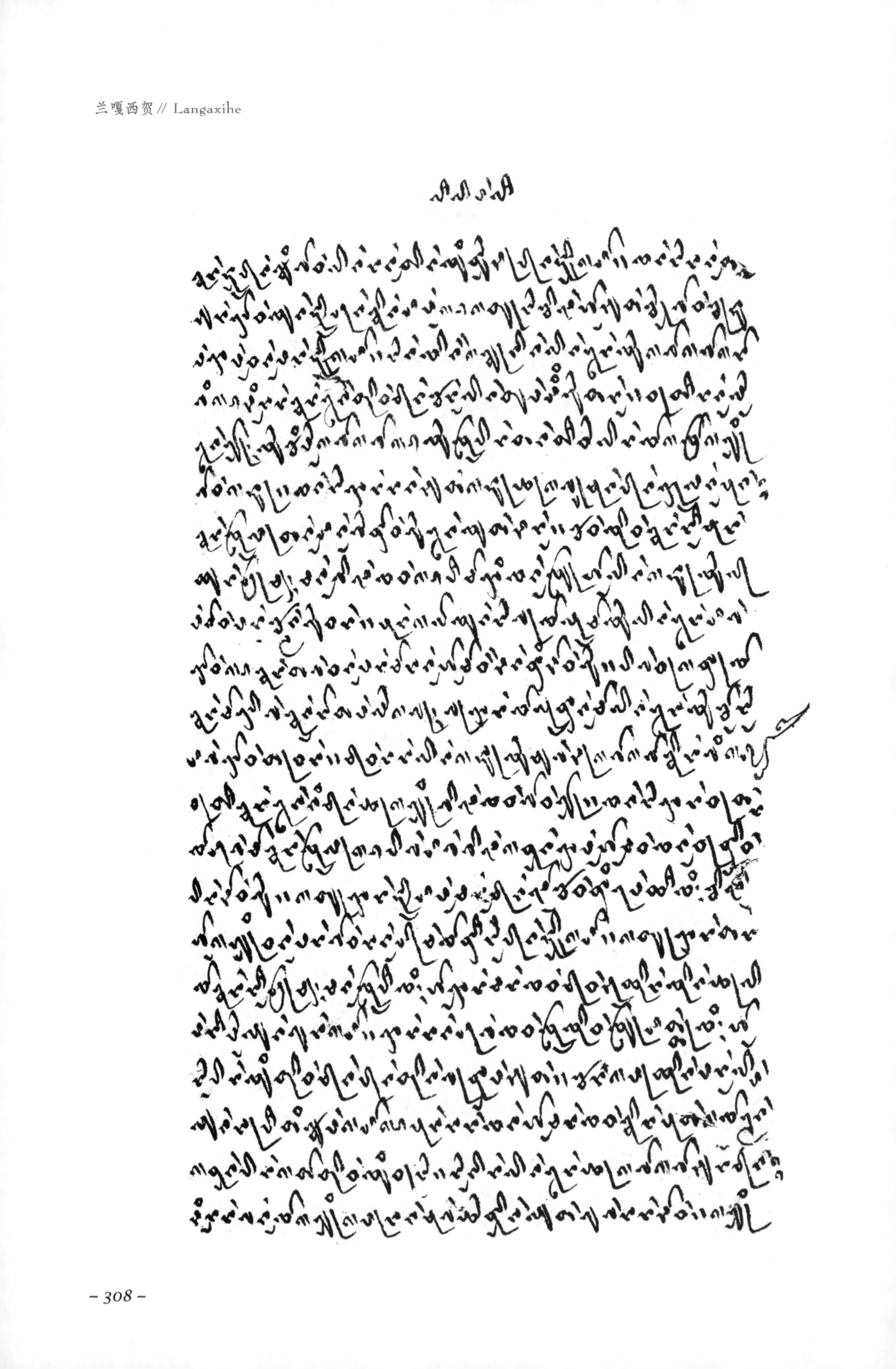

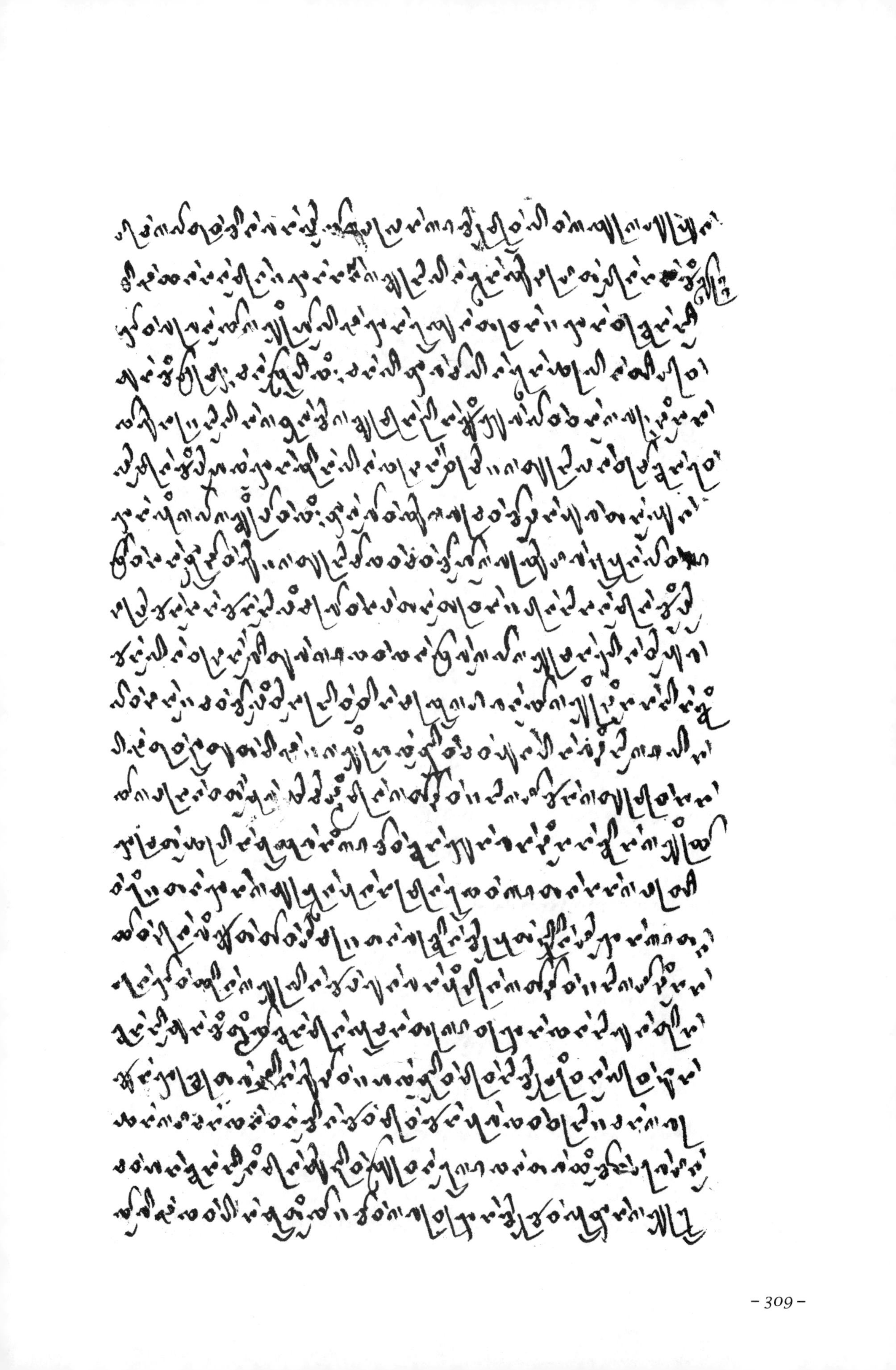

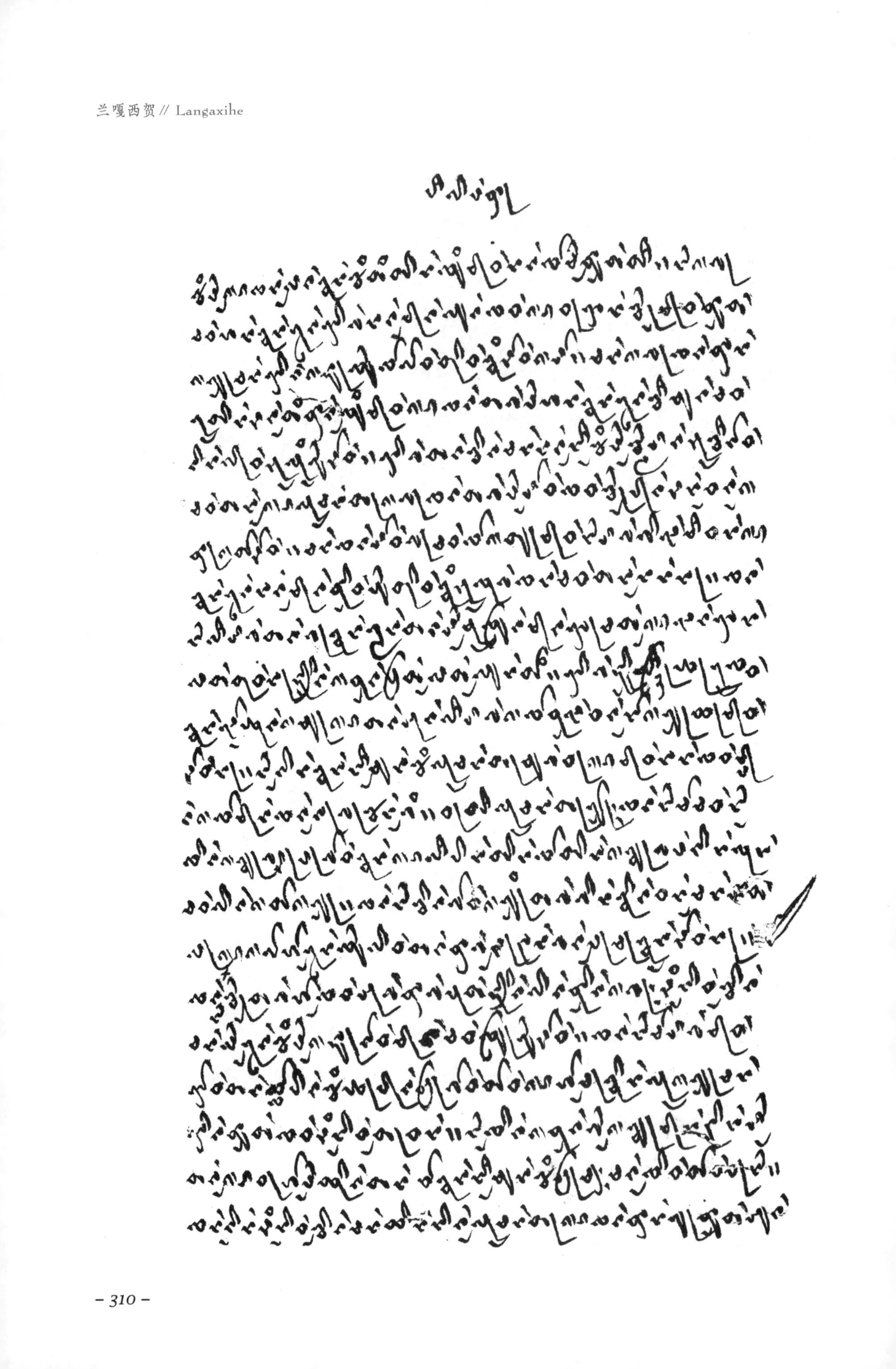

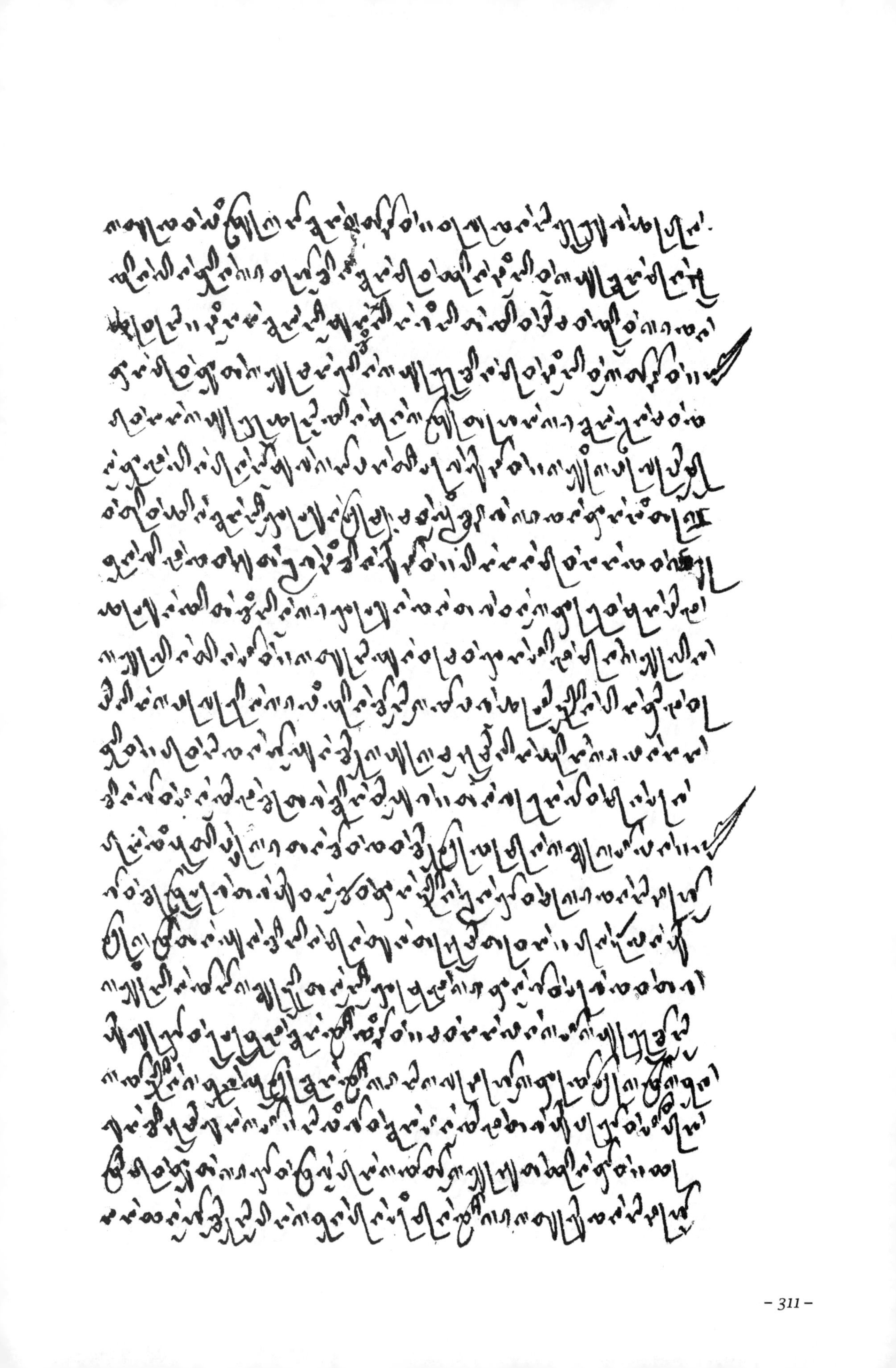

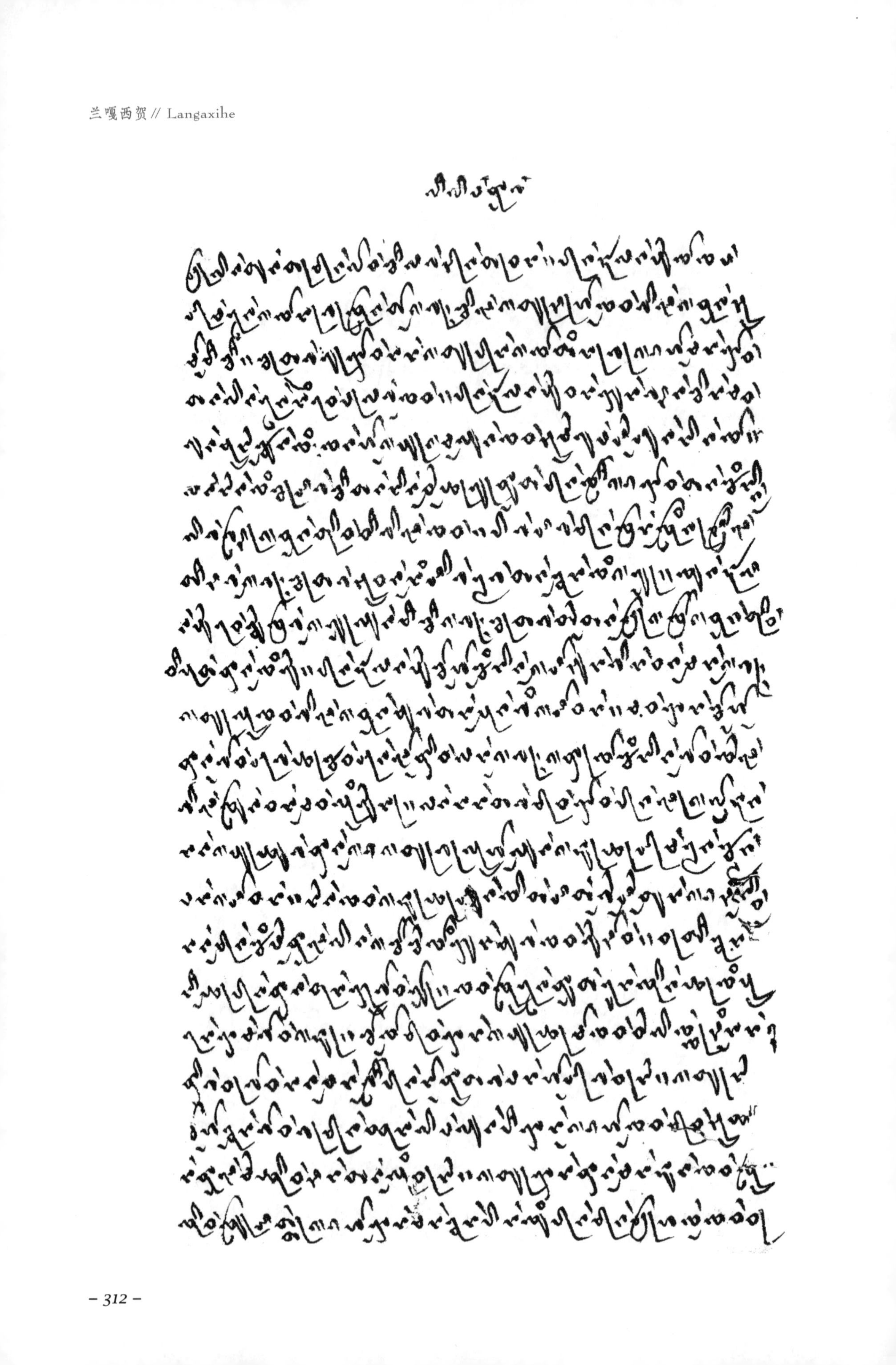

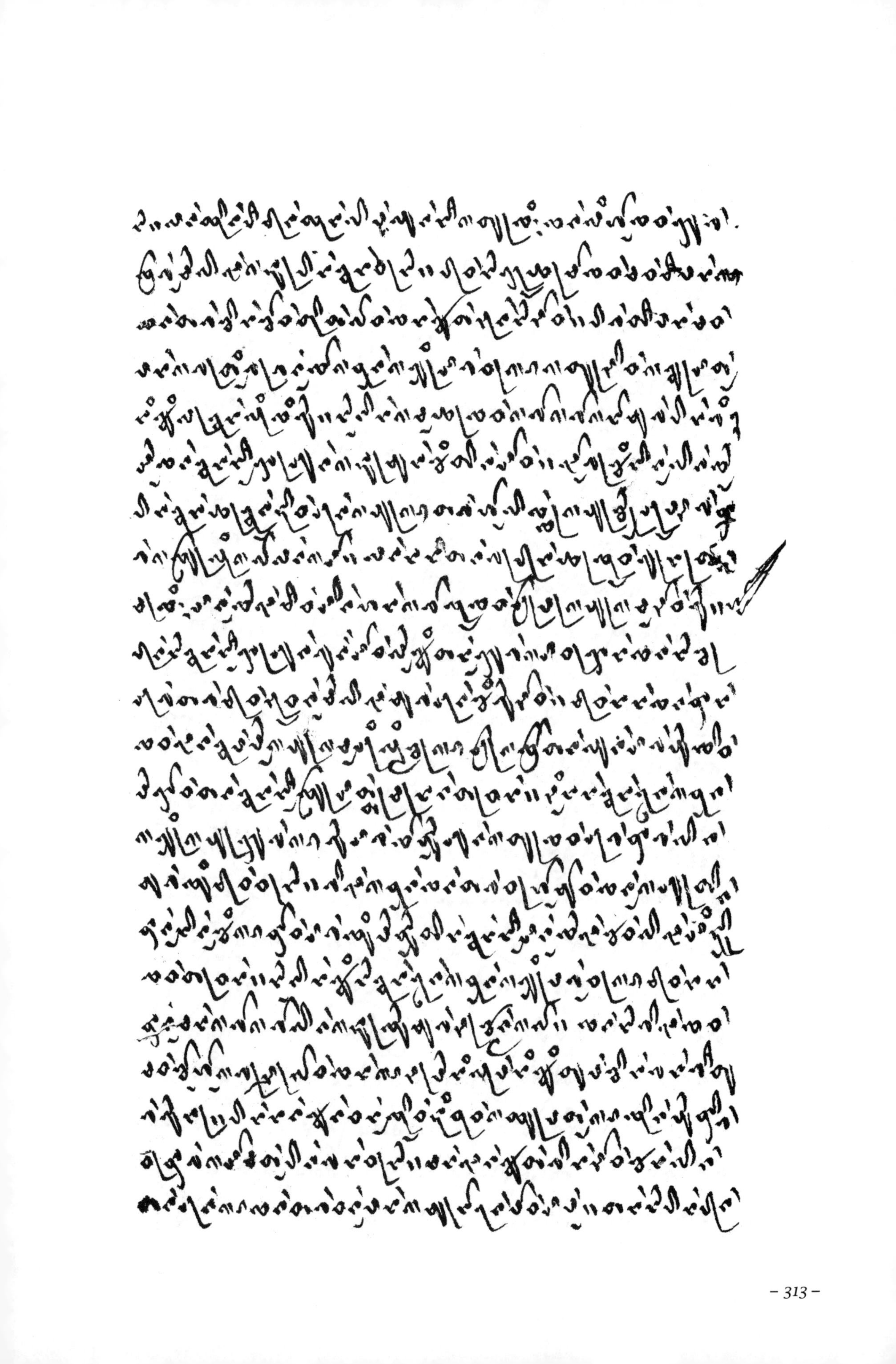

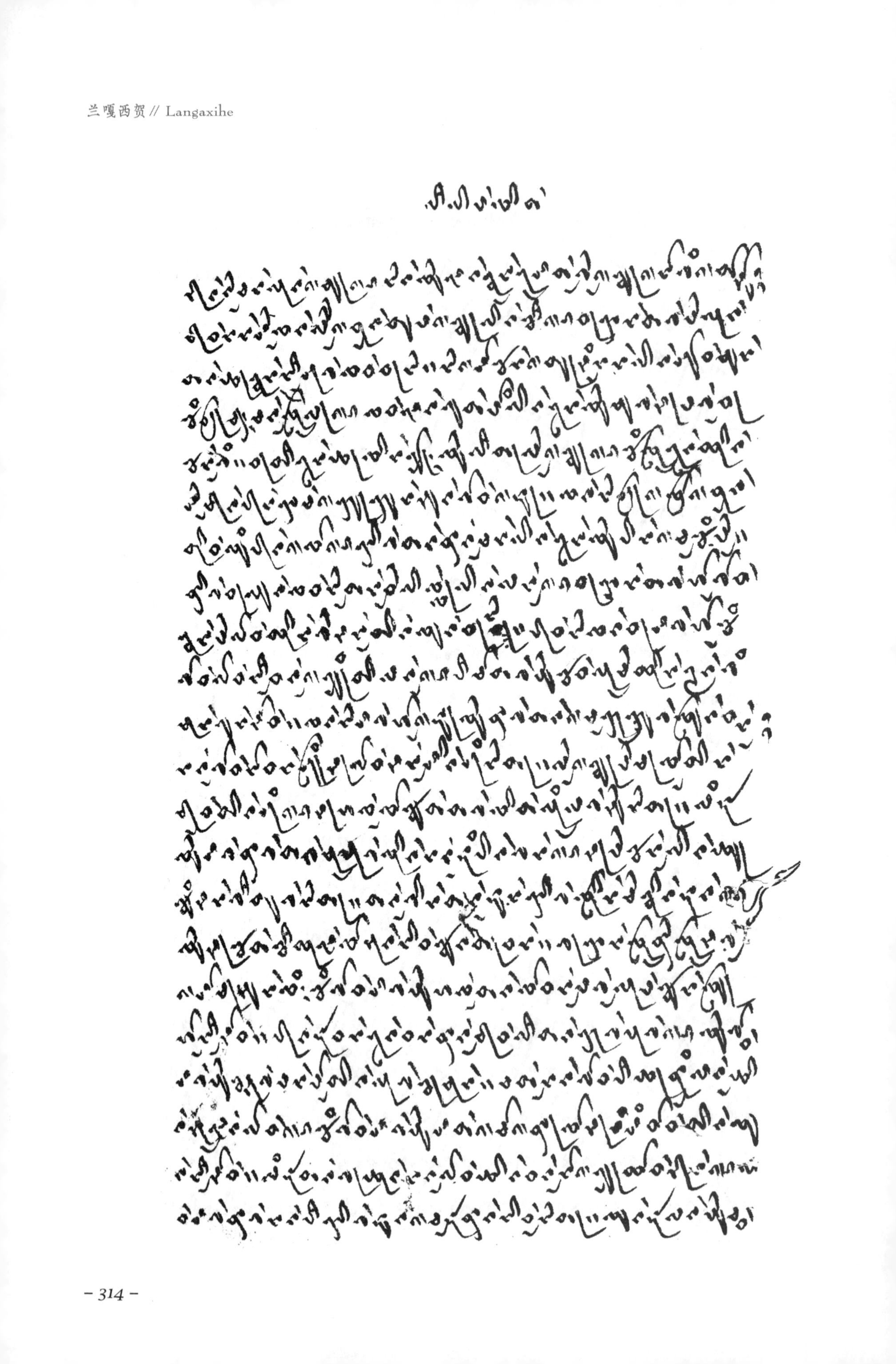

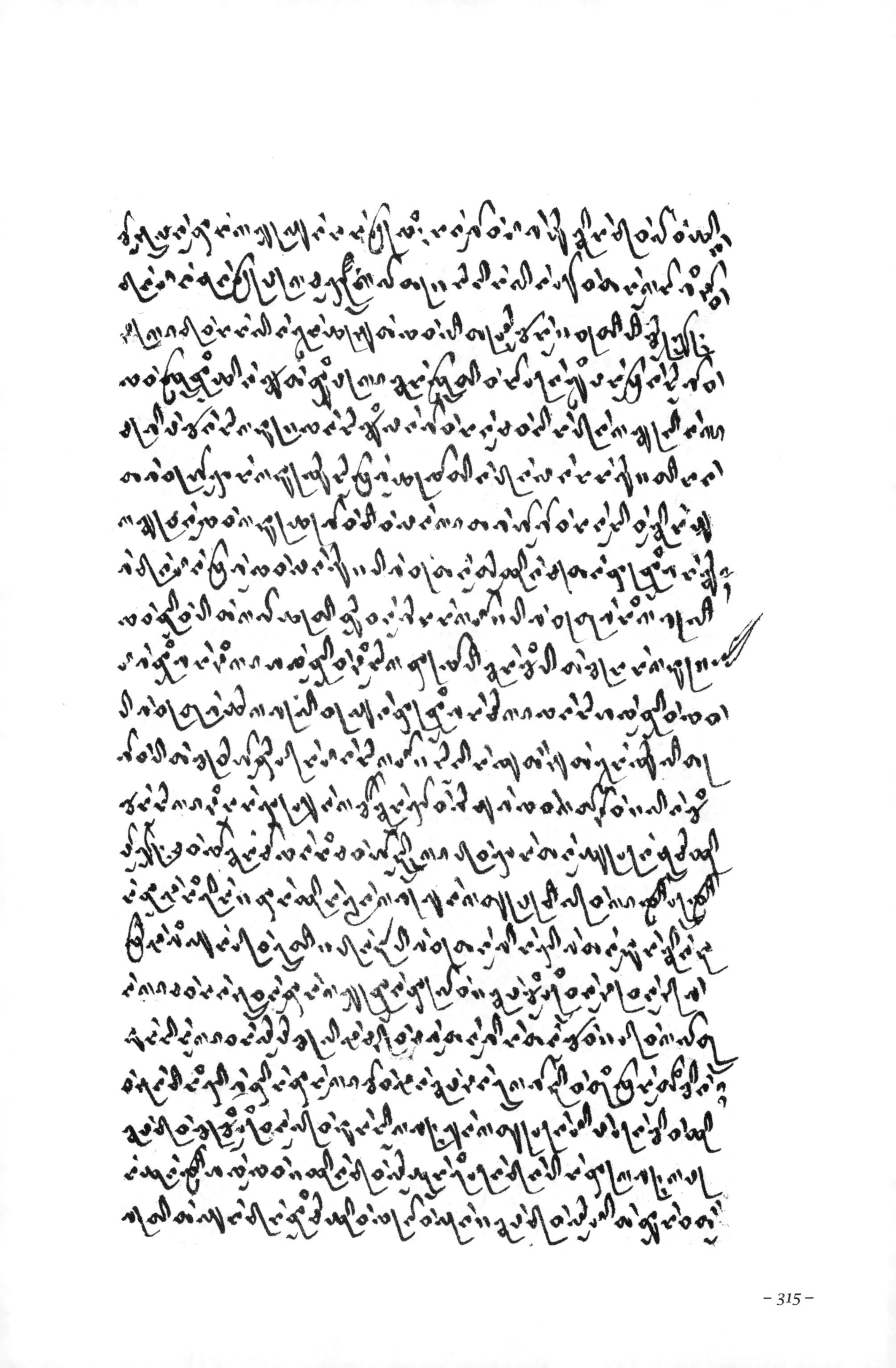

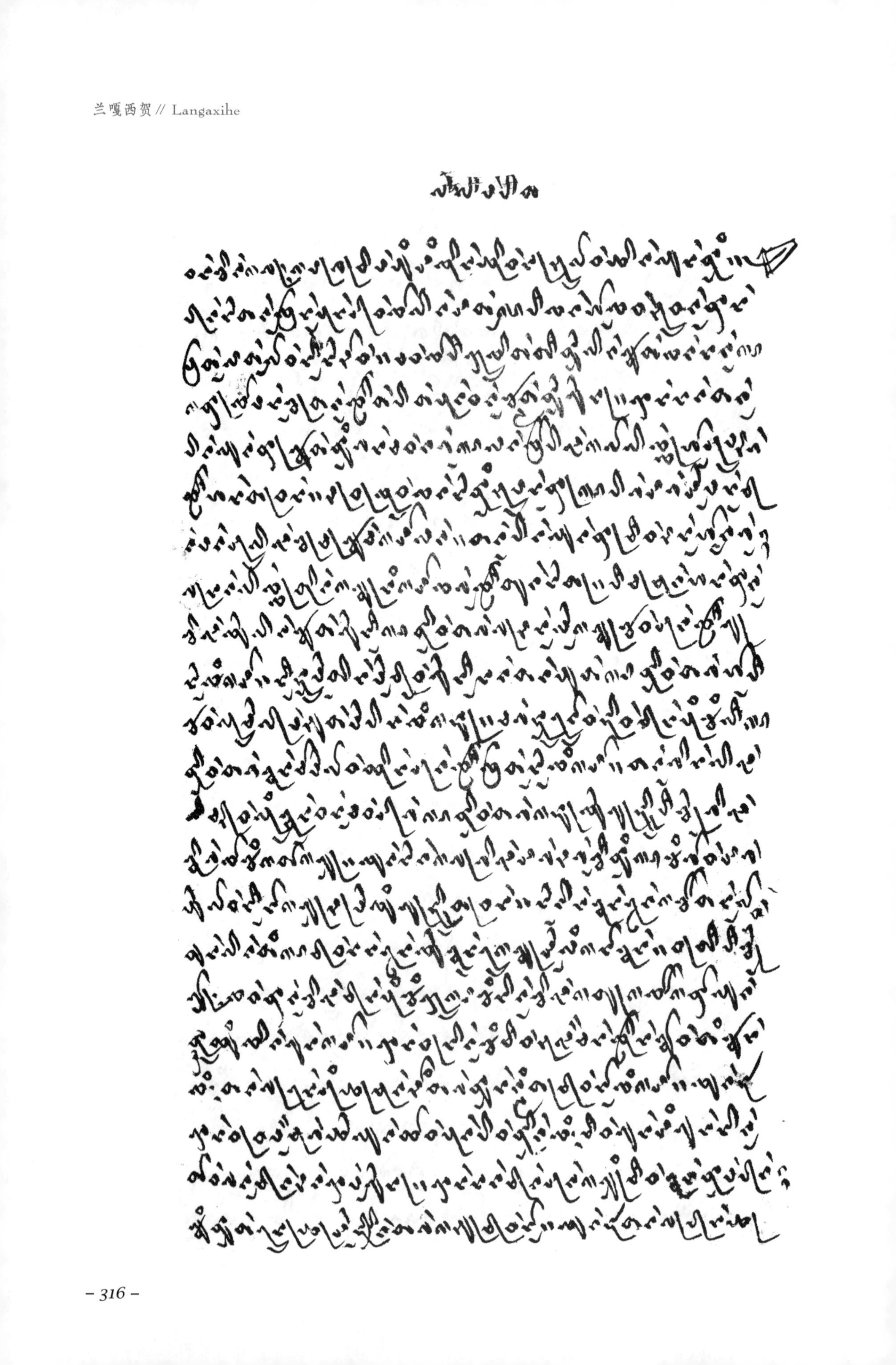

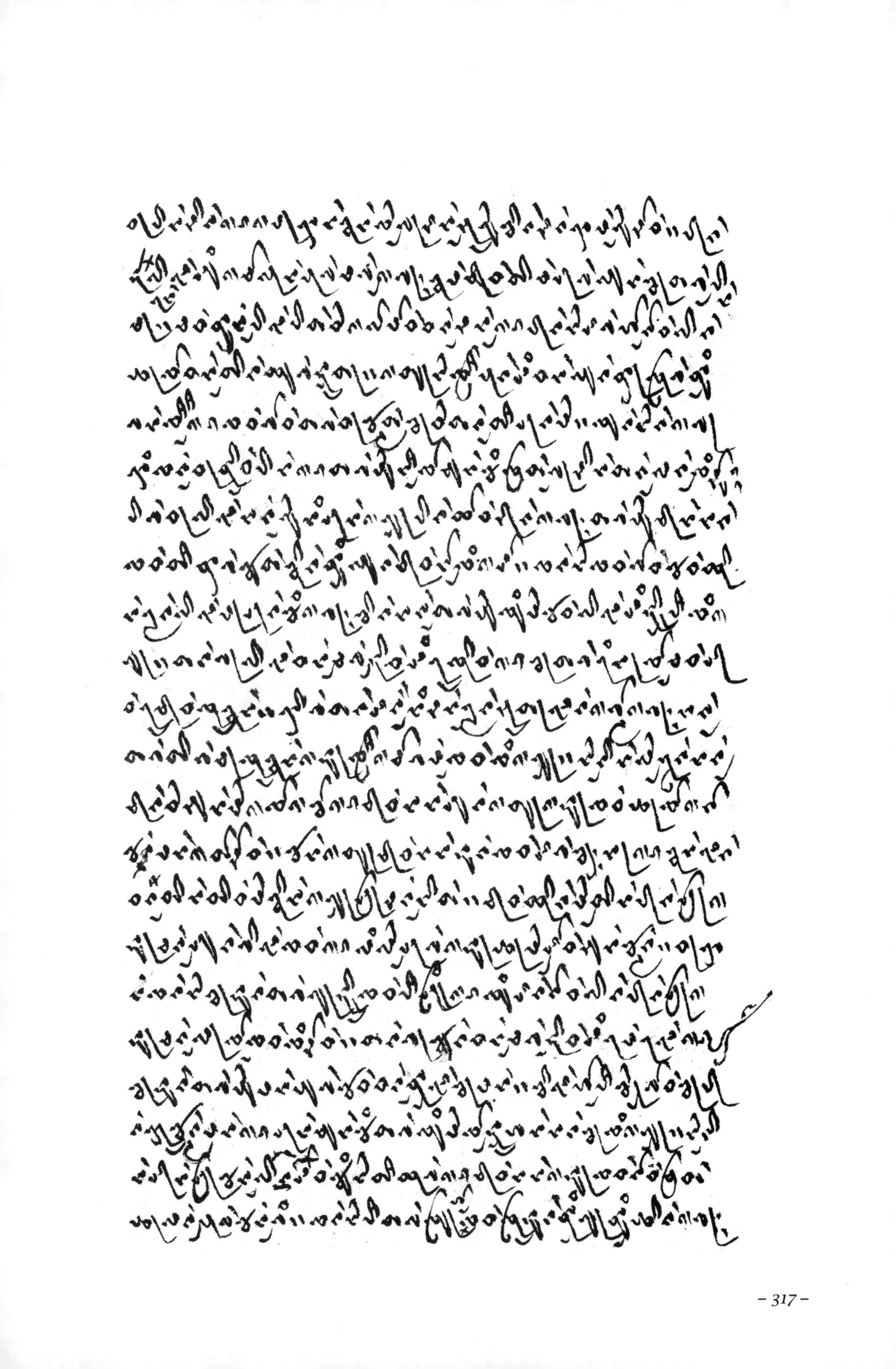

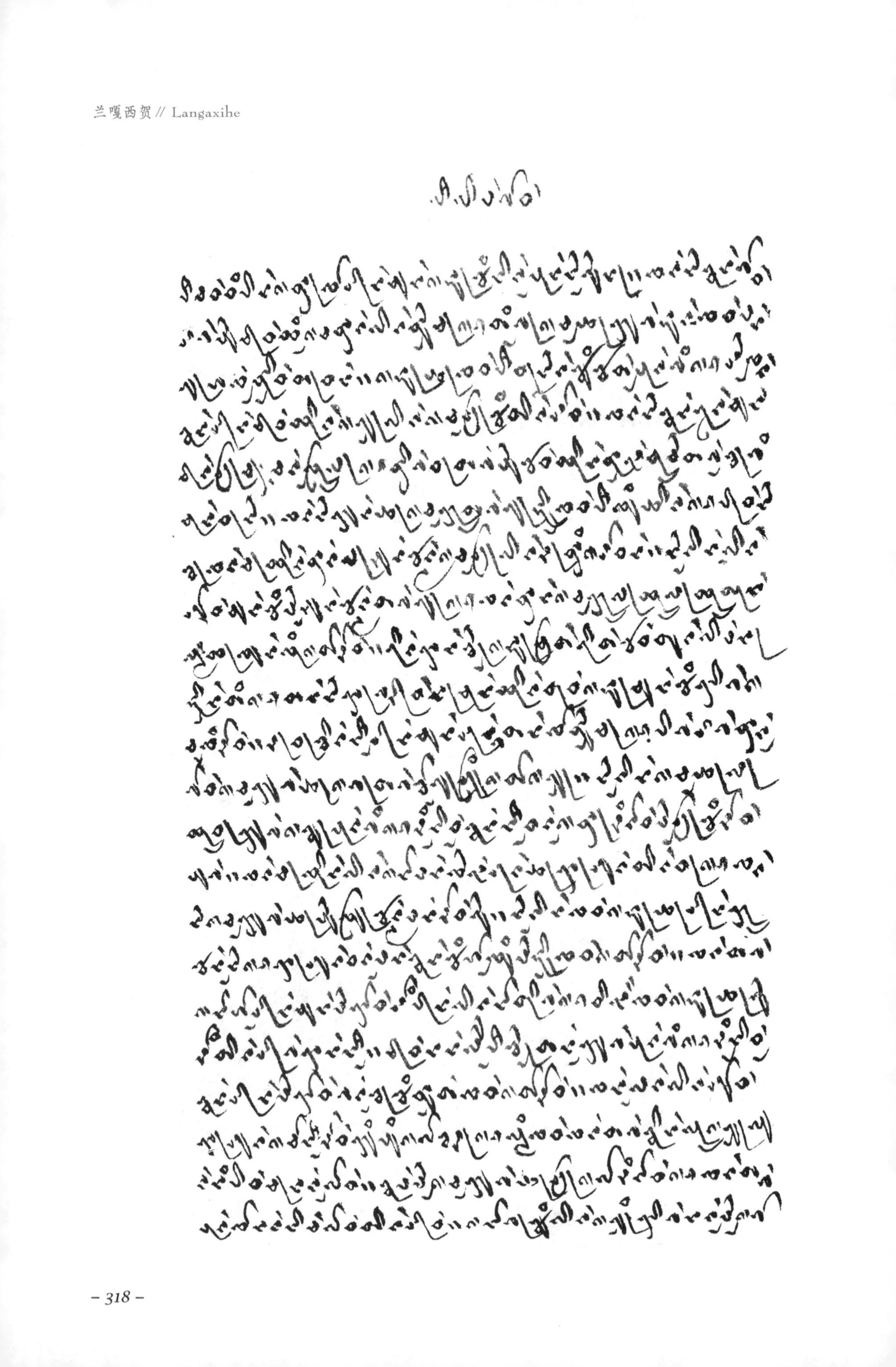

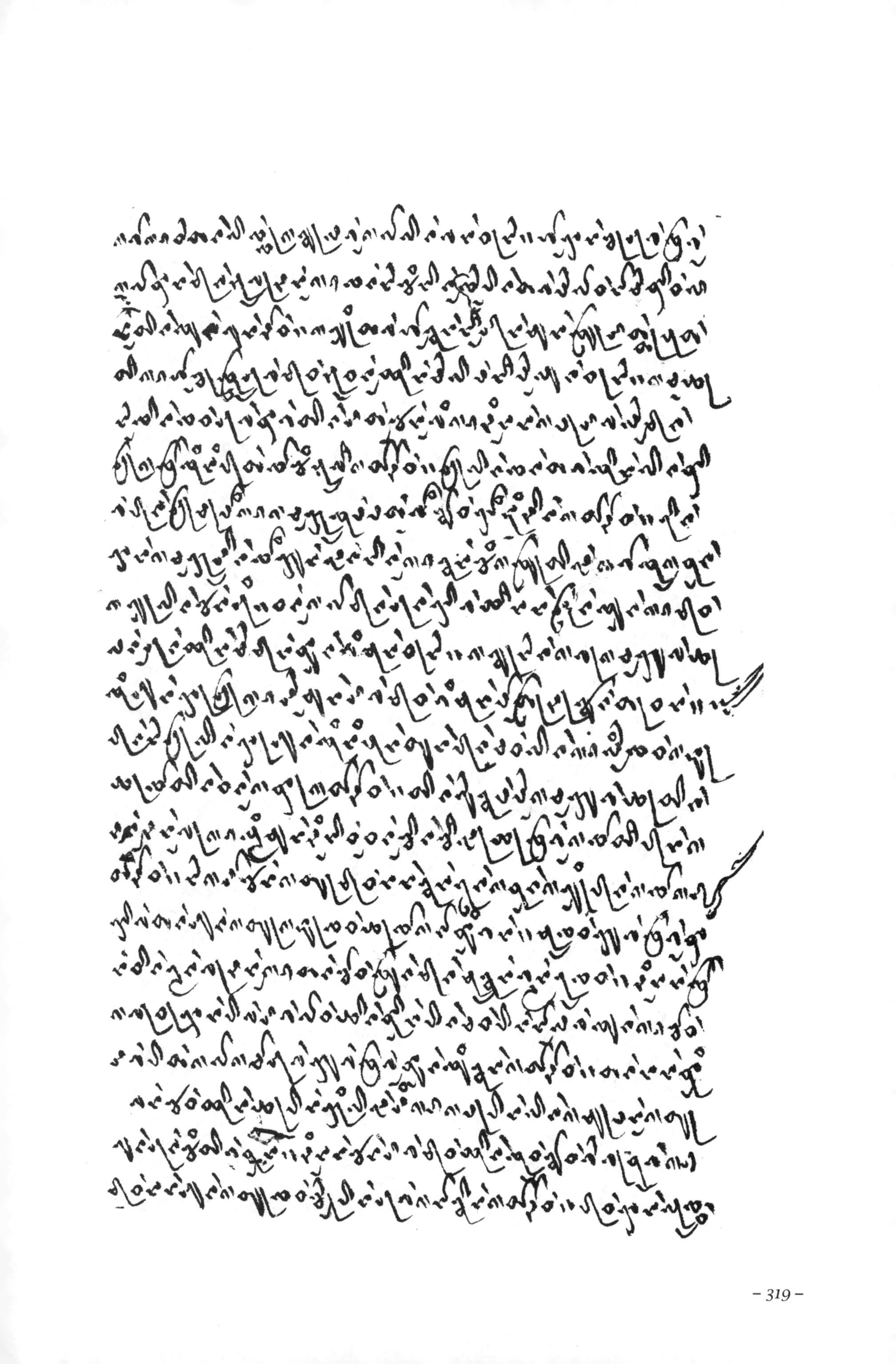

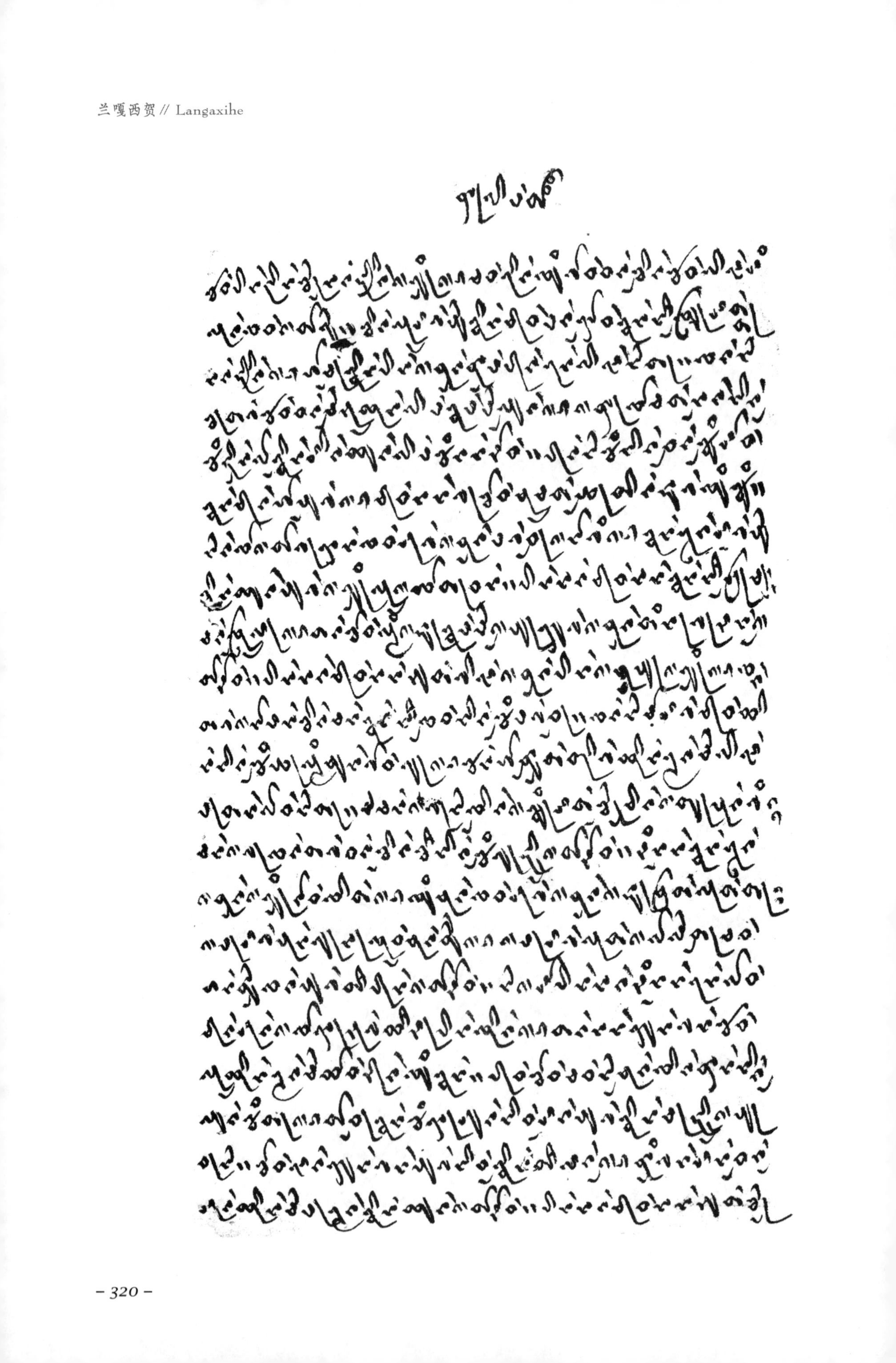

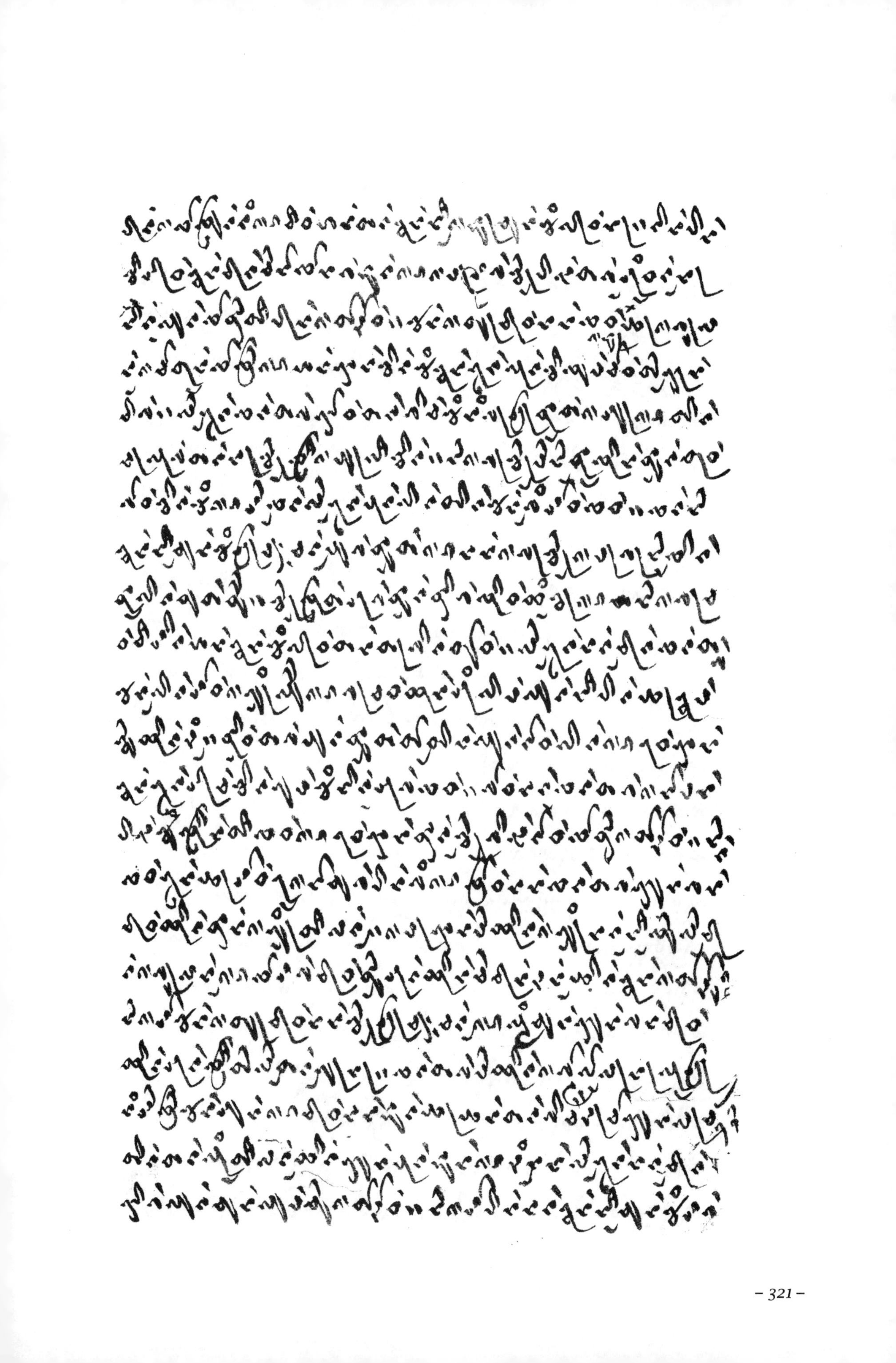

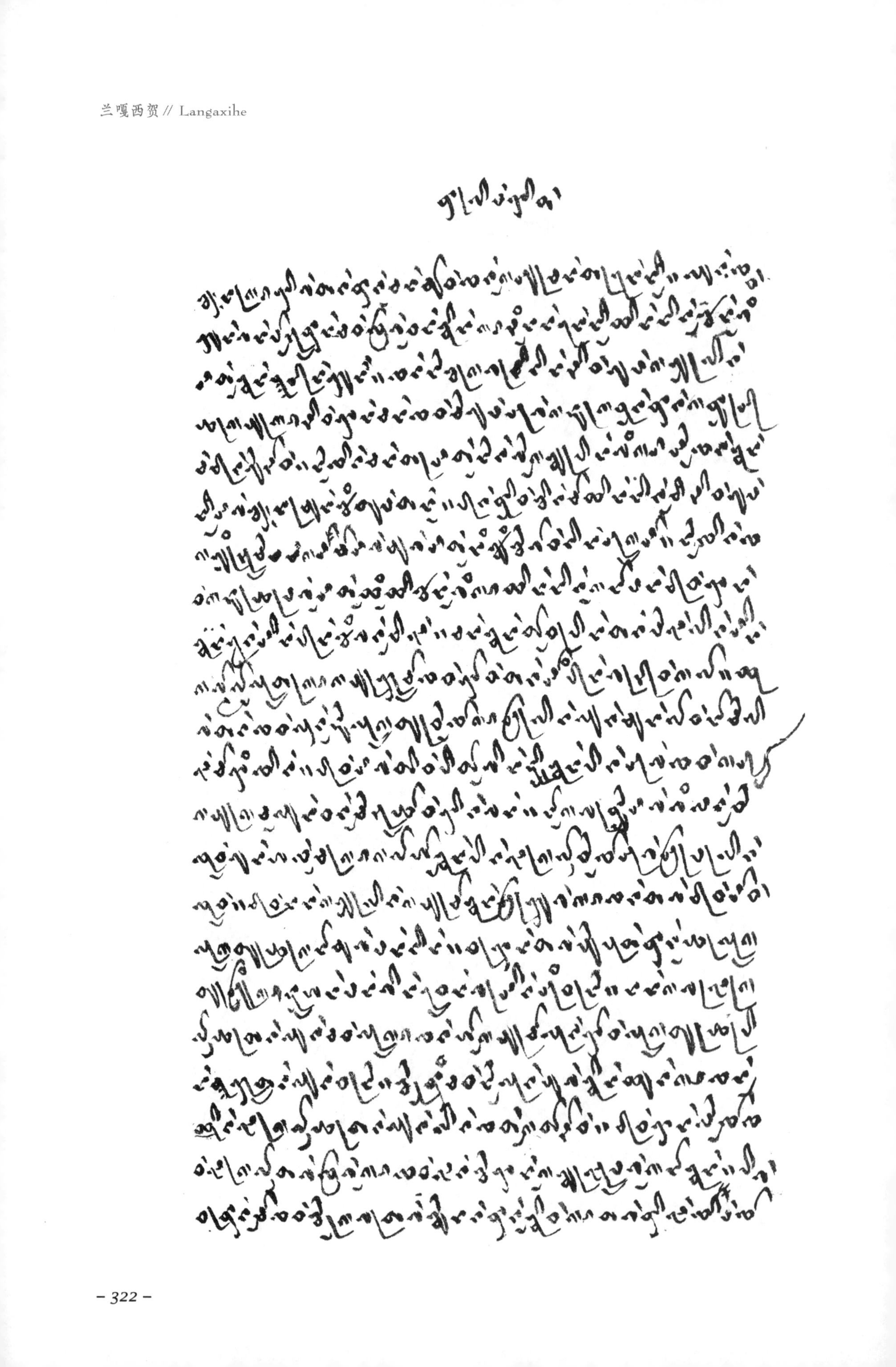

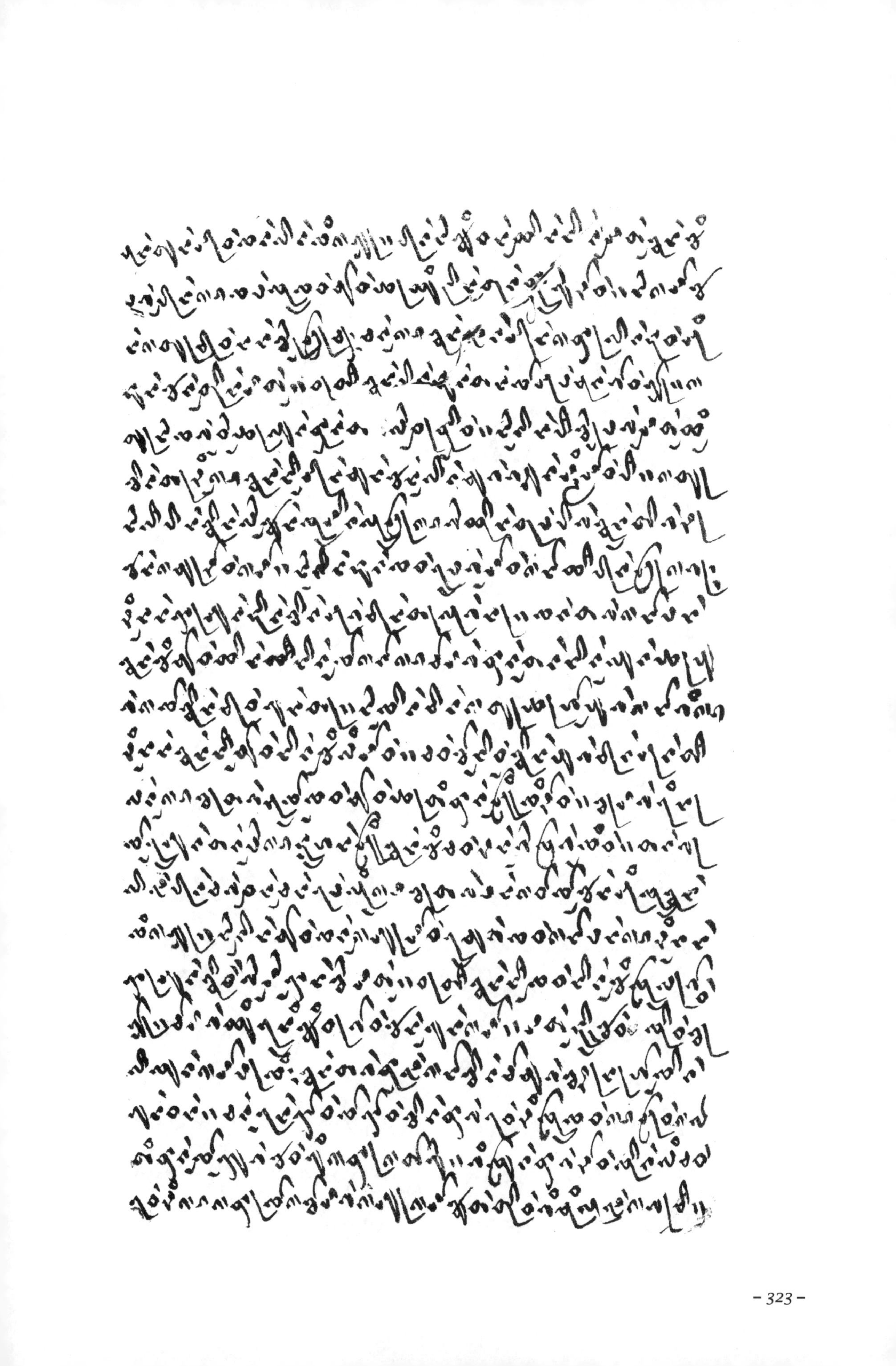

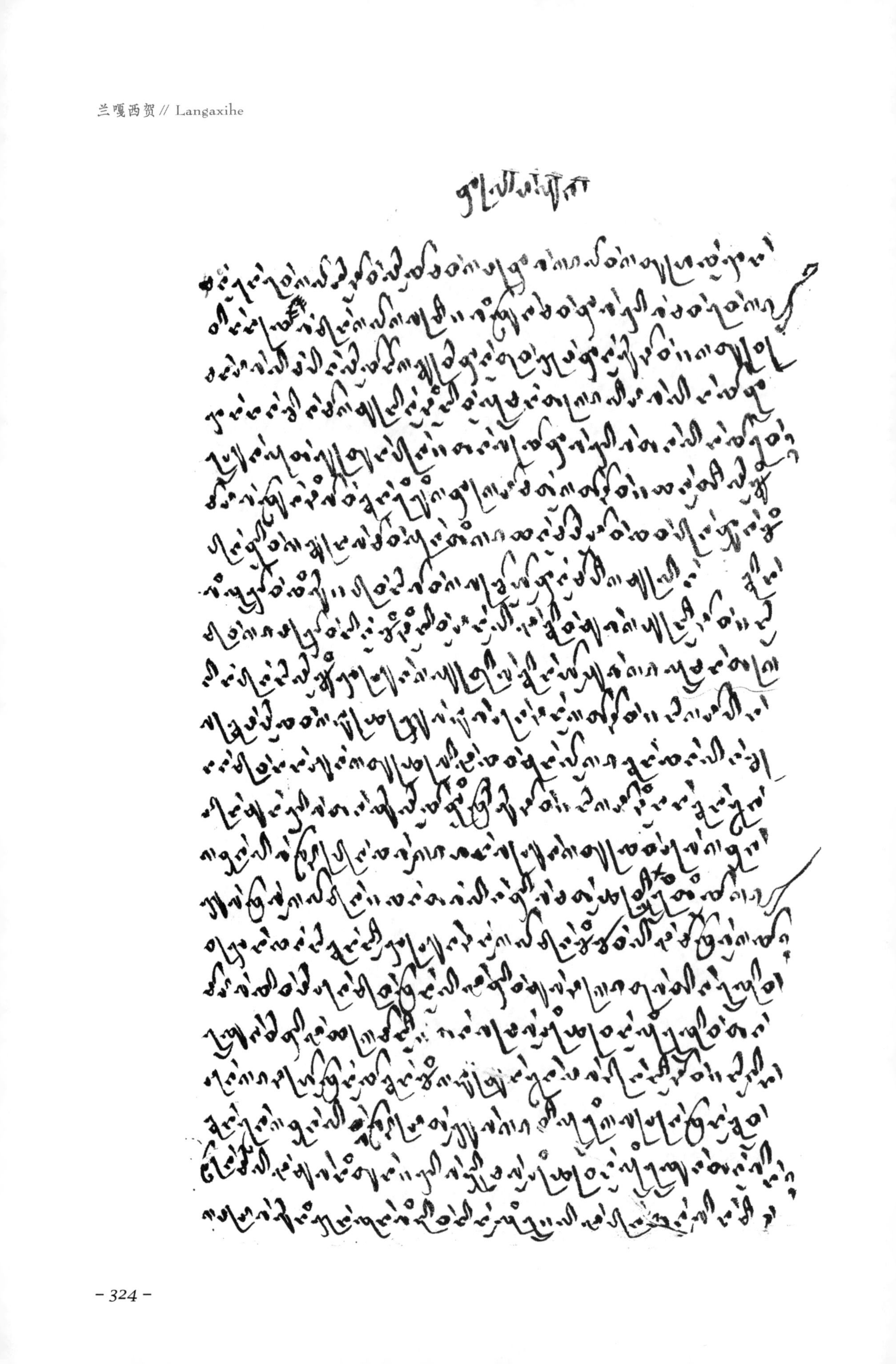

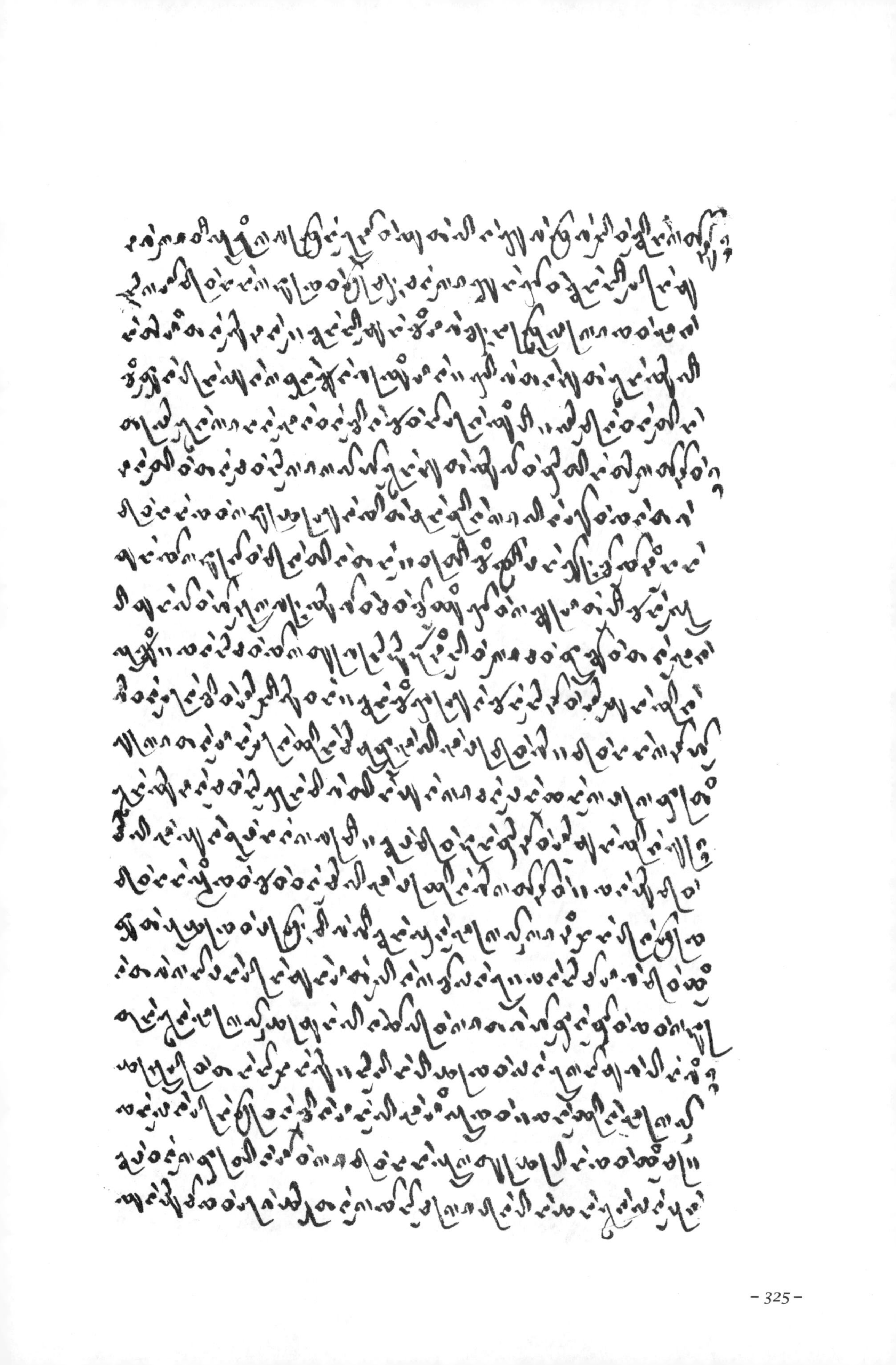

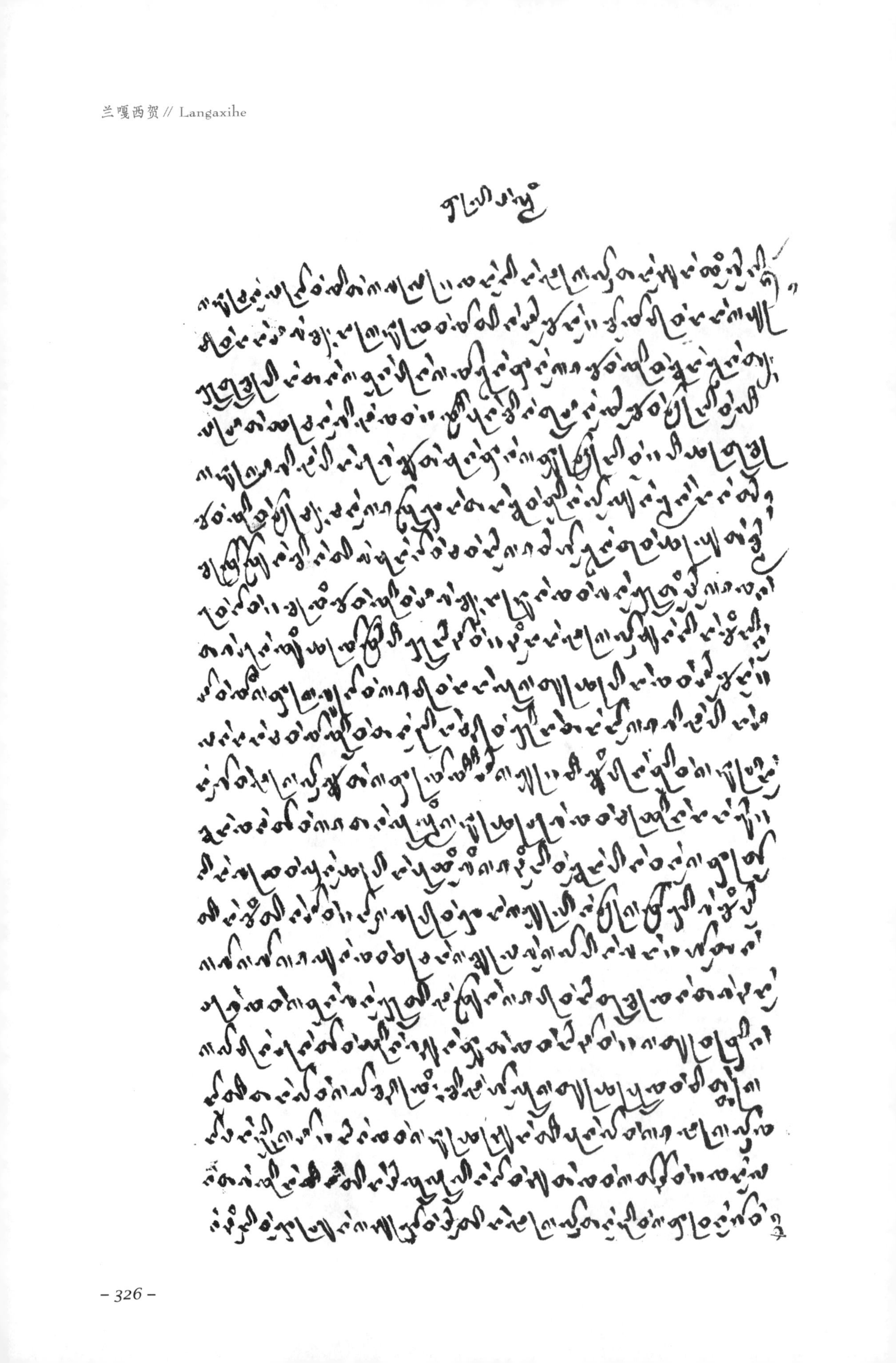

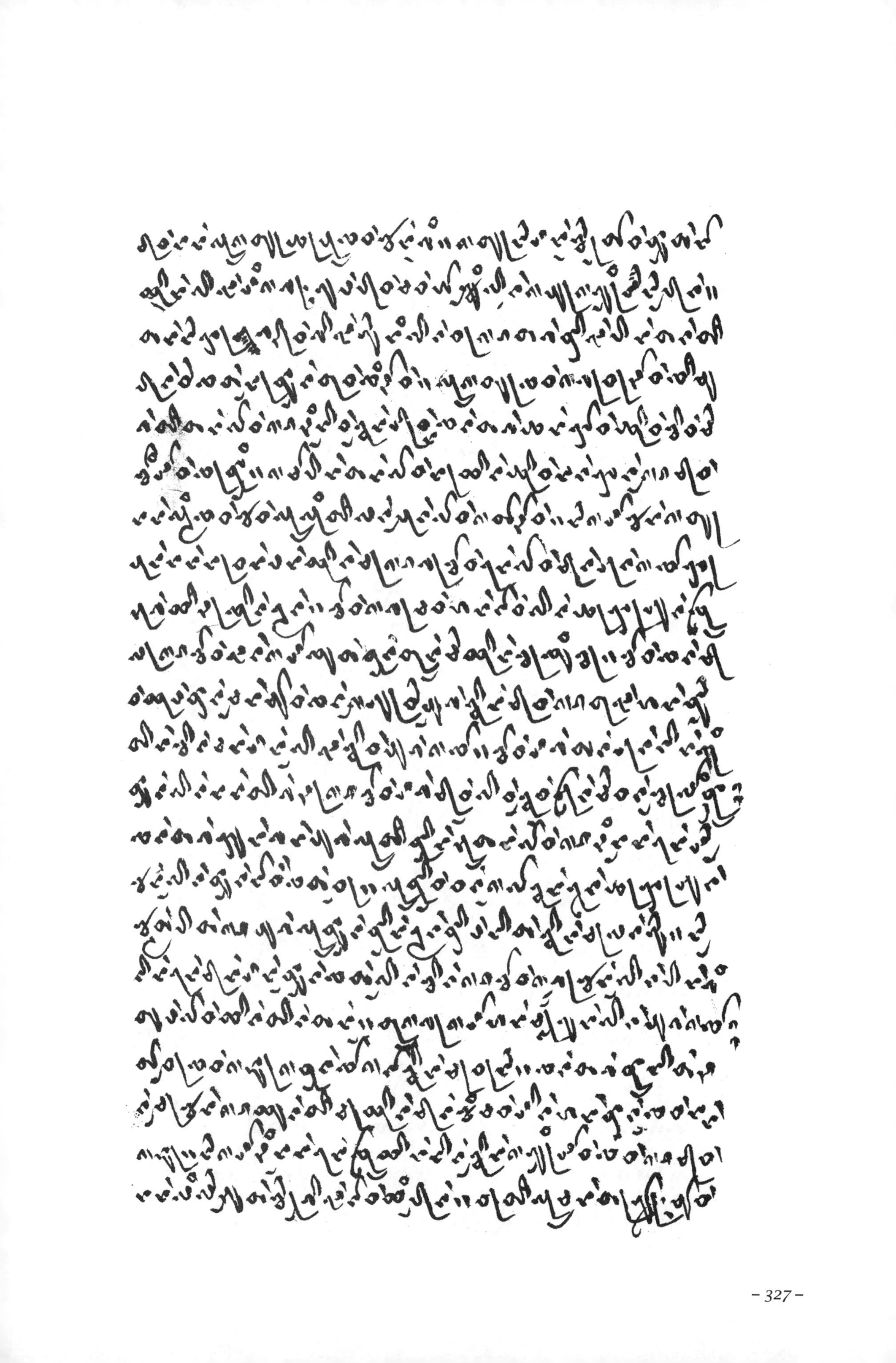

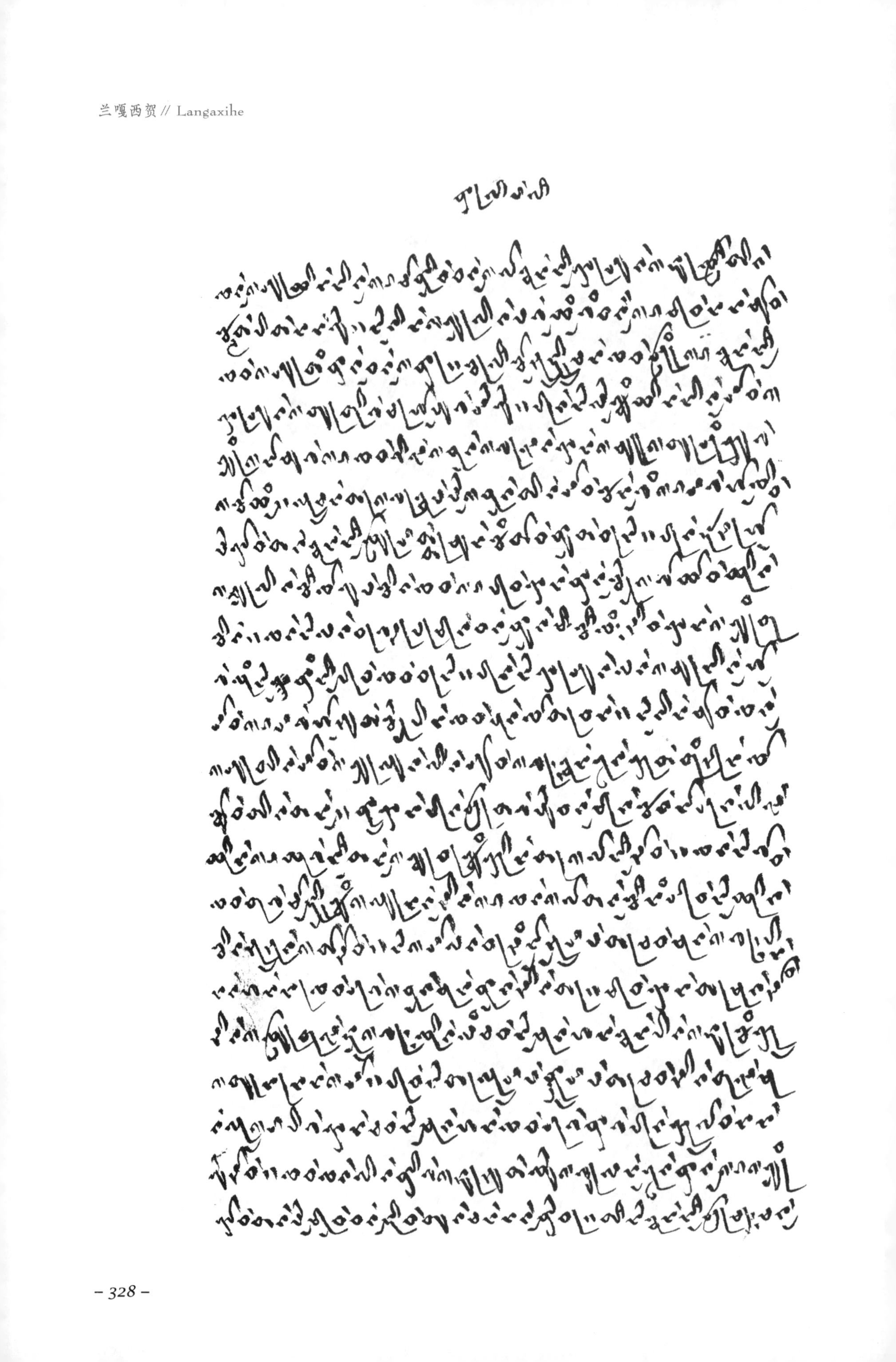

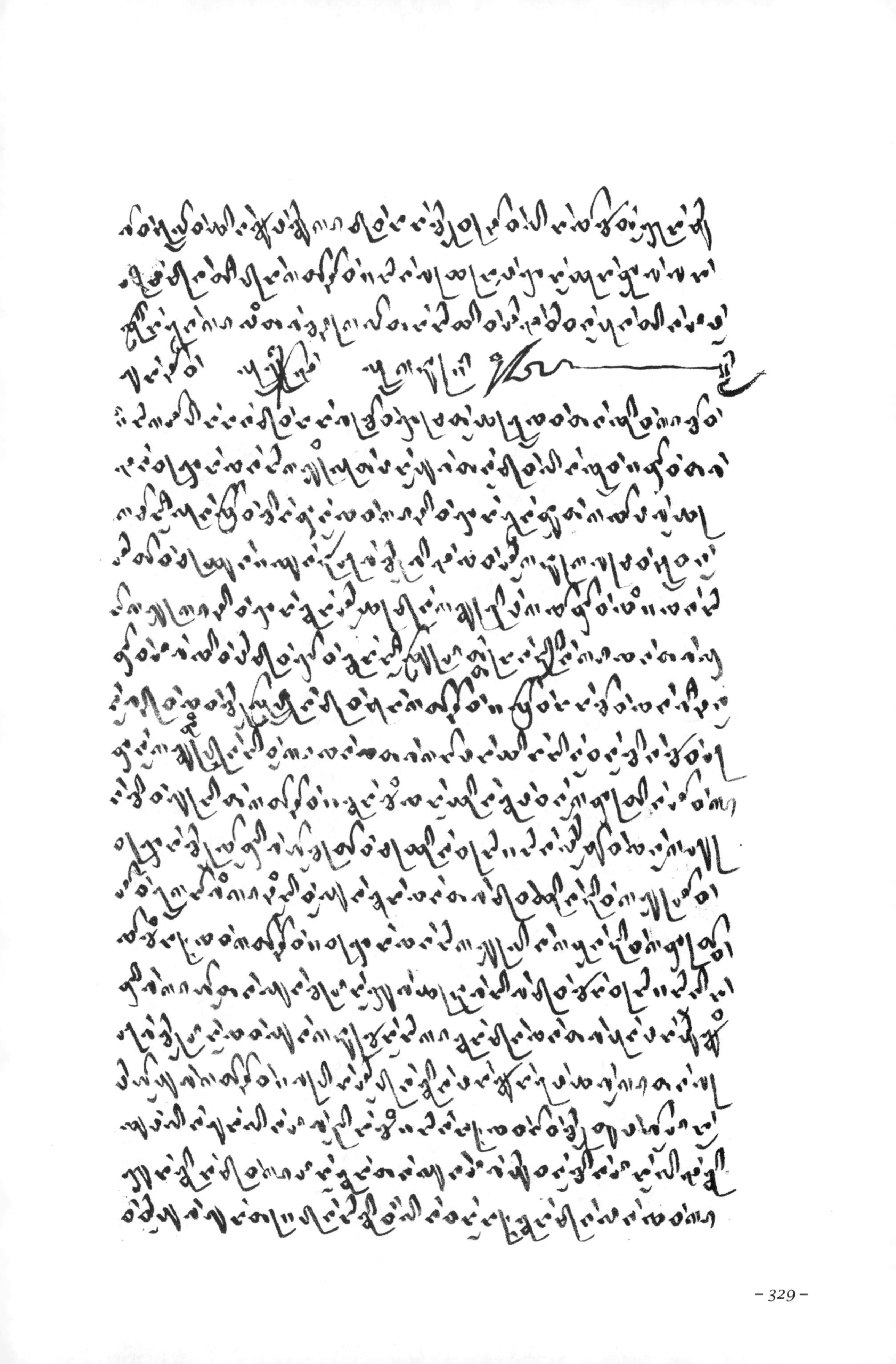

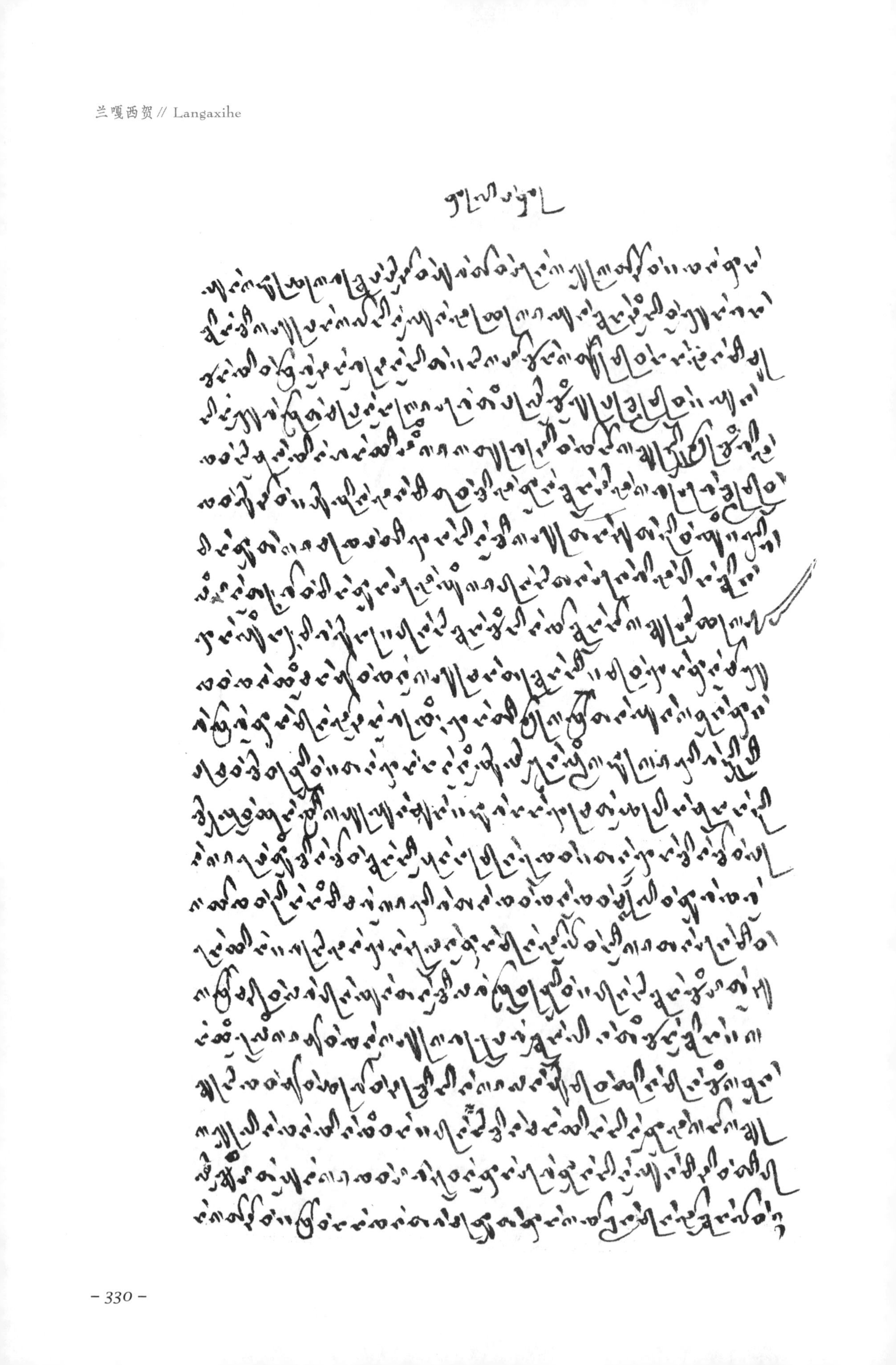

[illegible]

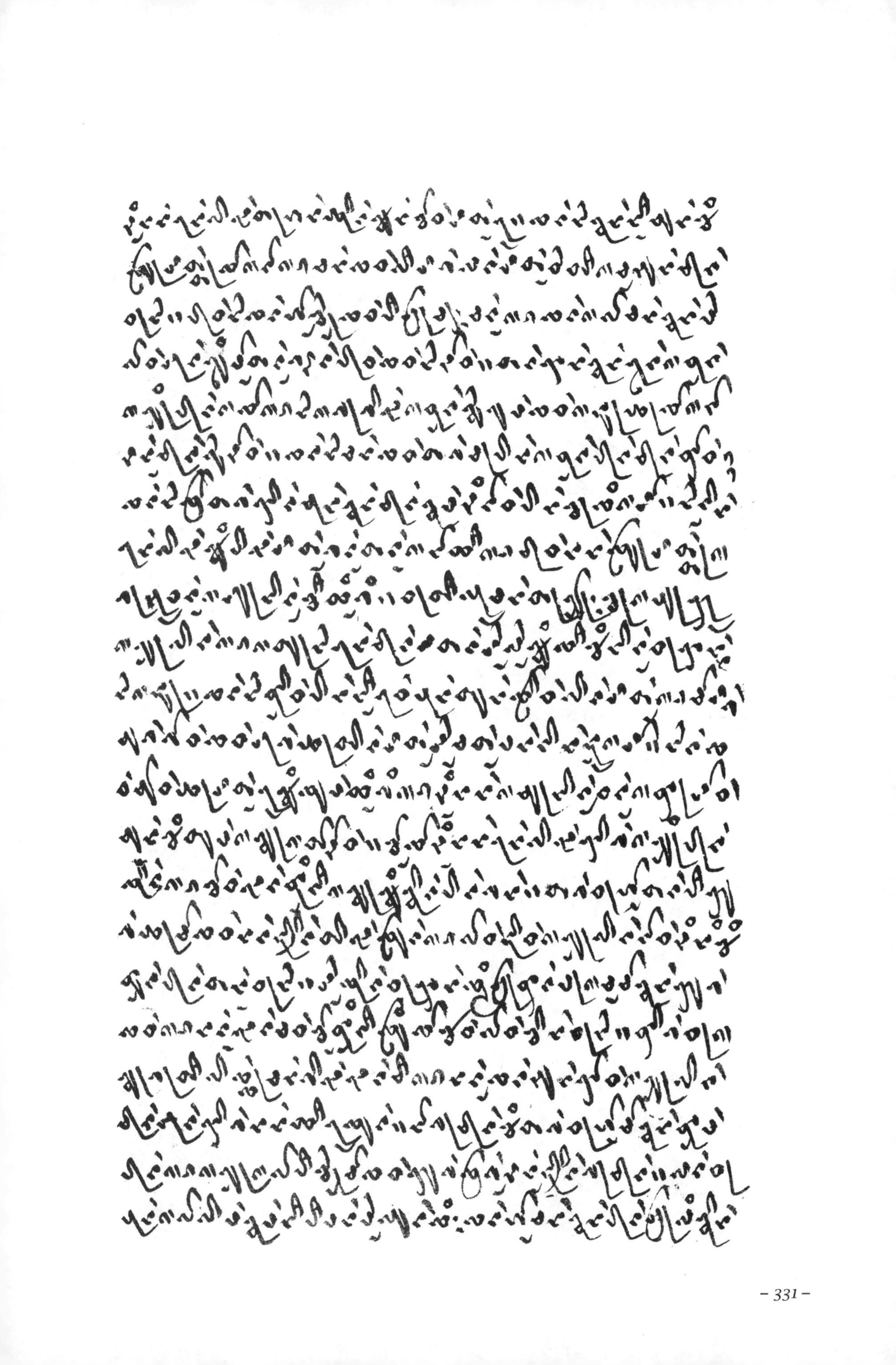

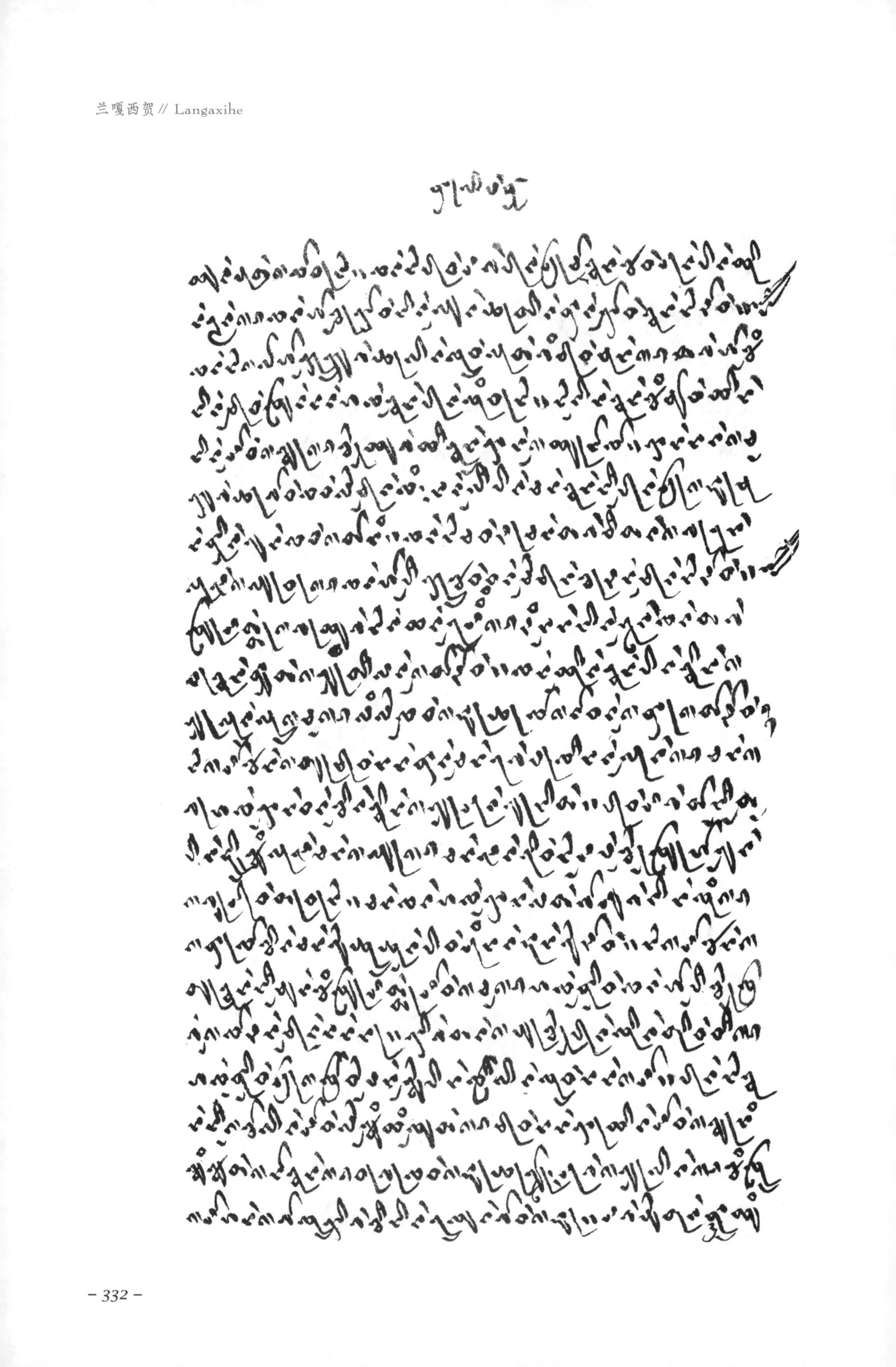

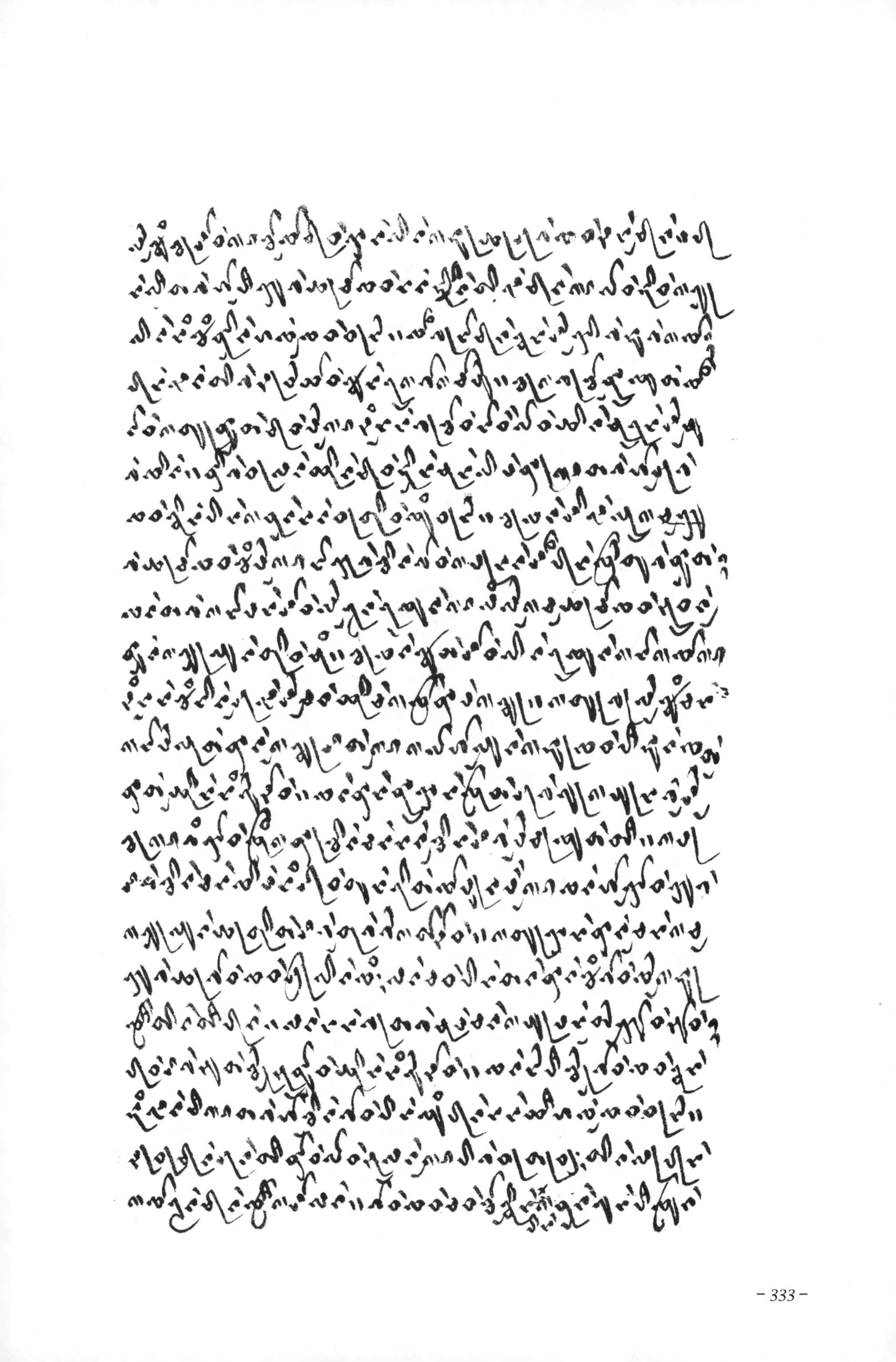

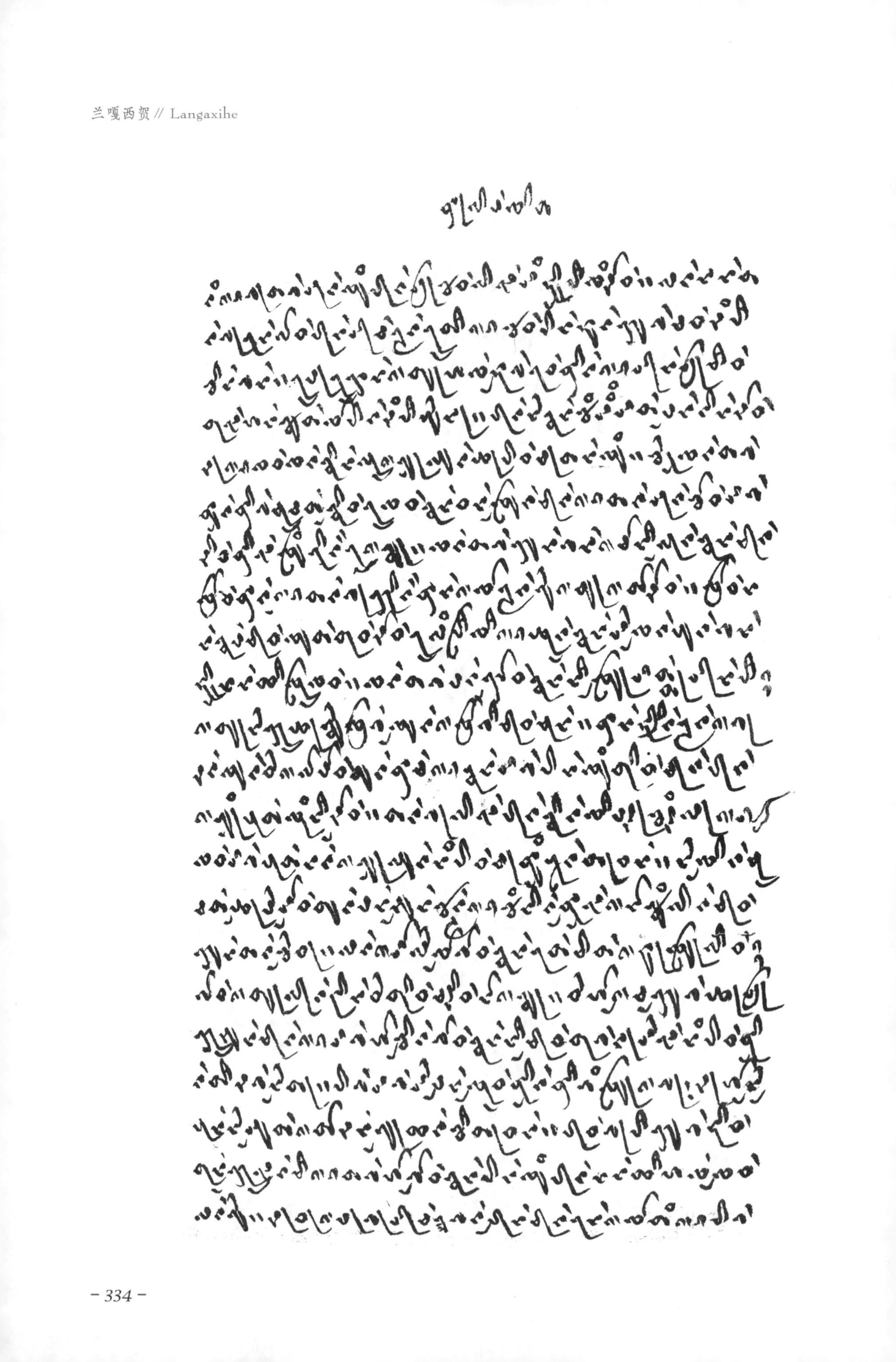

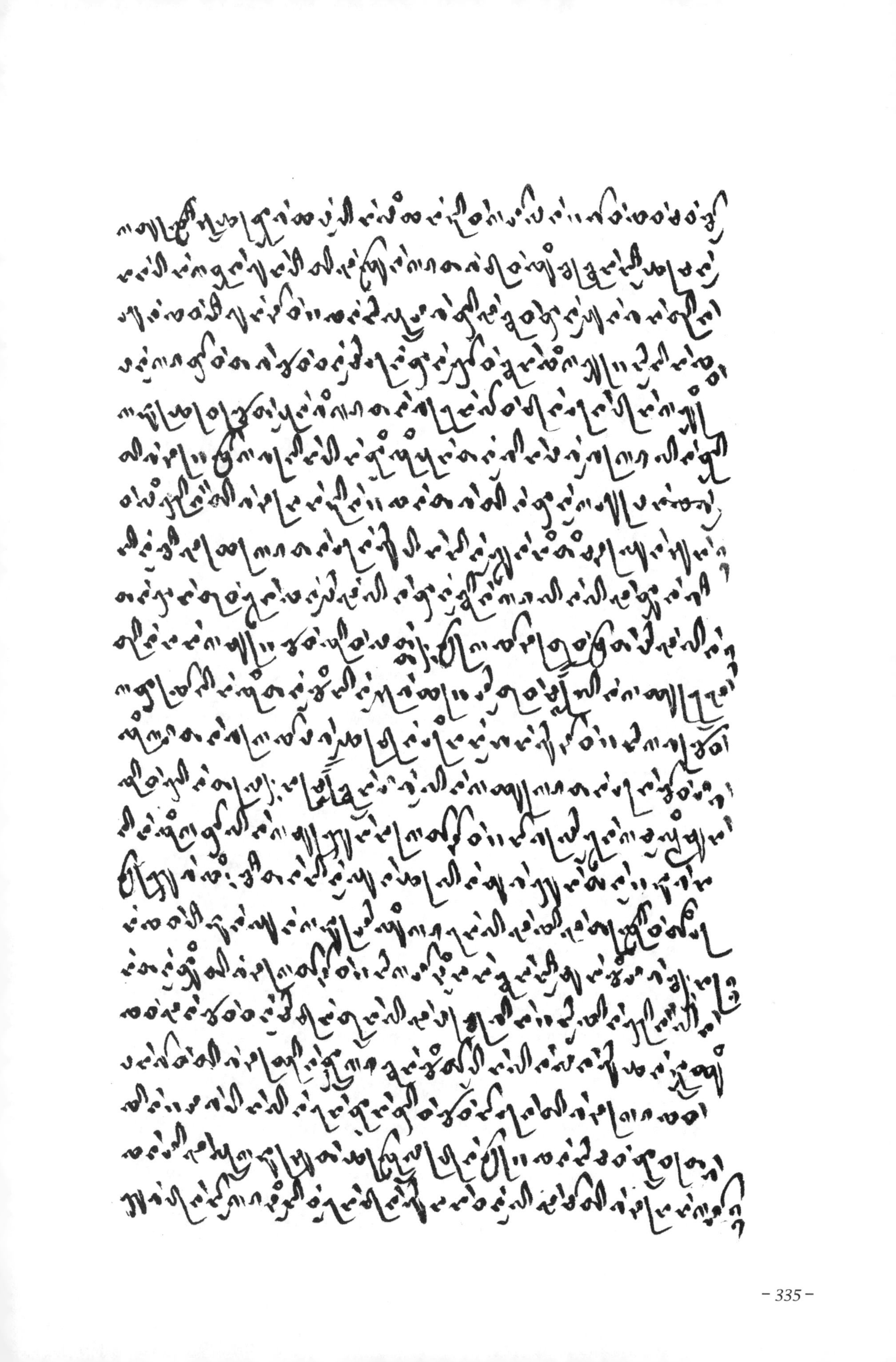

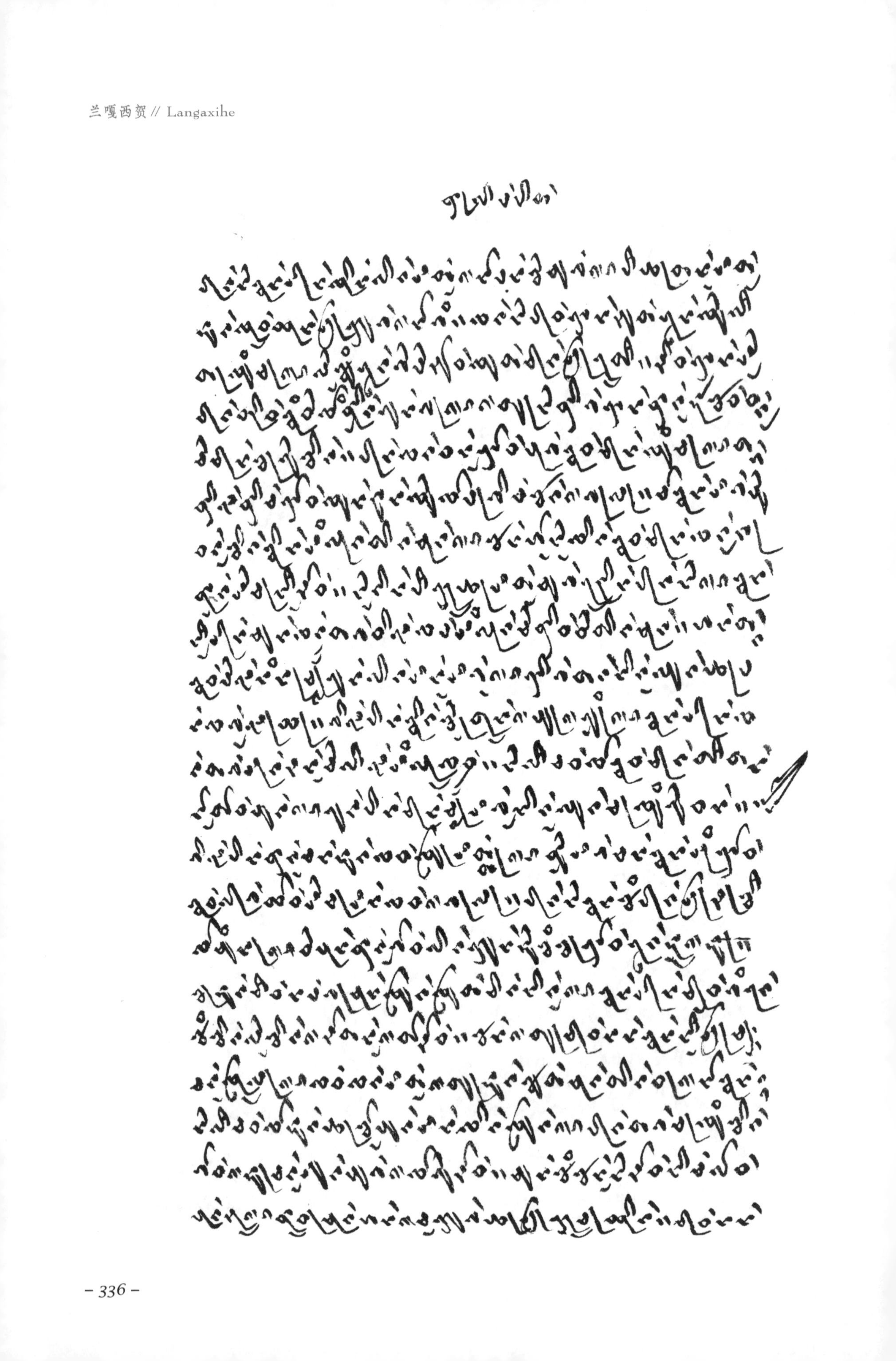

[illegible]

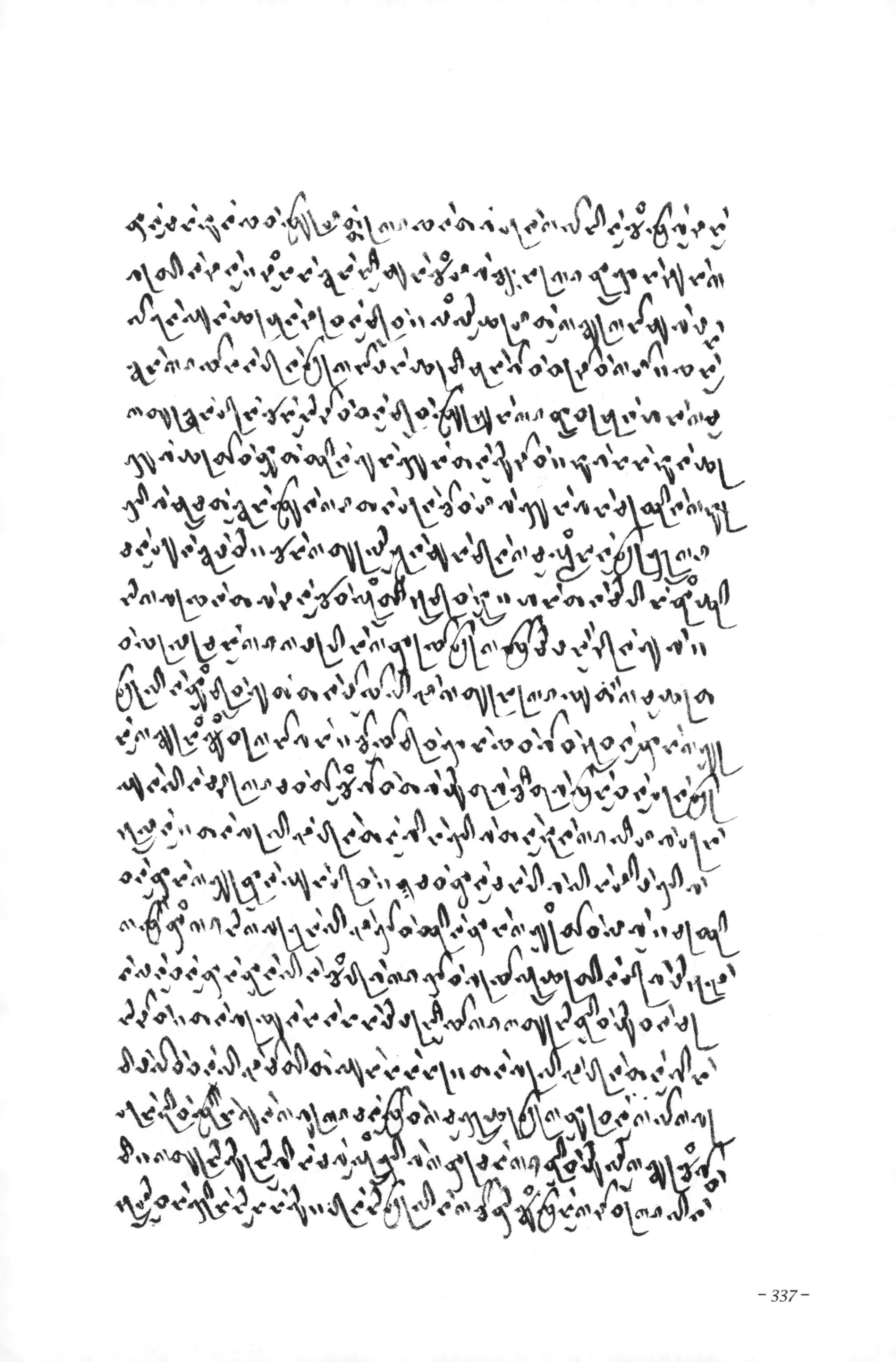

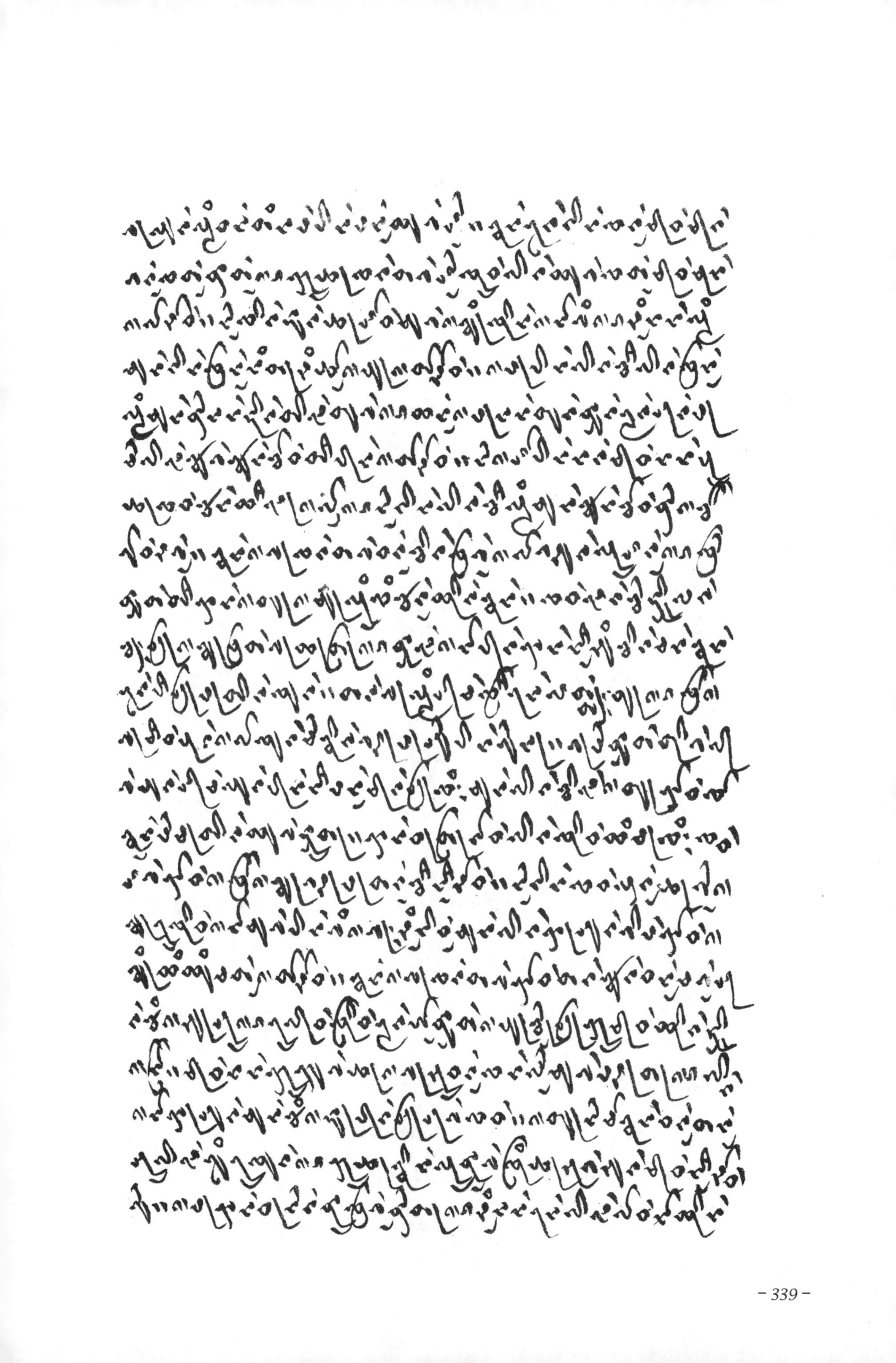

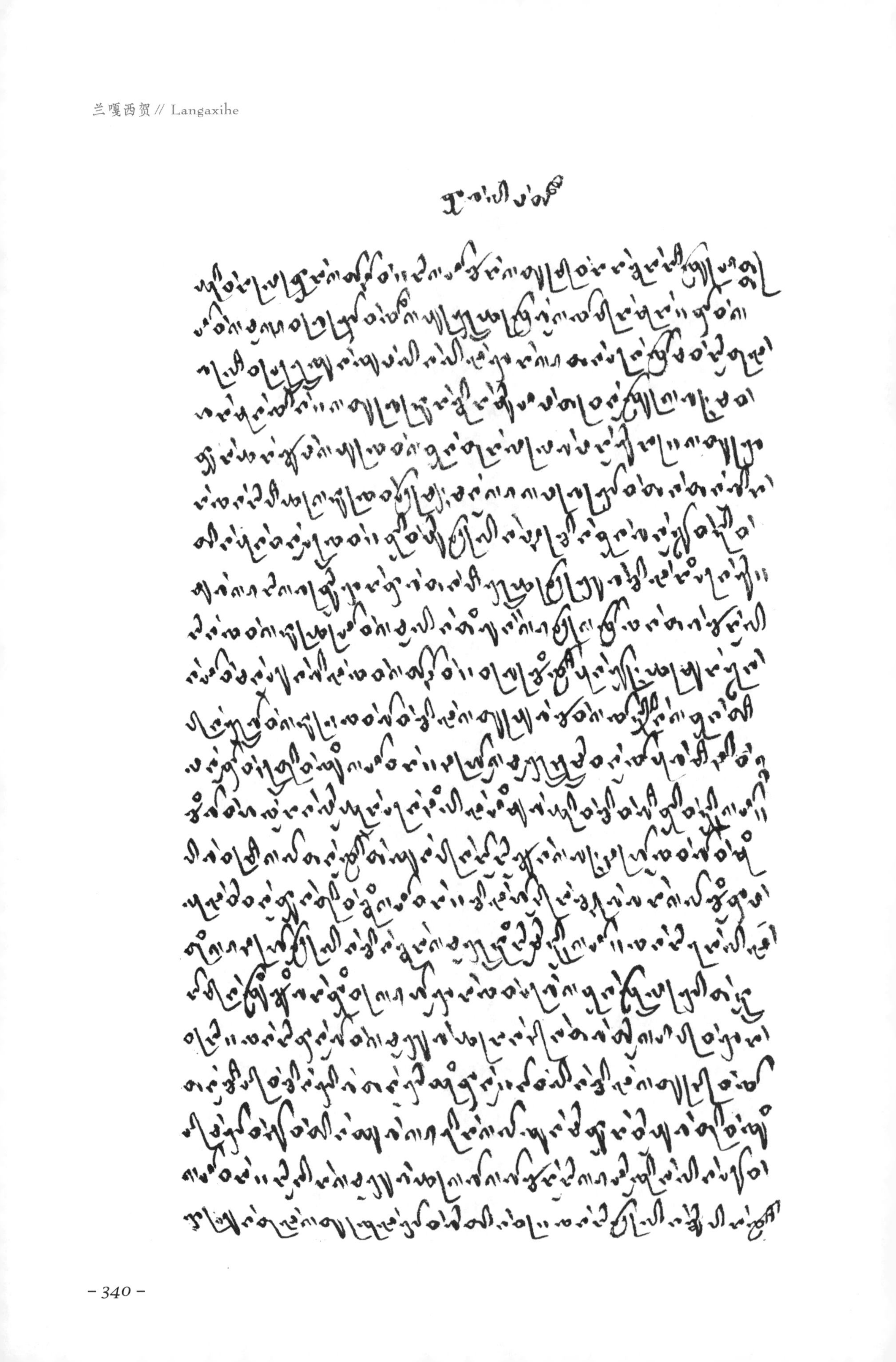

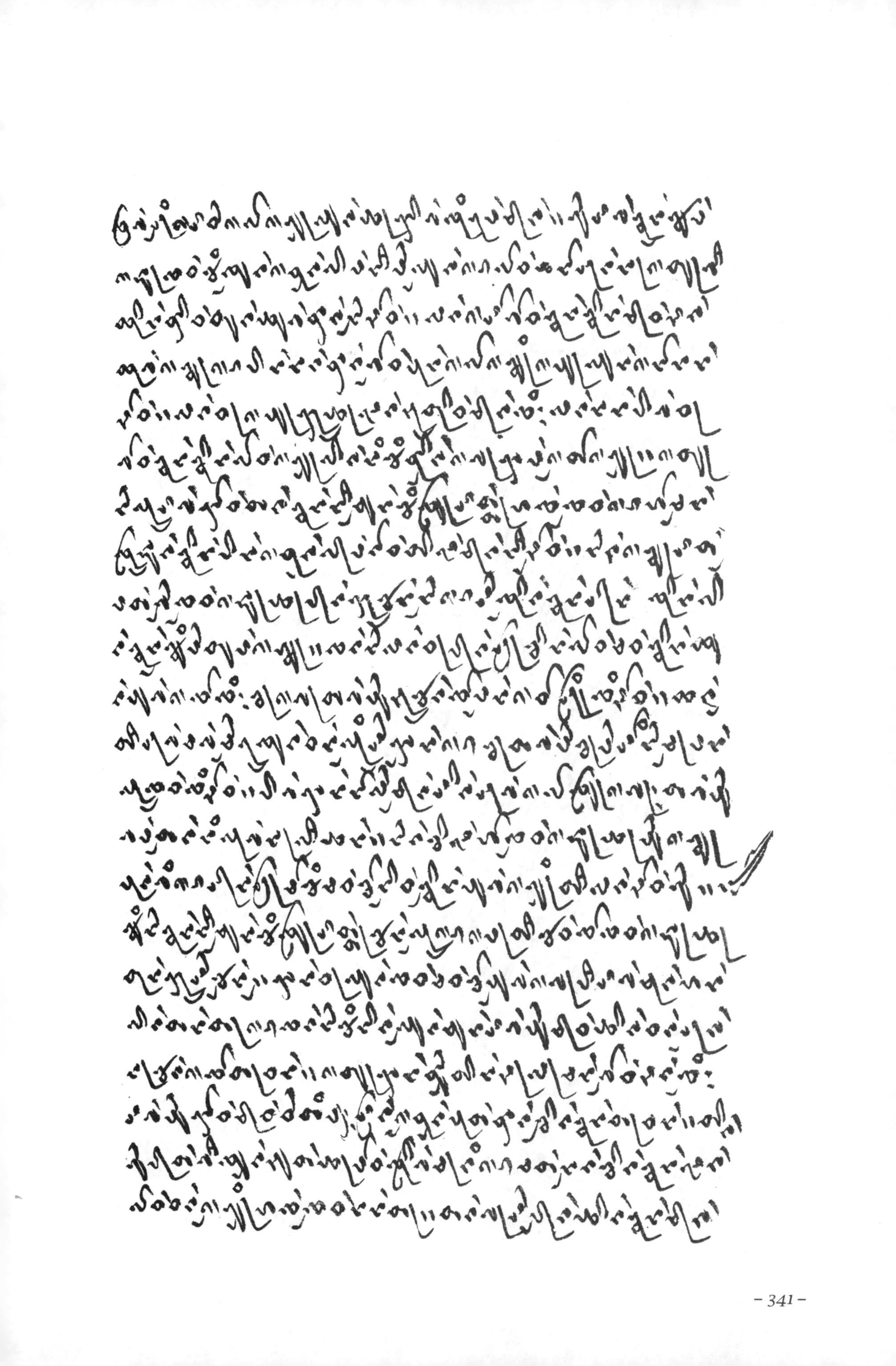

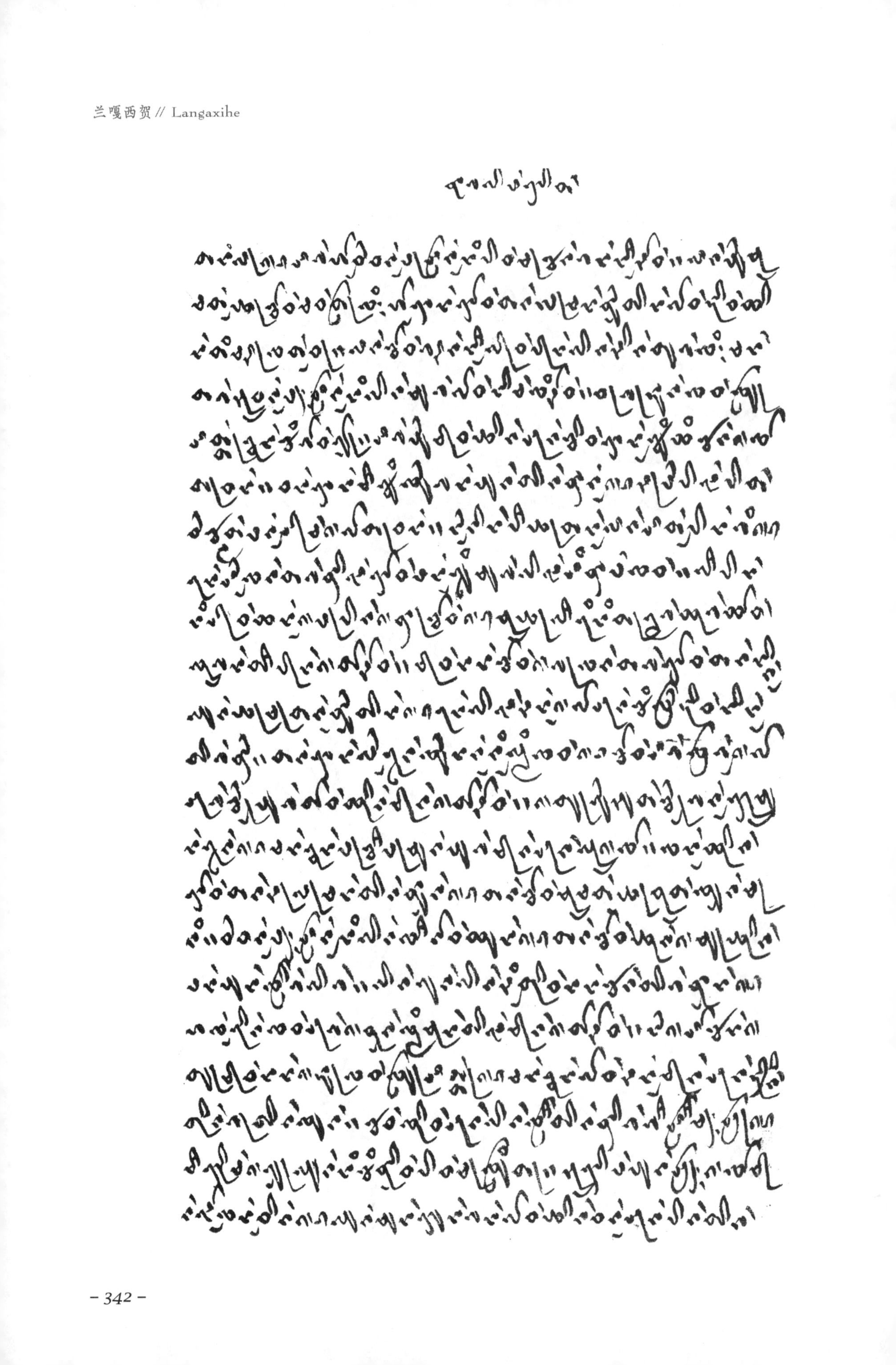

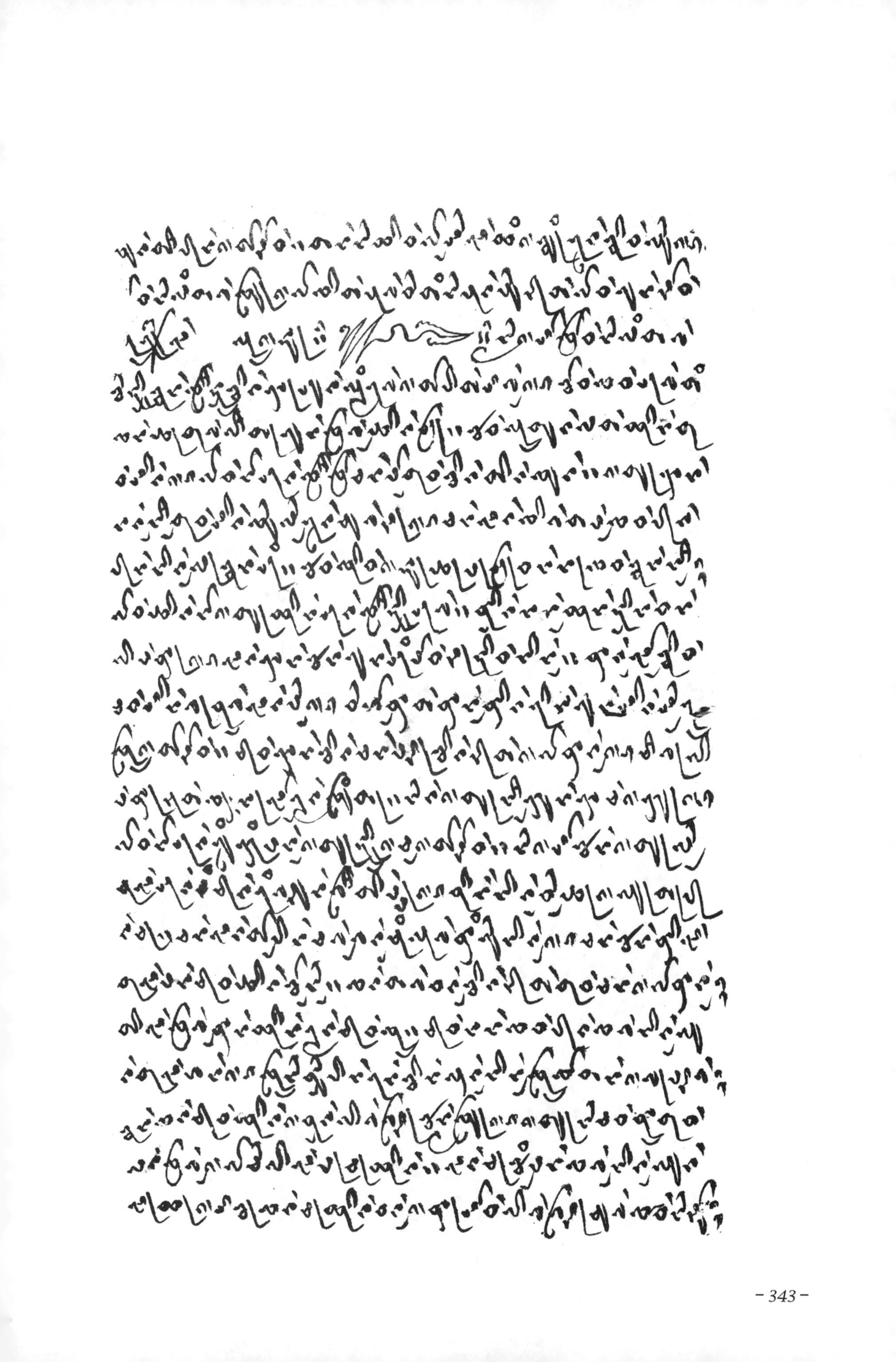

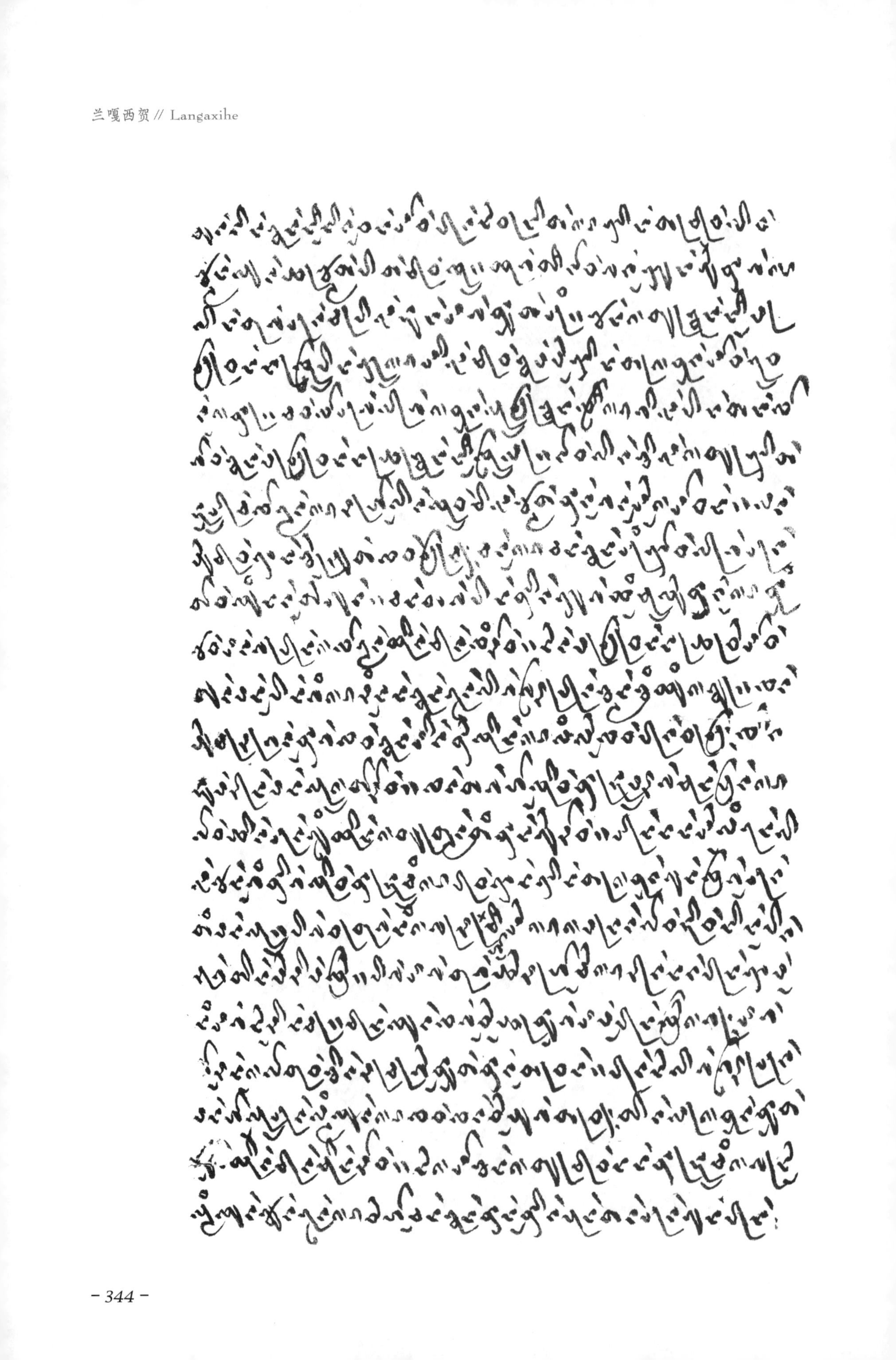

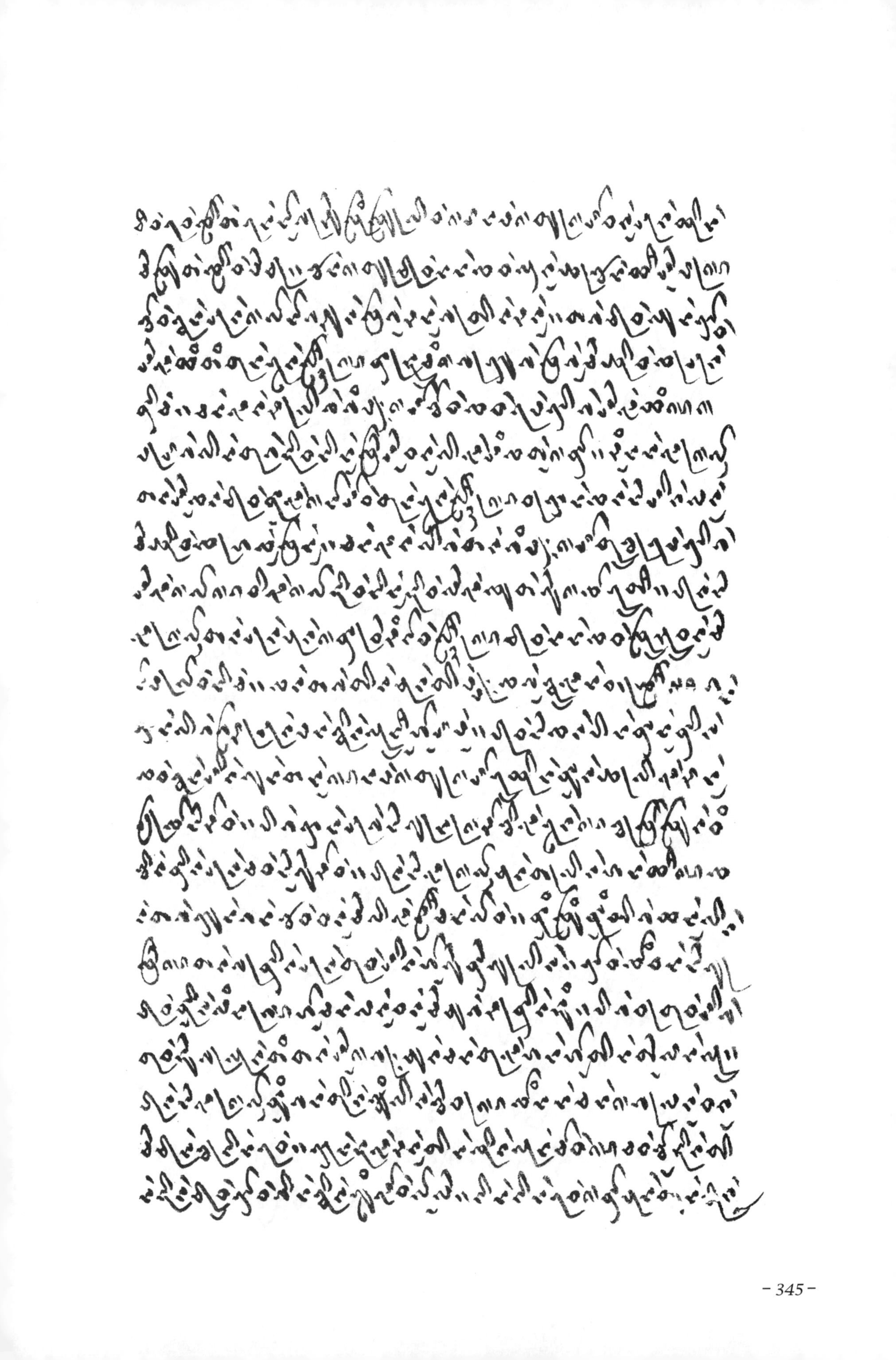

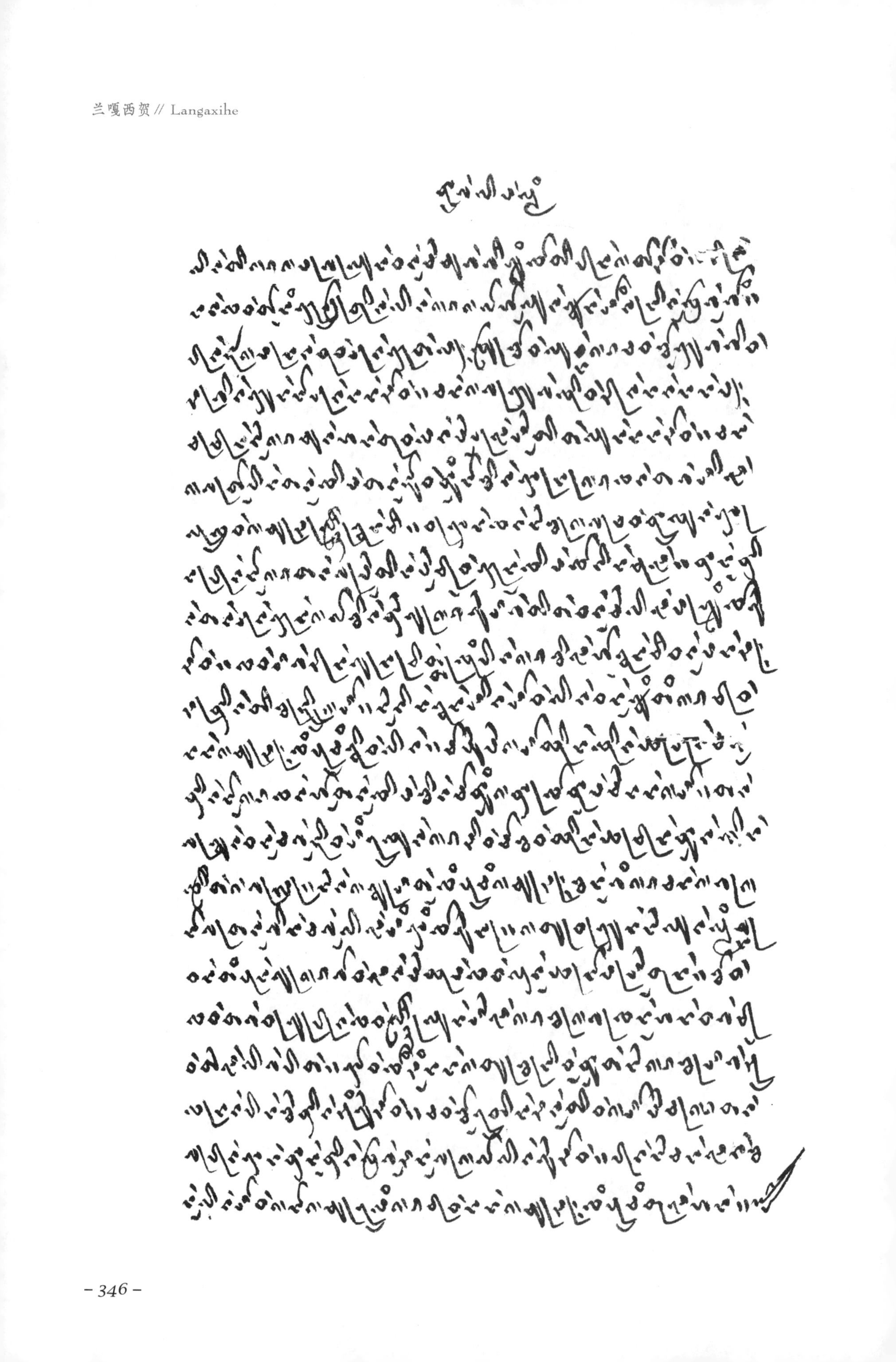

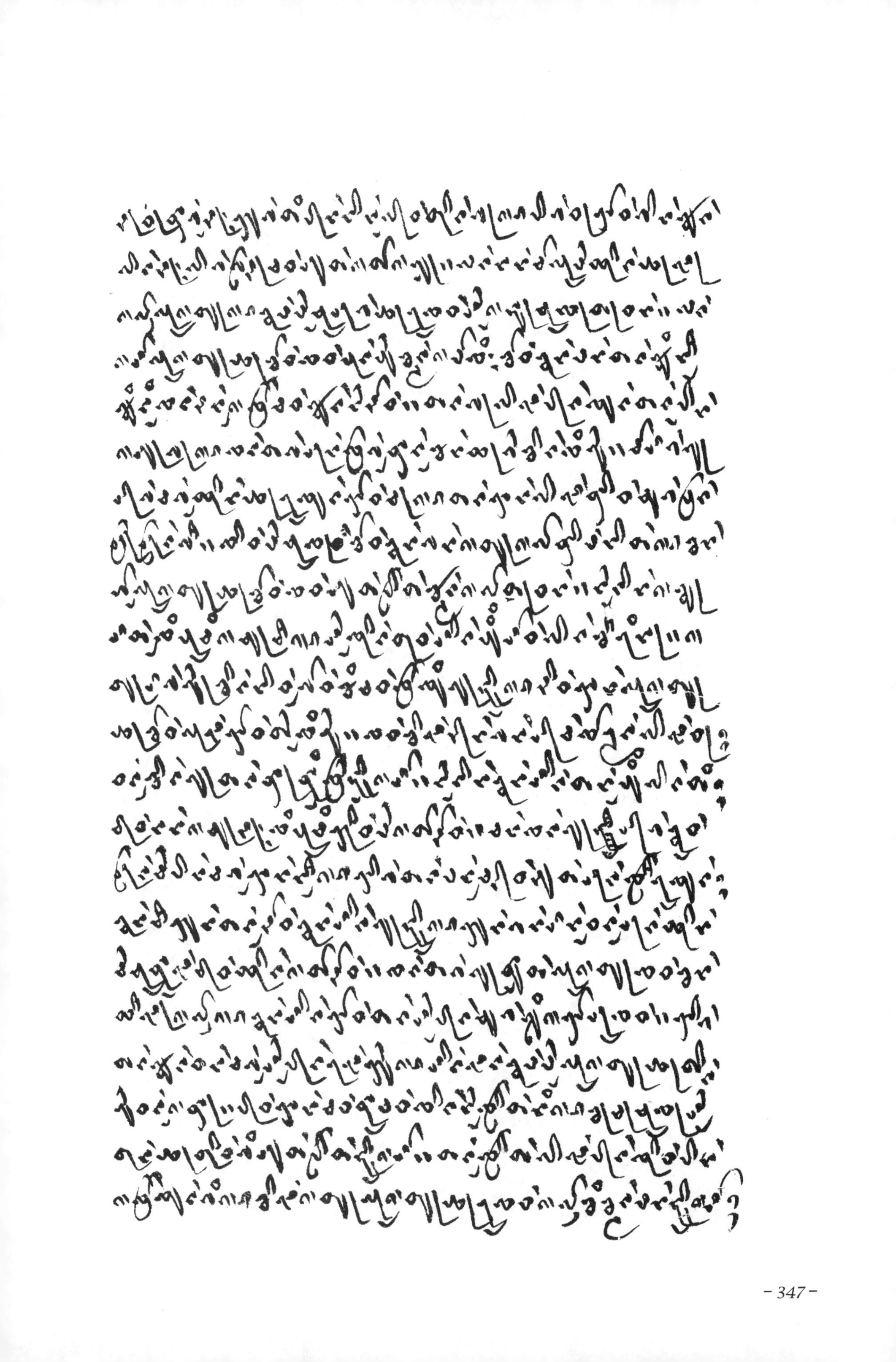

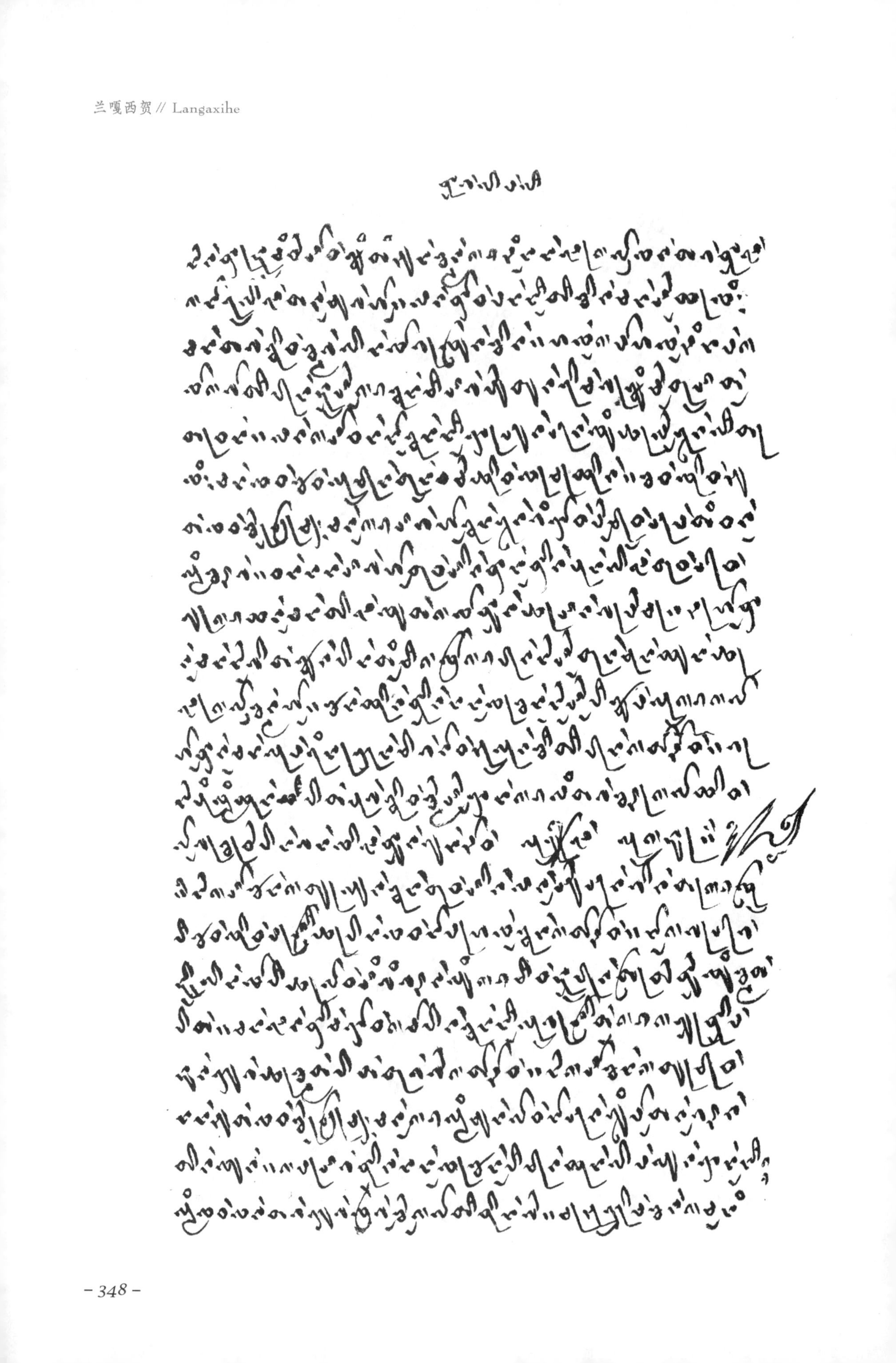

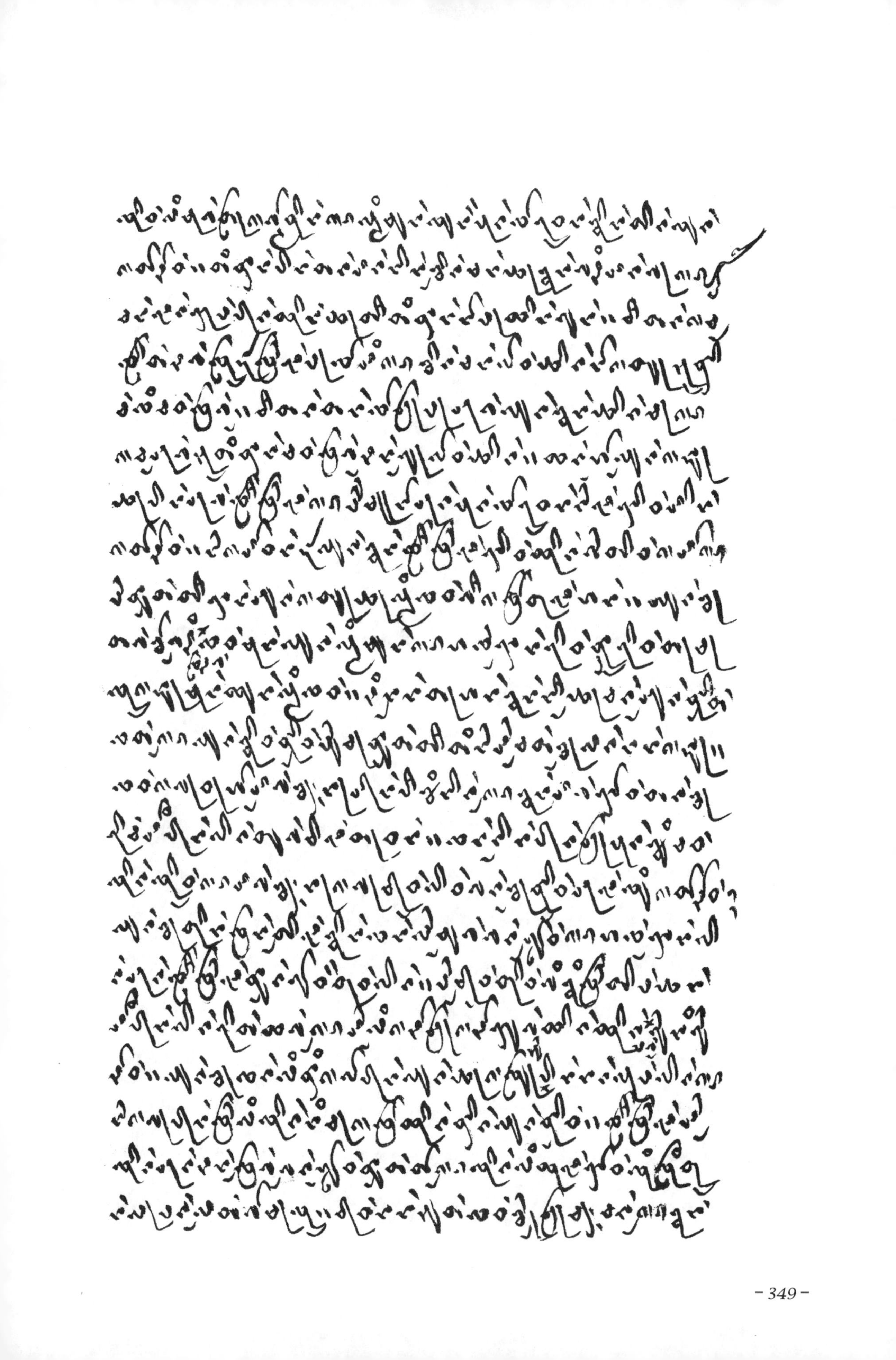

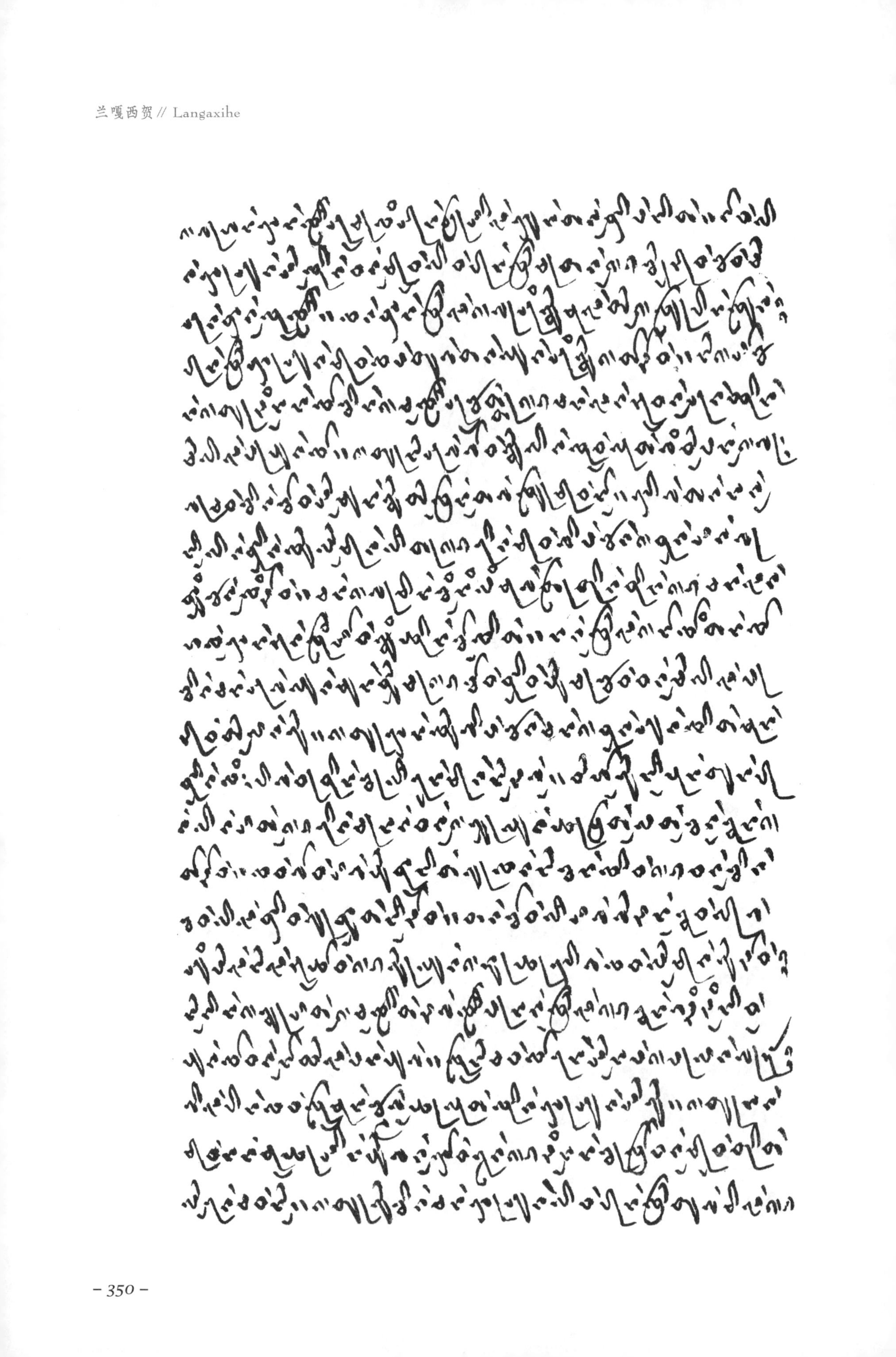

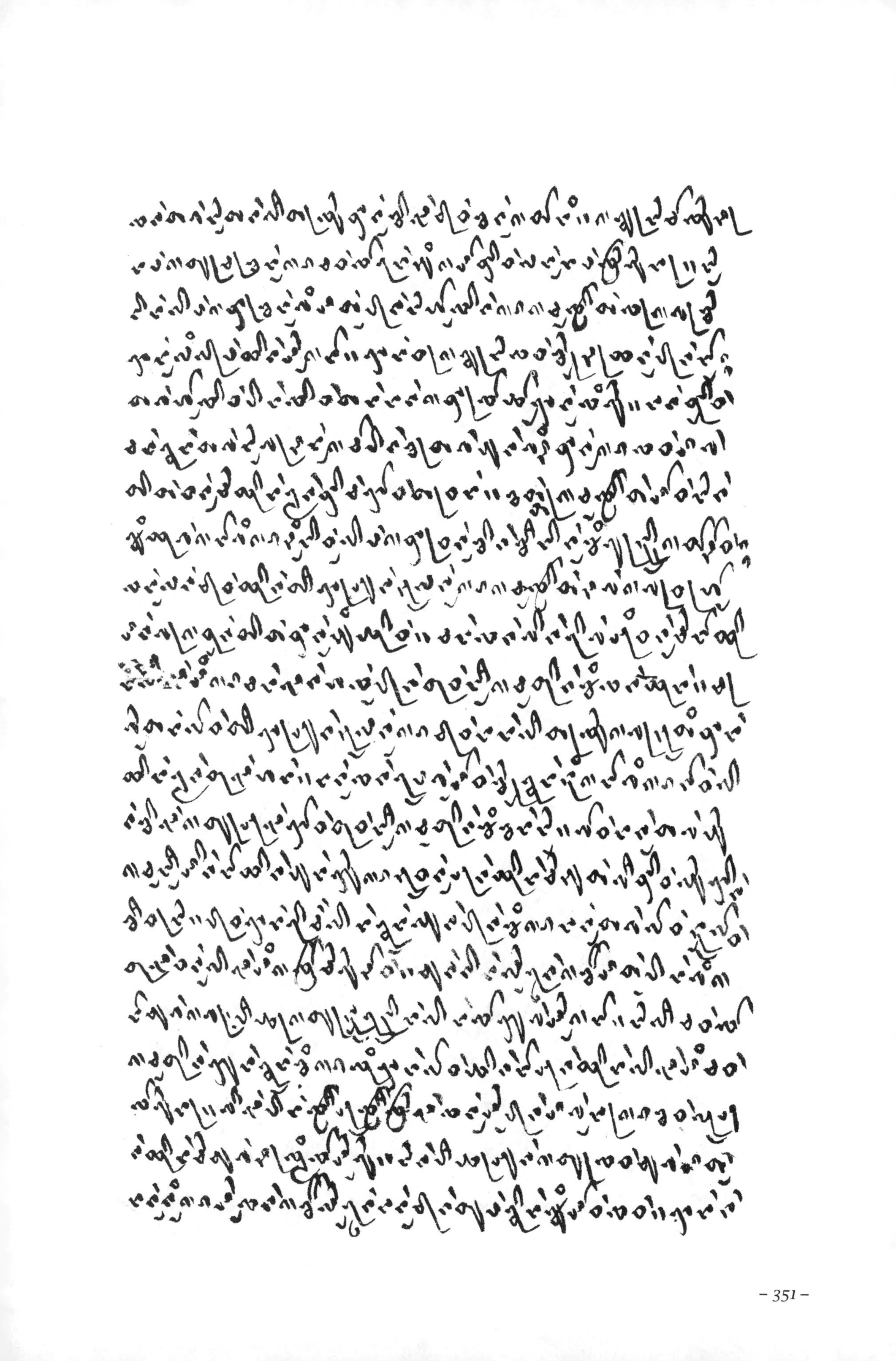

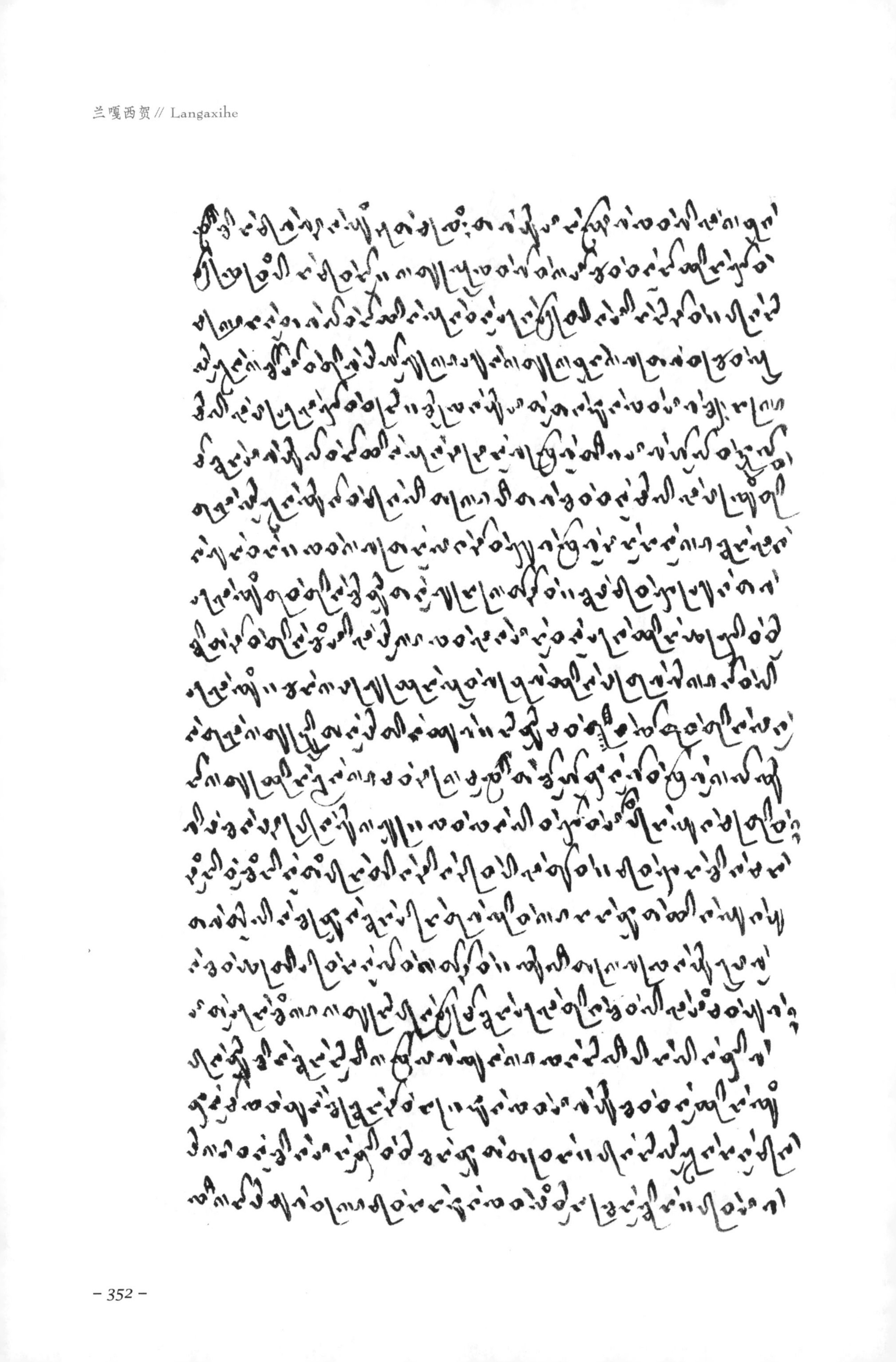

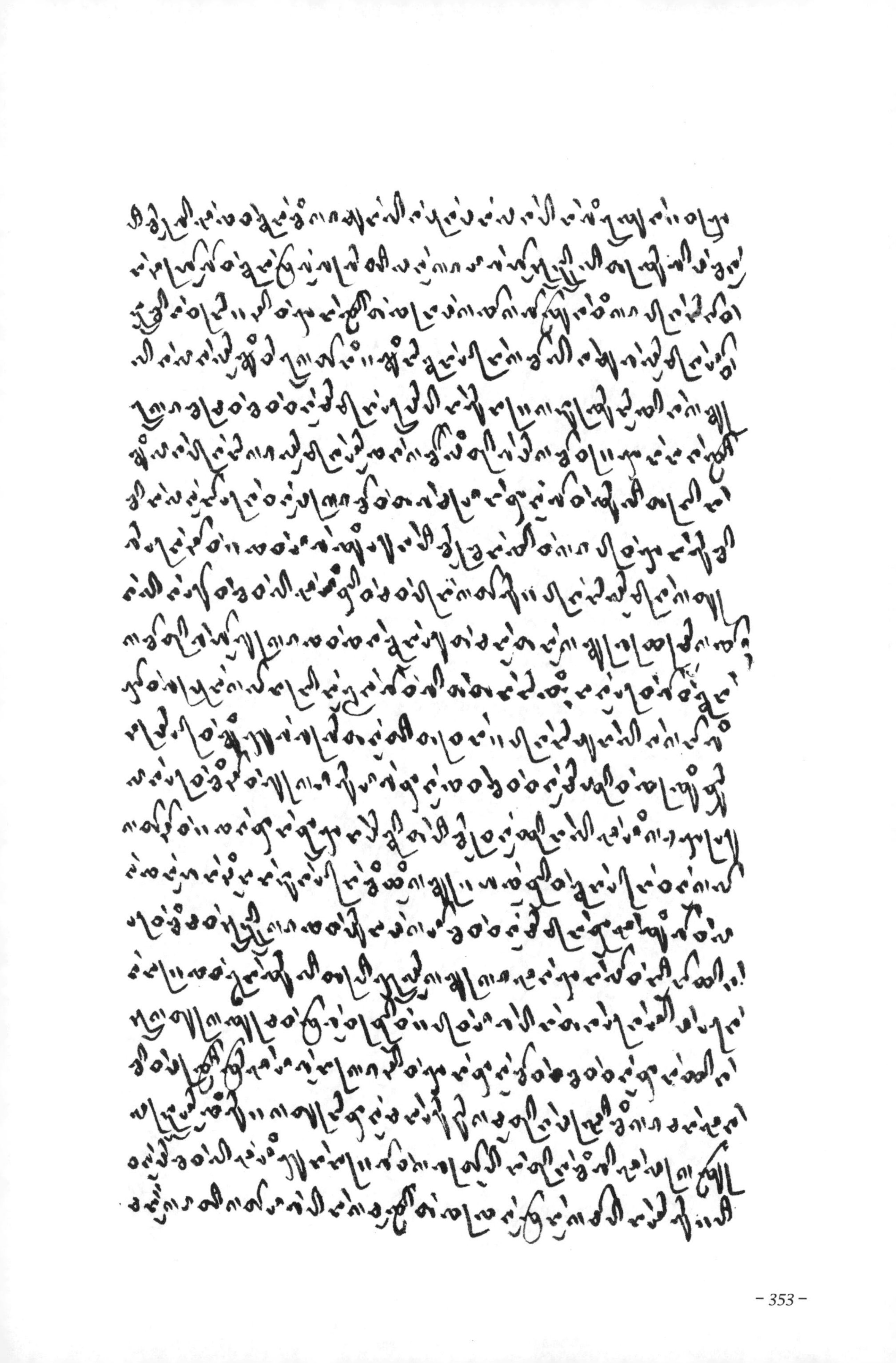

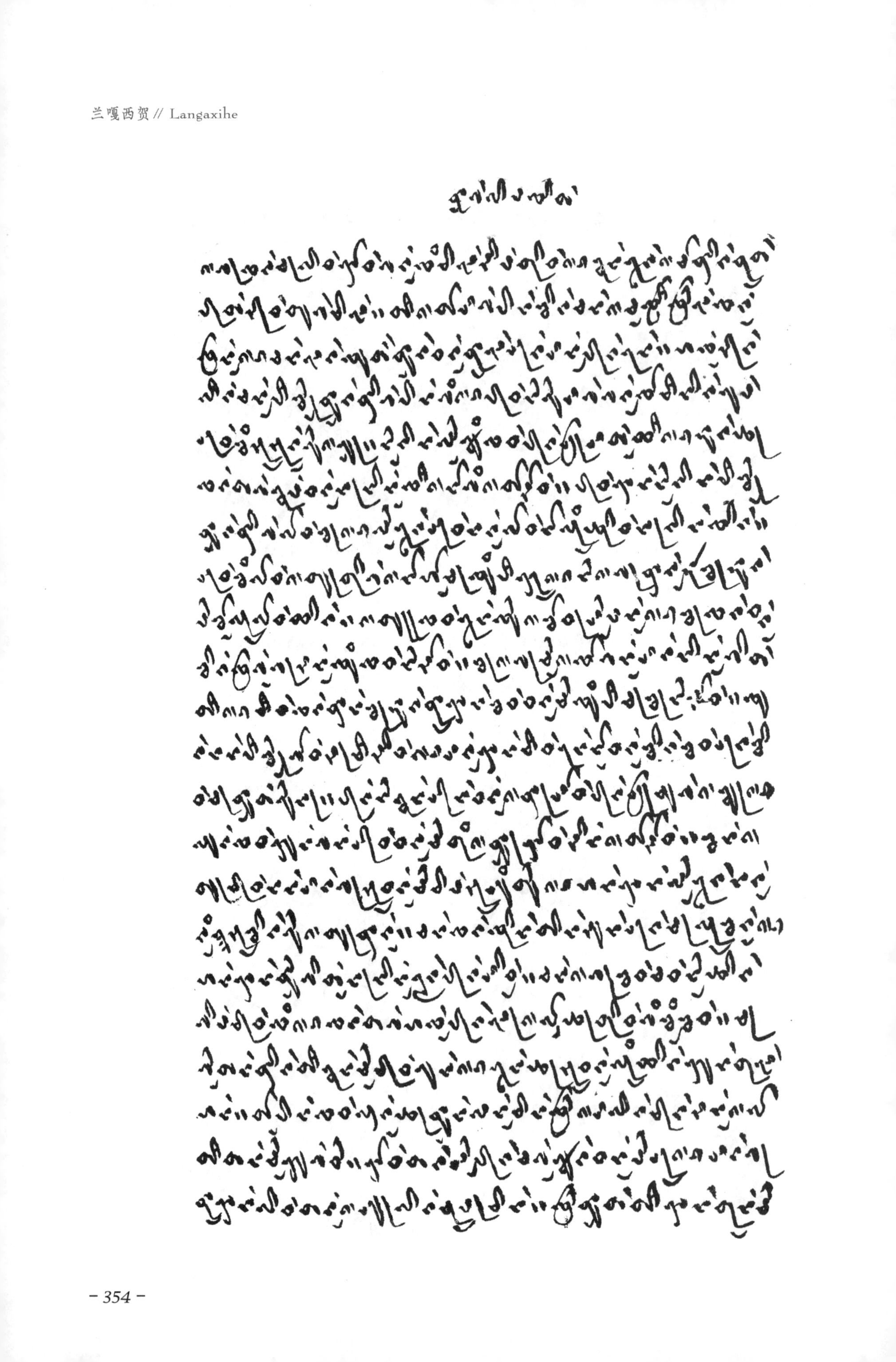

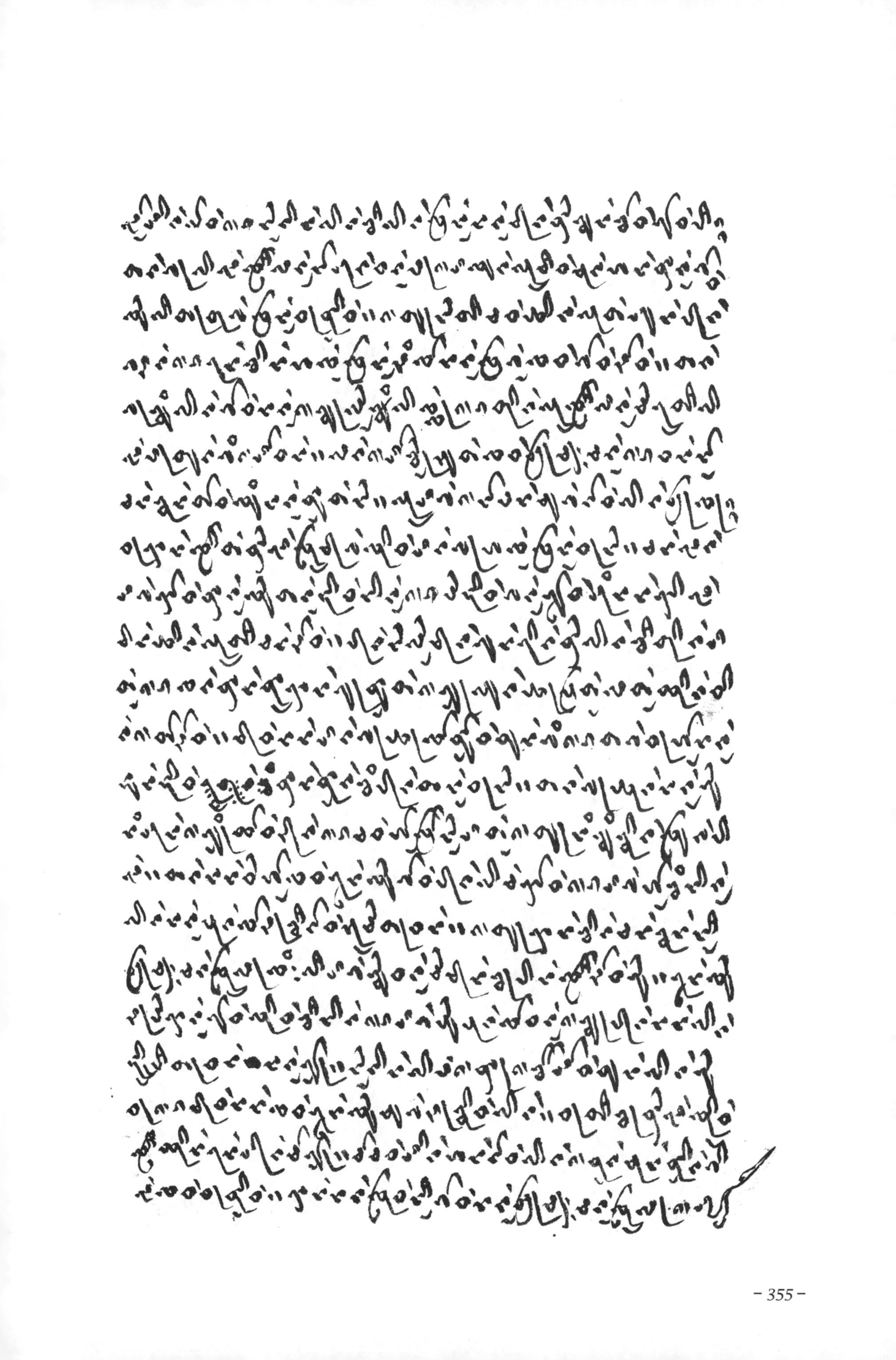

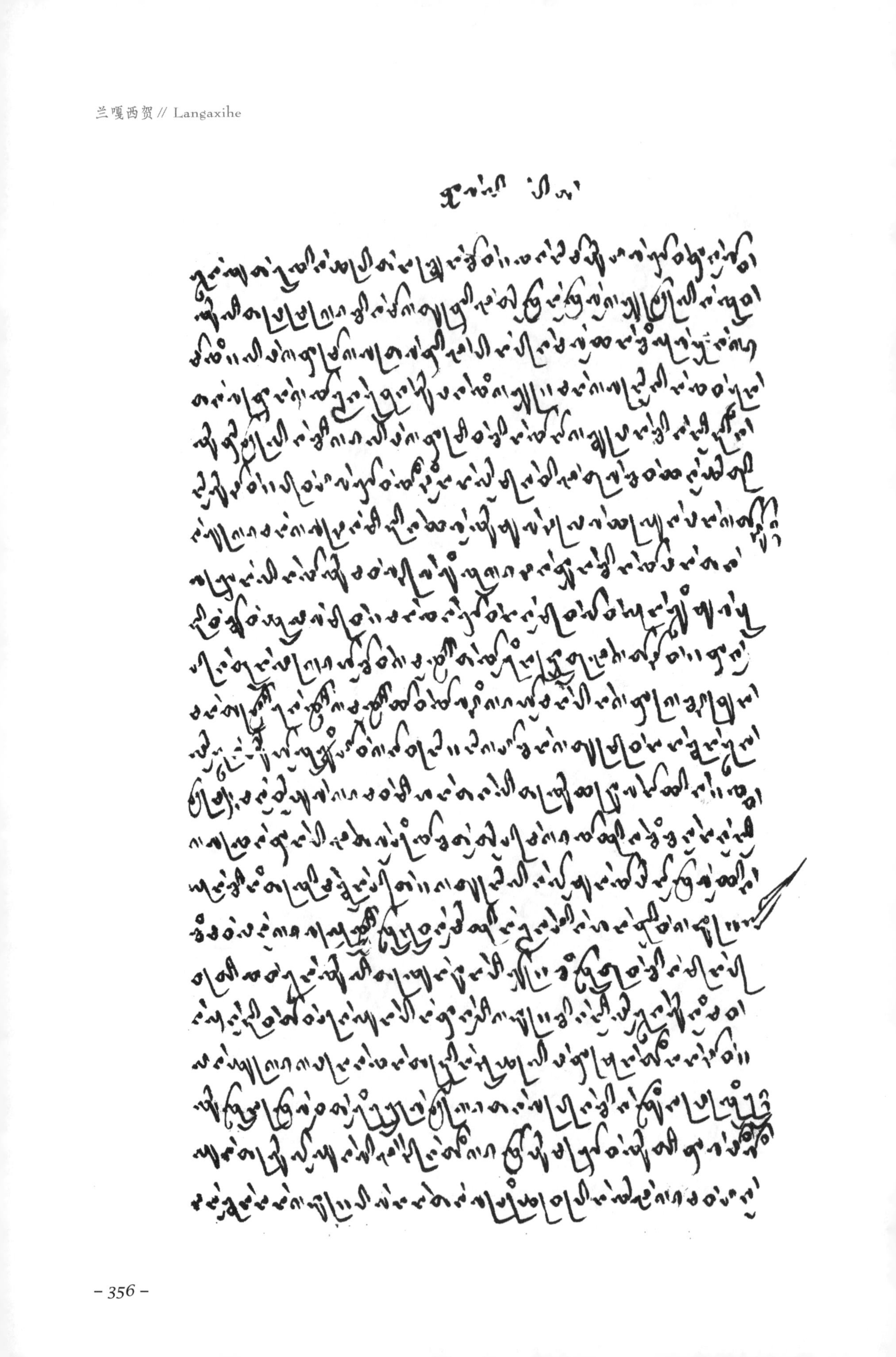

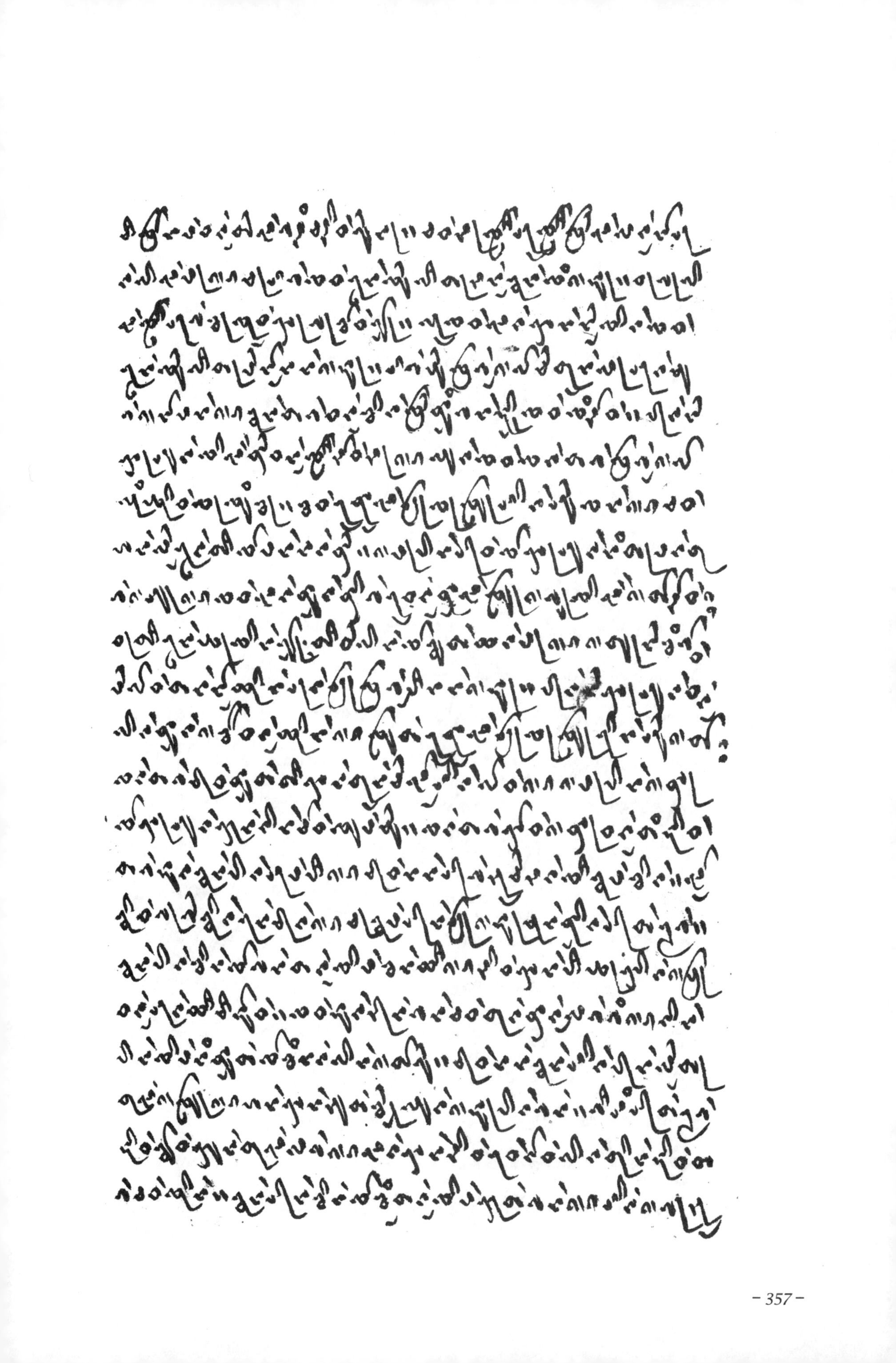

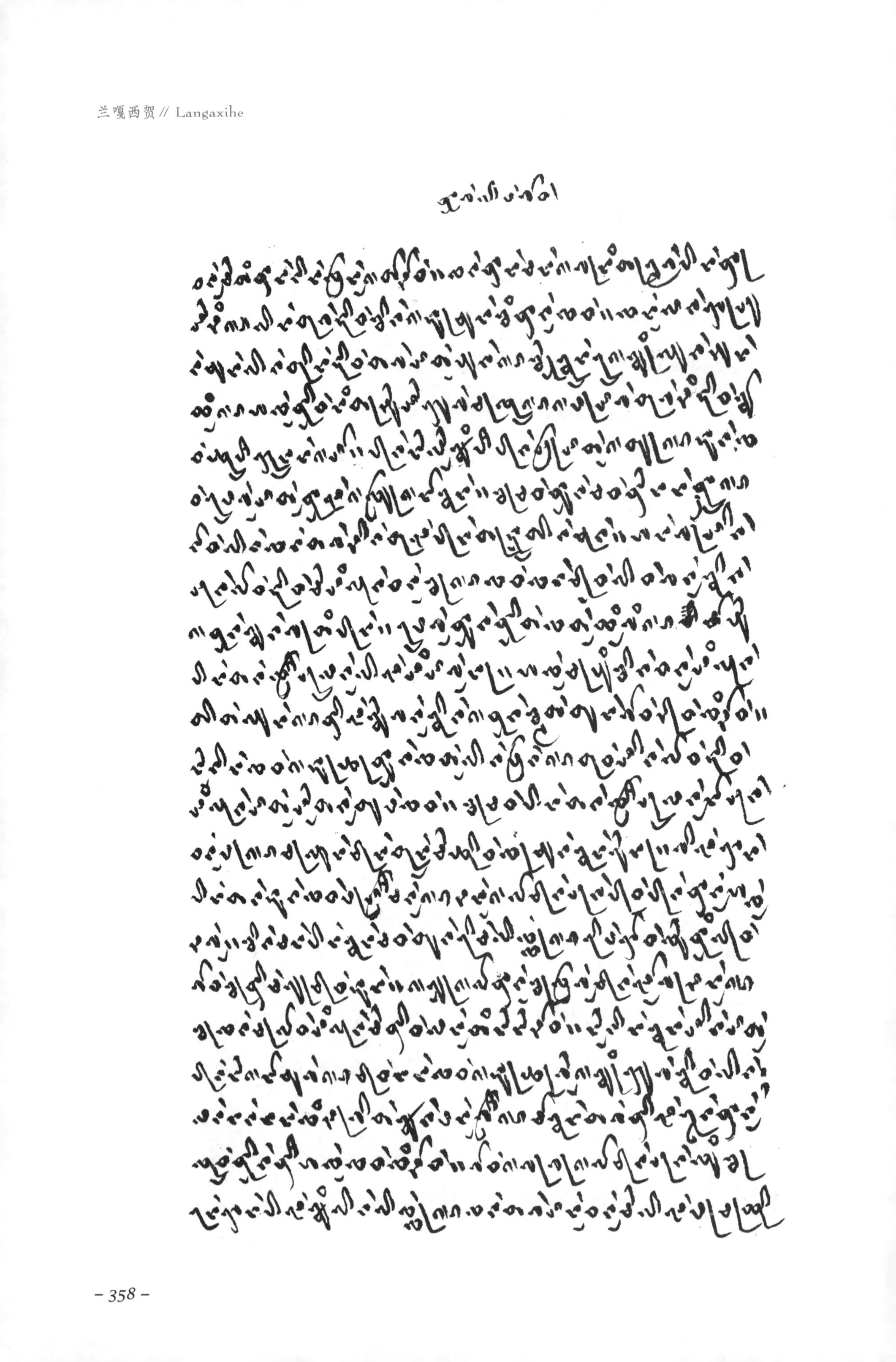

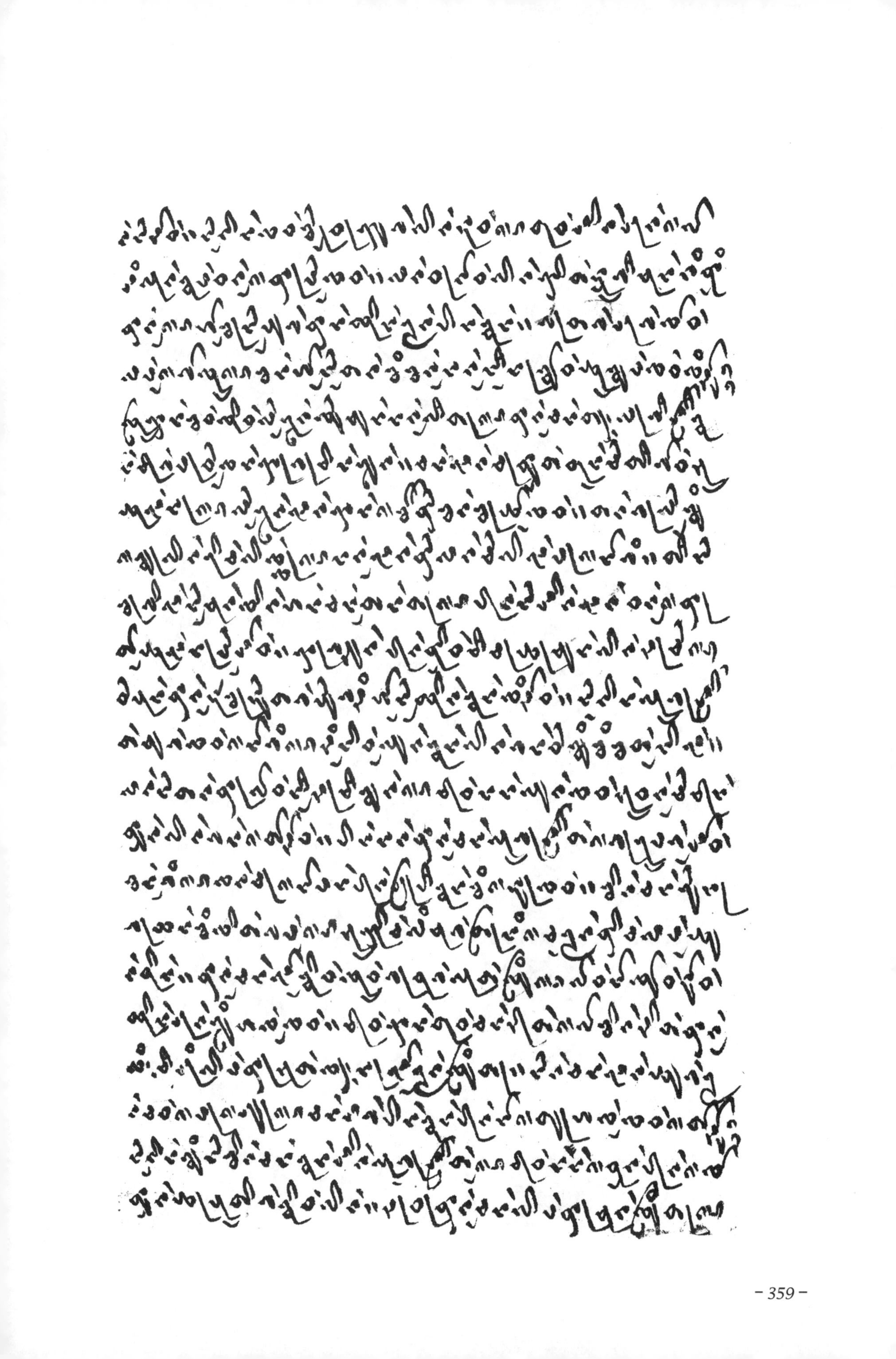

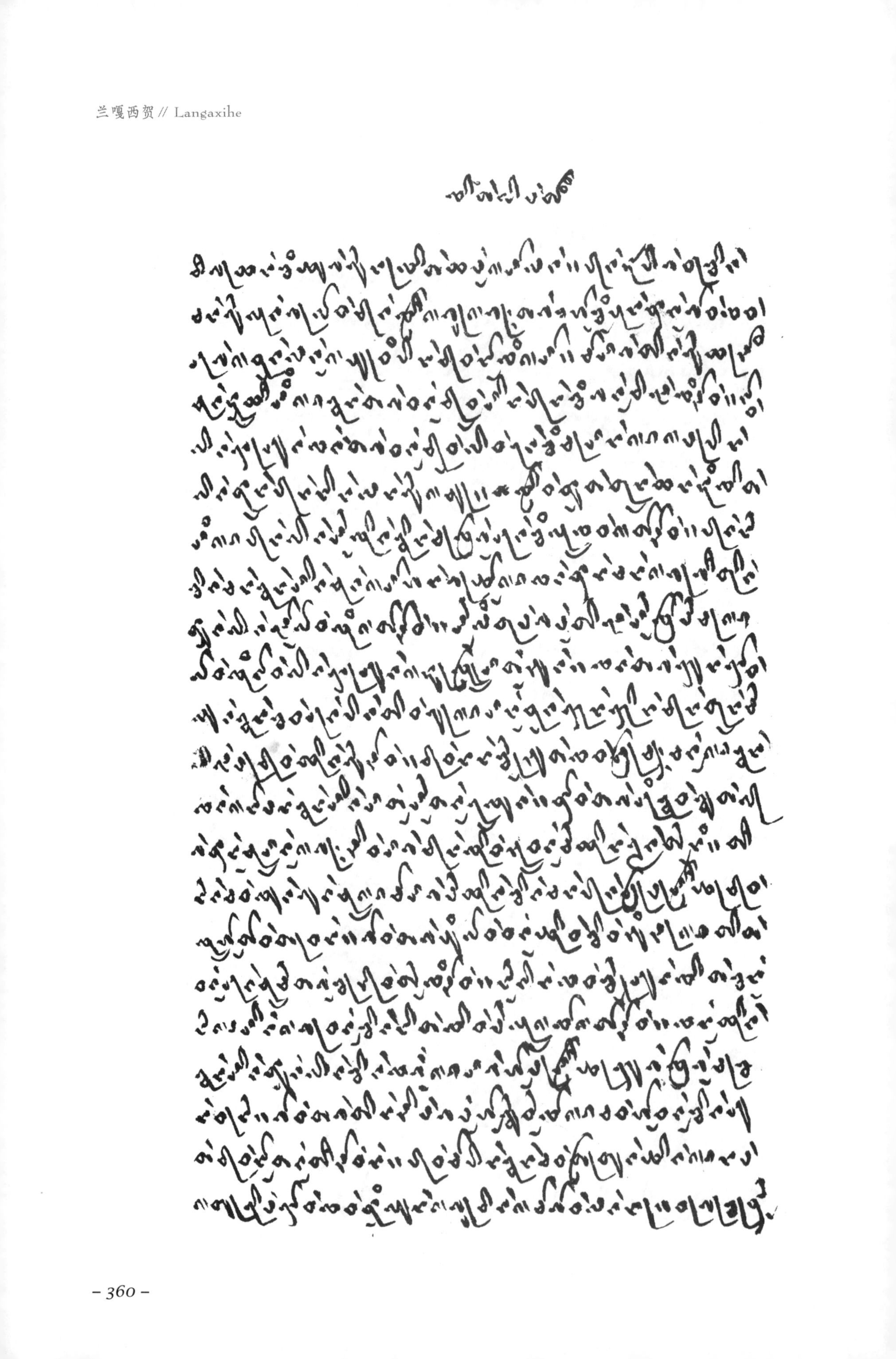

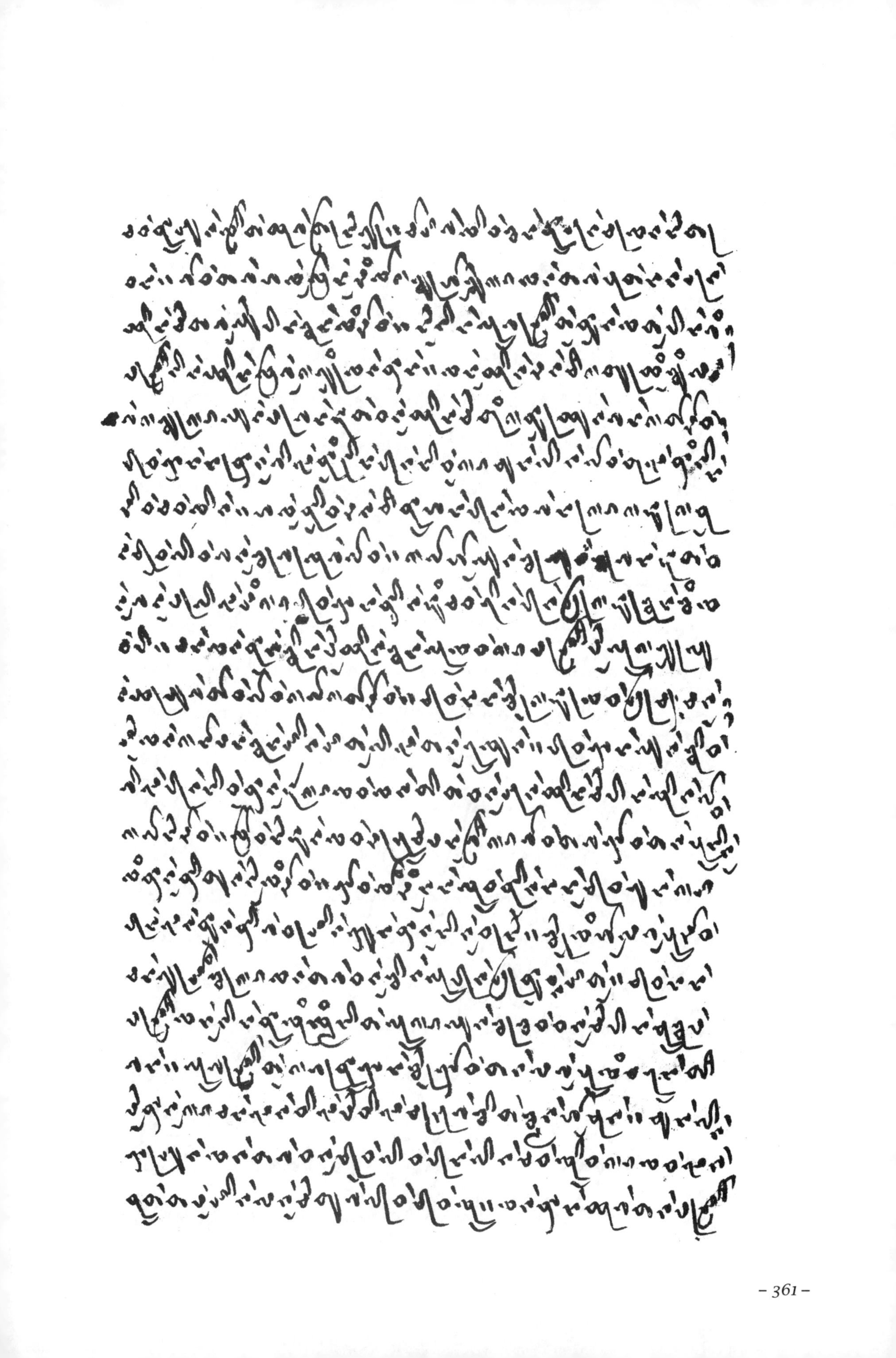

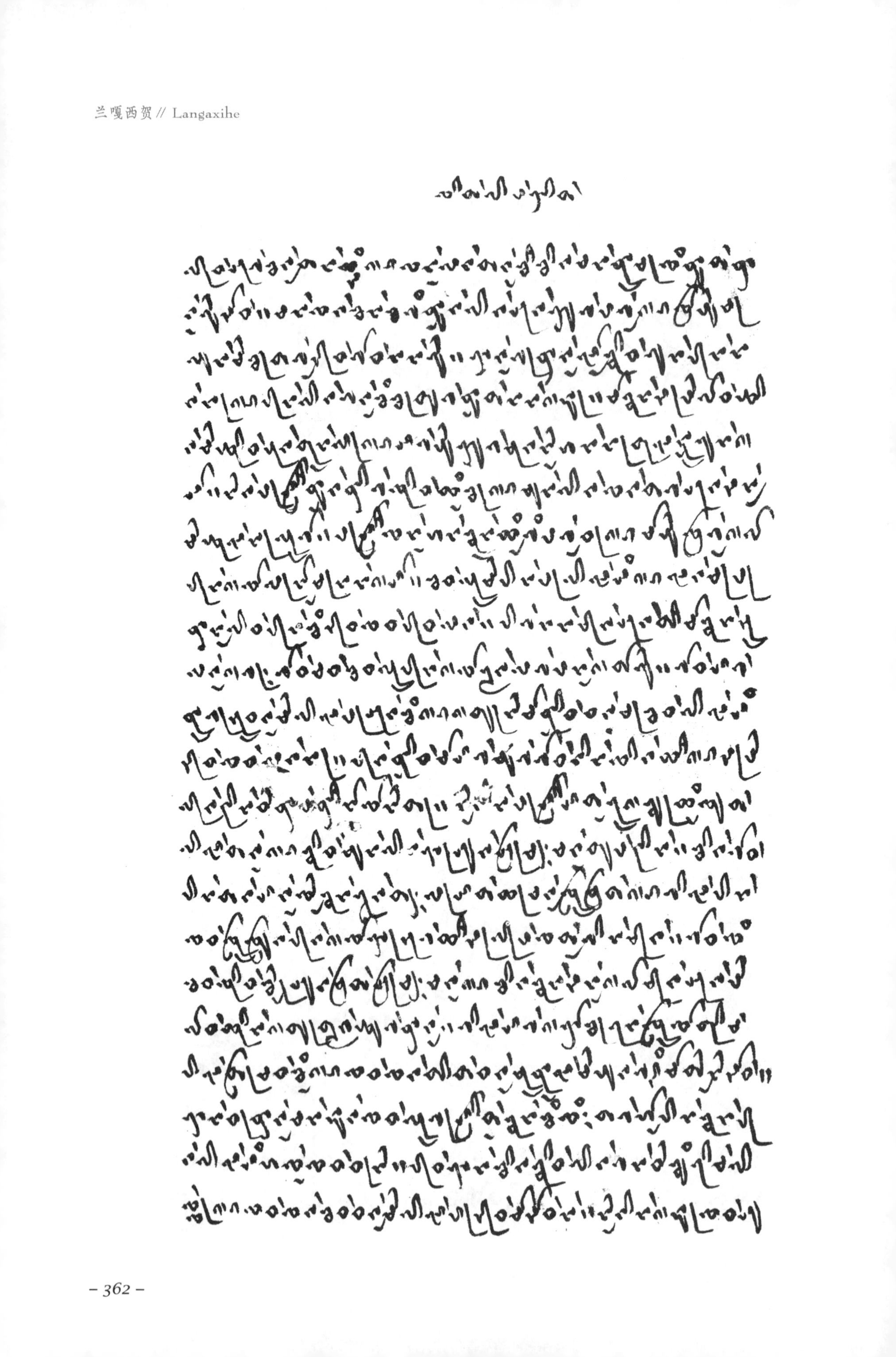

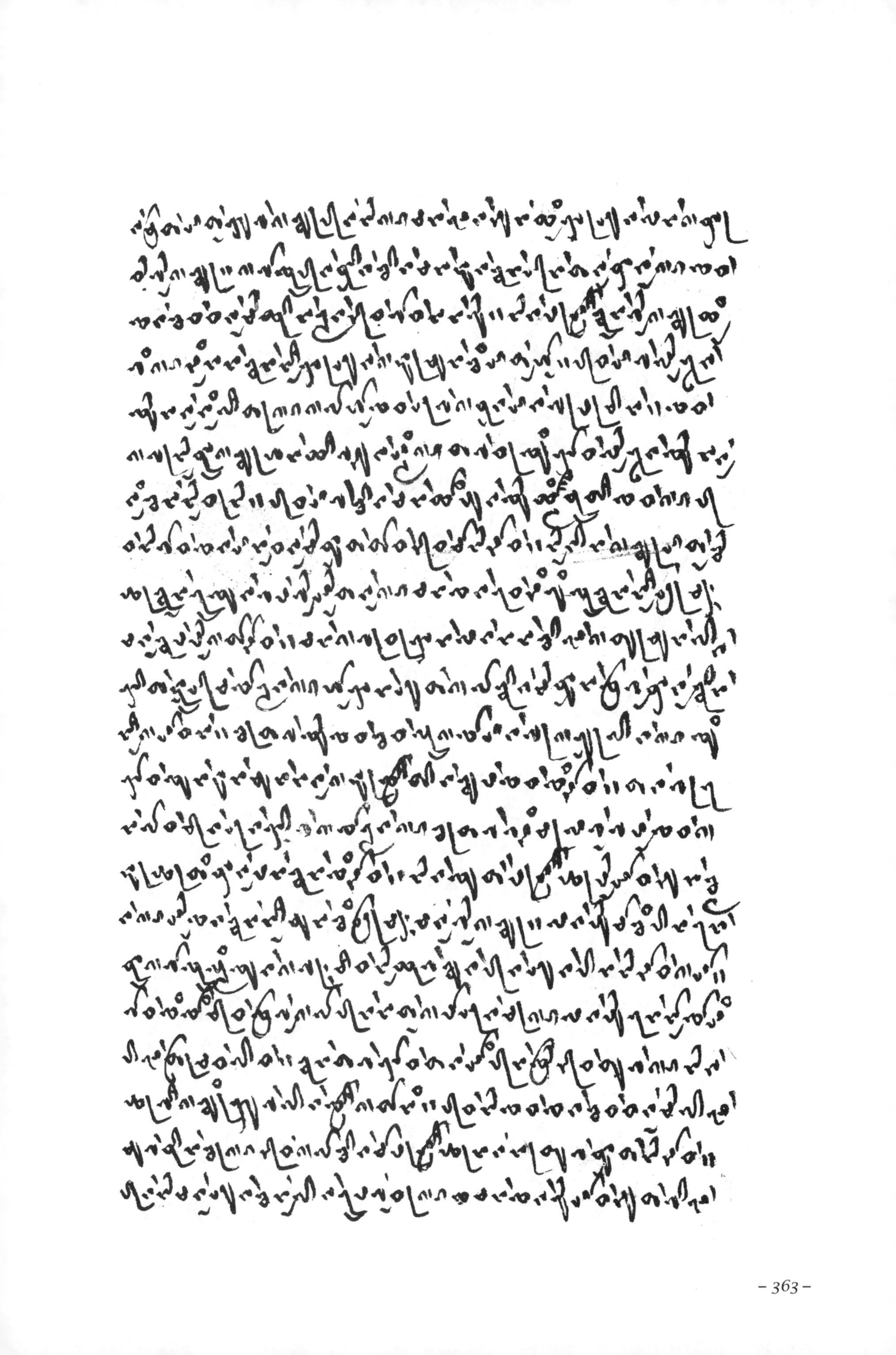

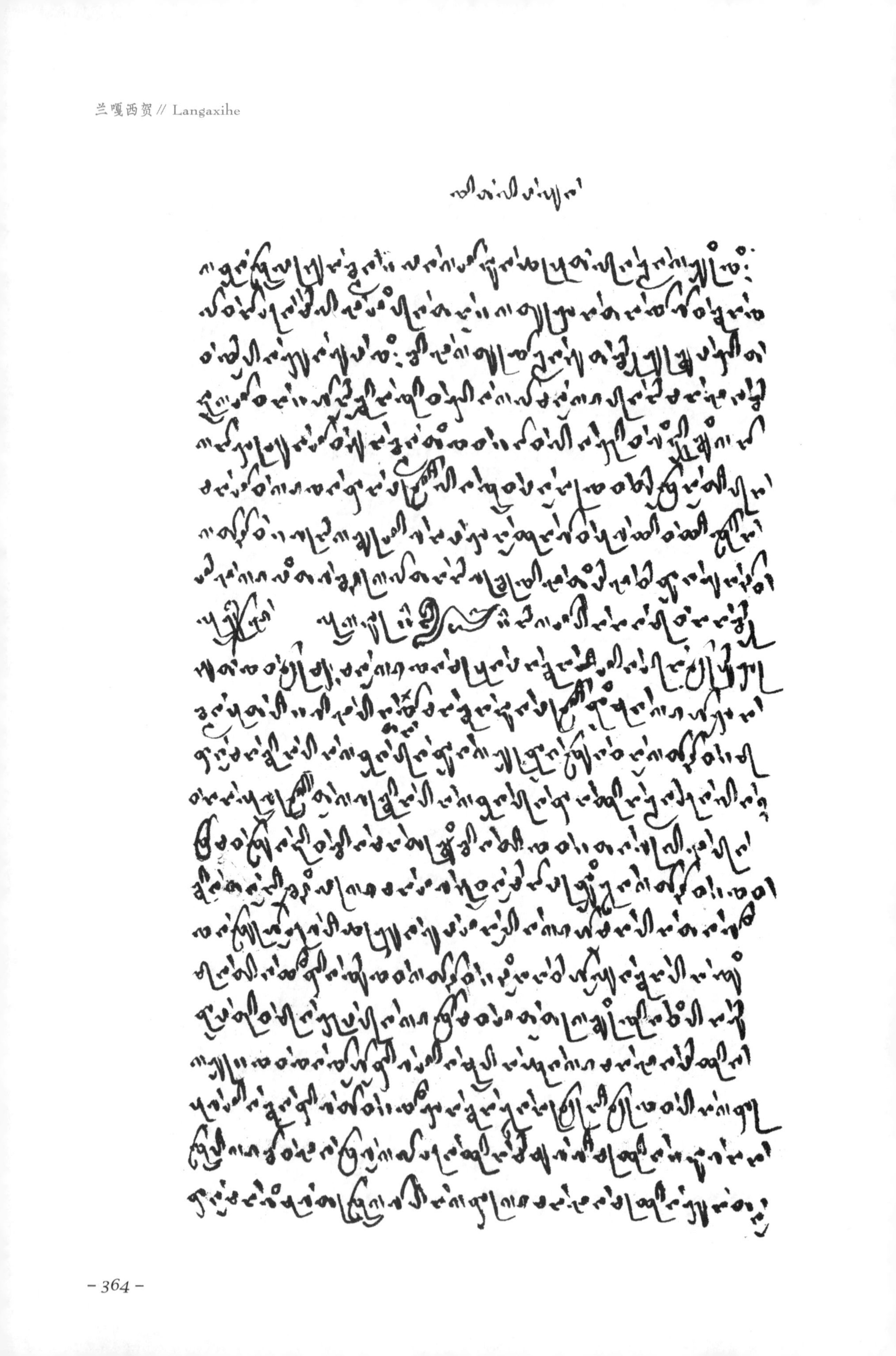

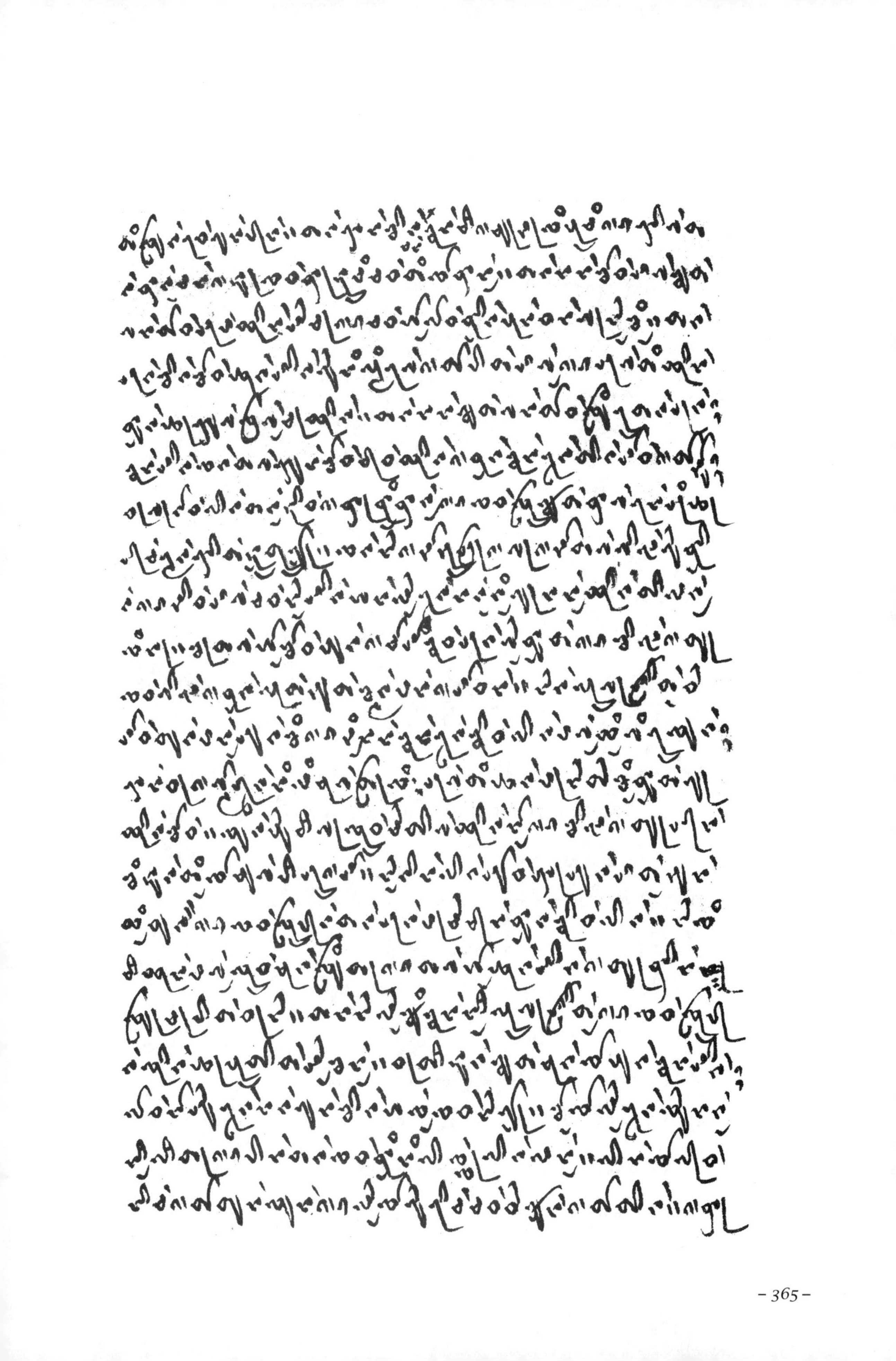

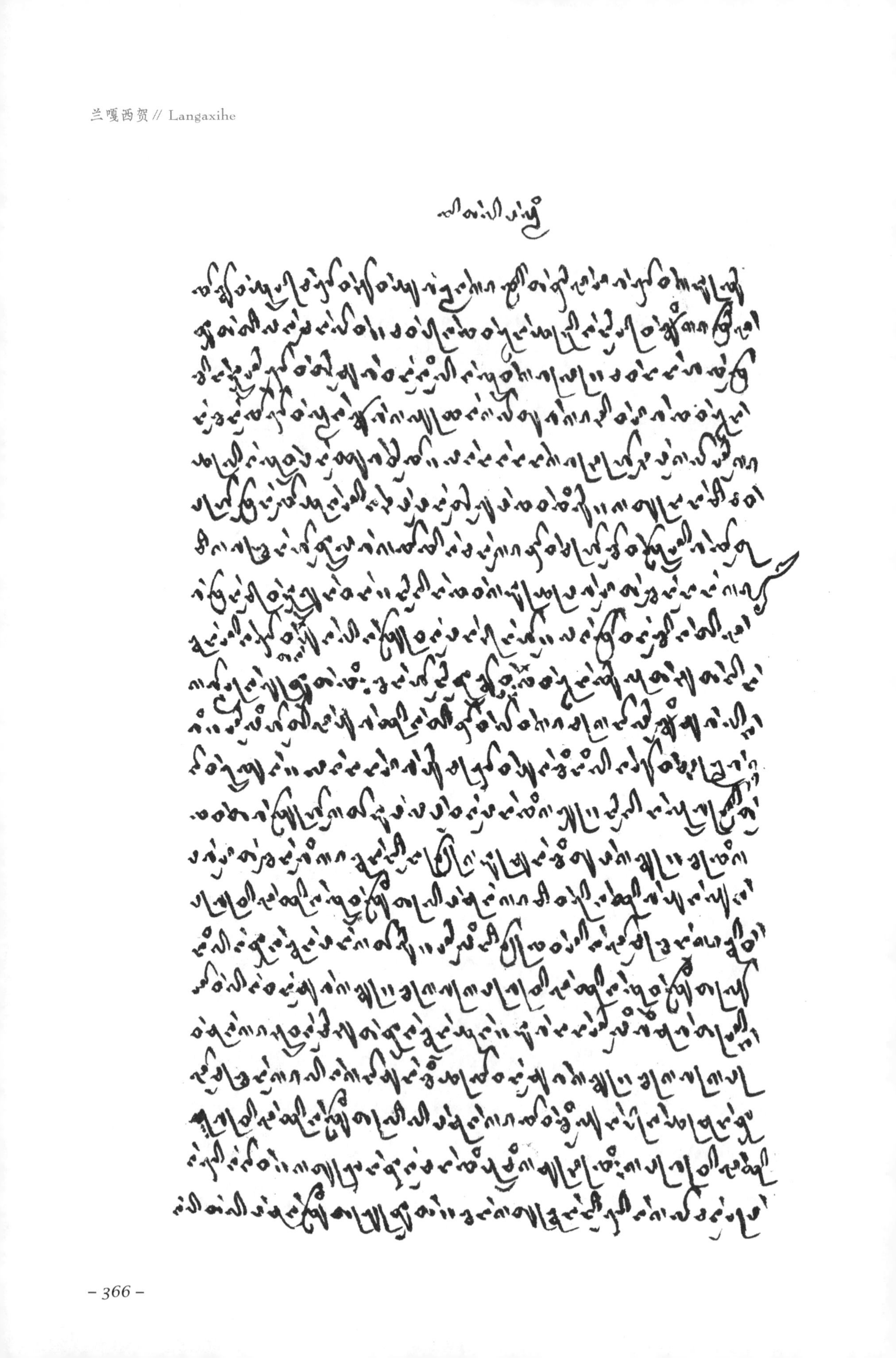

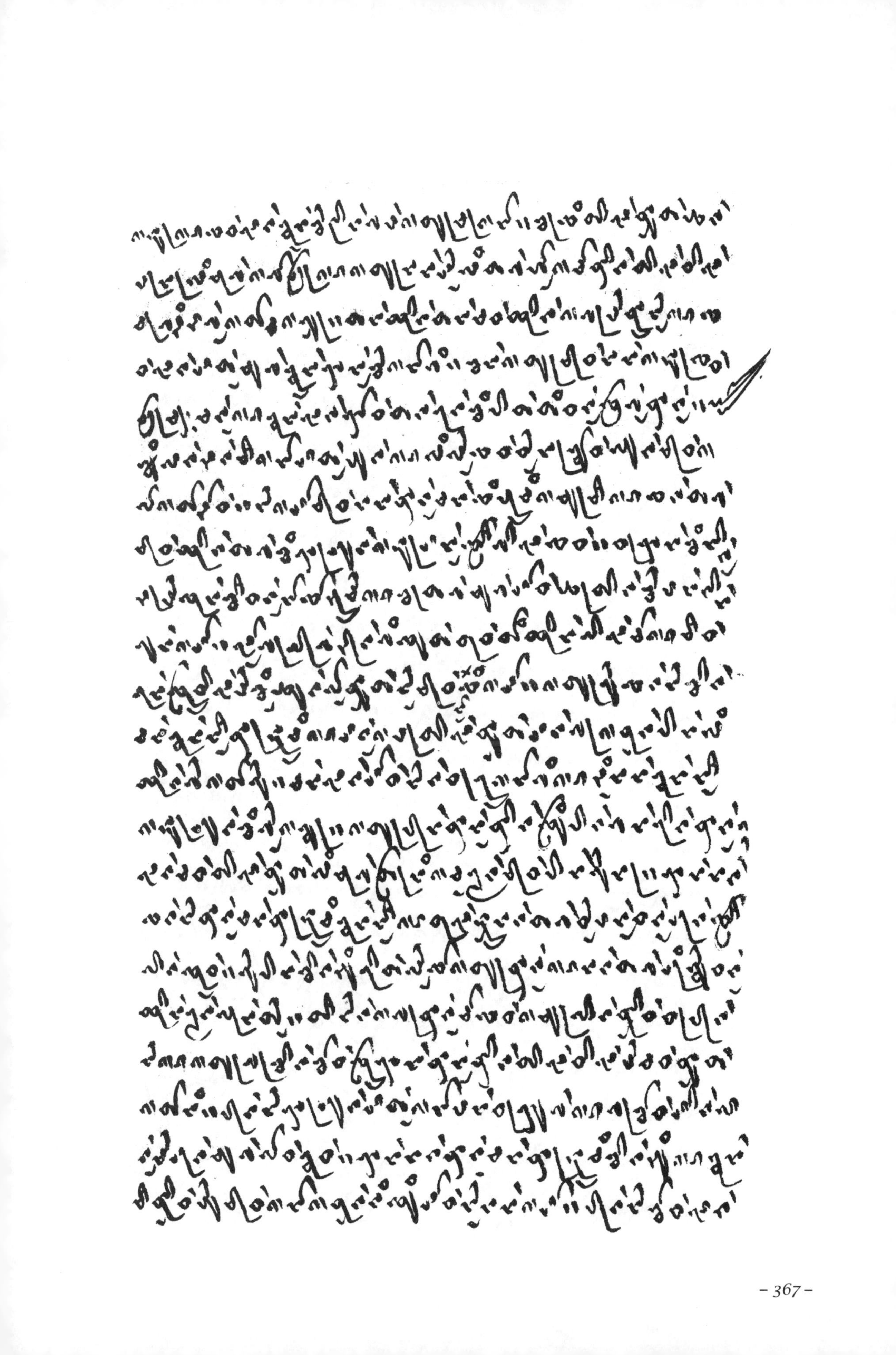

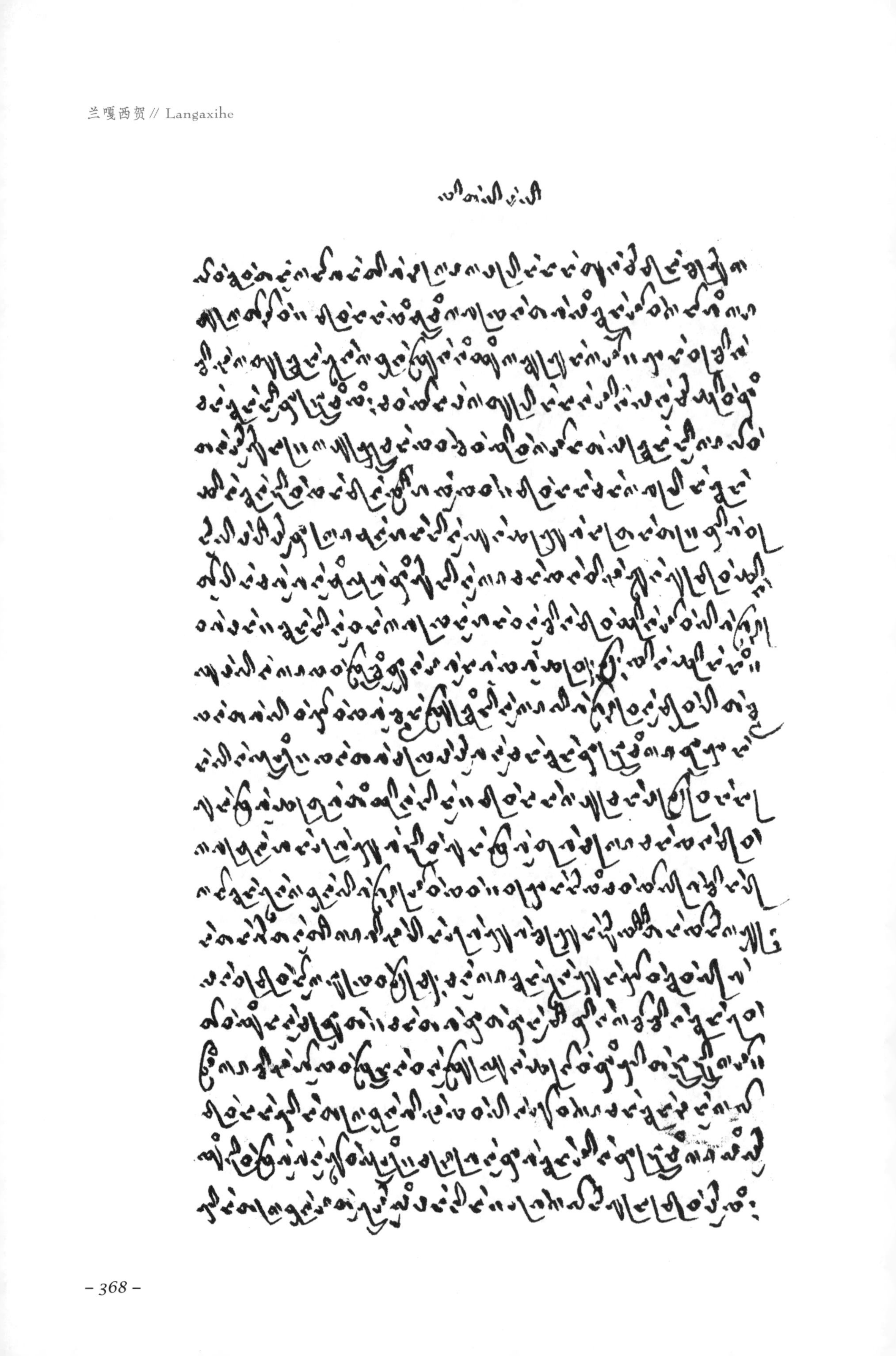

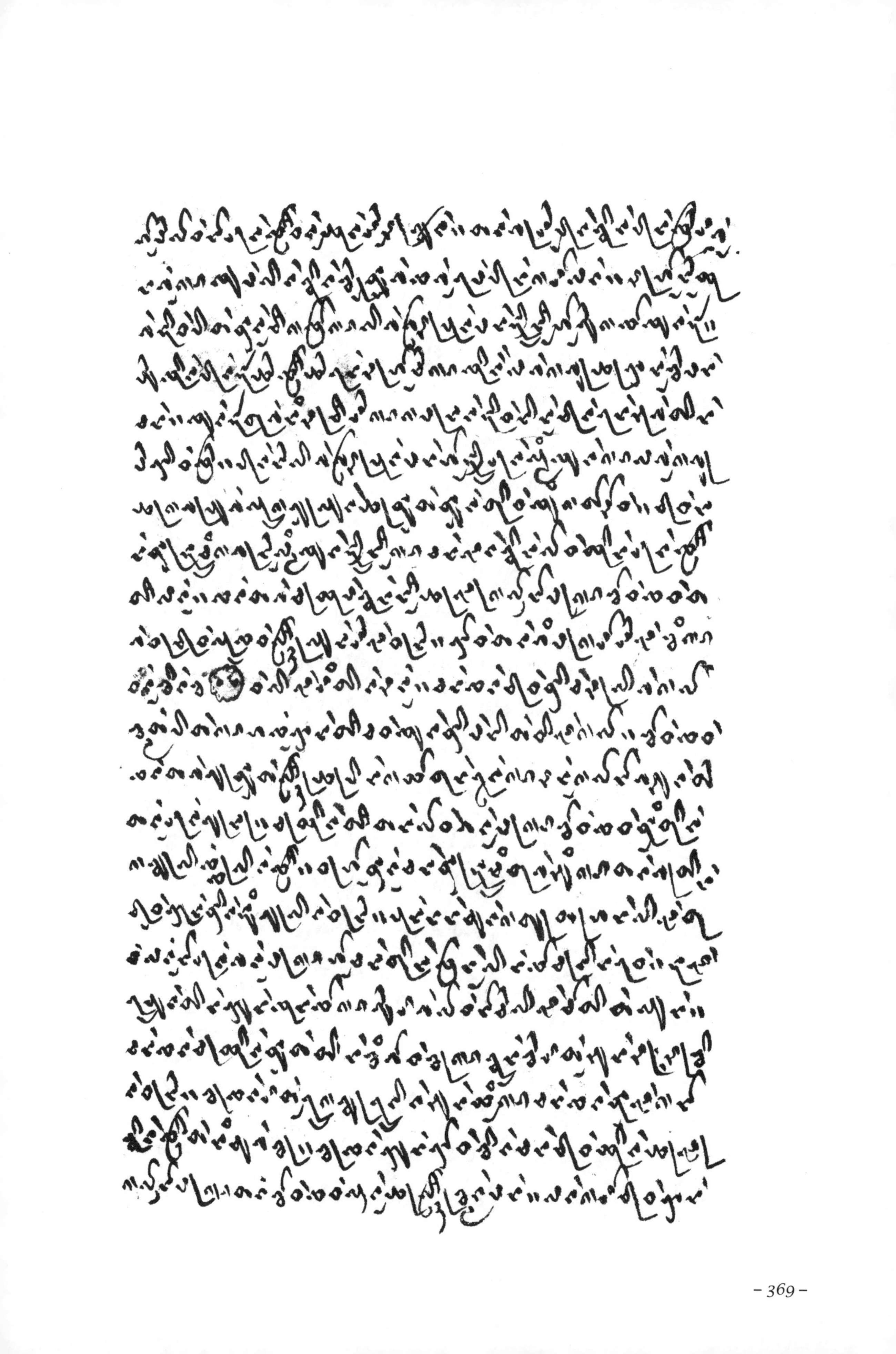

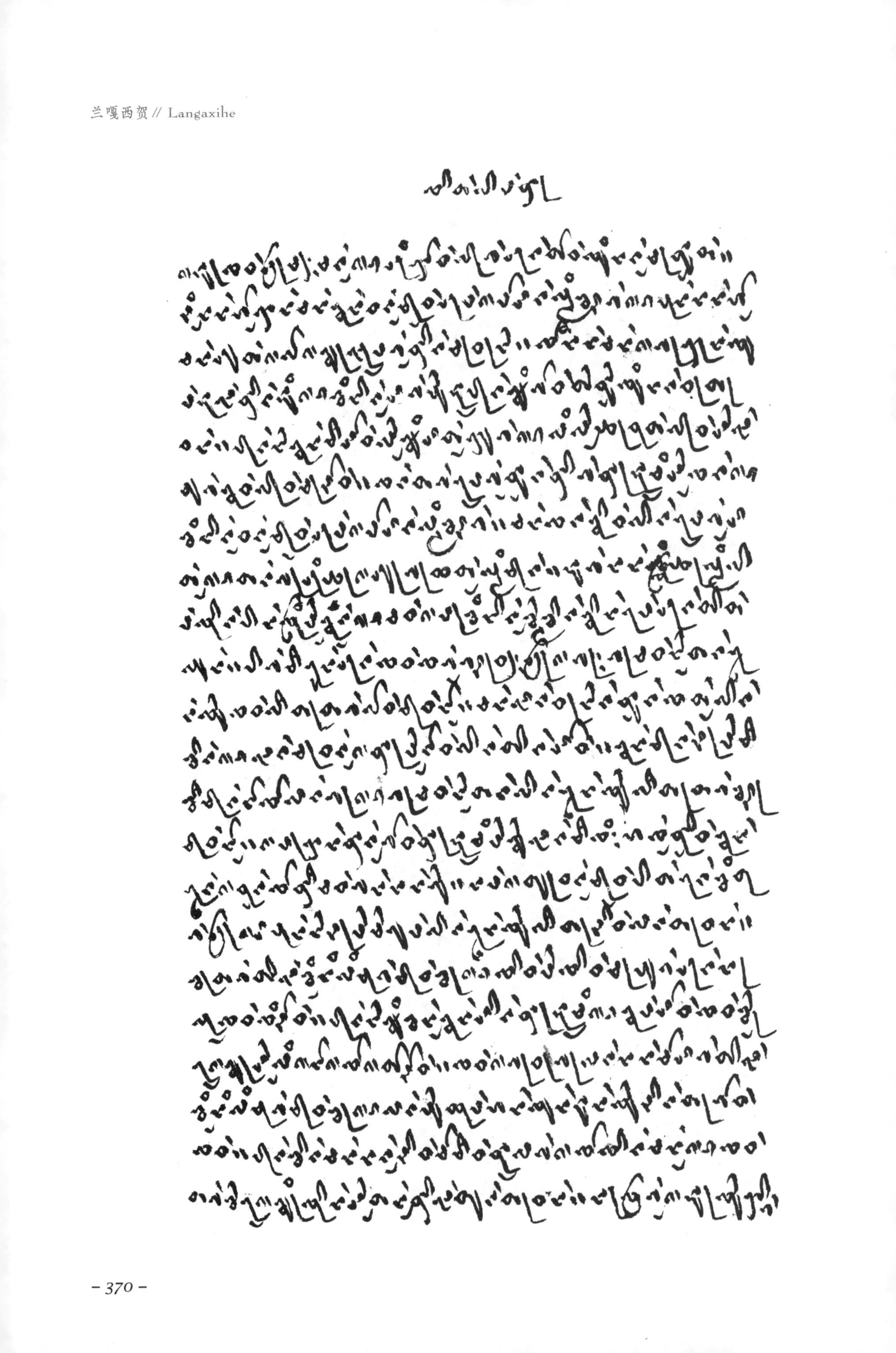

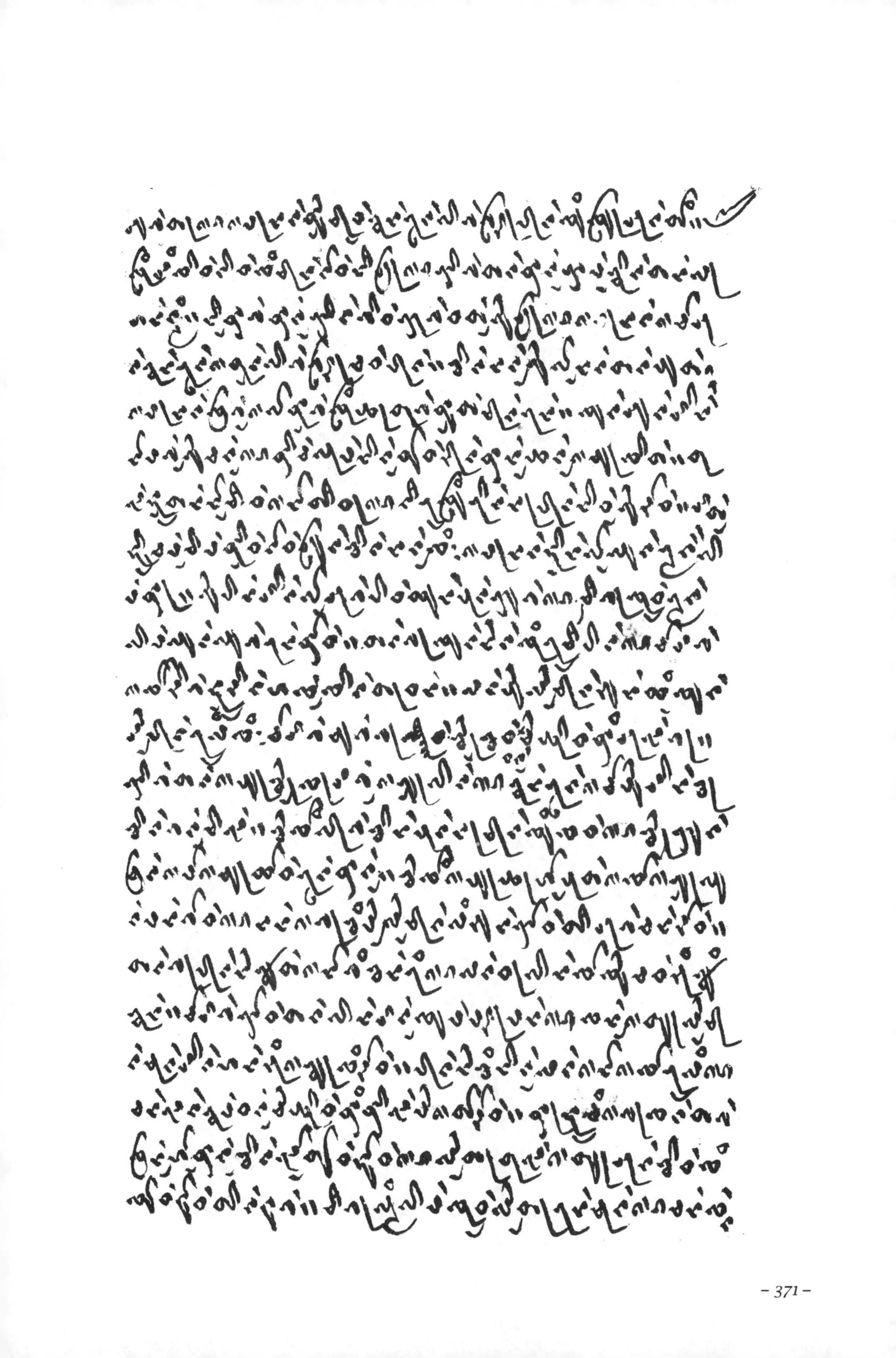

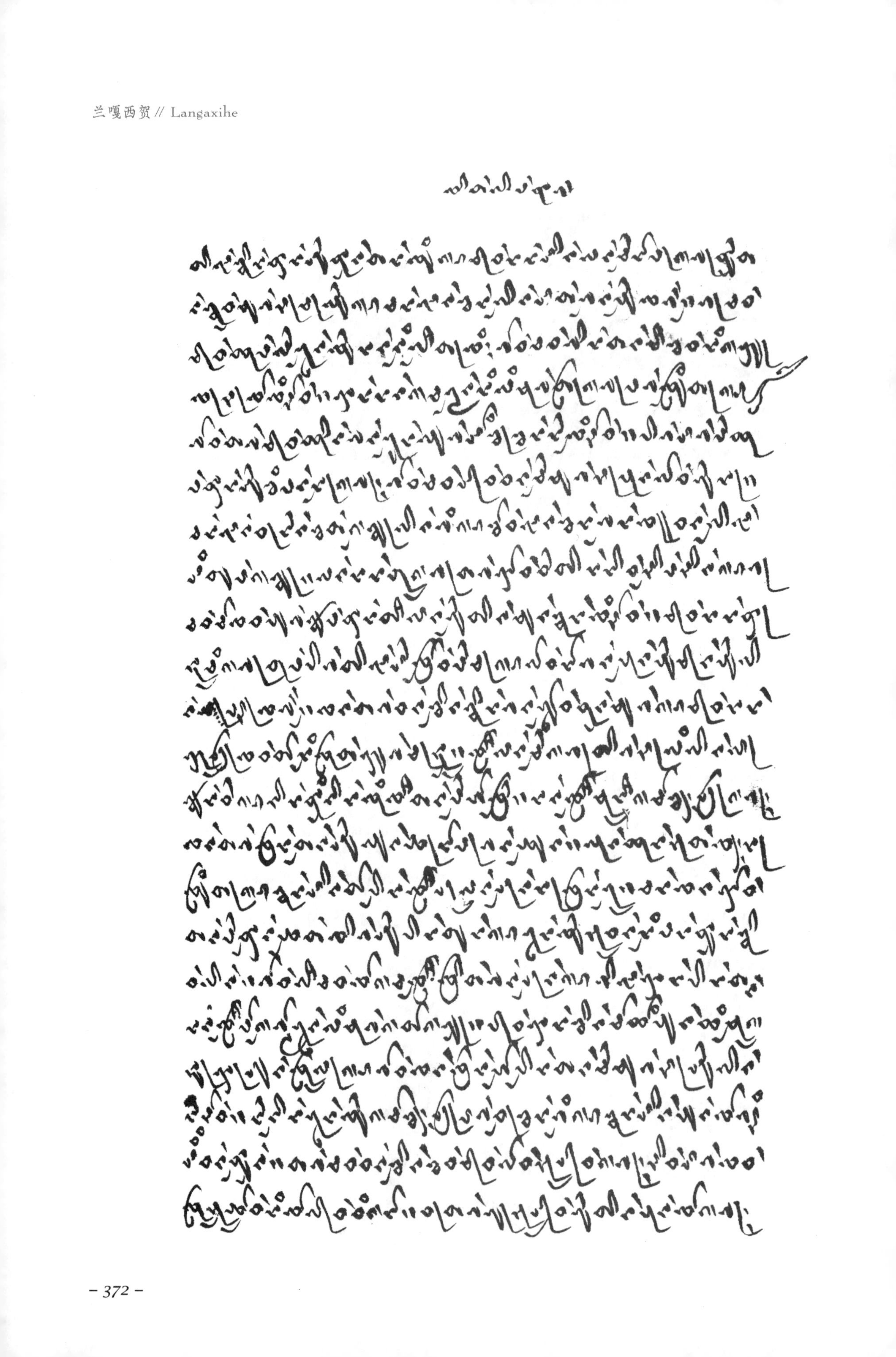

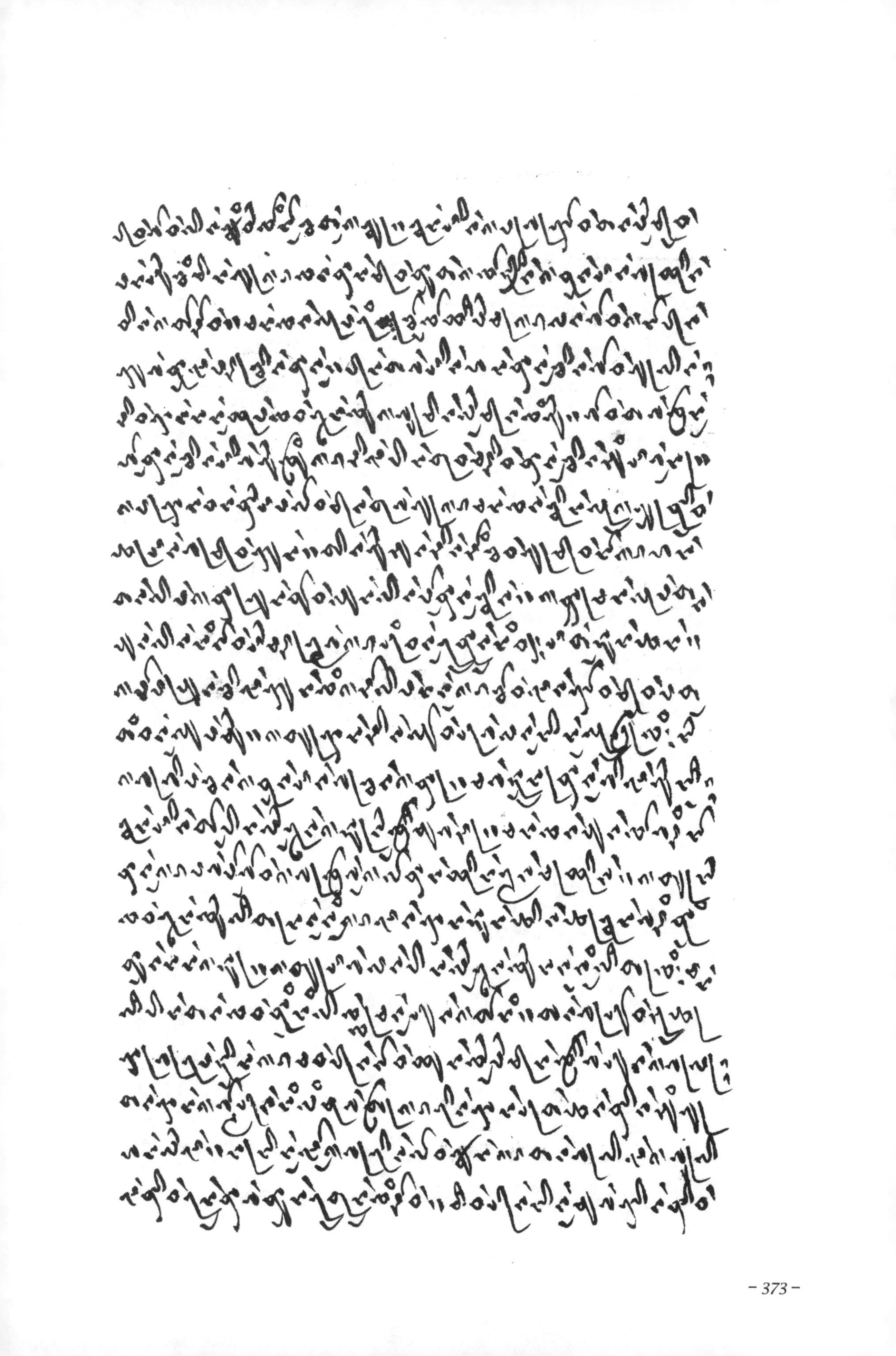

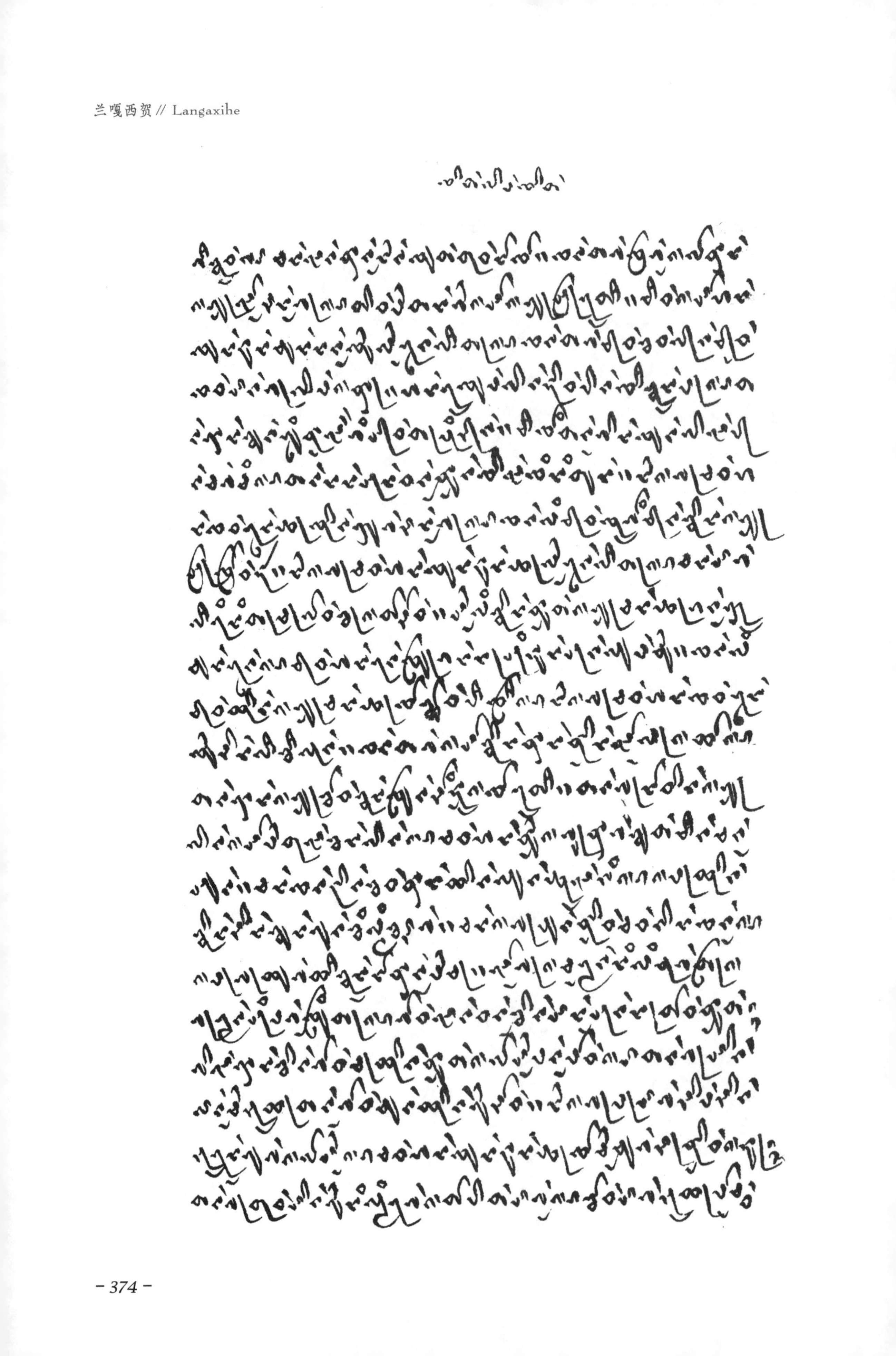

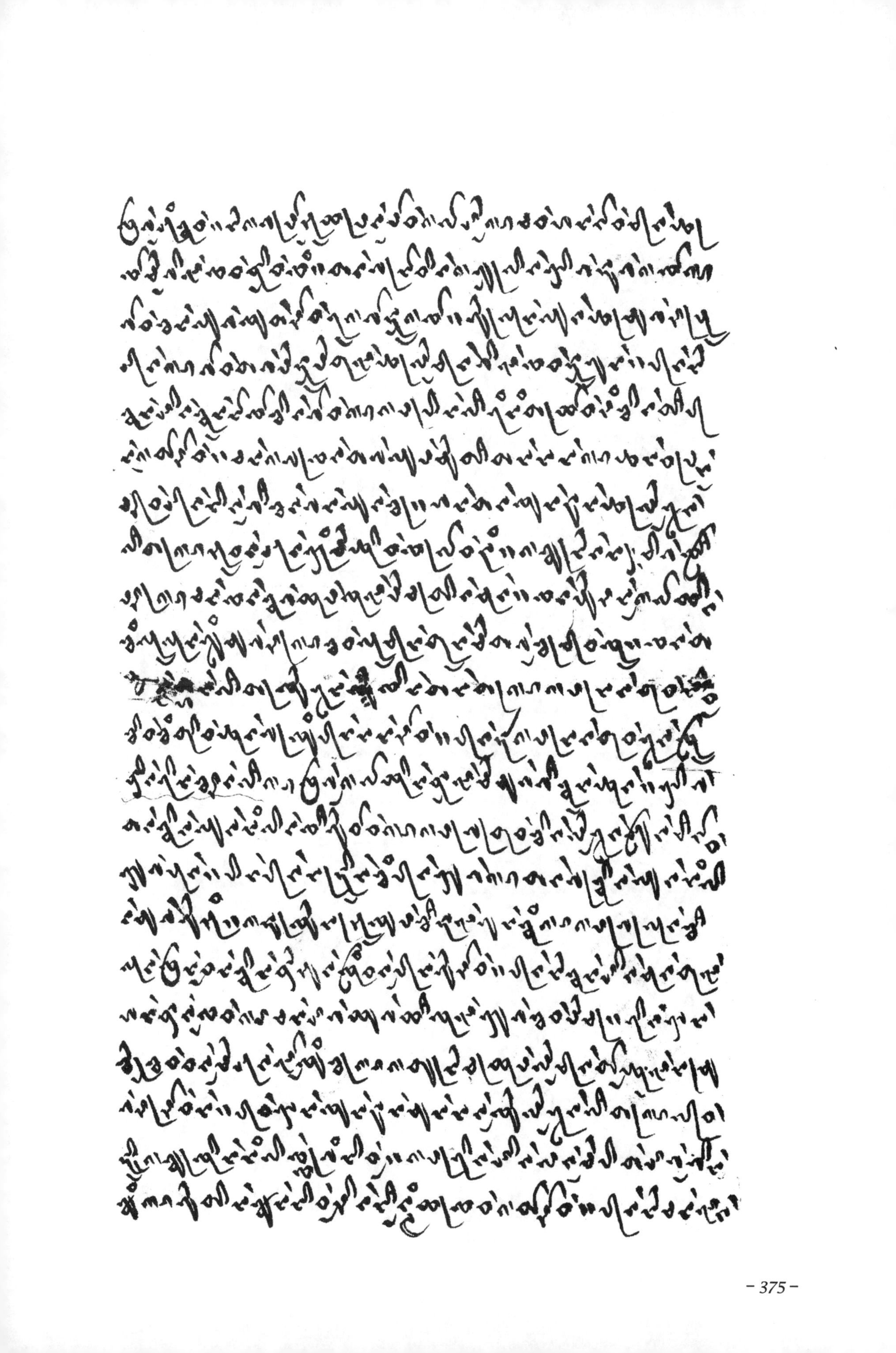

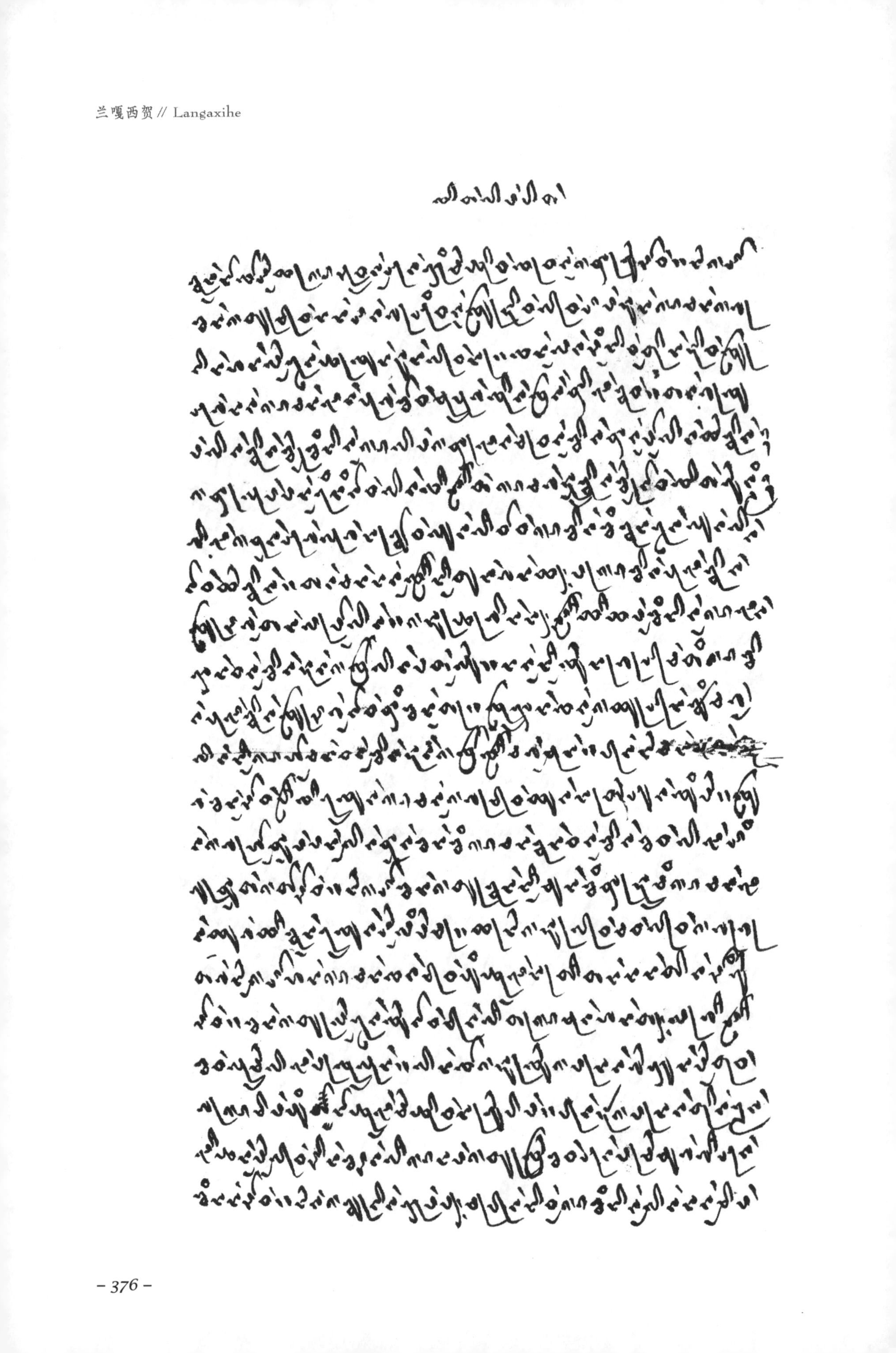

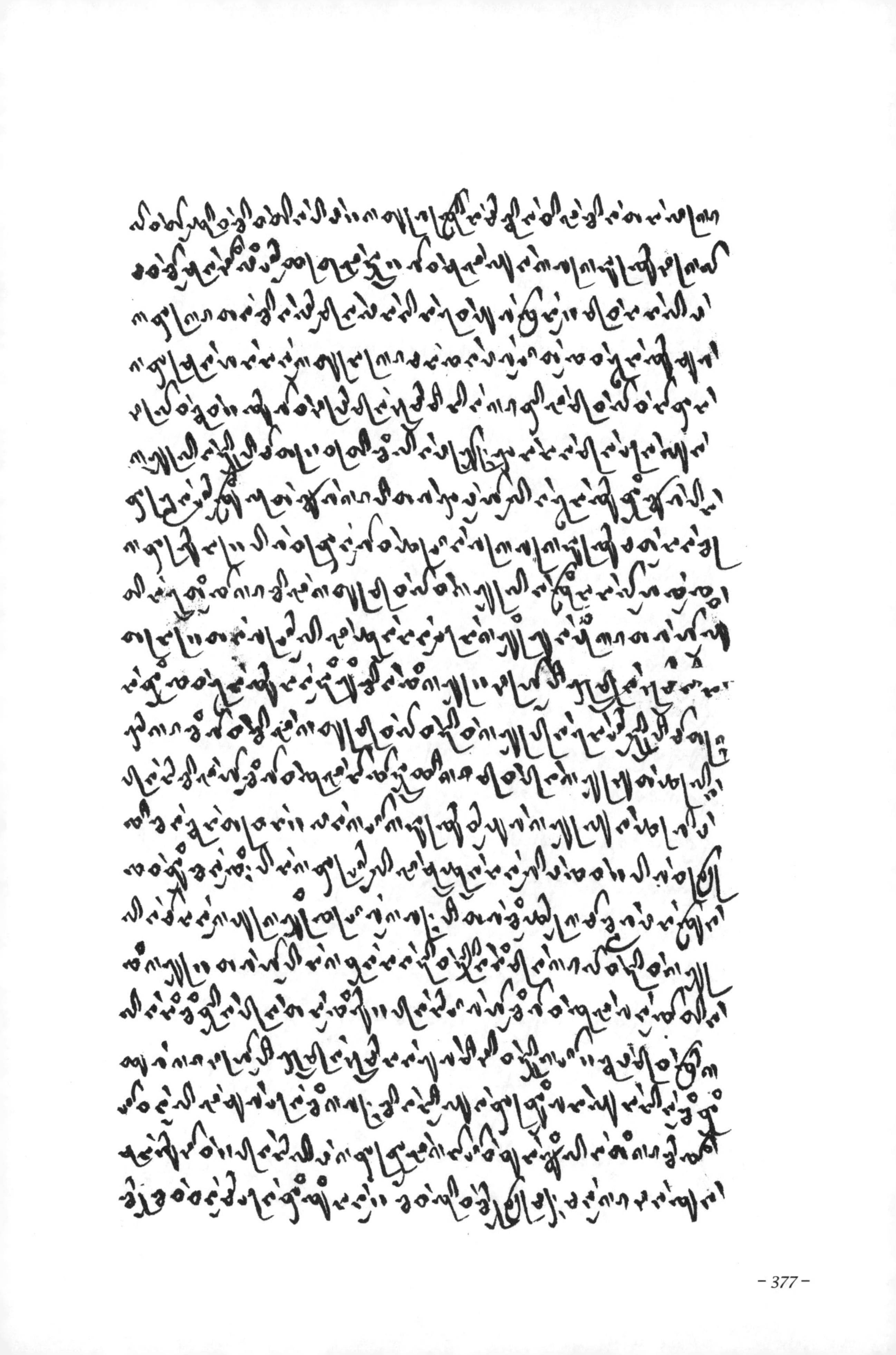

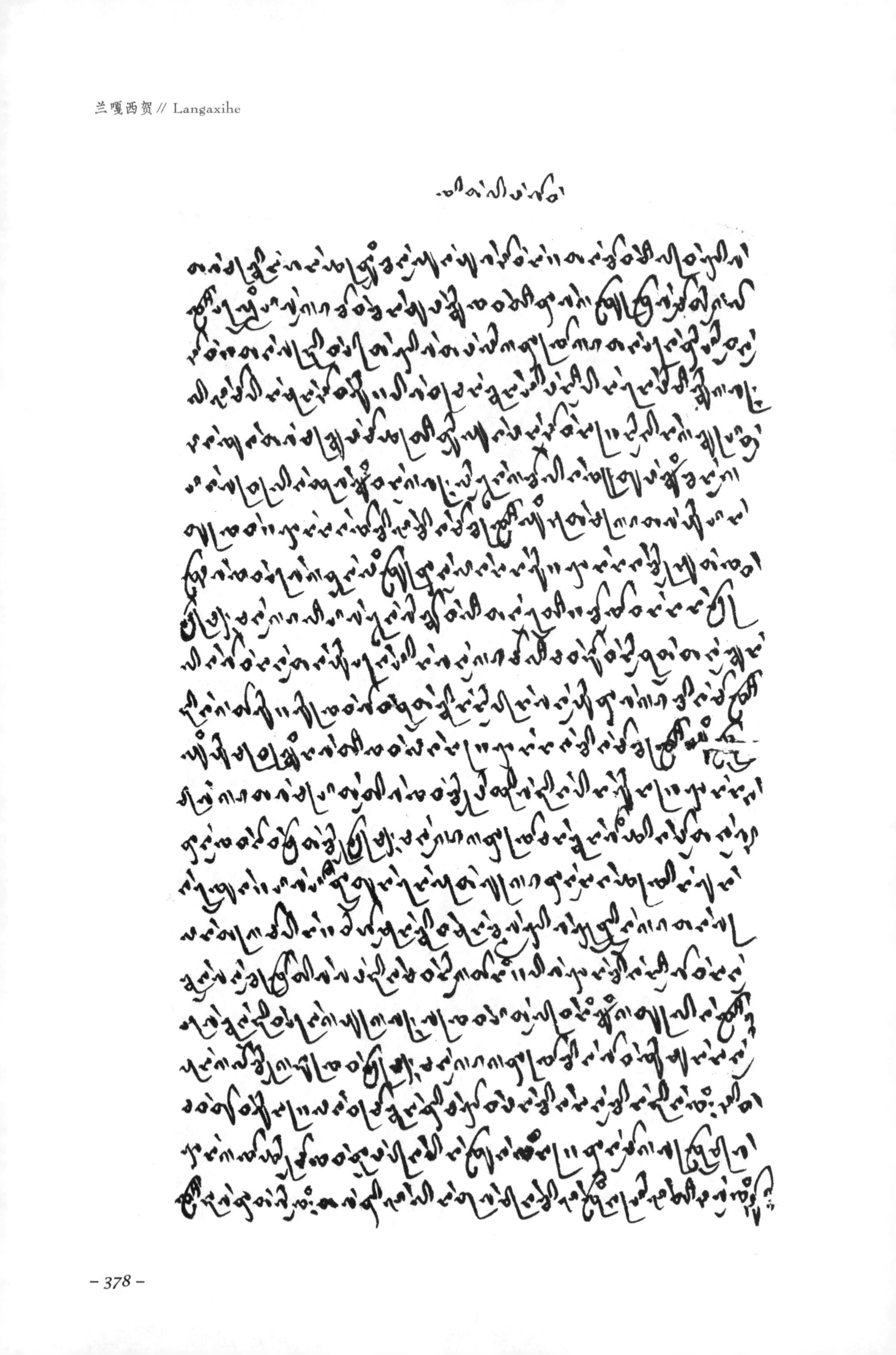

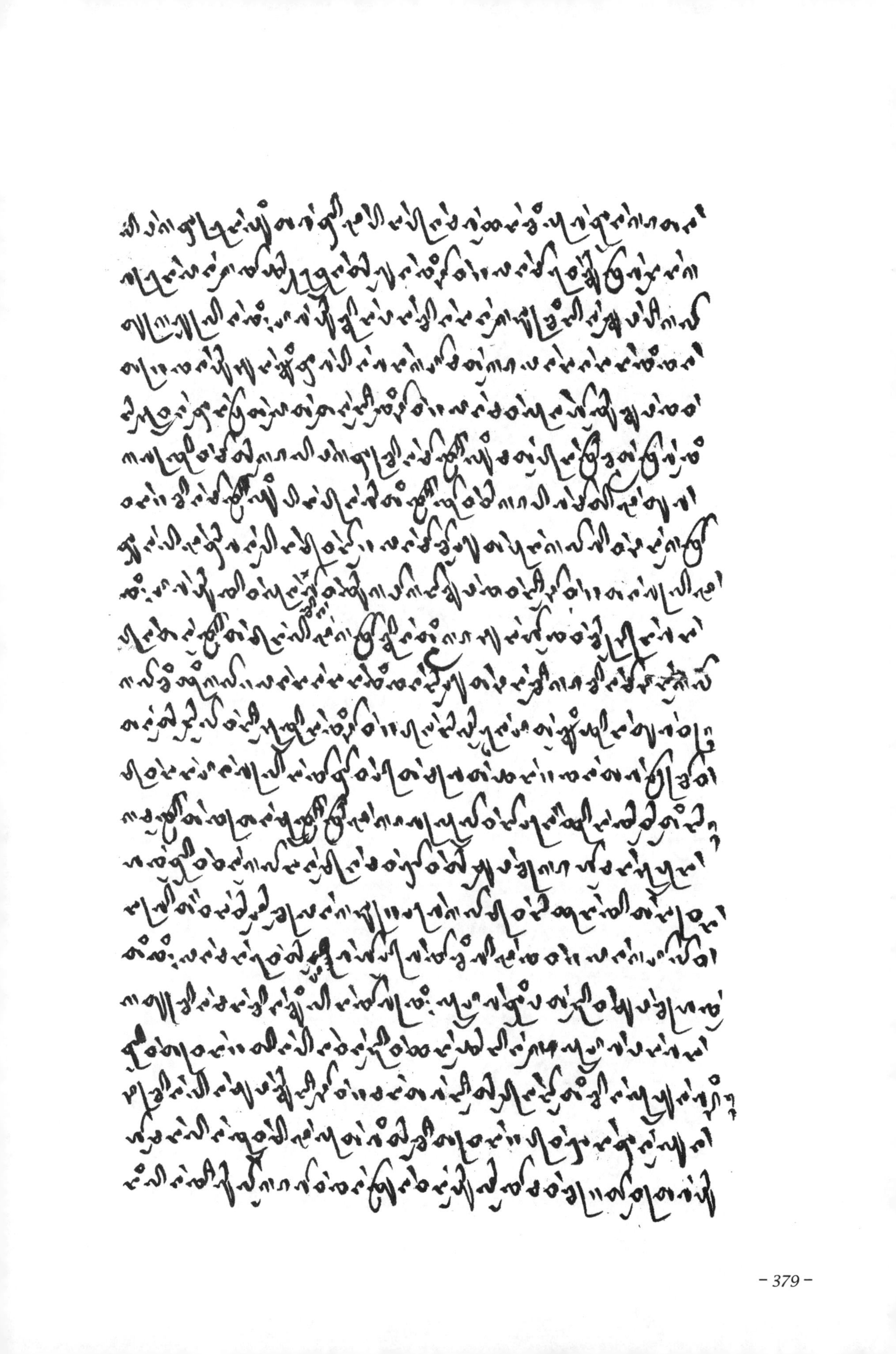

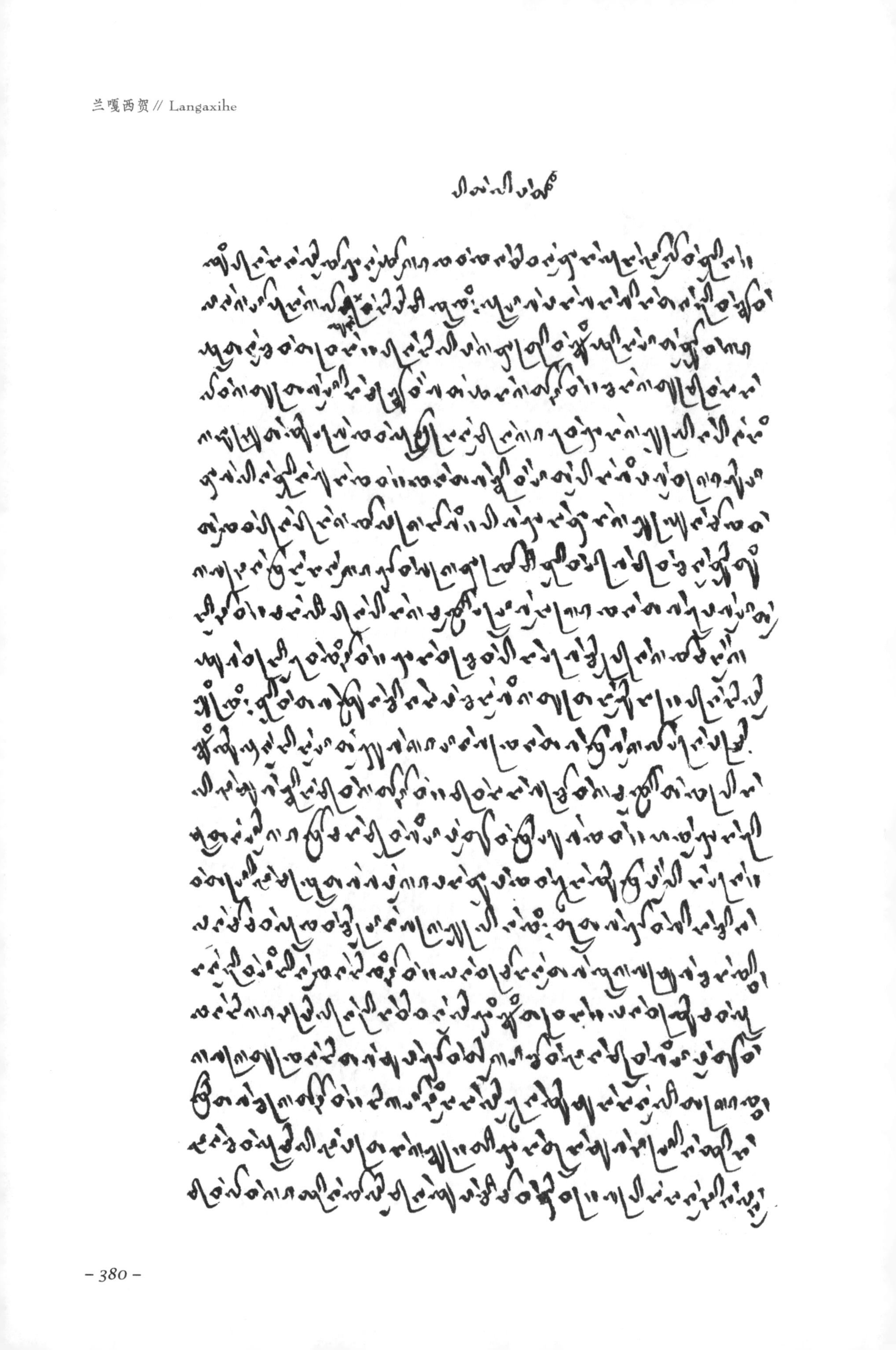

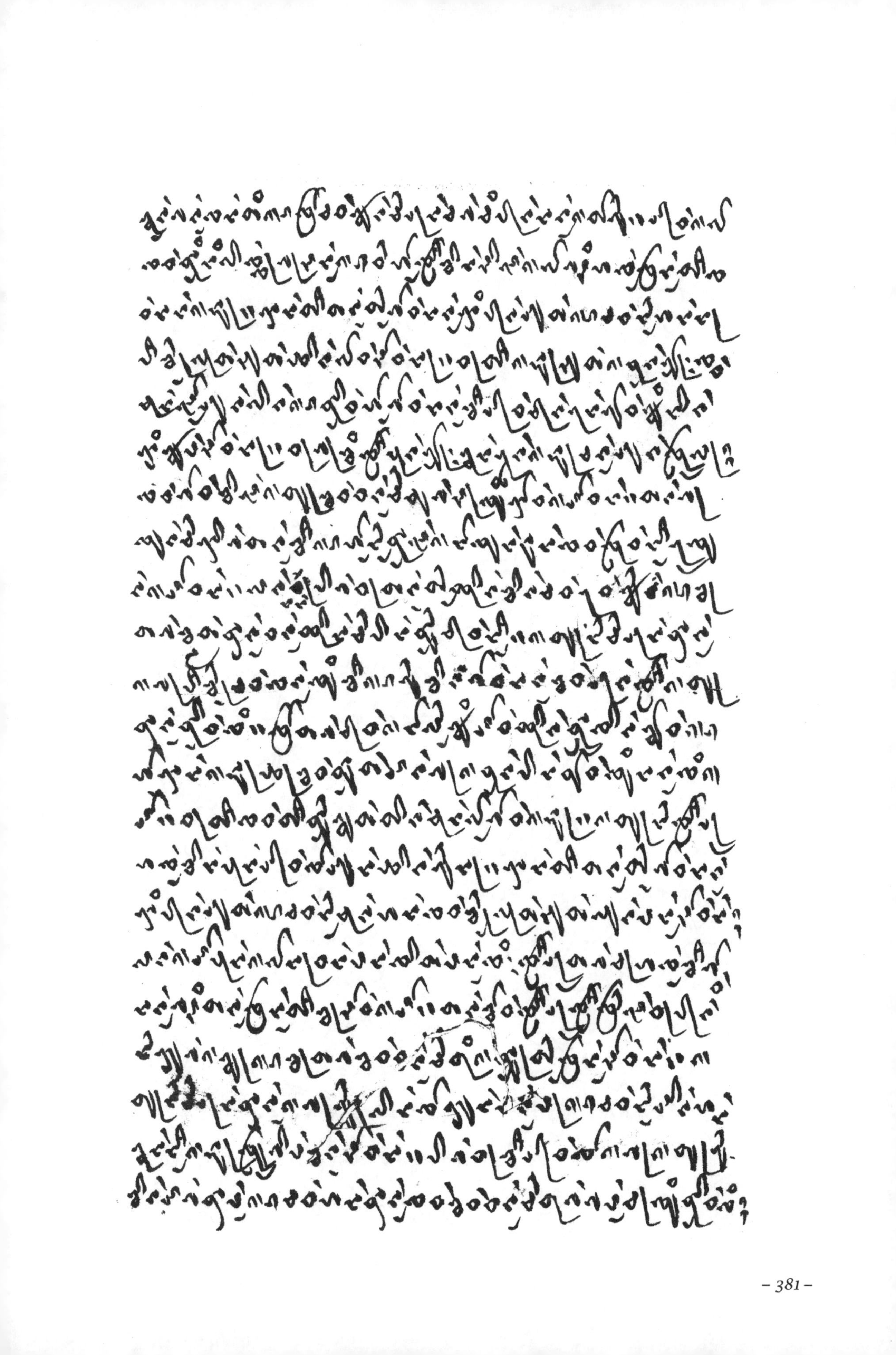

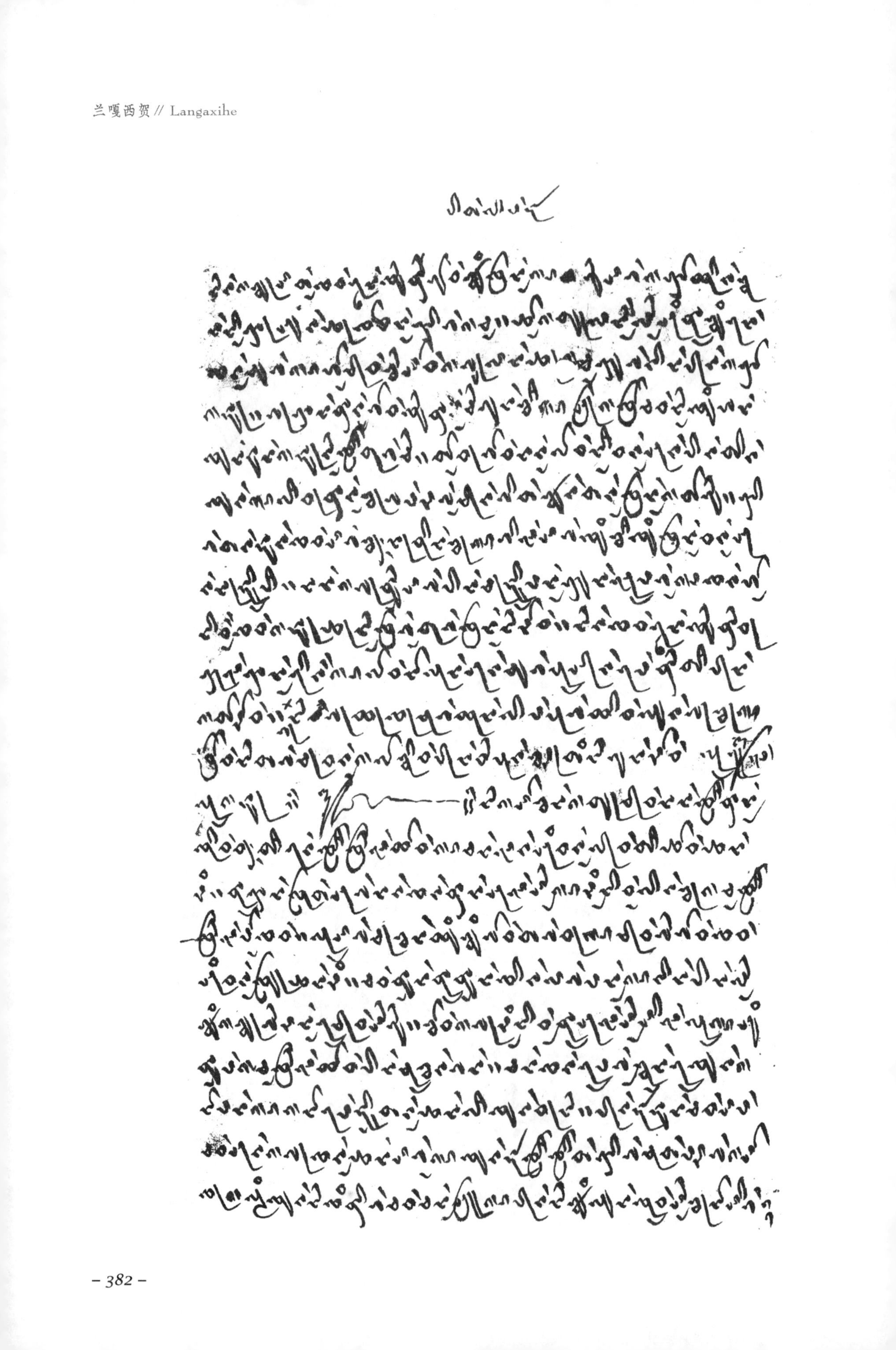

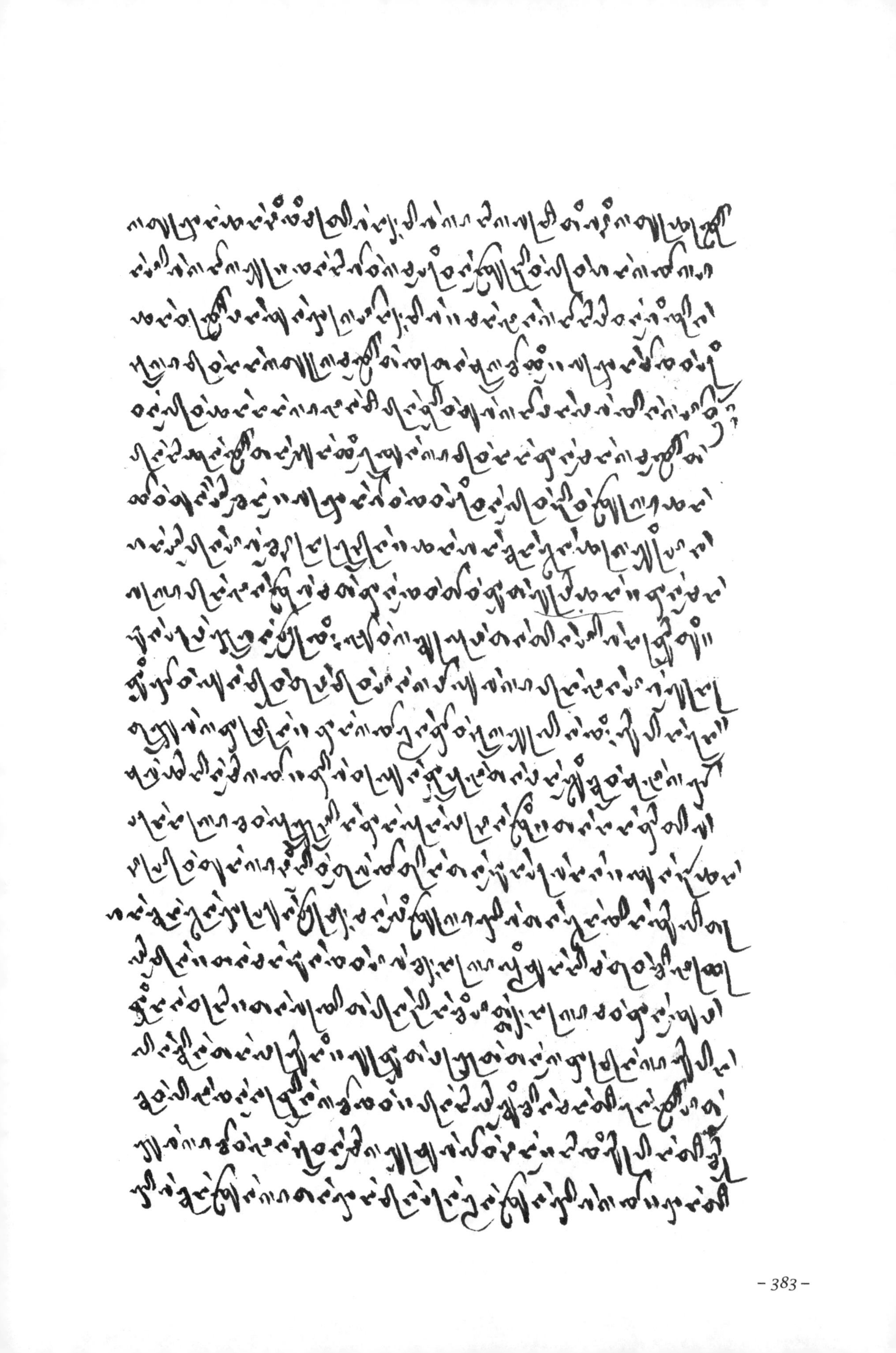

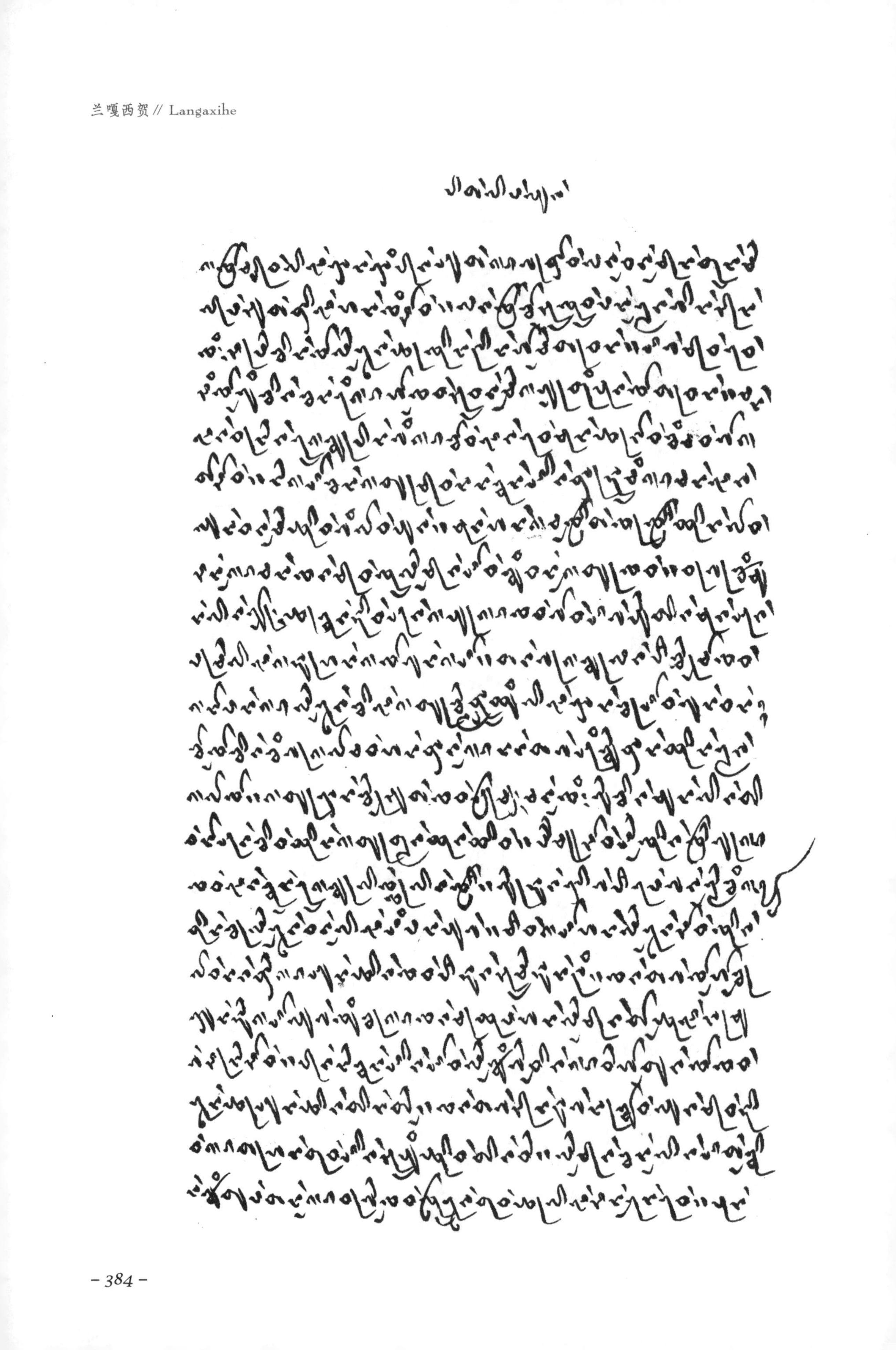

[illegible]

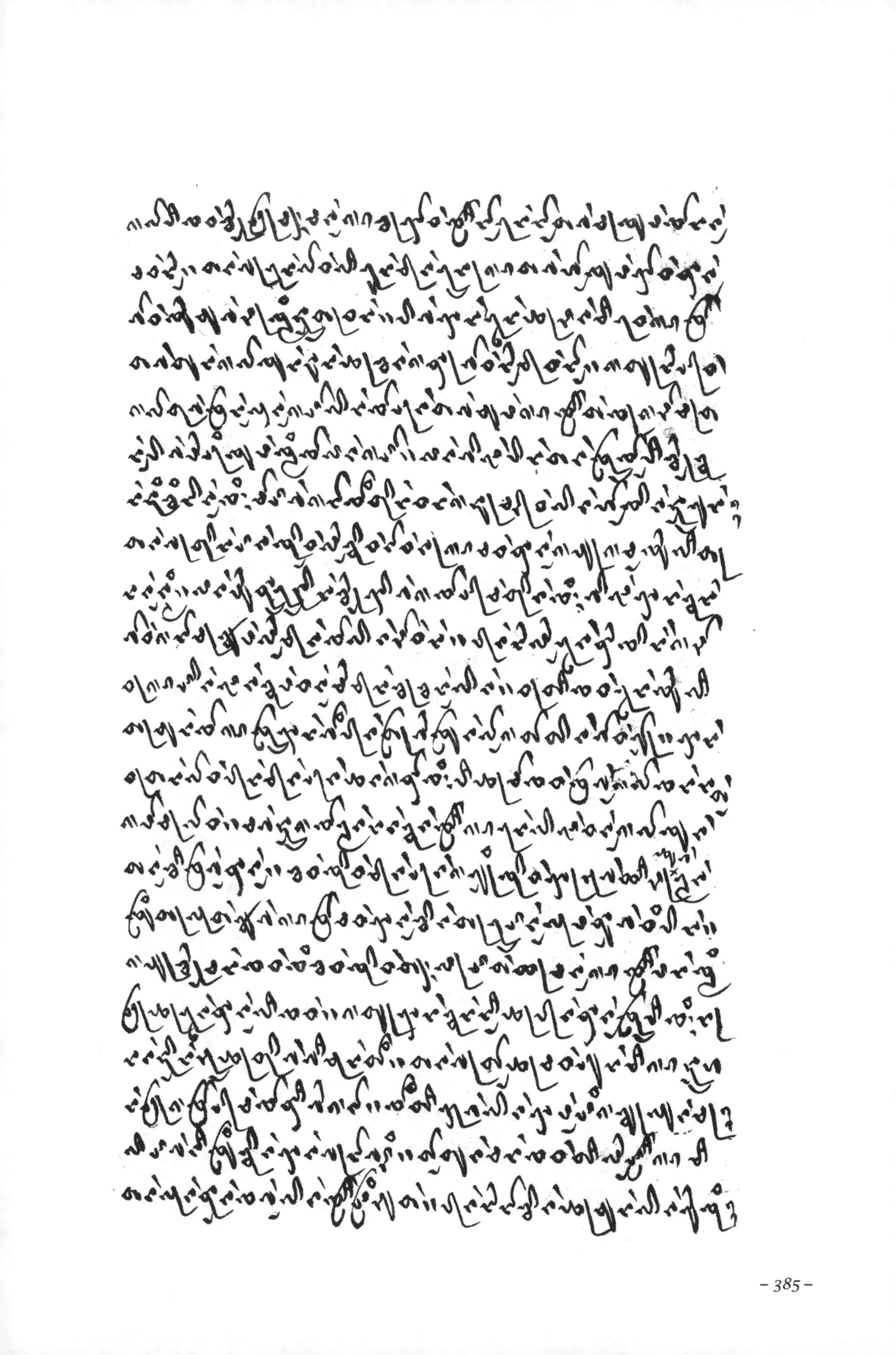

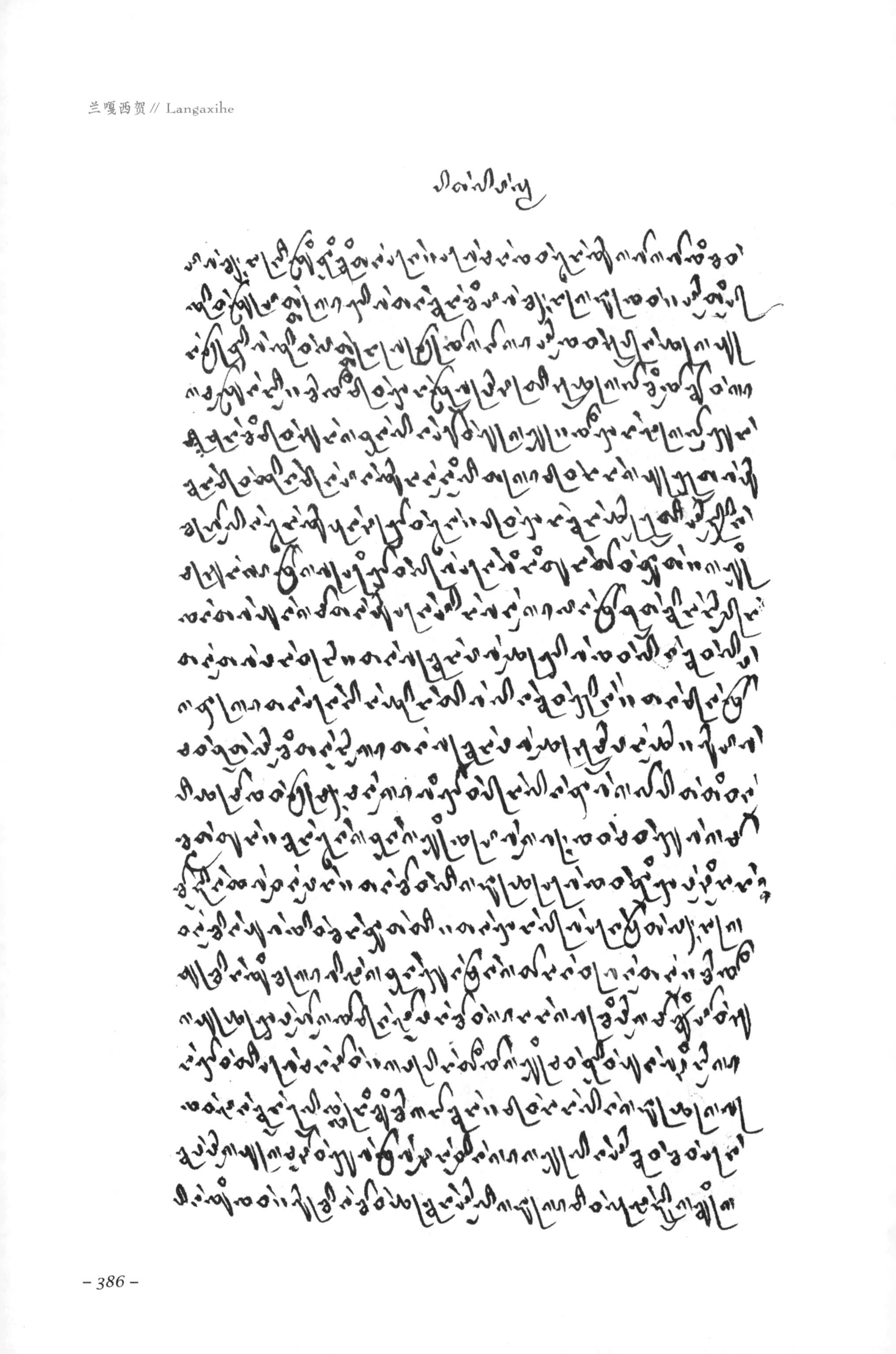

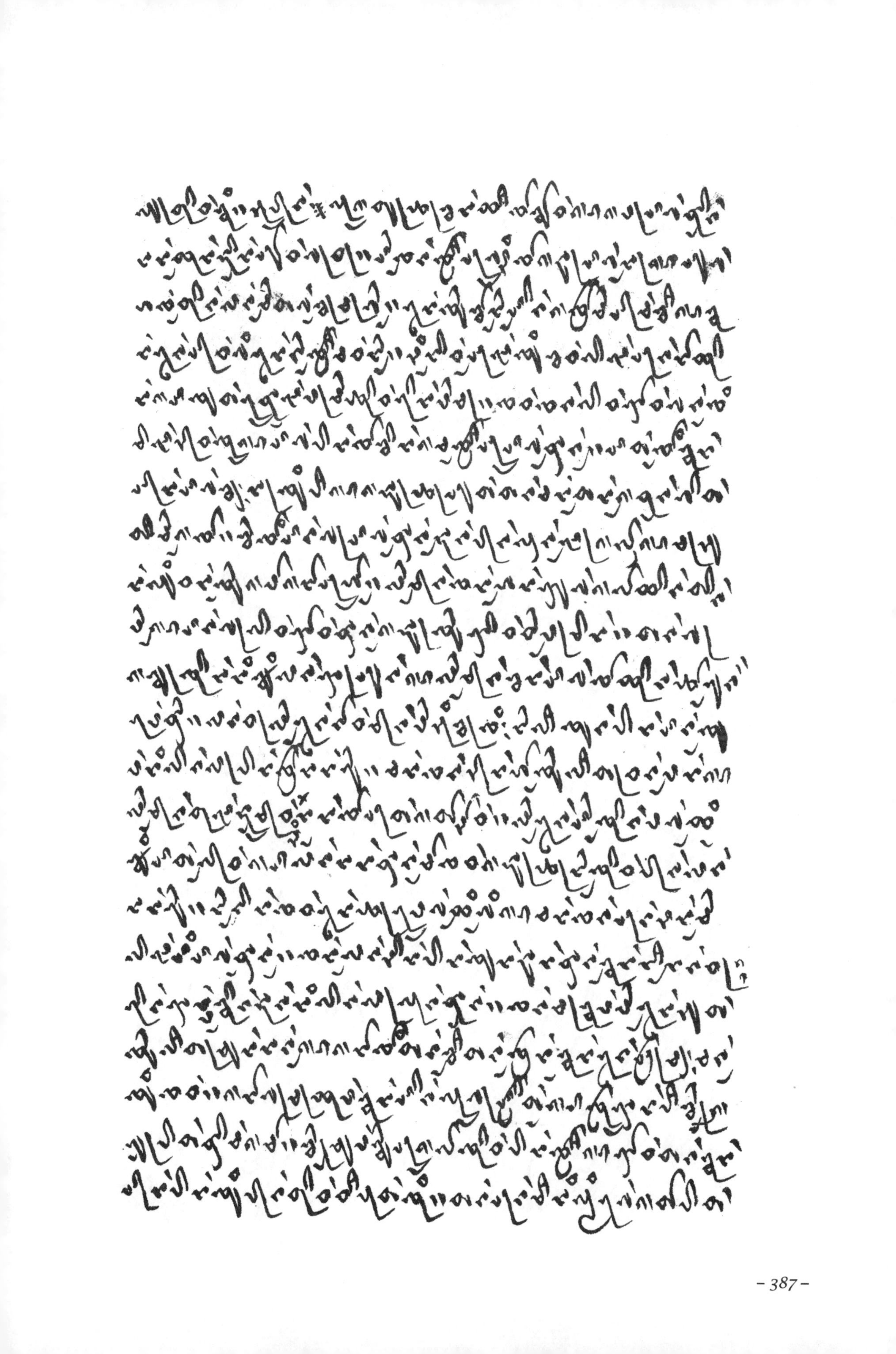

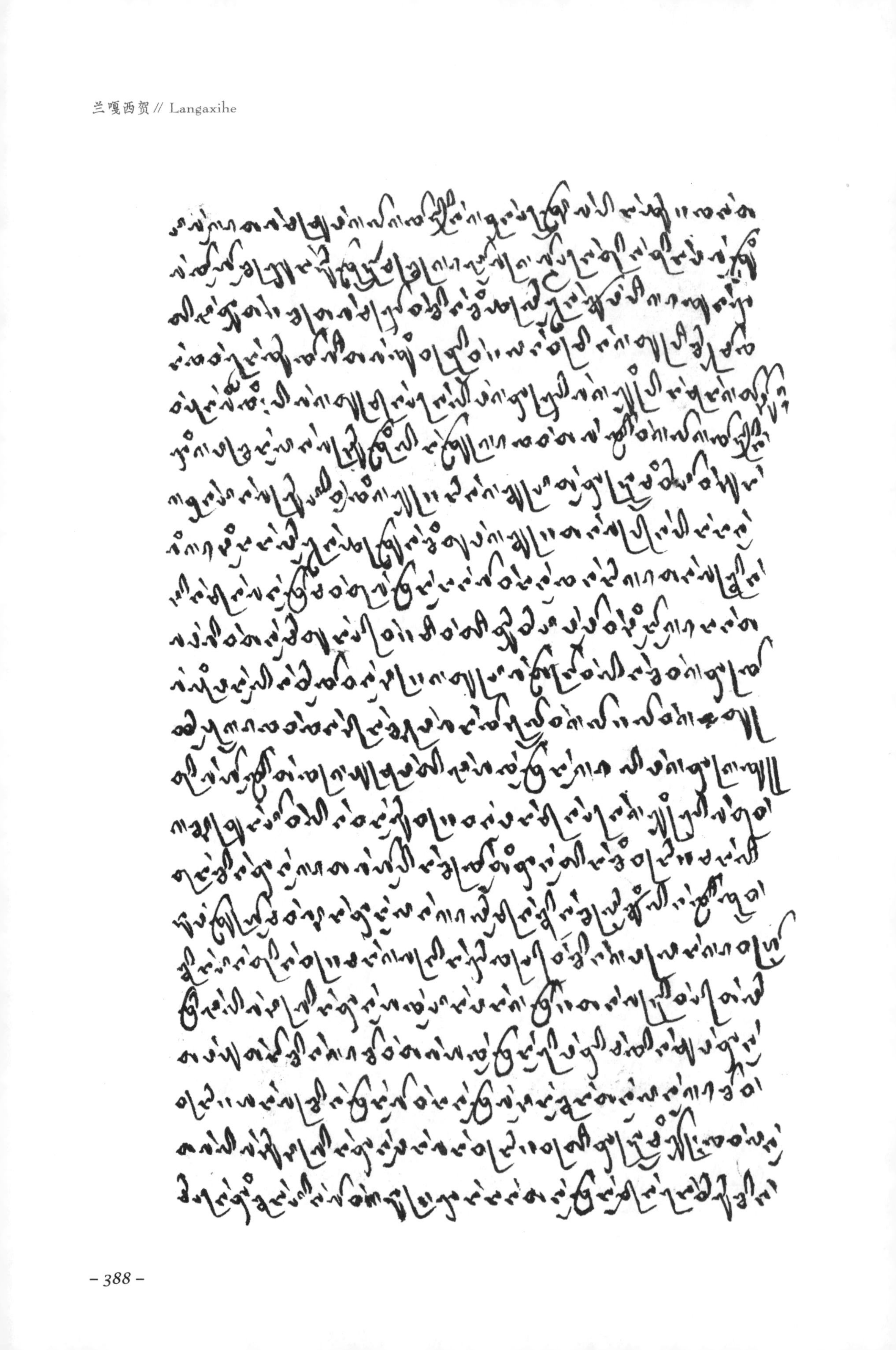

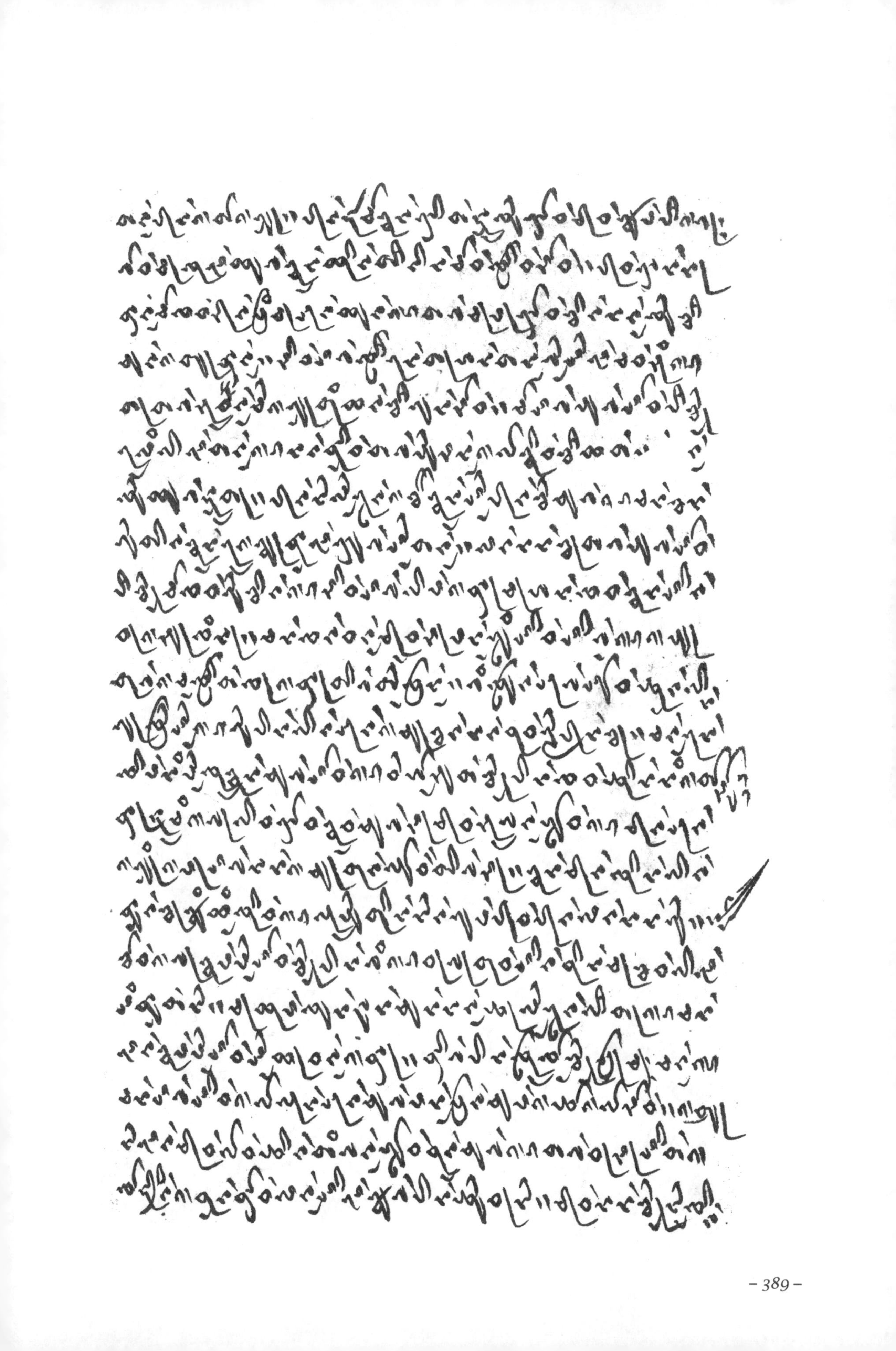

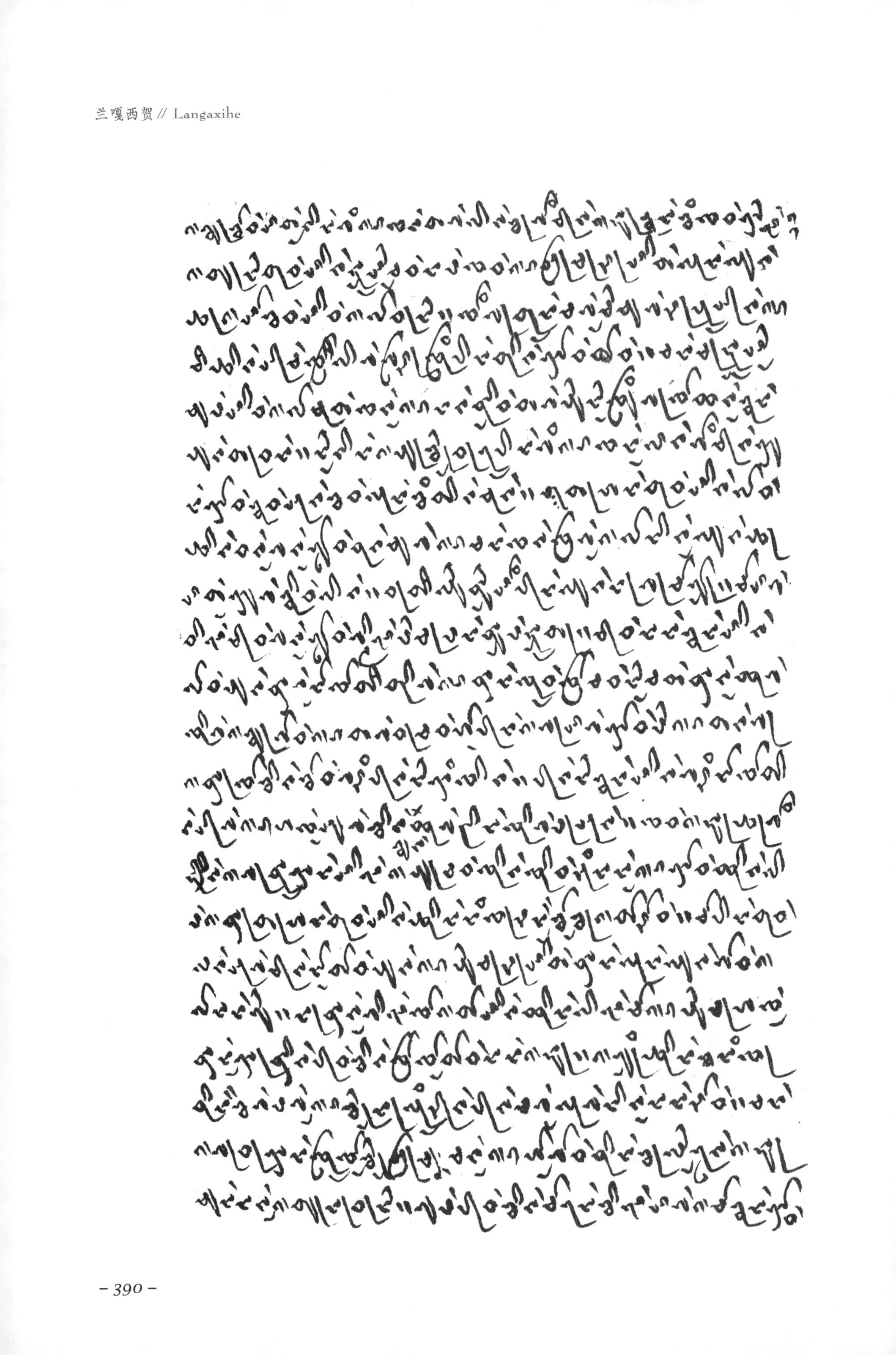

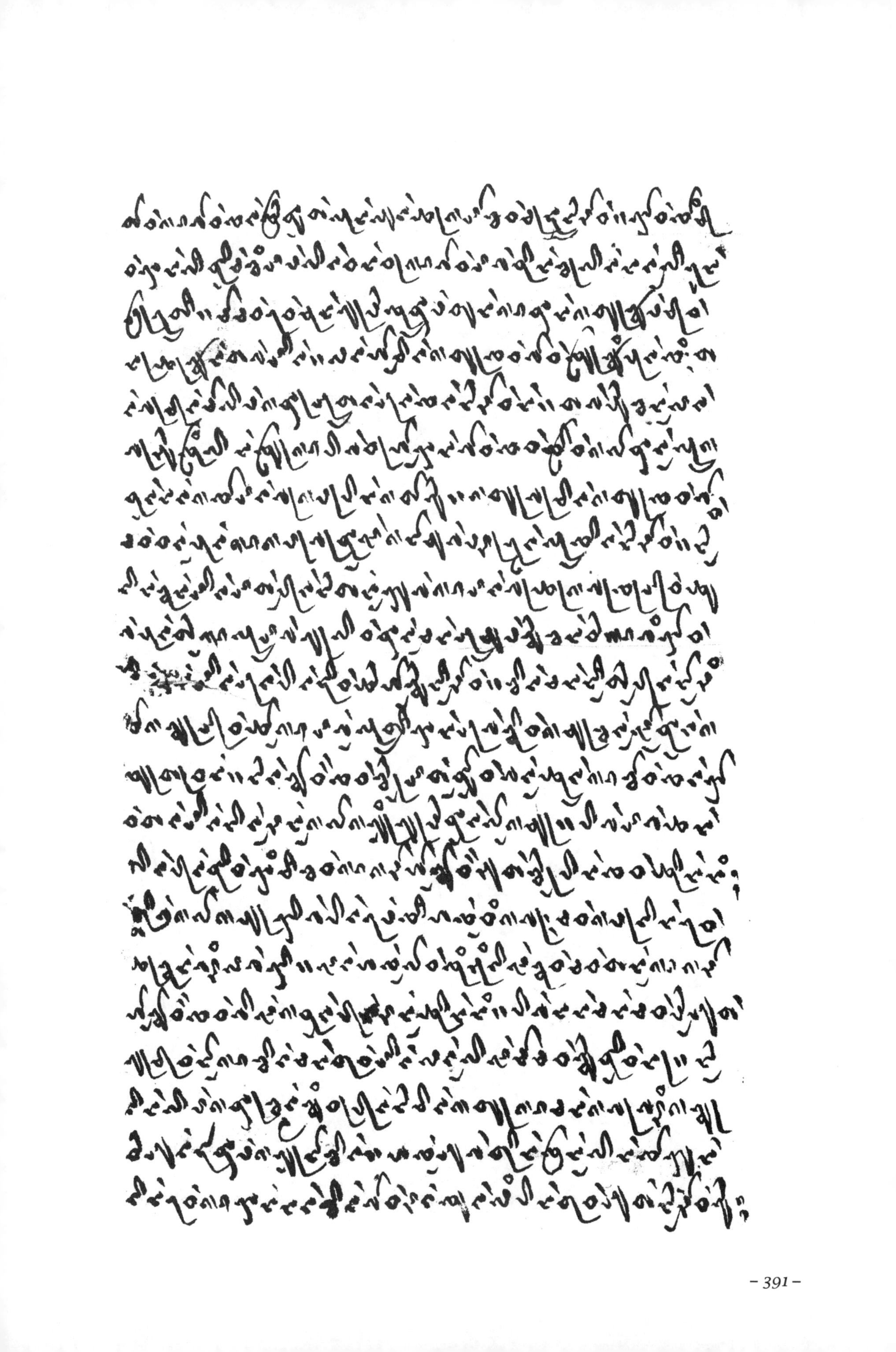

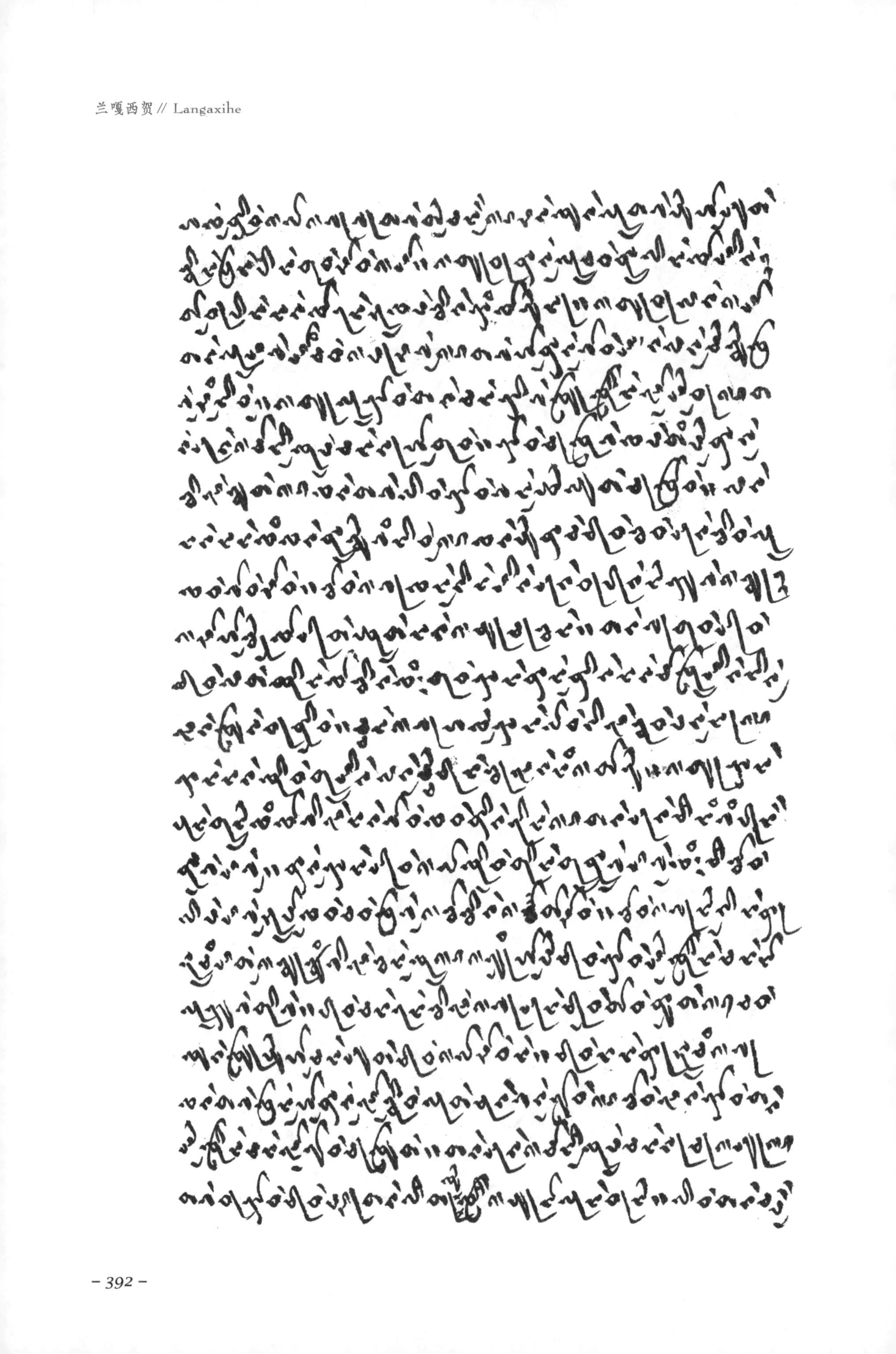

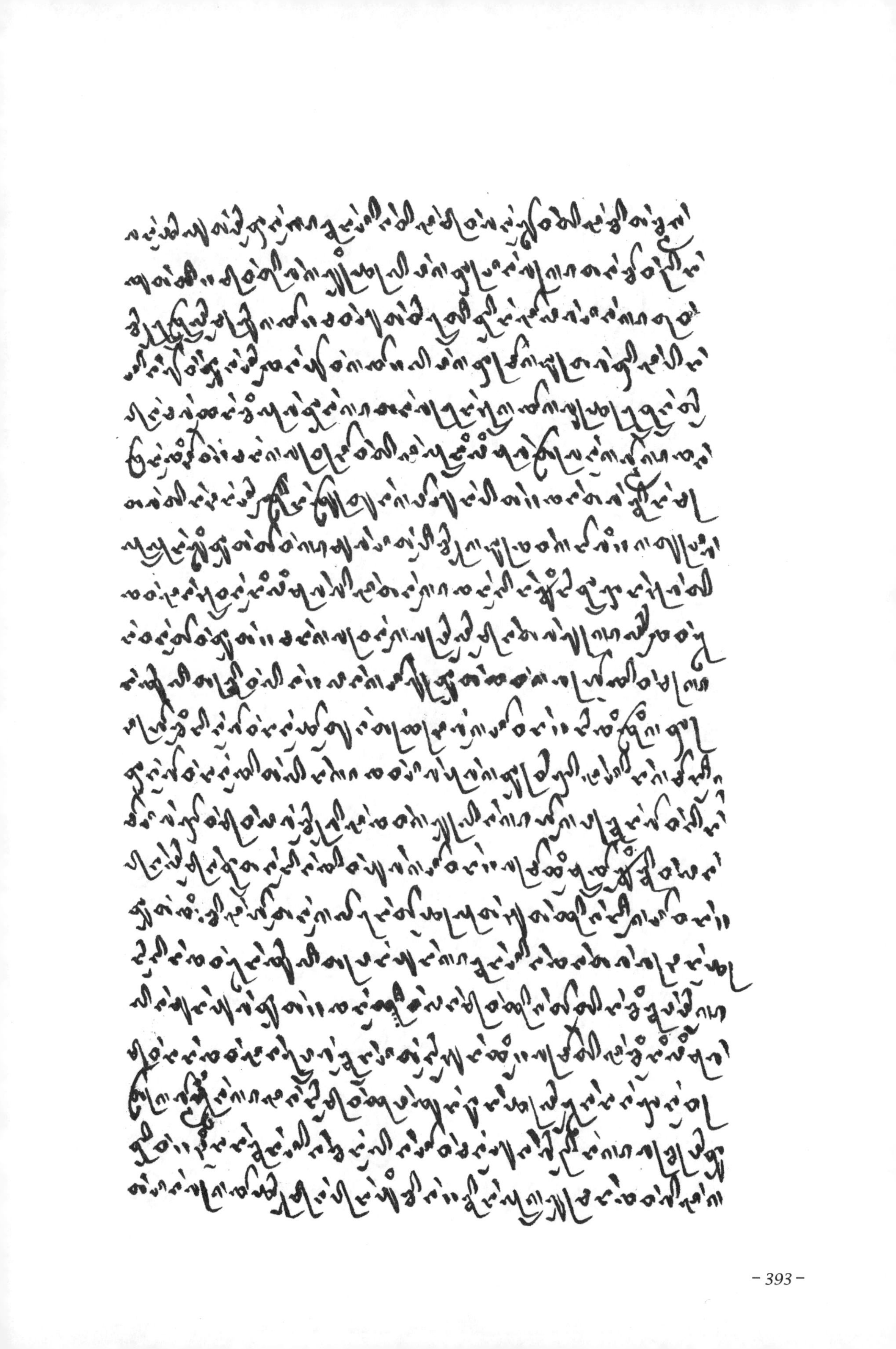

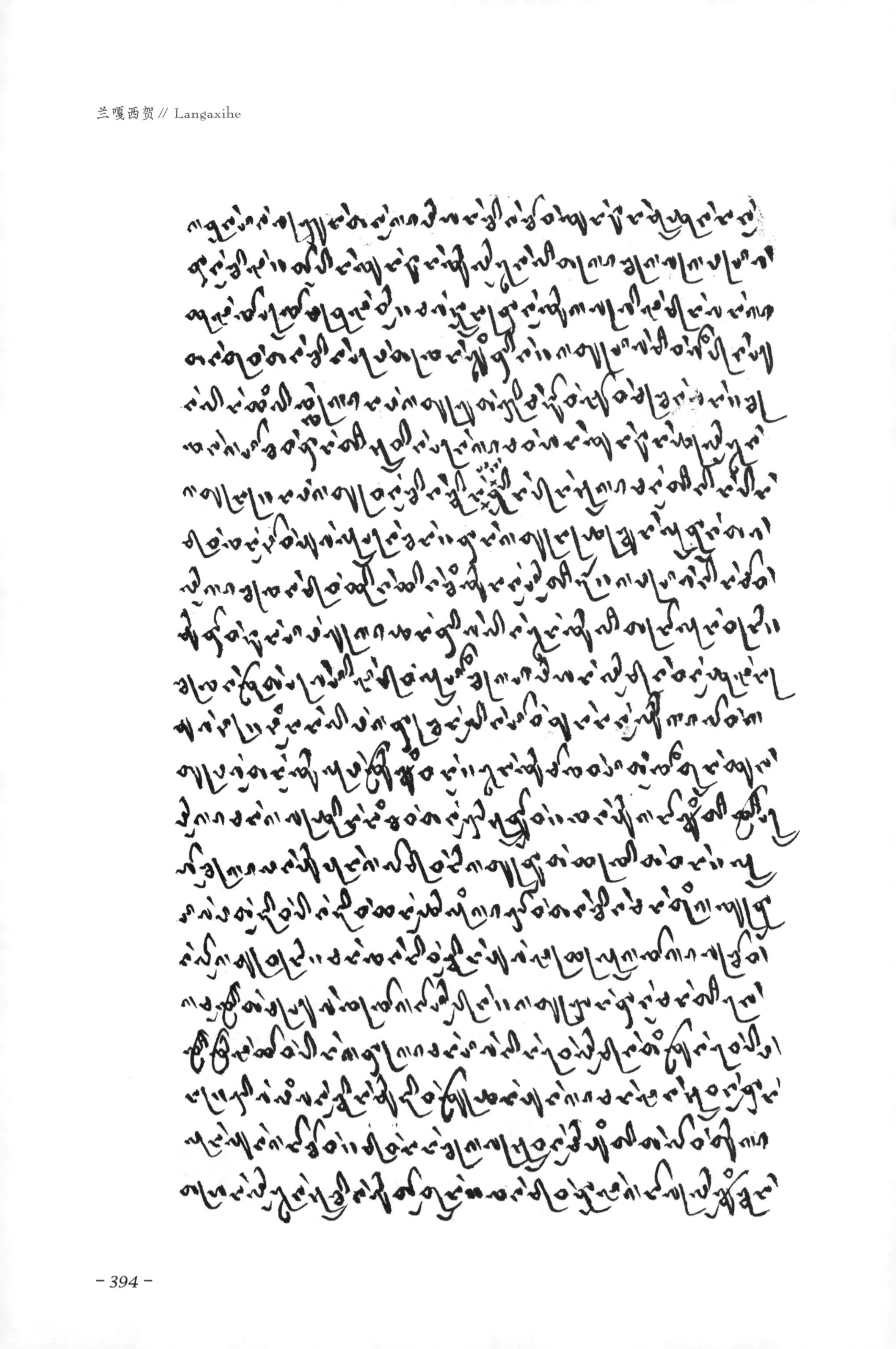

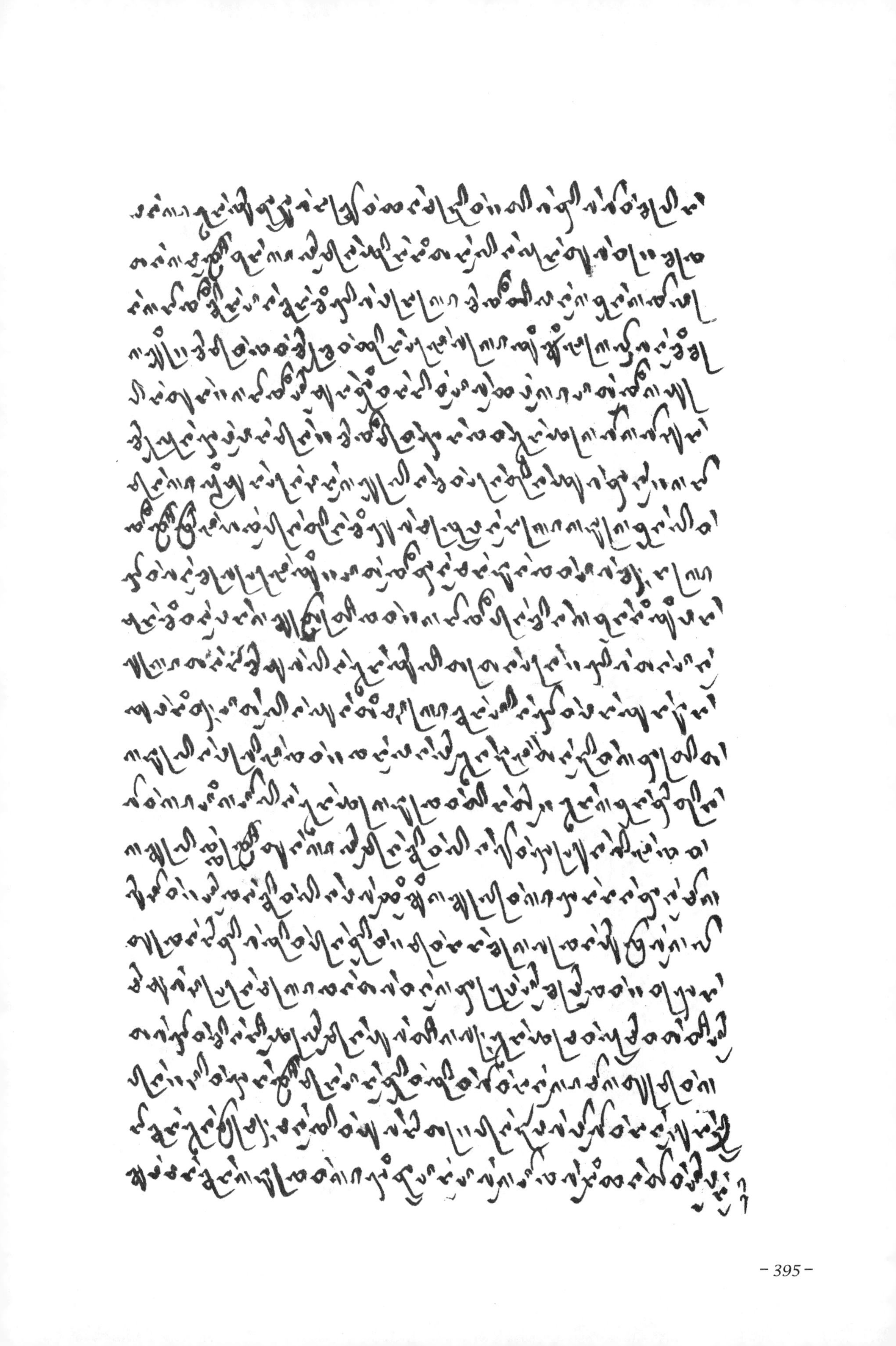

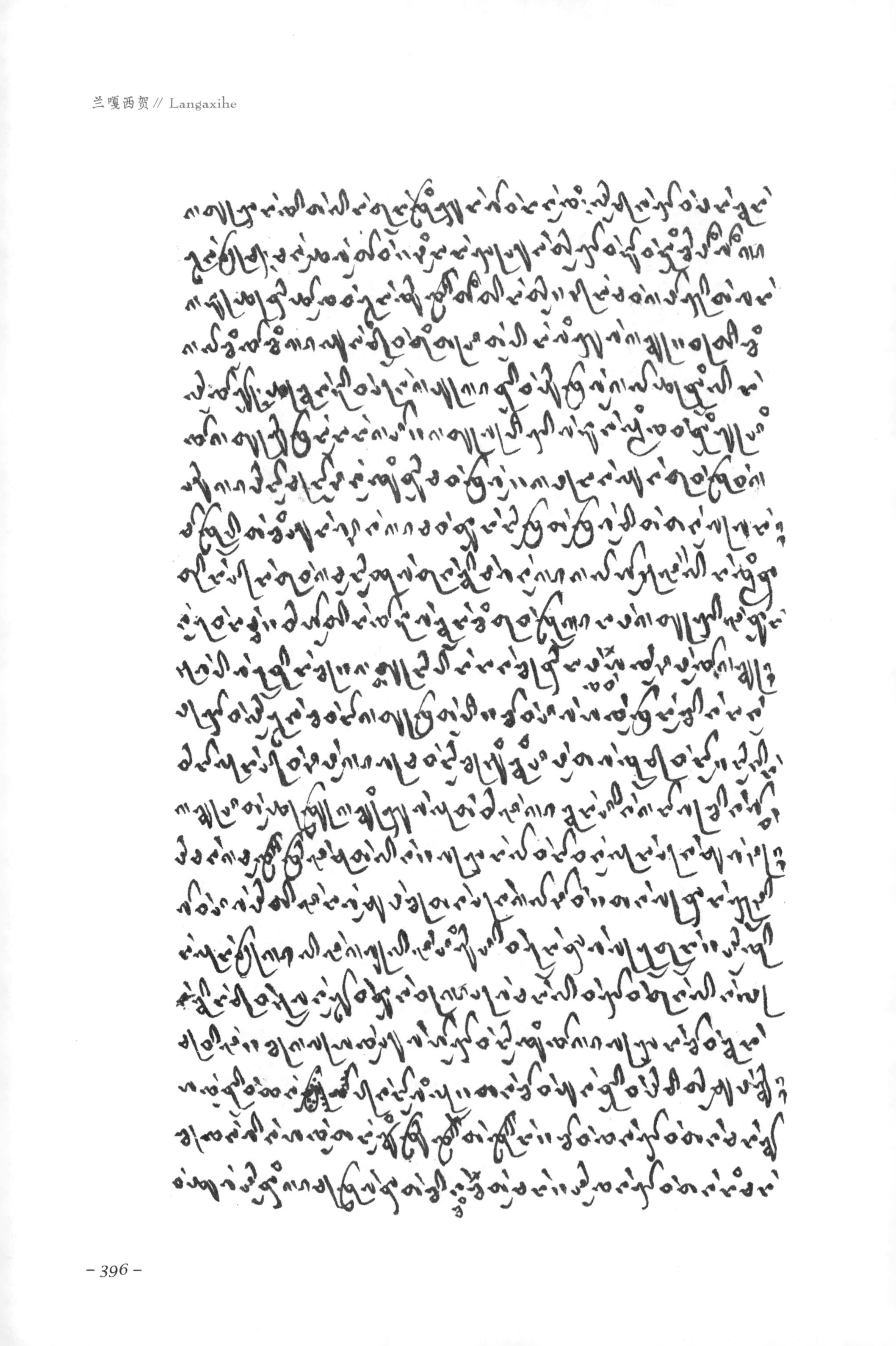

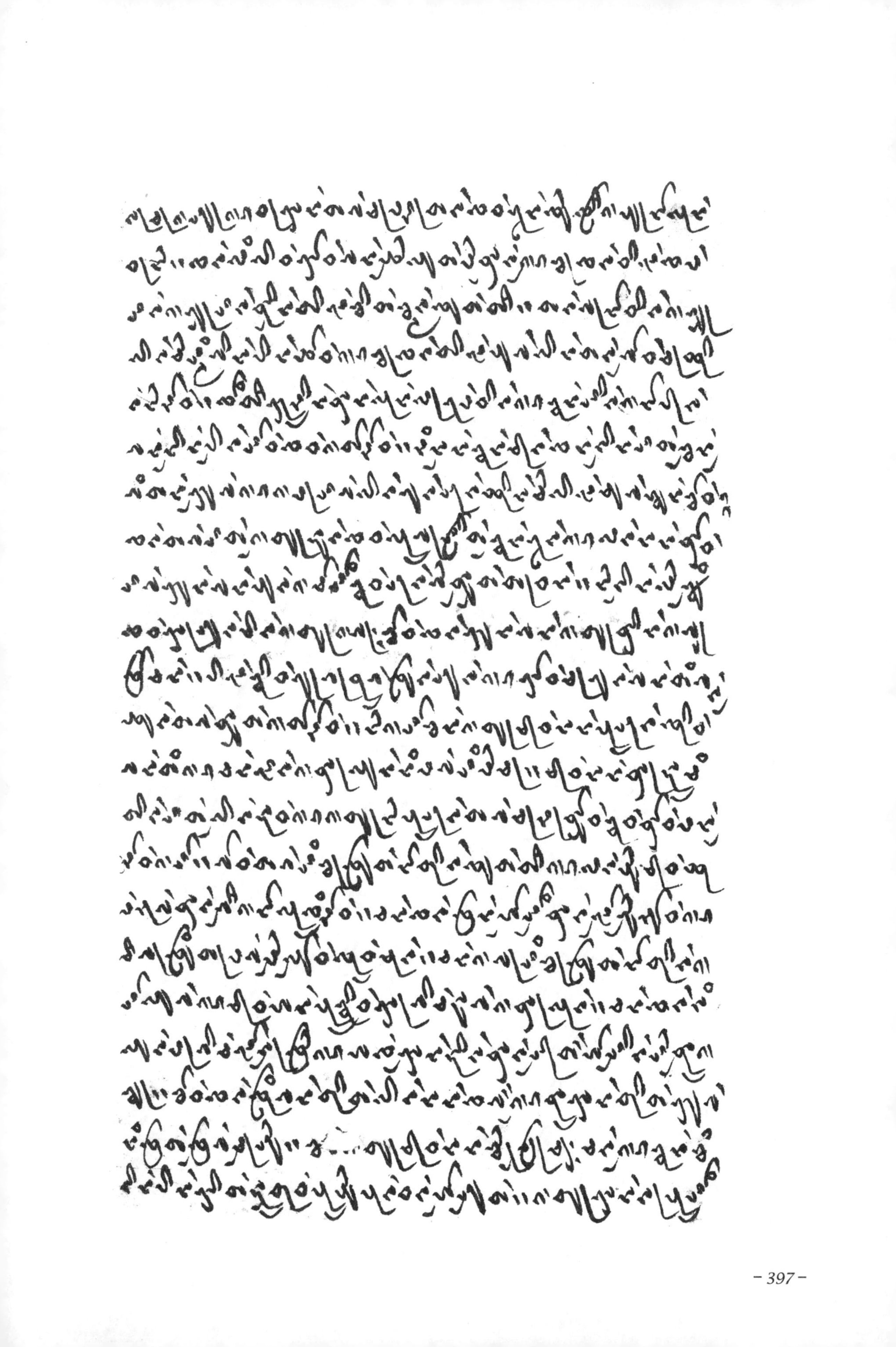

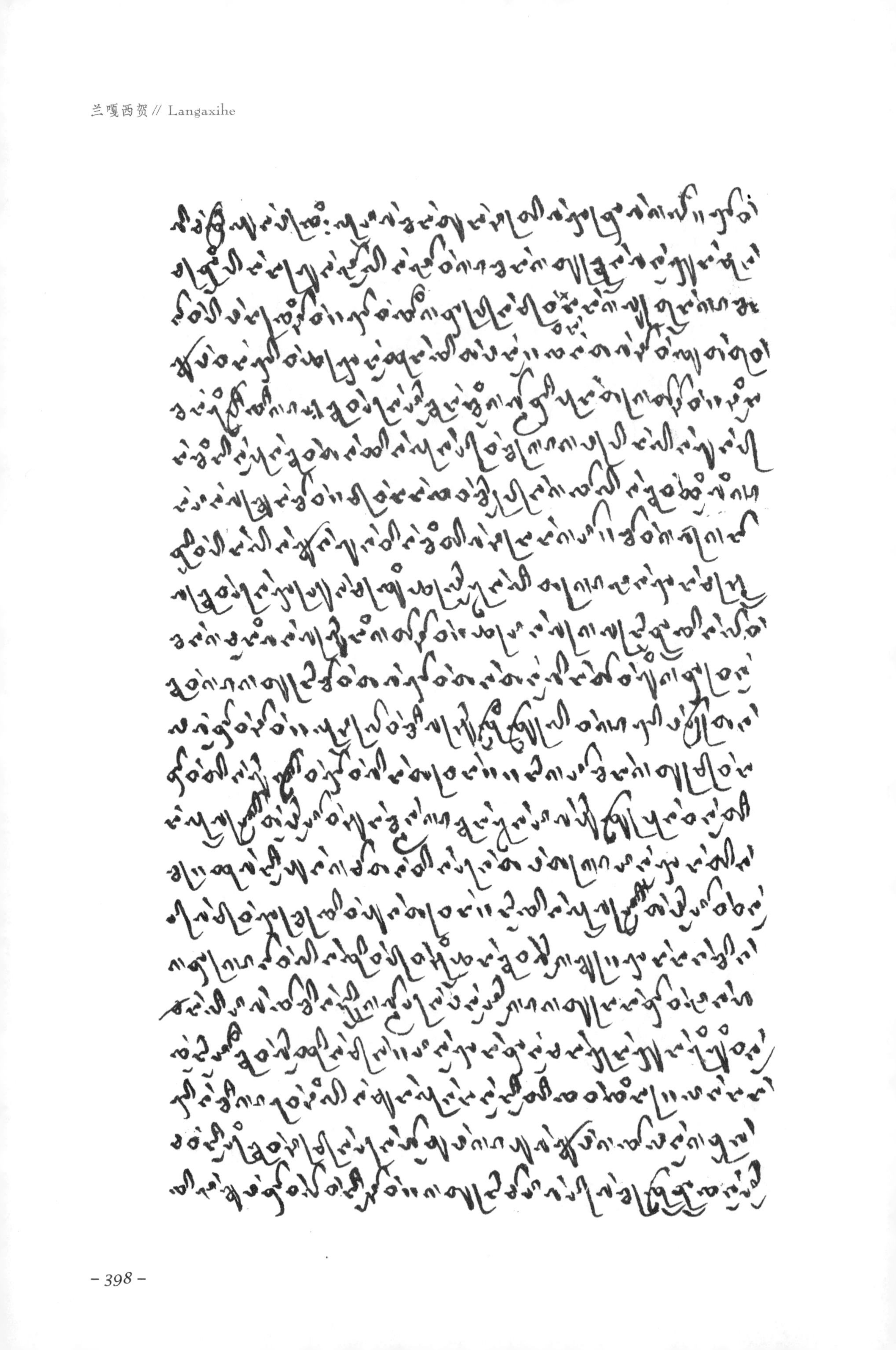

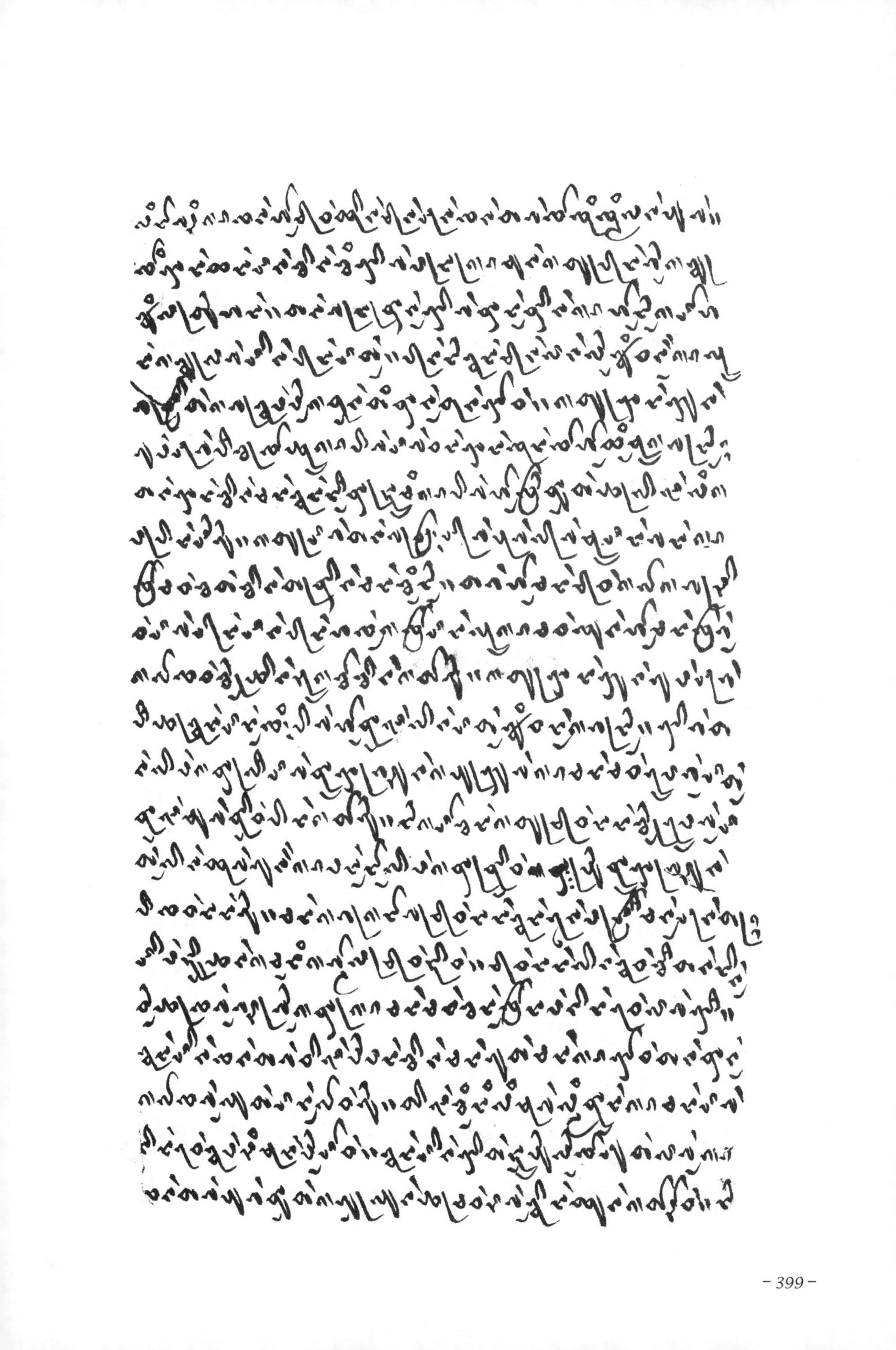

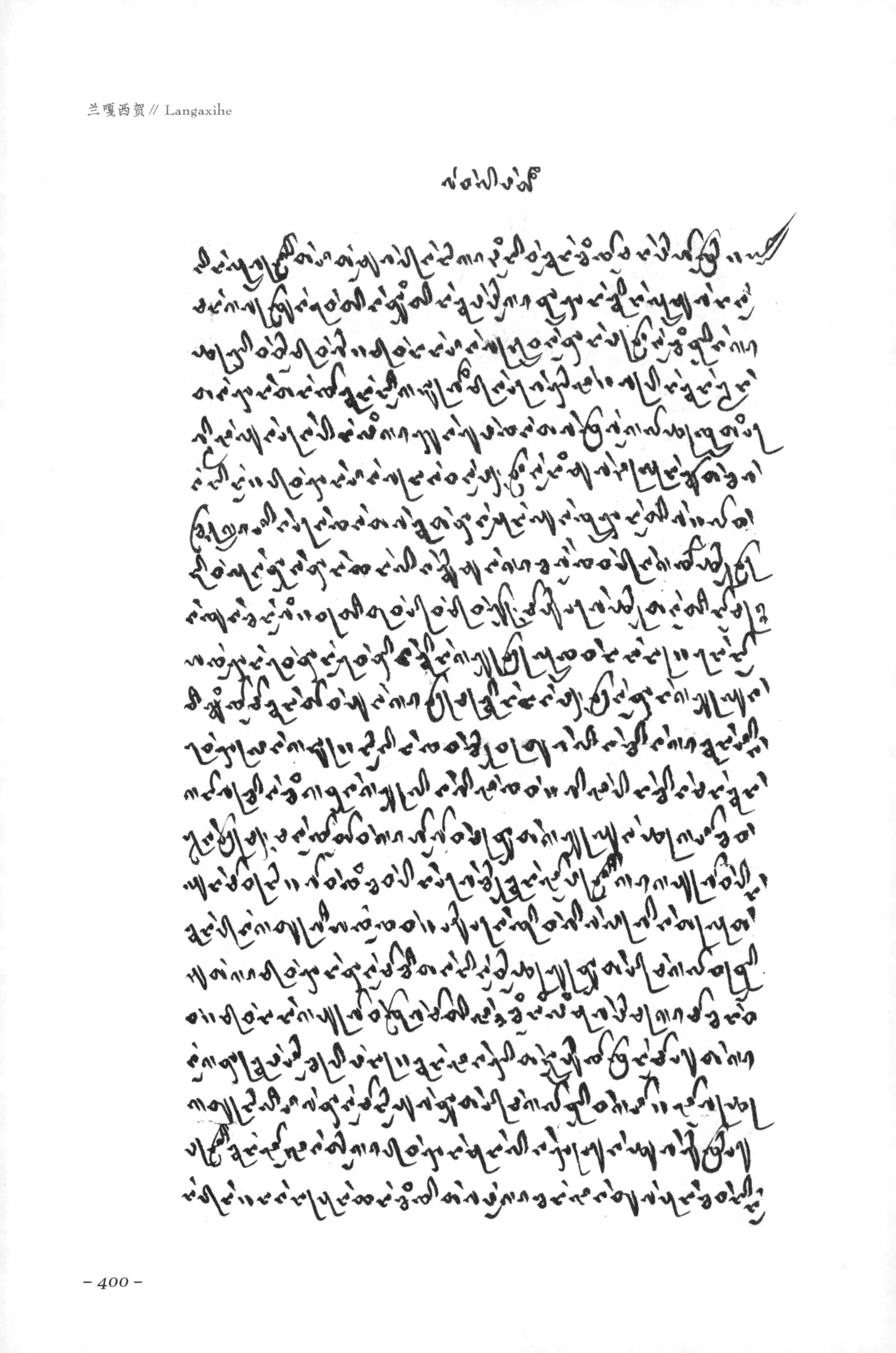

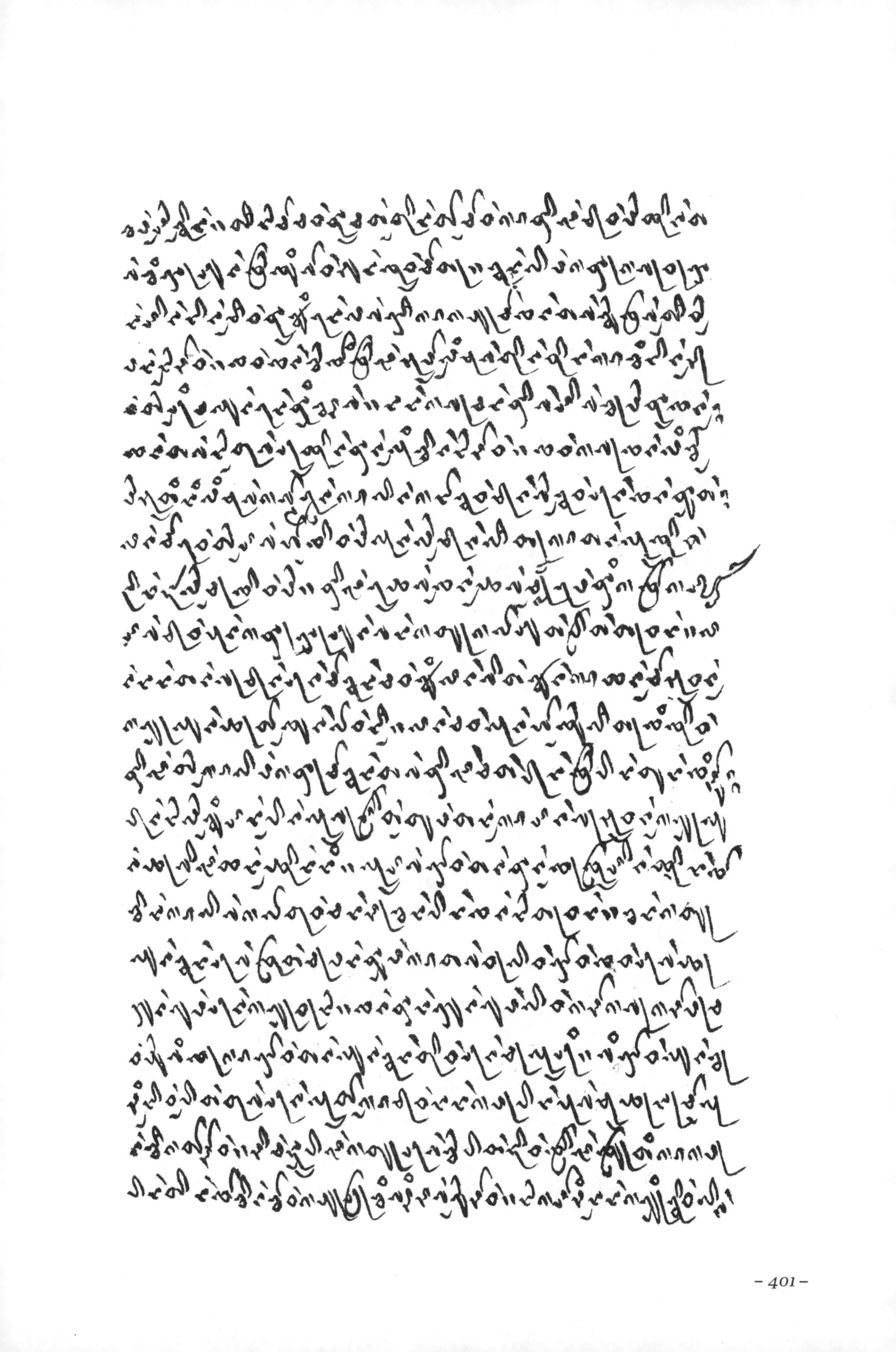

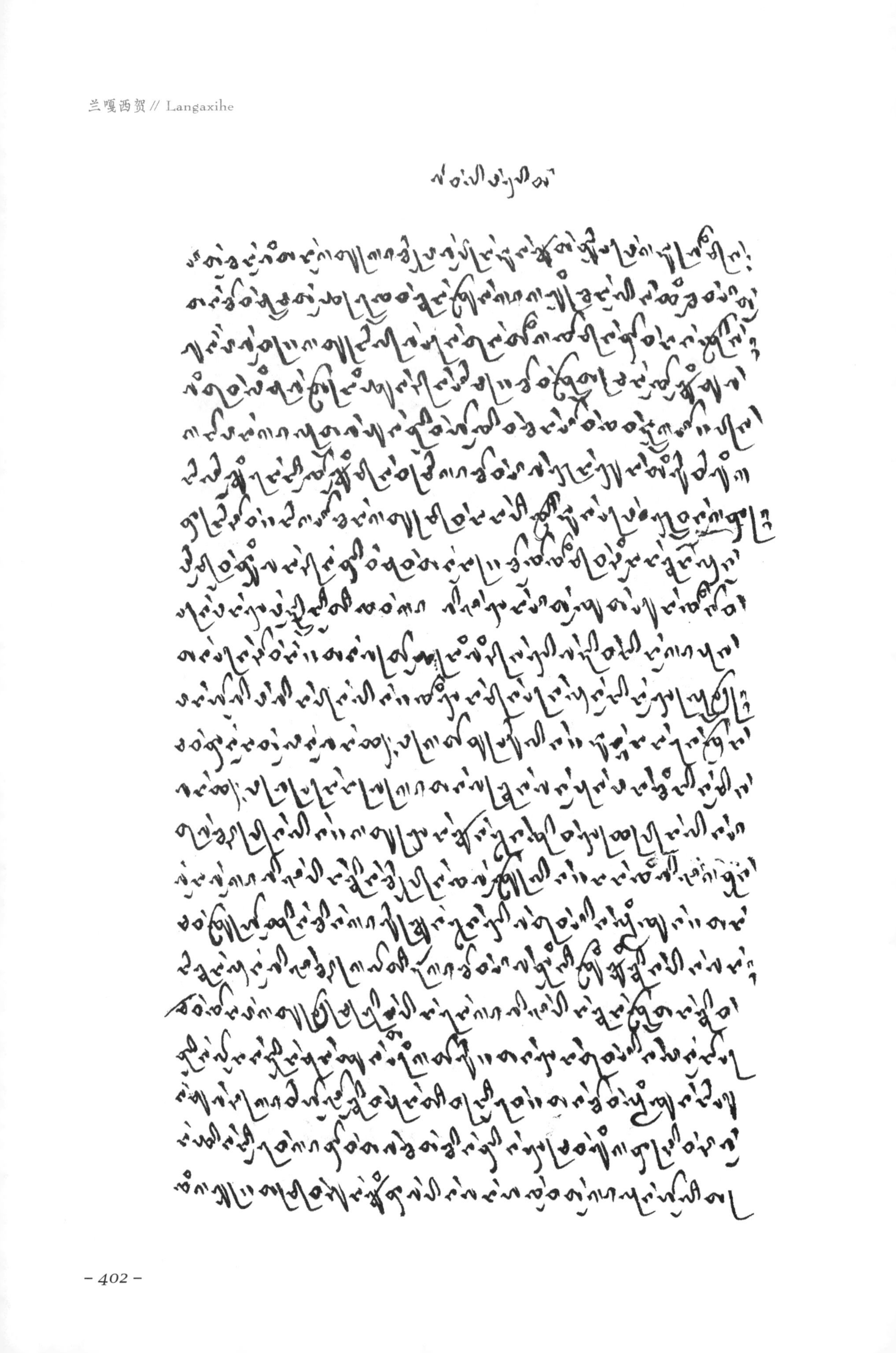

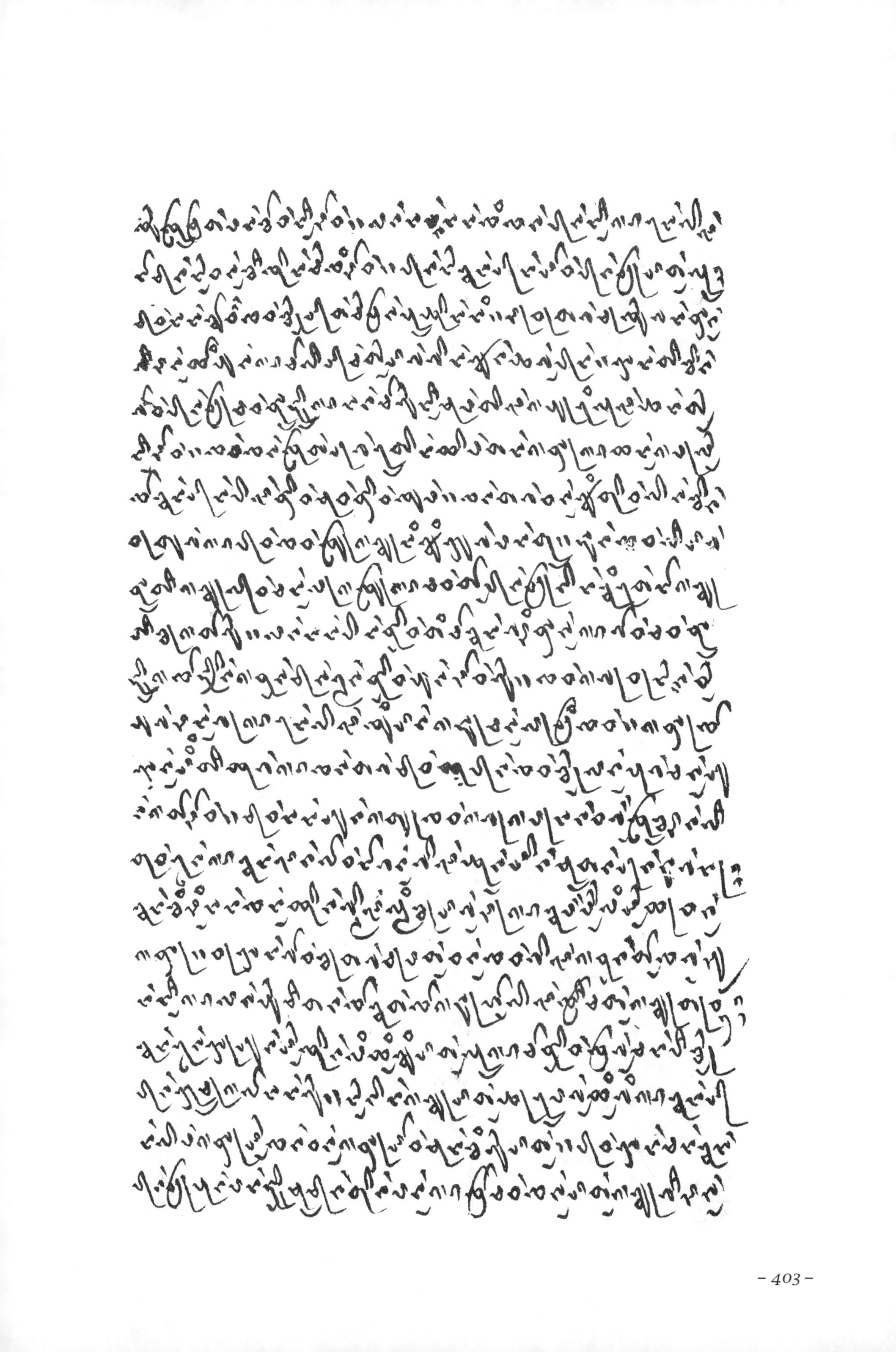

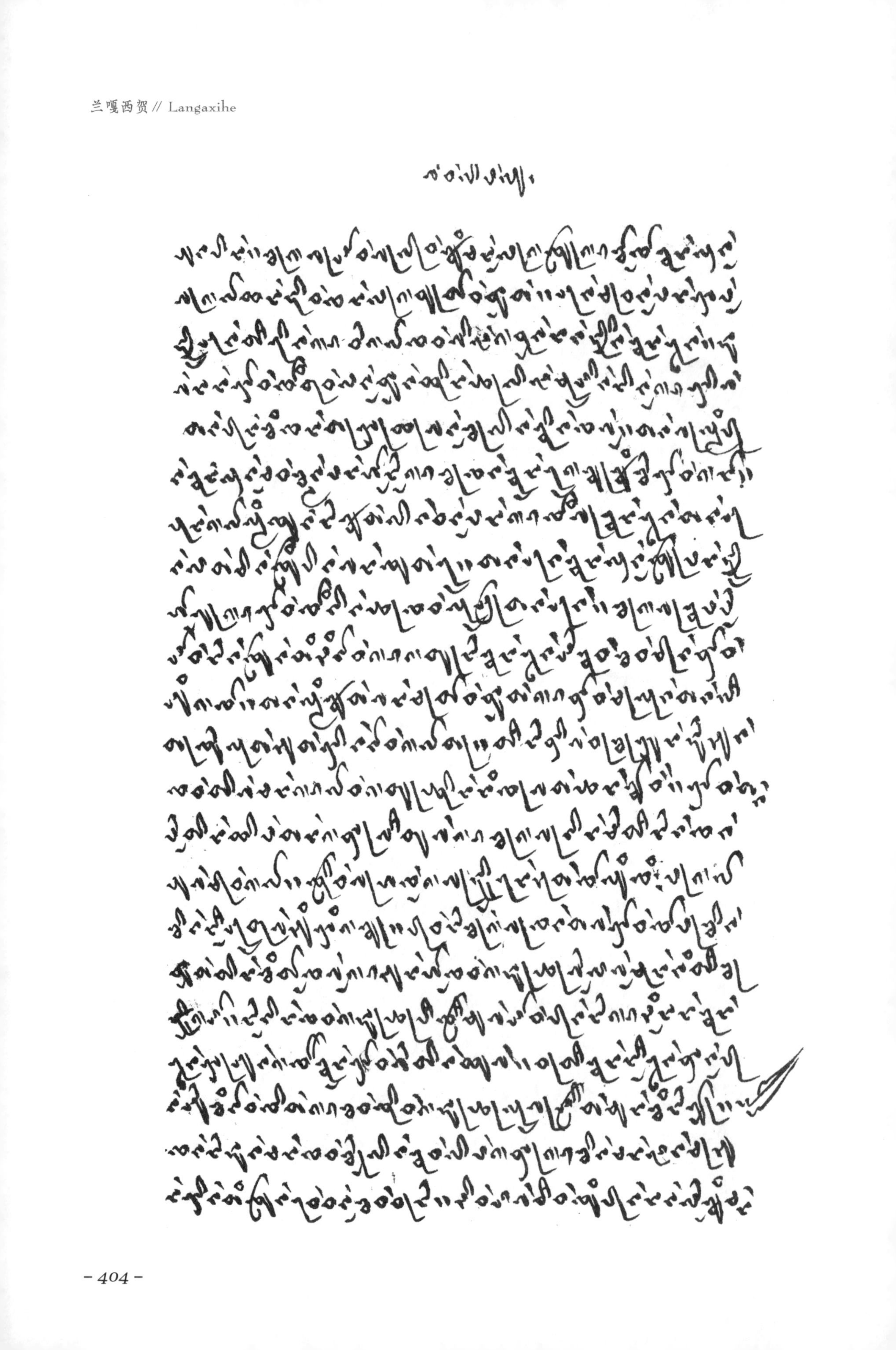

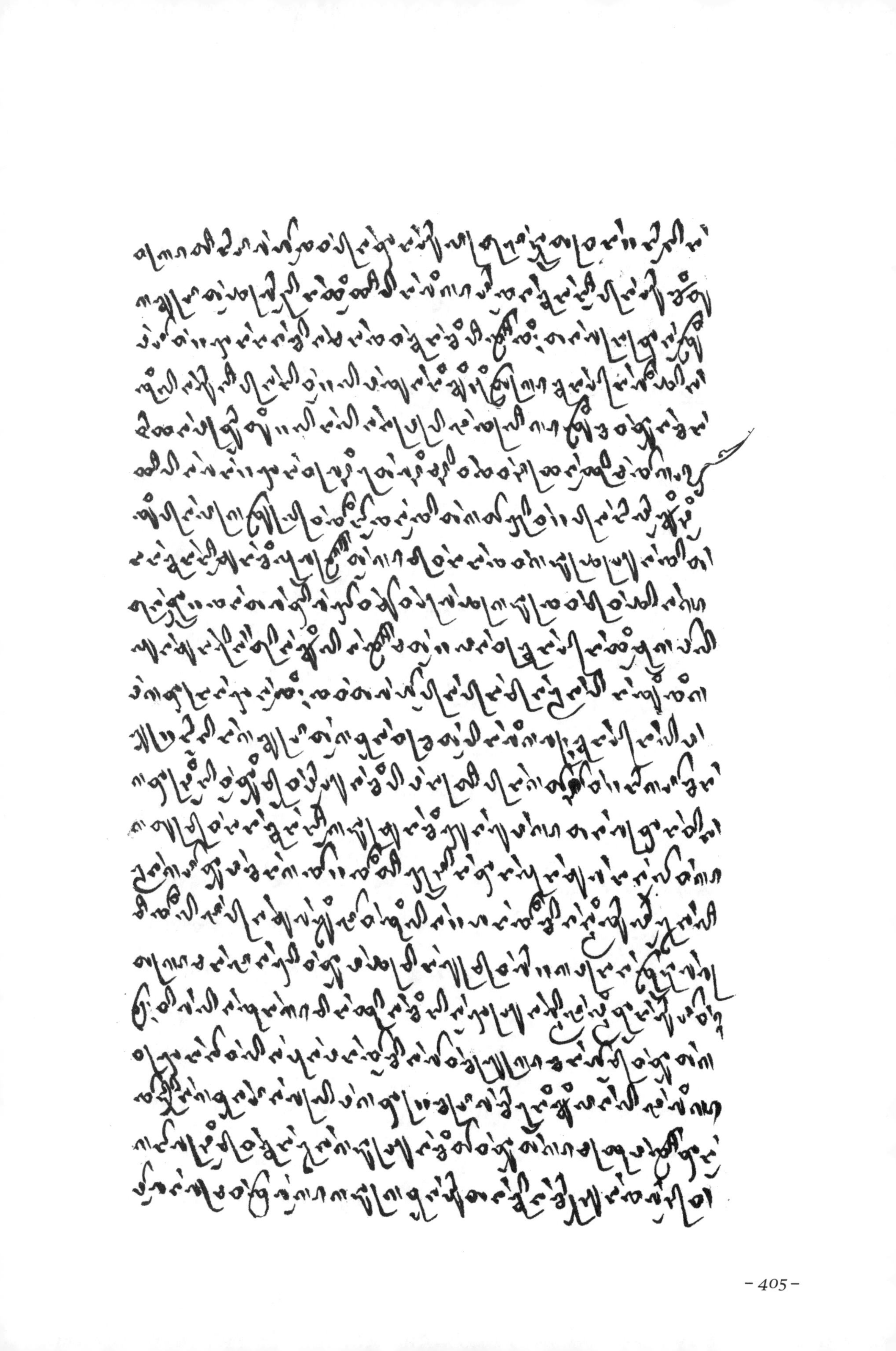

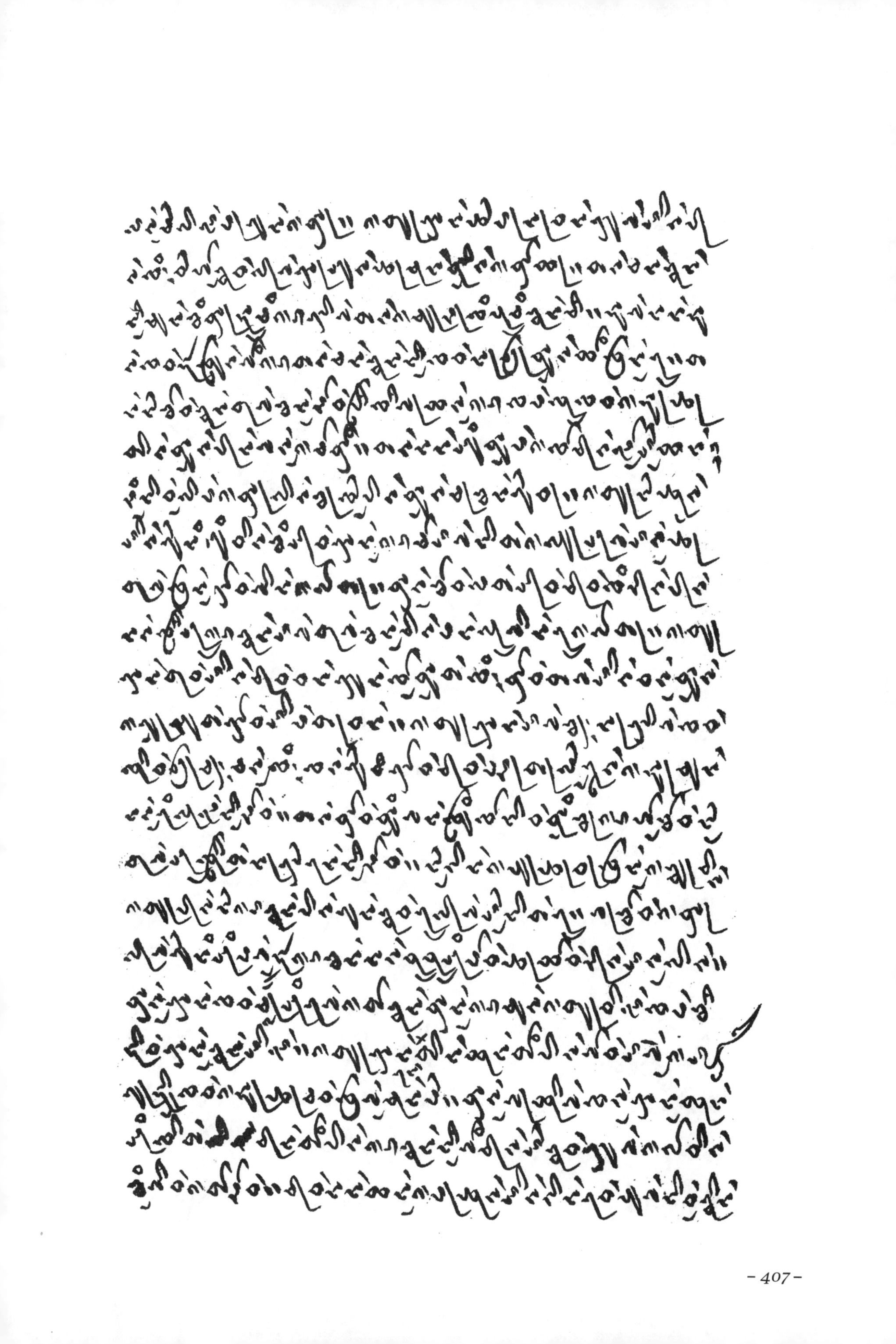

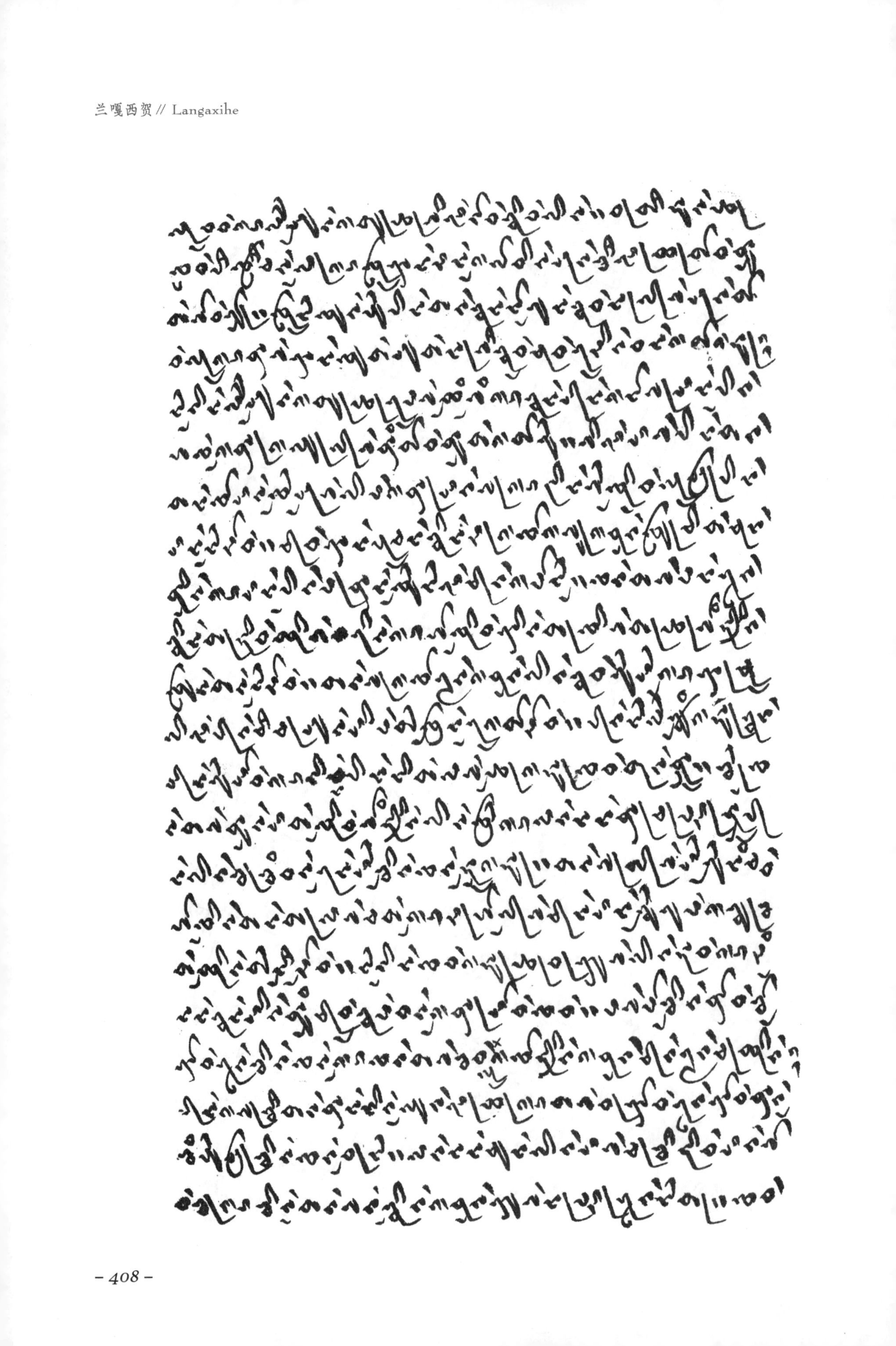

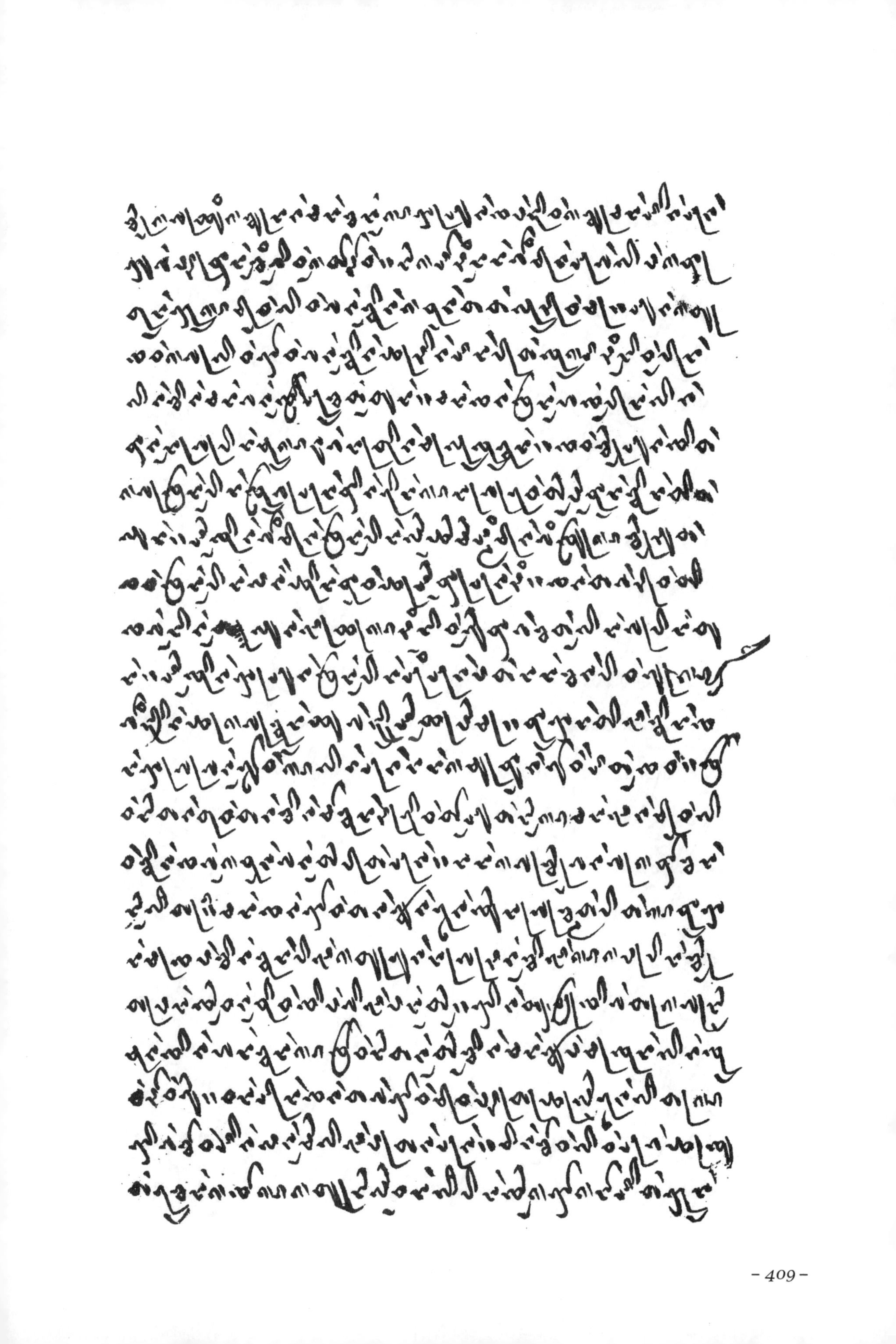

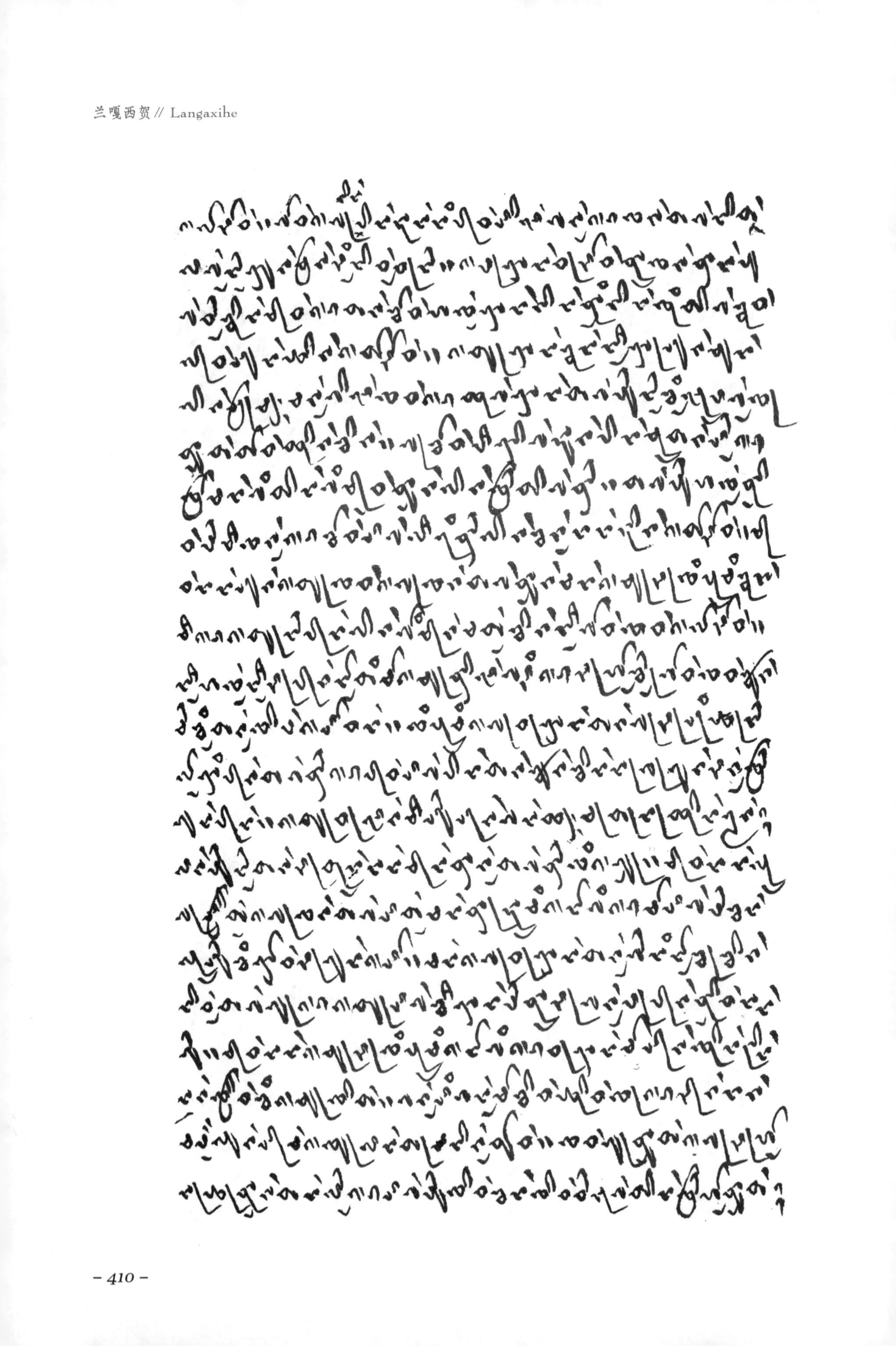

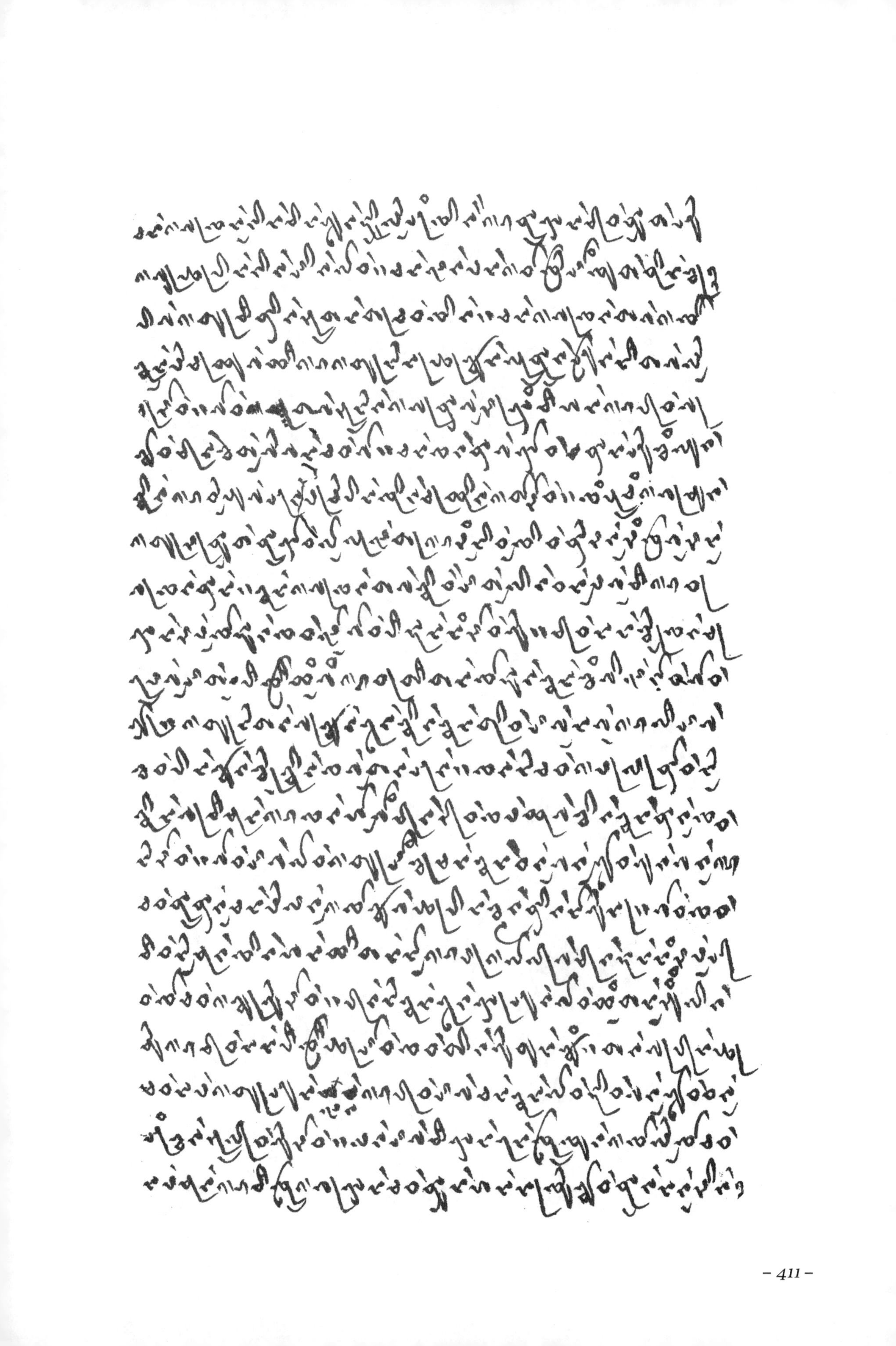

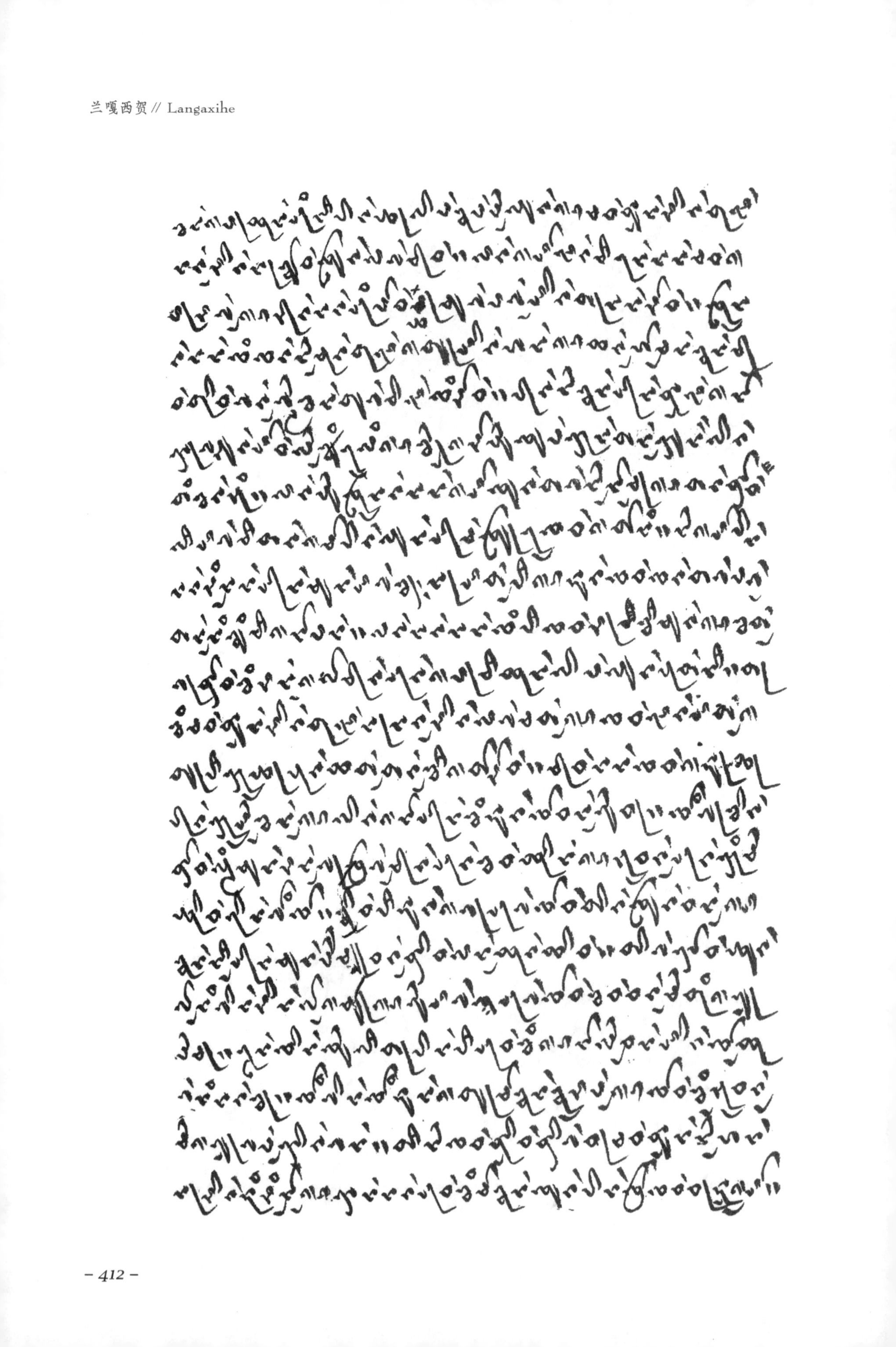

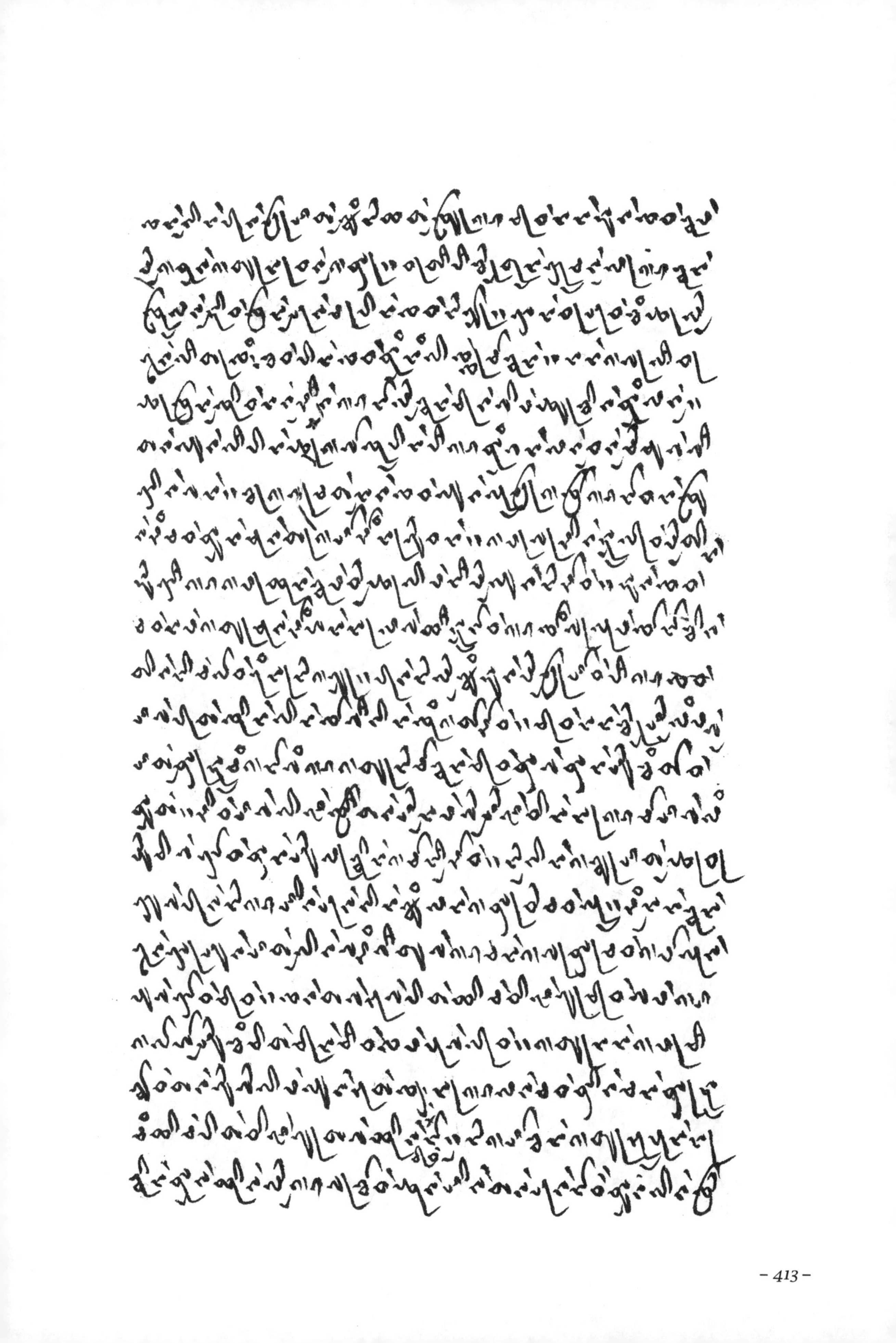

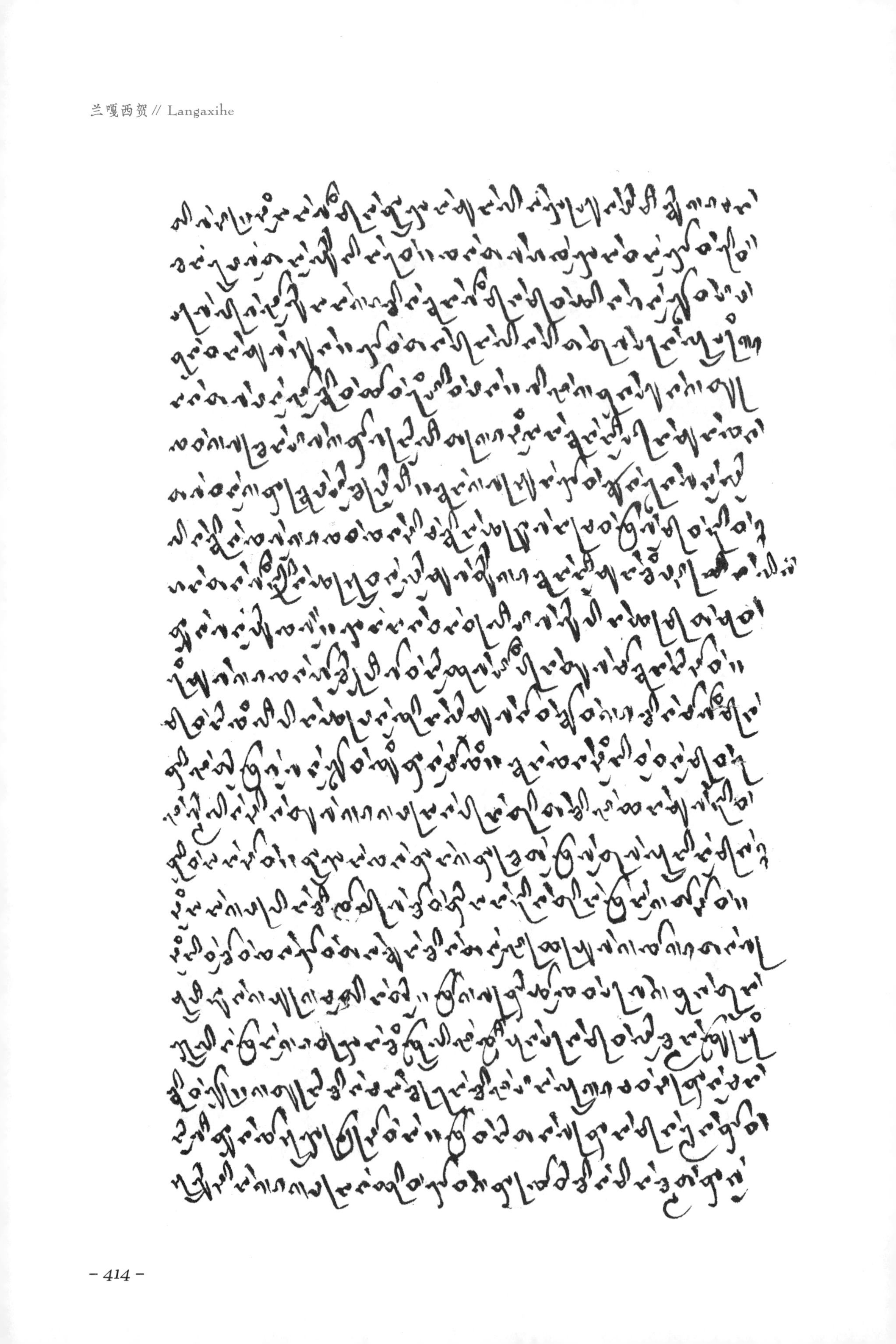

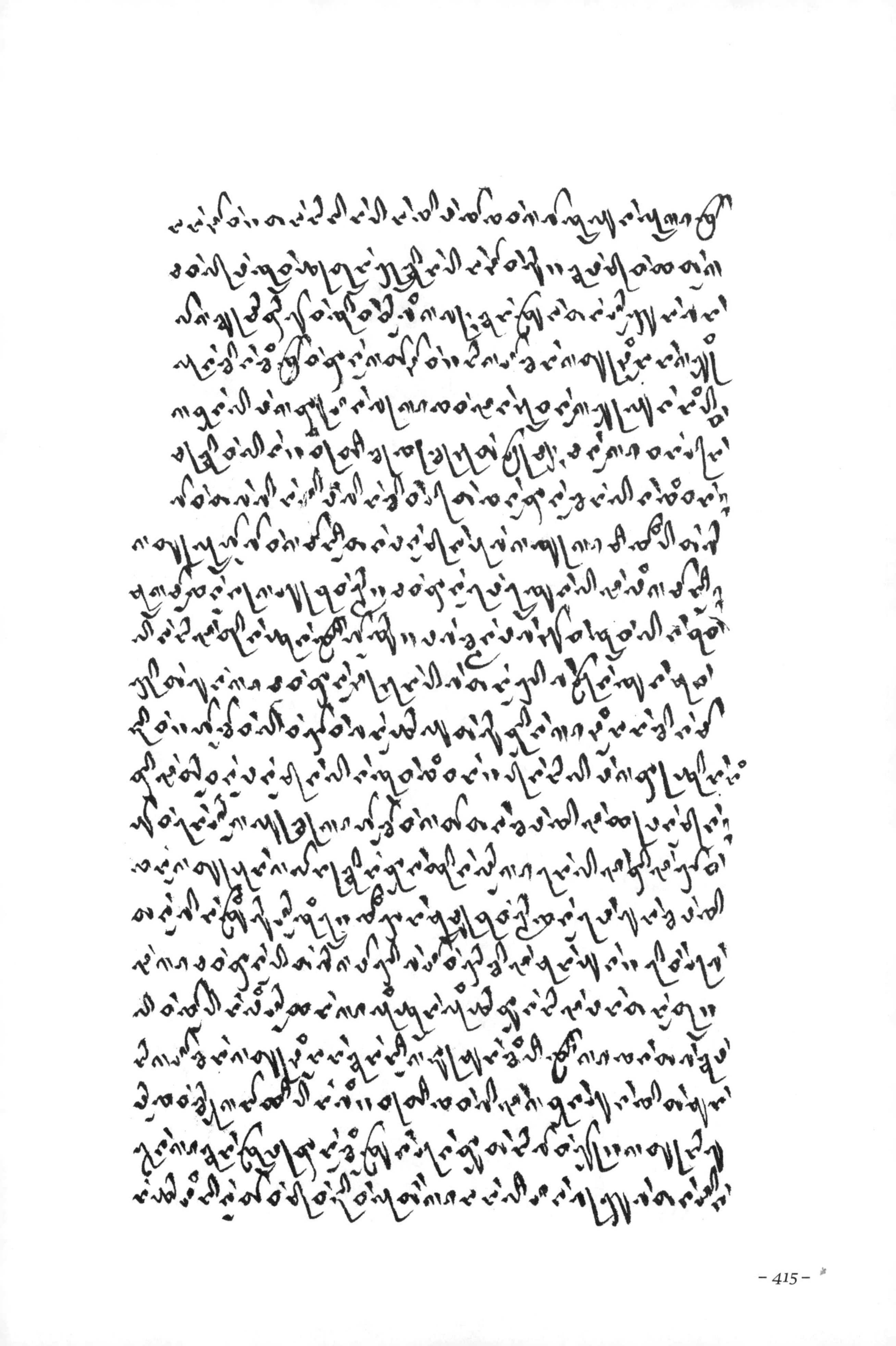

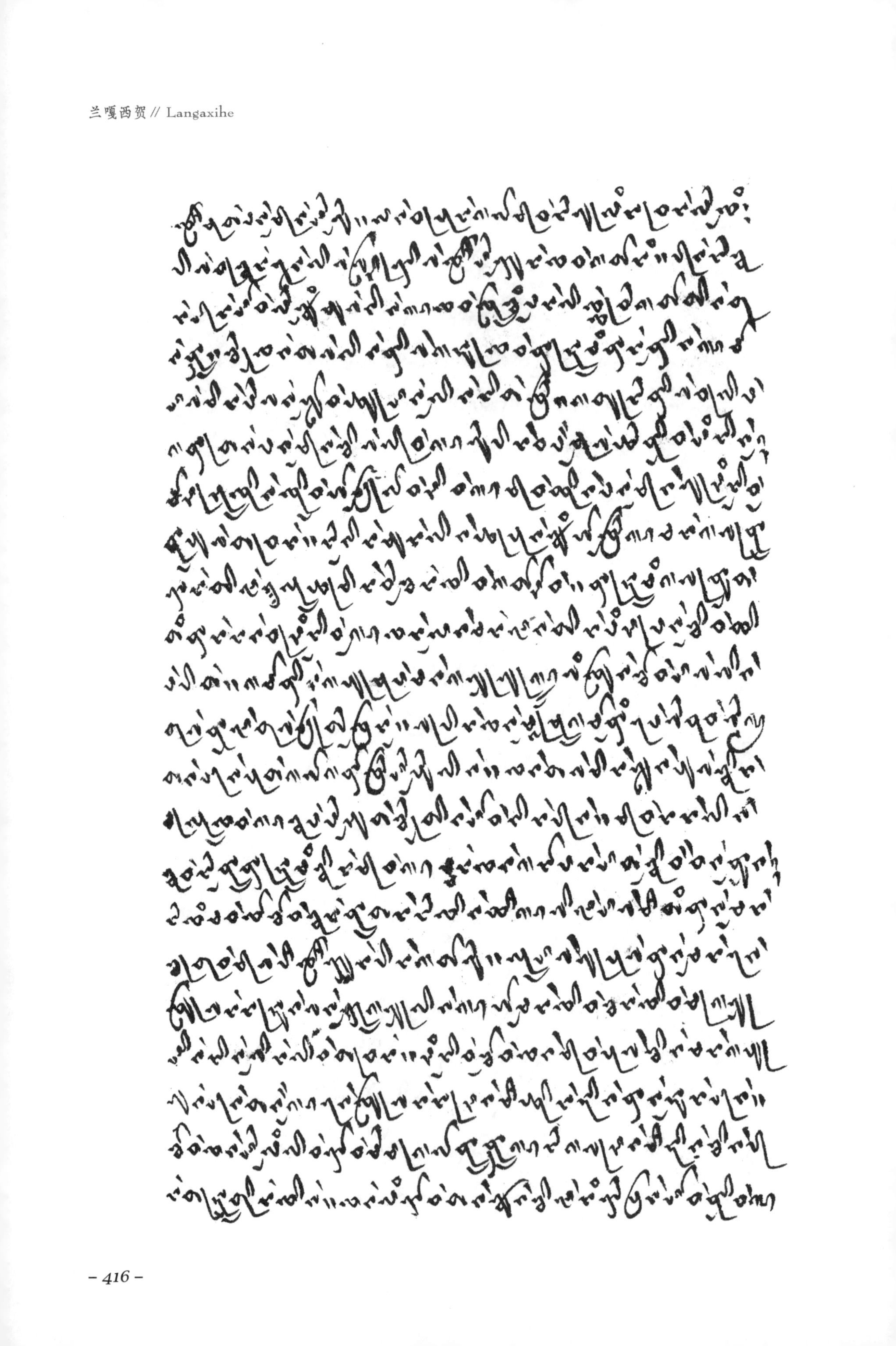

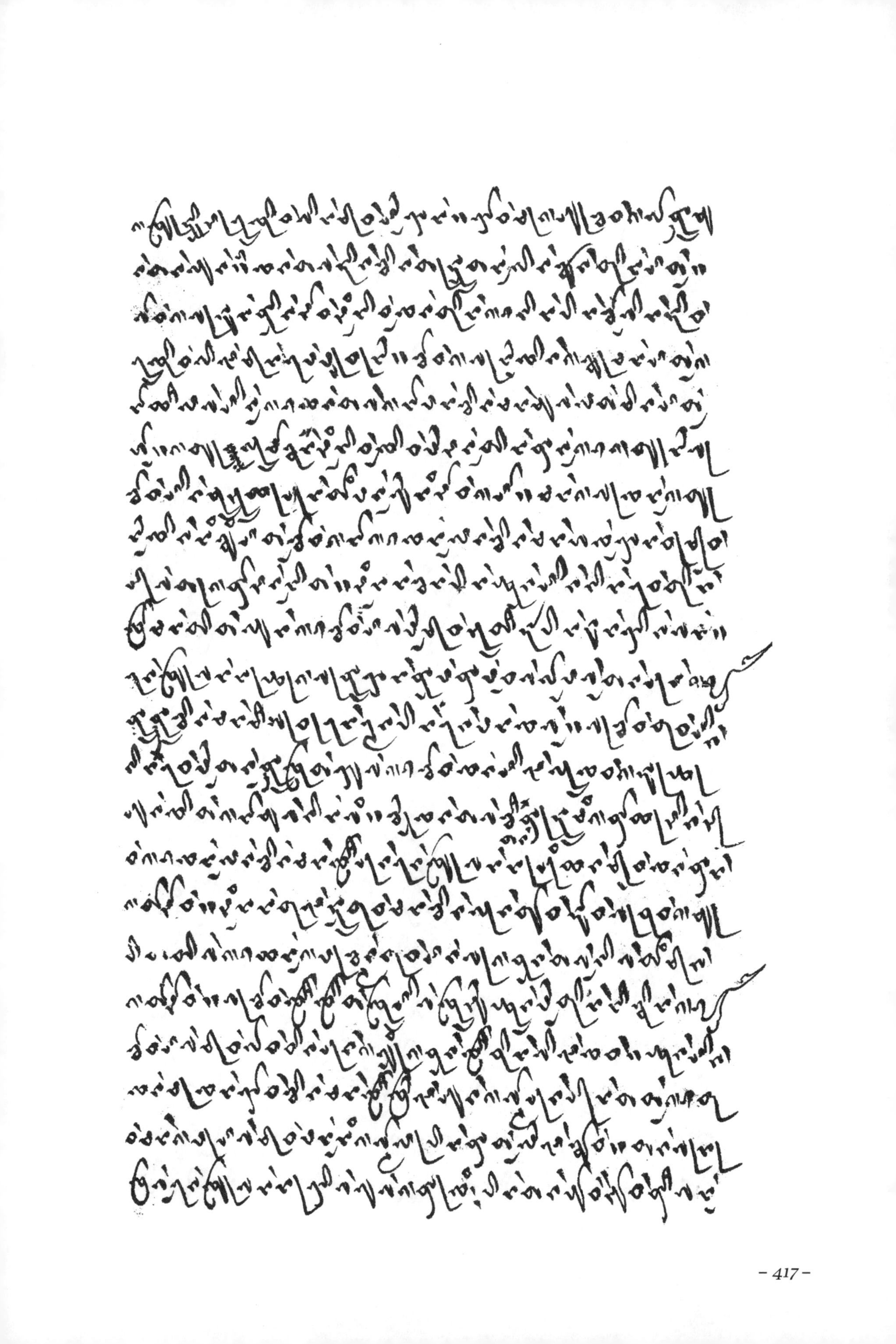

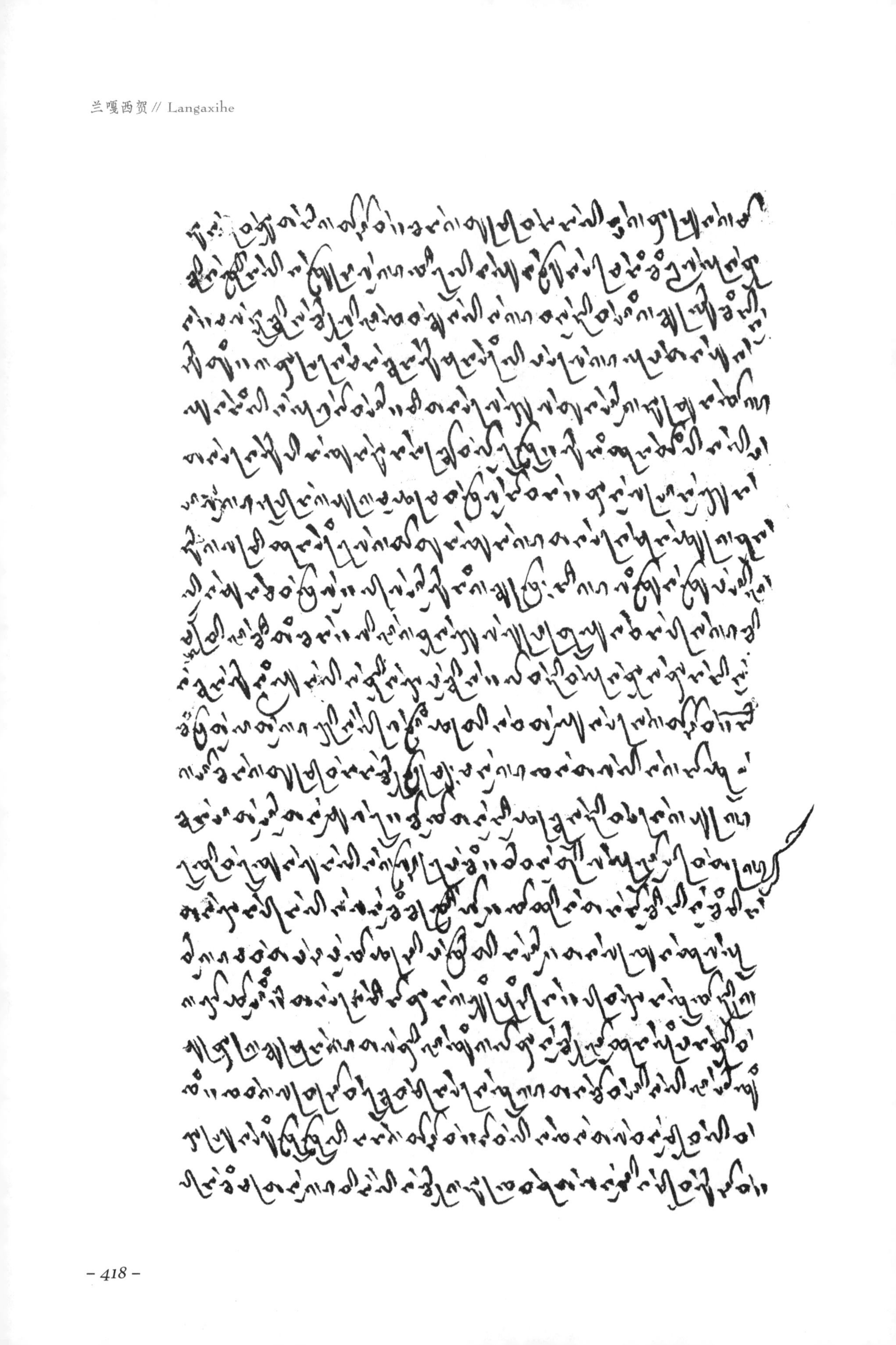

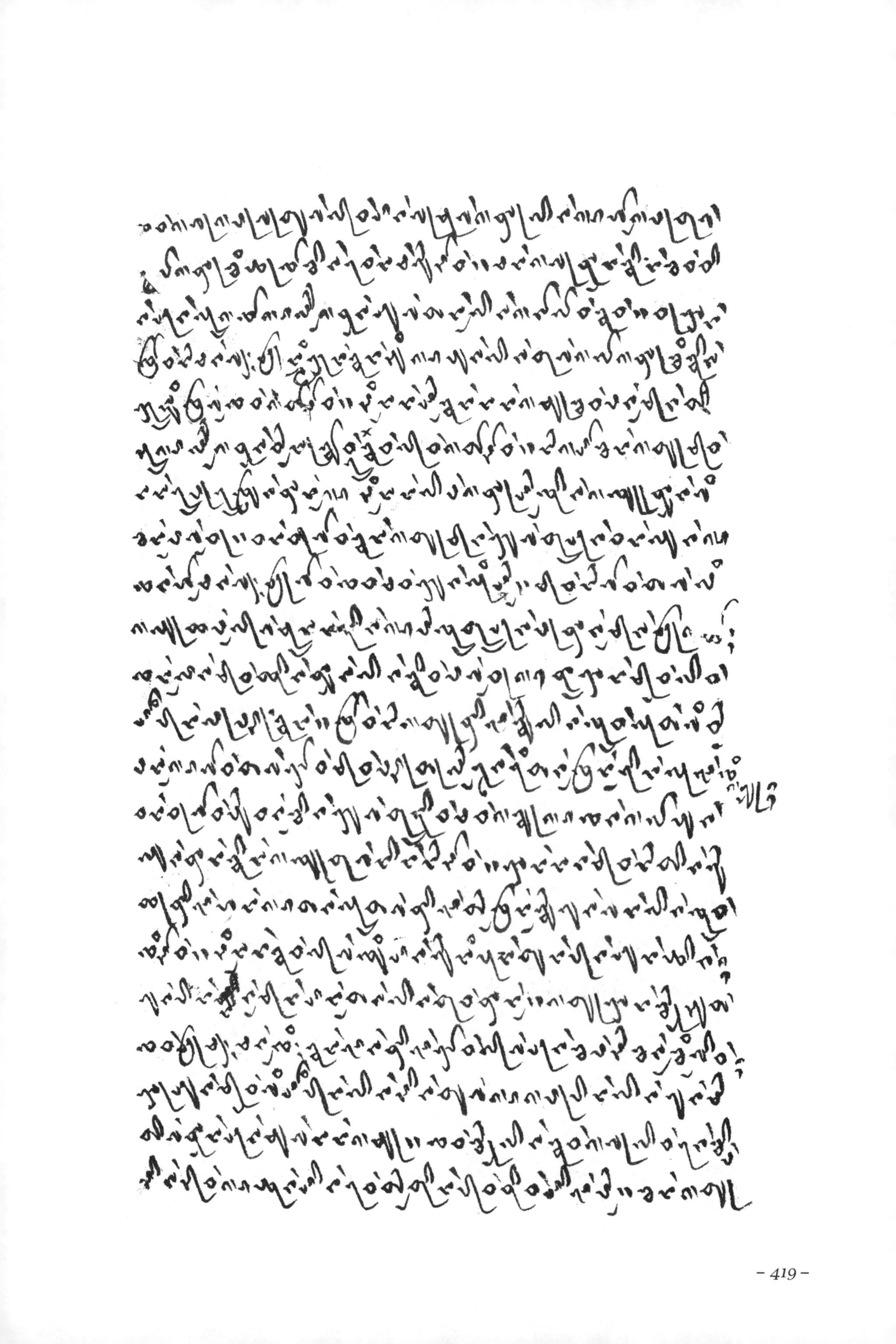

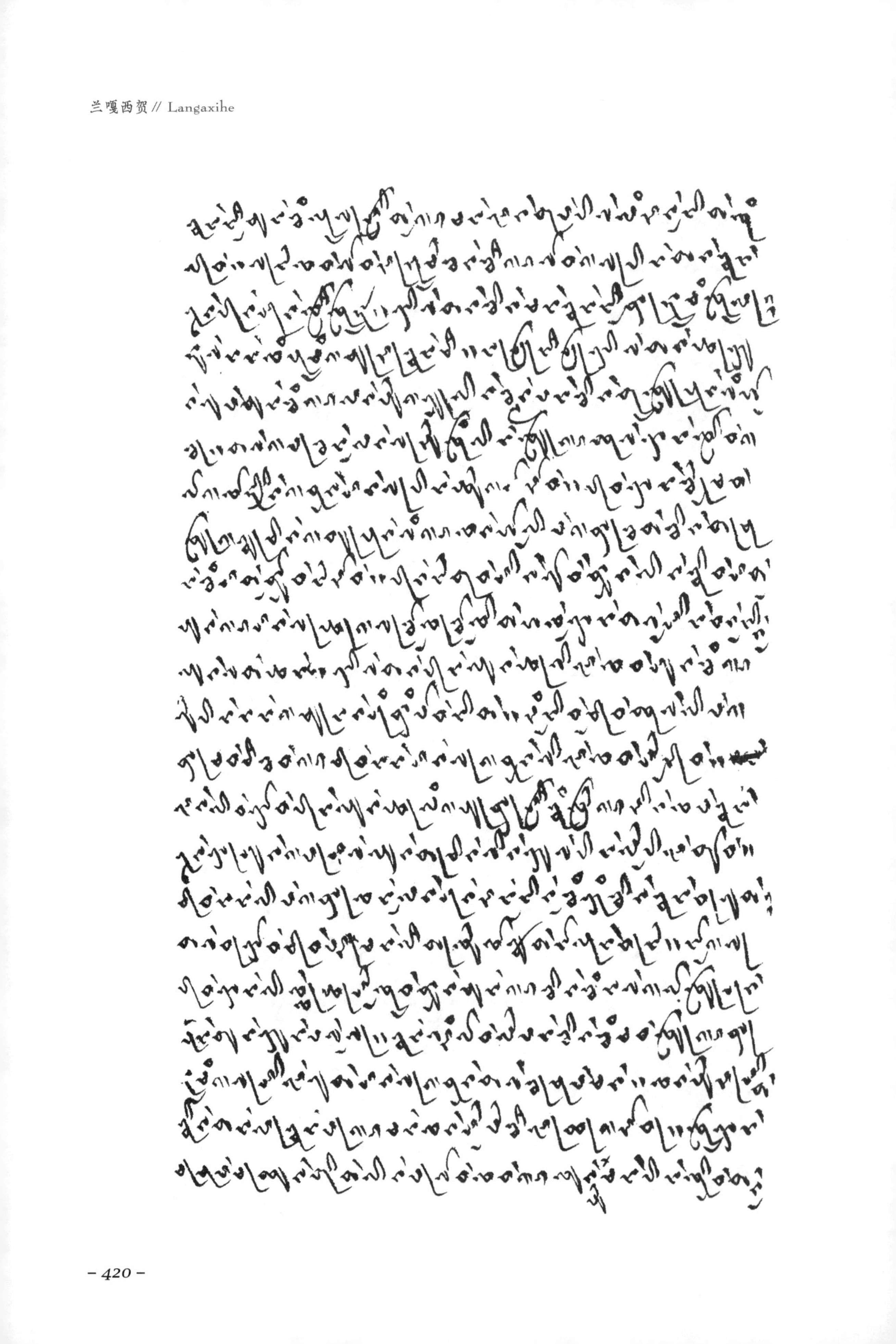

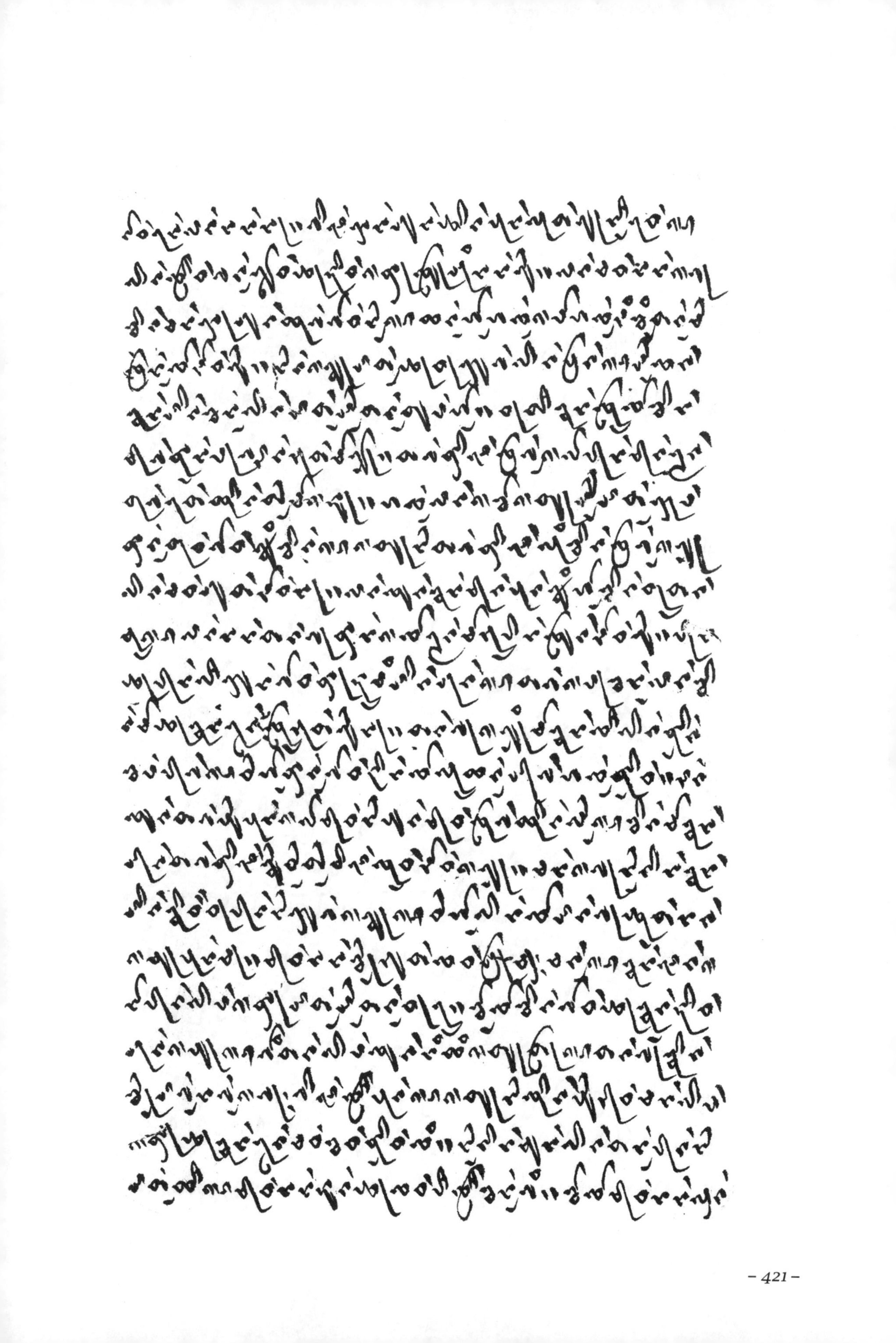

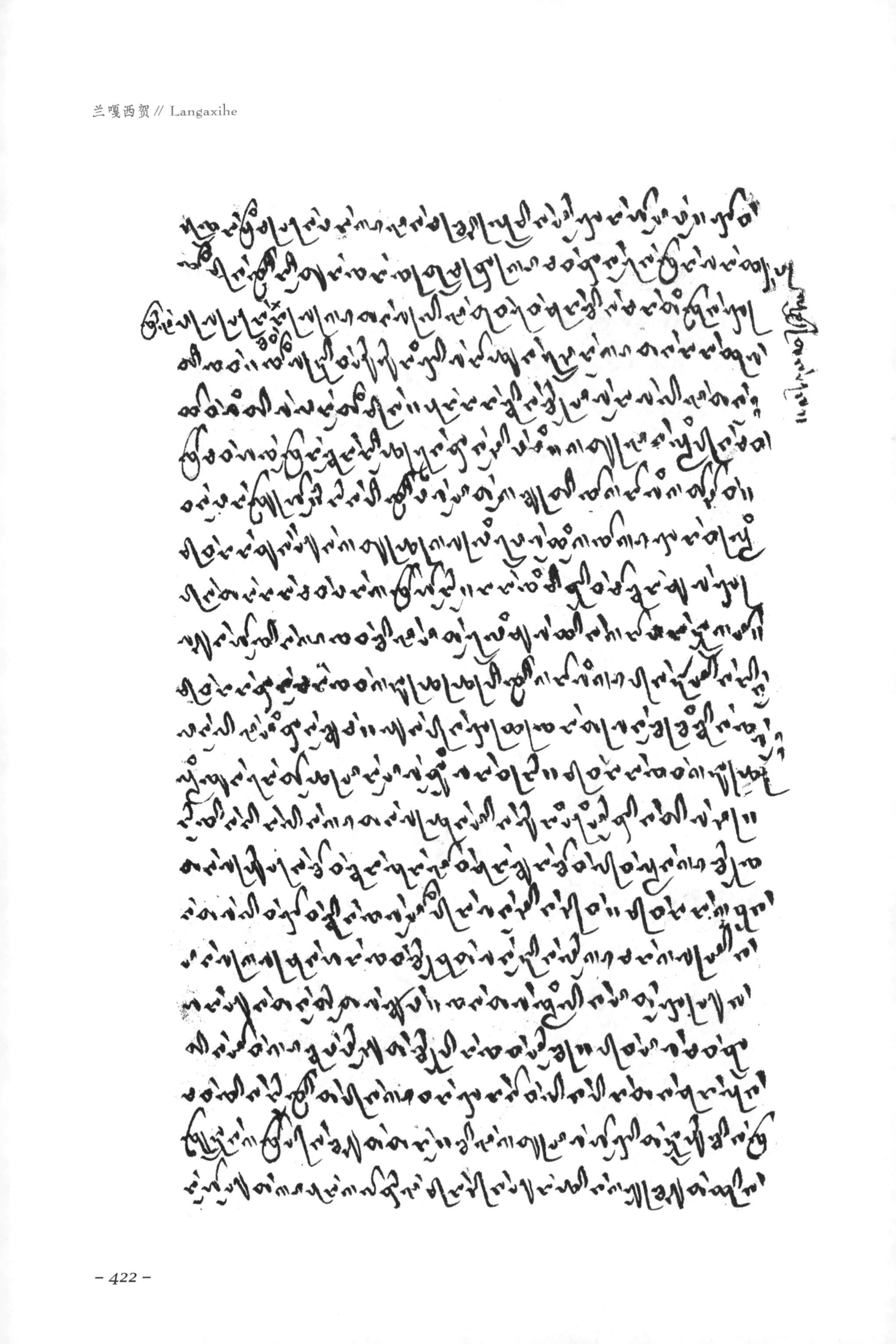

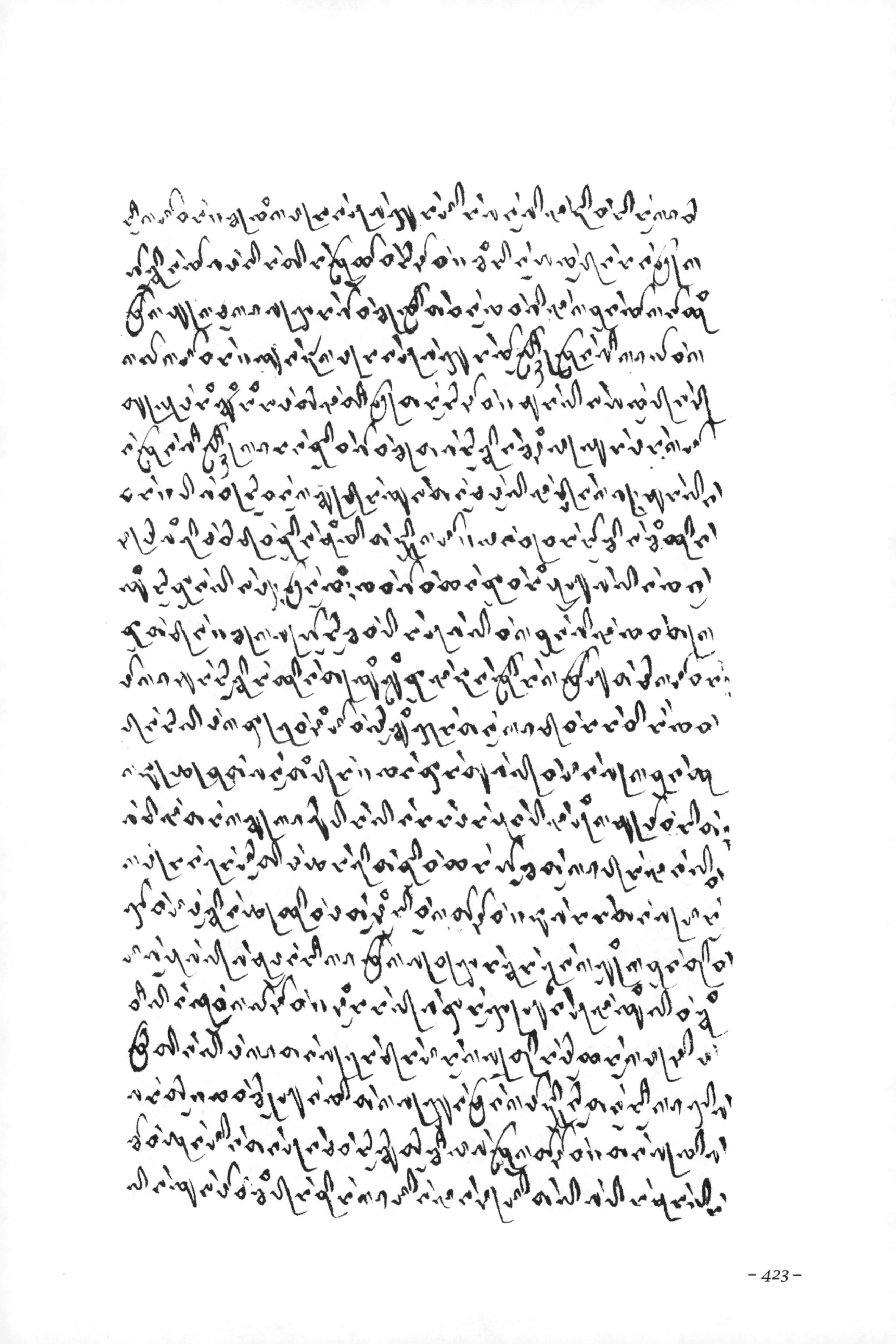

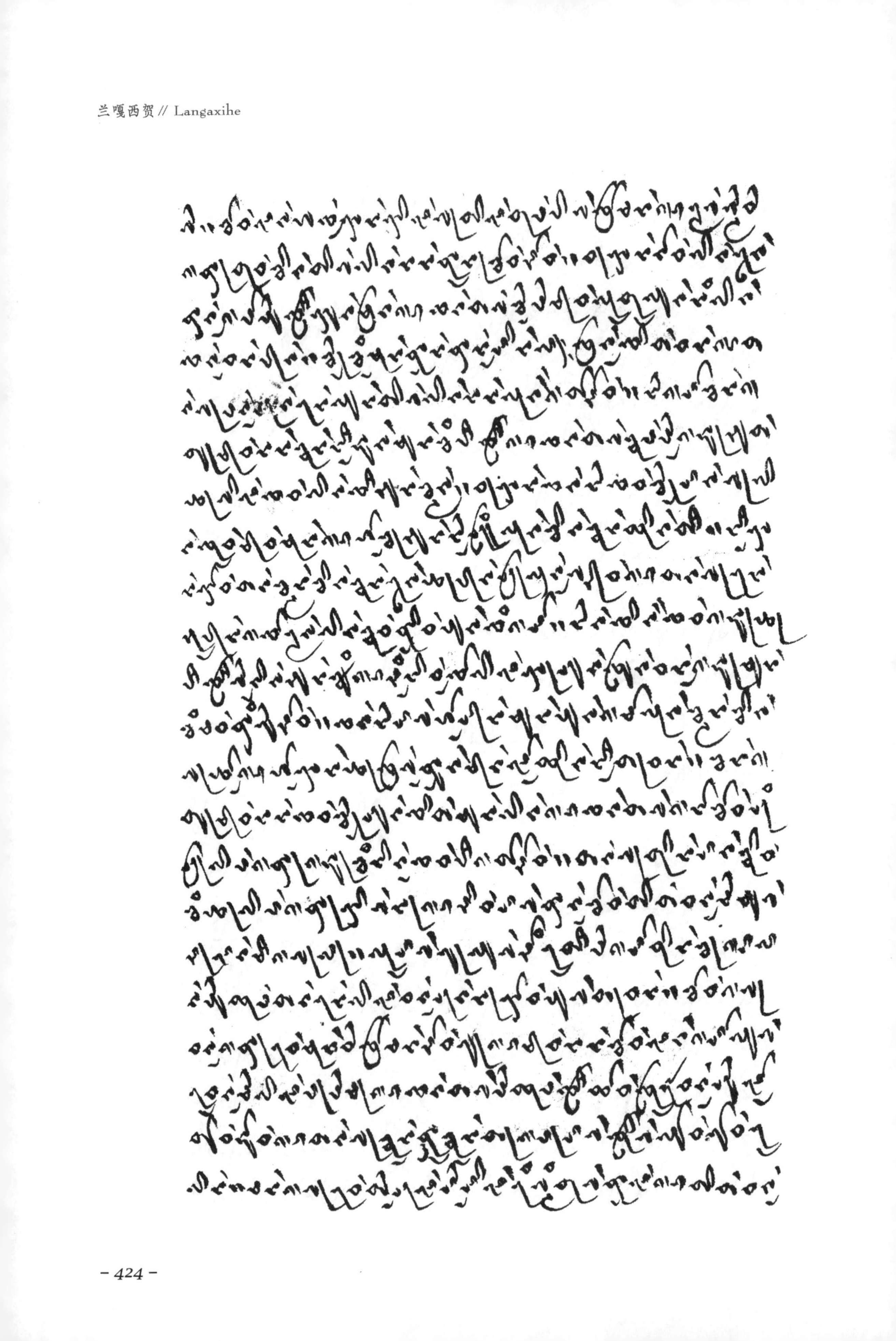

[illegible]

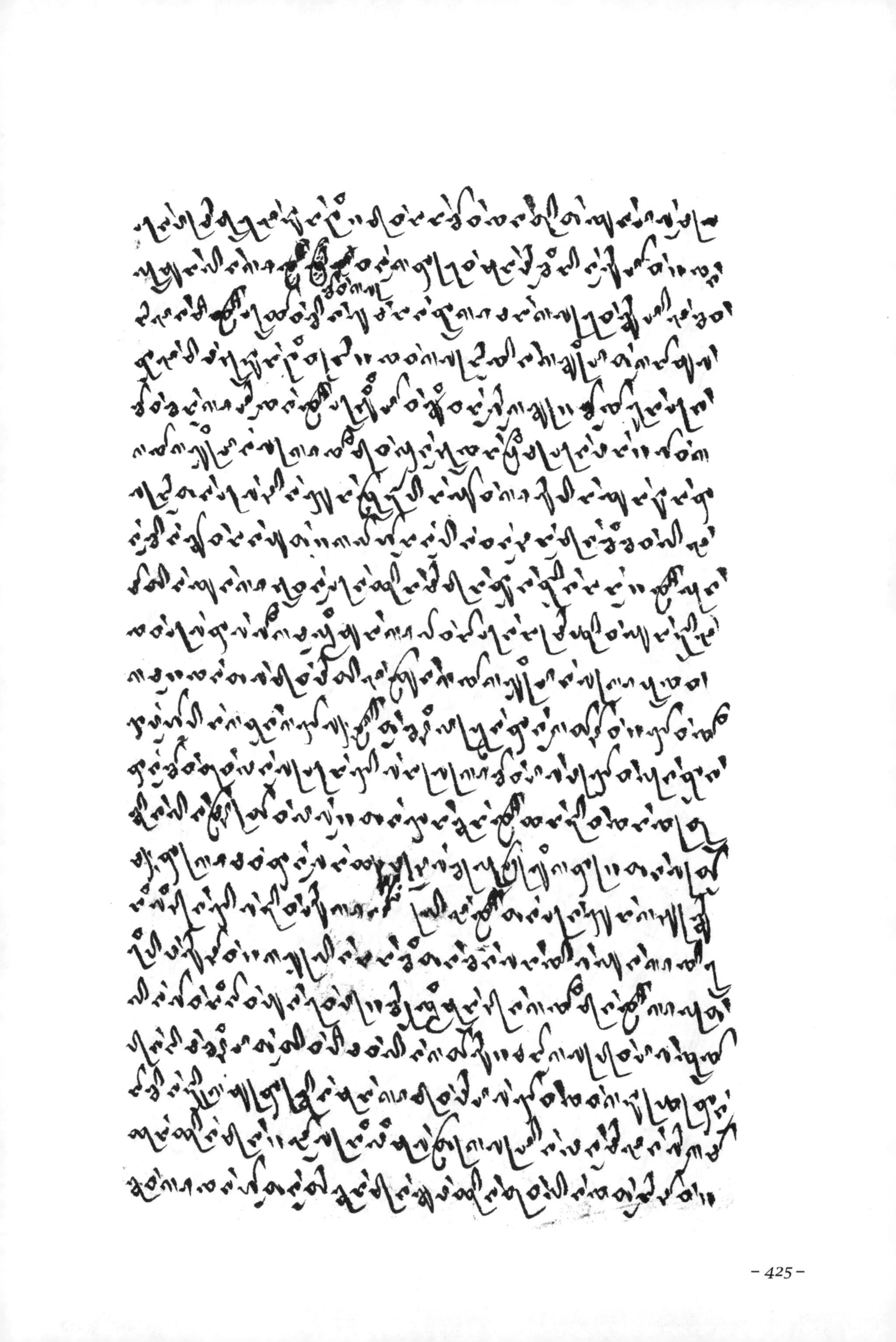

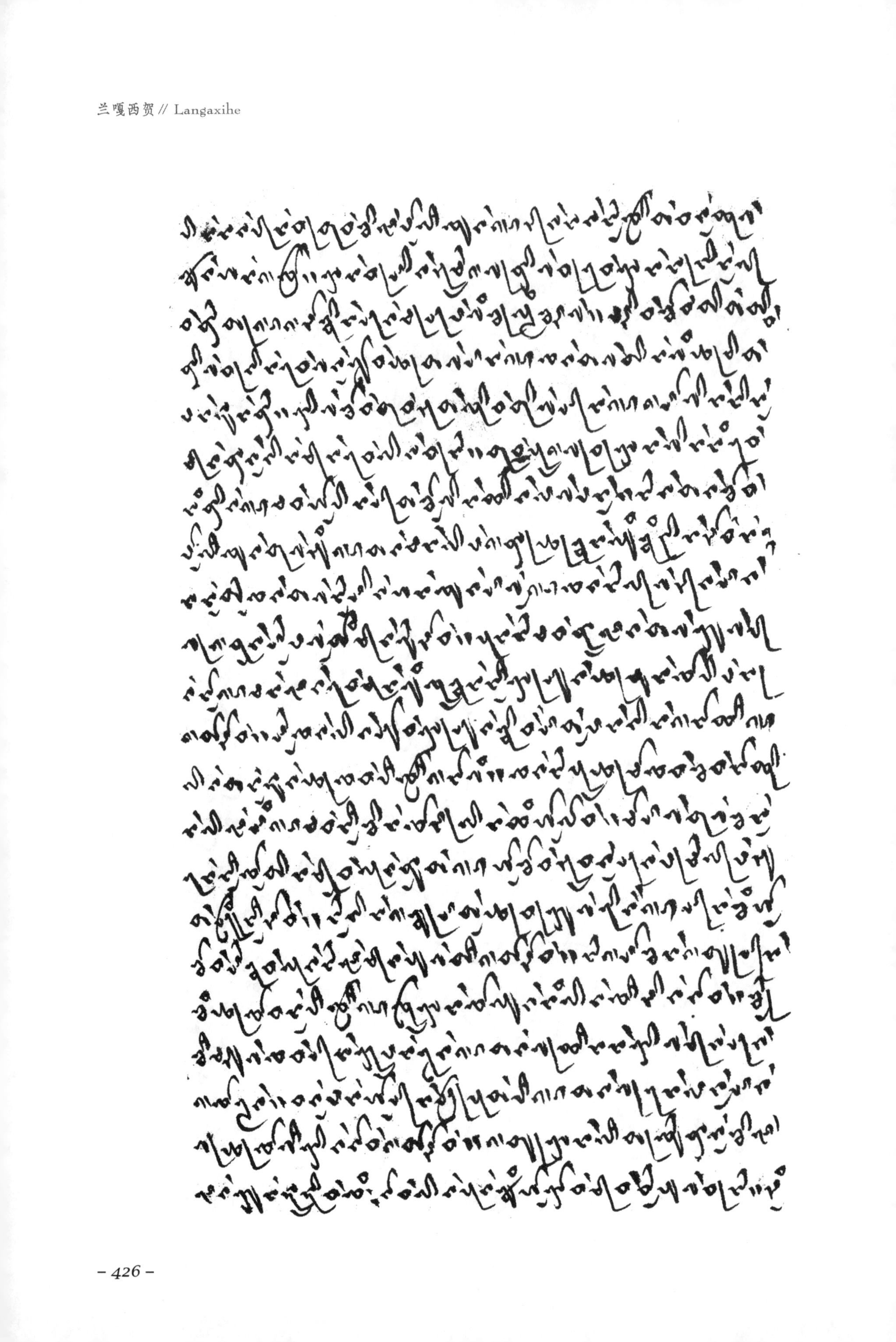

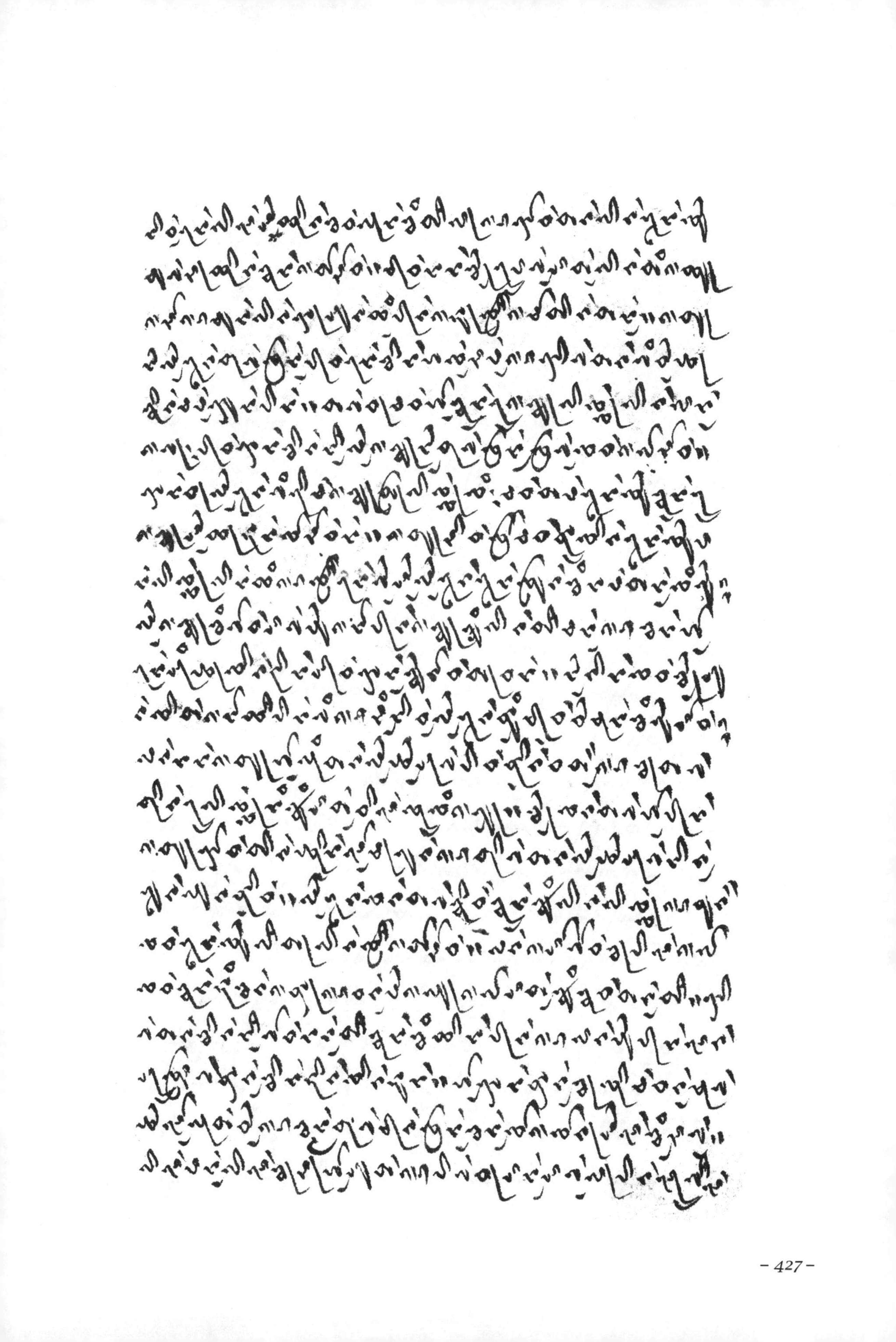

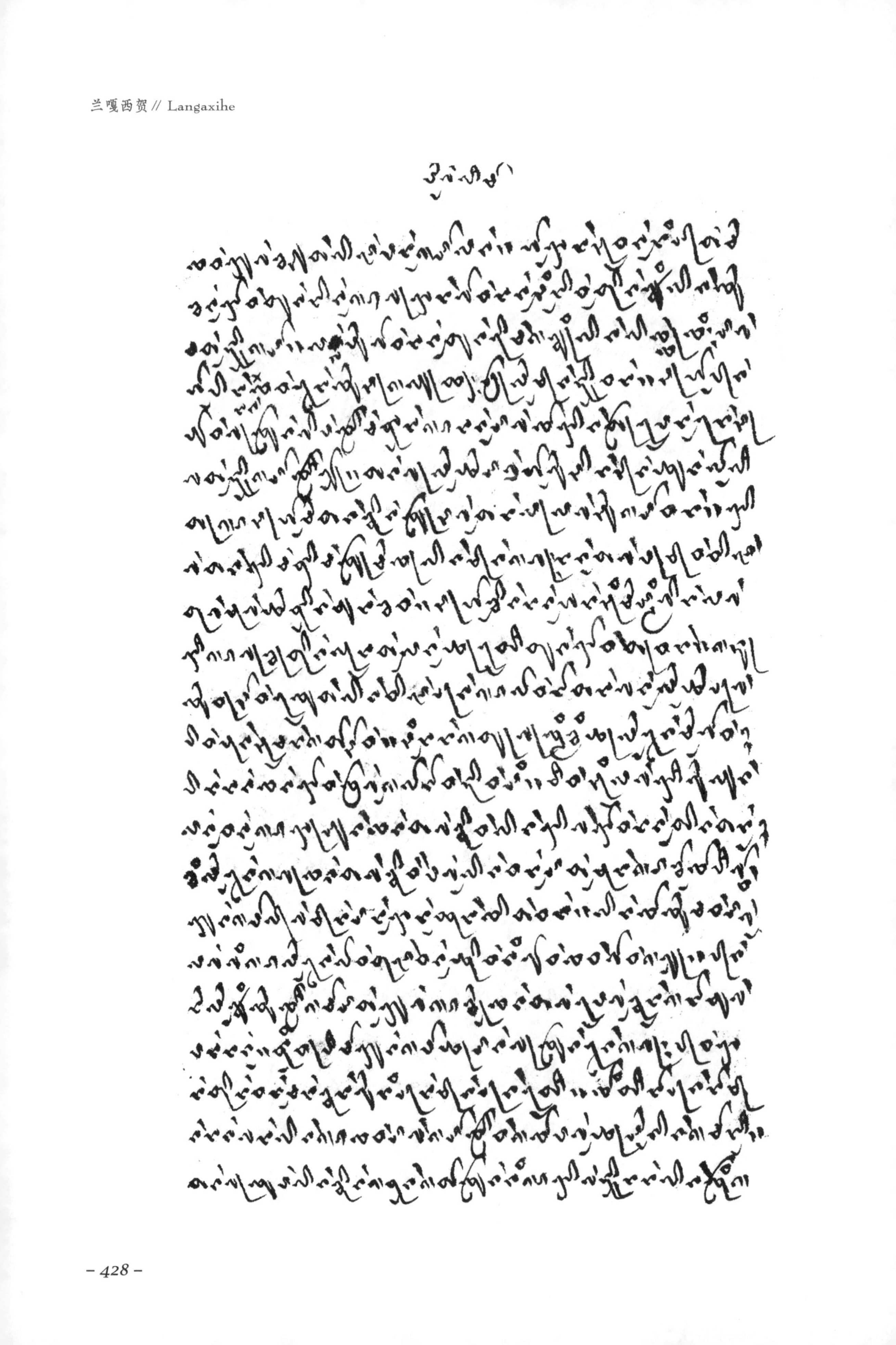

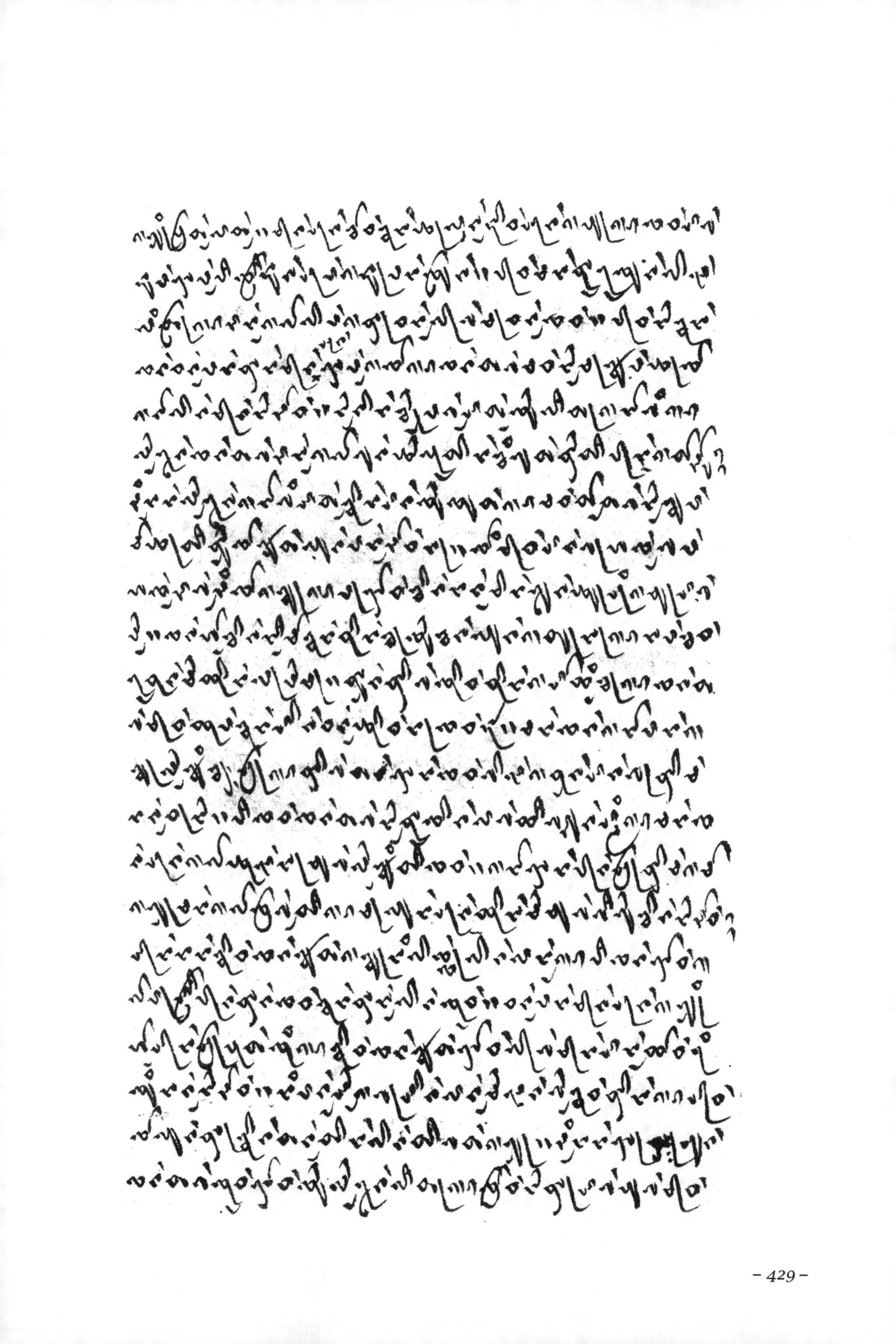

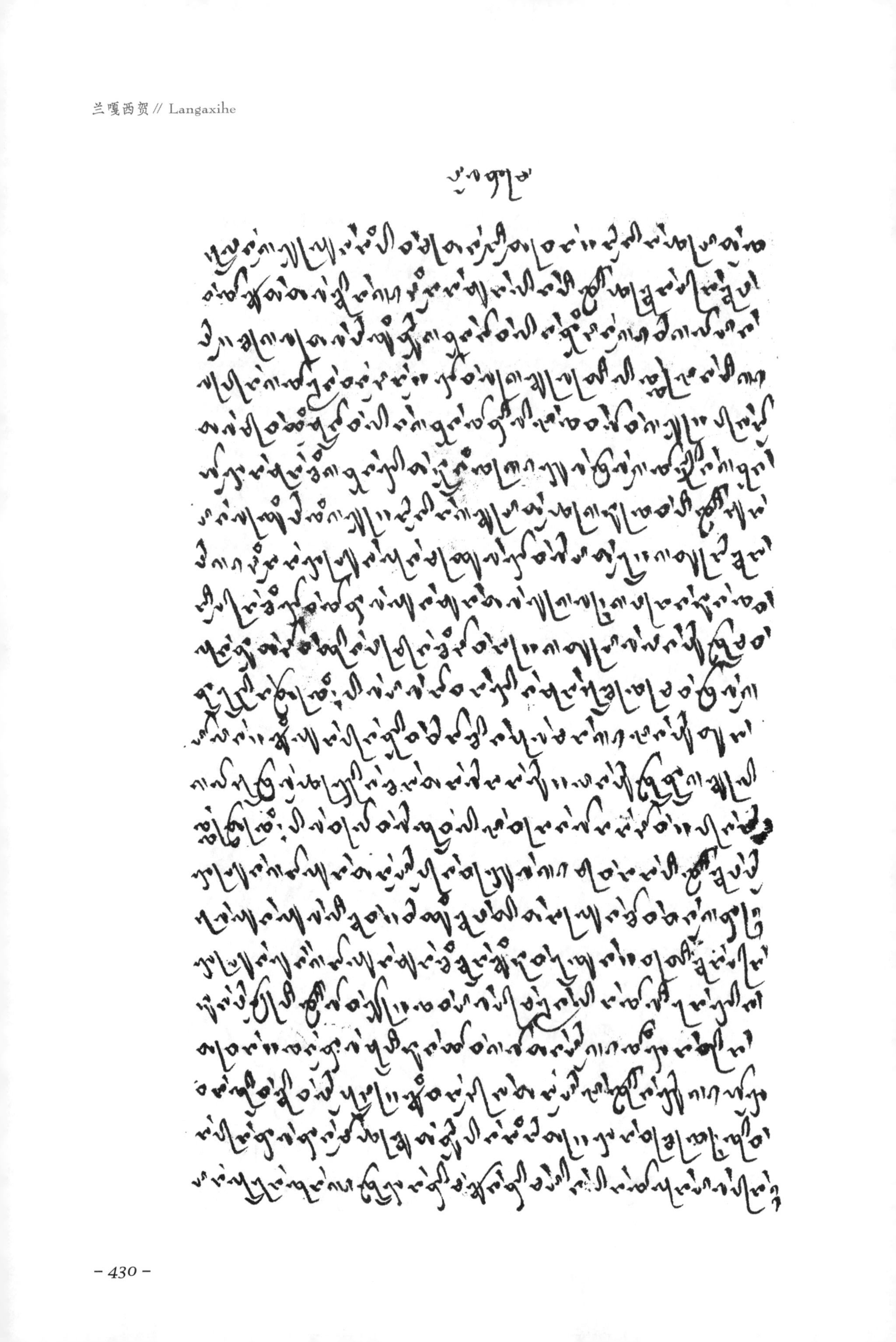

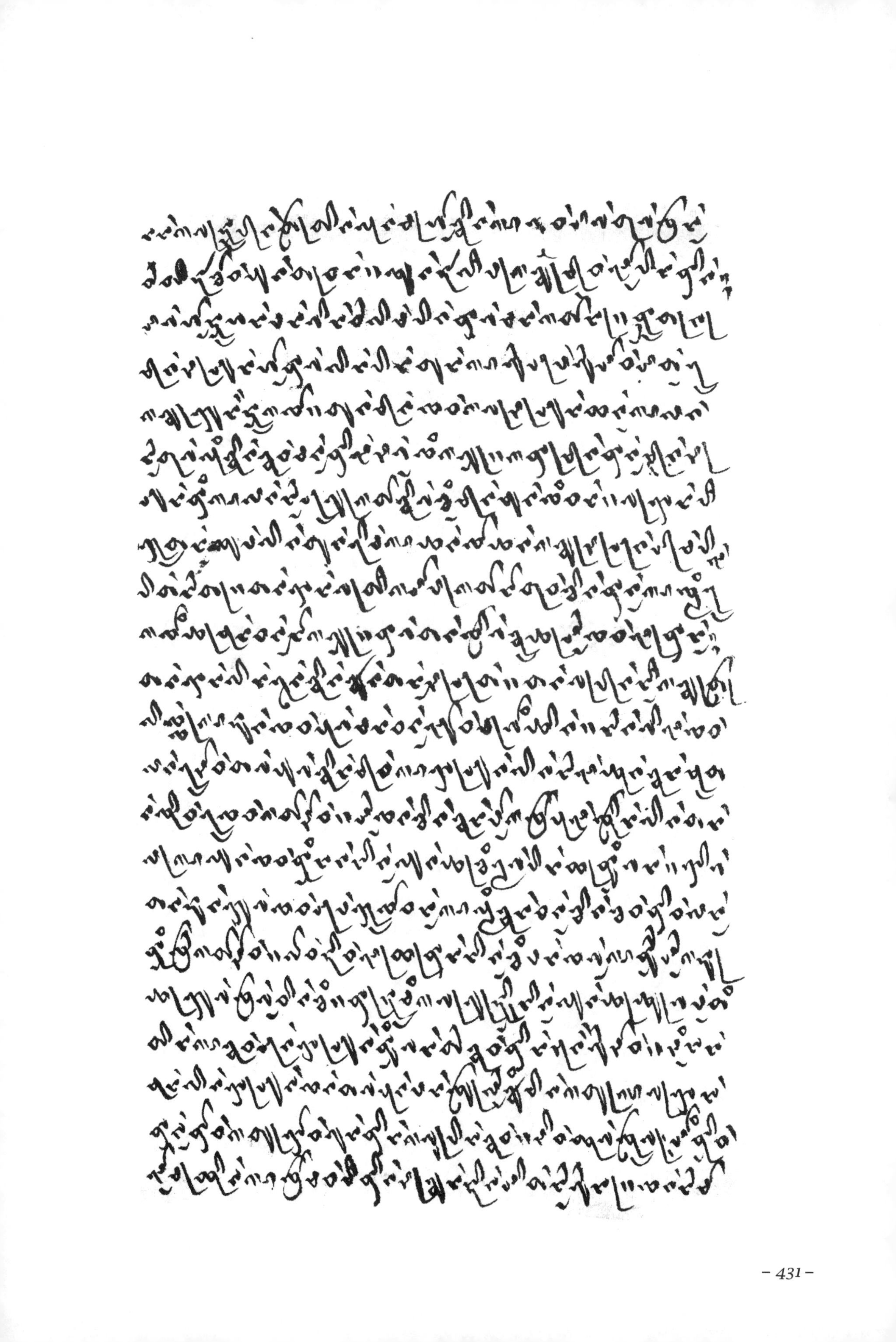

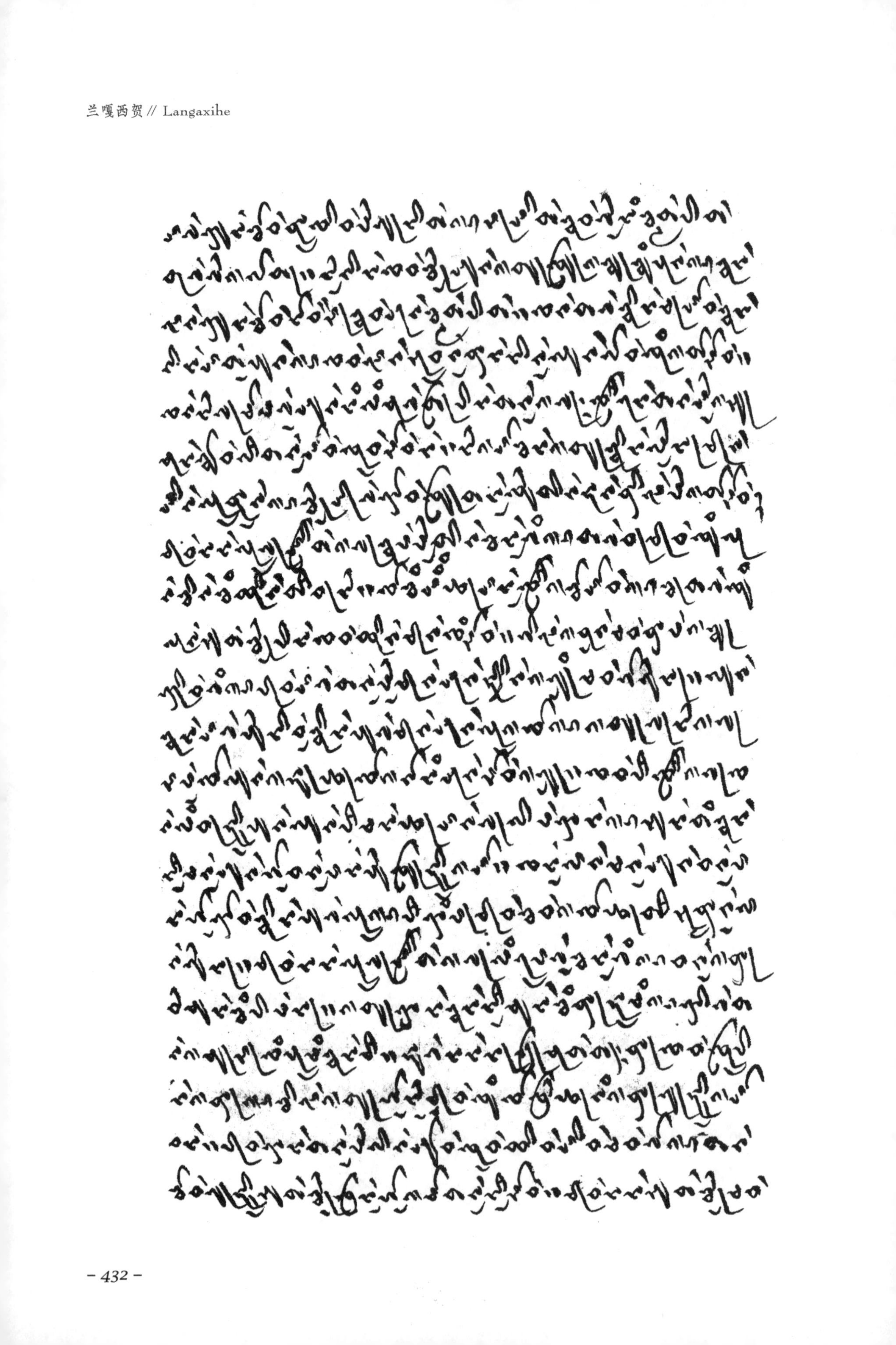

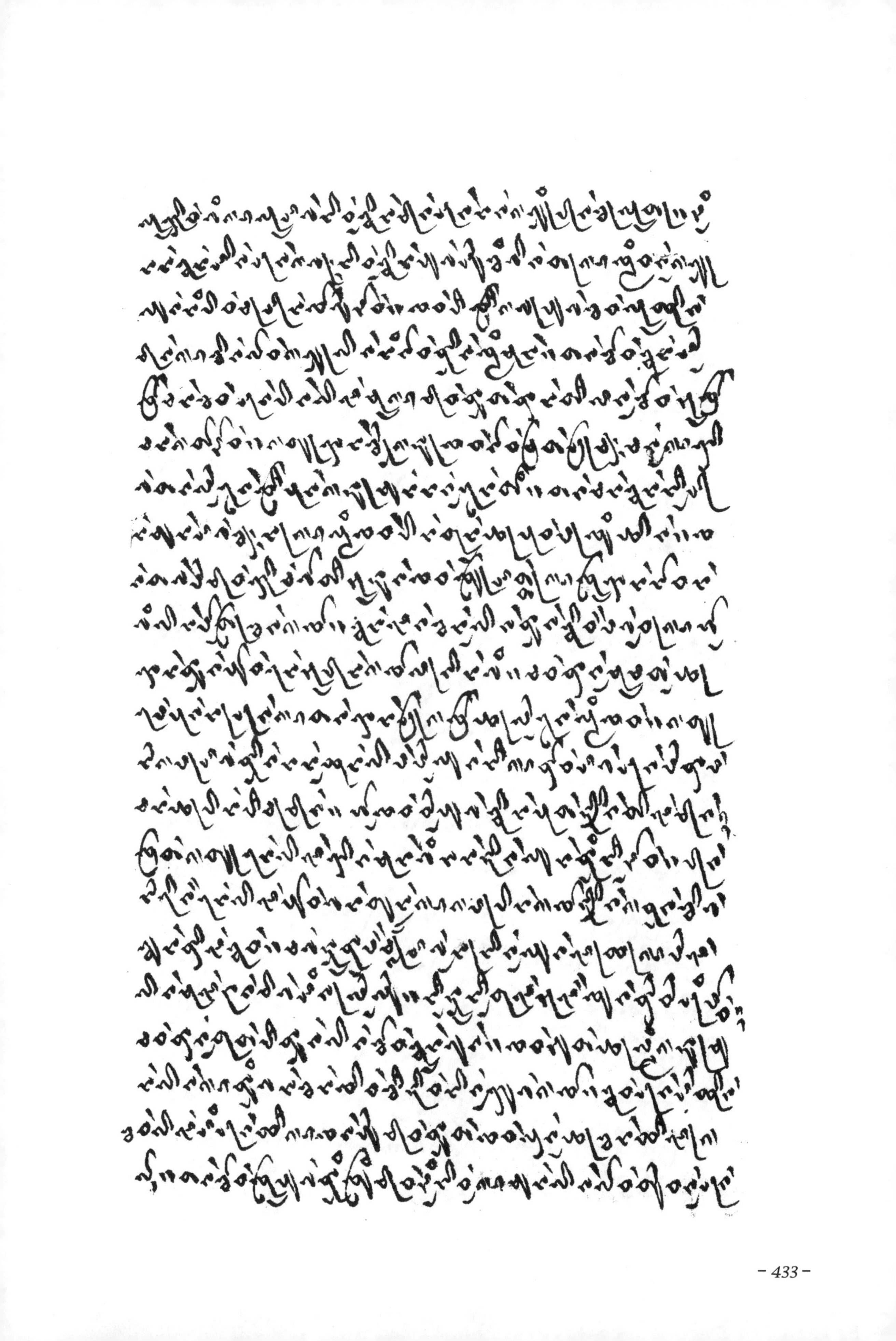

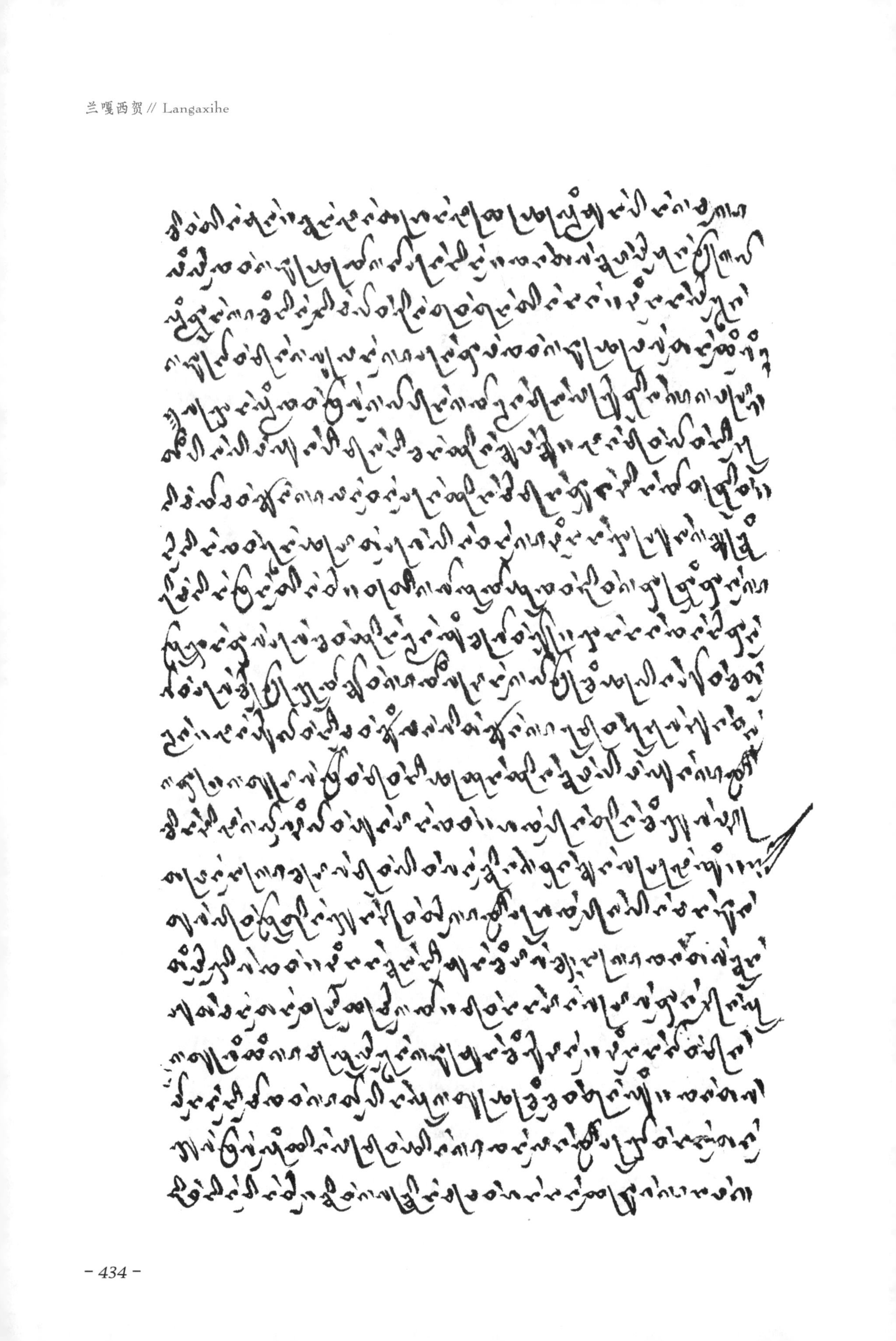

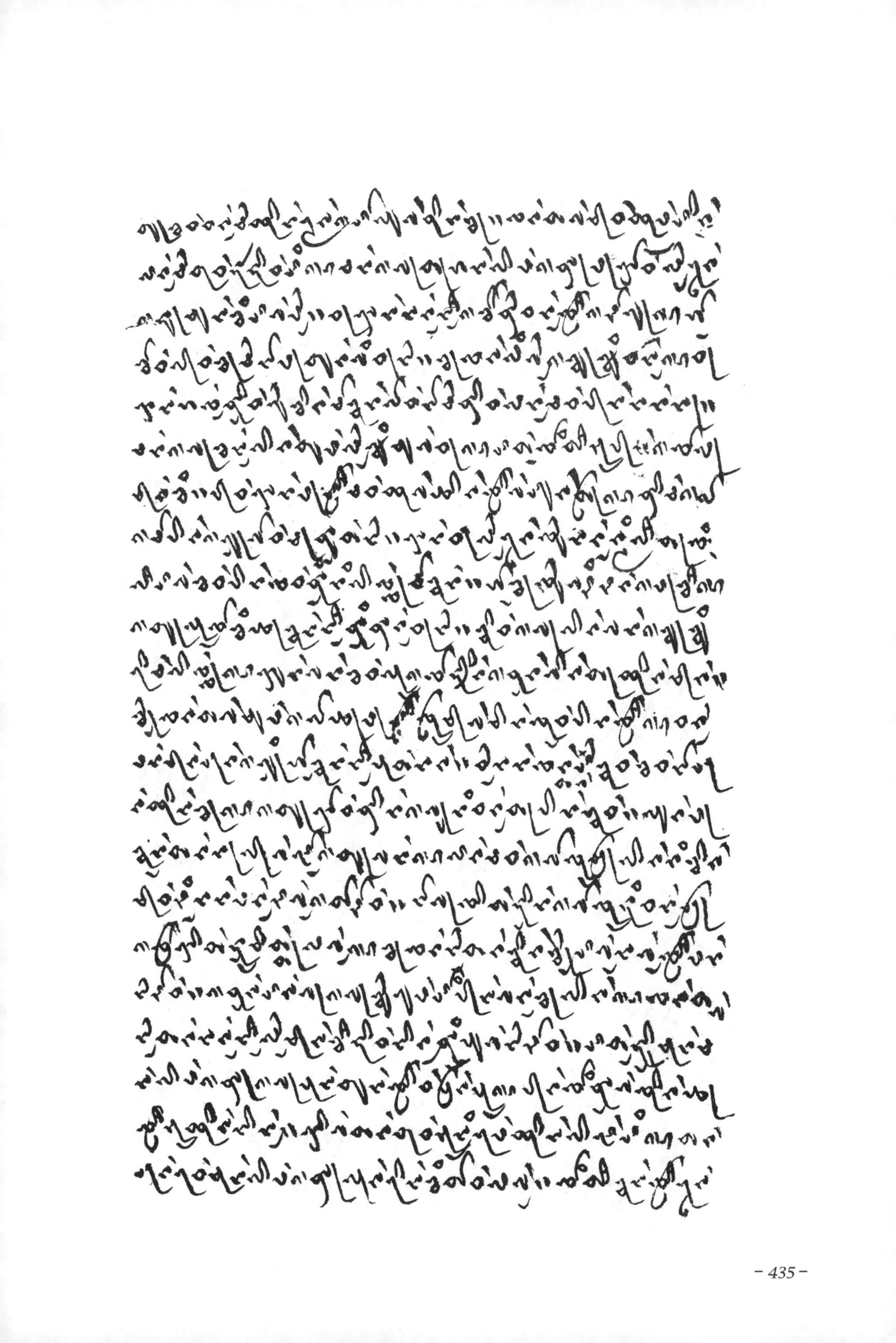

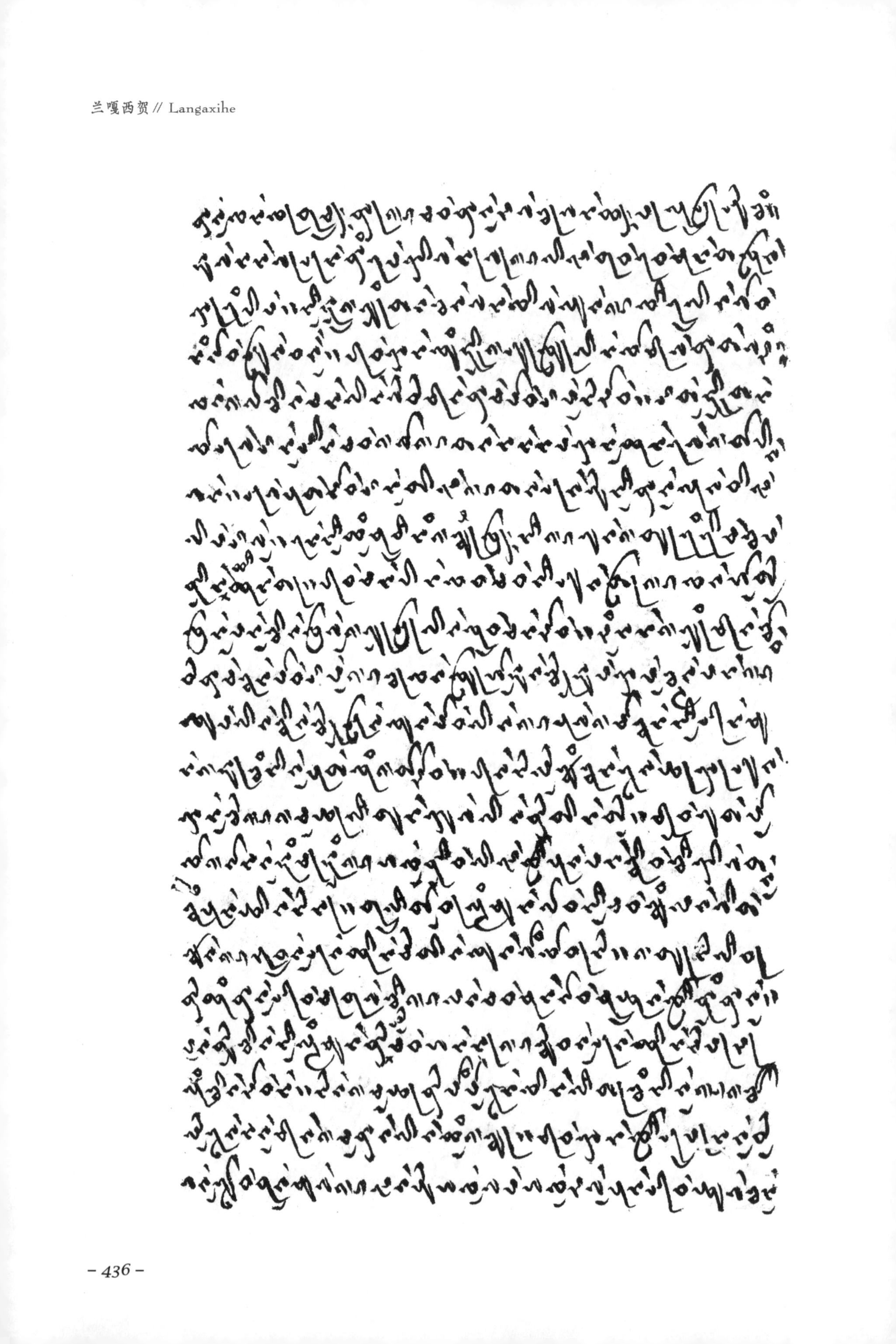

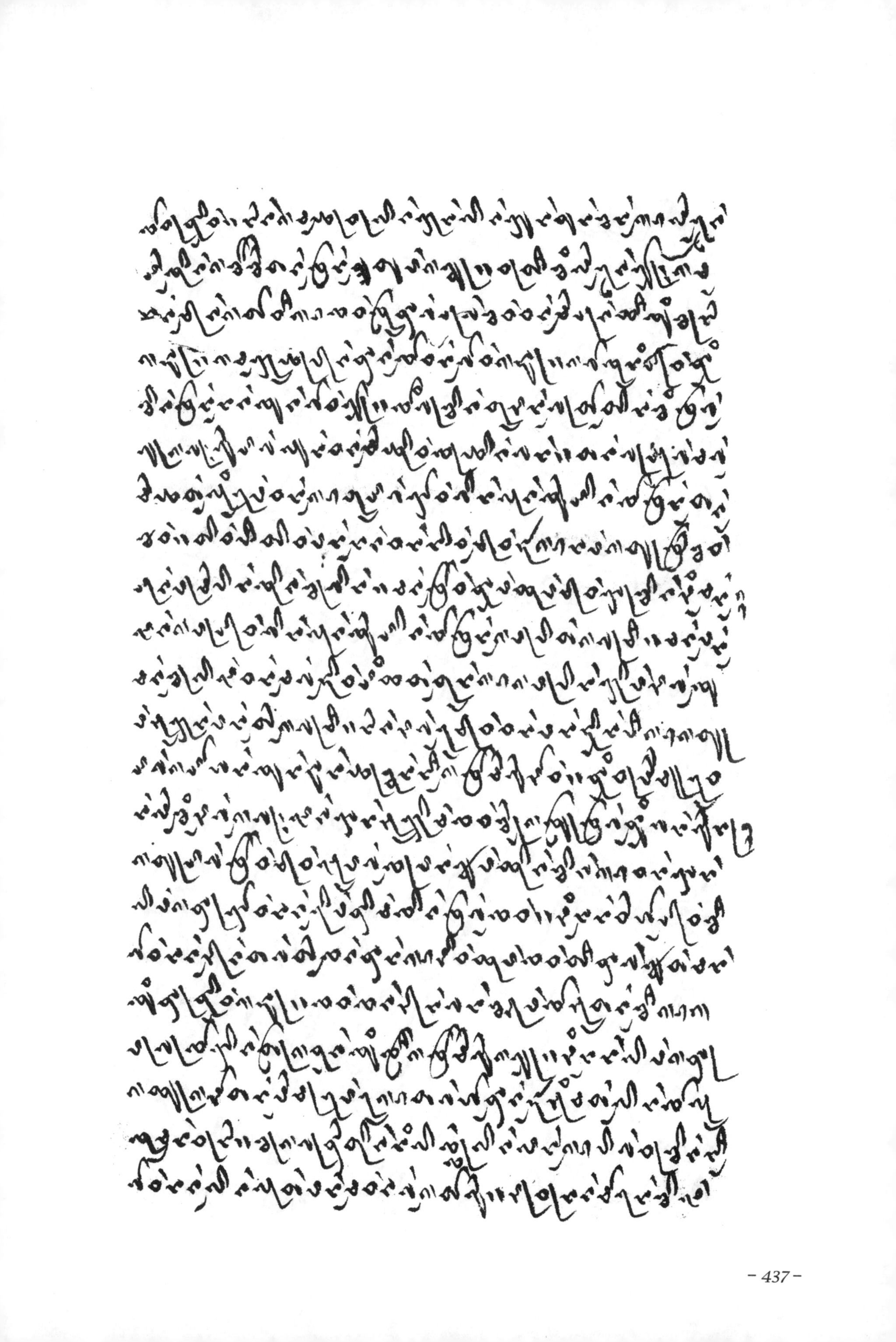

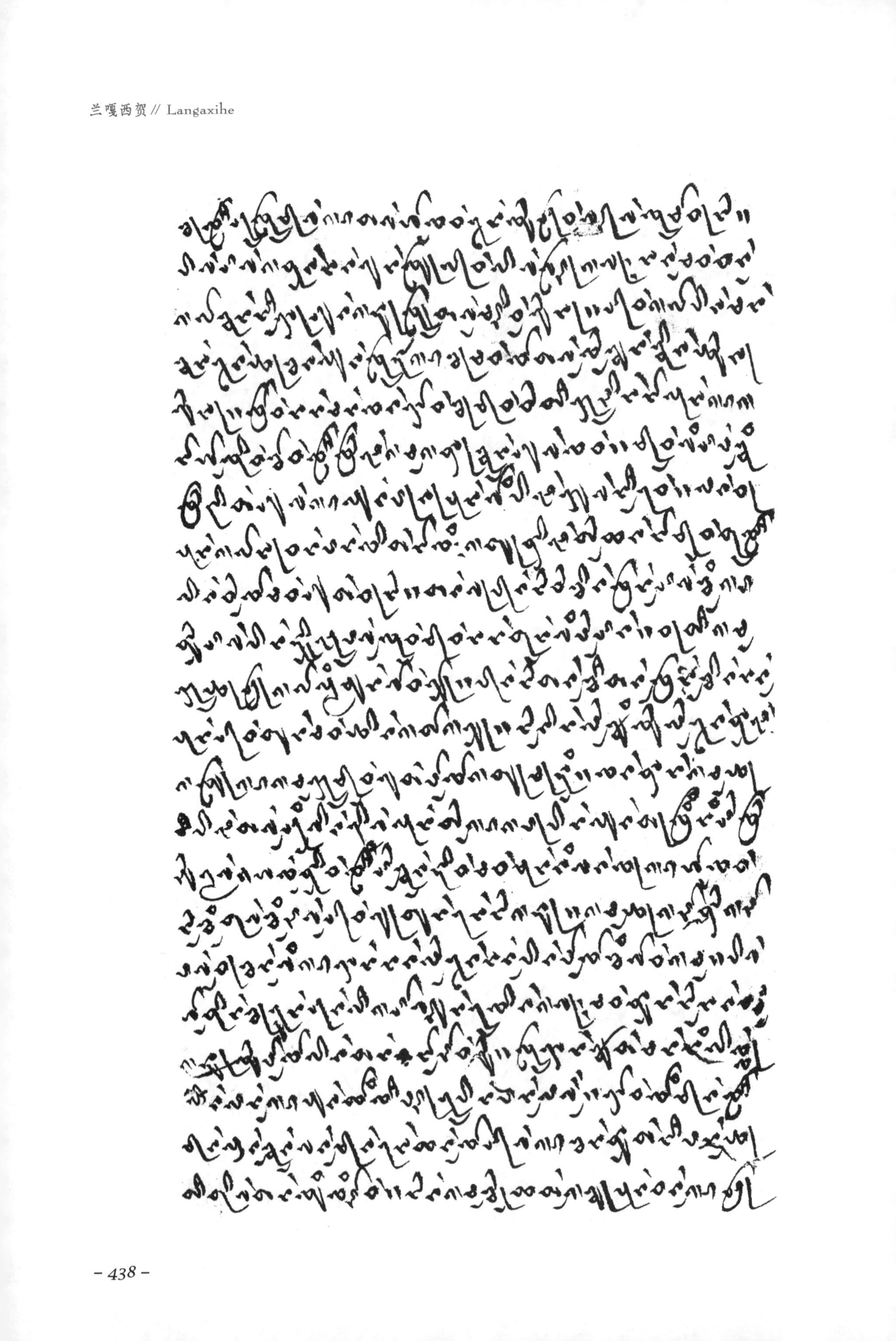

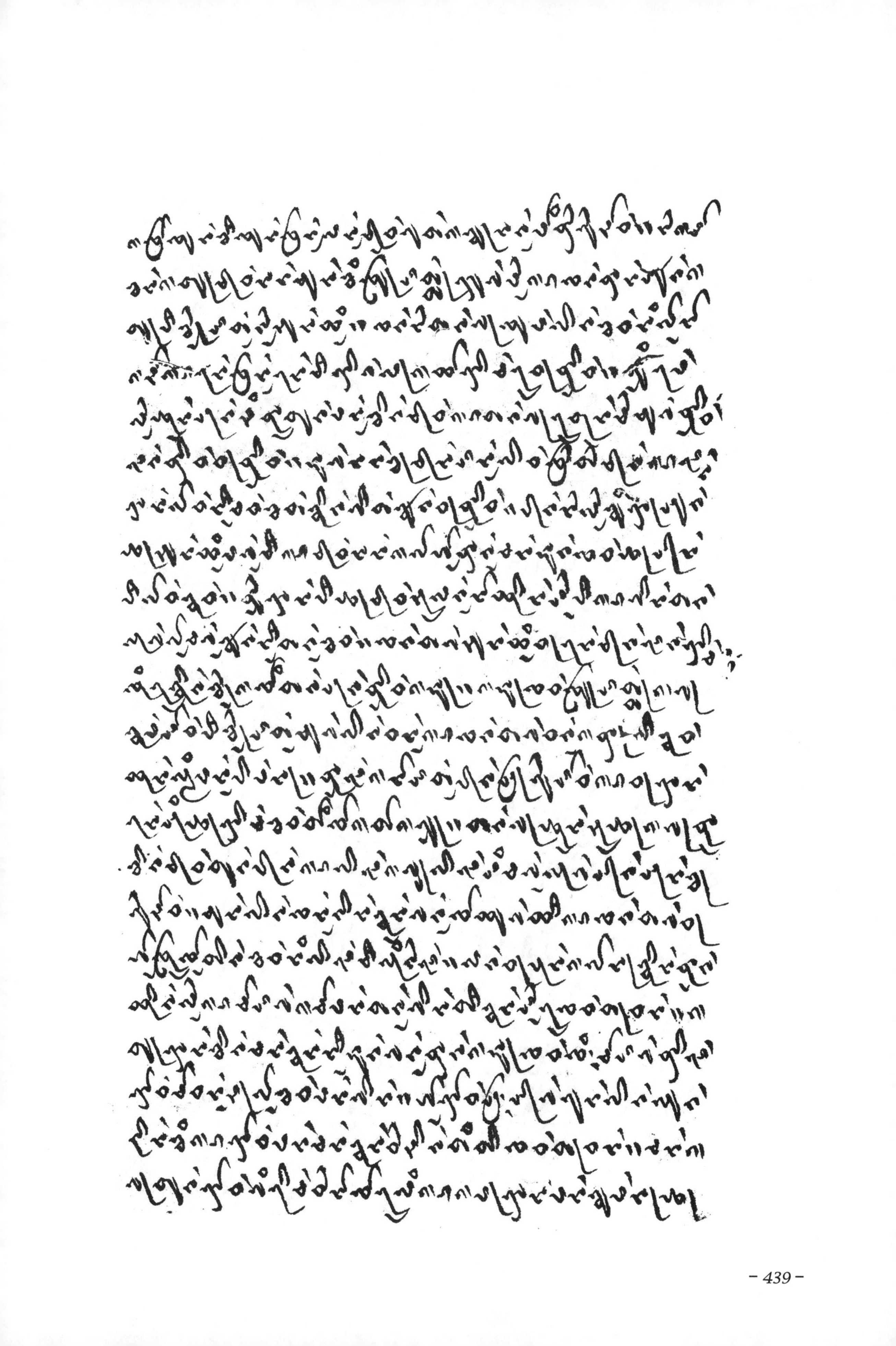

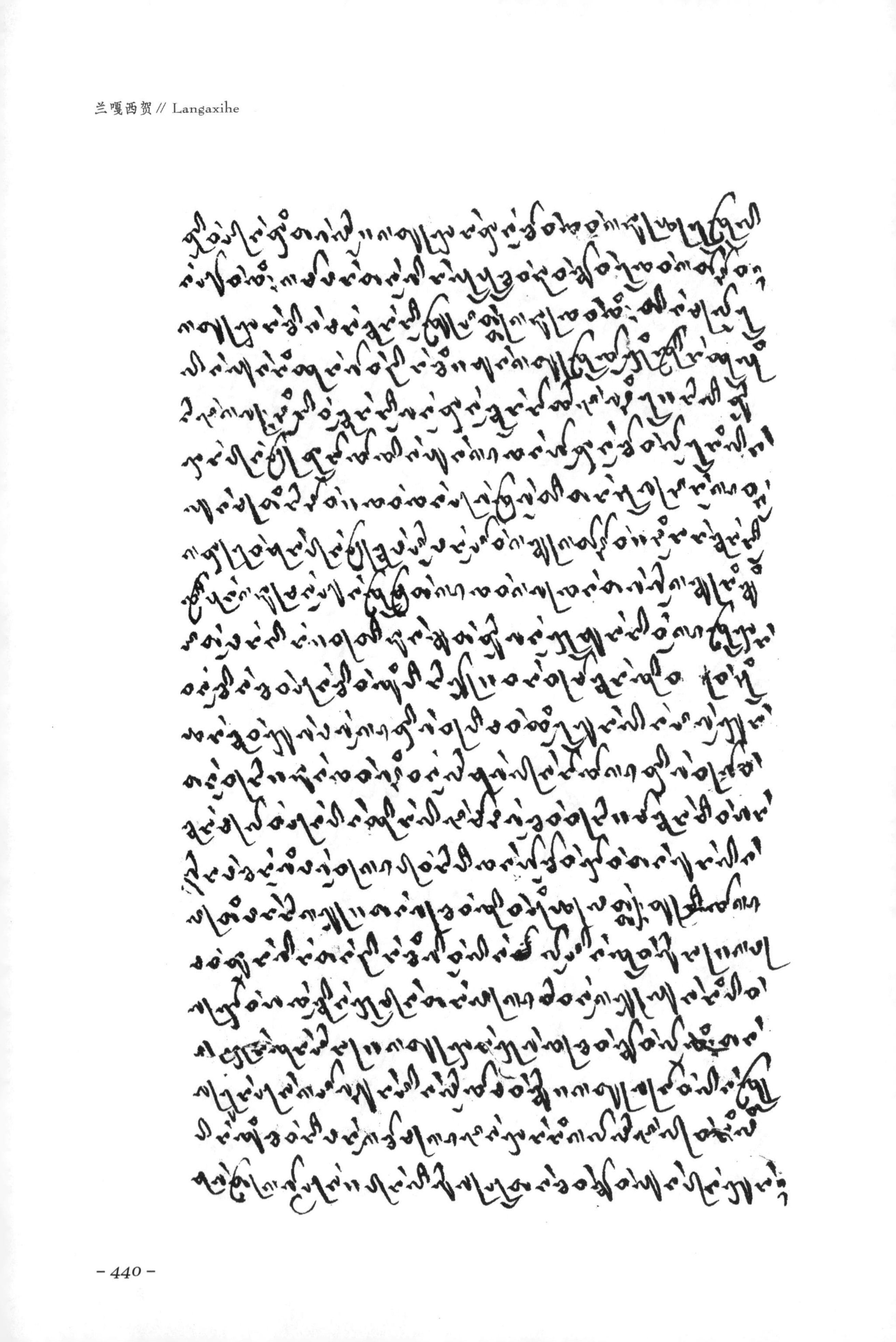

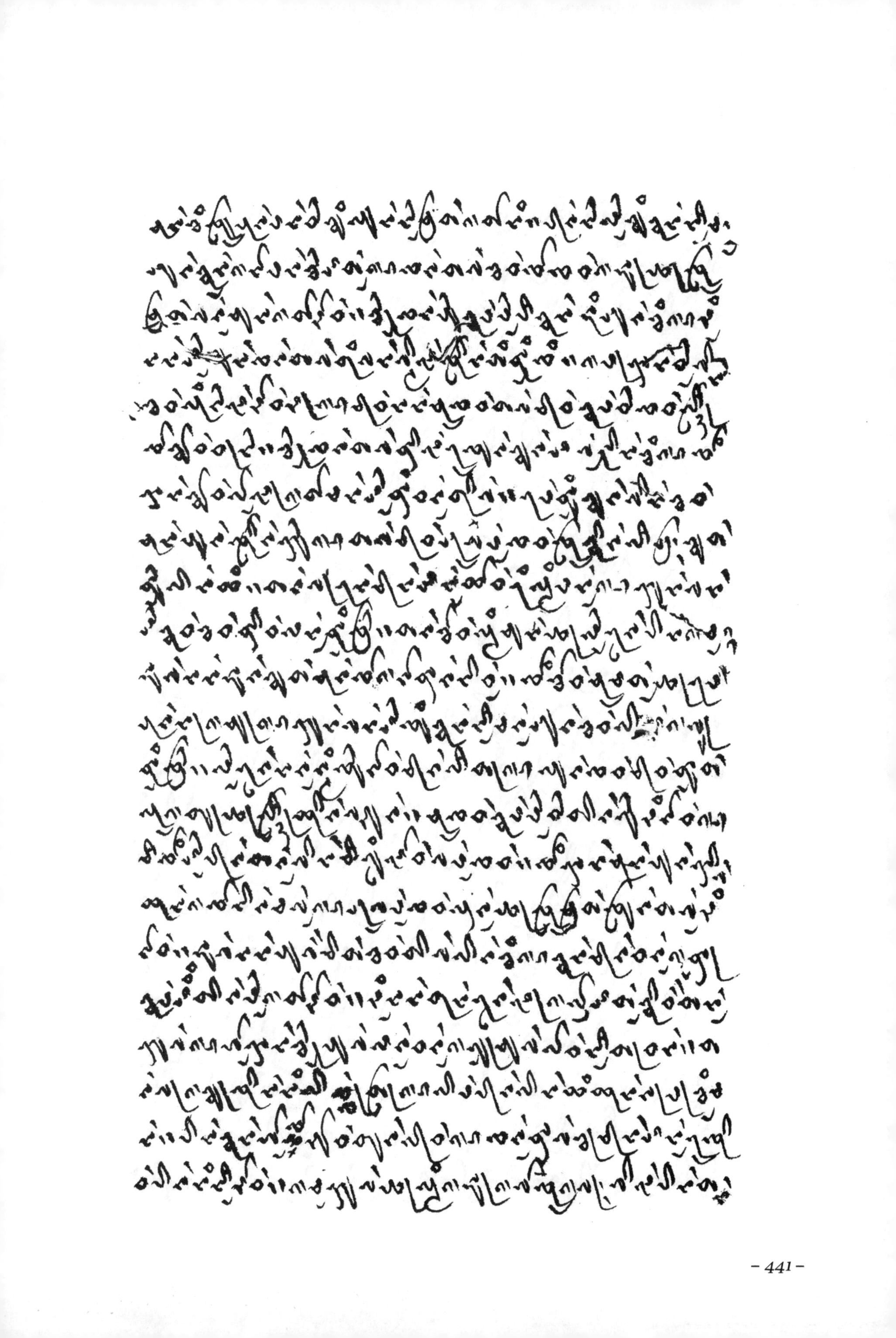

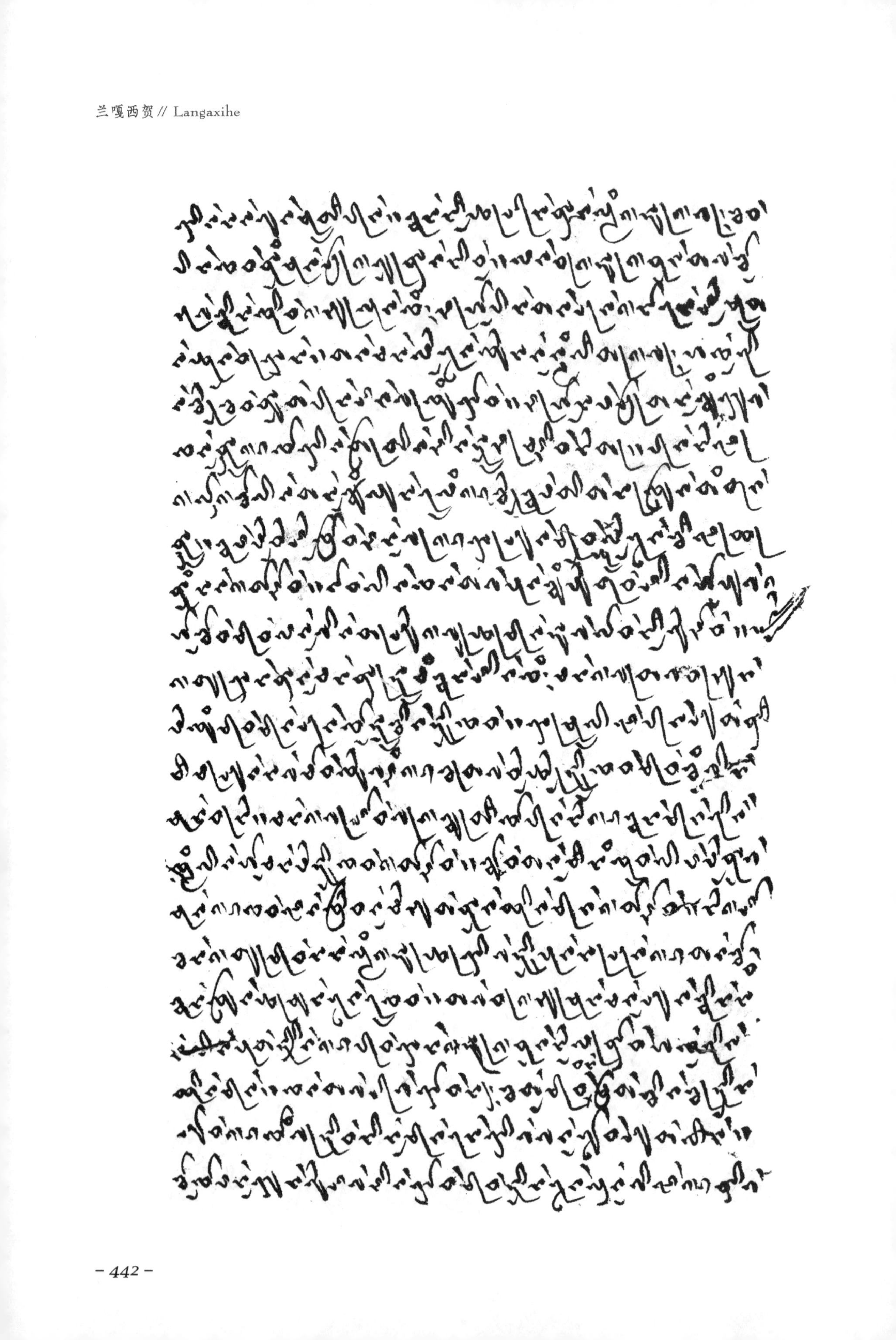

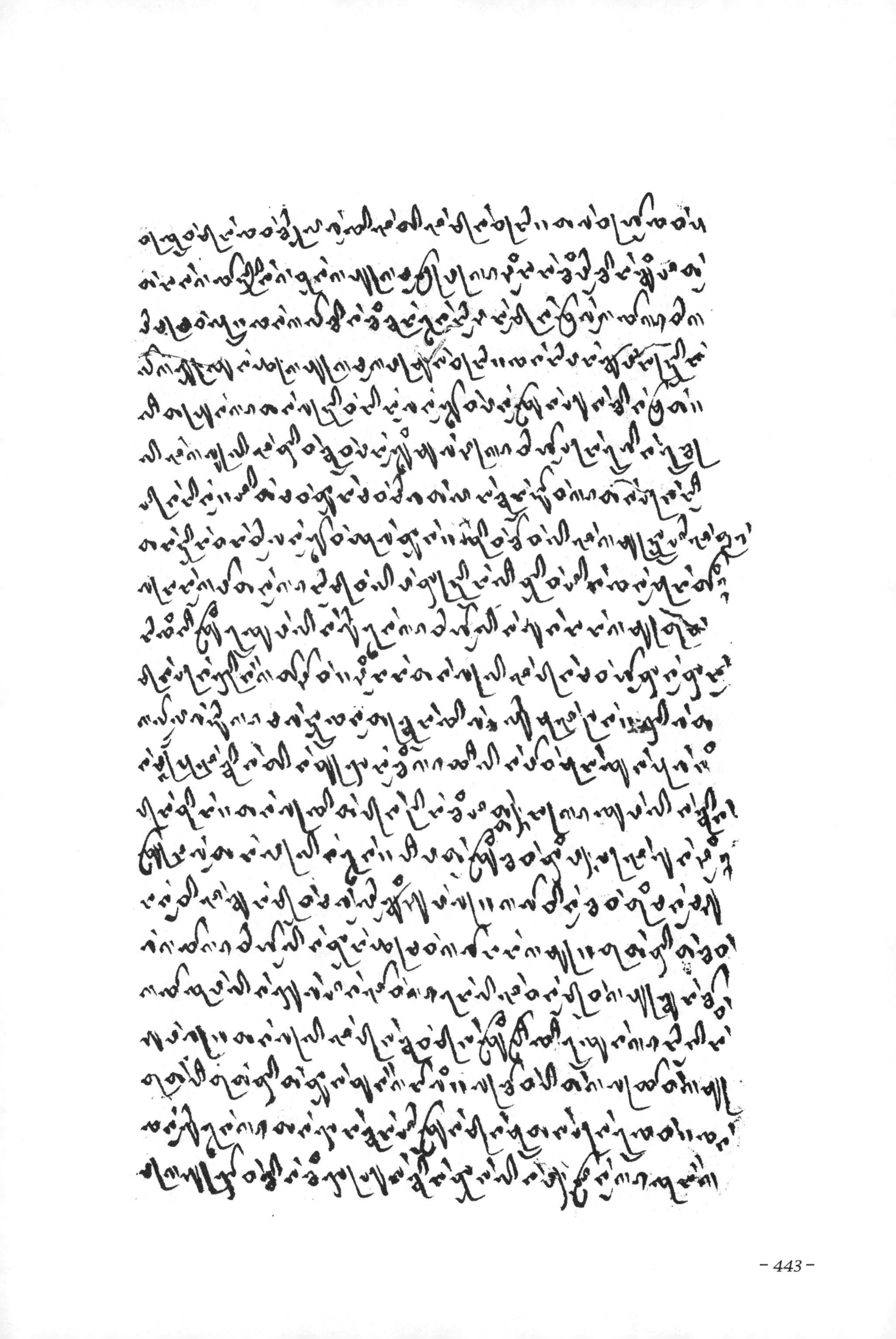

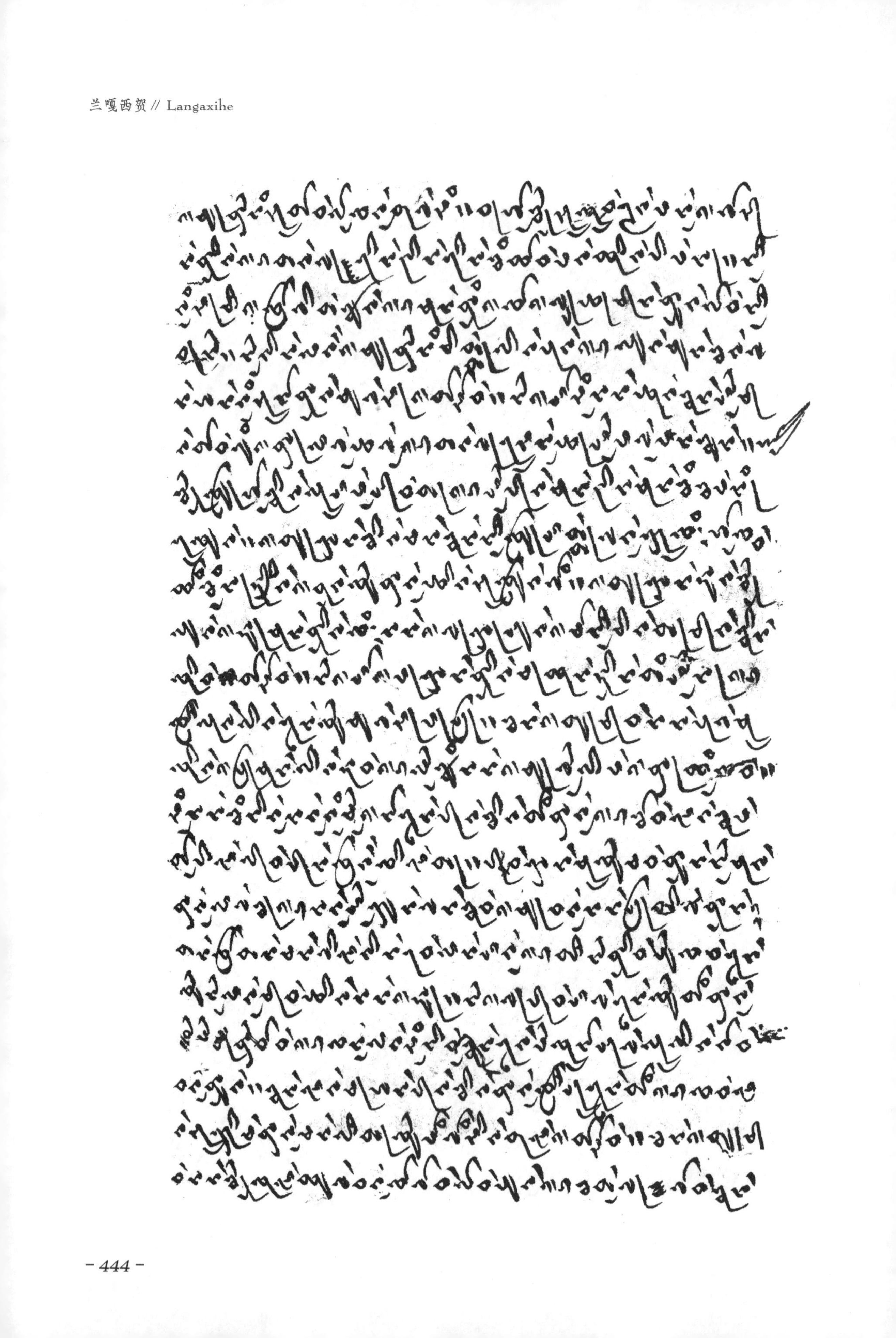

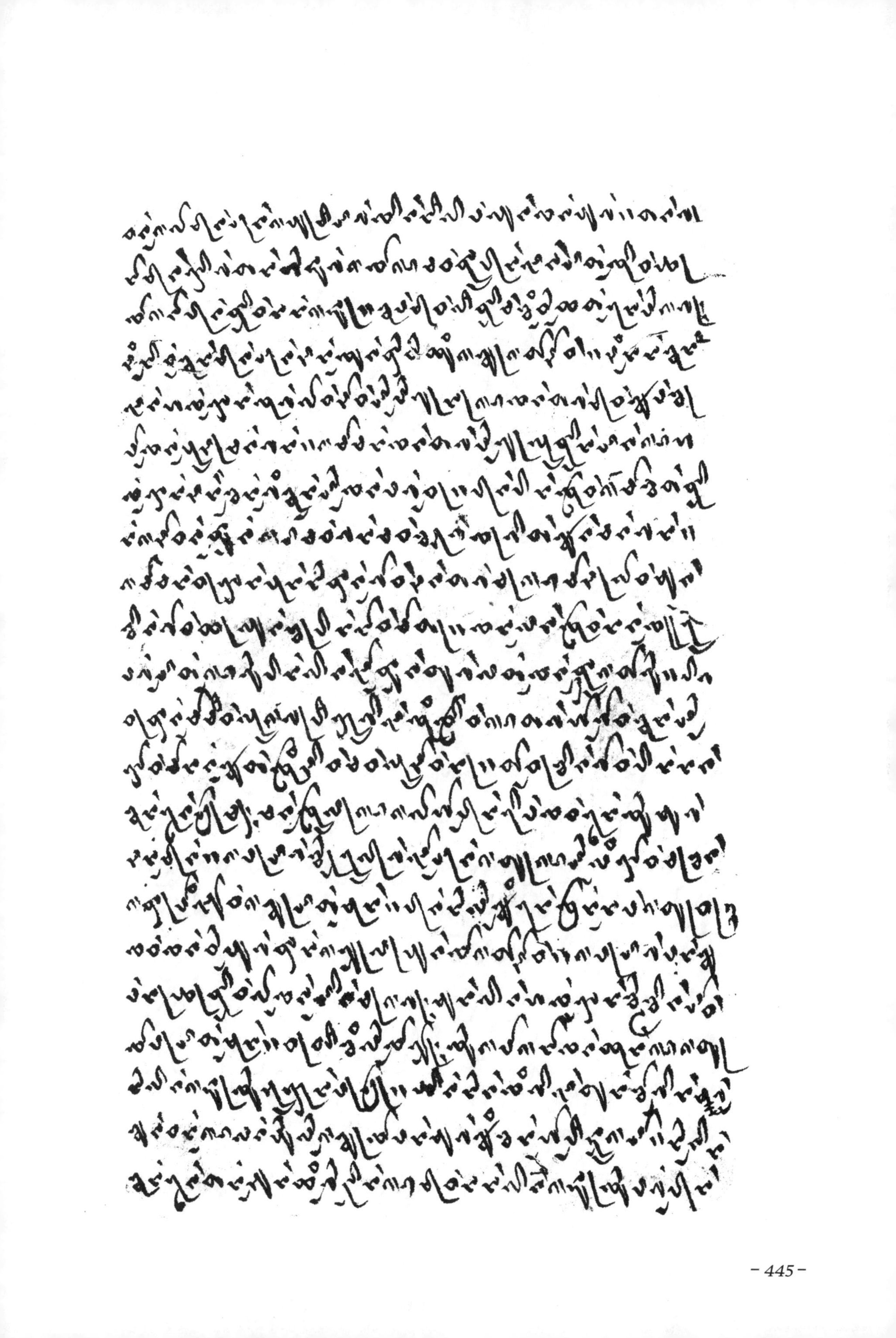

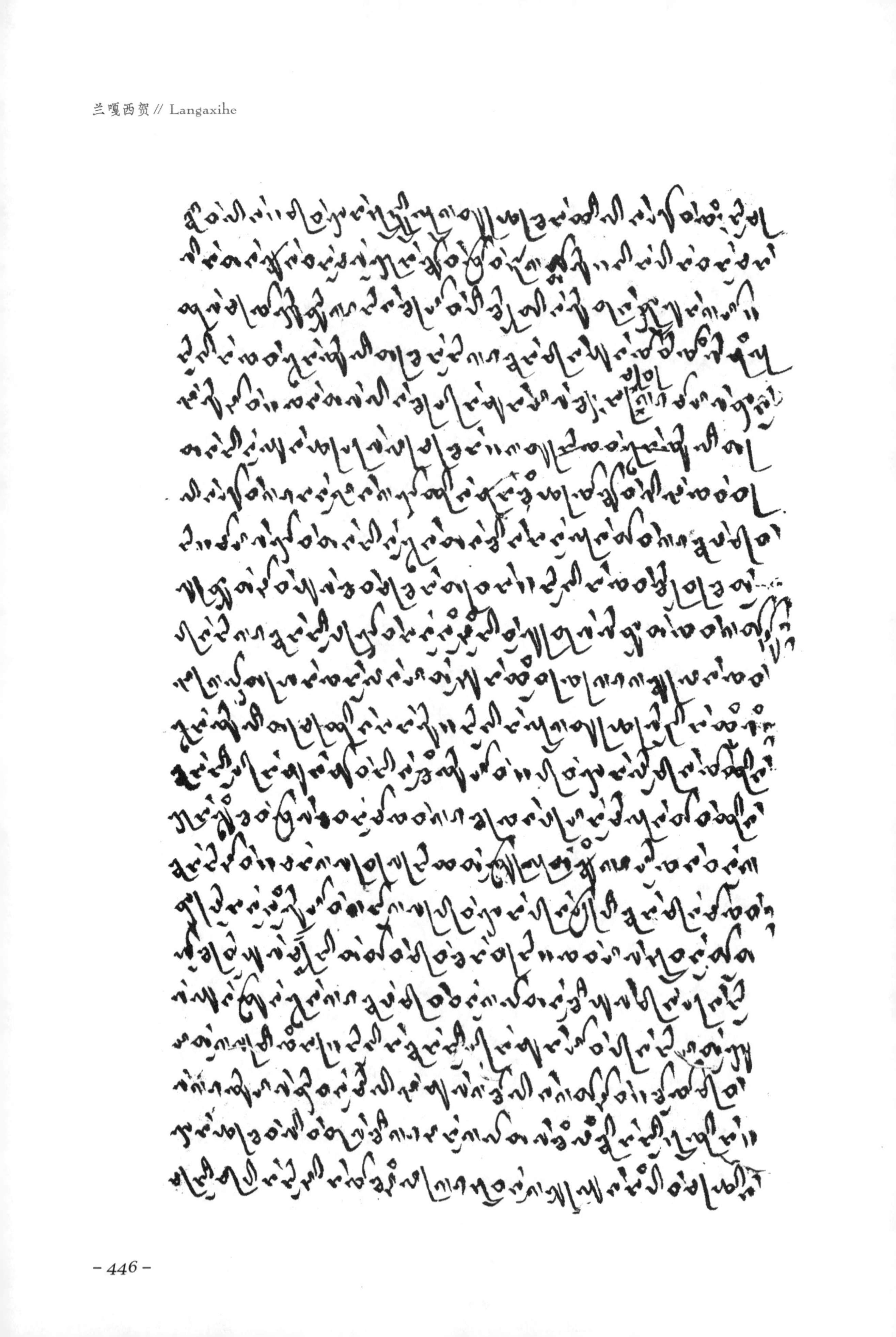

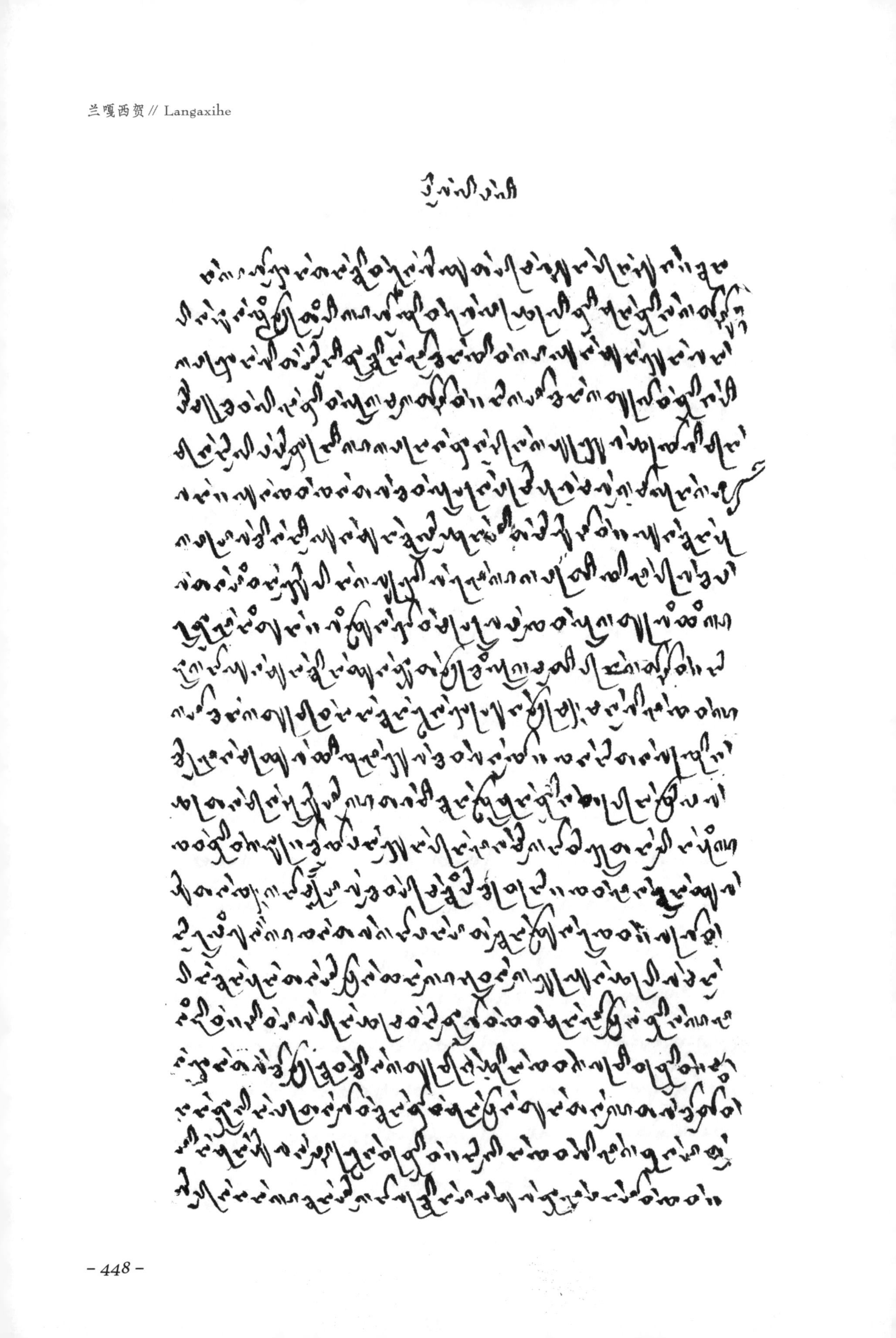

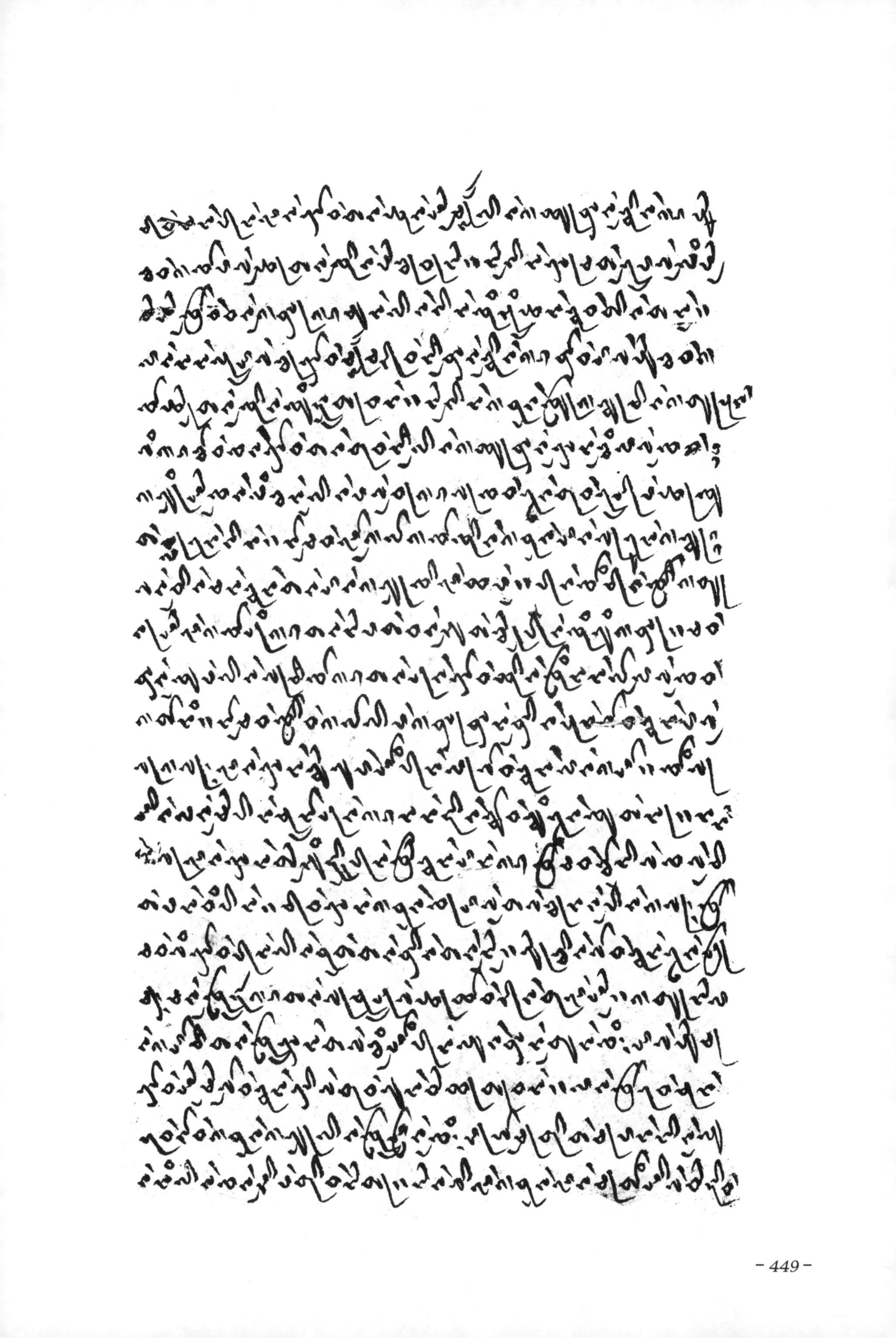

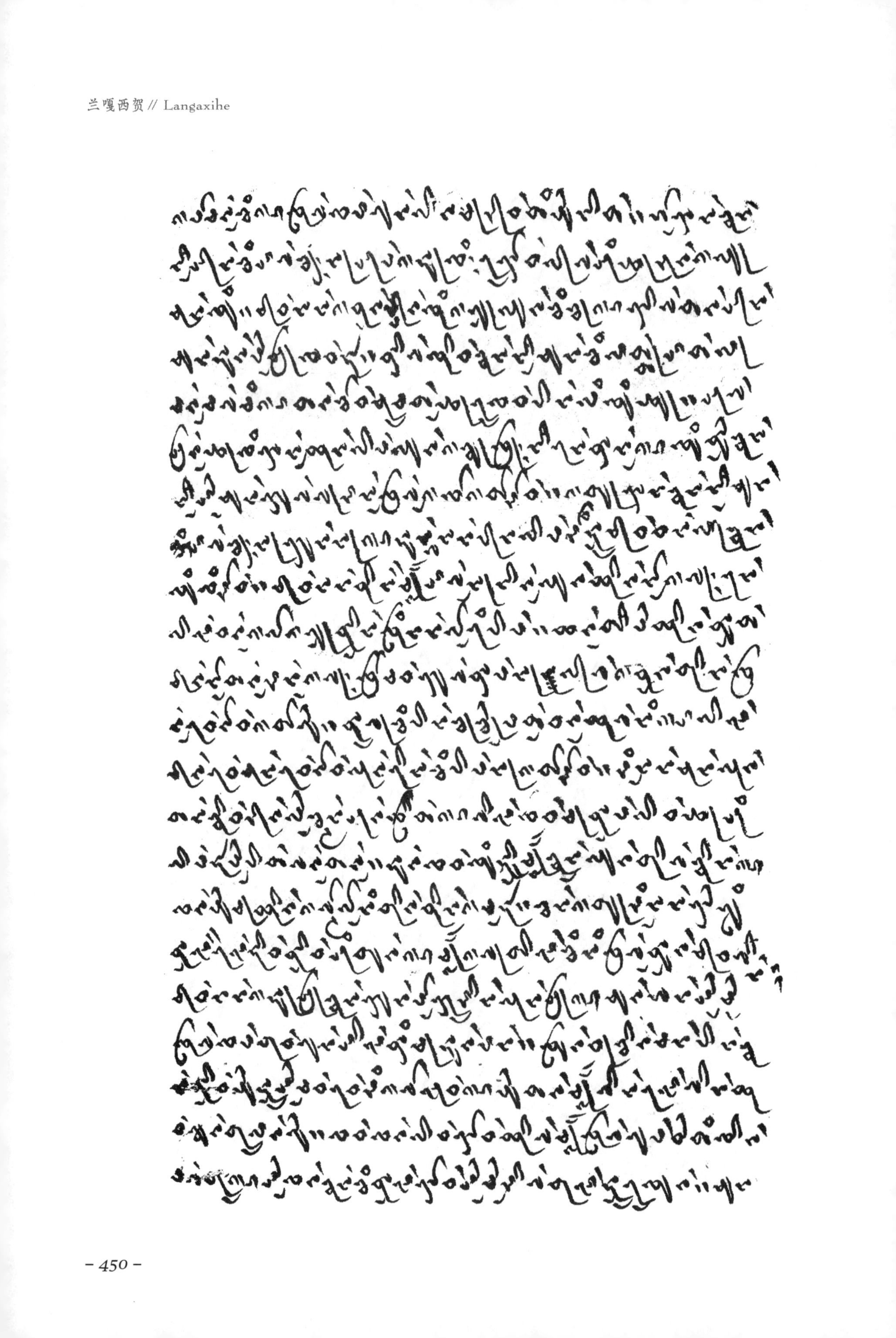

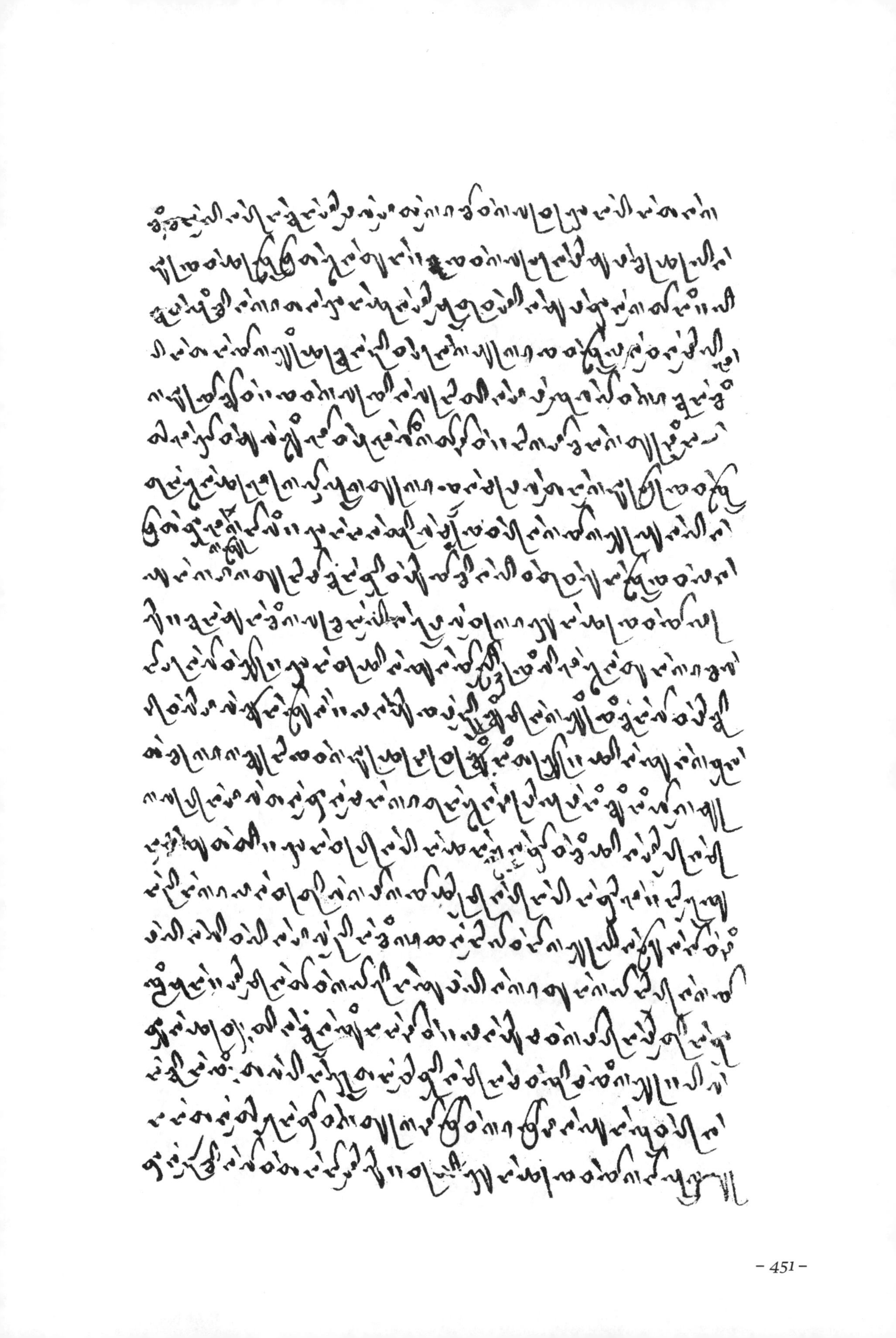

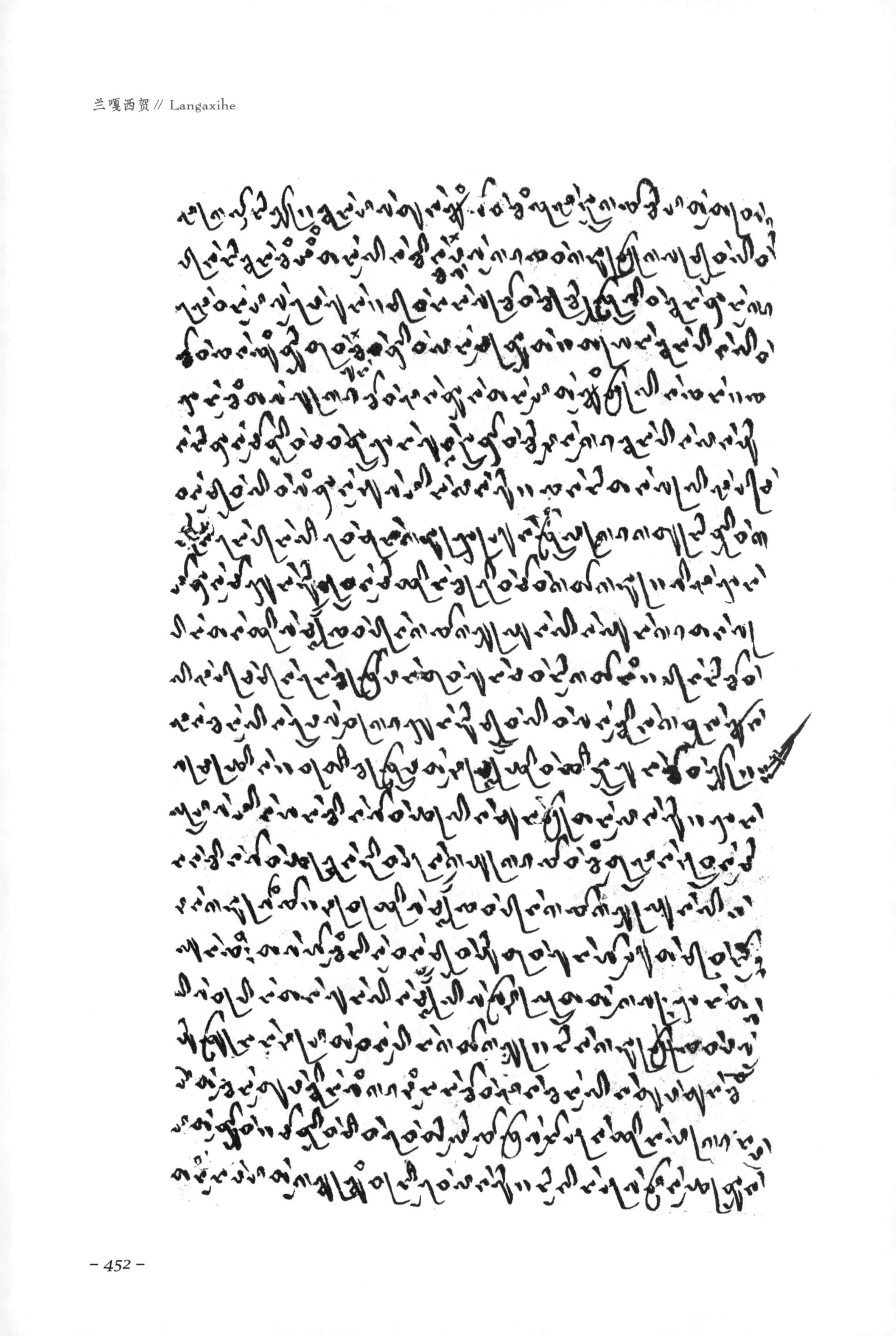

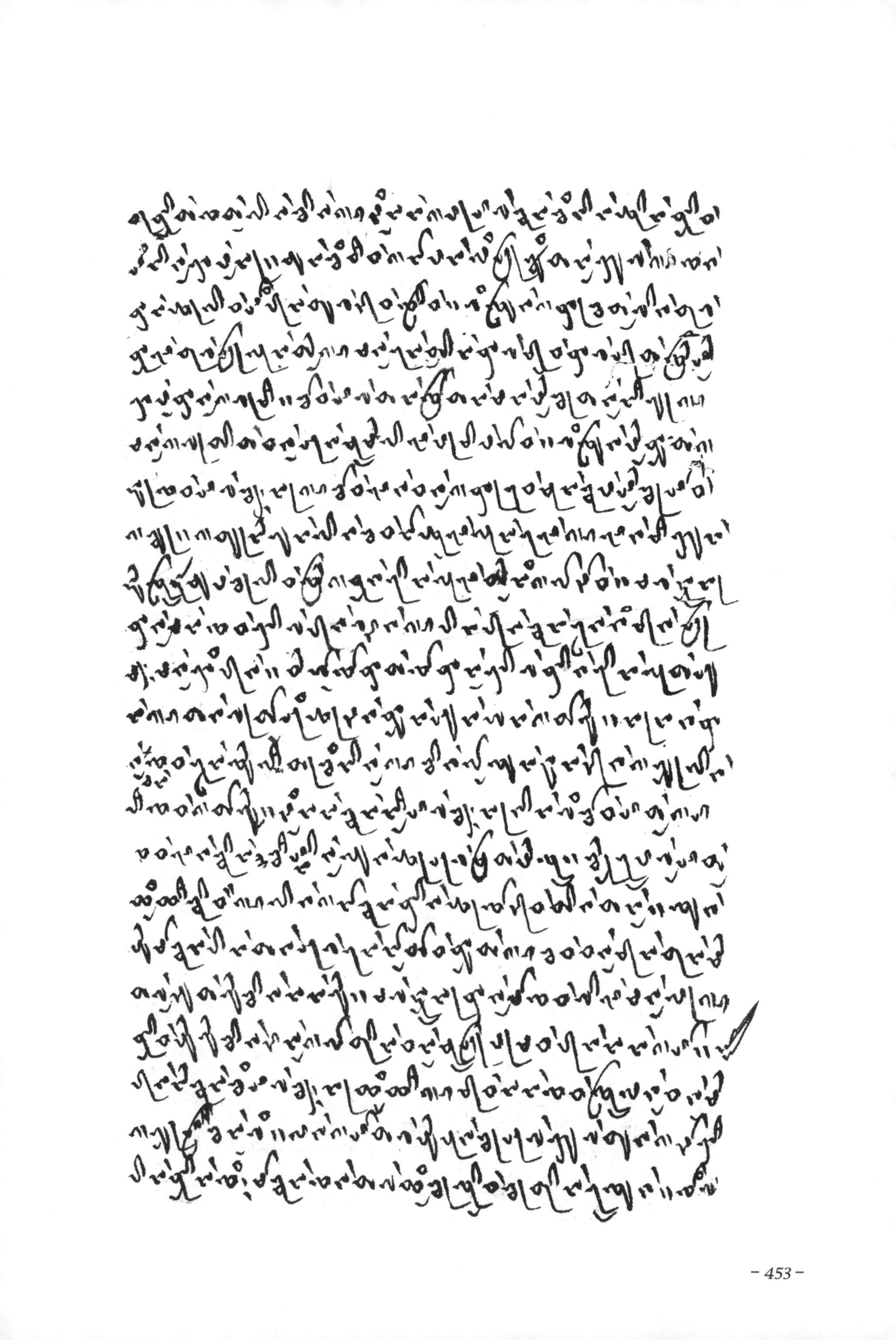

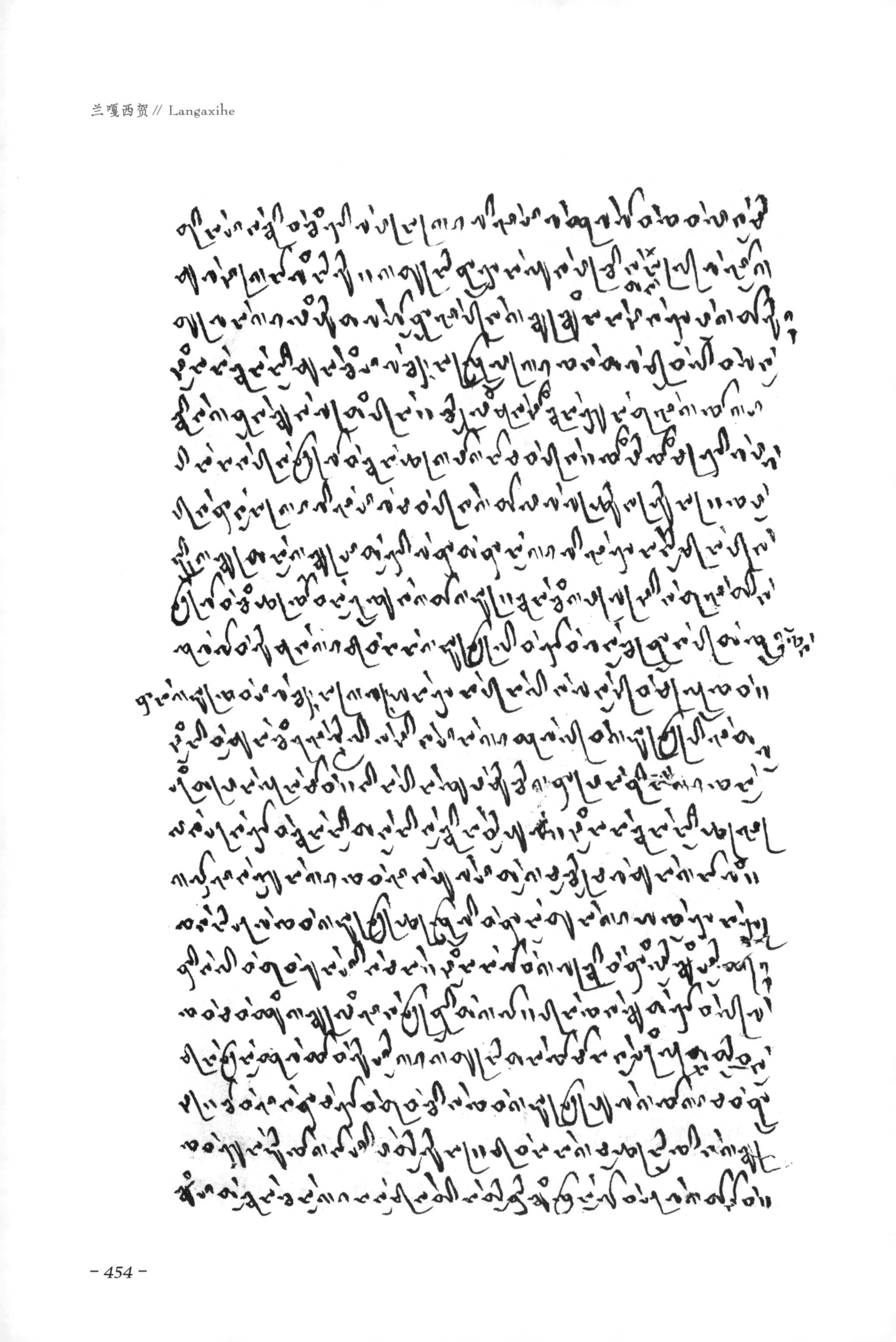

[illegible]

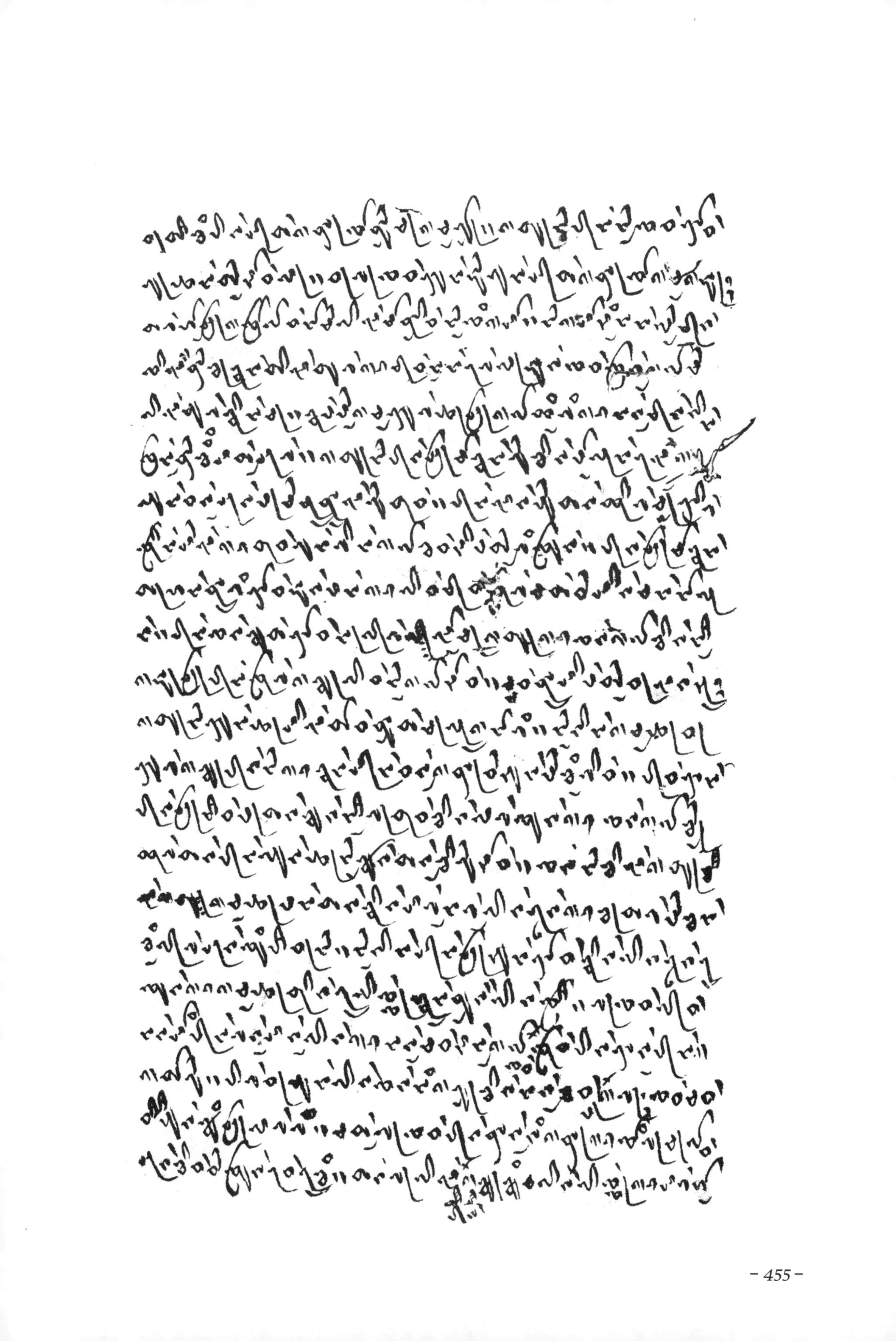

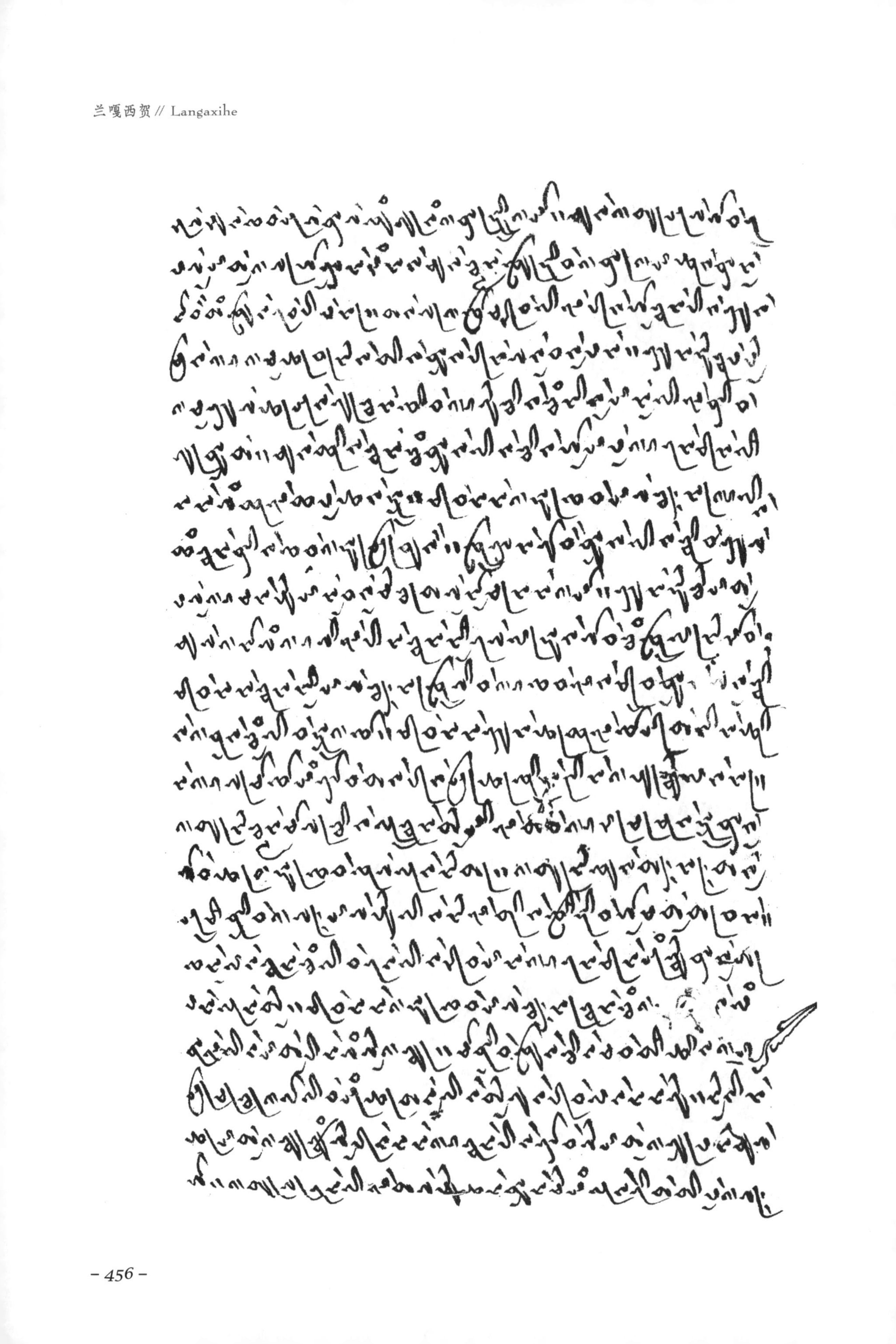

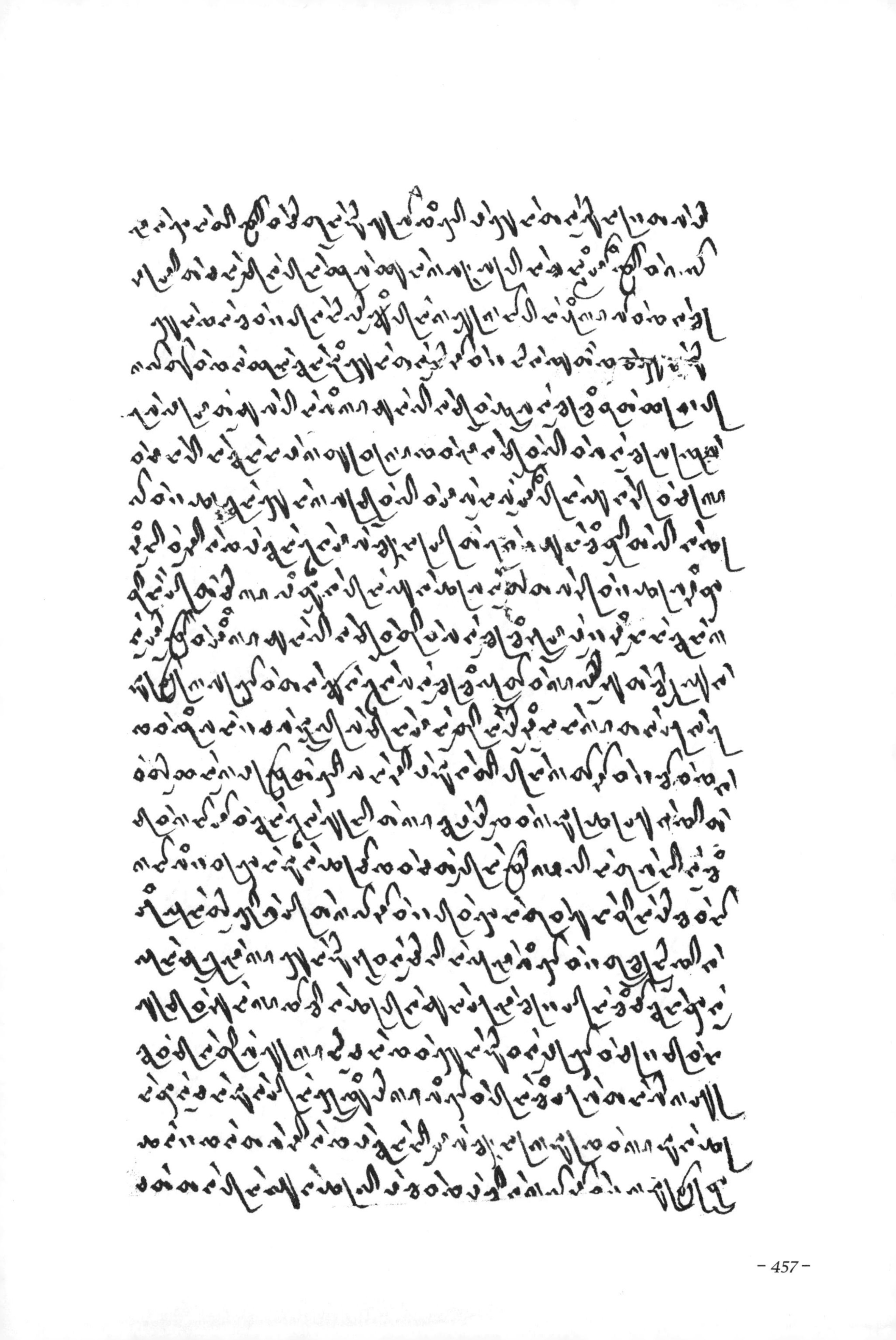

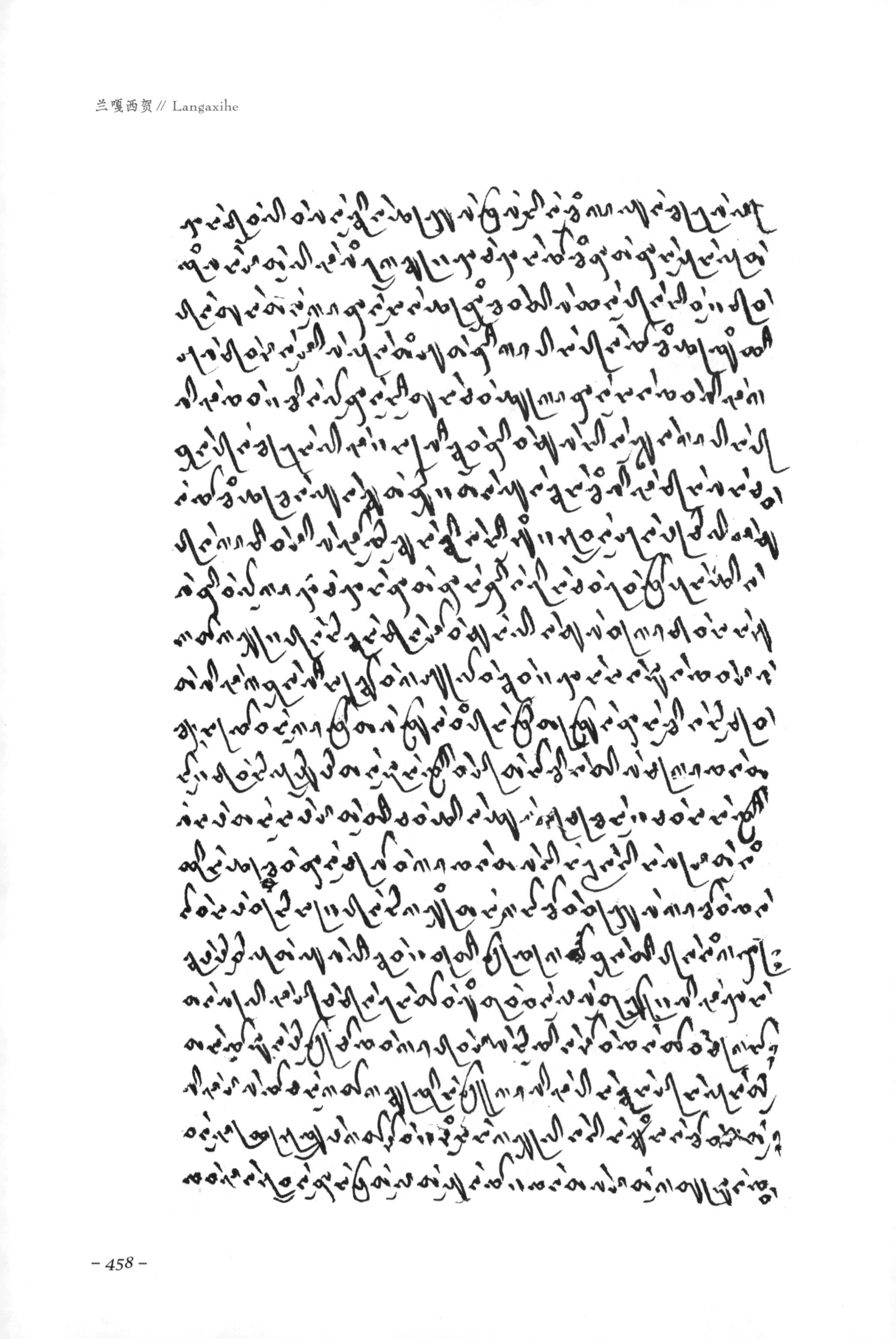

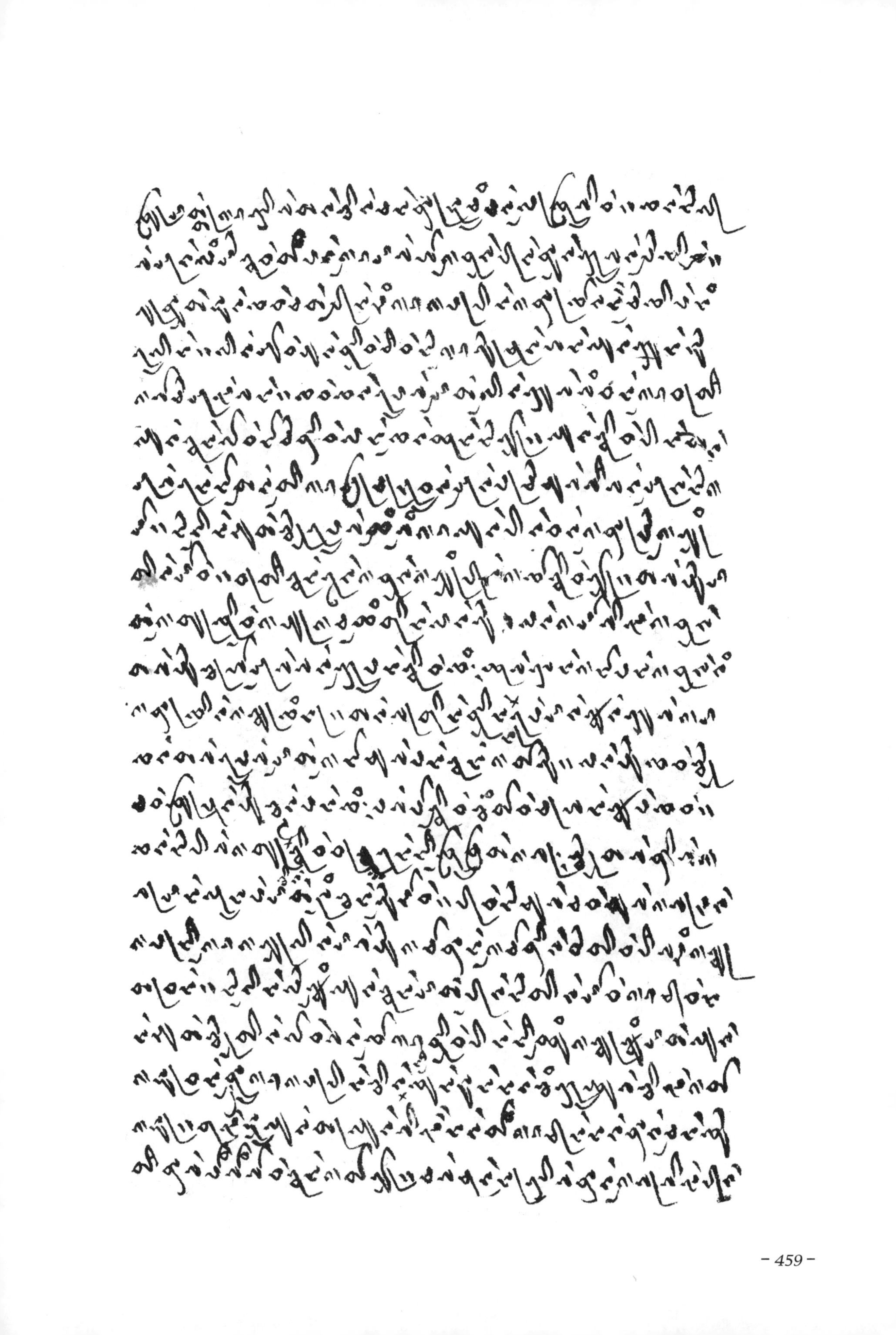

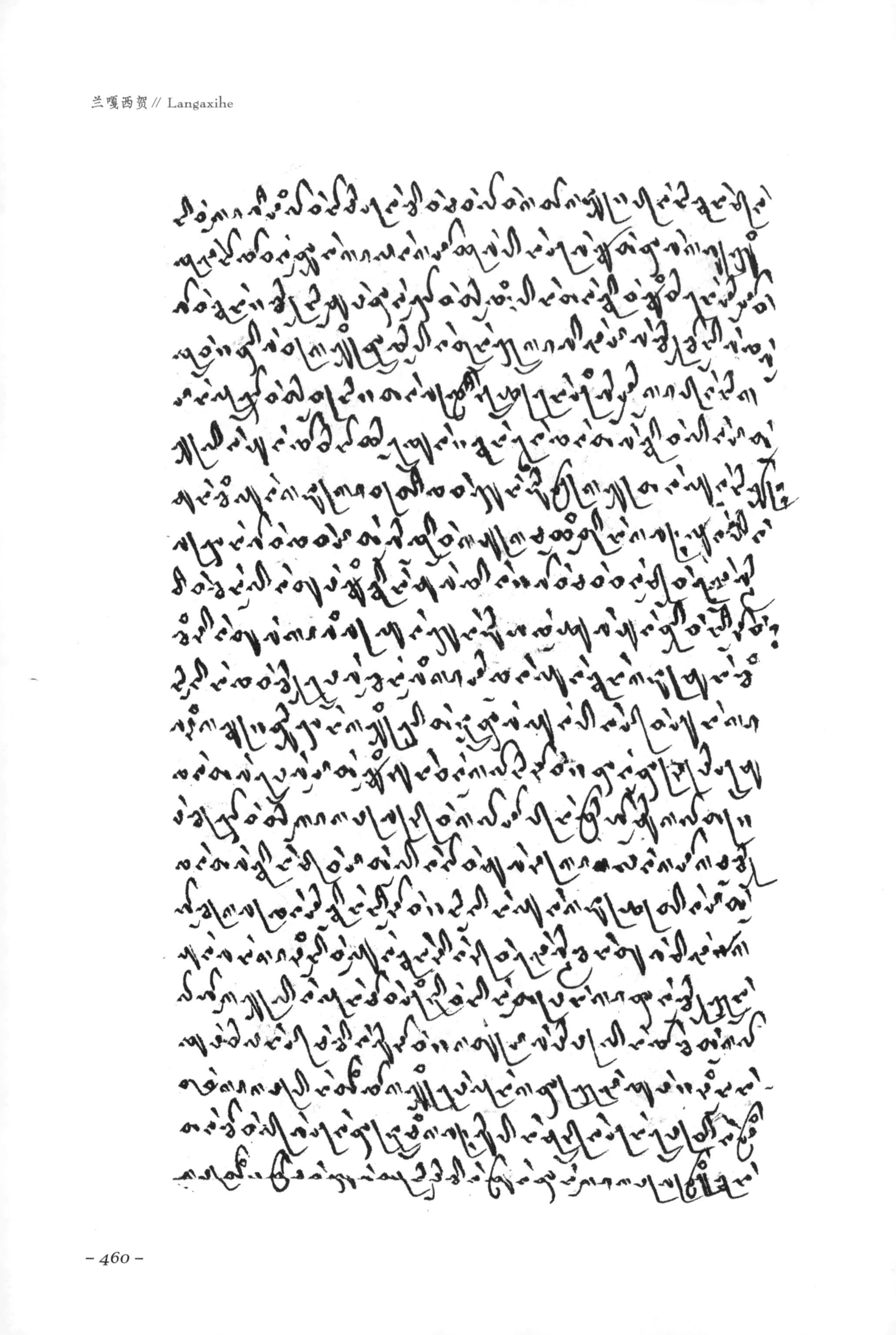

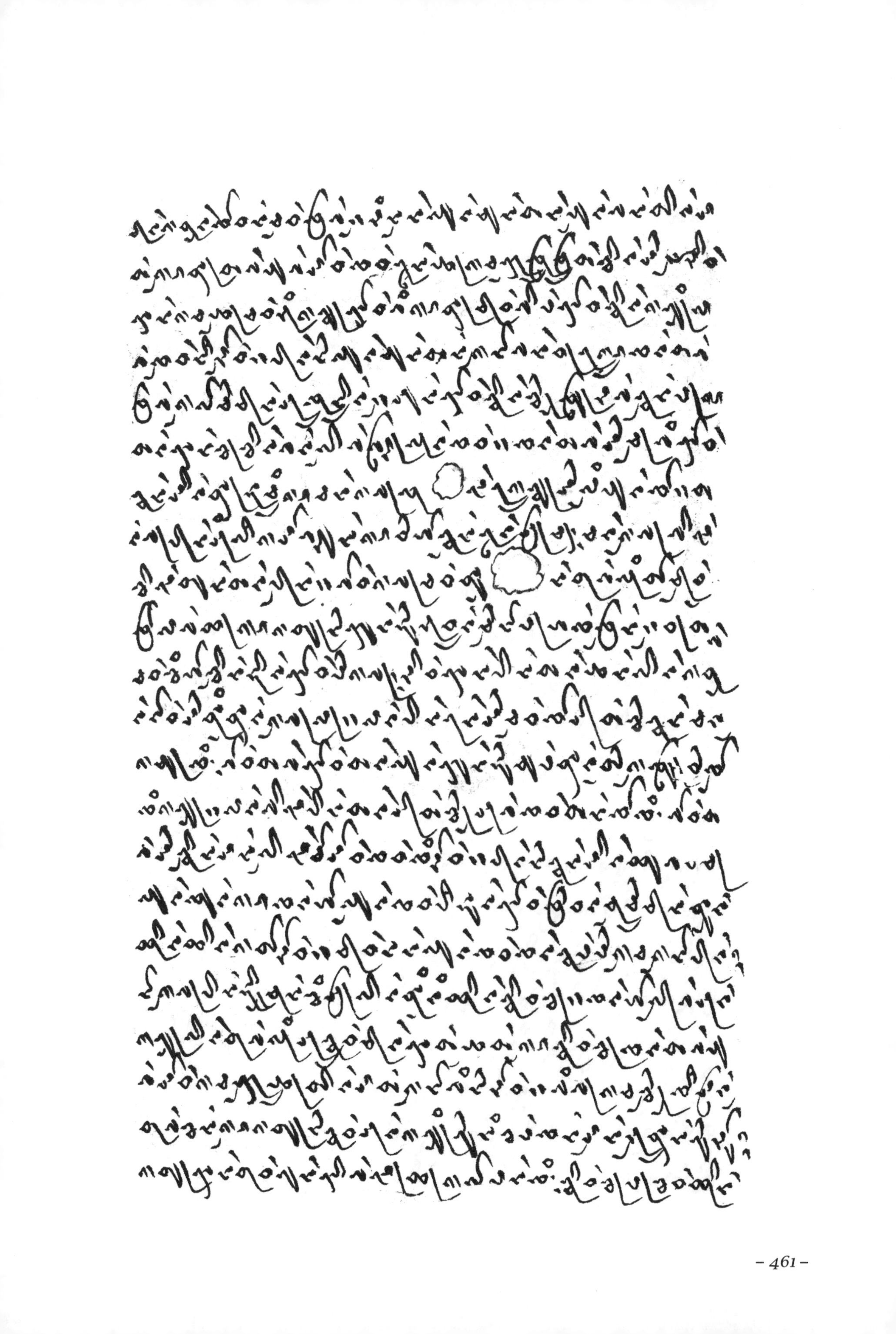

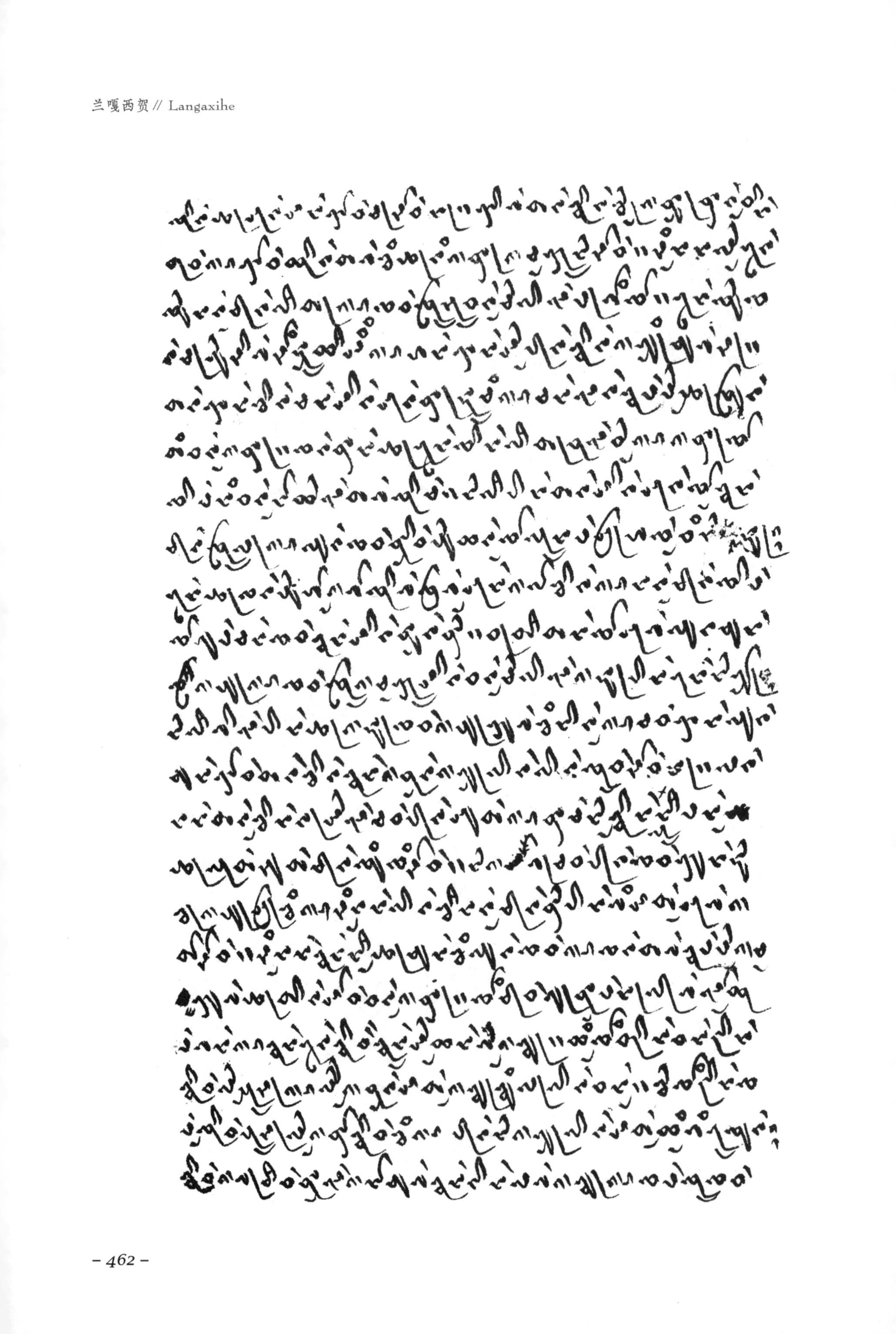

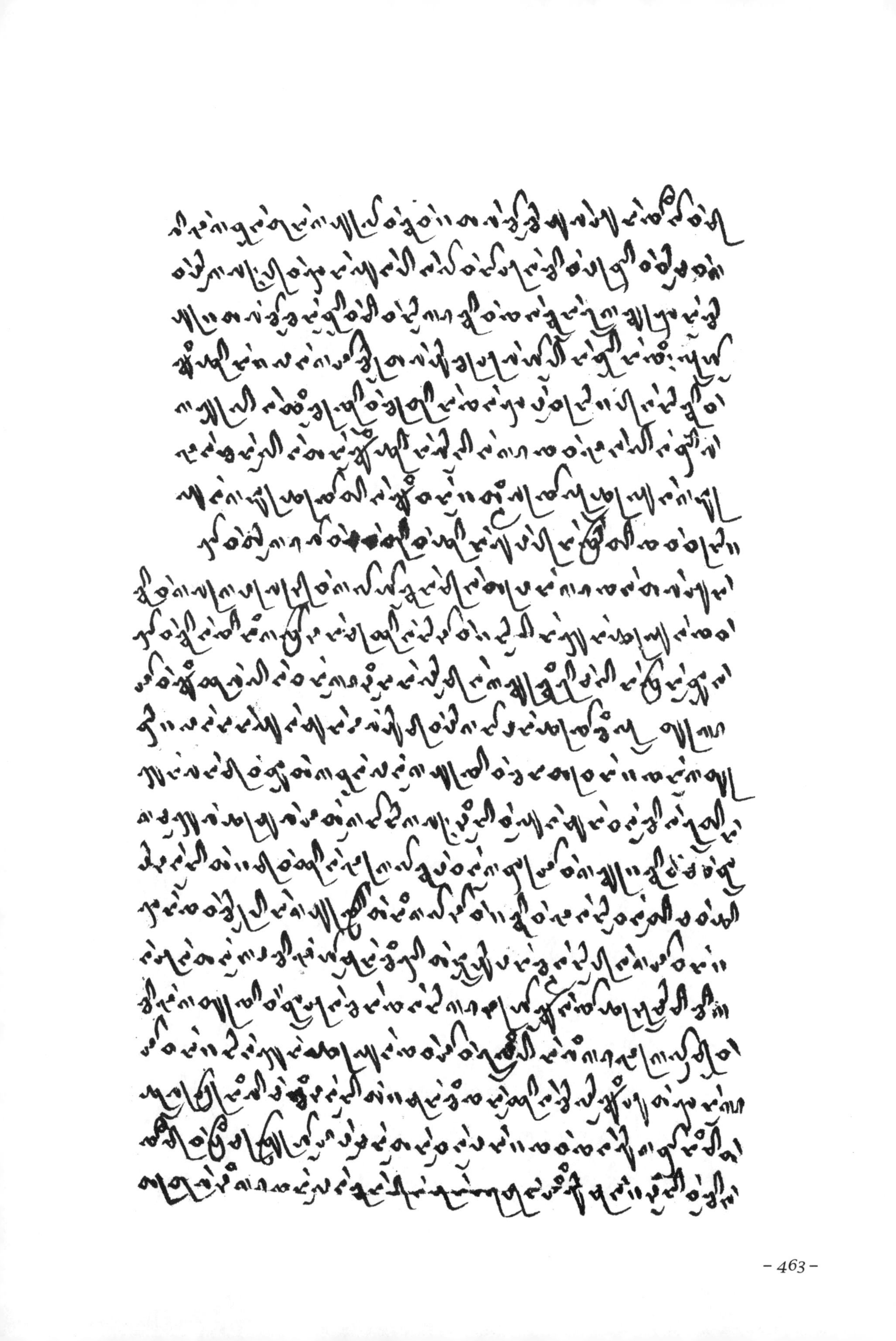

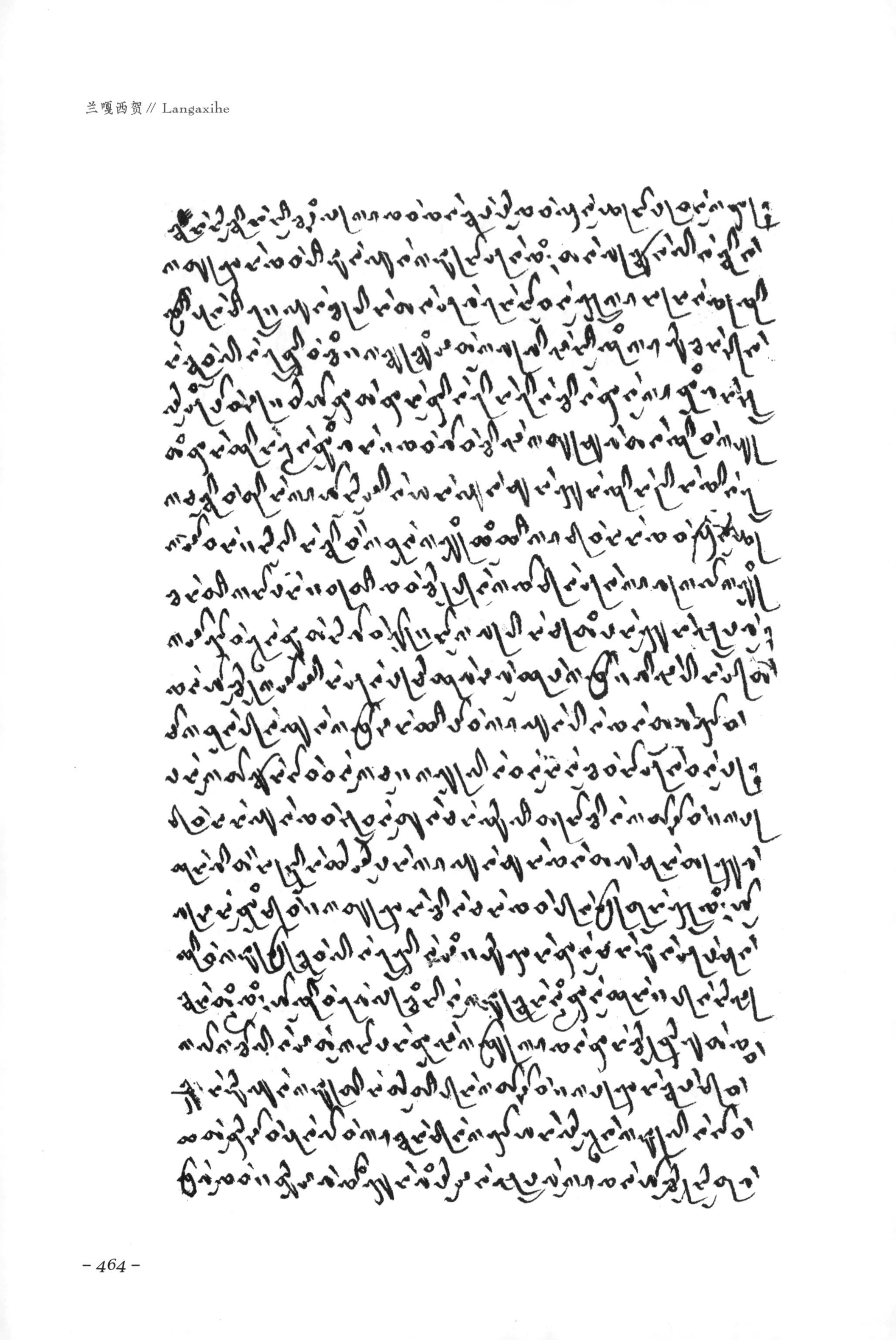

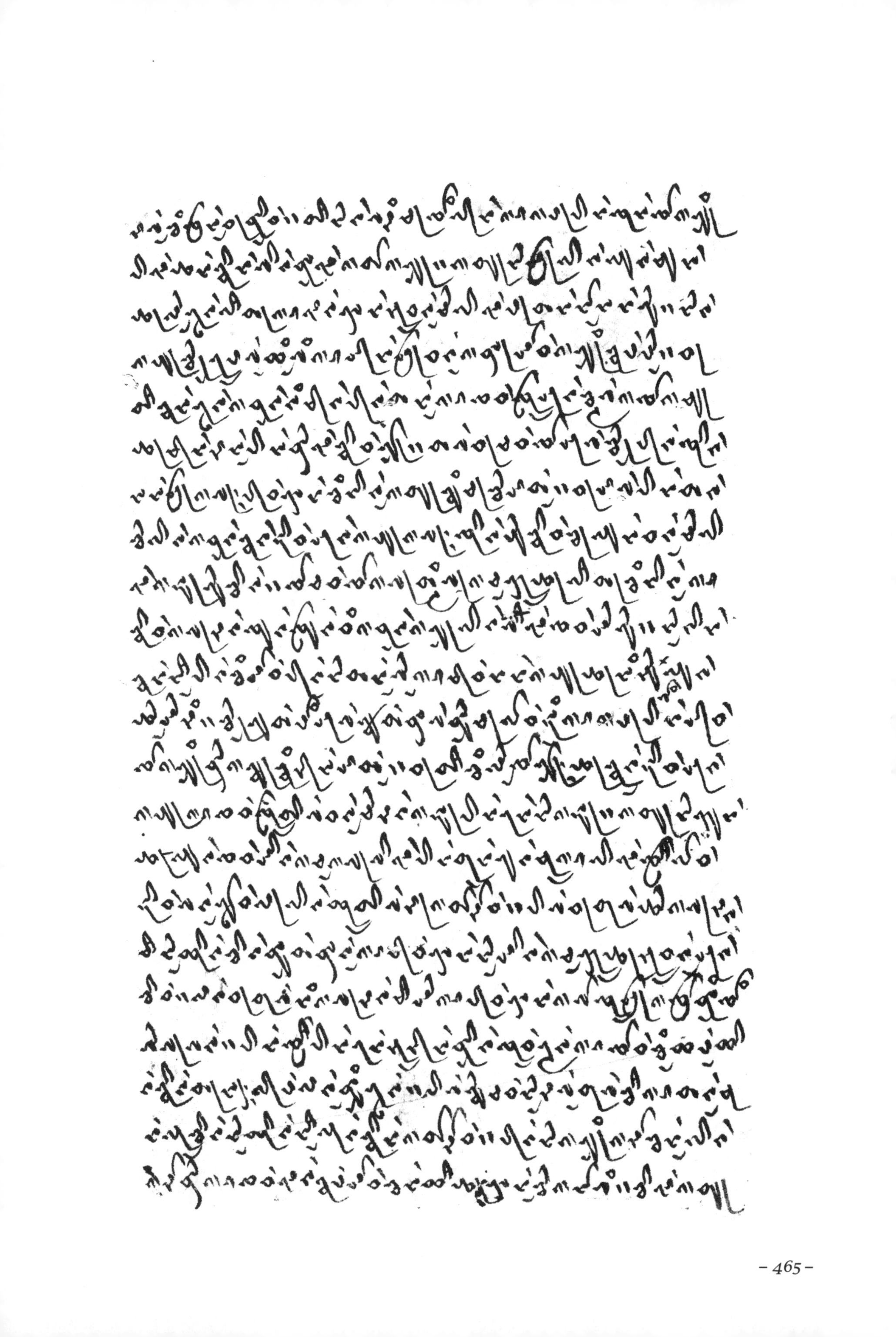

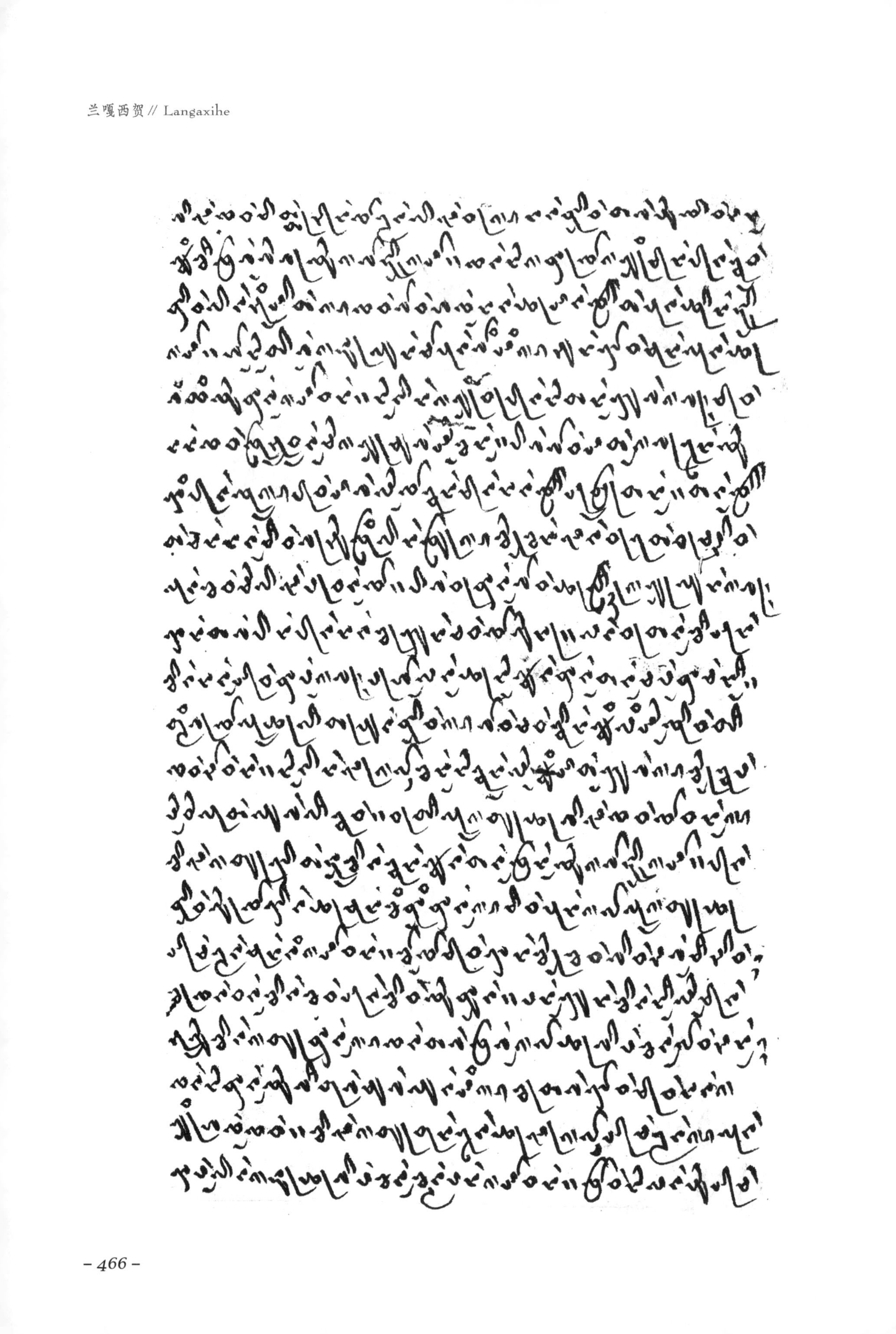

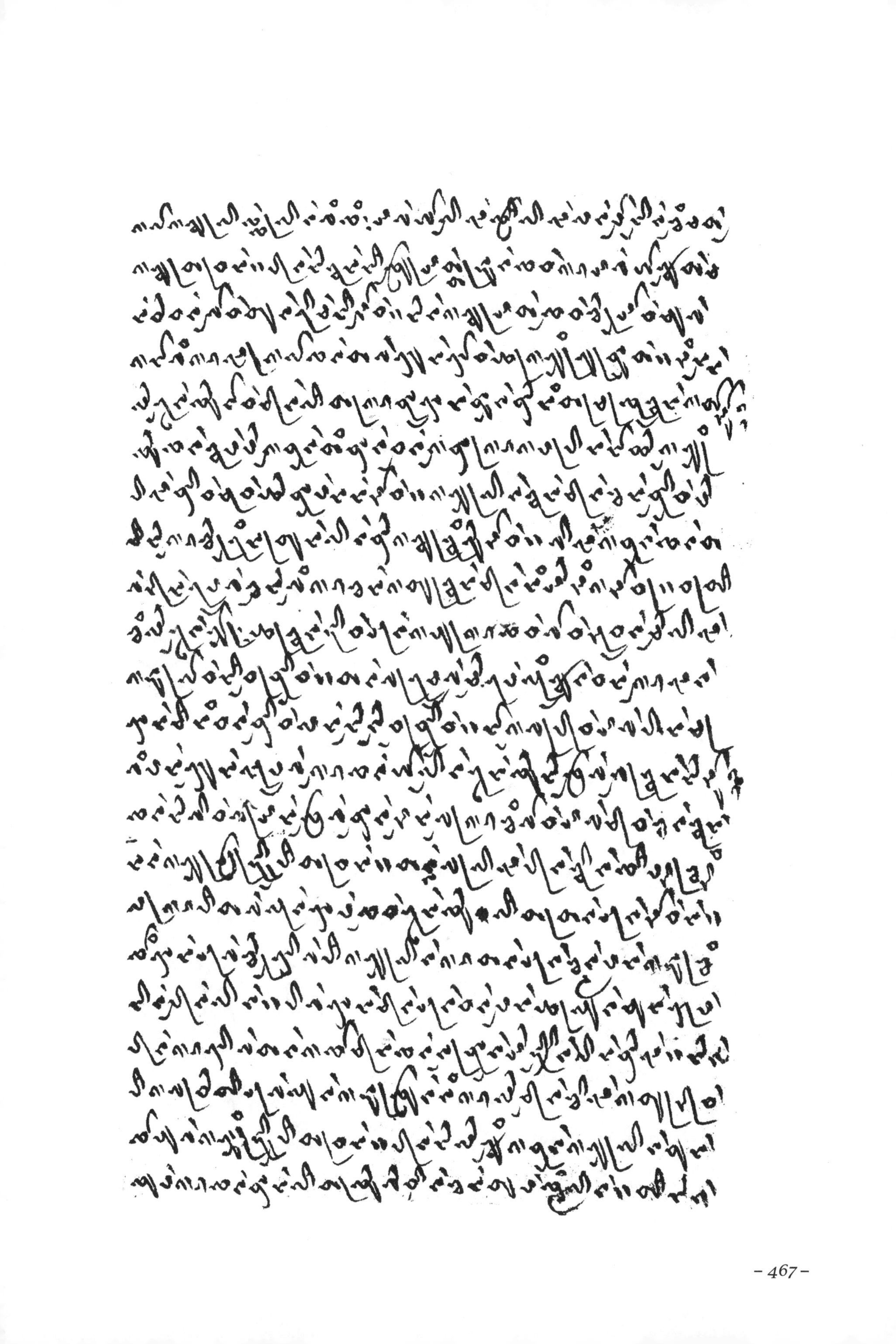

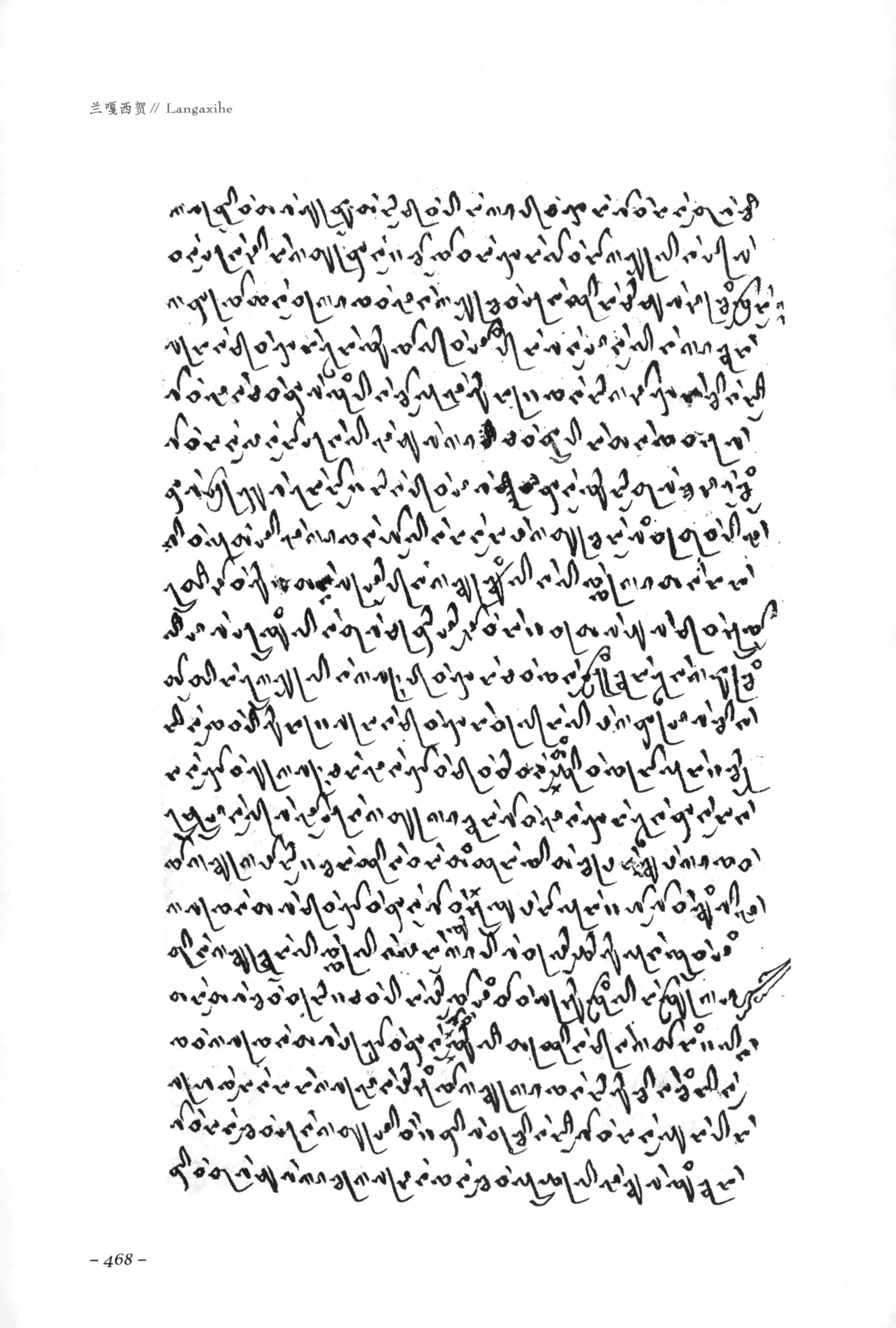

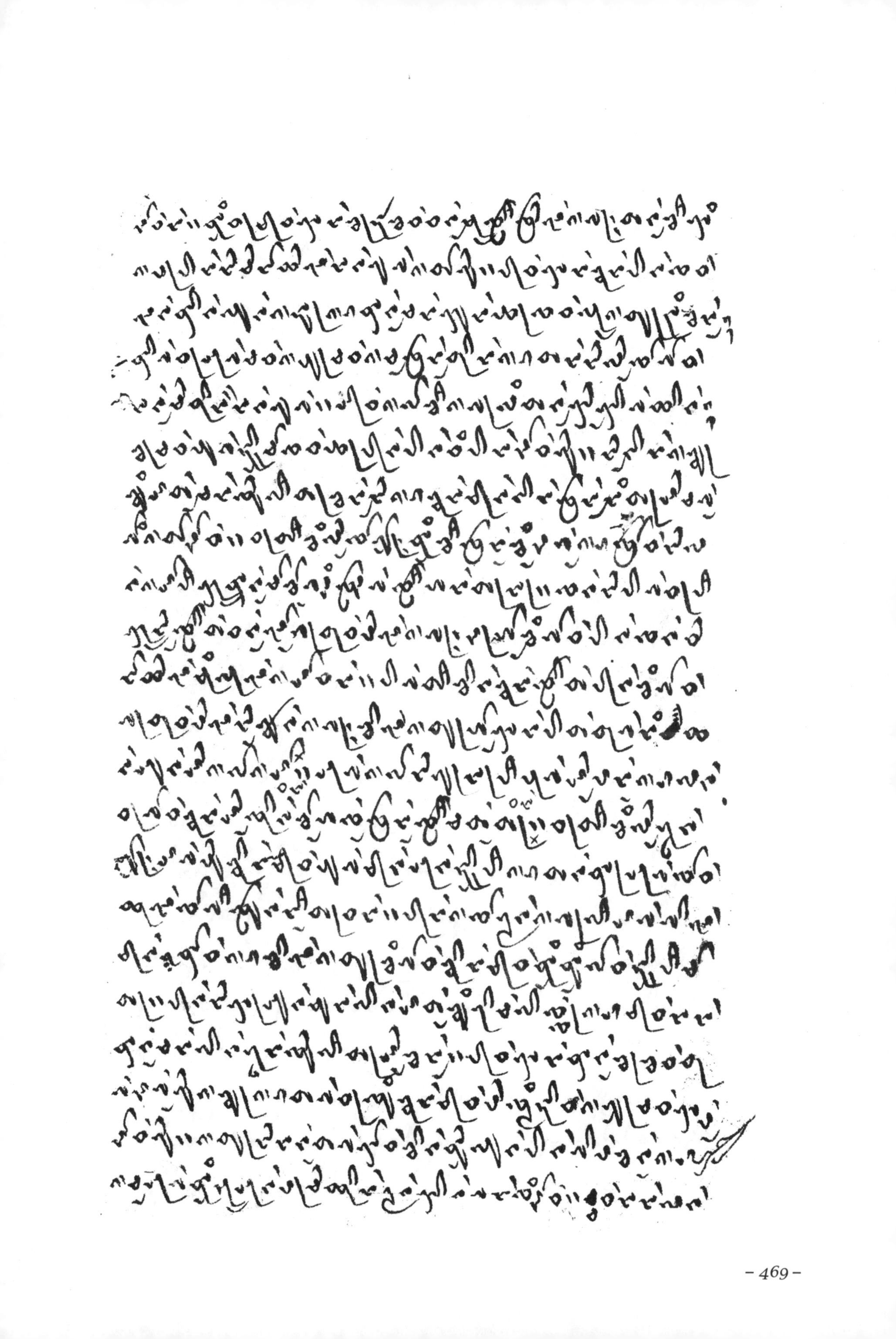

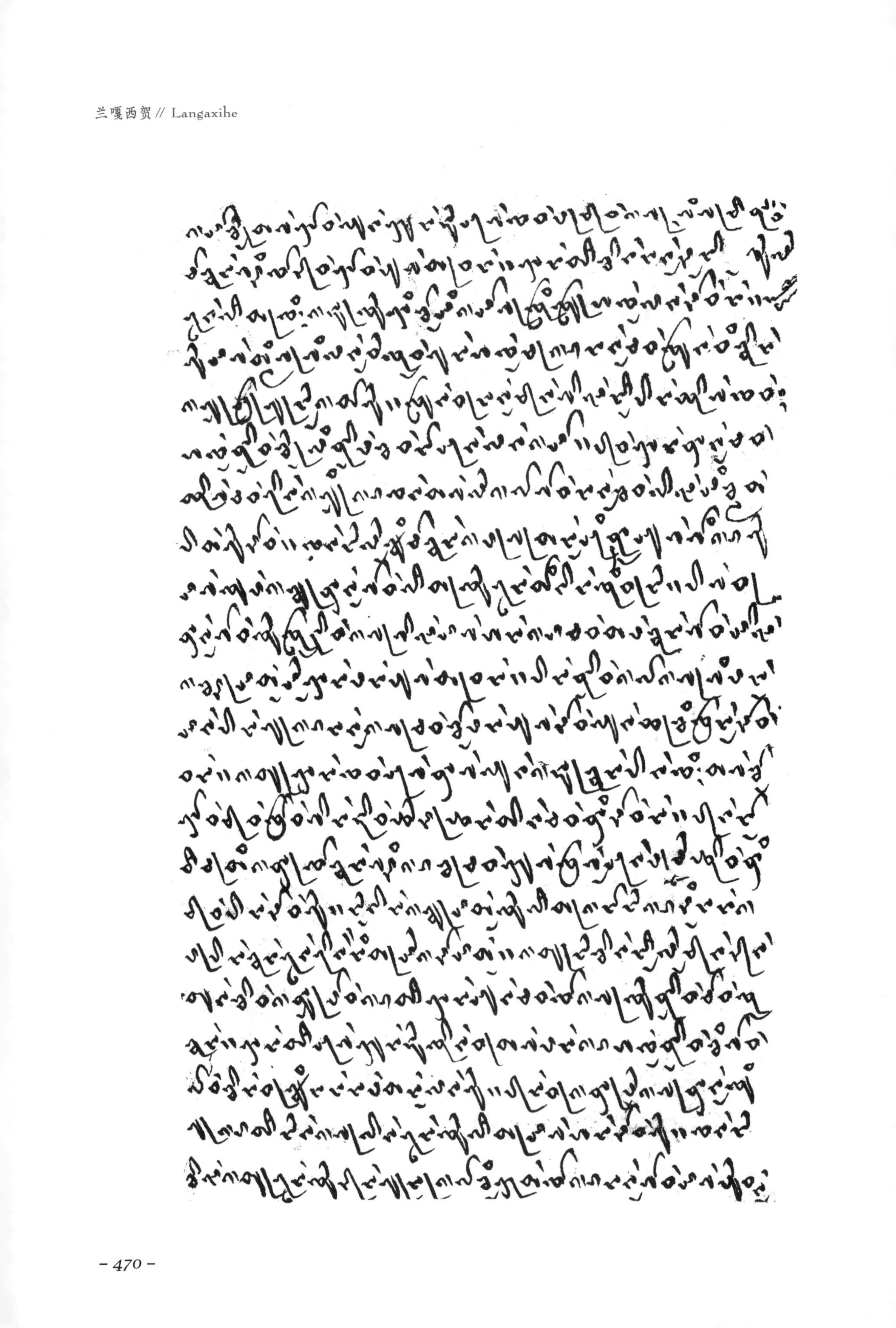

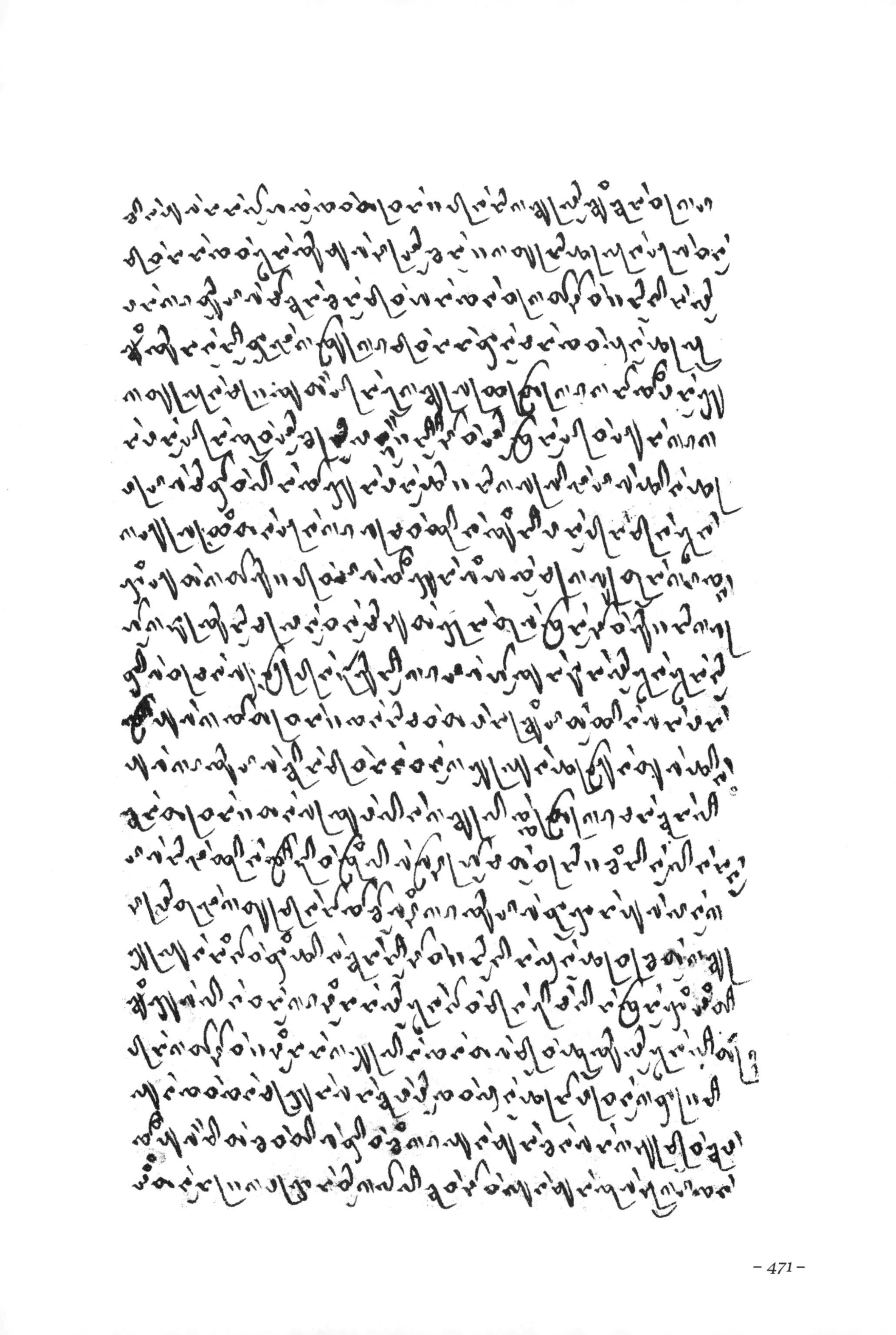

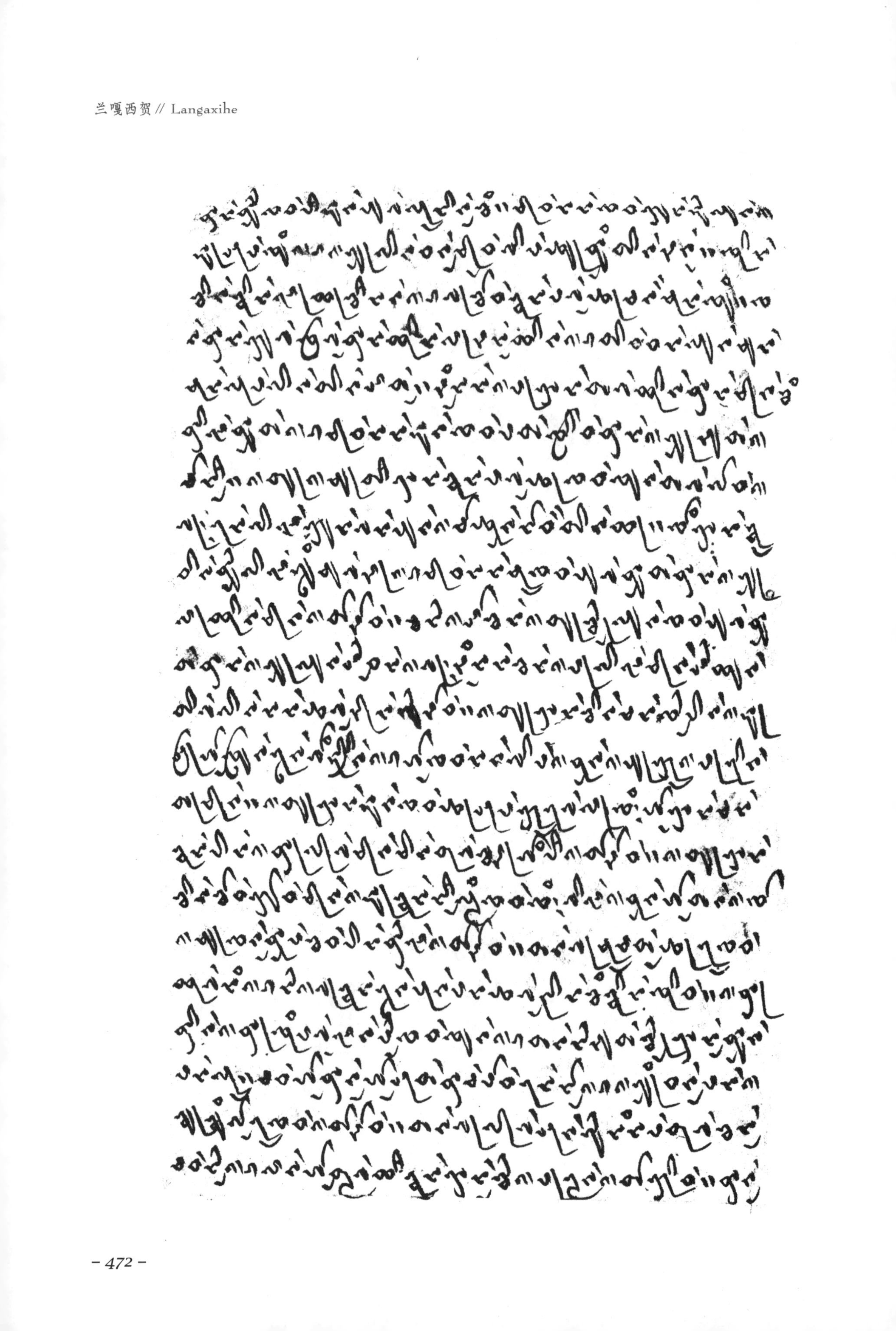

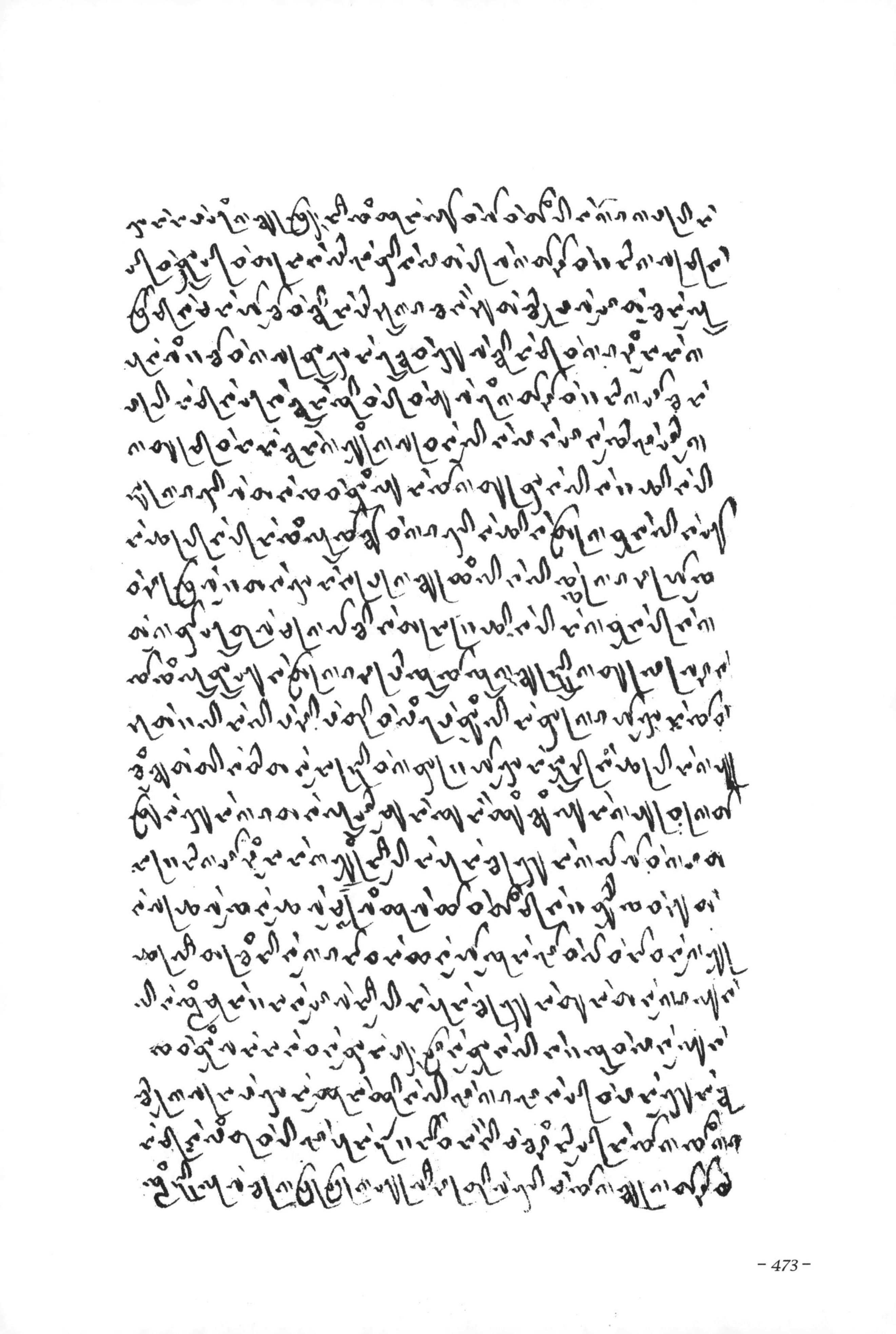

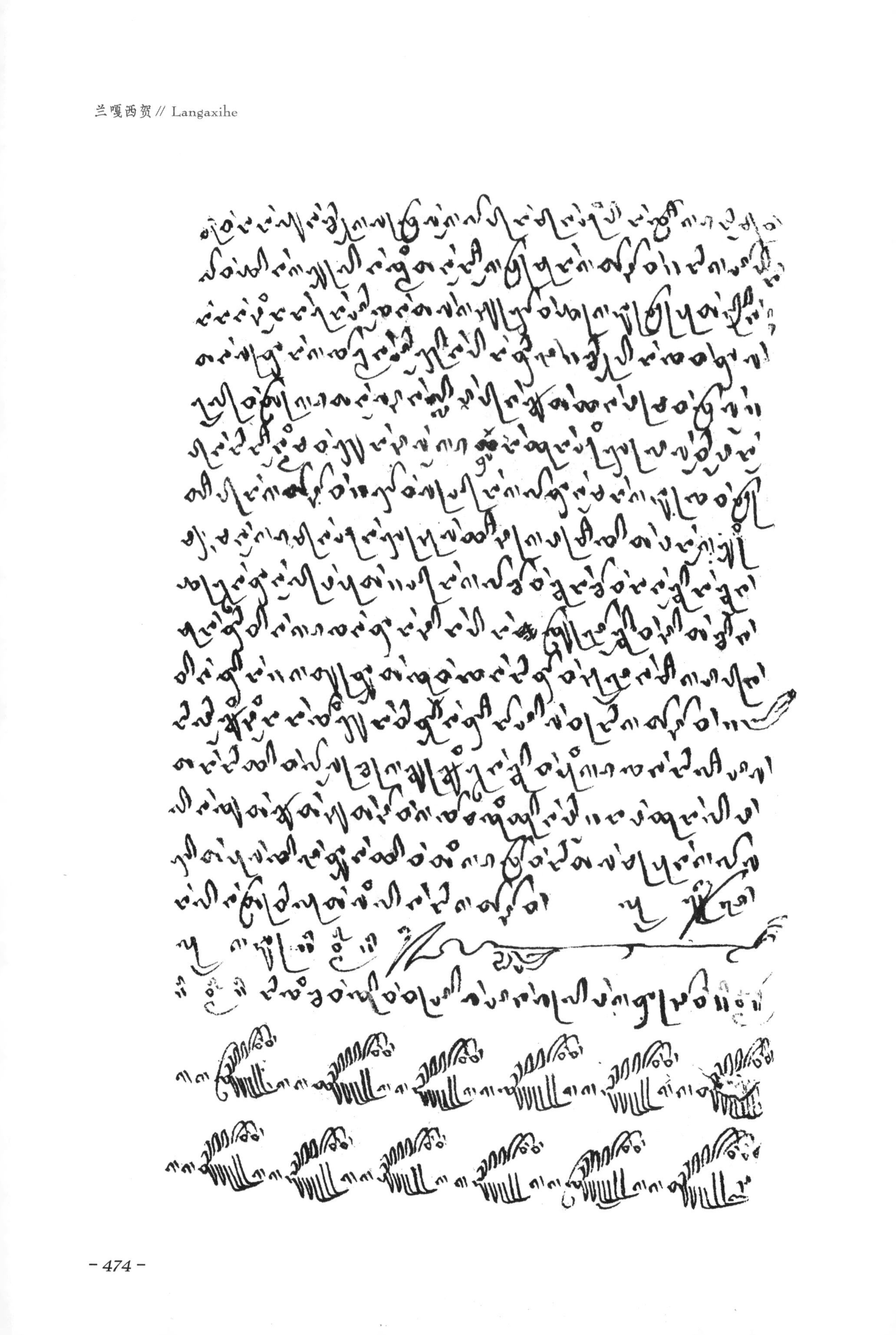

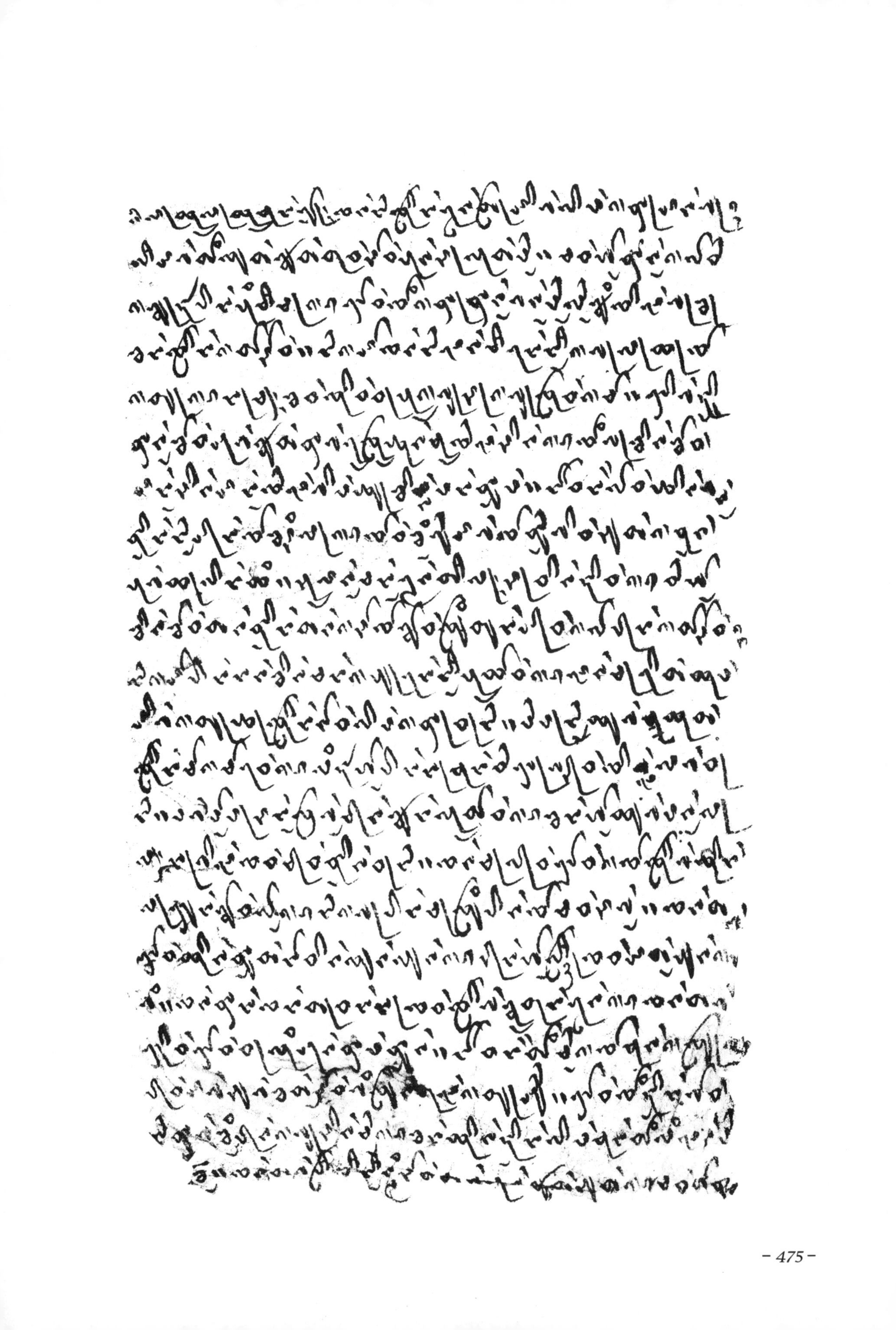

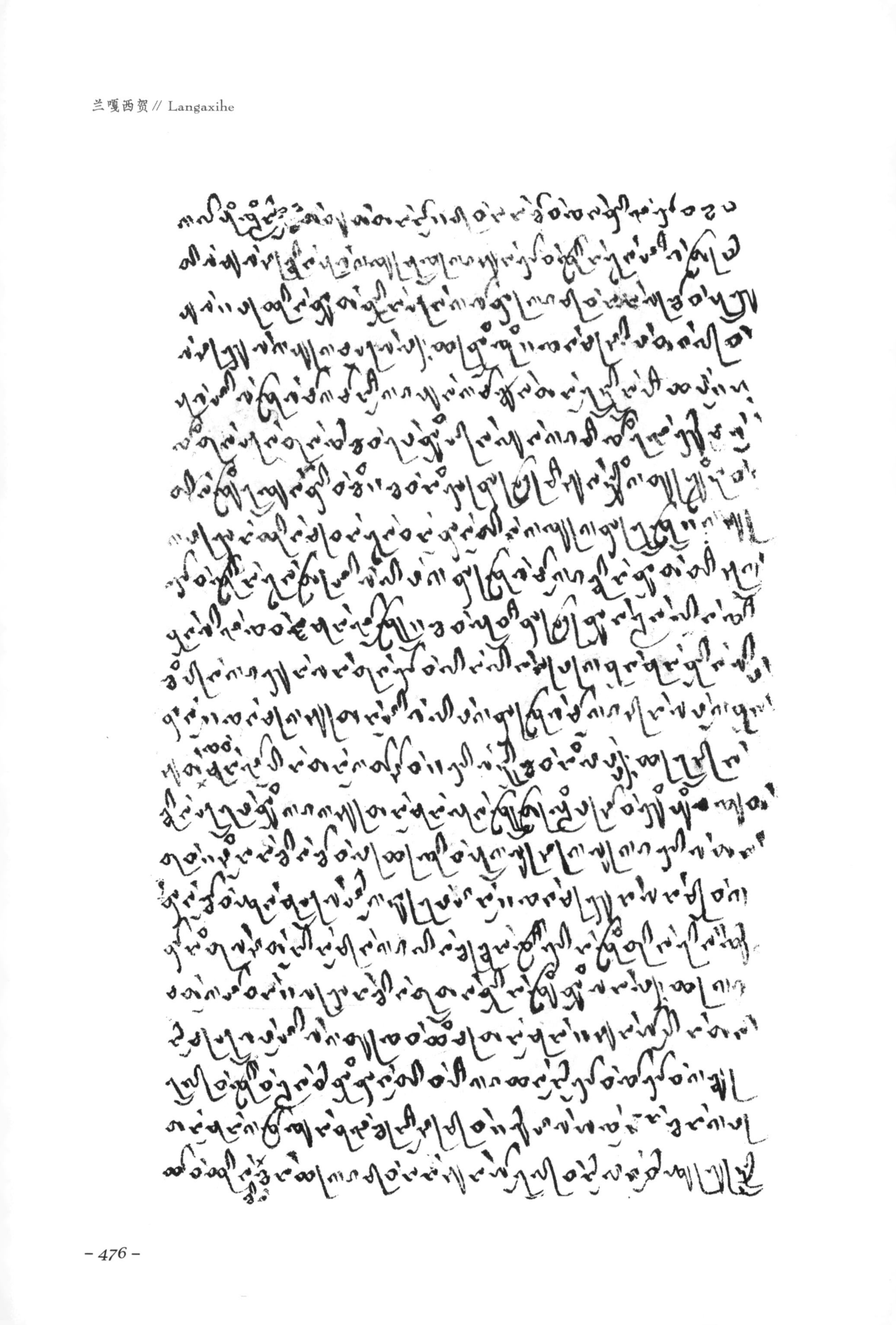

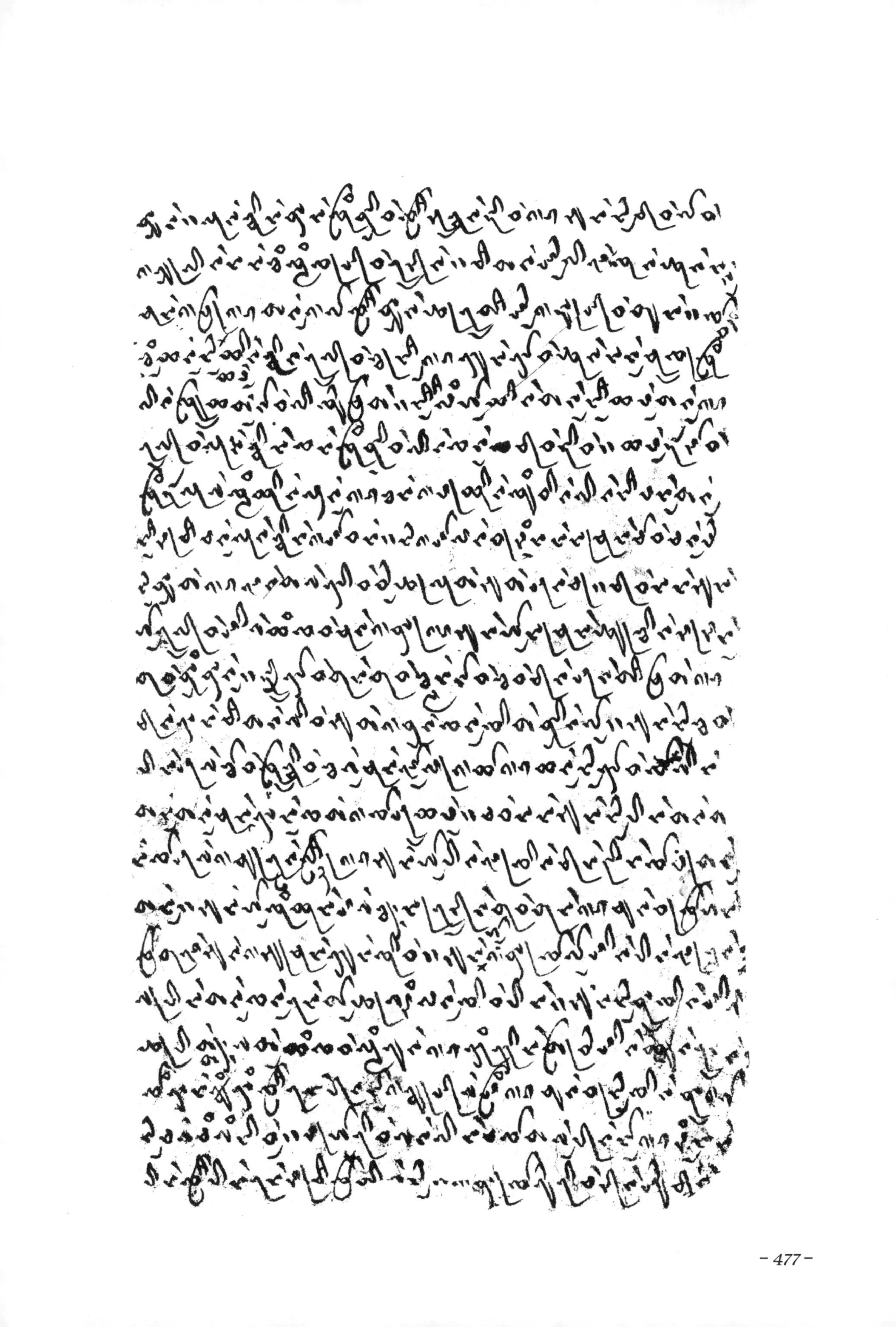

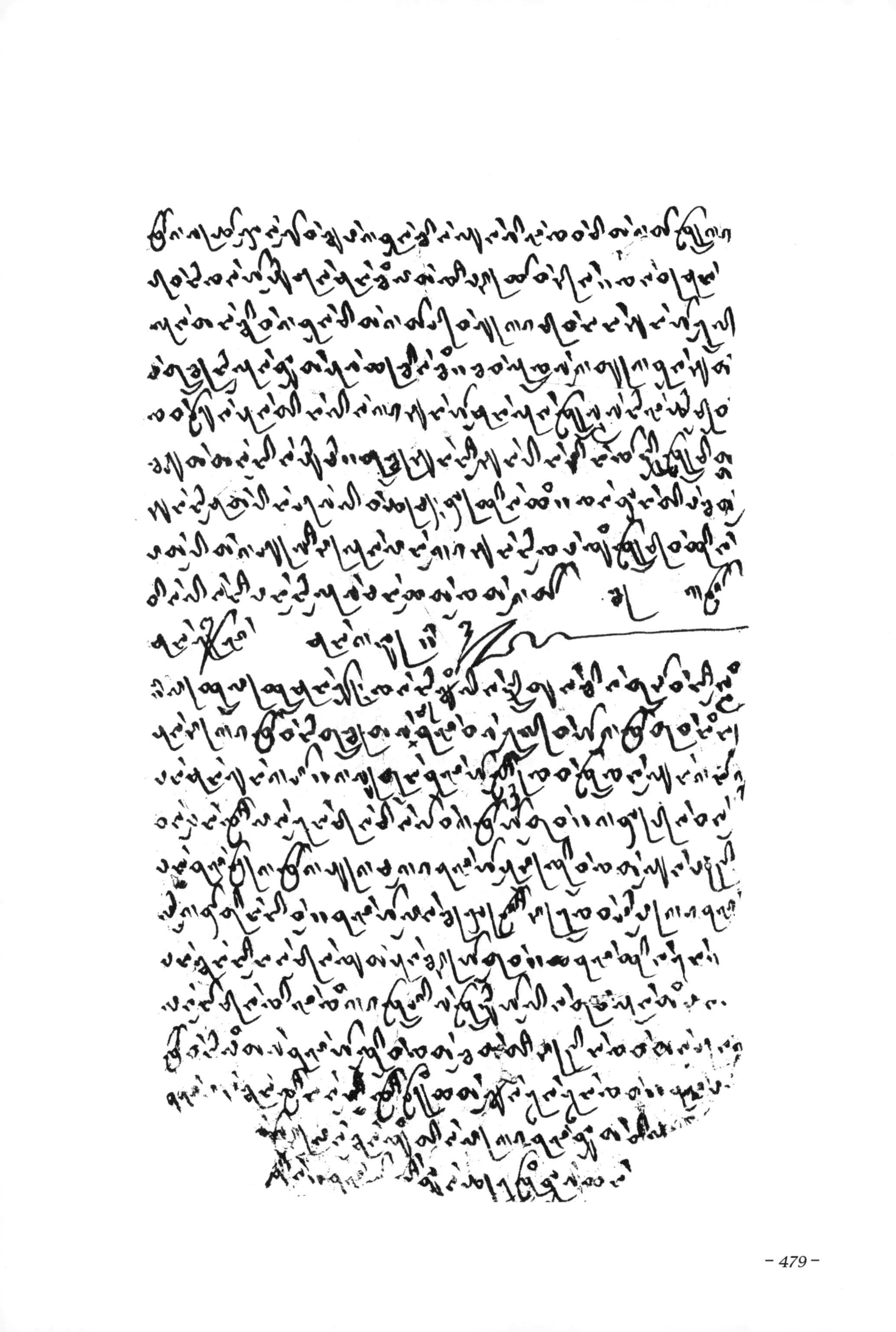

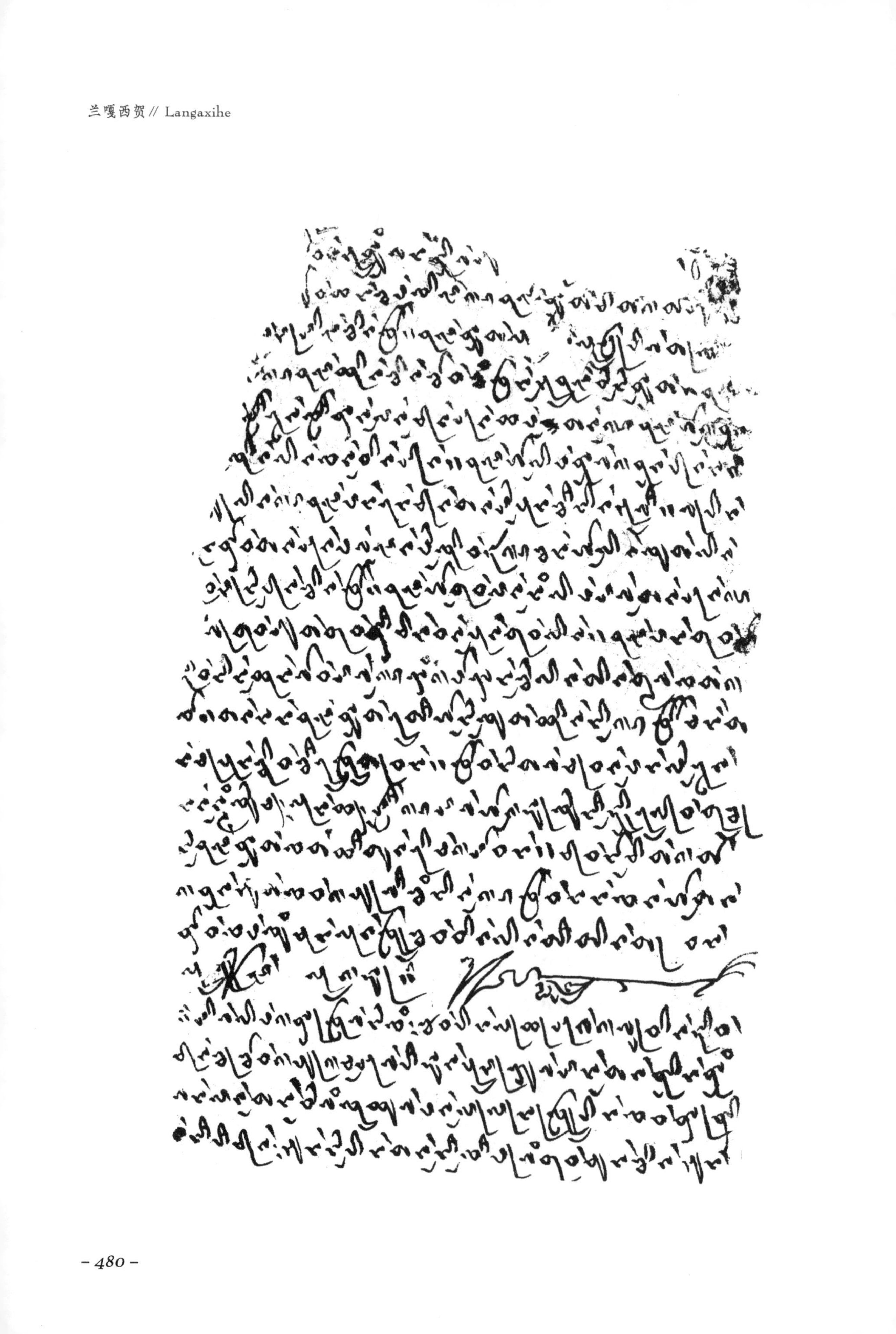

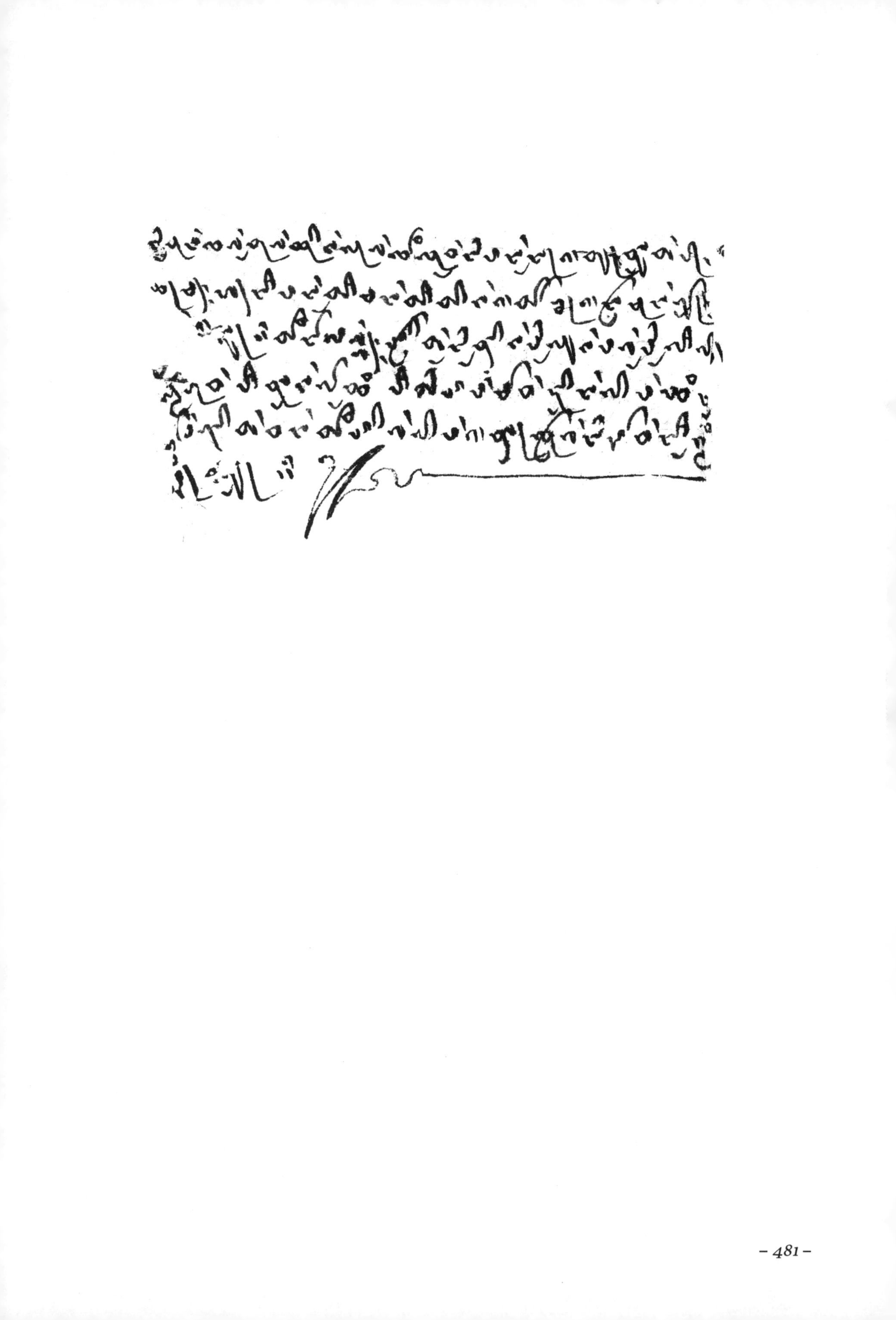